The Curse

Of

Beckett's Wood

R. E. Witham

Strand Fiction

First published 2020 by Strand Publishing UK, Ltd.

Registered in England & Wales Company Number 07034246

Registered address: 11 St Michael Street,

Malton, North Yorkshire, YO17 7LJ

info@strandpublishing.co.uk

www.strandpublishing.co.uk

Paperback edition

ISBN 978-1-907340-24-6

This book is dedicated to my lovely wife Andrea

Table of Contents

The Curse of Beckett's Wood

Part One

Chapter one - Arrival

That blistering day it seemed as if the hill would never end. The clumps of trees that bordered the road obscured the view and gave him no indication where the upward gradient would level out or at what point he would be able to relax. The last seven miles had been like this all the way, a persistent incline, not a steep slope, but a gradual, energy-sapping ascent. He contemplated getting off the bicycle and walking but, he knew from experience, such a move would lead to yet more exhaustion so he pushed on. Lost in his idling mind he thought how similar a bike ride could be to life. There had been times in his own existence where he had had to struggle forward with no end in sight. Recent times. Now he was free, locked in his own micro world, a simple world where the only problem to overcome was the arrival at the top of this hill and the glimpse of a brand new horizon.

Still climbing he passed the sign for a crossroads. He had already made his mind up to keep going ahead even though he was tempted to see where each of the approaching lanes might lead. The need to continue forward was overwhelming. As the road became steeper his face took on the contortions of a grim mask and it was only the markings on the road that caused a brief smile to flicker over it. In big white mocking letters, set upon the tarmac a few hundred yards from the crossroads, was the word SLOW. As he stood up to power his machine ahead, push by push, he knew that he could not have gone much slower. The crossroads passed. This was almost the last conscious thought that crossed his mind for some time. The hill dominated his thinking as it tried to wear him down and defeat his spirit. Gripping the handlebars tightly he surged from side to side, his

1

hips and thighs bearing down on the pedals, stretching the chain to what seemed like breaking point. The joints of the cycle creaked rhythmically threatening to snap the bolts that held it together. Saliva trickled out from the corners of his mouth with every grunt. He was not going to let this hill beat him.

The road started to meander through a more densely wooded area. It was dark and cool in this tree tunnel. Each turn brought into view a different spectacle. Somehow it made the fight easier taking on the hill in ever more attractive ever-changing sections. After crawling round the umpteenth bend he beheld a sign half hidden and strangled by brambles and leaves. It read: EMPTON please drive carefully through our village. A few yards on the road finally began to give in to the gasping cyclist and levelled out. As he allowed his legs to ease off he entered an attractive and quaint collection of houses - old properties that looked as if they had stood in the same plot of land for centuries.

The village was on two levels. There were the cottages and houses through which he was passing and on a hill to his right, just visible behind the oaks and sycamores, there was a large manor house and the sinister outline of a church tower leaning at a slight angle. Trees of all kinds and bushes were dotted everywhere. It was a beautiful place and a just reward for the miles of backbreaking toil he had put into getting there.

Now that the road had become perfectly flat he allowed his muscles a small luxury. For a few yards he stopped pedalling so that he could freely roll along the road and catch his breath. With the back wheel ratchet clicking contentedly he coasted to the village green shaded by a giant chestnut tree. Its shadow also fell across the Golden Goose, an odd little pub set between two equally odd thatched dwellings. What better reason to stop he thought. So he put his tired legs to work for the short distance that remained to the welcoming tavern and reached the pub's white railings in no time. It was the first opportunity to lift his weary frame off the saddle in three hours. Parts of his body had become numb. Nothing though could prevent him from seeking out that well-earned pint and he walked in through the cascading roses over the entrance in a kind of cowboy stagger. How good it was to be alive he felt like shouting.

2

Just as in the tree tunnel the inside of the Golden Goose was cool and dim. Its therapeutic atmosphere was made up of decades of tobacco smoke impregnated into the furniture and wooden beams that smelled as if they had been soaked in bitter and mild. The place was empty though evidently open for business. He glanced around as he made his way to the bar. He noticed at once that the pub was divided into two parts. On the left there were six tables. The chairs had been leaned forwards so that they rested on the tabletops. An old upright piano with the lid closed was at the far end. To the right he could see the walls lined with benches. Fastened to the far wall was a dartboard and in the corner neatly stashed away was a swing skittle game.

Dead ahead was the bar and it was there that he caught sight of himself in the mirror. His hair was streaked back from his forehead and his face was lobster red. A time honoured grandmother clock patiently measured the passage of life with its slow metallic beat that resonated from her wooden body. It was twelve minutes past eleven.

For a while that was all he could hear. Besides after three hours of hard graft on a bike just to stand still and be quiet for a moment was enough. It was while he was taking a particular interest in a framed black and white photograph on the wall that he heard the clattering sound of empty bottles being rattled. Then there came the noise of an almighty crash.

"You bastard," came the deep shout of a man from somewhere below the ground.

There followed the stamp of boots on wooden steps.

"Ellie, Ellie, where the bloody-hell are you my girl?"

Like some pantomime genie appearing from a trapdoor, a rounded figure wearing an apron emerged from the cellar behind the bar. He was sucking his thumb, his eyes screwed up in pain, fresh blood on his hand.

"Ellie, where've you bleedin' well got to?" he caught sight of his first customer at the bar as he ran by, "Beg pardon Sir. Be with you in a moment," and he squeezed through the narrowest of doorways into the back of the pub, shouting for Ellie.

There followed a distant argument that the cyclist could only just make out. The man had obviously found Ellie who sounded more

3

like a small child than a woman. The voices became louder but no more distinct. He strained to listen, to hear what was being said. Then he heard a muffled slap followed by the cry of a girl. After a few more mumbling words from the man the sound of footsteps made their way back towards the bar - slow heavy ones accompanied by light and more rapid steps.

"You'll find a brush and pan down there my girl," he ordered, "and be careful with the broken ones. Put the bits of glass in the orange box and don't take all day. I want you to give me a hand. We've got a busy day tomorrow."

The girl slid past the man as they got to the business end of the pub. As she made ready to descend into what the cyclist assumed was the cellar, she looked at him with eyes that he seemed to recognise. It was something in her expression that brought to mind something he had almost forgotten. The moment passed as quickly as it had arrived. She defiantly wiped the wet track of a tear from her face and miserably disappeared from view.

"Ah, sorry about that Sir. What'll it be?" said the landlord, gripping a red stained handkerchief round his hand.

"Oh make it a pint please, bitter."

"One pint of best bitter coming up," he said as he drew the handle down and the sparkling liquid frothed into the glass.

"Are you okay?" asked the cyclist.

"Oh that. Just a scratch, that's all. She will leave her blessed dolls down there though. I swear one of these days they'll kill me. I'm always tripping over the damn things."

He finished pulling the pint.

"There you are Sir. That'll be two and six."

"Two and six?" said the cyclist, trying to catch the humour.

"Two shillings and sixpence," reiterated the landlord in a matter of fact manner. What's up ain't you got enough or summin?"

The cyclist dug into his jeans, and examined the coins and notes in his hand. He had twenty pounds in notes. Four fivers, but as far as coins were concerned he had three pounds seventy-five pence. He handed over a two-pound coin.

"You had me going there for a bit," said the cyclist, dropping it into the landlord's wrapped up hand. The old chap was about to pop

4

it into the till, but not being able to grip properly, dropped it on the bar. The coin rotated into a slowing spin.

"Bloody hand," cursed the landlord. Then, trying to bring a bit of humour into his clumsiness, he shouted, "Heads or tails?"

The cyclist, who was beginning to find his host's ways warmly eccentric, replied, "Heads," instantly.

The landlord's good hand slammed the coin down on the bar. The slap brought the spinning sound to a dead halt.

"Let's see then," he said, "if you win, I'll give you the pint. How's that?"

"Great," said the biker, "what if I lose?"

"Well that would be an entirely different story," whispered the landlord, an unpleasant glint in his eye. He slowly lifted his hand. The cyclist bent down to have a look.

"Well, well, well," said the man behind the bar, "heads it is, here, you can have your two and six back," and he handed the coin back to him, smiling, "Enjoy your pint, sir."

"Thanks," he said with an uncomfortable sense of relief and took a long drink.

Soon half of it was gone.

"I'll be back in a mo," said the landlord giving a friendly nod in the direction of the trapdoor, "I'll just nip down and see how Madame Lazonga is getting on down there."

The biker took another long swig from his pint as the old chap climbed back down the ladder into the cellar. He was about to put the coin back into his pocket, when he became aware that it had a different feeling in his grasp from when he had taken it out of his pocket. It was enough of a feeling to make him take a second look at it. The fingers in his left hand opened like the petals of a morning rose, revealing the silver coin resting in his palm. It was a real half crown. He took a closer look. There was no doubt about it, he could see it was minted in nineteen thirty-seven. This was either a trick by the landlord, or he was cracking up. Cracking up was not an option. Surely those days were behind him now.

Outside, through the leaded window, a bleaching sun had flooded the village green with the brightest light. He gulped down the last few drops of beer and went to get a breath of fresh air. The scene was blazing with a brilliance that he had never known. Even when his eyes had become more accustomed to it the images he saw seemed to be like looking at an over exposed photograph. Only the barest form of trees and houses could be made out. The light was hurting his eyes even though he was squinting to see properly. It was as if a host of suns were burning in unison. Unable to bear any more he went back inside to the cool, dark shade of the pub. An invisible balm seemed to soothe his eyesight as he passed by the roses and in through the door. It was a minute or two before his vision readjusted to the lack of light once more. By the time he got back to the bar he could see just about everything - everything that is except colour. The whole scene was in monochrome. The brown case of the grandmother clock was now a dark shade of grey. The beams in the ceiling were black. Even his reflection in the mirror was like looking at a black and white picture of himself. His head slowly surveyed the interior of the pub. There was no pain in his eyes but he wondered if the light had done some damage to him. Maybe his retina had been harmed by his exertions on the bike. Maybe the hill had taken it out of him. Maybe he had overdone it a bit. Everything was in black and white. There was no question about it.

Just to make sure he was not imaging all this he reached into his trouser pocket and pulled out his money to take another look at the coin. There seemed more money there this time, great sheets of paper and heavier coins. Feeling an unhealthy curiosity to see what was going on he spread the contents of his pockets out on the bar. The whole lot was in pounds, shillings and pence. Money he had not seen since his childhood. There were four huge five-pound notes, three crumpled pounds, a torn ten-shilling note, and two half crowns. The notes were well used and dog-eared with faded handwriting on some of them in fountain pen, numbers mainly. All in all he worked out that it added up to twenty-three pounds and fifteen shillings. As he stared with disbelief at the items of antique currency he was sickened by a sense of unease. He felt as if the unthinkable was happening again.

The heavy plodding sound of boots climbed up from the cellar. The landlord was speaking to the little girl in a fatherly way as he

6

pulled her up behind him clicked the light switch and shut the trapdoor.

"Cor, come up on the pools have we sir?" he said, noticing the cyclist staring at the money. "Fancy another?"

The cyclist scooped up the cash and rammed it into his pocket.

"Thanks. Er, no, I'll have to go, I'm afraid," he said.

"Go?" said the landlord. "But you only just got here. Not that it's any of my business or anything."

The cyclist caught sight of the little girl peering over the bar. She was smiling. She was smiling at him. Willing him to stay. There was something about her face that he knew. It was a familiarity that had no explanation. He had that feeling the minute he first set eyes on her. For someone he had only met that morning he seemed to have an unexplainable acquaintance with this little person.

"Course, we're happy for you to stay for dinner," said the landlord. "They'll all be here in a quarter of an hour or so any road."

"Sorry?" said the cyclist, jolted from his trance.

"Half eleven on the dot. They're a wild bunch, mind. But they know how to have a good time. Why don't you stop and join 'em?"

"Pardon?" he asked the landlord.

"The blokes from Bofindle Farm. Every Friday, bang on eleven thirty, pints and pasties all round. What do you say? After all, what 'ave you got to lose?"

He felt cornered and uncomfortable, and a reluctant answer formed into words.

"Oh, all right then."

"Good. Then you've got time to get another in before they get here. Bitter again is it, sir?"

The cyclist, unsure if the ale was part of the reason for his weird colour blindness, opted for a non-alcoholic lager.

"What kind of a drink's that?" said the landlord leaning over the bar towards him. Then his face lit up as if he had just understood a joke, "Ah, I get it. You want a drink of water, right?"

The cyclist dared not argue.

"Yes a glass of water would go down a treat."

"I expect it would, but this ere's a pub. You want water then you'll have to nip down the village pump. You can have one of my glasses if

7

you like, but mind old Mrs Cartwright don't catch you at it. She'll rip your head off as look at you if you touch her precious pump. Dedicated to her dead husband it is who put it up forty odd years ago. I have to go with a couple of buckets when she trots up the graveyard with new flowers. We all do. Otherwise Sir, it'll have to be a pint of my best bitter."

The cyclist agreed against his better judgement and in a short while a rich dark liquid with a frothy head had been exchanged for a half crown.

"You'll excuse us I'm sure, but we've got a wedding in the village tomorrow," said the landlord, "and the reception's going to be here."

"Right. Well, I mustn't hold you up. I don't suppose you've got a newspaper to read, have you?"

"Newspaper?" said the proprietor in a raised voice. "Don't make me laugh," and he headed chortling through the narrow doorway into the back of the pub.

The cyclist was once more alone. He was still unable to see any colour. In fact his vision had changed further since his return to the inside of the pub. Things remained in shades of black and grey, but there was softness to the images entering his eyes now. The sharpness had gone and he was looking through what appeared to be a slight but even mist.

He glanced out of the leaded window as he sat down with his drink. The sun had almost reached its zenith and there was not a breath of wind in the huge trees that filled the village. Looking through the glass he realised that there was no more brightness. It was sunny all right but the blinding light that had hit him outside was gone. He was witnessing an idyllic summer's day. He decided to venture out once more to see what would happen. The sun sat in its celestial cradle and birds twittered in the trees and flew about in the warmth.

Leaning against the railings was his bike unaltered except for the lack of colour. What was to stop him getting on it and leaving the place? He could explain the colour blindness and the softening of the image. Or at least they were medical conditions that could be explained. It was the money that troubled him. That could not be explained away. Something had changed him in the village of Empton

8

and he felt it had to be changed back before he left. Anything short of that he reasoned would mean that wherever he went he would still be attached to the place.

He sat on a cast iron seat, painted white he assumed, and drank his pint in the warmth of the soon to be midday sun. The view was a splendid one. There was a road that led from the village green back to the hill from which he had come, with about eight or nine stone built cottages on each side. Each of them were separated from one another but somehow seemed connected by masses of vegetation; bushes, brambles, trees and hedges. Then right in front of him was the green. It was a triangular piece of grass - grey grass. Slap bang in the centre was a massive ancient-looking chestnut tree. It was almost as if the tree had been the first occupant of the hill and had ordained that the village should have been built around it. A lane ran between the green and the pub joining up with the hill road on the right. Looking left the lane rose up past the fabled pump of Mrs Cartwright, continuing past a small shop and assorted cottages curving eventually to the left out of sight. Just before it disappeared the cyclist could make out a slight entrance to somewhere, or possibly it was another small lane, it was hard to tell. To the left of the green behind the huge tree there appeared the remains of a derelict house smothered by overgrowth, its empty windows bearing a poetic resemblance to the vacuous eye sockets of a skull.

Bitten by curiosity the cyclist was just about to put down his empty glass, remount his bike and have a look when he heard distant voices. Presently a handful of rowdy individuals came into view down the very lane he was about to explore. He decided to stay put.

A huge ball of a man over six feet tall and three feet wide led them - a character of great mass and energy. Behind him were two burly figures, the workhorses of their species, each sporting thick Kitchener-type moustaches. Following in their wake were five boys, thin-armed creatures and brimming with laughter. They each wore dusty trousers and soiled shirts covered by weathered, open waistcoats. The big man was the only one not wearing a hat. The two burly fellows had bowlers on their heads, whilst the young whippersnappers wore a dismal collection of wide brimmed canvas headgear. The whole group was so wrapped up in itself and the constant banter of in-jokes they were sharing that they stormed past the cyclist and invaded the dark interior of the pub. The peace and serenity was replaced by the chaos of life.

Now the cyclist felt like a real imposter. He made up his mind to hand his glass in at the bar, bid the landlord farewell and nosy round the area.

"I'd forgotten about you," said the landlord, "You stoppin' for a pasty, or what?"

"No thanks," he replied, "I'm going to have a look around. Take in the countryside and all that."

"Did you hear that Will? He's refusing our hospitality," said the landlord to the big man.

The big man lowered his bulk and examined the little cyclist. He spoke with a whispery, gravelly voice.

"You don't want to do that, young feller. I think you're going to say yes please landlord, ain't you?"

The others fixed him with their gaze. Arguing was not an option.

"Very well then," he said.

"Sorry if my hearin' ain't what it used to be, but I couldn't quite make out yes please landlord, if you don't mind me pointing it out like?"

It had been a very long time since he had been pulled up on his manners and, like a child who could feel the embarrassment of a telling off, he gave the correct reply, and, as if the incident had never happened, the landlord announced quite cheerfully.

"One meat and potato pasty coming up, sir."

The big boss man slapped a giant hand on the taller of the two men.

"Right. Now that that's settled, how about a tune on the old Joanna, George?"

"*One Man Went To Mow*, Will?"

"You read my mind, George old feller," and he slapped his other equally large palm on the cyclist's fragile shoulder. "You'll soon pick it up my friend."

As soon as the cyclist's pasty arrived they took their food and drink to the tables near the piano and the pub was filled with music. It carried on like this for quite a while. The pianist slapped the keyboard with his sausage-like fingers displaying a surprising degree of dexterity. A wide repertoire of plinky plonky tunes flowed continually as the landlord fuelled the entertainment with beer. The pianist kept glancing over his shoulder every now and again in order not to feel left out of the jollity. After one such glance, as the final green bottle fell off the wall, he caught sight of the cyclist who by now had immersed himself in the fun.

"He ain't bad you know. We could use him," said the pianist.

"You got any songs of your own, young feller?" said the boss.

The cyclist did not know what to say.

"You ain't shy are you, Mister?" cut in one of the boys who was promptly clipped around the ear by the older man.

"Don't you cheek your elders my lad," he was told.

"Do you know the *Londonderry Air*?" the cyclist asked the chap looking round from the piano.

The chap lifted his bowler and scratched his head.

"*Danny Boy*, you might know it as *Danny Boy*," explained the cyclist.

An immediate smile shot across the pianist's face and he swung round to face the keys. Out flowed the most exquisite introduction to the piece by way of proof. As the intro blossomed into the recognisable tune the cyclist added his golden tenor voice, somewhat nervously at first. The combination was a joy to the ear. The landlord and Ellie came to the bar and stood spellbound. The others were equally transfixed.

As the last words finally faded away the pianist added a gentle flourish and finished off with a single high plink of a note from the far right of the keyboard.

"Well, I never!" said the boss after a few seconds of silence, "Now that's what I call singing. We ought to have him in the choir. What do you reckon boys?"

There was a landslide vote that he ought.

"I'll think about that," said the cyclist.

"Well you do that. We're looking for…" and he drew closer as if imparting a secret, "new blood."

Then as quick as a flash he told his band that it was time to go. They all bid Harry the landlord goodnight, blew Ellie a kiss and they were off, nattering to each other just as they had done when they

11

arrived. The cyclist cast a coy smile across the two at the bar. They smiled back politely as Ellie began to collect up the glasses.

Outside the green was cast in the shadow of the tall trees on the right. The sun had arced out of sight except for the flickering of light sparkling through the shimmering leaves now rustled by a gentle breeze. He felt no effect of the beer at all. Normally he never would have consumed so much without intoxication and, knowing from his youth how he ought to be feeling now, he was secretly pleased that he had been able to hold his liquor this time.

He reached for his bicycle to take a tour of the village before moving on only to find it missing. Without his bike he was no longer the cyclist. His identity had been removed with the disappearance of his machine. He had spent three months building his bicycle from scratch. It was his baby. He had even welded the frame together himself. Its construction had been more a labour of love than a mechanical process.

A wave of panic set in. How was he supposed to continue on his journey? Who had taken his bicycle? Where was it now? Why had it gone? What was he going to do? He wondered if the farm workers had hidden it as a prank. Maybe it was hidden behind the chestnut tree in the middle of the green. He was half way there before the thought finished flashing through his mind. It was not there. The sense of loss grew worse.

It was then that he caught sight of the old derelict cottage. Its broken windows and kicked in door stared back at him in the half-light like a troubled face. If the house did possess a tortured soul as it appeared to, then the torment transferred that instant to the man - the man who used to be the cyclist.

He glanced across at the pub. He could see Harry and Ellie busy at work in the warmth and safety of the Golden Goose. The broken cottage by contrast was dark, cold and sad, and the doorway was like a weeping mouth. As the sun sank, the image of the cottage's face took on a more defined reality. It was the perfect place to hide a bicycle for a prank, he concluded and, with not a little trepidation, he walked towards the gate strangled by brambles. It was slightly ajar which added credibility to his theory.

Once in the remains of the garden he was overcome with apprehension. Dead leaves spun in a tiny vortex near the gaping doorstep that was smothered in bird droppings. His heart and nerves were on full alert as he peered inside. Instantly a startled rook flew out of the house towards his face and swooped over his head, brushing his hair as it did so. The man tried to scream. No sound came out.

When he had finally steadied himself and breathed a calming sigh he took another look inside. The smell was full of death and decay. Damp plaster mixed with the smell of weeds and the decomposing bodies of dead birds. An unsafe looking staircase dominated the entrance hall. Evidently once imposing, it now stood littered with chunks of ceiling that had fallen from above. Behind the left of the staircase was a doorway. The damaged door lay flat on the ground in the doorway itself. On the left of the hall there was another door, panelled and still in place, as there was on the right also. Judging by the piles of bird shit that littered the floor it was obvious that they had not been opened for some time. His bike could not be behind them nor was it in the hall. Maybe it had been carried through to the room beyond the doorway behind the stairs. He stepped inside.

His shoes skidded slightly upon the slippery floor before regaining purchase. Looking down he could see that a layer of mud and bird mess was almost two inches thick - a slimy black and white carpet that squelched with every step. About halfway across, with the smell becoming unbearable, he came to the conclusion that anyone coming this way would have left tracks as he had. With some relief that his quest would no longer be necessary he decided to head back for the front door and to clean his shoes on the green.

How the door had closed itself so quietly behind him he could not say. He had heard neither squeaking hinges nor slam nor click. Once back at the main entrance he tugged and pulled on the doorknob. It was on old door built with a simple latch that lifted above a lock. Its construction was rough and ready as if it had been the product of the local smithy. In a frantic effort to get out he thumbed the lever that raised the latch. The clicking of this incessant, frantic action went on for a minute or so. With laboured breathing he stooped slightly to peer at the lock. Through the gap in the door he could see that shaft of the lock was rammed tightly into the frame. Someone had locked him in. He immediately cursed the farm workers.

From this stooping position he caught sight of one of the dead birds near his feet. It was the remains of a rook its feathered coat devoid of its shine and it had no eyes. As it lay there with its gaping, silent beak, it began to move. The bird remained completely stiff, even its claws were unbending, yet its body rocked awkwardly from side to side in a slow undulating motion. He kicked it away with the tip of his filthy shoe. A couple of feet away it came to rest. It had landed the opposite way up revealing a nest of writhing maggots. He felt sick to the stomach.

Without a moment's thought he forced open the squeaking door to the right of the staircase. The carpet of bird sludge was there too. In the gloom the room appeared to have once been a library and what little light there was came in from a broken sash window. He climbed onto the sill and kicked away the rotting frame that crashed into the brambles where a garden used to be. He was just about to climb out when he happened to notice something on the floor of the room. About halfway across there began the unmistakable lines of bicycle tracks in the slime. They led to a door at the far end. There were also disturbances caused by feet and the door had left a segment of a clearing in the bird droppings from when it had been opened.

The desire to find his bike was strong, but not as strong as the one to get out of the house. He dropped into the vegetation and scrambled through the prickles to the gate. For the next ten minutes he scraped the mess from his shoes and breathed in the freshness of the late afternoon air.

It was a hard thing to face up to, but it was all happening again just like last time - though the events themselves were different. Even though he had managed to get out before he had not actually escaped at all. He thought back to the previous time. He was sure that he had left everything as he had found it. He was certain that there had been no loose ends. He had even left like a bit of a hero.

Maybe that was it. Maybe he should not have left like a hero. Was it possible that he should have restored himself in the minds of the people there that he was just an ordinary man? Was there to be no stone left unturned? If that was the case then he had to make sure that every single thing was cleared up before he left Empton.

It was beginning to get gloomy. The tall trees that filled the village brought darkness to the green an hour or so earlier than the flat lands. The cottage defied him to return. He promised the place that he would in the morning. Meanwhile he had to find somewhere to stay.

Nine ghostly peals from the church bell rang muffled across the village as he arrived back at the pub. The air had cooled. Inside, Harry and Ellie were busy in the back. Amidst the clattering of crockery and the clinking of glasses he could hear Harry humming Mendelssohn's *Wedding March*. Harry eventually heard him knocking on the bar and shouting hello.

"Ah, hello," said the man, "sorry to disturb you, but I wondered if you had rooms?"

"Rooms?"

"Yes, well, a room, somewhere to stay. For tonight?"

Harry thought for a moment then leaned over the bar.

"I might have, for a feller in your predicament. Cost you five bob though."

"Breakfast thrown in?" asked the man.

"Reckon I can run to that, none of your fancy stuff mind. Bacon and eggs and a cup a tea."

"Done," said the man.

"Florin up front," said Harry, seizing the moment.

The man pulled out a fist full of coins and Harry counted out two shillings.

"You've got quite a voice there," said Harry, "you ought to take Will up on his offer now you're staying."

"I used to sing in a choir in my younger days," said the man, "ended up singing tenor when my voice broke."

"No more to be said then. He'll be in later. I expect he'll take you to see the vicar, him being on good terms with His Reverence."

"Oh, I see," he said.

"Any road, I imagine you'll be wanting to see your room?" said Harry, calling for Ellie.

"Ellie my love, show this gentleman up to old Aunt Rose's room."

15

A look of terror flashed across her perfect features. She gave Harry an imploring look.

"Now let's not be having any more of that," snapped the landlord, "I told you not to listen to Mr Elkington and his nonsense."

"George told me she was a witch," said the girl.

"Well she wasn't a witch, you hear. And it's Mr Elkington to you my girl. Now show our guest to his room and don't dawdle. Any road, it's about your bedtime, ain't it?"

Ellie lifted her big eyes towards the man.

"This way," she said.

Holding a lantern in her tiny fist they made their way up the creaking stairs to the first floor. She lifted a latch on a white door that revealed more steps, much narrower than those they had just climbed.

"It's up there, on your left," said Ellie pointing.

She stooped down to a small sideboard on the landing and took out a candle, lit it and fixed it to a holder with a few drops of melted wax. She handed it and a box of matches to the man.

"Thanks," he said, but she was gone.

There was no carpet on the stairs and his shoes resonated loudly on the wood with each step. At the top before him was the door, the door to old Aunt Rose's room.

At first, as the door swung open, he could see nothing but a black hole. The candle, once thrust inside, revealed an attic room with a single bed at one end and piles of discarded items at the other. Evidently it was used as a storeroom. He headed for the dormer window and looked out onto the green. Now higher up he could look down and see the outline of the manor house and the church on the hill. Through the trees lining the hill around them he could see a glow, a silvery grey light piercing the branches. It was the rising moon.

It had been a long day and not at all as he had expected. He closed the dusty curtains, stripped to his underwear, crawled into the old bed and was asleep in seconds.

Chapter two - The Search

He had always loved Saturday mornings and this was Saturday morning. He could not be sure though if he loved it like he once did anymore. As he emerged from sleep he was disappointed to find that the monochrome vision had persisted through the night and he had woken up to another black and white picture - this time of a dusty cobwebbed room full of junk. The rafters showed the anatomy of an old roof displaying the carpenter's cleverness and skill.

Outside the birds were breaking out the morning chorus. He felt a little cold and got dressed quickly. Yawning and stretching he stepped towards the window he had peeped from the previous night and flung it open. The morning sun had risen just over the trees that only a few hours ago the moon had been hiding behind. There was not a trace of wind in the air, almost as if the day was holding its breath in anticipation. Below on the lane and across the green in front there was a trail of bits of newspaper leading to the huge chestnut tree. Most of the fragments of newspaper in fact were there around its trunk. It was a complete mess. Lying on the ground surrounding the tree was a piece of rope. It all seemed very unusual. For a village so orderly in its rural grime, this untidiness seemed uncharacteristic and out of place. He closed the window and made his way downstairs.

It was obvious that he was the only one awake as he made his way down to and through the eerie silence of the bar. The public area resembled the aftermath of an explosion. Tables had been upturned, and there was broken glass everywhere. In amongst the debris he could see pages and pages of torn newspaper. He picked up a sheet and glanced at the date. It read 14th July 1955. Another piece was from the *Daily Express* of 27th July the same year. He walked towards the door and found it locked, though the key was still in the keyhole.

Once outside he followed the trail of paper to the tree, and to where a rope lay. That was all there was to it - masses of newspaper, damp with dew and the rope. He did not know what to make of it. For a while he stood there, thinking. Then, as the church on the hill rang out six pathetic clangs, he realised just how early he had risen.

Feeling more awake, he could see that he was back at the spot where he had cleaned his shoes the night before. The broken cottage had lost its spell in the new day. It was just a house in need of repair. It was also a house in need of investigating and he was soon fighting his way through the thicket to the back garden.

The overgrowth there was so wild that it was impossible to imagine how the garden used to be. Flagstones disappeared under a tangle of grass and brambles away from the house, suggesting a path through a lawn perhaps. There were no other clues. Then something caught his eye. It was a glint of metal behind a shrub strangled with vines. A broken gate lay smashed off its hinges a few feet away, disintegrating. The top of the gate's framework came away in his hands and he used this piece of wood to smash and hack his way towards the metallic sparkle. It was like finding a shipwreck once he'd arrived. Discarded on the wild grass was the frame of his bicycle, complete with chain hanging over one of the back spars. Thankfully there was no damage to it, except that the wheels were no longer there. It was a cruel discovery and he reasoned that the rest of his machine could not be far away. With every slash of his baton of wood he became more demented in search of his wheels. All the while he was praying that the nuts to the axles were still attached but search as he may they were nowhere to be found.

By now he had fought his way to the end of the garden and had come across a waist high wall. Rounded capping stones suggested that it had once been an attractive perimeter to the garden. Beyond the wall there was an area of sparse woodland leading away up hill towards the church and manor house. He went back for the bike frame, tossed it over his shoulder and scaled the wall into the ferns that graced the floor of the birch tree wood. His head scanned from side to side hunting for the arc of a wheel or the shine of a spoke. Glancing down he could see where the ferns had been freshly trampled. Now perhaps he could track the wheels down by following the trail. Bending low with head down, carrying the cycle frame in one arm and the piece of wood in the other, he felt certain that his search would soon be over. Only the next thing he saw was a pair of dirty wellington boots planted firmly in the undergrowth. It gave him such a fright. He stopped dead in his tracks. For the briefest moment he was afraid to look ahead.

As his head rose up he beheld an elderly woman dressed in a long greatcoat and a headscarf covering her hair. She wielded what appeared to be a couple of weapons - daggers or small swords. Only they turned out to be nothing more than gardening tools - a hand-held spade and fork. Her face seemed to be made of roughly hewn stone, like a sculptors trial piece, quite formidable. Like a reptile she fixed him with a robotic eye void of any human feeling.

"This is Holy ground," she said. Her voice was deep for a woman, with a trace of the effects of habitual smoking.

"I beg your pardon," he said.

She pointed up towards the manor house and the crooked church, just visible through the trees.

"All this belongs to God. This consecrated ground, this churchyard and the vicarage, all God's."

"I see," he said.

"Only the Lord sees," barked the woman, as if she was reprimanding him for some grave misdemeanour, "he sees everything."

She caught sight of the bicycle frame as he brought it to rest on the fern carpet. He noticed her avert her gaze from him and glance at the body of his bike. He took his courage in both hands and spoke to her.

"You haven't seen any bicycle wheels around here, have you?"

"Ask, and it shall be given unto thee. Seek, and ye shall find," was all she would say.

He wondered if she was playing games with him. It began to cross his mind if the whole village was in on the act.

"Okay," he ventured.

"Could you show me where my wheels are?"

"Not me, you stupid man," she scolded, "God, you must ask God. Go to the church. Repent and ask his forgiveness. The answers to all your questions are to be found in the church," the grubby hand clutching the small spade motioned towards the ancient building on the hill, "now, unless you are about the Lord's work this day, be gone."

19

Somewhat taken aback by the force of this woman, he did as he was told, headed back to the wall and trampled through the garden back to the newspaper-strewn green. He even managed to reach his room before anyone had woken up and he hid the frame in with all the junk at the far end.

It was a while before things began to stir, but eventually there was the sound of a hacking cough coming through the floor of his room. This was joined by the noise of creaking floorboards and other muffled clattering. The landlord gave one last vile cough and shouted for Ellie to get up, then proceeded to rumble down to the bar. The man used this opportunity to leave the attic room and play along as if he had just got up himself. As he neared the ground floor he heard the landlord's feeble cry.

"Oh, my godfathers. Oh, bloody hell."

The man arrived at the bar to see the landlord holding his head in his hands, not daring to look at the mess.

"What's happened to your pub, Harry?"

"Don't ask."

"You had a break in or what?"

"Huh, a break out more like," he said. "Oh my bloody head."

"Do you want a hand to sort it out?"

"Nah, Ellie'll see to that, but thanks all the same," he said, warming to the idea of gentle conversation.

"So what happened?"

"You mean you didn't hear it?"

The man shook his head.

"Once I'm asleep, that's it."

"Well, you missed a blinder. It was great," and he tried to massage the back of his aching neck as he spoke. "It was Daniel's stag night, a smashing night. All the usual village tricks and all that."

"The place resembles a war zone," said the man, wondering what the usual tricks would have consisted of.

"Oh, the mess. That's just horseplay. It's tradition," he gave a little laugh. "We get the bridegroom completely plastered, you see. Then it's off with his clobber, wrap him up in newspaper and tie him up to Old Methuselah out there," he pointed to the door, but meant the tree. "It's been known to find them still there in the morning. Want

20

to have a look?" He was just about to say that he knew he had escaped when he shut up just in time. "The bugger's gone," the landlord said when he stepped into the morning air. "Well, I'm blowed."

They both stood looking at the tree for a brief moment. Then the landlord stretched, yawned and coughed again.

"Any road, I reckon you'll be wanting your breakfast now, won't you?"

The eggs and bacon once consumed put a spring in his step and, when he had slurped his tea, he bid the landlord good day and went for a roam around. He decided to take a look at the little entrance that led from the lane to the left of the pub. When he got there he discovered that it was the main path to the church. It was a winding, partly gravelled drive, uphill through a mass of thick, black yew trees. Another smaller path led to the manor house, or rather the vicarage, as he now understood it to be.

The church was a strange piece of architecture. Judging by its weather-beaten skin it was by far the oldest building in the village. Its bulk had sat upon the hill for so long it was sinking into the ground and listing at an unhealthy angle. The tower looked to be the earliest part, built without finesse. It was more like a stack of stones for keeping the cow's hay in than a structure capable of holding a timepiece and a bell. Four newer pinnacles looked to have been added at a later date, but these had also suffered the ravages of erosion.

The simple nave was the newest part, its stained-glass windows unmistakably Elizabethan. Each window was very squat as the church walls were no more than fifteen feet tall. He passed through a mass of crooked gravestones, each one sinking into the ground as if they were trying to imitate the holy building. Finally, there he stood at the main door, a great studded and ornately hinged portal made of black wood. What was it about this door? Why did it have a resonance somewhere in his mind? He stood back a few paces to take in the whole of the old stone porch. The arch across the door was finely decorated and, where the curve of the arch terminated on each side, at about eye level, there were two carved faces. The weather had rendered them the epitome of early experiments in plastic surgery. Grotesque as they were they tinkered about with his long forgotten archive of buried memories. Even the boot scraper planted in the smooth doorstep on the right evoked the same feeling.

Behind him a mass of crows cawed in the trees, calling like a coven of demons, taunting him in the high branches. He reached for the large round iron handle and could hear the latch echo throughout the interior of the church as he turned it. He pushed open the heavy door and went inside. The interior commanded reverence. A combination of cool air and mustiness set this place apart from any other. This was not a building that people lived in. Rather it was a place they came to. Apart from those times it was a lonely building.

Nor was there anything sophisticated about its features. The stained-glass designs did not depict any biblical story. They were merely made up of broken bits of other windows. In some shapes there was a head, or an angel's wing. There was even the hand of a saint, or possibly Christ himself, index and middle fingers raised and the other two bent in blessing. How he longed to see it all in colour. How he wished he could see the myriad shades projected on the floor as the sun shone through these glass collages. The pillars that divided the wings from the central nave were incredibly thick and out of proportion due to the low roof, the apex of which could only have reached twenty feet or so.

Heading for the small altar through rows of seats, he came to a rough wooden screen and went through it, climbing over a shallow step. On the left there was a tiny organ with a double keyboard and three simple stops. Pews, presumably for the choir, lined both walls. Stopping short of the altar he turned and faced the opposite direction. It was then he noticed the flowers. Eight hanging baskets, fixed by brackets to the eight pillars, bristled with blooms. A great deal of work had gone into making the church look as beautiful as possible. Then the penny dropped. The wedding. Instantly he felt he should not be there and made swiftly for the door. The church had provided no answers at all, but then again, he had not asked any questions. Perhaps he should have prayed, he thought, as he shut the door behind him.

With time on his hands, he went for a walk in the warmth towards the fields that flanked the churchyard. A well-worn gate led to a pasture where a small herd of cows were grazing. Beyond the pasture there was another field separated by a hawthorn hedge. He crossed the stubble grass, trying to avoid the cowpats, and reached an excuse for a five bar gate in no time at all. A crippled looking oak tree was bent over it, giving the appearance of being in agony at having the gate's hinges impaled into its side.

He clambered over the gate and ran across the meadow. In minutes he had reached the edge of an escarpment, a continuation of the hill he had ridden up the day previously. The land dipped away at his feet, revealing a view that went on for miles and miles. The man was halted in his tracks and shielded his eyes with his hand. Before him he could see a blanket of fields, hedges and distant villages. Far away there was even a town. Only the more distant objects were in colour. He turned his head to see the oak tree behind him. It was like looking at a scene from an old film. He swung round to face the glorious scene of spreading countryside once more. Far, far away the colours remained.

The stubble was thick and uncomfortable to sit on but it was easier to think sitting down. Not everything had been changed. Was it worth spending every penny so that he would have no old currency left? What if he just kept on walking towards the distant greens and browns and blues, what would happen then? Deep down he knew he would have to find the rest of his bicycle, fix it and leave that way. It was the money that was the real sticking point. A bike could be repaired but how was it possible to change old money back into decimal pounds and pence? No, he would have to spend it all.

Hours must have passed by like this. As he lay back in the summer day, his thoughts were interrupted by the sound of the church bell. Its continuous clang could only mean one thing. The wedding was underway. He got up to have a look but immediately thought better of it. He did not know these people. What could possibly be gained by his looking at them and what pleasure would he get from watching their private moment? Before he knew where he was he had entered a densely wooded area to the left of the oak tree and the gate. A lightly worn path hinted at a way through. As the tired bell repeated its mournful peal he lost himself in exploration.

There was always something about a wood. The trees were ideal silencers, resisting the movement of sound and deadening all but the closest noises. He could hear his own breathing in the cooler air. It could not escape into the wind as it had in the field. Big as it was the wood was an intimate place where privacy was easy to come by. The thought of the wood as somewhere to hide in played with his mind, and if a person could remain hidden, surely other things could also. Why not the wheels of a bicycle?

He resolved to continue as far through the trees as he could and made a sweeping search of the undergrowth for a sign of anything that looked remotely man-made. The further he walked the more disconsolate he became. Nature was all around and the only sign of man was the whisper of the trail. There grew a sense of regret at ever thinking about the wood as a hidey-hole.

The path had been moving in a gentle but constant curve to the left. Almost by surprise a fork in the road appeared, or rather, a junction. The path was more defined and worn wider than the one he had been tramping through. The side leading left headed slightly downhill suggesting that it may have led back to the village. The other path meandered through the wood gracefully rising as it disappeared from view. With the day free to spend how he liked, he turned right.

He had only covered half a mile or so when he saw it. Twenty yards or thereabouts from the path, in a clump of leafy rhododendrons was the silver rim of a wheel. It was pure luck that it had attracted his attention. He leaped over the muddy dyke that ran parallel with the path and seized the precious object. It was unquestionably his, he recognised every mark on it. Filled with delight he saw that the nuts had not been thrown away and had merely been loosened to pull it off the front forks of the frame. Surely the back wheel was not far away.

Any joy he felt was short lived though. The frenzied hunt that followed bore nothing but frustration. Breathless, he stood still with the wheel secured under his arm and looked around him. The wood seemed to go on forever. His other wheel could be anywhere, tossed in a bush perhaps and hidden from view. It could even be close by and he would not have known. It was with a great deal of reluctance that he resumed his way along the path hoping that the final piece of his bicycle had been discarded further on.

As the snaking trail weaved almost imperceptibly downhill he heard the distant bark of a dog. The trees began to thin out with every step until the end of the wood came into view. There opened up before him an idyllic rural scene, a black and white Constable painting complete with cumulonimbus clouds hanging over an English farm. The trail carried on across a field and headed straight for the house. It was a simple two-storey building with a lean-to joined on. A mighty tree spread its shade over more than half of the roof and a small garden ringed by a picket fence created an image of perfect rustic contentment. Two barns built side by side huddled close to the house forming with it an L shape to the farmyard. One was a sturdy brick structure with giant wooden doors in the centre, the other built of corrugated sheets in the Dutch barn tradition, the latter three quarters filled with hay.

The intermittent barking of the dog was emanating from somewhere behind the house. He felt himself being pulled towards the place. The barking dog broke the almost magnetic spell. Dogs had always been a matter of bad luck. He had never got on with them. So he turned to re-enter the wood and began heading back to the village, with all hopes of ever finding his wheel fading with every step.

Chapter three - The Picture

It came as some surprise to find that the path led not back to the village, as he had supposed but spilled out onto a country lane. There was no signpost so he chose left and continued at a steady pace through the thinning woodland. After a while the road broke into the open air and began a slender course downhill. Below him he could see the village - a spreading mass of treetops with roofs hidden within. Three cosy wisps of grey smoke curled out of their chimneys as they poked out of the foliage.

The realisation that he had come full circle did not become apparent until he passed the entrance to the church. Directly ahead stood the fiercely guarded pump of Mrs Cartwright and the pub further on. The latter was festooned with bunting and balloons. Two horseshoes painted silver-grey hung from the doors. Despite the decorations however the place was deserted. He assumed everyone was at the church.

An even greater effort had gone into the trimmings inside. All except for want of a pine tree it looked just like Christmas. Even the tables had been laid out neatly, all covered with tablecloths and cutlery. It was a complete transformation from the mess the place had been earlier that morning. At the far end there was a long table bedecked with the finest lace cover and an elegant three-tier cake. The icing was as pure as virgin snow. In pride of place, standing right at the top, was a bride and groom ornament made from a couple of pegs and dressed in bits of material to look the part. What was most touching was how they had made the most of their meagre resources. Once more he felt like an impostor spying on a scene where he did not belong. He made quickly for his room hiding the wheel next to the frame secreted within the planks, picture frames and bits of broken barrels.

He sat on the creaky bed and became lost in thought. There was a lot to think about. As he flipped over on his back to stare trance-like at the crude rafters above he heard the pitiful clanging of the church bell outside trying in vain to herald a celebration. The clanking went on interminably. He could almost picture the crack in the bell's side killing any chance of a sweet peal ringing out in clear Christian tones. The noise was uncultured and ugly. More to the point it soiled his mind and imposed its own thought deprivation. After about half an hour of this torment he decided there was nothing for it but to leave. He leapt to his feet and made for the door. Almost as if by coincidence there was silence. For one fleeting moment the idea that the bell had been toying with him flashed through his head. So he sat down again, defying the mournful sound to start again. It did not.

It took a while, however, for him to realise that the silent bell meant the wedding had taken place and that the ceremony was over. The congregation would be on its way. Now he had to get out. The last thing he wanted was to be trapped in his room, blocked by the mass of people that would soon form the reception. He straightened the bedclothes and left the attic room. He had acted too late. Ellie was standing at the foot of the wooden stairs looking up at him in her pretty dress as he shut the door behind him.

"Harry wants a word with you," she said in her childish matter-of-fact way, "and you've not to dawdle," then she turned and ran off.

A wave of curses stormed inside him. This was not what he wanted at all. Already he could hear the noise of a gathering downstairs building up momentum as the pub filled up with the bustling wedding party. Burdened with reluctance he made his way to the bar wondering why Harry wanted him so urgently. The landlord could sense that something was wrong as soon as he clapped eyes on him.

"Bloody hell. What's the matter with you?"

"I don't think I should be here, that's all. This is a private party. I don't belong."

"Don't talk such rubbish. You're the entertainment," said Harry flinging his arm round his shoulder. "Besides, these are all friends of mine, so what's the harm if I say it's all right, eh?"

"Entertainment?"

"*Danny Boy*. That's what we ought to call you. Only the groom's name is Daniel, so maybe not, ay? You will sing it for us again, won't you?"

The way those flashing teeth formed into a smile the question ceased to remain one and took on the appearance of a command. The man nodded his agreement indecisively.

"Good. That's settled then. After the speeches and the cake," said Harry.

The pub was heaving with people and stifled with noise. Most were dressed in austere Sunday-best clothes that smelled of mothballs. Soon was added the smell of beer, pipes and cigarettes. They all mingled with the aroma of perfume that reminded him of his childhood and the way women used to smell when he was a boy. He made his way through the pub, pint in hand to the walled garden at the back. Even this garden, with the loganberry bush in the corner and the decaying bricks in the wall, seemed to possess an echo of some sort. Somewhere in the centre of a tangle of guests were the bride and groom. A photographer was becoming demented as he tried to organise everyone.

"Bride's relations!" he yelled through politely gritted teeth. "Bride's relations!"

As he observed what looked like a scene from a Laurel and Hardy film unfolding he sensed that Ellie was standing beside him. She had a silver horseshoe in her hand, dangling from a grey ribbon. He looked down and could see that she was waiting for her chance to present it to the happy couple. At that moment the body of the photographer slammed into him.

"Excuse me, please," came a terse request from the poor man as he manhandled his tripod and camera, "but you're in my way."

He moved out of the way, apologising. The photographer took up position.

Ellie moved forwards. The crowd thinned.

The man stood just behind the photographer and his tripod.

The crowd parted.

The bride and groom were revealed.

All went silent.

Ellie arrived.

She presented the gift.

She turned and looked at the man.

She smiled the smile.

It was a smile he knew.

He stood.

He looked.

Time stopped, briefly.

He stared at the bride and groom.

They were his mother and father.

This was their wedding.

Click.

In the very instant the camera had snapped the shot, he had watched the familiar picture from his parents' wedding album arrange itself like a jigsaw puzzle being assembled by an unseen hand, almost choreographed. In the centre stood his mum and dad looking so young it was hard to believe they were real. On either side were youthful but stern versions of his vile Auntie Emily and Uncle Gerald. Then there was the face of Ellie, smiling that smile. Now he knew where he had seen it before. He had just watched the picture being made. Then the moment was gone and the photographer was shouting for the groom's father and mother. As he watched and stood rooted to the spot, the young nubile girl, who would one day be his mother, caught his eye. She smiled at him. No vision could have been more beautiful. He turned and fled.

Chapter four - The Secret

He was gasping for breath when he finally stopped sprinting. He ran away like a child who had become overwhelmed by events. He half expected a grown-up to come and put a kindly hand on his head and ask him why he was so upset. The child within had been reborn and he felt like having a good cry.

He had left the pub heading right and turned right again following the continuation of the lane that came up from the hill. He had passed a number of stone houses, an old war memorial, then reached an old weathered bench crumbling into the grass verge. He was now out in the open with fields on each side. The village looked like the most peaceful place on earth as he glanced over his shoulder and its grey and white image added to that timeless notion. The lane heading away rose gradually uphill and without reason he walked to where it disappeared over the top. His mind had been stripped of reason. It was in a state of shock.

The image of the reception replayed itself in his head over and over like a haunting tune, tormenting him like the spirits of a bad dream. That familiar, old photograph stuck to the black pages of his parent's wedding album, it was something he had seen many times. His recollection of the album was that of a magical book his mother had loved to show him. He always liked the one with the little girl in it. He imagined that they had posed for it for ages to get it right. The snapshot was motionless, almost a recording of statues. He had just watched it happen in a fleeting moment and had witnessed its fragile transient creation. Yet, despite the lack of care in its arrangement, it had always struck him as a beautiful photograph. Ellie's smile in particular was picture perfect - pretty little Ellie.

"My God," he said out loud. "Auntie El!"

His mind reeled as he realised that the little girl at the pub was the teenager who babysat him as a boy. He had grown up to love Auntie El as he called her. His muddled thoughts flitted back to the album. He could picture his mother taking the album out of the cupboard. A bundle of memories rushed back as if being released from exile. Memories of how they would study each picture together at the table. When he was very small she would point to people's faces and ask him who they were. This was how he learned about his family, at his mother's side. He recalled the photographs taken outside the church. Now it all fitted together perfectly. The doorway of the church, even the boot scraper, he had seen these things before in the album, the album of black and white images.

By now he had arrived at the brow of the slope. Further on an old stone poking out of the verge near the road bore the words EMPTON 2 MILES carved roughly into it. There was nothing else ahead, though, except more fields and hedges punctuated by trees on either side of the road. He felt tired. It was a type of exhaustion not directly of the body but of the mind. His brain was clutching for straws blowing in a fog. He went back to the album and mentally recalled all he could from it. He must have been eight or nine when he was last allowed to see it. Or had he been older? He had never known his father in life, only through these pictures. He used to dream of his dad coming back from wherever he had gone. Now he had seen him in the flesh for the first time, his daddy, his daddy Danno. Everyone referred to him as Danno. He recalled immediately what the landlord had said to him, that he, the entertainer, should be called *Danny Boy*, but that he could not because the groom's name was Daniel. It was all too much to take in. The mental tiredness numbed his body the more his brain tortured itself. As time passed by all he wanted to do was sleep - anything to escape. He had been standing, thinking for ages when he became aware of the trembling in his knees.

After walking for a few more steps it was all over. The black and white was gone. It was now just black. It was black for a long time.

"Gimme that brandy, he's coming round," said the voice of Harry.

He began to force his eyes open. His head hurt. The room was dark, save for a glowing fire and three flickering candles.

"Here, sip this," said Harry, placing a small glass to his lips.

The tiny drop of liquid sent fire into his throat and seemed to bring his body surging back to life.

"What's going on?" he mumbled in a whisper.

"Now don't you talk yet," said Harry in a fatherly tone, "You've just had a nasty bump on your head, that's all," and he gave him another sip of brandy.

"Where am I? How did I get here?"

His words emerged from beyond a mist of swirling semi-consciousness.

"All in good time," said Harry. "Doctor'll be here in a mo."

"Doctor?" there was panic in his tone.

"You want to thank your lucky stars it ain't going to be the vicar," said Harry. "If you'd hit that bloody milestone square on, you'd have been a goner for sure. Now, no more talking 'til the doc gets here."

The doctor patched him up later on that evening and prescribed plenty of bed rest. Harry and Ellie helped him to his room and made sure he was comfortable. It all felt out of sync. The little girl copied Harry at the other side of the bed as they both tucked him in. She was too young to be doing this and he was too old. This went against all the memories he had of her. She should have been an older girl and he should have been a toddler. It seemed impossible to reconcile. He capsized into a state of sleep with the inside of his head in torment and the outside in pain. The exhaustion dragged him into a calmer world and he found some temporary peace for a few hours until daybreak.

The strange night ended with the sound of the church bell. The pain remained, pulsing with each heartbeat just above his left temple. He reached to feel the bandage wrapped around his head and quickly recollected the doctor's visit. It was Sunday morning, the village Sabbath. He got to his feet and made his unsteady way to the window.

31

The fresh air was like a drug, cool and intoxicating. He felt dizzy and he steadied himself on the window ledge. Across the grey swathe of the green a small lady was walking with rapid steps towards the derelict house. She wore a knee-length coat and a neat, furry bonnet. Despite the fact that it was summer she had white gloves on. A handbag was draped over one arm and in the other hand was a book. With the most amazing turn of speed she reached the broken house, headed towards the corner opposite Mrs Cartwright's and made her way to the entrance to the church drive. He had never seen anyone walk so fast. It was almost comical.

He turned back to his bed and sat on the corner at the end. The pile of junk was still there - a heap of fascinating uselessness. His bike parts were still there too, hidden, and he knew with even more conviction that he must get away. All that had happened before, the wedding was now unimportant. The money and the colour-blindness, he would have to live with them unresolved, but the wedding had taken things too far. As he relived that moment with the photographer the desire to escape grew ever stronger. His head was like a pressure cooker and he was forced to lie down. Up until Harry came to see how he was after church, he had drifted in and out of sleep countless times.

"Well, you're still alive then?" said the landlord as he sat on the end of the bed.

"I'll survive."

"Reckon you're up to talking, or shall I come back later?"

"I could do with getting shot of this bloody headache."

With little regard for the man's plight, Harry yelled downstairs to Ellie for some aspirin and a glass of the precious water from the pump.

"So what happened to you giving us a rendition of *Danny Boy*, that *London Air* whatnot? You left a bit sharpish?"

"Oh, I wasn't in the mood. I fancied a walk," he lied.

"You can't say that when you're in the choir you know," protested the landlord. "You'll have to sing whether you want to or not. Huh, not in the mood, my eye."

The pain was too much for him to argue. He swallowed the pills that Ellie had brought and was then left alone. The ache began to

32

ease off after a while. All he could do was lay there and plan. Plan a strategy. He tried to think where his other wheel might be by employing a half-baked scientific method. He concluded that everything pointed towards the farm on the edge of the wood. Somewhere close to the farmyard or maybe in one of the barns, that is where he would find the wheel. Then it would be a quick reassemble and he would fly back down that hill. He even toyed with the idea of heading down one of the lanes leading off the crossroads that he had ignored on the way up. Everything rested on finding his wheel.

Monday morning arrived. He had slept through most of the day and not even heard the church bell, calling people to Evensong. He sat up and felt only slightly sore. The bandage had gone. Evidently someone had called in during the night to change his dressing and had obviously thought it better to let the air get to the wound. With his body hanging stiffly on his still sleepy bones he lowered himself downstairs, finding contentment in the smell of frying bacon as it wafted on the air.

"Well, if it ain't Lazarus," mocked Harry

"I had to get up," he said.

"You hungry then?" Harry asked.

"Oh yes. It smells great."

"Just a mo," and he set Ellie to work laying the table.

After breakfast, and a wash and brush up, he went through to talk to Harry and to thank him for the care he had received. The bar was empty when he emerged from the washroom. He called out but no one was home. Feeling somewhat revitalised, he ventured outside. In the garden, confetti was still lying on the grass. He stared at the old wall for some time. He felt strange that he should know a piece of brickwork with its tiny window set in it so intimately, and yet here it was standing before him, like an old friend.

Monday was a quiet sort of day at the pub. He spent the day helping Harry with light odd jobs on his return from the brewery. At about teatime, Harry felt that he had been polite for long enough.

"So, what made you run off like that then?" he said as they both polished the pump handles.

The question had been waiting to arrive.

"I just fancied a bit of a stroll."

"Stroll? Stroll my arse. You left the bloody wedding like shit flying off a shovel. You owe Danno money, is that it?" probed Harry.

"Danno, money?"

He had not expected this.

"He don't take kindly to people messing him about. He can be a nasty piece of work when he's a mind."

"I've never met him before. How could I owe him anything?"

"So what made you take off like that?"

He decided to revert back to his original argument.

"If you want to know the truth, it's weddings. I told you I didn't want to stay. Let's just leave it at that shall we?"

Harry allowed the sentence to sink in for a moment and then the phantom penny dropped.

"Ah, I see. Silly me. Nursing a broken heart are we?"

"I'll get over it, in time," he said, glad that he had got the landlord off his back.

He decided to end the day not long after this conversation and bid Harry goodnight as he climbed the stairs for an early night.

The following morning, feeling recovered, though brandishing a scab-covered bruise on his forehead, he set off determined to find his wheel. As he passed the pump, bound for the lane up to the woods, he almost crashed headlong into an elderly lady as she stepped out of her cottage. As he turned round to apologise he saw it was the same woman that he had met near the church. The way she eyed him up, he almost convinced himself that he was up to no good. Neither of them said a word in the end. Most of the communication was done through eye language, with her doing most of the talking.

Once back in the wood he retraced his steps toward the farm, still looking for the glint of a wheel rim. The place was hushed at that time of the morning. The birdsong had quietened down to a mere smattering of chirps. He made his way along, not rushing, so as not to miss a sighting. Every now and then a breeze would rustle over the high branches and mimic the sound of the sea up above. Down below only the slightest trace of the wind could be felt on his face.

On one occasion, however, the air carried with it a sound. Being quite indistinguishable he stopped dead to listen. It varied in strength and, though never loud, rose and fell with the gentle gusts. It bounced off the hundreds of trees giving it a hollow quality, quietly echoing. As far as he could gather the sound was coming from a place off the beaten track but up ahead quite some distance away. He headed in the direction of the strange pining noise, stopping now and again to get a fix on it. He had a mental picture of an animal in a trap - maybe something snared and crying in its death agonies.

Now the sound could be heard without the aid of the wind. It sounded more like a person, akin to the cries of a child. He thought of Ellie in an instant. He had not seen her that morning and he became quite worried. Breaking off the path he charged through the undergrowth, ripping through bramble tripwires and homed in on the crying that was now perfectly clear. As he rounded a fallen tree he came upon a woman sobbing, wailing privately, with her head in her hands. Startled by his sudden arrival she turned round. He stepped back startled by her face. It was his mother, or rather the girl who one day would become his mother.

It was an intense moment. There was too much to take in. Words would not form in his head, let alone his mouth, his eyes were doing all the work. His mind became overheated with the growing list of questions it needed answering. Before him was a pitifully beautiful sight. He was looking at a woman in her late teens, slim like a screen idol, dressed in a light summer frock with buttons running down the front. A slightly dirty apron was tied round her waist and she had wellington boots on her feet. The top three or four buttons on her dress were undone and, in her sitting position on the ground, he could see down into her cleavage where a white bra cradled her small breasts. He looked away ashamed. He knew that he was not supposed to be attracted to her but he found it impossible not to be. He wanted to hold her, to show her that he loved her despite all that she would become. He wanted to forgive her for the future. He wanted to protect her and slap her all at the same time. Here was someone who would give him life and who would poison it in time - and yet she was mummy, the person who would care for him throughout those countless illnesses, and childhood dramas. She would in some time to come, bake his favourite cakes and tuck him up in bed - but she would also be the one who would take tucking him up in bed a stage too far. She would be the one who would have him walking on eggshells as he tried to steer clear of her temper. Here, she had not yet evolved into that person, and maybe a touch of kindness would go some way to making sure that she never would.

The girl dried her eyes on her apron and got to her feet. She was embarrassed and continued to wipe her face long after it was necessary. He too felt the awkwardness, rooted as he was to the spot. The couple of seconds this had taken to enact had seemed like an hour. At length some words spilled out of his mouth.

"I heard a noise. I thought it may have been Ellie," he said.

"How do you know Ellie? She don't like the woods," said a younger version of the voice he knew so well.

"Are you all right?" he said, finding it hard to believe this was actually going on.

"I'll get over it," she said looking down.

He wanted to know exactly what it was she would be trying to get over but he held back from prying too hard. He tried a safer question.

"Do you need any help? You've not hurt yourself, have you?"

"I'd better get back," she said, turning her head towards the path.

"I'll come along with you," he said, "if that's all right?"

She flashed a glance at him.

"I mustn't talk to strangers," she said. "Besides, I don't think it would be a good idea for anyone to be seen with me."

"Why not?" he asked

"It just wouldn't, that's all."

He could see the fear in her face, like a shadow passing fleetingly across her eyes. Someone had caused this in her. He made a guess.

"Because of Danno?" he put in.

Her eyes widened.

"What you been hearing?" her voice seemed charged, electrically.

"Nothing, it was just something Harry said," taken aback somewhat by the change in her.

"Well he's one to talk. His misses ran off with another..." her voice trailed off before she said another word.

36

His curiosity aroused, he nevertheless dismissed it and played safe again.

"Do you live far?" he asked

"Bofindle Farm," she blurted out, and straightaway wished she had not.

"The one on the edge of the wood?"

There was no answer. She was eyeing him up.

"You're the man I saw at the wedding, aren't you?" she said after a brief moment, "Look, I've got to go."

Like some frightened deer she ran off as best she could in her black wellington boots, heading towards the farm he had seen a few days ago. He tried to follow without appearing to give chase but with the bends in the winding path she was soon gone. The only clue to knowing that she had arrived home was when he heard the distant sound of a barking dog coming from the farmyard beyond the wood.

It was a confusing walk along the path to the wood's end. His earnest hunt for the wheel had been submerged in layer upon layer of other interlocking thoughts. He was only awakened from his robotic stride by the brilliant brightness of the world outside the trees, revealing the view of the farm across the open field. Somewhere in the mangle of the buildings there, he was certain his wheel would be found. He had always suspected the farm workers, but he would have to be sure none of them would see him, not to mention the resident dog. How he hated dogs. He leaned on a weathered and long-abandoned gatepost watching and waiting in the warm, white sunshine.

Nothing happened. He had not even expected anything to occur, though he felt restless that nothing did. He wanted to see people come and go. It would give him an idea of their movements and help him to gauge when it was best to cross the ocean of arable space that separated him from the farm. Or else he might see someone take the dog out to do some work, or for a walk maybe. As the minutes stripped away his patience he saw the light-grey wisp of a smoke trail begin to emerge from the farm chimney. A fire had been lit. It was a sign of permanent residence, an indication that someone was staying put. Could it have been his mother's work, he thought? Did it matter? It seemed to and it irritated him.

By now he had sat himself on the grass that skirted the field's edge, spying on the inert farm with his back against the crumbling gatepost. The place held a fascination for him. There was an odd kind of remembrance deep inside him far stranger than he had at the church. It was a sort of knowledge buried far down in the core of him. He could not help himself but be drawn to the place, and yet he lacked the courage to cross the field and defy the risk of getting noticed. He toyed with the idea of returning at night, bringing a torch, a lantern perhaps, but with some discomfort he could visualise the place at night and he knew it would be a bad plan. His nerves would not stand it he felt - and then, of course, the light from a torch would bring more attention to him than his body would have done in the daylight. It would be harder for him to see anyone creeping up behind him too if it were dark.

As this was going through his mind his body had risen to its feet and was cautiously stepping over the stubble field like a commando. The decision to go had been made without his consent and he felt a little annoyed that he had actually set off. About halfway across, with the farmhouse looking bigger, he felt the sense of dread grow at what he was doing and how exposed he was. He was particularly worried about the silent dog and was convinced it was aware of his approach. He flattened his body to the rough ground almost prostrate. All was quiet, much too quiet.

Cold dew that had collected in the hollow straw stems of the stubble flicked out onto his clothes as he walked. His trouser legs were wet through already. He looked up from the soil. There seemed to be a long way to go. In a low crouching motion, head down again, he changed direction and made for the Dutch barn instead of the house. A farmyard smell began to invade his senses as he came up against the metal structure - a concoction of hay and pig shit. He was in a nervous state of alert, ever apprehensive about the damn dog. The barn was a largely open building containing silage and bales of feed for the winter. He stalked three sides of it before admitting that the wheel was not there. It was a fairly thorough search despite his concerns. He was not planning to have to make a return trip. At the far end of the barn was a small lean-to shed made of corrugated iron. Its door was rusting but there was no lock. He was just about to creak open the door and have a peek inside it when he heard footsteps coming from the house. He let go of the door handle of the lean-to and raced round towards the bales of hay in the barn to hide. It was impossible to see who it was. The old brick-built barn in front obscured the view but he could hear its great wooden doors being opened and a second or two later closed quietly.

It seemed quite a while before he decided to leave the comparative safety of the hideout behind the straw but soon he was skirting the back wall of the other barn. It was not long before he reached the edge furthest away from the field. The building was long and thin and he quickly arrived at the front of the barn, nudging his head round the corner to sneak a look at the huge oak doors.

Almost dead ahead was the farmhouse with its garden, such as it was. Washing hung limply on a line and a rough wooden prop pushed it up in the middle. Resting up against the house walls was a motley collection of garden implements, hoes and spades and the like, and just to the left a small shed, about three feet high. It was too small to be of any use to anyone he thought, unless of course a very small person used it. It was not until he saw the chain, fastened at one end to a metal post and the other end disappearing into the open doorway of the shed, that he realised it was in fact a kennel. The shock caused him to gasp a breath. He put his hand to his mouth before he had a chance to make a sound. The sight of a strong looking chain though brought some reassurance as he crept up to the towering doors and edged open a crack big enough for him to slip through.

Inside it was dark and musty. Even the air seemed antique. The floor was one of earth scattered with trampled straw. He could not see anyone, though he knew someone had just gone in. An ancient-looking tractor was parked at the side near a workshop area comprising a greasy, black bench strewn with oily tools. He hid behind one of the tractor's huge rear wheels and listened. All was quiet.

It was clear that the barn had another, if not several, floors. He could not see the roof, just planks nailed to light grey beams that made a ceiling for him and a floor up above. In front of this was a rough wooden staircase, very wide, with a makeshift banister leading upwards. Beyond the stairs was a row of dividing walls made from thick, heavy wood - four or five on each side of the building. He imagined that cows or horses would have been stabled in these sections though he was not aware of any livestock being there. Maybe that is where he would find his wheel, he thought.

Carefully, he moved past the bottom of the staircase and reached the first of the left-hand-side stalls. It was empty just as he suspected, with neither sign of animals nor bicycle parts. He was just about to peer round to the next stall, when he heard a noise, very quiet coming from upstairs. He listened again. It was like a deep, heavy sigh, a groan almost - a few seconds later he heard it again. He had to listen hard but there it was. He could hear a long, drawn-out moaning sound, as light as a whisper.

The gap in the big doors was beckoning his timely escape. So was his curiosity. It was either back to the woods or up the stairs. The choice was simple. The decision was not. He took a long look around him. He knew someone had entered the barn. He had heard it. Who then was making the noise? Was it the person he had just heard come in? He had to make sure that there was no one else downstairs. He could not see anyone. The sound continued as he quietly placed one foot in front of the other making for the handrail to the steps.

With the lightness of a gymnast he climbed the stairs. The noise from above grew slightly in volume and its rhythmic beat more frequent. He could even hear his heart thumping in his rib cage and his nerves tightened as his head came level with the first floor. What he saw was a ramshackle mess, a dumping place where all the odds and ends of farm life were thrown out of the way. There seemed to be no order to it. The place lacked any form of discipline whatsoever. Broken bits of ploughs had ended up there, awaiting repair he assumed. Old boots with no laces looking forward to the same treatment he imagined. There seemed to be so much rubbish he could not take it all in. Still the sound persisted, like the deep moan of a dreaming dog, low and guttural. The noise was emanating from a large bundle of old sacks. And in the middle of the great heap he could see a head - the head of a woman. She was lying on her back, gently nodding back and forth to the undulating moan.

40

With a brief backward glance down the stairs he managed to rise to his full height and hid himself behind the carcass of an old piano. Now he could see more clearly. He could make out the back of the woman's head and her bare shoulders. Her dress was undone but not removed. She held a photograph in one hand, creased as if it had once been folded in half. The other hand reached down between her legs, rubbing gently up and down. She was beginning to pant with every movement and every moan. The dress was the same as the one his mother had worn when he had seen her earlier that morning.

He felt rooted to the spot, trapped, unable to move and get out. He crouched down further, wishing he could shrink to infinity. The rubbing and groaning increased with almost animal ferocity. She called out a name half weeping half squealing.

"David, oh David," she said through quickening breaths.

Then, with what sounded like a cry of pain she began to thrash about on the sacks rubbing herself with tiny, rapid movements. She continued for a minute or so, finally collapsing into the heap, sobbing like a heartbroken child.

He ducked down further, as he watched her get to her feet and fasten up her dress. It was the girl who would become his mother, he could see clearly. She tied the apron around her waist, dried her eyes and brushed the creases out of her clothes. Then, after putting her boots back on, she carefully folded the photograph in half again, kissed it, and slid it between the floorboards under the sacks. He held his breath as she walked past and tiptoed back down stairs. She did not see him and she was soon gone. He let out a sigh of relief.

It was a while before he collected enough nerve to get up. And even though he was anxious to get out, he could not resist the temptation to look at the photograph. He gently eased it out of the tight slit she had hidden it in and opened it out. It was a picture of a handsome man, taken on a summer day out in the fields. He was standing, arms folded confidently and leaning back in a grandiose fashion, legs apart, and a big grin across his face. He had no shirt on, and his braces hung down the side of his hips. He flipped it over, to see handwriting. In neat copperplate, it read: To my happy Lot, ever yours, David.

41

Lot, he whispered to himself. His mother's name was Charlotte. Everyone called her Lotty. To this David looking back at him from the picture, she was his Lot, his happy Lot, and he tried to imagine all the scenarios that had brought about this peculiar event up here in this old dirty barn.

Chapter five: The Visitor

A horse and cart was parked outside the Golden Goose when he got back from the farm. A boy was holding on to the bridle trying to keep the horse calm, as Harry and an older man were loading the cart up with old rubbish. He could hear them chatting as they clattered and arranged the contents.

"Kids. I can't see them havin' any kids Harry," said the man, dusting down his overalls.

"Well, I know what you mean Tom, but 'er dad would've wanted 'em to. He'd have made a marvellous grandad if he'd lived. Poor Arthur."

"I hope he gets what's comin' to 'im one day," said old Tom.

"It's all turned out the way he wanted," said Harry. "It's 'er I feel sorry for."

They both stopped work and looked studiously into the cart.

"Right old chap, is that the lot then?" said Tom.

"Reckon you could manage any more?" said Harry.

Tom lifted his cap and wiped his brow.

"Suppose I can just about manage to take that broken bicycle off yer 'ands I reckon. Not that I'll get much for it you understand, it being in bits and all."

The conversation was interrupted as he arrived on the scene.

"What's going on, Harry?" he said, his worry showing through at hearing the mention of a bicycle.

"Well, good day to you too," rebuked the landlord, "Never 'eard of 'ello, or 'ow-dy do, ay?"

Once again he sensed the clip behind the ear, as only Harry could deliver.

"Who's this then, Harry?" put in Tom.

"Him? He's me lodger. Pays me half a crown for the attic, he does. It's him what give me the idea."

"You mean to tell me you old bugger," said Tom, "that I'm paying you fer this lot, and you're going to cash in on the space left behind as well?"

"Business is business," smiled Harry.

The mention of the bicycle being removed from the room had created real anxiety. He felt like protesting, but he knew Harry's odd ways by now and, against his own feelings, he tried a polite approach.

"Sorry Harry, I couldn't help overhearing. Were you talking about the bike upstairs?"

"I'm getting rid of some old junk, if you must know. Been there years. Don't remember where the pushbike came from though, but it's all got to go."

They all took Harry's lead and craned their necks up to the attic window poking out of the roof.

"Am I to go and get it then?" Tom piped up.

It was his last chance to say something.

"Look Harry, the cycle belongs to me," he blurted out.

"There's only a frame and a wheel," said Harry. "You don't know what you're on about."

He knew that there was nothing for it but to own up. It would mean admitting that an unknown someone had got the better of him, that he was in an embarrassing situation and exposing himself to ridicule.

"I know it's not all there. I'm looking for the front wheel. Someone's idea of a joke, very funny, I'm sure."

He tried to interject an air of humour in his voice, attempting to sell the idea that he was taking the theft in a spirit of geniality. The two men were not convinced.

"Well, what the bloody hell is it doing up there in my bleeding attic? It's not a bike shed up there, you know."

He tried to explain the events of the last few days to a disbelieving pair of bewildered old men and a boy.

When he had done storytelling Harry said, "Ah, but can you prove it's your bike?" then flashing a fleeting glance at Tom, "You've got to prove beyond doubt that it's your property, else how am I going to know that it's really yours, ay? I'll have no thieving in my pub. What if the real owner comes back for it?"

He felt insulted. It was his bike. Why should he have to produce proof to get back what was his anyway, and Harry was keen enough to sell it for scrap to this Tom, he thought? Thieving was all right, so long as he was the only person doing it. Then again, just what proof did he have? He could not even say what make of bike it was. It was as unique as he was. He knew every weld. He could recall sawing each piece of steel tubing, but remembering any identifiable markings was going to be nigh impossible.

"It's got a saddle bag," he suddenly recollected, "with a puncture kit inside it."

He gestured with his hands to give them an idea of its size. He could tell that they all thought he was an idiot. He waited for Harry to say something

"I haven't got all day," interrupted Tom. "Am I taking it off you or not?"

"Hold on down here a mo, Tom," said Harry, "we'll soon have this settled," and he charged through the door, shouting, "come on young feller, follow me."

He trailed like a lost soul behind the landlord who behaved like a bull raging through his very own china shop. They arrived in the attic room, now cleared out except for the bed and the two pieces of the bicycle resting on the wooden floor. His eyes homed in like magnets to the seat of the bike where his saddlebag was attached. Only to discover that it was not there. For a second or two he stood in the doorway like an angry fool, even though he knew full well that he was in the right.

"Well, it was there last time I saw it."

"Yes, of course it was," said Harry, with a false friendliness that he was in no mood to hide and he leaned out of the open window to Tom below. "Get yourself up here, Thomas old chap, and give us a hand, will you?"

44

He now felt in a desperate pickle. Inside he was a mass of jangling, tightening springs working against each other. There was no way of avoiding a confrontation. He was no good at arguing. His nerves were not built to deal with situations like this. He was not equipped to grapple with the complications that people created, but he had to say something, do something - but what? As he racked his brains and fiddled with the change in his pocket, he tried to bring to mind other aspects of his machine that he could use as proof. Although now, he had to admit, it was a little late in the day, considering they were looking at the chief exhibit sprawled on the floorboards. Any so-called proof now would be meaningless. The question of what to do was solved by the jingling of the coins and rustling of the notes in his pocket. Hiding his worry he walked up to Harry who was closing the window.

"How much is he giving you for this heap of scrap then?" he asked.

"That's none of your bloody business," retorted Harry, sensing a deal coming on.

"Well whatever it is, I'll raise him," he was going to say a fiver. "I'll raise him a whole quid."

Tom's footsteps could be heard approaching. He instinctively knew that Harry would inflate the price and take advantage, and he knew also that Harry would have to make his mind up before the old man burst through the door and give the game away. He could see the burly man weighing up the state of affairs, like an old gambling master.

"Six sovs and she's yours," he said quietly, and as if to add insult to injury he added, "once again."

He dug into his pocket, not quite knowing how much he had been ripped off and dangled a well-used tenner, insisting that they settle up later in the bar. Just as he put the note back, Tom staggered in, half exhausted from the climb.

"Sorry, Tom," said Harry, "seems this piece of junk does belong to him after all."

He gave his old pal a friendly slap on his back.

"Look, it's been a busy morning, come downstairs and have a pint old son, you've earned it!"

As he picked up the pieces of his bicycle Harry turned to him.

"And you can find a bloody home for that heap of shit too. There'll be no place for it up here when I've made this attic into two rooms."

So during the remainder of the week, true to his word, Harry brought in a couple of jobbing builders – reeling in a favour, he called it. The craftsman, Bill Cornwell and his son erected a stud wall thereby dividing the attic into two. When it was done each room shared half of the dormer window. A second door at the top of the narrow staircase was hung at ninety degrees to the old one, which gave access to the newly created room. On Friday morning old Tom delivered an iron bedstead, along with a mattress that had evidently seen better days. By the time the sheets and blankets had been laid over it though, the room began to take on the appearance of a real bedroom.

Mrs Eversage from across the green came in and made the place more like home. She was one of Harry's oldest friends and, if body language and innuendo was anything to go by, she shared more than just an interest in interior decorating. Ena Campbell, a frail lady, who spoke with only the slightest trace of a Scottish accent and was fond of gin, tagged along like a chaperone and accepted the position of Doreen Eversage's gopher as if it had been her reason to be born.

"So, how are you going to attract people up into your bedrooms then, Harry?" teased Mrs Eversage.

"Not the same way as I would to get you up there Dorry, you old saucepot."

"And how would that be as if I didn't know? Swank off that bulge in yer trousers, ay?"

"That's my little nest egg, is that," said Harry, pretending to look proud.

"Ah, is that what you call it then? Well come over 'ere yer daft bugger. I'll give you a taste of inflation, so I will," and they both fell about in fits of laughter that seemed to know no end.

When they had calmed down and wiped their eyes, Harry said, "I'm going to put up a sign in the window."

"What, to let me know when you're feeling a bit fruity?"

"It's an idea, is that," he chuckled, "but no, just one word will do it."

"What word you got in mind, ready?" asked Mrs E.

"Vacancies," said Harry, "vacancies."

As this conversation was going on the front door of the pub swung open. Harry looked round.

"Ah, the cyclist," he said. "Well, it would be if he had a bicycle, that is," and he manufactured a forced laugh.

The humour hit him like a dig in the ribs.

"Don't you pay no attention," said Mrs E, in a mother hen voice. "He's like this with everyone. Here, let me buy you a drink."

He had learned by now not to refuse any hospitality and a glass of dark grey beer was soon frothing from the pump. The contents went down his throat to the incessant chattering of Mrs Eversage, mostly on the subject of hotel guests and some of the horror stories she had picked up from her time in Canada, a country she referred to again and again. She warned against gypsies, vagabonds and motorcyclists. She advised Harry on how to use left over food from breakfast and gave him detailed instructions on how to make all manner of meals from discarded scraps. She went on, and on, and on, and Harry could not get enough of it.

The only thing to shut her up was the timely arrival of the farm workers. They burst in teasing one of the youngest boys on his lack of muscle as they headed straight for the bar. The little chap took it in good humour and he beamed with his sense of belonging, as his hair was ruffled almost affectionately by his work-mates. In the middle of the bunch was Danno, big and heavy-set, looking as young and fit as a draught animal. His hair was thick and very dark, longer at the back than any of the other men. The leading feature on his face was a brow that hinted just slightly of early man, but somehow only served to make him more handsome, or at the very least, worthy of respect. He certainly commanded it from all those around him.

He had never seen his dad in three dimensions before. Even at the wedding he had only seen a recreation of the photograph he had seen countless times. Now he was able to watch how he walked and talked and the way he behaved as a living thing. Danno was better groomed than the other men by far. Whilst they were grimy from a day's work

47

he was different. He wore a suit and a chain hung from the waistcoat and he wore shoes not boots. It was clear that he had not toiled in the fields like the rest of them. The most noticeable thing was the large bag that he had draped across one shoulder. It was a canvas sack with the words ROOKE'S BREWERY stencilled black in upper case letters on it. He lifted it and brought it with a thump on the bar. A silence fell. He looked Harry in the eye.

"There's twenty in there. Will that do you?" he said.

Harry opened the bag and peeped inside, looking but not counting. A faint smell of musk escaped from the opening.

"Aye, twenty will do just fine Danno."

He put his hand in the bag and like a macabre magician pulled out something. It was a dead rabbit, freshly killed like the rest. Everyone watched. Everyone waited. There was hush. He put it back in the sack.

"Right then. It's pints all round, aye?" he declared, to the spontaneous joy of all those present.

Danno looked over the heads of the farm hands as the pub came to life once more, and caught sight of the big boss man.

"Hey Will! Where's old George got to?"

"Call of nature, sir," said Will respectfully.

"He's too fond of nature that one," said Danno. "What he needs is a good bit of flesh sitting at home like me. He wouldn't need to go and get friendly with the bushes then, ay?"

Everyone in the group, except the young lad, realised the joke and fell about laughing. The laughing was forced and unnatural. It did not do to ignore Danno's humour. Sitting quietly in the corner out of sight, someone did ignore it. He took exception to his mother being called a piece of flesh even by his dad, but he kept his own counsel.

George finally arrived, edging timidly into the room. A riotous uproar greeted him. His rough face reddened. He realised that they knew what he had been up to.

"Come on George," said Danno, "let's get them fingers busy on those ivories this time, eh?"

"Yes sir," said George, like a thief who had been caught red-handed. "*One Man Went To Mow*, is it?"

A cheer of agreement went up as he sat down at the piano and raised the well-worn tune.

"One man went to mow, Went to mow a meadow, One man and his dog, Went to mow a meadow."

Was it really a week since he heard this tune being played and this song being sung? He found it hard to believe that seven days had actually passed since his bicycle had been removed. Looking at each and every one of the assembled revellers singing their hearts out, he knew that it could have been any one of them who had pinched it. He wanted to accuse them all, but he also knew how they would pick on him if he did as much as mention his bike. It was clear that he would have to save face and say nothing.

Each new song required yet more beer. The combination fuelled the volume and, with Danno in the chair, that meant singing with as much gusto as possible. It was he who was due the tribute. It was compulsory to enjoy Danno's indulgences. He constantly surveyed his happy band looking for dissenters. No one dared catch his suspecting eye. How hard they worked at the fun. Even Harry, grateful for the gift of twenty freshly killed rabbits, was keen to keep on the right side of his patron. He pulled the pumps and lent his baritone voice to the proceedings as if his life and livelihood depended on it.

The songs ran in exactly the same order as they had a week before. As the *Ten Green Bottles* met their fate, Harry began to search around the bar. He finally found what, or rather, whom he was looking for in the corner of the room sitting quietly almost out of sight.

"Gentlemen, gentlemen," he said in a raised voice, being careful not to actually shout.

"Gentleman. Well, you're all in fine voice, I might say. How on earth can we thank our benefactor for this most enjoyable afternoon?"

A boozy cheer went up. It was a mechanical response, not an answer.

"Well gentlemen, we just so happen to have in our midst one of the finest tenor voices in the county, even in the land, I dare say."

The helpless figure in the corner cursed Harry for his words, and cringed. He pleaded inwardly to be spared what he knew was coming to pass, but the landlord was in full cry.

"My lodger here," Harry announced, gesturing towards the victim, "has a most beautiful song that I ever did hear. He calls it the air from London, or summin, but you'll all know it as *Danny Boy*. Come on lads, let's hear it for the young feller, a round of applause everyone, if you please."

The victim seemed to be rooted to his seat.

"Jump up," Harry ordered politely, "look lively there."

His body raised itself almost by an unseen force. Even as he reluctantly got to his feet and passed through the room full of over exuberant farm hands, George had wasted no time and had begun to play the sweetest introduction the song had ever had. By the time he arrived by the side of the piano it was time to sing.

He had sung the song a thousand times or more. He knew the words as if they were old friends. Every inflection, every tone was at his command. There were places where he added force on the mountainside, and there was pianissimo when the pipes, the pipes were calling. Incredibly George seemed to be in a telepathic connection with him. For a rough farm worker he had an amazing musical gift and the two of them gave a performance that hushed the room and brought the makings of tears into the eyes of these hardened labourers.

Danno soaked up the attention at first. His ego had been inflated by Harry's supposed gift of a singer with an apt song - but as he watched the spellbound faces of his workforce he became uneasy. For once, someone else had control of his men. Another person had their affections in his grasp in such a way that he could not comprehend. The proud smile was in danger of withering away and was replaced with a forced grimace. The teeth shone through the upturned mouth but his eyes burned.

"*Oh Danny Boy, Oh Danny Boy, I love you so.*"

As the last line melted into the final piano flourish, the singer caught his father's eye in the crowd. He knew hate when he saw it. Through the false grin it seemed to be there in abundance. The energetic applause that followed only served to compound this sense of deep dislike.

It was the men who ultimately saved him from this discomfort. They warmly shook their employer's hand and in so doing returned their loyalty to him, repairing his bruised ego in the process. Their action was enough to enable him to step towards the singer. Danno squared up to him and looked him up and down. It was an unnerving moment. Then he took his right hand out of his trouser pocket and offered it to him to shake.

"Well, you can sing, I'll give you that," and then the cold grin widened as he tightened his grip. "Aye, but can you drink?"

He had never imagined his father to be like this. All the stories he had ever been told gave him the impression that he was a hero - a hero with a kind heart at that. He had to admit to himself he was scared of this man.

"I'll have a drink with you," he said, remembering not to refuse. "Thanks."

"A drink he says, boys," Danno said, looking back to his gang of workmen. "He'll have more than one, won't he lads?"

The swell of opinion was expressed in a rowdy cheer and the beer began to flow. By the early evening the workers who had remained to partake were decimated. They lay sprawled over the tables, some lay on the floor. Save for Harry and Ellie, only Danno and his rival were awake, Mrs Eversage had long since gone home, but the tables had been turned. He lost count of just how many jars he had demolished, but he matched his father pint for pint. Danno was barely conscious, whereas he felt as normal as if he had only been drinking the water from Mrs Cartwright's pump.

"I'm not pissed yet you know," slurred Danno, who evidently was.

"Me neither," came the nervous reply, delivered with such polite conceit. "Fancy another, a brandy perhaps?"

"You buying?"

"Why not?"

Harry fixed both of them up with a glass of brandy. Down each throat they went.

"I can keep this up all night long, singer man," said Danno

"You'll join me in another brandy then?"

Harry was all ears and the glasses were refilled. Danno threw his head back and down went the drink.

"Tell him Harry. Tell him I can drink anyone under the table."

Harry did not know whether to reply or not.

"Tell him you bleeding shit, tell that little singing bastard I can out-drink anyone."

"He can you know," stammered Harry. "He can drink anyone under the table."

"Yeah, Harry," barked Danno almost incoherently, "you line up half a dozen beers each. You've got your sodding rabbits."

Harry went and did as he was told. He ordered Ellie to stay in the back and then brought the jugs of ale to the table and lined them up.

"Just you watch now, little songbird."

The drinking began. Danno gulped the beer like a man dying of thirst. His opponent tried to keep pace with his jars of tasteless liquid. Harry watched. He looked at Danno protecting his title - his famous, meaningless drinking crown. Then he turned his attention to his lodger. He could see he was playing a dangerous game.

"I hope you know what you're doing, my lad," he said.

"Just having a friendly drink. That's all."

"I think you know what I mean," warned the landlord.

"Course he knows, don't you singer boy? You going to fall down to the floor," the words were barely comprehensible.

They finally emptied the last glass at about the same time. Danno's eyes were out of control in their sockets as he tried to form speech.

"Let's chase them down with another brandy, Harry."

Harry had never seen the like of it before. He was given a handful of silver coins and he filled up the two glasses once more. The brandy had to be virtually fixed into Danno's hand. He was by now talking gibberish, holding on to the very idea of a drinking competition with a tenuous grip.

"Bottoms up," he said quietly, as he raised his glass to his lips and sipped. Danno crudely swallowed it down and sat very still for a few minutes, gazing forwards, looking but not seeing anything.

Within two minutes of the brandy entering Danno's system he was out cold. He collapsed on to the table then slithered to the floor in a heap.

"Well, I'll be buggered," said Harry. "You better watch your step from now on old son."

"I'm going out for a walk," he replied.

It was a pleasant Friday evening as he left the pub's smell of stale beer. Outside it was a summer evening with air full of nature's perfumes that kissed his face and calmed his soul. He breathed it all in whilst Harry's last words buzzed round in his head. He passed the old chestnut tree as he headed down the lane towards the hill that had brought him to the village a week ago. He half made the decision to carry on walking, to descend the lane and keep on going to the world of reds and blues and greens, but he had arrived with a bike and he would have to leave with it, surely? He turned his head to see the pub. The lights in the Golden Goose had just come on, and somewhere inside was the man who would one day be his father. He knew there was going to be hell to pay when he came round, so why not keep going? He stood there for quite some time trying to decide what to do.

In the end he put one foot in front of the other and began to trek down the hill. The early evening dusk was diminishing the light everywhere and the overhanging trees that formed the road tunnel made things even darker. An old sign in the verge, draped in thicket and brambles, came into view. He was looking at the back of it. He could see the rusty brackets holding the sign onto equally worn posts. The sign was rectangular and laid on its side with a half-moon shape rising from the centre of the top edge. He was soon past it and could see its grubby white face. The sign's black edge was encrusted with cats' eyes. So too were the six large black letters that spelled out the name of the village EMPTON. The whole thing was made of cast iron - each letter moulded to stand proud. In the half circle at the top were three other initials, equally moulded WCC. He studied it for a few moments. The last time he had passed the sign it displayed the words Please Drive Carefully Through Our Village written beneath the village name. He began to wonder just how far this transformation extended. Maybe the world of reds, blues and greens no longer existed at all anymore. Yet he had seen colours on the far distant horizon the day he went to the hilltop, so he decided to resume the march.

He had only gone a few steps when he heard whistling and then the tramp of regular foot strides coming up the hill. It stopped him in his tracks. Looking downhill he watched the bend in the road to see who would come whistling round it. The tune turned out to be the *Radetzky March* and, in perfect step with the beat of the music, a figure

53

emerged from the gloom. It drew closer, ever closer. The dark figure was female. He leaned against the sign and waited. As she finally caught sight of him she stopped whistling and slowed her march to a walk. She was the first to speak as she closed the distance between them.

"Heck of a hill that one," she said with an attractive voice.

"You want to try cycling up it," he replied.

"Ah, a cyclist, ay?"

"Sort of," he said.

She had now arrived and she stretched out her arm to shake hands.

"Hi. Well that makes me a sort of hiker then. Pleased to meet you."

He could now see her face and he was not ready for what was to greet him. She was nothing short of a goddess, a movie star in the flesh. She radiated beauty. Her perfect features changed his curiosity into a startled awkwardness. Her body was sheer perfection too. She wore a white shirt that could barely contain the swollen shapes therein. A rucksack, complete with rolled up tent and sleeping bag, clung to her back and the straps over her shoulders only served to display matters even more provocatively. Below she wore light grey shorts made of denim that clung tightly to her thighs and left nothing to the imagination as to what existed between her legs. It seemed an embarrassing few seconds before he held out his own hand and he returned her polite greeting.

"Have you come a long way?" he asked her, regaining some of his composure.

"I feel like I've been on the go for years," she laughed, "my feet are killing me."

He looked down to her walking boots. Two of the shapeliest legs fitted into them. It was hard to believe that things so naturally sensual could ever feel pain. She looked to the side of him and read the sign.

"Empton. Well, at least the map's right. The guidebook mentions that there's a pub here. Is it any good?"

"It's okay if you like the rural life," and before he knew what he was doing he said, "Do you fancy a beer?"

"Well thank you very much, I think I just might. You know, I really think I'm going to like Empton."

54

With all plans of escape now evaporated, they climbed back to the village and were soon nearing the Golden Goose.

"Oh, look!" she said with touching excitement as she caught sight of the sign in the window, "they've got vacancies. I suppose they mean a room and not a job?"

"It's half a room, actually, but he'll charge you full whack. Just watch old Harry in there."

"Oh, it's Harry is it, on first name terms already? Been here a while have you?"

"I arrived a week ago."

"So what happened to your cycling holiday, then?"

"I'm still hunting for my stolen bicycle, sorry to say. You really have to be on your guard you know. They're a bit odd round here, them being a rural lot you know."

"Oh well, never say die, ay?"

And they went inside.

Chapter six: Devices And Desires

In the dim warm light of the bar she looked more overpoweringly beautiful than she had done outside. Her hair was dark, though not too long, and her face was silky smooth with perfectly shaped eyes and lips that shone like precious stones set in a satin cushion. He was smitten. He could not help it. That is the way it was from the minute he first saw her in the lane. He could not help wondering what it would be like to kiss her. He imagined it as he looked at her. Her sense of life and the obvious enjoyment she had of it infected him to the core.

Ellie was helping Harry to collect glasses from the tables that appeared to be strewn with what looked like corpses. Danno was still on the floor, his once clean suit now covered in dust. The girl found the sight amusing after she got over the shock. Harry stopped what he was doing as he heard the two of them come in.

"Looks like you've had a shoot-out," she said.

"No miss. More like a drink-out, you might say," said Harry.

"Ah, I see. Nobody won then?"

"Oh aye. There was a winner all right," he said nodding towards the cyclist.

She fixed him with an admiring stare. He would have been happy to look at that smile forever.

"Well, well, bumped your head in the process, I see," she said glancing at his head wound. "You'll have to let me in on your little secret, won't you?"

He could not think how to answer so he gave a short laugh. She turned to Harry.

"Your sign says vacancies. How much?"

"Half a crown to you miss," he replied, rubbing his hands like he was washing them. "That includes breakfast. Bacon and eggs and coffee or tea."

She slipped the rucksack off her back in one complete motion and rested it against the bar. Then she took out a small purse and handed over the large silver coin.

"Have you got anywhere I can freshen up?"

"I've only got a scullery. My girl will rig up a sheet to give you a bit of privacy. Will that do?"

"That will do very nicely indeed."

Harry called Ellie to get a sheet.

The young woman lifted herself onto a stool and sighed with exhaustion.

"Are you still up for that drink?" she asked remembering his offer.

"Oh, yes. Sorry. What would you like?"

"A beer. Not a half but a pint. A whole pint to myself, thank you."

"Two pints please, Harry."

"You're some feller, I'll give you that," and he leaned slightly towards the lady as he pulled the drinks. "He's just drunk Daniel Harper under the table, and he's still as sober as a judge. Sings like a canary too."

The name Harper hit him like a brick. At least now he knew his surname.

"A cyclist and a singer," she said giving him that playful smile, "and just what other talents do you have, I wonder?"

She giggled quietly as she watched him struggle for an answer. She was happy toying with him like this.

The glasses of ale were soon on the bar. She was thirsty, as thirsty as he had been on the day he fought the hill. Some of the beer spilled from the side of her mouth as she drank hurriedly. A trickle ran down her upturned neck and disappeared from view into her shirt. He watched the passage of the droplets and wanted so badly to follow them. When she had finished she was gasping for breath. He even found the sound and motion of her laboured breathing almost too much to bear.

"You not drinking then?" she said looking at his still full glass. "No wonder you're still sober. I think I've discovered your little secret."

Just to prove her wrong, he drank. It did not take long. It never did here.

"Do you fancy some fresh air, a bit of a walk maybe?" he suggested, hoping she would say yes.

"Walk!" she exclaimed. "I'll have you know I've been on my feet for most of the day. What I need is a wash and then it's to bed."

Oh lucky bed he thought.

"Right oh! I dare say I'll see you in the morning then?"

"Up with the lark, that's me," and she shouted through to Harry to enquire about the scullery.

He came through and told her it was nearly ready. So she got up and made her way past the bar.

"Well then. Goodnight," he said.

"You too. Sleep tight."

Some hope with just a stud wall between us he thought.

The twilight was almost past when he stood outside once more. It was colder. Above him the black sky was punctuated with pinpricks of white light. The brightest of the stars were making their appearance. He did not know where to go now. Maybe he should delay any escape until tomorrow. Tomorrow now had promise of an altogether different kind. Before he knew it he arrived at the church on the hill. The place was full of peace. With a few more paces he made it to the oak tree and leaning on the gate there he could see other pinpricks of light, man-made light from far away places glowing softly yellow.

The horizon where the tiny lights could be seen was very far away - forty or fifty miles on the other side of a great valley. At walking pace it could mean ten or twelve hours without a break to reach it, and once there, then what? More walking? He could average fifteen miles per hour on his bicycle, faster for the first few downhill miles. He could reach the world he understood in three hours or thereabouts. For the sake of a front wheel, it was quite possible. The wheel, where was the wheel?

No amount of thinking could alter the fact that the only practical solution was the salvaging of the last bit of his machine. He would have to stay and hunt it down. Then there was another more recent reason why he should stay. So that was it then, decision made. Find the wheel and see what transpired with his newly found friend. Or was it the other way round?

He left the dark shape of the oak tree swaying in the night breeze and tramped back to the church. He passed the old building and came to the path that led to the vicarage. His curiosity pricked, he went to explore where the gravel drive headed slightly downhill to a large house. He had admired it the first day he entered the village. A grand Georgian affair built on an almost square plot, the front entrance graced by a mock Greco/Roman pediment held up by fluted pillars. The front door was tall and thin - two doors in fact. One of them was slightly ajar allowing light to spread out in a wedge over the gravel. One of the ground floor rooms also glowed with a weak, grey light. The curtains were not drawn and he could see shelves full of books suggesting a library or a study. He made his way to conceal himself behind a rose bed and looked through the window.

Inside could be seen the vicar still dressed in his cassock. Even in the dimly lit room he could clearly see his dog collar. The vicar was standing in front of a large chair talking to someone. He could only see the back of the chair but it was plain to see that whoever was sitting there needed help or comfort by the way the vicar behaved. He knelt down and put his hand on the person's shoulder and took out a handkerchief. The person took it. The talking continued. This went on for a while but then the person, a woman, rose from the chair and sought to embrace the priest. He held her like a father would, patting her back. The person was his mother. The embrace was not an intimate one and did not last long. He moved to grip her shoulders and held her at arms length. His lips were moving and his head nodded now and again emphatically. On one occasion she nodded back rapidly, as if in agreement. It was like watching a silent film what with everything being in black and white.

With a sense of determination they both left the room and the study light went out. Seconds later they emerged through the door and crunched their way over the gravel to what looked like a garage, which is just what it turned out to be. As the priest opened the garage doors the back of a large black car was revealed. His mother remained on the drive whilst the churchman squeezed down the side of his car and started the engine. As soon as it had been reversed on to the gravel path and stopped his mother jumped in and off it rolled towards the village. He followed on foot half running.

From the end of the church drive he could see the shiny black Rover stop outside the Golden Goose. The two occupants got out and entered the pub. Less than a minute later his mother, the vicar and the landlord carried a comatose Danno into the back seat of the car. The priest shook the landlord's hand and then he held the door open for his mother and they got back in. He concealed himself in the shadows as he watched the car speed past him and head down the lane towards Bofindle farm.

He felt pangs of sadness to have witnessed the past few minutes. Sadness mixed with something akin to guilt, or self-consciousness at least. He was not meant to have seen any of this. It was not so much the fact that he had been spying on the vicarage, nor watching his drunken father being bundled into a car. It was that he was not supposed to be here in the first place watching these events unfold. What he had seen was a time before his own life, yet here he was seeing it first hand and he was somehow involved. After all, it was he who had caused his father to pass out. His mother's distress had infected him once more, like it had done in the woods. He tried to imagine her home life in that grubby farmhouse. What was it like to be a piece of flesh? What would her morning bring when she awoke.

Then, in his own selfish way, he wondered what the morning would bring for him, when Danno remembered how he lost his crown.

From his hiding place he watched the remainder of the drinking party stagger out of the pub's door and head off in various directions. It was time to go back and get to bed too.

"My, oh my," said Harry as he walked back in. "Welcome home the conquering hero."

"I've just seen him being driven off," he said. "He's still out cold, isn't he?"

"Oh aye. He's ripe for a bear's head come daylight," said Harry with a wicked chuckle.

"Best I keep out of his way then, don't you think?" he asked, searching for reassurance.

"He'll either want your head or he'll be filled with admiration and pay you some respect, he will. And I wouldn't like to bet either way," he looked at the worried face before him and could not help himself. "Actually, I reckon the odds are on you getting your head ripped off." |

At the look of horror staring back at him Harry burst into a self-satisfied belly laugh.

"Mind you," he added, "that ain't all you've conquered tonight, my lad."

"It ain't, I mean, it isn't?"

"Oh no. Her upstairs, the raving beauty, she's been asking questions about you."

"She has?"

"What kind of questions?"

"The sort that means only one thing."

"One thing?"

"Aye lad. I reckon she's got her hooks out for you."

"You're pulling my leg, Harry."

"You mark my words, if she ain't."

Another face now looked back at the landlord. It had changed from worry to apprehensive excitement in less than a moment. Harry sighed with an amused grin that stretched from ear to ear.

"Fancy a nightcap before I lock up?"

"I fancy getting into my bed Harry."

"Funny, that's just what she said too," he replied, enjoying the humour of the moment. "Sleep well."

He climbed the stairs to the sound of locks being locked and bolts being shot as Harry closed the pub for the night. The nearer he got to his room the stronger the smell of scent. If it had been designed to send men crazy with passion then it worked.

Sleep well, Harry had said. He could not. He stared at the newly painted wall at the foot of his bed knowing who lay on the other side. The night was warm. Even the bricks and the wooden structure of the inn had absorbed the heat of the day. The stored heat in the building made the room act like an oven. All that was covering him was a single sheet and, apart from a layer of perspiration, he was naked.

Even in his room, he was aware of the demons that danced in the girl's perfume. They taunted him and painted pictures of her lying naked on her bed just as he was. Another of their spells cast them on the same bed together. He could feel her hips, run his hand up her waist and across up to her breasts. The magic of the aroma was so powerful that he could feel her nipples under the palm of his hand as he stroked her. As he moved it down across her belly, her back arched with the pleasure she was receiving from him. Now descending he could feel her pubic hairs with his fingers. He was now in the garden of the Holy of Holies. It was a moist garden and she placed her commanding hand on the top of his wrist and pushed his hand further down. His finger sank into her, sliding with no resistance into that wet warmth only a woman can give. The perfume made him look into her face, a face he could not help but love. Her eyes beautifully caressed his heart and soul and drew his mouth to hers. Her lips engulfed his own as if to melt him and every time he caught her breath against his face a fresh wave of ecstatic pleasure energised his whole being. He moved his body so that she was beneath him. He felt her naked heat on his chest and thighs as he moved over her. His eager penis searched out the blessed place as he held her in his arms.

Then an owl screeched outside. In an instant the vision had turned to dust and except for an aching erection there was nothing at all to show for it - but she was still behind the wall and the demons would not leave him be. They continued to torment him in other ways. They paraded Harry's words before him, repeating how she had been asking for him and that she had got her hooks out for him. The spirits of the scented bottle even suggested that he should see if her door was open. It would be a sign, a sign of invitation. Even if it was not open, he was cajoled into the notion that it would be the right thing to knock gently on it and wake her. Yes, they cried, she is waiting for you.

He had not realised that his heartbeat had quickened considerably until he sat upright. He caught sight of the iron bar between his legs. The skin there was so tight it had become uncomfortable. He drew his trousers on and made for the landing. There before him was her door. He touched it, but it did not move. He pushed a little harder with the same result. As if by someone else's will, his hand had become a fist and was poised, knuckles turned forwards to knock. He reached back to strike and stopped. A whispering voice of reason was begging him to stop. What right had he to proceed? Had he not invented it all, but the demons fought back with reasons of their own. They danced in his mind and spoke about how it was not a figment of his imagination that he was attracted to her and it was not a trick that she had liked him. What was the harm in pursuing discovery? Had not all man's great achievements been reached by breaking into unknown territory? Knock. Go on man. Knock.

He must have stood there for several minutes, engaged in this almost three-way conversation. In the end, the indecisiveness of it all took away the purity of the vision. It was madness to think that she would ever have agreed to invite him in and make his imaginings come true. He felt stupid and annoyed at himself. Back in his bed he tried to sleep. A mist of tiredness did settle over him by degrees, and eventually managed to put him out of his misery.

Singing interrupted his sleep, and he opened his eyes to find it was Saturday morning. He loved Saturdays and the young feminine voice made the expectation of the day even greater. She was la-la-ing the tune and he could only hazard a guess that it was the folk song *Linden Lea*. He fluffed up his pillow on the headboard and sat up to listen. It had to be the sweetest way to wake up, he admitted. With some satisfaction he was pleased that the demons had not won the night before. Maybe now he could get to know her properly and let nature take its course in both of them. Maybe they could explore the unknown territory together.

Arriving first downstairs he made for the scullery and got himself clean. Ellie was already busy there having just washed her doll's clothes in the stone sink.

"Where's Harry?" he asked.

"Out the back, skinning rabbits," she said in her quiet childishness.

"Is he going to be finished for breakfast?"

"Spec so," she said, and ran off to hang her washing on a low twig on a tree.

He watched her stand on tiptoe to reach but could not quite make it.

"You need to grow an inch or two," he said, walking out to her, tenderly picking her up and lifted her up to the real washing line. "There you go. They'll be dry in no time up there."

She quickly began to peg out the three little knitted dresses as her feet dangled high above the ground. As the girl was busy he became aware of a presence nearby. He turned his head to be greeted by the smile from heaven.

"Nice to see a man who likes children," she said.

She stood in the doorway, leaning on the frame, with a small bag draped over her shoulder. To him she was loveliness personified. Everything about her, the way she looked, the way she talked, even the way she simply was, had him besotted. He smiled back whilst Ellie finished her job. As he put her back on the garden path the child looked up to him with that smile, the smile from the album.

"I'll give you a shout when they're dry, then," he said to her.

He went up to the woman and asked her if she had slept well.

"Hardly slept at all," she confessed, "at least for the first couple of hours. You'd think I'd have dropped off straightaway after a day's walking, wouldn't you. But it was too hot up there. I heard you arrive though."

"Went for an evening stroll. It's nice up on the hill near the church, especially at night."

"Really. Maybe you could show me. After breakfast, perhaps."

"It would be my pleasure, madam."

He gave a slightly theatrical bow of the head to humorously emphasise just what a pleasure it would be. In his heart he was glad he had not gone into her room during the night. She was too special to be rushed. This way, he thought, she would grow to like him and, as time passed they would be able to take things at their own pace. If his vision of the dark night was meant to happen at all, then it was better to develop this way in the light of a warm summer's day.

Breakfast was duly provided. Harry used the occasion to embarrass, and tease him with innuendo and suggestive remarks generally on the subject of romance. The woman found the whole matter rather comical and thought the shy way he tried to deal with Harry's leg pulling quite touching. Even the victim of the ribbing could not fail but derive some pleasure from the landlord's jibes, once he realised it was possibly helping to cement his new friendship.

The village was busy that morning. A large carriage, pulled by a couple of dark grey horses was filling with people near the green. They saw Mrs Eversage and her friend walking up from their cottages together, each clutching a voluminous shopping bag. They were deep in conversation and did not hear the greeting he gave them as they climbed aboard. The driver, a mournful looking soul, made a clicking sound out of the corner of his mouth as soon as they sat down, and the horses' hooves hit the road. The chattering party, bundled in two neat rows in the carriage, headed for the lane that led to the memorial and the fateful milestone.

They watched it vanish behind the pub as they made their way to the church. Soon they had passed the old building and crossed the gate by the oak tree. A few more paces and they had climbed the fence beyond to where the hill fell away, revealing the entire view. The air was clear. There was not a trace of haze, even in the distance, not even any clouds. Far away the colours remained.

"What do you think?" he asked. "Worth yesterday's climb?"

"I had no idea from the road. I couldn't see for the trees everywhere. It's beautiful."

"No," he said. "You're the one who's beautiful."

The minute he said it, he wished he had not. Only at breakfast he had decided to take things easy and here he was now rushing headlong out of control.

"I think I can see Salisbury Cathedral, look over there," she said, seemingly in a world of her own.

She obviously had not heard his remark. He had got away with it. He promised himself to guard against any other outbursts. With his hand shielding his eyes he followed the line of her pointing finger and could just make out a pale golden spike rising from the far horizon. The distance was impossible to judge but, if she was right, it was the first piece of geographical information he had had since he arrived. Salisbury, Wiltshire, he murmured to himself.

"Well, that's the view done. Any more places of interest?" she asked.

"Not really," he said. "There's a wood, full of wildlife, but that's about it."

"Oh come on now," she said in disbelief. "There has to be something to have kept you here a whole week?"

"Don't you worry," he said. "Once I've got my wheel found and fixed back on, I'm back down that hill."

"You'd go back the way you came?" she said, bringing her delicious eyes to bear upon him. "Not me. It's onwards and upwards for me."

She took a deep breath of morning air. He loved the way she could fill her chest like that.

"So, where's your next port of call?" he asked.

"Oh, anywhere north of here, really," she said. "The ultimate goal is John O'Groats. That's if I don't go and spend daddy's money all at once. It's supposed to be a camping trip. Guesthouses are out of bounds he says, but what the heck. I've had a fortnight of tents. A girl's allowed a few little luxuries along the way. What do you say?"

"Who says guesthouses are out of bounds?"

"Oh, that's daddy. He does."

"He's made you go on this trip, then?"

"He said I need a goal in life. So I said all right. I'll walk from Land's End to John O'Groats, how's that for a goal? It's no great hardship really. I love the outdoors, camping, walking and all that."

65

"Some dad. Actually letting you go on your own like this," he said.

"What do you expect from a retired general? He looks upon me as a son with an extra big chest," she laughed, but then the smile vanished. "My Mum got blitzed when I was only little, see? So I've been brought up just like a boy by a father who only understands men."

He was mildly confused by all this and began to view her differently. On the outside she was all the things he felt a woman should be, fit, shapely and charming, everything in fact required to turn a man's head and keep it turned. But inside she was pure steel, cold like a bayonet. She oozed femininity on the one hand, but was clearly as determined as a soldier on the other. The confusion permeated through to his plans for an assault on her heart, or her body at any rate, and again he thanked his lucky stars that he had not knocked on her door during the night. It was quite possible that she could have knocked his head off had he gone in and tried it on with her. Privately though, as he considered his own existence, he envied her energy, her life and her freedom.

"Do you want to see the woods, then?" he said at last. "Squirrels and birds everywhere."

"I'll give it a miss if you don't mind. I rather think I'll make a start on my next leg. I reckon I can put in a good twenty miles after that bed and breakfast."

She sensed the cold front pass over him. His heart chilled. She was taking the sunshine away.

"You never know, you might bump into me again on the road, if you find your confounded wheel," she said with an air of mild indifference.

"When do you plan to get going?" he asked.

"Well, it looks like it's going to be a fine day. No time like the present I suppose."

They made their way back past the church and arrived at the Golden Goose. Within two minutes she was back with her rucksack slung over her shoulder. They strolled past the old war memorial and the roadside seat. After a couple of miles they reached the milestone where he had fallen. Here was an appropriate place to say goodbye.

He knew his heart was not breaking, but the pain of impending loss ached inside him. He wished she could stay. He knew she had to go.

"A kiss for luck?" he said, taking his chance.

She slid the rucksack to the ground and stood close to him.

"Why not," she said, pressed her lips to his and placed her warm hands against his face.

It was not a passionate kiss and it did not last long, but it was given tenderly. Even when it was over and she said goodbye and disappeared over the rise in the road he could still feel her. Her kiss and her presence remained. She had etched herself on his soul. It seemed like she would remain there forever.

Chapter seven: The Job

Even as he turned to face Empton he knew that something of his self had gone over that hill with the girl. She, on the other hand, would not have been aware of it in the slightest he concluded. Even now, as she undoubtedly marched further away, he was clear in his own mind that she had made no place for him in hers. He had the feeling that by the end of the day he would be consigned to the dustbin of her memory - but some part of him had left with her. With that kiss she had partly absorbed him, like a portion of his ghost. The rest of him wanted to follow, only it was the sensible part, the bit of him that always weighed things up, that had been left behind. The sensible mind said that everything revolved around finding his wheel - it had become his private emblem of freedom.

His sense of frustration sank deeper the closer he drew to the village. Even the black and white view of everything was getting on his nerves. The monotonous monochrome was gradually sapping his spirit. He longed to see the world in colour like he once did. He was sick of the masses of shades of grey.

It was a slow walk along the country lane. He seemed to have lost his vigour. Now and again he stopped dead in his tracks. It was as if he had misplaced himself somewhere. He imagined how the girl would have felt if her boots had been stolen. She would have become the walker unable to walk. Would she then be free? Would she still be looked upon as a walker, free to go or stay? Her boots made up some of the person she was, in the same way his bicycle made up some of who he was too - and that is how it felt. It was not simply a case that something of his was gone. The only way to describe it was that part of him was missing. Just as she would not have been the walker anymore, he no longer felt like the cyclist he once was. She had gone and taken her freedom with her and his sense of being trapped deepened.

He was so lost in thought that he did not even hear the rhythm of a horse's hooves behind him until the sound had almost drawn level. He looked around to see the old man Tom at the reins of a pony and trap. Ellie and Harry were behind him. The trap was full of produce, mostly foodstuffs. He could see masses of vegetables and fruit.

"You said somethin' to offend her then?" said Harry from his high position.

The landlord could see the vague look on the walker's face.

"We just passed her on the road back from Wexby market. Your girlfriend."

"She's off to Scotland, walking holiday. And she's not my girlfriend," he said trying to hide his misery.

"What's she want to go to bloody haggis country for?" Harry said with a sneering laugh.

"Land's End to John O'Groats. Looks like you'll be putting your vacancy sign up again."

Harry's grin dropped. He was dumfounded that such an important consideration had failed to cross his own mind until now and the look on his face could not hide how he felt about all the half-crowns he would be losing.

"Any road, you want a lift back?" he asked after a moment.

He said yes please and jumped up, squeezing little Ellie into the middle of the seat between him and Harry. Somehow the contact of people had slightly warmed him and he felt a primitive glow of faint happiness as the horse dutifully pulled them along.

The day was warming up. The small carriage created a dry curtain of light grey dust that hung in the air behind them as they plodded slowly back to the pub. They reached the village in time. Tom helped Ellie down when they pulled up alongside the Golden Goose and everyone helped to take the provisions inside. When he had finished helping out, he could not make his mind up whether to go to his room or wander around some of the places he had not visited yet.

The warm day outside beckoned with summer promise and so he bid good day to one and all and headed for the great outdoors. With a determined stride he was soon past the church gate and climbing up away from the village towards the place where he had emerged from the wood that day. Only when he reached that opening in the trees he carried on along the lane.

Everywhere was densely vegetated and the cool smells all around were a heady concoction of scents from flowers and leaves. The chirping and quiet twittering of birds created their own atmosphere of calm. Eventually the trees on the left-hand side thinned to reveal fields rich with wheat waving in the light air behind a low hawthorn hedge.

He came to a gate in the hedge and stopped to rest. As he watched billions of ears of corn perform a ballet in the breeze it occurred to him that here was perhaps the best place of all to hide something like a bicycle wheel, at least until the harvest arrived. The thought made no apparent lasting impression, partly because proving such a theory right would have meant a mammoth search of acres of heavily cultivated farmland. There were no guarantees that even after such a painstaking survey that the last part of his jigsaw would ever be found. He left the gate dismissing all notions of tramping countless fields and carried on down the lane.

Now and then he thought he could see something glinting out of the corner of his eye. When he went to look it either turned out to be a curved wet leaf reflecting the sun or the sparkle from the little dyke that ran along the outside of the wood on the right. He got the feeling that he was being deliberately taunted, both by nature and by man, and he still could not get the girl out of his mind. There was frustration that his wheel remained lost, and there was frustration in the way the girl had stirred up his desires. He found it hard to tell which was the greater.

As the road curved gently right he finally came to the end of the wood quite abruptly. A single dirt track ran from the right-hand side of the lane, flanking the wood's end and, from an old wooden post, a weathered and rusting metal sign squeaked softly as it swung from its rusty hinges. He could see that no professional sign-writer had made it, but could clearly make out the words Bofindle Farm. The black letters had an abandoned look about them as they clung to the remains of a flaking white background. Far away, at the bottom of the gently twisting track he was able to see the shapes of the two barns, from behind which a smoking chimney poked out. Now he knew where the lane led and his belief strengthened that his wheel was there in the farm somewhere.

He was heading down the track before he knew it. Each step tightened his state of nerves, prising his eyes wide open like a wild animal ever watchful for other people. With a heightened stare of alert he swung his head to look behind, fearful that someone should be following. At any moment he was poised to dive into the wood's end and disappear into the undergrowth. Then he remembered the dog and he wondered whether or not he should turn back. He was halfway along when he saw figures in the distance emerging from behind the barn. There were five of them. He crouched, bolted and was hidden in a matter of seconds. He shrank into a tight ball. It seemed ages before they marched past the bush that shielded him. It was hard for him to see anything, so thick were the leaves, but he heard them pass and the sound of their feet tramping in unison receded until he felt it safe to emerge once more out onto the track.

All became quiet and at length he carried on. About three-quarters of the way along the track the trees at the end of the wood made way for a field. He could see that it had recently been mowed. The field was quite large, a big square of land, and was flanked on three sides by the wood. There was no time to stop and stare. With an ever-quickening pulse he made it to the Dutch barn where he hid once more within the hay bales. It was only when he caught his breath that he realised the field was the same one he had crossed a week or so before.

It was a while before he felt comfortable enough to leave the shelter of the hay and begin the job of rummaging around in the barn.

The search proved fruitless. Even when he remembered the lean-to and eased open the clattering tin door as quietly as he could, all he discovered for his pains were lengths of rope, pitchforks and two worthless-looking wheelbarrows. There was no sign of a wheel at all.

He wanted to hit out at something. He underwent a rage inside. It was anger, anger that he should have to be putting himself through this nervous torture and, though he accepted that he was going to have to visit the brick barn once more, his nerves wanted no part of it. It was only the picture in his head that kept him going, the picture of a gleaming bicycle wheel. He could see it in his mind. He could see him grabbing it, running back to the Golden Goose, taking the other pieces out of the coal shed behind the pub, fixing it all together and cycling off never to return.

By the time all this had gone through his mind he was slipping through an ample opening in the barn door and, as he gently heaved the door closed behind him, he saw that the dog was not in its kennel, or at least the chain was not there. It was only a brief moment of silence, just enough to listen for signs of life. There were none. The first thing he did was to check the animal enclosures. One by one he looked in the cattle mangers, kicking the straw away with his foot, waiting for the clunk of a metal rim to be heard. Nothing. All he could hear was the scream of frustration that he wanted to yell out but could not. After ten minutes of rummaging around he gave up. He had been up the stairs before, so instead he made a thorough search of the workshop and the area around the tractor. There was nothing there either. That only left the house, an altogether different prospect. He went to one of the great wooden doors, put his shoulder to it and heaved. As it opened the sight of Danno and the dog greeted him. Their eyes met. A chemical reaction took place in a fraction of a second, a bad reaction.

Danno was half dressed, his whole body and face twisted by illness. The dog, a black bullmastiff, looked no happier to see him either. It could sense the fear that he was unable to hide. The top of its muzzle was wrinkled concertina-like, revealing its front teeth and long white canines. It tried to growl from the pit of its throat. Only it was prevented from doing this by the tightness of the chain that restrained it. Danno looked beyond him into the interior of the building, searching for a clue as to why this man was poking around on his farm. He then focused his bloodshot stare on the intruder.

"What the fuck are you doing in my barn, singer man?" said Danno.

There was no reply. He could not speak. The terror and shock were acting like a drug rendering him speechless. The dog managed an ear-splitting bark. He almost jumped off the ground with fright, as if a bomb had gone off nearby.

"Well, I'm waiting," Danno spat out.

He could not believe this was his dad speaking to him.

"I was looking for you, as a matter of fact," he blurted out feebly.

"So, you've fucking found me. So what?"

"I was wondering if…" the words were tumbling out of his mouth by themselves. The need to create a reason for his presence in the barn other than the real one was taking his tongue on a journey it had no control over and, pressurised by his own nervousness, he completed the sentence, "If you had a job?"

"Job? What sort of sodding job?"

"Helping out, you know, on the farm."

Danno cradled his head in the palm of his hand. He looked like he was going to be sick. When he finally looked up again his face was like a death mask.

"Never mind a job. I'd like to know your fucking secret?" he asked after a couple of steadying breaths.

He was not sure if Danno was referring to the lost bike or what.

"I don't know what you mean. Secret?"

"Yeah, what's your secret? How come you don't feel like a pile of shit?"

It suddenly came to him like a flash. He had virtually forgotten about the night before. The absence of any ill effects of his own had given him no cause to recall it. If he was to be honest he did not understand the reason for it either. The poisoned eyes waited for a reply. Desperate to give a reason he recalled some advice he once received and thought it might provide a welcomed light-hearted answer.

"The secret to staying sober," he said, "is never to drink from a wet glass."

Danno's face managed a flicker of a smile.

"Pratt," was all he said, but the friction between them had eased, very slightly. "So what job could you do on a modern farm then, Caruso?"

"I'm good with machines," he said.

"Oh yeah. What kind of machines?"

"Any kind. I'm a bit of a tinkerer."

"Oh aye?" said Danno, thoughtfully. He began to scratch at the stubble on his chin, still thinking and moved his nauseous gaze deep into the barn. "You see that tractor behind you?"

He knew it was there but he turned round to look at it anyway.

"Yes," he said.

"Reckon you could tinker with that. Think you could get her running?"

"I can have a go."

"There's a fiver in it for you if you drive her out of here under her own steam."

"What if it needs parts?" he asked.

"I'll get hold of them, just tell me what she needs. I'll get 'em. Deal?"

"Deal," and they shook hands to the sound of a growling black dog at the foot of his master.

Inside the barn they both beheld the tractor. It was a Fordson, though he had no idea what colour it was. He judged its age to be from the thirties. The motor was a simple four-cylinder engine. There was rust everywhere. A snapped fan belt hung limply at the front, giving at least one reason why the thing did not go. Looking deeper into the power plant he was unable to find a starter motor. He was just about to add that to the list of parts he would need, when he noticed a crank handle resting on an ornate cast-iron driver's seat. He picked it up and rammed it through the hole at the front of the machine. With a grunt of effort the pistons moved. The sound of the compression was like an old man gasping for breath after a long sleep, but at least his guts sounded ready for action.

"Is she a goer then?" asked Danno.

"All depends," he replied, "I need to make a list of bits. Have you got any fuel? This old thing runs on petrol and paraffin."

"Like I said, you just tell me what you want. I have ways of getting everything I need around here."

"I bet she needs an oil change too."

"You leave all that to me. Your job's to get the old bitch working again, all right?"

"Yes, but what about tools?"

"Help yourself to what's on the workbench. I'm going back to the house."

"I don't suppose you've got some paper and a pencil, have you?" he asked. Judging by Danno's questioning expression, he felt he needed to qualify the request. "So I can write a list."

"Look, follow me to the house and wait outside. I'll find you some scrap paper."

Danno chained the dog back up to its iron spike when they crossed the yard, and the animal flopped lazily back into its kennel. The inside of the house, as far as he could see, was dark and dismal. He was looking down a long hallway. There were doors on either side of it and at the far end he could see a pantry through a door that had been left half open. He heard muffled talking.

"Thought you'd have finished that by now," came Danno's voice.

He could hear his mother's reply but was unable to make out any words. A few more inaudible bits of conversation wafted in and out as Danno moved further inside. Listening intently he moved right up to the open doorway. There were more words, distinguishable this time.

"It's that cyclist from the village. I'm getting him to fix that old Fordson."

"Oh, good," replied his mother.

"Good don't come into it Lotty. I'm paying him a bleedin' fiver."

As he peered beyond the doorway he heard something heavy being brought down on a table. The next second the young face of someone he would one day call mother looked round from a door on the left. She seemed tired, but her face lit up as she saw him. He smiled back instinctively. It was a very fleeting moment as the sound of Danno's voice had her darting back into the room to continue with her work.

"Here we are, paper and a pencil. Now sod off into that barn and get busy."

The door was closed firmly behind him and he walked past the sleeping dog towards the old brick barn to do as he was told.

It had been a long time since he had worked on an engine, though this one was a fairly simple affair. The spark plugs were easy to get at, but how easy they would be to get out would remain to be seen. He walked around the engine like a doctor familiarising himself with a patient. How long it had rested in the barn was hard to tell. He imagined the day it was brought in. His mind contained a picture of a horse towing it through the big doors as the farmer of the day kicked and cursed it for packing up on him.

The magneto looked in good nick. The distributor, on the other hand, looked incapable of sending the required surge of electricity to the plugs. The arms were misshapen and the whole thing looked as if it had borne the brunt of an impact of some sort. He would need a new one that was certain. At least he knew now why the damn machine would not start anymore. Still, there was a lot more to do besides fitting a new distributor, so he rolled up his sleeves and went to examine the workbench.

By mid-afternoon he had got the blackened spark plugs out and had tried to remove the cylinder head, without luck. He could only guess that the valves were encrusted with carbon too. If so they would require regrinding. The sump drain had come free with some energetic hammering. The engine was almost as dry as a bone. The dipstick had shown no oil but he expected there to be a small amount in the belly of the crankcase. He was just about to remove the equally dry radiator when the barn door opened. Expecting to see Danno appear to check on progress he was surprised to see his mother, Lotty, walk in with a sandwich and a cup of tea.

"I thought you'd be hungry," she said, warmly.

"Come to mention it, I am actually," he said.

"It's only a bit of chicken left over from last night's dinner."

He wiped his filthy hands on a rag and took a bite. Last night's chicken or not, she could tell he was enjoying it.

75

"How's it going?" she asked, then added. "What have you done to your head?"

"Oh that? It's just a nasty scratch. It's healing up now," he turned to face the partly dismantled engine. "As for this old thing, it's hard to say at the moment. I've seen worse though. The main bits look all right. I don't think it was properly looked after though."

"It belonged to my dad," she began. "He got too old to care for things. In the end he couldn't care for anything. If it hadn't been for Danno, the farm would have had to be sold to one of the big county farmers."

"How long's it been in here then?"

"It was making noises. One morning, about two years ago, he couldn't get it going. It's been here ever since."

"So why's Danno never tried to repair it himself?"

"The Harpers own many of the farms around here. There's never a shortage of tractors and machinery, so he doesn't really need this one. Mind you, he's often talked about getting it going, just for the heck of it."

"Well, let's get it going for your dad, shall we?" he said, realising at the same moment that he was referring to the grandad he never knew.

She smiled a weak smile, as her eyes fought the tears that were determined to come.

"That would be nice," she managed to say.

"Can I ask you a question?" he said.

The tear she was wiping away prompted him to remember the time he saw her in the wood. She looked at him knowing it was going to be a personal question.

"You can ask," she said.

"Look, I don't wish to pry, but are you all right now?"

"Please don't ask. It's complicated. You caught me on a particularly bad day in The Beckett."

"The Beckett?" he asked.

"Beckett's Wood. Everyone round here calls it The Beckett."

"How is it complicated? I wanted to help you know. You seemed so upset."

"I was, but there's things you shouldn't know. I think I'd better go."

"No, please don't rush away. I'm sorry. I had no right to be so nosy."

He was now looking into the most exquisite pair of eyes he had ever seen. For a brief second, he forgot who she was or who she would be. The eyes, once taken together with the face and the shape of her mouth had a beauty not of earth but of heaven. It was some time, a couple of seconds perhaps, before he realised that she was gazing back at him in almost the same way. He felt as if they had both become magnets and were being pulled together. An electric charge was building up in him and he could only guess that the same was happening with her too. The dog barked outside.

"Bye," she said abruptly, and left.

Over the course of the next four days, he stripped, cleaned and re-assembled the old workhorse. Danno came in now and again to see how it was all going. As often as not he dropped off items that were on the list. Bit by bit the tractor was granted the blessing of a resurrection. An understanding bordering on friendship developed between the two men. As the days passed Danno invited him into the house for a midday meal. He was made welcome and the odd experience of being entertained by parents who did not recognise him as their child gradually waned until it felt strange no longer. The more he got to know them as they were in their younger years the less they became the iconic figures of mother and father.

Finally the great day dawned. One of Danno's other tractors pulled the museum piece out of its exhibition hall just in case the thing exploded and demolished the barn. Once out in the sunshine its two fuel tanks were topped up with their respective petrol and paraffin and the caps screwed on. She was ready. Her cooling system was no longer leaking and fresh engine oil filled her veins. With a twist the valve to her petrol tank was opened. The farmyard was unusually busy that morning. Most of the workers made sure they had jobs nearby just to see what would happen. As he reached for the starting handle he was struck by the impression that he was lifting a ceremonial sword - *Excalibur*. He carried the bent iron bar and thrust it into the hole in the front of the grille at the bottom. With a twist it slotted into place. Three hefty turns drew the mixture into the cylinders. Now the fourth one was ready to do the deed.

He spat on his palms, grabbed the handle firmly and yanked it round violently. It almost started. Breathing heavily, he glanced round at the audience who had stopped whatever they were doing to watch the performance. He found the compression point again and whipped the handle round once more. Only this time the punch of pistons firing continued. He slid the handle out of its hole and stood up to a farmyard filled with applause. In the centre of the clapping throng were Danno and Lotty. Once more Danno had to watch as the cyclist received his accolade. Lotty's face was brimming with pride. After waiting a while for the engine to heat up, he opened the paraffin tank and turned off the petrol supply.

"All right, all right. You've all seen a tractor working before," shouted Danno over the music of the engine, "The deal is that it has to run under its own steam. Remember?"

He had not paid too much attention to the gearbox during the repair. The gears felt like they were engaging properly when he first fiddled with the clutch and gear stick. The question was would they transfer the power? He was soon on the seat ready to find out. He rammed his foot down on the clutch pedal and shoved the long rod into the first gear position. In that instant he jumped out of his skin when he heard the angry grating of grinding gear teeth. He tried again. Same result.

He could not understand it at first. His foot was firmly pushed down on the clutch, so why would the gears not engage? He knew the connections from the pedal to the clutch were all right. It all pointed to the clutch itself. He had not been able to undo the nuts to check it during the repair but the betting was that, after years of neglect, it had seized up tight. A thin layer of rust had probably welded it to the gearbox he imagined - but how to free it, that was the question.

Somehow he would have to find a way to force the two plates that formed the clutch apart. After some deliberation and amid jeers and taunts from the congregation he decided to take drastic measures. If he could force it into gear, and the engine did not stall, then he could ram the tractor against something solid. If all this was done with the clutch pedal depressed, then the resistance holding the clutch together would be overcome and the plates would be freed.

After looking around he saw the perfect thing to ram against. It was a large conifer at the edge of the wood. If that would not do it nothing would. Grabbing the gear stick in both hands he tried to manhandle it into first gear. There was an ear-shattering mess of a noise as gear teeth collided. He wondered just what damage he was doing to them. So he tried to ease it into reverse. At last the gears meshed and the tractor lurched suddenly backwards towards the field and the wood beyond.

With his neck craned round he aimed for the great tree. The speed was not very fast but it was hard to steer over the uneven field. As the distance between the tractor and the tree trunk closed up he braced himself for the impact. He only just remembered in time to push down on the clutch pedal. Suddenly there were only six inches to go then came the titanic collision. As the tree cracked at the roots hundreds of startled rooks exploded out of the canopy of the trees in fright. The driver was jolted back and would have been thrown off his seat, had he not been holding on to the steering wheel tightly, but the most incredible sound was the bang of the clutch freeing itself. The plan had worked.

All that remained was to see if the thing had been broken by the sledgehammer treatment. He noticed everyone waiting to see if he could return or whether they would have to fetch him out with their own tractor. Shoving the machine into first gear he pushed down on the accelerator and the revs increased. Now for the moment of truth as he gingerly lifted his foot off the left-hand pedal. With delight he could sense the bite. Suddenly the tractor jolted into life, lurched forwards and careered back over the stubble field towards the farm. Great tyre tracks printed themselves behind him, directly over the ones he made on the way out, as he bounced helplessly on the cast iron seat.

Approaching the house and the gathered spectators he took it out of gear and pulled on the brake. After a small skid she had stopped, her engine running almost perfectly except for the slight tell tale sound of tappets that were not set exactly right. He threw the switch to the magneto and the engine chugged to a stop.

"I don't know about steam Danno, but she's a goer."

"I'll grant you that," he replied, and he reached into his waistcoat and pulled out a large piece of white paper. It was a five-pound note.

"Thanks," he said as he stuffed it into his pocket.

"Don't mention it," said Danno. "How are you with windmills?"

"No idea," he said, taken aback.

"Time to find out then," grinned Danno. "There's twenty quid in it for you if you can get that fucker working."

"Fine then, count me in."

"Look, I've got to go now. Drop by tomorrow morning. I'll take you up to Maltoft Hill. If you like challenges, you're going to love this."

They shook hands and Danno left with a gang of four other men. Lotty waved pathetically as he went.

"Well done," she said flatly, before going back to the house. She looked burdened with the cares of the world.

"I wish your dad could have seen it going again," he said in an attempt to brighten her up.

"Yes," she replied without conviction.

"What's up?" he asked, finding it hard to see her this unhappy.

"It just seems like an anti-climax now. You'll be off to Maltoft and we won't see you much. I won't see you much."

"I didn't know you cared," he said trying to be light hearted.

"Then you don't know a great deal, do you?"

He was lost for words.

"It's been nice having you working here, that's all."

"I've enjoyed myself too. I liked it when you came into the barn for a chat."

"I don't get to do that with many people. I'm going to miss that most of all."

He could see it in her face that she meant every word.

"We don't have to stop all that, do we?" he said.

He watched her heart sink at the suggestion and her shoulders appeared to slump under the invisible weight of her husband. Her spirit seemed trapped in some sort of emotional quicksand.

"Look, I won't be working for him all day. I could see you wherever you like, if that's what you want. You choose a place where you feel safe. You name the time. You don't have to worry."

She raised her face and took a deep breath.

"Meet me in The Beckett, this afternoon," she said as if she had got it all planned out, "There are things you have to know."

With that she ran into the house and left him there to walk back to the village with just his thoughts for company.

Chapter eight: The Woodman

He felt pleased with himself as he reached the lane that led back to Empton. It was a condition tempered by a sense of being mildly perturbed. He sank into a reflective mood as he walked and thought about the last few days and the reason he had gone to the farm in the first place. He used every opportunity to search out the last piece of bicycle during his time there, to no effect. Even when he went to wash his hands, on the occasions he had been invited to the house for food, he took the chance to peer round doors into rooms. As far as he could tell the wheel was not there either. He imagined at first that the house would be the hardest place to investigate. In the end, as things turned out, it proved to be the easiest. Not that it made any difference to the final result.

No, what disturbed him more than anything was the integration that was taking place. What was he now? Before he had arrived at the village he had been nobody, a complete stranger. Now he was recognised by name as a cyclist and a singer - henceforth he felt he would be known as the tractor man. It seemed only a matter of time before he would be revelling in the title of the windmill king. The roots of his presence there were sinking into the fabric of the land, unwelcome roots that could possibly hold him with the power of shackles.

As he approached the pub he could hear shouting. It was Harry's voice, deep and angry and loud. Now and then he picked up the sound of a high-pitched quieter voice. He ran up to the front door and burst in to find Harry holding up a doll in one hand and a broken bottle in the other. The back of his shirt was ripped and there was a bloodstain on his shoulder.

"And what if the whole case had fallen on me, you stupid kid, then what?" boomed Harry.

"I only left Molly down there for a rest."

"And how many times have I told you not to leave bloody dolls down there?"

"It's only one doll. You should have looked where you were going."

The bottle and the doll were slammed down on the bar, and Harry's spade-like hand was flung out like a whip. The back of his knuckles and fingers slashed across Ellie's face. In an instant she was hurtling towards the scullery, senseless.

"I'll have no bloody cheek off you my girl," he raged.

Then Harry looked round to see who had just come in.

"What the hell have you done to her?" he said to Harry.

"If I've told her once, I've told her a thousand times," said the landlord.

"And you think disfiguring her face will teach her?"

"They've got to learn discipline."

"So you give a lesson in violence and expect her to learn right from wrong, is that it?"

"I don't need you giving me lectures on how to bring up a child."

"That's not bringing up, that's knocking down."

"Maybe, and maybe not, but anymore out of you, and I'll give you a taste of the same. I'd advise you to bloody well mind your own damn business."

Ellie sat up in the small doorway, unable to speak. Harry left the bar undoing his blood stained shirt as he went. As the landlord was heard climbing the stairs, Ellie was helped to a chair.

"Let's take a look at you," he said.

He gently moved her jaw. She flinched as he touched it, quickly moving her head away in pain. He did not know what to do. Should he find the doctor who had patched him up when he knocked himself out? Where would he begin to look? The little girl put her hand to the side of her face, but she did not cry. The look in her eyes was that of a fighter. She appeared to be summoning up an inner strength, like someone who had been through all this before. He took hold of the little doll, Molly, and gave it to her. There was a flicker of a smile. Then she carefully lowered herself off the chair and went to sit in the corner of the back garden by herself - and there she settled herself, defiant, waiting for the bruising to appear and the hurt to fade. Waiting to grow up. She seemed to have become accustomed to this kind of life. As he watched her leaning back against the brick wall he found it harder to deal with than she did. There was something heroic about her, coming from within, and he felt a complete coward as he stepped away, through the pub and out into the street.

Walking aimlessly, he recalled what Lotty had said about Harry and how his wife had run off with someone. It must have been under the utmost pressure that a mother should have left her child. What could those circumstances have been, he wondered? Who did she run off with? He tried to imagine Harry bringing little Ellie up all by himself. Maybe he had been a violent husband. Maybe she had not been the wife he had expected. Just how many times had Ellie had to bear the brunt of Harry's temper? Sweet little Ellie, how could he do it?

By the time his mind had snapped out of its thoughts his legs had taken him deep into the wood and there he found it easier to contemplate matters in the midst of the tall trees. Their slender, perpendicular trunks rose like those of cathedral pillars. The spreading branches high above resembled the kind of vaulting found in the ceilings of churches and minsters throughout the land. Even the hollow sound of air moving through these living timber columns created the same atmosphere as that of a transept. Instead of the majestic growl of a mighty organ there sang the choir of the Almighty in the shape of birdsong and the quiet hum of tiny insects. But he was aware of a kind of constriction, as if the world was imperceptibly closing in on him - not here in the wood, rather in the village and the places connected with it.

For a few moments he sat upon the stump of an old conifer and looked around. He was completely alone. He had wandered a long way since entering the wood, most of it in a kind of trance, his mind deep in thoughts and questions. He now realised, as he took the weight off his feet, that he was lost. The last half hour had been far from the pathways, an ever-changing course through brambles and thick clumps of broad-leafed bushes. He remembered passing the fork in the lane that offered the route to the farm but now he was in a place worse than a maze. Whichever direction he looked in, everywhere looked the same.

He was neither worried nor concerned. Here he could hide away from people and all the complications they brought about. In any case, there was time enough to find a way back. After a brief rest he carried on, now brandishing a stick that he wielded like a machete, cutting through any vegetation that got in his way. Striding on like some jungle explorer he covered a good distance, until he was brought up sharply in his tracks.

Through the trees there loomed a dark shape, quite large, a structure of some kind. Visible through the gaps in the mass of trees he could see the shadowy bulk of a black building. It was purely an outline. He continued clambering on. Each tree he passed revealed more of its shape and he was less than fifty yards away by the time he realised it was a house - a house in the middle of the wood standing in the centre of a large clearing. What a bizarre sight it was, burned to the ground, its walls smeared with the black whip marks of smoke. Remains of timber rafters poked upwards from each wall. Once they had met to form a roof - now their blackened stumps could only resemble the ribs of a creature that had been burned to death. Debris was scattered all around. The front door, strangely unaffected by the affects of the inferno, had crashed inward and now lay with the outermost side facing upward in amongst the charred rubbish that littered the floor of the dwelling. All the windows were smashed both on the ground floor and upstairs.

He had now reached the tortured house. Stepping carefully over the charcoal fragments he peered in through a hole that was once a window. The ceiling had gone and he could see where the roof tiles had crashed violently through and taken the first floor with it. A mess of shattered pieces of slate covered the ground, but apart from the badly seared stumps of floor beams poking from the inside of the walls, the house was nothing more than a shell of four sooted slabs.

He wondered how long it had been like this. Had it stood here for years, long abandoned? It was impossible to tell by looking. Rainwater had seen to it that all dust and filth had been washed away. The burnt rubbish had been cleaned but a jumbled, irreparable mess remained.

A narrow line of flagstones led to a small shed on the left that had also been consumed by the flames and, although it was not attached in any way, its proximity to the house had sealed its fate. A metal bench lay on its side in the middle of its black remains - a vice still bolted to it. For some time he stood and stared. It was a spectacle, like an unearthly sculpture, that somehow deserved to be stared at. The dead house reminded him of the decaying birds in the broken cottage. Here, in the middle of the wood, was the corpse of a dwelling. It was a sad sight to behold.

The time had come to leave he felt. With a sense of reverence he walked from the house making his way on the path that continued across the small clearing until it reached the trees. Here the path stopped, being at once overrun by brambles and ferns. Beneath their shade the ground was worn and, with a flick of his foot, he could make out the faint trace of the path as it cut through the denser woodland. With a final backward glance at the dead house he turned to see where the path would lead.

The path was hard to follow. It was obvious that it had not been trodden for a long time - years perhaps. Eventually after a painstaking plod he reached a defined track. It was a relief to have a way to go at his feet and, although he still felt lost, there was a sense that the track led somewhere at least. The sun had reached a high point in the sky. It was shimmering through the leaves that rippled in the breeze high above him. It was a loose indication of where south was and, since he believed that he had been heading in this general direction most of the time, it made sense to make his way in the opposite direction. Turning left on the track took him away from the sun, north, and he felt confident that he was making for a part of the wood that he would know.

This assumption lasted for the first mile or so. He persisted in turning his head to catch sight of the sun and, whilst it remained roughly behind him, he held on to the blind belief that he would at some point recognise some feature or other. As each moment passed and nothing familiar materialised, he became more troubled that he was getting evermore lost. At last he stopped and looked about him. The scene behind was more or less the same as that in front. The first fluttering of panic began to make its nest in his mind. Peering up to the canopy high above he even contemplated climbing to the treetops to see if he could spot the village - the church perhaps. It was a crazy idea that he abandoned as quickly as he thought it. No wood went on forever and he told himself sternly that the path would eventually lead somewhere. With that he fell into a march, briskly striding along the dusty way going somewhere.

After an hour or so he was still walking. His stride had slowed to a stroll, and he felt as if he was in a never-ending setting. That was until he heard voices. His pace quickened. So did his heartbeat. With sweat pouring off him he arrived at a thinned out section of trees - the path at once being absorbed by a clearing of sorts. Cutting through this sparse area was a road. A proper one, a real country lane and, as he reached it and looked both ways, he could see the roof of a house to the right some way off. Roof, house, people, directions, this logical progression created a happy ending in his head and he was off there like a shot.

The roof turned out to belong to a row of dilapidated, terraced cottages, six in all. Some children aged about seven or eight were playing in one of the little front yards and he went up to see if they would help him. Their game, a cross between cowboys and Indians, and doctors and nurses came to an abrupt end as they saw him approaching. The four boys and two girls eyed him up with deep suspicion. The girls ran inside. The boys on the other hand pulled faces, not purposefully rude but in that time-honoured way, which boys do when they are faced with something new. He arrived at the cockeyed picket gate to the garden and took in the sight of these scruffy urchins.

"Is your mum or dad in?" he asked.

"Are you the rat catcher?" asked the boy with the darkest hair.

"No. I just need to talk to your parents."

"We ain't been doing no trouble. It wasn't us what did it," squawked the smallest child.

The dark-haired boy dug him in his side and mouthed a reprimand to shut up through clenched teeth.

"I'll get mum," he said, eyeing the blabbermouth with an intimidating flash as he went.

His mother was brought outside into the sunshine. She squinted at the brightness of the day as she dried her soapy hands on a flower-patterned towel.

"Who is he mam?" said one of the girls. The mother ignored her.

"Can I help you?" she said with great politeness and insincerity.

"Hopefully. I'm trying to get back to Empton. I'm a bit lost to be honest."

"Empton ay? What way did you come?"

"Through the woods actually."

"Blimey, you've had a walk ain't you?"

"A bit. I thought I'd never get out to be honest. I lost my bearings near the burned-out house I think."

With that the woman's face dropped. Her eyes widened and her smile vanished. Like a mother hen she bundled the kids into the grubby house and then spoke to him from the doorstep.

"You ain't got no business going near the woodman's house, and we don't want our kids' heads fillin' with all them kind of tales. Now, you be off. You'll find a signpost at the end of the lane."

She pointed in the direction he should go, back towards where the lane cut through the woods. Then she quietly shut the door and flicked a corner of the grubby lace curtains to make sure he was going to walk away.

It was not what he had expected. He was left feeling mildly shocked but he had been given some directions at least, so off he went. He was weary, though more hungry and thirsty than plain tired. He had memories of cycling over a hundred miles in a single day so a walk in the country should have been easy. Strangely it was not. It had seemed a long day since the starting of the tractor. The tractor. It was the old machine, or the thought of it that suddenly reminded him of what Lotty had said about meeting him in The Beckett. She had said this afternoon and that, as far as he could make out, was now. He put a spurt on and soon reached a junction in the lane, complete with its signpost set in the grass verge. Three white wooden slats poked out of a lopsided concrete post peppered with lichens all over. The one pointing in the direction he was walking said Tunby one and a quarter miles. To the right he could see that in seven miles he would reach Rembleton. With a lightened heart he headed left and knew with certainty that within a couple of hours he would reach Empton, now eight and a half miles away.

It should have been a pleasant stroll. The sun warmed the side of his face and the countryside was brimming with life and fullness. Even without colour there was an elemental beauty everywhere. It was like marching through a Francis Frith postcard *Country Lane In Summer*. But that was the problem. No matter how nice it looked, even in black and white, perhaps especially in black and white, he knew he should not be here, and the more at home he felt within the postcard and the more he became absorbed into the world that existed in this pretty part of England the worse it would be. Now though, even after a few days, he was beginning to be accepted. There was something seductive about it. It lured him in. The part of his make up that wanted to know what would happen next if he stayed began to dominate by curiosity. It begged him to remain. It was if he was succumbing to a gas, a sweet smelling poison gas that made the prospect of dying a pleasurable expectation. There was a kind of contentment as he drifted deeper into the world around him, yet he knew from a whispering voice from within that it was wrong. It was a voice that grew ever quieter and the uneasy thing about it was that he knew in time the voice would die.

He was snapped out of his daydream by the sound of an engine behind him. He turned to see a car, an Austin Seven, black, chugging its way along the lane. It slowed and finally stopped. He thought the driver was going to ask for directions. He was ready with I'm a stranger round here myself kind of remark, but he was wrong.

"Good afternoon," said the driver. "I thought it was you. How's the head?"

He touched his forehead, wondering how on earth this total stranger knew about his fall.

"How did you know about that?" he asked.

"I'm Fletcher, Dr Fletcher. I patched you up. Fancy a lift?"

"Very kind," he replied, and climbed in and onto the soft but somewhat cracked leather upholstery.

It was a cramped little machine, the Austin Seven, the most basic of cars and, as he closed its door, he became submerged into the smell of leather mingled with that of petrol and engine oil. It seemed to sway from side to side as it trundled along the uneven lane on its narrow tyres. The doctor had clearly mastered all of its quirky characteristics. He was evidently very good at getting a good tune out of this particular old fiddle, timing the changing of the gears with perfection and perpetually adjusting the steering wheel, as if it was a matter of balance to keep the poor car on the straight and narrow. He spoke with a different accent from the rest of the rural folk in the village and, though he obviously belonged, it was plain he had originated, or at least had been educated, elsewhere. There shone from him a rich seam of friendliness, a good humour, mixed with a deep intellect.

"You've healed up very well, I must say. Any pains, blurred vision and the like?"

"I had a headache at first," he said, "but I'm perfectly fine now. Thank you for asking."

"Don't mention it, nasty things, bumps on the head. You have to watch the old brain box after a wallop like you had. You don't feel giddy or anything of the sort, do you?"

"No, honestly doctor, not even a dizzy spell to speak of. I wouldn't have ventured this far if I'd felt funny."

"Wonderful," said the doctor with a sense of satisfied pride. "And you have ventured a fair distance, haven't you? That's good, the exercise will build you up, and anyway, it's a nice part of the world around here."

"Oh, I'll say, especially at this time of the year."

"How far did you get, Rembleton?"

"Not quite, I got to a row of cottages outside Tum…" he could not remember the name on the signpost.

"Tunby," put in the doctor, "Yes, they're the labourers' cottages. You know, they live in filth and yet they're as fit as fleas," he said with a chuckle.

"I came across them by mistake. I'd come through the woods. I got a bit lost actually and came across an old burned out house."

The doctor's smile vanished in an instant and he slammed on the brakes bringing the car to a dead stop in the middle of the lane.

"You haven't told anyone else you've been there, have you?" he said in a voice that would have been a shout had he not been whispering the words.

"Only a woman at one of the cottages."

"No one else?" his tone was like an interrogation.

"No one."

"Well keep it that way. If I were you, I'd pretend that you never saw it at all, understand? Never go there again. Do I make myself clear?"

He did not know what to make of it, let alone how to reply.

"I just ended up there, that's all," was all he could say.

"Do I make myself clear?" the words had force.

"Yes, perfectly," he paused as the words hung in the space between them. "Well no, not perfectly as it happens. It was only a ruin. Anyone would think it was haunted or something."

"It's something," said the doctor trying to regain some calm, "Something you should steer clear of. The least you know, the safer it is for you. Don't go there again. Don't even talk about it to anyone," the doctor's face managed to break into a kindly smile. "Look, people's welfare is my business. Think of my advice as a prescription for safety. Okay?"

The patient smiled back through an expression of perplexity.

"Okay," he replied, unconvinced.

He was in the village of Empton in no time at all. He bid the doctor farewell as he got out of the car near the green and watched him turn the corner and disappear in the direction of Wexby. The timing could not have been better. The church clock struck three. Lotty, he said to himself and made for the woods.

It was an easy stroll along the arboreal path to Bofindle Farm. He felt he knew every twist and turn now. This was no longer exploration. It was just a trip. The kingdom of trees was losing some of its mystique as a sense of familiarity grew. Within a few minutes he reached the spot where days before he had heard the sound of Lotty crying. He wondered if he should trample over the brambles to the exact location where he stumbled upon her. But who was to say that is where she would be, or exactly where she would meet him? Should he go to the old gatepost at the wood's end? There seemed more merit in staying put. It seemed safer. She would have to find him, providing she remembered to come at all. There was a fallen conifer nearby and it made a convenient, if not a comfortable, bench.

As the music of the wood relaxed him he turned his mind to the cottage, the woodman's cottage, the burned out remains, the labourer's wife, her reaction, the doctor and his reaction. He had seen a burned house that was all, but now it was something far too terrible to speak about. It intrigued him but it frightened him more. He could see the blackened cadaver of the cottage in his mind's eye. Its memory took on a whole new sinister appearance. No longer would he think of it as a house that had once caught fire. It now represented the unthinkable and that, in itself, seemed to be far worse than the worst he could imagine.

He was lost in this state for an incalculable amount of time. It was the distant sound of footfall on a dusty path echoing through the trees that pricked his ears. Instinctively he sank for cover beneath a tangle of leaves, but it was Lotty. She had remembered after all and she walked straight past him. It amused him that she failed to see where he was hiding and, like a genie popping out of a bottle, he likewise popped out from within his secret lair.

"Lotty," he said with the quietest of yells.

She swung her head round coming to an abrupt halt. Her look of surprise gave way to an excited smile. He was glad that she looked pleased to see him.

"Quick, follow me," she said, running into the depths of the vegetation. He caught her up in no time.

"I'm supposed to be picking mushrooms," she said. "I nearly got caught out by Ernie Gladstone, so you'll have to help me pick some to make it look real."

"Right," he replied, realising once more how difficult it was for her to have any kind of life back at the farmhouse.

She strode on with a purpose, he trailed behind like an apprentice, and then, just as abruptly, she stopped, looked about her and knelt down. The trees were closely packed hereabouts, a dense part of the wood. It was dark as the leaves up above deprived the place of sunshine. Spread out on the ground was the city of mushrooms. He half expected to see the king of the fairies fly out from under one of them and introduce him to all of his people.

"You have to know where to find them," she said as she picked them and placed them into the pocket of her apron. "Pick the broader ones, the others will grow in time."

He felt as if he was being given a lesson in mushroom picking. It made him laugh.

"What?" she asked, somewhat energised by his laughter.

"It's nothing," he said, feeling caught out. "I've never picked mushrooms before."

They knelt together as if in prayer. Picking the damp grey discs. Soon they had got enough. That is when they looked at each other in a way that changed everything. Nothing was said. It was all in the look. More than all the works of Shakespeare passed between them without a word being uttered. In the darkness, alone, the moment had purity. There seemed to be so much to explain. He remembered that she was going to tell him things that he ought to know. Now she already had. On her feet were the boots of a farm girl, silly and at the same time practical. Her eyes had a majesty that belonged not on a farm but in a golden palace. He handed her his mushroom. She took it from him. Their hands met, grubby from the picking but warm and alive. The mushroom dropped to the ground as their fingers became intertwined. She drew him closer. He could feel her breath on his face. The move was slow and deliberate and their lips as they met melted into each other as completely as two raindrops touching. The taste of her mouth had all the flavours of woman - intoxicating, exciting and soft. Her tongue danced inside his mouth urging his to do likewise. Their breathing became heavy and his penis grew hard and uncomfortable in his trousers. The hiking girl had been nothing compared to this. This was no vision of heaven. This was heaven itself.

As they lay on the springy floor of the wood she reached down to his trousers and undid them. His penis found its liberation in the fresh air and as she caressed it in her hand he stroked her smooth legs and found his way up her dress and into her underwear. It was already damp there. Damp and warm. She arched her back to let him take them down and soon he was able to plunge his fingers into her. As they kissed he could feel the vibrations of her groans against his own mouth. By now she was rubbing him towards the point of no return. Going out of his mind with the madness of it all he climbed between her cold legs and with no effort thrust himself into her. The warmth and tightness of her was too fulfilling. He felt the rush spring from within the depth of his belly and speed up through his hips and groin. With one explosive shudder he filled her womb with his offering.

They stayed in that position for several minutes, still kissing. She stroked the back of his head as if comforting a child. Then they flopped to one side and stared up at the leaves high above them. The madness faded by degrees as they lay there, the madness that had made this event seem like the right thing to do. It was the experience of it all that protected the purity. Her eyes and smile, her eagerness to have him, rather than him chase after her, the whole thing had been of beauty, pure beauty. When she reached for his hand and squeezed it, he knew that the madness had been right.

"That was…" her voice was hesitant. "That was your first time, wasn't it?" she paused to see if the question had angered him. She felt safe to go on. "I'm right, aren't I?"

He wondered how she could possibly have known.

"Is that important?"

"It is to me."

"How did you know?"

"I just knew that's all," her face broke into a teasing smile. "It wasn't bad for a first time."

"Oh," he sounded deflated.

He did not want this incredible moment to be measured. To him this would always be the best no matter what came afterwards.

There was a long silence, just the sound of their breathing, now settled, and the surf-like sound of the leaves catching the wind that ran over the dappled roof of the wood. He rolled towards her after several minutes had passed. He wanted to hold her, to protect her and stroke her hair and kiss her again. He found that she was crying.

"What's the matter? What have I done wrong, what's wrong?"

"It's not you. It's everything."

"Everything?"

"Oh, you can't possibly understand. I'm not sure I understand it all myself."

"Understand what?"

He waited for her to reply. It was like being a spectator at the bursting of a dam. Her defences or at least the protection of some deep secret was crumbling. It was as if she had kept the dam walls together until this moment, until she met the right person to flood her secret with and her tears were just the precursor to the deluge.

She buried her head in his shoulder, shuddering with held-back sobs. Then the words came. They were barely distinguishable, her voice now distorted by crying. He held her close and kissed the top of her head.

"There's no love between us, you know. No love at all," was all he could make out.

There were references to her dad that made no sense and David whoever he was. All the time his shoulder was moistening with the spilled tears that were now in full flow.

When she had let it all out she breathed a long sigh, held his face in the palms of her hands and kissed him. It was a loving kiss, full-bodied and from her heart. Their lips parted and he beheld her dampened face. The dam had burst and it made no sense. Tears and gibberish had gushed from a hidden depth and without sense there came questions, many questions.

"David, who's David?" he asked.

She found it hard to answer but managed to say something about getting engaged and wanting to marry him.

"So why didn't you? Where is he now?"

"I don't know. I'll never know, he just disappeared."

"Disappeared?"

"He just didn't come back to me. To this day I don't know why. It was about the time that Danno began to talk to dad about the farm."

"Did Danno come to the farm a lot then?"

"My dad was very poorly at the end and Daniel Harper was the only person able to give his farm a future. They did a deal," she said.

A crude and sketchy picture of all this was building up inside his head as he probed her further.

"Did this David think that you were seeing Danno behind his back?"

"I don't know," she said. "He should have known I wasn't. I loved him. I really did love him. He knew how to be gentle, like you."

Her tears tried to return. They lodged in the back of her throat and choked her words. He could do nothing but hold her and speak softly.

"So why didn't your David talk to your dad about the farm, especially if you were going to tie the knot and all that? Couldn't he give it a future?"

"Oh he didn't have the money," she sniffed. "He had a decent job though, well for around here anyway. I'd have been happy with him, I know I would."

"And what job did he do, this David?" he asked.

"Oh, he was just a woodman," she said.

Chapter nine: The Windmill

The Golden Goose was quiet and hushed in the night. Laying in his bed his body was still but his mind raced. It raced through thoughts at speeds that pushed his brain to the limit. Sleep wanted to rest him. His head would have none of it, but sleep proved to be a persistent salesman and soon it was morning.

As the machinery of his consciousness built up momentum, a flickery film of the day before was projected onto a screen inside his head and concerns were flagged up in tandem. He wanted to know how Lotty was and what kind of night she had had with Danno. He wanted to know more about David the woodman. Had he burned to death? Was it his cottage? How come Lotty had married Danno? Why had she chosen this life or did she have it chosen for her? Who could he ask?

This was not so much a list of questions as a bombardment. Then he remembered that he was supposed to meet Danno at the farm - he had mentioned a windmill. How was he going to be able to look him in the face after what he had done with his wife? He had not given much thought to Danno's malevolence yesterday. Even though he was now on what could best be described as friendly terms with him, there was more than a little mistrust and rather more fear, but he would have to go.

Harry was still in a sulk after their disagreement over his treatment of Ellie. Breakfast was a process, a contractual obligation. The eating of it was pretty much done in the same vein. Then he was off down the road to Bofindle Farm.

He could hear Danno's voice shouting orders to his men as he approached the barns. His guts tightened. He could almost hear the blood rushing through the veins in his ears. In the farmyard stood a heavily damaged lorry. It was an old Commer, a flatbed rigid with severely bashed-up wooden side panels. Its engine was already running with a deep mechanical and repetitive purr.

"Fuck me, he's made it," said Danno with the smile of a crocodile.

The others, three older men, quietly laughed siding sensibly with their boss.

"Sorry I'm late," he said, knowing it was the wrong thing to say as soon as he said it.

"Well, you're here now. Get into the cab."

He clambered into the filthy, throbbing interior of the lorry. There were bits of receipts scattered here and there, old fish-smelling newspapers, an alternator with wires hanging from it and loads of soil on the floor. Danno hoisted himself into the driver's seat and with a stroke of his arm cleared a mass of crap off the dashboard, sending it tumbling to the feet of his passenger. The passenger looking behind him watched the three others jump into the back amongst a mass of scaffolding poles and fix the tailgate into place. The one nearest to the cabin slapped the palm of his hand on the back window and within a second the vehicle was shaking itself to pieces as the revs increased. The diesel engine growled like a mechanised lion and once in gear it propelled them jerkily along the track he had just walked down.

Conversation was impossible over the engine noise and the deafening rattle of the lorry's vibrating body and chassis. He was glad to have an excuse not to speak. How he would ever have made small talk with this man, this husband, he could not imagine. Besides it was early morning. No one was in a mood to chat.

The old vehicle had seen many years of hard work and despite its decrepitude gave the impression, albeit grudgingly, that it was prepared to give many more years of faithful service. The initial route was familiar until they passed the signpost he had seen the previous day. The lorry rattled on towards Rembleton and continued on through the long stretched out village until there was countryside around them once more. They rumbled and crashed along winding lanes lined with thick bushy hedges, overgrown gateways and dense patches of trees. Not too far ahead he could see an escarpment largely blanketed by trees that gave an impression of a giant fluffy heap of broccoli heads. Just visible, on the top of the ridge where the trees did not reach, was a monument of some kind, a great mound quite distinguishable, like a diminutive church spire on the crest of a hill.

Danno waited until the lorry had begun its climb up the gentler part of the rise. With the poor beast beginning to strain under the burden of hauling them to the top he pointed at the odd structure and shouted over the snarling engine.

"Maltoft. The windmill. Can you see it?"

"Yes," he yelled back.

That was all the conversation they had the whole way. By sheer persistence they managed the steep climb and as they emerged from the forested part of the hill they came to a fork in the road. The signpost was old and broken having only one directional arm attached to it. Pointing to the left it only displayed the letters OFT followed by 1m. The shaking vehicle curved left and followed the cryptic instruction. All around cows and sheep grazed on steep pastureland. Old buildings were dotted here and there in the fields. They all looked as if they had undergone partial demolition. Roofs were missing or at best only half of their tiles remained in situ. Masses of weeds and grass grew so thick around the base of their walls that it

97

looked as if they were keeping the buildings from collapsing into the dirt.

Slowly the gradient eased out and the sight of the ravaged windmill came into view. Danno had been right about a challenge. The windmill was a mess. There were not even any sails on it, just a crumbling old tower with what looked like a headlined dome on top. The resemblance to a phallus was quite remarkable. The lorry pulled off the road that led on to the barren village of Maltoft now only five hundred yards or so away and shuddered its way down a deeply rutted track to where the lifeless windmill stood. There it was, stubborn and defiant and broken. He felt hopelessly unequal to the task of repairing it as Danno pulled the brake on and the engine shook to a convulsive rest. With his ears now ringing after the noise he stepped out of the rust-ridden cab into the sunshine and looked at what was once a working mill. He did not know whether to laugh or cry.

He knew straight away why a tower of this sort had been built up here on the ridge. A constant wind tugged at his clothes and jostled his hair. The building seemed to peer down at the puny humans walking down on the ground watching the wind make fools of them. It gave the impression that it was an old grandfather sagely casting an eye on the youngest generation of his family, knowing that they had seen nothing of life, not like he had.

The brick walls had been painted black, or so he assumed the colour to be. It was flaking off the bricks in most places revealing crumbling masonry and mortar. He tried to guess at its height, a hundred feet perhaps. At least he could see that it had four floors by the ascending rows of broken windows in the tapering sides of the tower. Right at the top poking out of the dome was the remains of a wooden gantry painted white. It had obviously been used for holding something heavy. The fact that he did not even know what it was for left him feeling stupid and inadequate, and the building seemed to know it. If it could have had a face it would be laughing at him. Even without a face the thing had a force, a will, even a life.

Being a structure that had working parts inside there was something tangible with a living entity. Here on the hill was a sick old man who just wanted another chance at life. Begging to have the force of the air enable him to be useful again. The old man's grandchildren entered through a padlocked door and, once in the dark interior, climbed a set of stairs to the first floor. It was his first time in a windmill. He was amazed at its wooden guts - heavy, mighty and built with an incredible precision. There was an abandoned smell, an aroma mixed with those of bird mess and damp, but pervading through all these unwelcome scents was the fine musty fragrance of corn and flour. It was not strong but it hinted that the old man was not finished just yet. Perhaps it was possible after all to bring the smell of a life's work back into this proud old mill. In the two minutes that he had spent inside this great, dilapidated building he felt a strong sense of affection for it and, despite his concerns about the tasks ahead, there was a relish in his soul that he was here and ready to make a contribution to its future.

"Where do you fuckin' start, ay?" sighed Danno, evidently overawed by the spectacle too.

"Search me," he said as he looked upwards to the floor above.

"The insides aren't bad. The roof's lead and it's kept the rain off. We're going to start fixing up the walls. Your jobs to figure out how all this fuckin' lot works and get it going."

"So what happened to the old place then?" he asked.

"Ah!" began Danno. "A story best told over a pint. Look we'll be finishing before it gets dark. I'll let Harry tell you all about it. You just help yourself and have a look around. Figure out what needs to be done and what you'll need. But be quick about it. Time's ticking on."

"You're in a hurry then?"

"Bloody right I am Caruso. I'm fucked if I'm sending any more grain to that bastard Wagstaff," he cast his eye to the mill. "I want this old bugger grinding my own flour by the time the harvest has dried out. Two months at most I dare say."

"So, where are the sails?" he said as a sense of foreboding came over him.

"Inside a barn up at Maltoft. There's only three there. The fourth was knackered. It's under a tarpaulin in the next field. Be all right for spare bits I reckon though."

Danno went out into the sunshine and yelled at the three old chaps to hurry up unloading the scaffolding in his own particular style.

Inside the stairs to the next floor beckoned him and the floors beyond. In no time he found he had reached the top. There he beheld a giant set of gears. One massive wheel standing almost vertically meshed its wooden pegged teeth into those of a slightly smaller horizontal wheel. He recognised it as a kind of differential - a gigantic version that was to be found on the back axle of a car. It was simply the transfer of power from the revolving sails to the long vertical shaft that drove the millstones - the millstones that would have rotated on one of the floors below.

A thick wooden shaft with an enormous timber boss at the end of it poked through a square aperture fashioned in the wooden shell of the dome at the top of the mill. He could see the square holes in the boss where the sail's main shafts would have been slotted. There was a mass of damage here. There were other bent and twisted metal rods and levers fastened to it that he considered being the means by which some form of control of the sails had been achieved. How they worked he had no idea. Exactly what he was supposed to do to repair them equally baffled him. He poked his head out of the square hole from where he caught sight of the view. He could see for miles and miles, right over to where the grey horizon faded away in the shimmering summer haze. Grey as far as the eye could see.

Gripping the gears he tried to pull them to see if they would turn. They were paralysed. The old man was crippled with mechanical arthritis. It all seemed so sad. He had seen enough up at the top now and soon he clambered down three flights of steps to the first floor. The single window in the wall there was boarded up and it was dark. He had not paid much attention to this area in his haste to get to the top. Here were more oversized wooden cogs, beautifully crafted. He could even see where the millstones had been removed.

Directly in front of him was a long, thick spindle with a wooden drum-like attachment halfway along it. A frayed piece of rope, about six inches in length, hung down from it dangling close to where a set of double trapdoors had been built into the floor. The shaft of the spindle passed through a lever of some sort and there was a small-toothed cog at its end. The little wheel could only have been a couple of inches or so from the main shaft of the mill where a large wheel with wooden teeth poking out of its rim had been precisely fixed into position.

He now knew what it was like to be inside a gearbox. He felt like an insect trapped inside one. The lever intrigued him. Even if the gears on the top floor had been petrified into place maybe this lever might move. So he pulled it down. It would not budge. He grabbed hold of the very end of the smooth, worn handle to increase the leverage. It moved. The spindle was attached to the other side of the lever's pivot and, as he pulled down, the spindle began to rise, pushing the cog at the end of it upwards. The cog eventually meshed with the large gear in the main shaft.

He imagined what would have happened if the mill had been working, if the shaft had been revolving. The main gear would have turned the cog and the spindle would have turned the drum. If a complete rope were to be passed through the open trapdoors it could be wrapped around the drum in no time and would be able to pull something up - something like bags of corn perhaps. That was all there was to it. This was nothing short of an ingenious crane that used the power of the mill to lift heavy bags of corn up to the grinding floor. Clearly the people who had put this incredible piece of machinery together were far from stupid. He was filled with a sense of admiration for these anonymous engineers of long ago.

Outside he saw the other men unloading the metal poles. The sound of the clanging tubes echoed all around. Danno saw him and came over.

"Bit more to it than a frigging tractor, don't you think?"

"There's a lot of work to be done, no doubt about it."

"Well, we're doing the brickwork and general repairs to the building. You're the machinery expert, so I'm relying on you to get the old bugger grinding."

"I don't suppose there's anyone around here who knows anything about these old mills, is there?" he asked.

"Oh aye," said Danno with amusement, "he's around here, isn't he boys?"

"Aye, Mr Harper. He's around here all right."

"Good. I need to talk to him. I've got a few questions that need answers."

"Well, you'll have to shout your bloody head off," said Danno mocking him. "He's in the fucking cemetery."

A screech of hysterical laughter from the men and their boss isolated him as an idiot - and isolated was how he felt. He realised that the only thing to be done was to keep his head down and examine the mill thoroughly and figure out how each part worked. He was going to have to learn the hard way.

By the time they were ready to leave he had come to a greater understanding of this great machine. He had visited the barn to see where the sails had been laid to rest. They were like giant louvre doors set inside a huge frame made of oak beams and impossible to move. A lever at the near end moved back and forth and altered the angle of each slat. This was how the miller regulated the amount of wind that the sails caught. He thought earlier that the pitch of the entire blade might have been altered. That is what he thought the remains of the metalwork he found near the great boss might have been for. This arrangement though was far simpler in a sophisticated sort of way and cunningly brilliant. He even saw a large circular fan, some ten feet in diameter, propped up against the barn wall. Danno said it had once fitted on the back. The broken gantry was up there, so that was another part of the jigsaw moved into place, but what the fan was for he had no idea. It was like this continually. A question solved here, more questions posed there. The day had been a long one and he was glad to climb back into the tin pot lorry and rattle down the hill back home. Back home to the Golden Goose.

How Harry was able to remain in a sulk for a whole day was beyond comprehension. The grumpy landlord hardly said a word as he was asked for a pasty and a pint. He delivered it to his resident customer without speaking. It was consumed equally silently. Then, with food and drink inside him, he felt even more exhausted and, even though it was still light, he climbed the stairs to his room and collapsed on the bed. There was no energy left even to think and he plummeted into a coma-like sleep that lasted until the dawn broke through the windows and woke him up, still fully dressed.

As he awoke his mind addressed itself with its concerns. He wanted to see Lotty again. He wanted her again, hungered for her. In the same instant the mill began to irritate his thoughts. The conflict of heart and mind continued through a strained breakfast and all the way to Bofindle Farm. As he tramped down the track to the barns he could hear voices resounding in the fresh morning air. He arrived to see the old hands waiting against the lorry enjoying a smoke. With perfect timing Danno emerged from the house with a parcel under his arm. In fact it was two parcels. Danno threw one to the new arrival.

"Sandwiches for you. Lotty was whittling about you getting hungry up at the mill."

He caught a paper bundle with the word pickle written on it.

"Hope you don't mind pickle on your ham," he snapped. "Can't abide the shit myself."

"No, that's fine, very kind of her, both of you. Yes, thanks."

"Yes, well that's enough of that, let's piss off to Maltoft."

By lunchtime a ring of scaffolding had begun to surround the base of the tower. The job was taking far longer than expected and had only reached fifteen feet in height. Danno's mood was darkening. He expected twenty five to thirty feet by midday. A cloud of exasperation now overshadowed the upbeat enthusiasm he had brought with him up the hill. The three older farm hands found many of the connectors stiff and rusty but Danno flew into rages whenever the poor, wretched creatures tried to explain this and other reasons for the delay. Instead of stopping to eat Danno grabbed his worthless bastards and left with them to get more scaffolding. He said he would be back in about an hour. So Mr Miller, as Danno and the rest of them now called him, was left alone with his gears and cogs and his ham and pickle sandwiches.

There was something exciting about being at the highest point in the mill. He gradually began to make sense of the view from up there. It was possible to see the expanse of woodland that spread down to Empton. The village itself was too far away to be visible but he could work out where it ought to be. Further on he could make out a hill descending away towards flat farmland. The glint of a river or even a lake caught his eye. Beyond these visions there was only a patchwork of grey fields diminishing into smudged strips, before merging into a haze of nothingness that mingled with a distant sky.

He opened his lunch whilst he was peeping out of the square hole in the dome. Without looking at it he took a bite. The ham was thick and moist, brimming with flavour but there was no pickle. This fact took a few seconds to sink in. When it did he drew his head out of his windy spy-hole and parted the rounds of bread. Sure enough there was no pickle, just a piece of paper. It had been neatly folded twice and there it was inside his sandwich with a written message - *Beckett Friday afternoon lesson two.*

He could not believe what he was seeing. His body froze. The blood in his heart went wild. Or was it blood? It felt as if jolts of electricity were passing through his veins. The words remained on the paper. He read them again and once more the surge of anticipation electrified him. Lesson two, Friday afternoon. How was he supposed to wait until Friday? He wanted her now, here in his secret den, high above the crazy world below. A lesson? What was he going to learn? What could she teach him? He thought of her, all of her. He wanted to be inside her, to come inside her once more. The five words on the grease-stained scrap had sent a wave of excitement into his groin that made him grow there. He was powerless to prevent it. Friday afternoon. It seemed like a lifetime away.

He thrust the note into his pocket but he could hardly eat the sandwich. All he could manage was the meat and he threw the rest of it out of the back where the superstructure of the shattered gantry was attached. The words of the note swam in his brain over and over. He held on to the wooden beams, which had once reached out to the large fan that now lay in the barn. The thought of her wrapping her hand around him down there sent his mind into a sexual whirl. He imagined her naked this time. He was drawing her nipples into his mouth and rolling them around with his tongue, whilst he thrust in and out of her. What was the lesson to be? The unknown tantalised him and created the most excitement of all. He felt suspended in an experience where time meant nothing. Up in the dome by himself, he had the feeling that he had stepped off the treadmill of hours and seconds. He was still, and the world was moving onwards past him.

He touched the note. His fingers caressed the corners of the paper. What a risk she had taken to get this message to him he thought. What if Danno had got the wrong sandwiches? That thought brought home the risk he was taking himself. She must have been certain of Danno's dislike of pickle. She must have been entirely certain that her plan was going to work. It was clear to him that she had engineered this very carefully and to what end? She wanted him that badly? As his eye wandered about the monstrous machinery he felt the paper in his pocket again. It was like touching a very precious part of her.

His eyes had been busy and, it seemed, another part of his brain had been at work. He realised with some annoyance that, whilst he had been staring at the tangle of wood at the back of the dome, he envisaged what the fan and the gantry could have been there for. It intruded like an unwanted impostor into his daydream. It nagged for his attention and he was forced to look closer to see if this flash of inspiration actually possessed credibility. He took his hand away from the piece of paper and went to look at the rim of the tower near the gantry where it met the dome.

All around the bricks that formed the top of the tower lay a circle of metal gears set in the centre of what appeared to be a small railway track. He pulled a couple of the dome's strips of cladding away to reveal a miniature set of train wheels, resting on the track supporting the dome. He guessed that this arrangement went all the way around. All that was missing was the pinion, a small gear that would have come from a drive shaft connected to the fan. This had to be the most ingenious marvel of them all, more impressive than the crane, yet just as simple. The fan's job would have been to keep the main sails facing in the direction of the wind, automatically. If the sails were doing that already, then the fan, being at right angles to them and the prevailing wind would have been unable to turn - but if the wind changed, it would rotate the fan and set the rack and pinion assembly in motion. The dome would turn on its track until the fan stopped. The only reason the fan would stop would be because the sails had turned to face the wind once more. It was a brilliant set up and the pleasure he felt from having figured it out was only eclipsed, by his admiration for the long forgotten craftsmen having figured it all out for themselves from scratch.

He was made to jump back on the treadmill of time by the distant rumbling noise of the returning lorry, and he sank at the thought of having to spend the rest of the day with the one and only Danno. However, he had the news of his discovery to report to him, so he assumed that would gain some approval. Retaining Danno's favour was more vital than ever now and, by the time he climbed down the steps to the ground the lorry was just pulling up the rutted track from the road. Danno was not there, just the three farm workers with a new load of scaffolding. He went to help them unload it.

"Where's the boss?" he asked.

They all looked at each other deciding who would take up the post as spokesman. It appeared to be a hard decision to make. All three were old men. He had not paid much attention to them before. Each of them looked worn out. Lines of care were etched into their weathered faces. They could have been three brothers for all he knew. They all had thinning grey hair and broken bodies alike.

"Where's Danno?

"Mr Harper, he comin' up later," said the one at the wheel.

"We've to get this lot up by the time he gets here, else it's the dog run for us," the one next to him piped up.

"Dog run, what's the dog run?"

"You don't want to know," said the driver. "At least we ain't got him here this afternoon."

"Aye," said the one on the far side getting out. "Better shit on by an angel than pissed on be the devil."

"I'll help you," he said.

"Fuck it you will," said the driver as he stepped from the cab. "He said we got to do this."

"I won't tell if you don't. We'll hear him coming, then I'll make myself scarce."

"It's a trick," said the last one in the lorry. "Harper's put him up to this. Don't listen to him boys."

"No trick," he replied, astonished. "Besides, I'm going to need all the help I can get later. I'll scratch your back if you scratch mine, and all that?"

"I suppose we're heading for a bitten arse anyway. All right, but the minute you hear his tractor, piss off inside, okay?"

"Deal."

The three old boys, Herbert the driver, Scrumps and Splash, as they liked to call each other, were real workhorses. He learned that they were not brothers in blood but were the same age and had gone away to school together. In every other respect they had a tight bond of brotherhood and he soon warmed to their wit and humour. He discovered that, just as they had done all those decades ago, most of the children in the local villages went to a charity school kept afloat by donations from kindly benefactors like Danno. He paid piss-poor wages anyway, according to Splash, so it was easy to see where the money actually came from. Herbert said that he used a carrot and stick form of management but had eaten the carrot himself.

The banter went on like this all afternoon. By the time the sun began to familiarise itself with the horizon all the poles had been used. The scaffolding was twenty-five feet high in a ring around the brick tower. It had been an exhausting few hours so he decided to go to the barn up in Maltoft to examine the fan, but mainly to distance himself from the men. He reasoned that it would help to make the scaffolding job look more like their achievement alone if he was out of the way. Eventually he did hear the sound of a distant tractor. It stopped outside the mill for a while and then it could be heard getting louder as it approached the barn. It came to a stop directly outside.

Danno strode through the barn doors as if he owned the place. His silhouette in the doorway, black against the brash outside, came closer to him. His voice rebounded off the musty roof and walls.

"So, what you been up to?" he said.

He thought he had been caught out, but held despairingly onto whatever calm he could find. Had he found out about the scaffolding he wondered, or worse still?

"The mill?" he offered, not thinking.

"No, the fucking daisy chain, course the bloody mill, prat."

"You see this," he said standing up and patting the palm of his hand on one of the fan's large white sails. "This is part of the mechanism that turns the mill into the wind."

"I fucking know that you arsehole. Everyone knows that's what it's for."

107

This comment came with the force of a slap across the face. He instantly felt stupid, betrayed, insulted and quite angry.

"You know how it works then?"

"Me? No. I'm not paying you so I can fucking tell you. That's your job to figure that out."

"I've figured it out."

"Good. Well don't go expecting a bloody medal then."

He was going to say he thought he would have been pleased that he had solved the problem of the fan, but thought better of it.

"I think I'm going to need a carpenter," he said instead.

"You're going to get four," he said without hesitation. "That's where I've been this afternoon, organising some joiners for you."

Danno looked disapprovingly at him.

"Are you sure you're up to this job, or what?"

"I'll get your mill working," he said, mustering up an imitation of enthusiasm from within his sagging spirit.

"Yeah, well, tomorrow maybe, it's piss off home time now, come on."

He stuffed his hand wearily into his trouser pockets and followed Danno out into the breezy dusk of the dying sunshine. The tips of his fingers felt the piece of paper in his right pocket. This experience alone created another kind of sunshine. As he watched the pompous figure of Danno clamber into his tractor he felt a curious cheerfulness wash over him. Somewhere in the depths of his soul he was glad he was able to deal a silent act of retribution on this awful man.

Chapter ten: Friday

The carpenters had been well chosen. They were a silent bunch, insular, more at home with wood than people. They had brought the most primitive array of tools with them: spokeshaves, adzes, deadly looking chisels and mallets, but they could make them work marvels and, with breathtaking craftsmanship, were able to turn the drawings of gears and cog pins into three-dimensional objects that actually did what they were supposed to.

Danno had told him to keep them busy, so he spent his evenings at the pub drawing out on paper the bits they would need the next day. During daylight hours he would measure and remeasure every aspect of each component that would require refashioning. Then at night, kneeling at his bedside like a child saying his prayers, he would plan out whatever was needed. Even if the part was too large to fit onto the paper, the carpenters could translate the scale. It was a team effort and the fact that some of the systems began to work reflected the pooling of skills from both draughtsman and craftsman.

By now the scaffolding had risen to the top of the mill as high as the base of the dome. The three musketeers, as he had dubbed the older men, were busy chasing the mortar between the bricks ready for repointing. There was a sense of anticipation in the air today. The fan was going to be hoisted into position and reconnected. It was a day full of possibilities and promise. It was Friday.

The fan had been brought out of the barn and now rested in the weeds at the foot of the tower. Its old, rusty, bevelled drive gear, now recently wire brushed and regreased, resembled a large jelly that had just flopped out of its mould on to a plate. From the top of the scaffolding the gantry had been repaired and made ready to accept the axle of the fan and its attendant mechanical connections. A raised section of poles had been erected to reach up to the angled gantry that jutted out from the dome at about thirty degrees from horizontal. From this dizzying height the fan looked like a giant daisy, white against the thistles, dandelions and nettles below. It looked fragile too and feather light. Nothing could have been further from the truth. Its constitution had been restored to its former glory and was now as robust as ever. As for its supposed lack of weight it was going to require four men to lift it off the ground and into position.

In amongst the weeds the axle, a long steel rod two inches thick, was in the process of being driven through the fan's central boss. Everything about this mill's restoration had been a delicate combination of savage brute force and precise engineering. This axle was a case in point. It did not want to go through the two-foot deep hole that had been carefully drilled through the boss to take it. In the end they had to bore a four-foot deep hole in the ground, place the boss over it and then sledge hammer the axle into place. Two taps and check, over and over until it was perfectly centralised. Then, with rope attached, the hoisting began.

Considering all the work that had gone towards this moment, it was all over in a matter of seconds. In half a minute the axle lay in its grooves in the gantry, ready for the securing brackets for the bearings to be bolted into place. This part of the operation, on the other hand, was not at all easy to achieve, as the breeze began to force the sails of the fan round. Left to its own devices it would no doubt have spun round at fantastic revolutions. Even so it took some time before its modest rotation could be arrested and tied fast by ropes.

The prop shaft was dragged up next, complete with its own bevelled gear on one end and the pinion gear on the other, each of which was heavily greased. The bevelled gear was connected to the one on the fan. The pinion gear sat squarely on the rack of gears that lined the top of the tower on which the dome sat. It was a moment of relief to see that the measurements had been so accurate. The height caused all concerned to be ever careful. It was with some trepidation that he tightened up the bearings for the drive shaft on the internal supports at intervals along the length of the gantry. The rack and rails capping the tower's rim had been greased the previous day. So too had the wheels that supported the dome upon it. All that remained was to dismantle the section of scaffolding that reached up to the gantry and to release the rope holding back the fan. Danno called up to the sweating team, who had made today's feat possible. He had been back to Empton and brought back a barrel. From their high position, they could see it on the flat bed of the old vehicle. It was not every day that Danno showed his appreciation. Like monkeys they descended the ladders at varying rates, all save one.

He stopped to look at the fine piece of machinery they had put in place, and that he had designed. It was a bad time for a celebration. He would have preferred the thing to have been tested and proven before any beer had flowed. It tempted fate, but it was symptomatic of Danno and his arrogant attitude. Up here, high above the noise and chatter of the men below, he enjoyed a moment of calm, almost as if he was looking for the first time at his newly born child. This mill was becoming his. He was forgetting it belonged to the swellhead below. It was he who had agonised over the details of its rebirth, not Danno. He felt that it should be him getting the beer in for the happy event. The moment hung in the air like a vapour. All the pieces seemed to fit. They did fit. The proud moment was up here, not down there with the empty gesture of beer and meaningless congratulations.

"Oi, get the fuck down here. I'm in the chair," came the vulgar invitation.

He left his baby and, with a sense of unease, descended to a dusty earth, inhabited by grateful, ill-paid workers ecstatic that Daniel Harper himself had deigned to proffer upon them free drinks. If it were not so pathetic it would have been almost funny.

"Here, get that down your neck."

He was handed a glass of grey beer.

"Down the hatch," he replied.

"Aye, it'll be down the bloody hatch for you if this bastard doesn't work."

He choked on each and every gulp. As Danno watched, his victim tried to appear calm.

"What do you think we should do to him boys if the thing fails the test. Any ideas?"

There was silence. Most people knew that these were not idle words. The persecuted one felt in no doubt either. He was getting fed up of the negative force of Danno's personality willing him to fail. He drank the dregs at the bottom of his glass and looked his persecutor squarely in the eye.

"Let's watch it work first Danno, before we make any further plans, shall we?"

He called to Herbert to climb up to the top again and give him a hand with the scaffolding. Herbert placed his half empty glass on the back of the lorry, quietly eager to use this order to defy his lord and master. He grabbed a couple of spanners and followed on behind.

Whether it was the climb or the high sun that did it, they were both hot and exhausted once they made it to the rim of the tower. The sky was void of any clouds. Above them blazed the white-hot disk of the sun, set in a flat, grey sky that should have been azure blue.

111

Even the wind, which had cooled them during the morning, ceased making the job of loosening the scaffolding brackets more tiring than ever. Each pole, once it had been taken away, was neatly placed on the running boards that surrounded the upper limit of the brick tower. Far below an expectant crowd waited to see if the fan would do its job.

At last the final pole was removed and the gantry was free to move. With a sharp yank of the rope securing the fan the slipknot pulled loose and fell to their feet in a random coil. The complete mechanism was now liberated. Several days of intense work finally ready to be proven and it would have been but for the lack of wind. The air was still. Like some stubborn, ethereal donkey it refused to make a move. The fan sat in its gantry hopelessly static. In a demonstration of wishful thinking he looked at Herbert, licked his finger and held it out to feel for a ghost of breath. Nothing. He glanced down at those on the ground. Danno was there amongst them arms folded, waiting.

"No wind up here," shouted Herbert.

"I know, I'm not stupid," Danno yelled back. "Get down. We'll call it a day. Bring some poles down with you."

They both grabbed hold of a couple of the smaller ones and backed down the ladders to the dust.

"Right," said Danno to everyone as he leaned against the cab of his lorry. "We'll have a tidy up, and then it's off to meet the boys at The Goose," then he shouted, "Caruso!" above the men's chatter. "All except you. I want a word with you first."

He came over to the lorry ready to explain that once the wind began the fan would rotate the dome.

"Let's get one thing straight," began Danno, as he arrived. "I'm the boss around here. If you make the mistake of undermining my authority and making wisecracks again in front of my men, you'll lose. Got it?"

He was just about to answer when Danno put the question to him once more, with increased force.

"Got it? People hereabouts play by my rules. You'll do well to remember that, singer man. Now piss off and help tidy up."

There was no point in arguing. He could not think how to argue on the matter, even if he wanted to, and winning a battle of words was by no means the best way to come out on top in any event. So he turned away and joined the others who were loading the lorry up with tools and other bits. By noon the place was as shipshape as it was possible to be. He climbed into the back of the lorry with Herbert and the others and left the sleeping mill to another day in its steel cage of scaffolding.

They stopped off at the farm and cleared the back of the old vehicle, moving the tools into the barn. He looked around to see if anyone was in the house. The dog was wide awake at the sound of all the noise and yanking at its chain, barking with intent to kill. There was no sign of anyone else at home. No one. No Lotty.

When all was done Danno announced that they were to jump on the empty lorry and he would give them all a lift to the pub. There was an over appreciative cheer at this favour and the boss filled himself up with yet more self-importance as they clambered aboard. The back of the rumbling flatbed was full of simple happiness. Herbert pulled everyone's leg. He knew all there was to know about each person, but no one minded at all, in fact it was a mark of belonging to have the piss pulled this way.

"And this one here," he began. "Mr Miller I call him. The only person I know who fixes up a windmill and turns the wind off at the wrong moment."

He smiled back as the men's laughter because he was being included for the first time in the friendly banter. As soon as they arrived at the Golden Goose and the engine had shaken itself dormant they could hear singing. It was Friday afternoon, his third Friday, though that thought never occurred to him for a moment. They all piled in. Danno led the group carrying the empty barrel. He brought it with a slam on the bar. Harry's face was on the edge of fright.

"There you go landlord, and let that be a lesson to you," said Danno.

The singing had stopped. Everyone was button-lipped.

"Very good," answered Harry.

"Right. We'll say no more about it, all right?"

"Just as you say Danno."

The boss turned his back to the bar to face his faithful men. There were those who had just come in with him and over in the corner was George seated at the piano. Will and the boys stood on ceremony around him.

"Right, pints all round is it?"

There was yet more sycophantic cheering. Such displays of artificial affection were a matter of survival in this small community, he observed. Harry meanwhile, putting on fake cheerfulness, filled up a long line of glasses and each man helped himself to one.

"Give us a tune then George, ay?" shouted Danno over the hum of his men's voices.

"*One Man Went To Mow*, Sir?"

"You read my mind, Georgie lad."

With that the weekly ritual began all over again - the same repertoire in the same order. The pasties were brought out of the kitchen and then there was the call for Mr Miller, as he was now cheerfully being called, to sing. To sing, yes, to sing. *Danny Boy*, that is what they wanted, but he thought for a second or two and then asked George if he knew *Ole Man River?*

"It's more for a baritone, but we'll have a go shall we?"

"What about *Danny Boy?*" said George, feeling uneasy.

"This one's about folks who toil all day in the fields, folks like you."

George flashed a glance around the room searching for a consensus.

"I'll sing *Danny Boy* after, if it'll make you happy," said the singer by way of compromise.

The pianist managed a brief smile at his soloist and placed his hands on the keyboard. Suddenly Danno's voice shot like cannon fire towards the duo.

"They've asked for *Danny Boy*. Who the hell are you to tell them what they'll listen to?"

All eyes focussed on the boss. His eyes were wild. Even George and Will were taken aback by such an outrage about something as innocent as the choice of a song. The singer could see it too. He could sense that it was nothing to do with a choice of music. He had deliberately chosen a song with references to *sweat and strain, and bodies all achin' and wracked with pain* in order to turn attention onto the

114

workers. The wild eyes were more full of tantrum than displeasure or anger and the boss, it appeared, did not want his workers to have the slightest sense of self. Power was what mattered, power, not only over the individual, but also of the mass.

"There's to be no slave songs on a Friday," he said with a calmer tone. He seemed afraid that his outburst could have been seen as a loss of control. "Any road, we don't care for rivers, do we boys?"

There was a ripple of strained laughter that trickled from an understanding of the reference. Mr Miller wondered what he meant but already the piano was playing and the exquisite accompaniment of the *Londonderry Air* was calming the ugly situation with every bar. The song was sung as if by an automata. George finished it off with his now famous plink. The pasties were eaten but the good humour never came back. The pub would always be a happier place without Danno in it.

It was time to leave. Soon there was just Danno and the singer left in the bar.

"Well, see you tomorrow, Danno," he said lightly, as he got up to go to his room.

Danno lunged at him like a tiger.

"What the fuck are you up to?" he whispered in his ear.

"Up to?" he replied, taken by surprise.

"No one defies me. Up at the mill this morning, songs about poor working bastards just then. I say what goes on here and if I say sing the sodding *National Anthem*, then that's what you bloody well sing. Got it?"

The words were spat out through clenched teeth.

"I was only…" but he was stopped from uttering another word as Danno grabbed hold of his lapels.

"Any more backchat, and I'll have to teach you a few lessons. Now fuck off up to your little hole and think about it," he pushed him back with a flick of the wrists, "and don't be late tomorrow," he barked as he walked out of the pub.

He sat clumsily down at a table shaking, trying to smooth down the creases in his jacket. It had rapidly become clear that he was going to have to treat this man quite differently from the others. In fact he came to realise that he was going to have to treat him like everyone else did. That is how they had survived Mr Harper - that is how they had survived generations of Harpers and their kind.

Harry came over to collect glasses and sat beside him. He had witnessed the scene from the confines of the scullery behind the bar. All his sense of grudge had been swept away by what he saw.

"You get on the wrong side of him and there'll be hell to pay. I've already warned you about him," he said with true concern "And I should know. I asked him to pay his bill this morning, Thirty-eight pounds, eighteen and truppence it comes to now, if you don't count the rabbits. He told me that he alone decided who gets paid and when and, to prove the point that he owns just about everything around here, he took a barrel of bitter with him."

"Does he have to control everything?"

"He doesn't have to," said Harry. "It's enough for you to know that he just does, that's all."

"How can he treat people like that and get away with it?"

"Look lad. It's like I've said the Harpers own all the farms hereabouts. You strike a twenty-mile radius around this here pub and it'll be a Harper farm. Bofindle was the last of the little independents to go. Charlotte was faced with losing her title to the land and buildings, or hanging on to it by marrying that... man," Harry moved closer across the table folding his arms on the beer-stained wood. "Arthur Gibson had run that farm since he was twenty-one, long before he was married. It had been a Gibson farm for years, hundreds of years it's said."

Mr Miller felt the suction of the story draw him in.

"Go on," he urged.

"Well, Charlotte, Mrs Harper, as she is now, poor cow, had been going with a woodman from near Tunby, a little hamlet up the road. There was talk that she was engaged to him. He stood to gain the farm if he married her, only there was a problem."

"A problem?"

"Aye, the matter of debts. Arthur had found it more and more difficult to compete with the Harper farms. Bofindle had been losing money on account of it being surrounded by all these bigger farms, so David, Charlotte's fiancé, as you might say, went to Salisbury to arrange a loan. We never saw him again. He was a lovely man, very funny, used to make us laugh all the time. Danno hated him. Hated how popular he was. He hated the fact that he was going to have the one great prize that he craved day and night for."

"Charlotte, you mean?"

"No you stupid bugger. Bofindle," Harry chuckled. "He was never interested in women. Cor, you should have seen how he treated his mother. Almost killed her he did with his temper. Mind you, his dad was no better. They've all got that nasty streak. Like I said don't you go upsetting him or any of them. You learn to play by the rules and you'll be tickety boo."

He wanted to ask about the woodman. The subject of this David character caused a sense of morbid fascination, even dread and he wanted to know more. Harry had not referred to the burning of a cottage to explain David's disappearance. Maybe he did not know about it. Or possibly he was keeping to the line that it was unwise to mention it to anyone. Saying that the woodman was never seen again was a safer version. He decided to tread carefully to see if Harry would open the forbidden door and talk about what really had happened. The doctor's words were still fresh in his mind and they tempered the way the questions would come to be asked.

"Where did you say this David lived?" he tried.

"Somewhere near Tunby. I was told he had a place of his own, I know that much. Not tied to the job or anything."

He wanted to probe further.

"Is it for sale then, this house?"

Harry looked across at him as if looking at a child who persisted in asking why all the time.

"How the bloody hell should I know?" he said with a severe tongue.

"I only asked."

"Well don't ask. In fact, if I were you, I'd forget all about the woodman."

"Why?"

"Y is a crooked letter that can't be straightened," he replied with impatience as he picked up the last few glasses. "You keep your mind on other things, you'll live longer that way."

Harry rolled into the scullery, glasses in hand, humming a meaningless tune. The bar was empty. So he wandered out into the afternoon air, laced with summer warmth and nature's smells. The roses that lined the doorway delivered a delicate concoction of scents, as did the trees and the grass. As if to underline the fact that Empton was a rural community, he detected the distant smell of manure coming from the nearby farms, nearby farms like Bofindle where Lotty was heading off to meet him.

Friday afternoon had at last arrived and lesson two was just a walk in the woods away, but what would be the price for these lessons he wondered. He had seen the effects of merely back chatting Danno. What about this lunacy? Was it worth it? Was it worth a walk in the woods? Or would it be a walk into stupidity, the worst kind of stupidity. My God he thought but she was a beauty and he could not fight the need to make love to her again. He had arrived at the wood's edge after all and penetrating deeper and deeper with every footfall.

The wood. It wore no cloak of mystery now. He easily recognised familiar features such as tufts of grass that he had once made note of, a collection of broken branches lying on the fern floor in the form of some avant-garde sculpture. None of the serenity had changed. He was just like a verger in a church. The surroundings possessed a comfort to him, a peace that was easily taken for granted. He walked for twenty minutes and then quite abruptly stopped.

He had arrived at the place. There was no one there, and, as if it was unable to bear the loss of such an expectation, his heart inflicted stabs of aching disappointment on itself. Such an ache only served to swell the yearning and magnify the desire for her. After nearly a week of putting up with the heavy hand he felt he could not face losing out on the sweetness that he felt was his.

Ever since he received the note hidden away in the sandwich, he had imagined that she would be there waiting for him. He had allowed images of this meeting to roll around in his mind over and over. Mostly he had run through the woods to find her there, half naked with her deep, dark, take-me-now eyes boring into his groin. He would ravage her there and then and she loved it. Now he was mad at himself for being so idiotic as to believe the actual event

118

would turn out so. In any case, the last time he had met her she was late. He would have to be patient.

A fir cone fell to the ground from high up in the branches and bounced in the undergrowth, disappearing. He took a deep sigh. It was as if this age old ritual had probably been occurring in these woods for centuries. The falling of the little cone set before him a different clock - the steady, slow tick of nature that seemed to make waiting for something full of goodness that much easier to endure.

He came off the path and sat to rest his back against the trunk of a tree. Somehow the peace and calm of the wood always won through. Another cone fell, landing close to his out spread feet. He leaned forwards to pick it up. What a marvel of natural achievement it was. Each tiny oar bent outwards from its stem was set in a perfect geometric pattern that reached its ultimate precision in the centre where its stalk had been attached. After working on the mill all week, he had to accept that the natural world was the master when it came to engineering.

As if to mock him further another cone hurtled from the heights and hit him squarely on the head. He immediately put his hand to his crown in needless protection. It had caused no pain, only surprise. He had not expected to be hit on his head. Then two fell together by his side followed by an odd noise behind him. He turned to see what the sound was, only to find Lotty throwing fir cones at him. She was trying to hold back her laughter, one hand pressed wickedly against her mouth stifling the giggles. He got up to chase her but she was quicker than him and they both delved into the depths where the trees were thicker and the light dimmer.

She was a woman of the forest. Her light and graceful sprint over the brambles and ferns was a result, not only of power and strength, but also of an instinctive knowledge of this arboreal landscape. He could not compete and, as fit as he was, he lacked her gazelle-like ability to bound and leap. It was all he could do to follow the breathless laughter that lured him towards thicker undergrowth. It was only by chance that he saw her dart into what appeared to be a cave-like opening seemingly gouged into the side of a mass of leaves.

He was not a runner and he was out of breath by the time he reached what turned out to be a tunnel created by mangrove-like

119

roots and branches that burrowed deep into a swathe of rhododendron bushes. From the dark interior, of what was a confusing labyrinth of such passageways, he caught the sound of her laughter. He crouched down and made his way towards the intoxicating voice. Further in he was forced to crawl on the soft humus that formed the tunnel floor. Then quite suddenly he came upon a chamber where the roots or branches had naturally separated higher up. It was almost possible to stand upright and, just visible, lying at the far end in an almost foetal position was Lotty her breasts rising up and down as she caught her breath. They were both panting. They were both wanting and, without a word they fell into each other's embrace and absorbed themselves in each other's lips.

Very little of the afternoon light was able to penetrate through the dense high conifers, nor past the thatch of broad leaves that formed the roof of their hideaway. In the dimness he watched her remove her boots. Then, kneeling as if she was facing an altar, she lifted her dress up and over her head and laid it on the soft velvety carpet. She was deliberate and slow, taking her time. Again she smothered his mouth with hers and then standing, her hands slipped off his jacket and undid the buttons of his shirt. He lowered his head to bury his lips into her neck and, groaning with the pleasure of it, she unfastened his trousers and they fell to his knees. As if partially freed from a spell he threw off his shoes and socks and stepped away from the fallen garments - and there they stood in their underwear beholding each other. Nothing was ever so perfect. He was in a high state of nervous excitement. Surely, he thought, it was not possible to be so aroused.

Her body was beautifully proportioned. A mass of dark hair graced her shoulders. Her petite belly rested on slender hips that curved in sculpted magnificence following a graceful line to her legs. She gripped his pants and pulled them down. There he stood naked before her. His end was stretched stiff as if to explode. She reached down and wrapped her hand around it, pulling the foreskin down and up and down again. He grunted at the pleasure of it. This was teasing on a scale that he had never known - but there was more to come. She removed her grip and reached behind her back. He watched as the bra jolted loose. One shoulder strap fell away, then the other. Finally the bra fell to earth.

They were staggeringly beautiful - full, round, almost liquid, with dark nipples that rested on the upper curves. He moved to caress them, he wanted to press her close to him and, as he approached her, she took his hands and placed them on the waistband of her knickers. They were cotton and elasticated. He slid them over her white rounded hips so that now they were both naked. For the first time their warm bodies merged into one as they lowered themselves to the ground.

As they kissed she took his hand and moved it past her belly and on past the tuft bush of hair. She purposefully selected his index and middle finger and showed him where to rub her. He could feel the place, the thing she wanted him to play with. It slipped in and out of his fingers, but every time he came upon it she became submerged in deeper ecstasy. His head reached down to the breasts that had now spread out flatter and, taking one of the nipples in his mouth, sucked and licked it with his tongue. All the while she was sliding her thumb over his soft, sensitive end, causing him almost to choke on the pleasure of it. Her fanny was saturated. His fingers were wet through.

"Get in, get in," was all she sighed.

It took no doing to plunge into her. He could feel the little part of her that he had been rubbing with his fingers now slipping on the head of his penis as it delved in and out. Each and every motion caused her to cry out as if in exquisite pain. He could feel a return of the feeling well up from his stomach just as before.

"God, oh God," was all she whispered quietly.

Her hips rose up with each plunge he made. They were as one in motion. He could feel that rush about to explode from him. He could see that she was about to have a fit. His hips pumped up and down wildly. So did hers in partnership with him. She felt luxurious underneath him. He cried out as his fluid filled her. She cried out for him not to stop. She cried out as if she was being dismembered, each penetration caused her to become almost deranged. He had completely emptied himself into her, and still she begged him not to stop. The sensation was hard to bear. He felt different, almost in an instant physically different. What he felt was pleasing but he sensed it was too pleasing to stand. He tried to continue but after a short while it was no good. Even pulling out of her made him feel as if he was going to have convulsions.

"Rub me, just rub me," was all she grunted.

His fingers became buried once more in the soft, wet flesh. He continued to rub her for several minutes before she closed her legs, exhausted. All that was left was the sound of their breathing, slowly settling down to normality. They curled up to each other for warmth and fell asleep.

It was either the cool chill, or the far distant bark of a dog that woke them. She turned over to face him. They seemed to have woken simultaneously. A carpet of black particles was embedded in her shoulder, and with a lover's instinct he brushed them off her. She began to shiver slightly.

"That's probably Danno home," she said listening for the dog to sound again.

He leaned forward to kiss her and wrap himself around her, to warm her.

"I can't, not now. If I hurry, I won't be missed. I can pick some blackberries on the way home," she said as she reached for her clothes.

"Blackberries?"

"Use your brain," she answered a trifle agitated.

"Ah," he said waking up, and remembering the day of the mushrooms.

Her clothes were on in the blink of an eye. She could see the slightly confused look on his face, forlorn, as she got to her feet.

"I hate to have to go back, more than you," she said.

"I don't know how you put up with him," he said.

"I have my ways."

"Ways? What's your secret?"

"He's like all men. They all want to know how brave and clever they are, even when they're not. Danno doesn't so much want a wife. He wants a nanny for his ego, not to mention the farm. But that's half in my name, so he hasn't got it all quite has he?"

"Don't you feel...?" he searched for a suitable word.

"Afraid?" she suggested.

122

"Well, worried he'll harm you, maybe."

"Dad said that he'd arranged things so that I'd never have anything to fear. He made a point of telling me that before he died. When Dad arranged things they stayed arranged. I think he got one over on Danno somehow. I only get scared when he's drunk. But the vicar helps me when he gets in a state. Look, I've got to go."

She smiled at him lying there, still naked.

"Hurry up and get your clothes on, I'll point you in the direction of the path."

"It's all right. I'll walk with you."

"Are you stupid?" she said sharply. "You'll set off ten minutes after me. Now come on. Get dressed."

Soon they emerged from their secret grotto into the comparative light of the dense wood. She stretched out her hand like Moses parting the Red Sea.

"Keep on in that direction. You'll come to a faint track. Turn right and you'll reach the path. Right again and you'll reach the village."

"But what about? Well, when will we...?"

"You still like pickle in your sandwiches, don't you?"

He just smiled, mostly at her ingeniousness. Then she smothered his lips with hers and vanished into the interior. Just then a fir cone fell on to the springy ground. He picked it up for a talisman and gazed at its wondrous geometry until it was time to leave.

Chapter eleven: Vikings

"Well, I'll be buggered," said Herbert, as if talking to himself.

He was standing uneasily on the rocking flatbed, holding onto the roof of the cab, staring at the approaching mill. As the lorry clattered towards the brow of the rise he turned to Scrumps and smiled.

"Look, she's turned."

Scrumps stood up to join him to see that the dome of the mill was pointing in a new direction.

"Stone the crows," he said, "she's done a quarter turn, ain't she Herb?"

Inside the cab, holding onto his ham and pickle sandwiches, someone else had noticed it too and had elected to say nothing - at least not yet.

They arrived at the old tower, now trapped inside its cage of scaffolding, and each of them got out to begin their jobs. It was a calm morning, a Saturday morning. He used to love Saturdays. Without saying a word he ran up to the tower and ascended through its workings to the top. He knew well the place where the fan's drive pinion had rested on the rack at the top of the tower's wall. The little gear had been above a stain of grease that was caused by his attempts to lubricate it. He raced to the spot excitedly out of breath.

A wonderful smile spread across his features as he reached the dark, oily patch. Above it now was the wooden wall of the dome. Ninety degrees to the right the gear had come to rest. He looked through the aperture that led out to the gantry where the fan was fixed. How he wished he could have seen it work. It did not seem enough just to know that it had. At some point in the night, a breeze had turned the clean white fan, and pulled the main sails into wind, if there had been any. He would have relished the clanking of the gears turning the white cap of the great dome. But the morning was still and a chilled mist hung in the air. He would have to wait. The only sound he could hear was the noise of footsteps approaching. The sound grew louder and by instinct he knew who was coming.

"Suppose you think you're a bit of a clever Dick now, ay?"

Danno's eyes were hidden under his heavy brow as he looked through the trap door. The question seemed to stem from them and not his mouth.

"I'm pleased that it worked, if that's what you mean," he said.

"Well that's the point," he continued. "It's not working yet, is it? Before your head swells too big, I ain't seen no fucking flour coming out of this mill."

"Aren't you even pleased that we've got the first bit working?"

"There's only two things that'll make me pleased," he said slowly, pausing for a brief moment to make sure his victim paid attention. "The first is getting one over on the Wagstaffs and their rip off water mill and the other is teaching you who's the fucking boss around here."

He could not think what to reply.

"Now get your arse out of my mill," and he disappeared from the trap door to organise his men.

All the joy that just a moment ago had lifted him, now drained away like shed blood from a stabbed heart. He clambered down the stairs with the poison of misery in him. As he approached the ground floor he remembered what Harry had said the previous afternoon. It did nothing to cheer him but it did colour the way he decided to behave that day. He would have to learn from those about him the subtle ways of surviving the Harpers - after all they had managed to do so, and so would he. When all was said and done it was a Harper mill. He emerged out into the misty morning. Danno was directing where the supplies from the lorry were to be delivered. He strode like a dominant male in a pride of lions. He did not have to be told he was at the top of the tree in these parts. He knew he had been born to it.

He walked over to Danno ready to eat a portion of humble pie.

"Just a bit too keen there, I'm afraid," he said.

"Keen eh?" Danno remarked.

"I just wanted to know if anything had been damaged up there, that's all."

"Better not have, Mr Miller, for your sake."

He realised he was not going to appeal to Danno's better nature - he had none.

"I need to make a start on fixing up a new sail and connecting them to a new boss," he found he was talking faster. "I'm not sure how we're going to lift them and rig them up to the shaft. There's some weight there."

"Am I paying you to talk or get this mill working?" said Danno.

He was about to answer back and only managed to control his tongue just in time.

"I'll get your mill working, don't worry about that."

"I won't," Danno said quietly. "Worrying about that is your fucking job. Now piss off and get busy."

He did as he was told like an obedient dog then went to find the four carpenters, getting his pencil drawings out of the lorry's cab on the way. The sandwiches were there, vulnerably left near the windscreen. He grabbed them and stuffed them in his pocket as if they were rags. He let a flicker of a smirk cross his face as he did so, knowing that there was more than sustenance wrapped up in the greaseproof paper. The irony of a scripture found its way into his mind, *man cannot live by bread alone*. A warm healing returned to his bruised spirit.

The morning wore on amidst the clamour of labour. The mist began to clear and the sun shed its white light everywhere on their colourless activities. As the carpenters finished setting up their stall the leaves of the poplar trees close to the village rustled gently. As the sound of their sawing grew ever more industrious so too did the swaying of the tall trees. Then there came a muffled clanking sound from high up, close by. The fan was revolving. He stood back, as they all did, to see the small sail spin and the great white dome rotate and point windward where the sails would have been to face the valley below the hill. The moment deserved a cheer. There should have been applause and handshakes. He felt a crushed sense of pride in his heart but it remained lashed down lest he should offend the lion king. It would have to be enough to know that his plans were solid. From that moment on he worked quietly helping his carpenters make sense of his scale drawings, keeping the sense of confidence he felt from seeing the dome spin on its tower secretly to himself, but inside his head, oh, there were celebrations.

The broken sail on first appearances seemed a delicate affair and, it was not until they tried to move it, that they realised just how incredibly heavy it was. This discovery threw up a number of problems. The most obvious one was that once all four sails had been assembled to a newly manufactured boss, how were they going to haul it up and connect it to the main shaft eighty feet or so above them? The damaged sail was lying in a mass of overgrown weeds in a field adjacent to the mill. It had evidently fallen and hit the ground with monumental force. Most of its injuries were at the far end where the impact had occurred and more than half of the louvre slats were

126

missing. Those that remained in place were either split or shattered. Only four of a full complement of twenty-five were intact and, of those, only two were able to move as they were meant to. A far greater worry concerned one of the two main shafts of the great sail. It was severely fractured. He looked round and presented his frowning face to the four carpenters. They each managed poor excuses for smiles and declared with professional pride that, even without the aid of drawings, they were still capable of fixing this giant wing as they called it.

With some enthusiasm they went straight to work and he had to restrain them from going headlong into the task without any understanding of the sail's anatomy. In an effort to explain something of the theory of the slats to them he led them up to the barn in the village. There he pulled at the connecting lever at the hub end of the sail. They watched the slats open and close. They were filled with understanding and, when the reason for the mechanism was explained, they all let out a collective, ah, yes, I see!

The morning passed quickly and noisily. The work was getting done - it was like a competition to see who could create the greatest din. As the carpenters worked on a new stretch of oak to repair the fractured limb of the sail, the men on the scaffolding hacked away at flaking mortar and tossed down broken pieces of bricks onto a heap of rubble building up below. Mingled into the industrious clamour came the intermittent outbreak of a whistled tune, or else it was a curse blasted at something that had gone missing or, as was more often the case, a lack of coordination between someone's hammer and a misplaced thumb.

Danno had left the site around mid-morning saying that he had need of the lorry and that he was going to be back later that afternoon. He gave instructions to Herbert that, come midday, if anyone wanted to walk home they were free to, Saturday being a half-day only. Nobody had bothered to bring a watch and Maltoft church had not been graced with chimes as Empton had. So they guessed by the sun when it was time to stop and eat. Once the noise had ceased and the work for the day was done, a group of three of the labourers headed down the hill to their village. They knew a way home across the fields and were quite happy to spend the afternoon wandering back to their pub.

Mr Miller, Herbert, Scrumps, Splash, two labourers and the four carpenters were left sitting on a pile of bricks at the foot of the tower. He reached into his back pocket for the compressed sandwiches. They had been flattened into wafers and it took some care to peel away the greaseproof paper with the barely discernible word pickle written on it.

"You ain't going to eat that are you?" laughed Herbert.

"He's going to write a letter on it," put in Scrumps. "It's as flat as a piece of paper, look."

Scrumps' comment was almost too close to the truth for comfort. He peeled back what was left of the bread, looking to find the note.

"He's trying to see if the filling's been squashed to nothing," said Herbert with more humour in his tone.

The ham was warm and sweaty and would have been completely unappetising had he not been so hungry. The bread was stuck fast to it. The job of finding the note was almost impossible. So when he decided to give up the search he was not sure whether to be disappointed that she had not written or to assume that it was there and that he was not able to get to it. He sighed with resignation and ate it all to the mock dismay of everyone present.

"So, who's for Shanks's pony?" piped up Herbert.

"All the way back?" said Splash. "Won't the boss be back soon?"

"You know him," replied Herbert. "Might cost him fuel to take us home. Besides we only have to make it to Rembleton. Jack Manders owes me a favour for those walls. He'll take us the rest of the way."

"You reckon. What if he ain't there?" Scrumps put in.

"That's the trouble with you, Scrumps, me old mate. You never look on the bright side, do you?"

"That's because I ain't never seen no bright side. Not since you started calling me Scrumps, any road."

"Well. I'm for a foot slog. Who's coming with me?"

As expected Scrumps and Splash agreed to go too. Mr Miller got up without hesitation, his sandwich resting now in his belly. Anything that helped to avoid Danno he thought was instantly deemed a good idea. In the end the carpenters and remaining labourers decided to stay and hope for the lorry to come back. Each group, the walkers and the waiters, said their goodbyes and soon there were four tramping down the hill, leaving the windmill behind - its body resembling Gulliver tied down by the Lilliputians, not with rope but by scaffolding.

At first they walked along in a shambolic heap. It was amazing how eventually they began to form into a group. By the time they reached the lower part of the hill they had become a squad of marching men. It was no one's decision, it merely happened, as the men kept in step the sound of their unified march on the road set up a perfect rhythm. It was a while before anyone spoke. Mr Miller eventually broke the silence.

"Why Scrumps?" he said, as they reached the level road. "Come to mention it, why Splash?"

"Go on Herbert," said Scrumps, "you tell it best. You tell him all about it."

"Oh my word. That's going back a bit, ain't it?" said Herbert chuckling. "Do you remember that old orchard up near Tunby? It's still there you know?"

"We know. We know," they said together.

"I love this story," said Scrumps, to their new friend. "Get on with it Herb."

Herbert's eyes misted over and took flight as if to another age. His two pals giggled like children about to be told a bedtime story. Then he began.

"I'm going back now, oh, forty-five years or more," he paused for a moment. "No, more like fifty. Well, the three of us, we grew up together. Like brothers we were. Still are, come to think of it."

The aura of his long vanished childhood seemed almost visible as the boy he had once been arose within him.

"One early autumn afternoon we all met up to have an adventure. We were about six or seven. We loved adventures. Most of the time we just walked around aimlessly waiting for an adventure to come along. Nothing happened usually but on this particular afternoon we decided to raid Tunby. We had been learning all about the Norsemen, the Vikings, so we decided to be Vikings and raid Tunby."

Mr Miller's face grinned as the silly story unfolded, enjoying every bit of it.

"Well, we got to Tunby, but we didn't know what exactly we were going to raid. We knew we had to steal something. That's what we'd been told the Vikings did, but we didn't know what to steal until we came across the orchard or rather the apples on the orchard trees. That's when our Viking blood got up and we set about to pillage the orchard there and then. Now the only trouble with the orchard was that a high wall made of stone surrounded it, and between the wall and the road there was a wide ditch full of stagnant water. We'd seen old fashioned castles and moats with Vikings attacking in the pictures our teacher shown us, so you can imagine we took the wall to be a rampart and the ditch to be a real moat."

"Tell him about the branches of the trees," urged Splash.

"All right, all right. I'm getting to that bit. Hold yer bloomin' horses. As I was saying, some of the apple tree branches overhung the high wall. That was our way in. I lifted these two on my shoulders and they reached for one of the branches. It bent as it took their weight but they had soon scrambled like monkeys over the ditch and across the wall."

"We scrambled like bloody Vikings, not flamin' monkeys, get it right," laughed Scrumps.

"They scrambled like Vikings over the ditch and the wall," he pretended to sigh with exasperation, "then they began to lob the apples over towards me. I stuffed them into my pockets, all the time keeping watch. We'd only just begun our Viking raid when there was a shout, a boy's voice coming from behind the wall. It was quickly followed by a man's yell, 'Oi you two, get down and come here,' he bellowed once more, and then there was a bang and instantly bits of lead shot were rattling through the branches. Well these two stopped being Vikings and raced out of that tree like a couple of frightened squirrels. The minute Scrumps here had hit the road I started running. Unfortunately Splash, bless 'im, got his braces caught in a spur in the bough. He missed the road and splashed into the stinking dyke. We ran back, grabbed him out of the water and legged it as fast as we could. Nobody ever found out it was us what pinched the apples but it was our first encounter with the Harpers. The boy was Danno's dad. The man who shot at us was his grandad."

"And you've been known as Splash and Scrumps ever since?" said Mr Miller.

"From that day to this," said Scrumps. "My real name's Alexander and his name is," he said cocking a thumb towards Splash, "Joshua."

"And did anyone find out about the raid?" said Mr Miller.

"Splash's dad did," said Herbert, "when he got home wet through. He found some apple leaves in his pocket and put two and two together. Took his belt to him he did and warned him not to do it again. His dad faced eviction from his tied cottage if the truth had been found out. His mum washed his clothes there and then and dried them in front of the fire so no one would smell the foul water on him."

"The funniest thing is that Danno has known us as Splash and Scrumps all his life and he has no idea why. None of the Harpers know why either come to mention it. There's little things like that what keeps us going," said Alexander.

"But was everyone that scared of the Harpers even back then?"

"You don't ever mess with them, believe me. They seem to hold the balance of life and death around here. You keep your nose clean and you'll be all right. I ain't seen no one come off the better when an Harper was concerned. Well, that is if you don't count these two pillocks here," said Herbert, and all four laughed as they marched along the lane.

The bonhomie continued until they reached the house of Jack Manders. In fact it was a forge with a house attached. An argument was in full swing inside the forge itself between a high-pitched female screech and a rather submissive tone of a man's deep voice.

"I ain't slaved over a rabbit pie for you to let it go cold," snapped the venomous woman.

"I can't help it if I ain't heard you. It's me hammer."

"It'll be your hammer all right, on your flamin' noggin if you don't come in this instant."

There was a clattering of tools on the floor and, from the depths of the dark workplace, there emerged a huge man in a leather apron and a tiny lady dressed all in black except for a sullied white apron.

They both caught sight of the advancing troupe. The lady beheld them through her tightened eyes, as a witch would have done. The giant man waved pathetically and attempted a smile.

"We ain't come at a bad time, have we Jack?" said Herbert.

"Er, no Herb. Grace was just telling me it's time for dinner. Wasn't you dearest?"

"And who's this, might I ask?" demanded the lady, nodding her head in the direction of Mr Miller.

"It's our Mr Miller," said Herbert. "He's fixing the mill up at Maltoft. He's the one who…"

The lady interrupted.

"The one who fixed Arthur's tractor. I know. I'm not chained to the range all day, I'll have you know."

Jack glanced to his friends making sure his beloved was not looking and cast his imploring eyes heavenward.

"I was wondering, Jack," said Herbert, "If you could take us home, when you've had your dinner like?"

"Be glad to boys. I need a new grottlehopper from the shop," he said, making sure his wife could hear him.

"Aye, and I've got a list of things you can bring home while you're at it," she said.

He quietly sighed with relief that he had been given chance to escape, even if it was at the expense of having to do some shopping. Ten minutes later he emerged into the sunshine and ran to the back of the forge. In no time at all a battered American Army Jeep, complete with a white star in the front, bounced onto the lane.

"Hop in boys," he shouted.

They all clambered aboard like a Flying Fortress crew and sped down the lane like the devil was under the bonnet. In no time at all they had whizzed past the turn off to Tunby and came thundering into Empton at the speed of sound. Except for the driver they were all doubled up in fits of excited laughter. Jack pulled on the brake beside the Golden Goose calmly smiling with pride.

"Time for a round before I'm missed," he said to his friends, and they all piled into the pub like a band of desperados.

Harry, busy behind the bar, looked up and saw someone he had not seen for ages.

"Well, I'm buggered. If it ain't Jack Manders. You ain't changed a bit."

"Harry, you old sod. You're still a fat bastard then?" and they shook hands as only old friends can.

Herbert explained to Harry about needing the lift home and Harry asked Jack how Grace was, in a knowing way. They passed a while going over trivial news and then Harry asked Mr Miller how the job up at Maltoft was going.

"We're fixing up the sails now. But the fan is working again."

"You reckon you're going to get it working on time?" said Harry.

"I've got the feeling I don't have a choice."

"You ain't felt nothing strange up there have you then?" said Harry in a sinister tone.

"What do you mean, strange?" he asked.

"Like you're being watched," explained Harry. "An unseen eye, you might say."

"Remember that mill up on Old Dyke Lane?" put in Herbert.

"Do I remember?" said Harry with a knowing look.

"Go on," said Scrumps in an eager voice. "Tell the story of Old Dyke Lane."

"Later," said Harry. "Come back this evening, and we'll make a night of it. How's that?"

They all agreed. Jack tried to agree, but everyone could tell that it was not going to be easy for him to get away, as much as he wanted to. They each drank their drink, patted Jack on the back and went their separate ways.

It had been a tiring morning. He had a wash and took advantage of forty winks whilst he had the chance. He lay on top of his bed, resting his hands behind his head, thinking of the mill and the tasks ahead. Herbert and the others had imparted a genial sense of his being part of them. It felt good to be accepted like that. Danno worried him, not least because of Lotty. What might happen if he were to put too many feet wrong but then whatever was perfect in life, he thought.

Gradually these notions lost their boundaries. Their individual properties, their entities were becoming melted down and merging with one another, the sense that each one had, or rather their essences were dulling. The sharp focus of each topic as an idea was by now a blurred piece of single thought that rolled around in his head, getting quieter and quieter, sleepier and sleepier. He was only just aware that he had drawn his arms from behind his head and rolled over when all his consciousness sank into the well of dreams. It did not last long. A little knock at his door propelled him uncomfortably awake.

"Who's that?" he said, deprived of the blessing of a good kip.

"It's me, Ellie. There's someone to see you. And you've…"

"I know," he yawned, "I've not to dawdle."

He ran his fingers through his hair, rubbed his eyes and followed her down to the bar. A man dressed in a smart grey suit was talking to Harry. He could not get a good look at him as Harry was blocking his view. It was only when Harry moved round to behold his lodger entering the bar that Mr Miller could see it was a vicar, or rather the vicar he had seen before when he had driven Danno home the night he had had a skin full.

"Ah, so this is your discovery," said the vicar, smiling.

"Pardon?" he said, looking at Harry for answers.

"I've been telling the vicar about your voice, your singing voice," explained Harry. "I always said you ought to be in the choir. Well, now's your chance."

"What we lack in the bass section we more than make up for with sopranos, if you follow my meaning," said the vicar.

"You mean you've too many ladies and not enough men, is that it?"

"Quite so, quite so," he replied.

"Go on, old son. You're a natural. You'll be amongst friends. You already know Mrs Eversage and George who plays the organ," said Harry.

"Well, I was in a choir once," he stared ahead, thinking.

It suddenly seemed a very, very long time ago, and somehow a long way away, in another world almost.

"Then you'll know a *Nunc Dimittis* from a *Magnificat*, won't you?" said Harry. "See Vicar, I told you he was just what you're looking for, didn't I?"

"Quite so," said the vicar, full of child-like innocence.

134

"Well, that's settled," said Harry. "Half past nine Holy Communion for you my lad, tomorrow morning. That'll set tongues wagging around the village and no mistake. You'll have a church full vicar by Harvest Festival."

"Splendid, splendid," said the vicar, finishing off his port wine before leaving. He turned his head round as he reached the door.

"See you tomorrow, Mr Miller."

Then he was gone.

"Looks like you could do with a drink yourself," smiled Harry. "Wait 'til I tell the lads tonight. You don't know it, but you've just gone up in the world my lad."

"Really?" he said, as he watched his pint being pulled.

"Oh aye," said Harry. "I reckon the Harvest Fayre will be happening here after all. And this pub will do a bomb."

"Harvest Fayre?"

"Yep, the Harvest Fayre," said Harry. "The location of the fayre had always been decided on which village had the best choir. It's been like that before I was born. It's all about who can bless the harvest with holy music the best, if you understand?"

"I think so."

"Look, the village choir that can sing *Harvest Home* or *All Things Bright And Beautiful* the loudest and the sweetest gets to host the fayre. And the village what hosts the fayre does all right in the money department. Folks will come from miles around for a proper fayre. It'll do the local economy no end of good, get it?"

"Oh now I see," he said.

"Penny dropped, eh? You're our very own secret weapon, at least your voice is. If we win the charter this year I might just let you stay here for free. There. Now how's that for an incentive?"

"But how do they know which choir is the best? Is there a vote or something like that? A committee maybe?"

"Ah, well, that's the exciting bit. Sometime in August none other than His Holiness the Bishop from Salisbury pays us a visit. A bit of a spot check, you might say. Only with you behind a pew, we'll be ready for him," Harry smiled a wicked smile. "I'd dare to say it's in the bag, old son."

"Well, I'll drink to free accommodation," he said with a grin, "Cheers!"

"Cheers!" said Harry.

The afternoon passed happily. There was contentment in the pub. The after taste following their row had long been laid aside and the two men worked in a cheerful state of cooperation until about an hour or so before opening time. Harry fixed up some food from left over pork pie, home-cooked ham and radishes. Ellie sat with them quietly and ate her meal with such practised perfection it appeared that she had been trained to do so. Then the doors were opened once more and the wait for customers began. It began and continued for some time, quite a long time in fact. He killed the dragging minutes by wandering around the bar looking at the old clock with its shiny pendulum swinging their lives away. He was drawn to one of the old photographs on the wall behind the bar. It was very faded and not very clear. Within its frame was an image of a village green covered with marquees and tents. In the foreground were five youths doing their best to keep upright on stilts. Each face was packed with happiness. Harry caught him looking at it.

"Recognise anyone?" he said.

He squinted and peered closer then flicked his head round towards Harry, and back to the photograph.

"That's you second from the left, isn't it?" he said.

"Yep, that's me all right. I was a mere lad of fourteen when my old man took that picture. Recognise anyone else then?"

He examined the other faces but it was hard to make out sufficient detail. He had to give up. Harry's finger pointed to the figure on the left.

"Well, left from right you first have Jack Manders. I thought you'd get him, what with him being so big and all. Then there's the handsome one, yours truly. Third along is Scrumps, then Herbert and tagging on the end is dear old Splash. We always hung around together. We called our gang The Vikings. Herb's idea."

"And what's with the tents in the background?" he asked.

"Well, you see, this photograph was taken in 1908. We'd decided to join the church choir as a lark that summer. There were some lovely girl sopranos there in those days. There was one particular one with the most amazing pair of lungs, as you might say, but anyway. We sang our hearts out when the bishop arrived knowing that the fate of the fayre rested with us. We must have been good because the next Sunday in church the Reverend Pritchard, as it was then, told us that the fayre would take place on our very own village green. That was the last time we ever held it at Empton. That big marquee is the beer tent. It was used as an overspill for the pub."

Harry was in full reminisce when Will and George arrived along with some of the boys from down the lane. By nine o'clock the place was full. Herb, Scrumps and Splash were present, as were Mrs E and her friend. There was a glorious cheer from them all when the sound of a jeep pulled up outside and a mischievous-looking Jack Manders came in.

There existed a strange peace in the pub that night, a relaxed and warm atmosphere. It was a Danno-less evening. When George was invited to bring a little entertainment to the proceedings he did so with a medley of old tunes that were seldom heard in his repertoire. As he floated effortlessly from one tune to another he craned his head over his shoulder and asked if anyone had any requests, or wanted to do a turn maybe. Harry seized his opportunity.

"Ladies and gentlemen, if you please, may I have your attention?" he began.

"Tonight, we have more than a turn to entertain you with, we have within our midst a saviour and it ain't Christ The Lord, so don't anyone panic just yet."

A ripple of good-humoured laughter filled the old place.

"You young-uns won't remember the last Harvest Fayre in Empton, but I can see one or two faces that do."

"Aye, and a bloody good weekend it were too," chimed up Herbert Ashcroft.

"Well folks," continued Harry, "happy days are here again," he turned to his lodger and wrapped a friendly arm round his neck. "Go on, you ought to tell 'em," he insisted.

There were a lot of faces to talk to, so he said it quietly.

"I'm joining the choir, tomorrow."

137

The old guard saw the implications of this immediately, especially those who had already heard him sing, and the cheers and applause became instantly infectious. It was an explosion of anticipated victory over Tunby. Quickly, spontaneously there was a call for him to sing. He was bundled to stand beside George who was seated at the piano amidst well meant backslapping and handshaking. The pianist and the singer exchanged the briefest and most knowing glance and spoke to each other, almost in unison.

"*Old Man River?*"

This too created well-received appreciation amongst the crowd. The demon of Bofindle Farm was away. It was time to let their guard drop, time to be real, time to enjoy. The piano prepared the audience for the song to come with the most endearing introduction and, in the deepest voice he could muster, he came in with a nod from George.

"*Ole man river,*
That ole man river,
He must know somethin',
But he don't say nothin'.
That ole man river,
He jus' keeps rollin' alon'."

All who listened were spellbound, even the young lads.

"*He don't plant taters,*
He don't plant cotton,
But them that plant 'em
Are soon forgotten."

The words had meaning for most of them who spent all their days on the land.

"*Tote that barge,*
Lift that bail,"

He sang with almost a boss's shout that had the ring of Danno about it.

"*I'm tired of livin'*
But scared of dyin',
But ole man river,
He just keeps rollin' along."

The piano played the last two bars of the tune again and finished with three of the choicest chords imaginable to round the song off. Mrs Eversage was quietly crying, holding her hanky to her mouth. Everyone else had been struck dumb. It was finally Harry who put his lone hands together and began to clap and soon the pub was bursting with applause.

Then, along with George, he led them all in a collection of well-known music hall songs that everyone joined in with *Down At The Old Bull And Bush, Daisy Daisy, It's A Long Way To Tipperary,* and a dozen or more. By now the candles and lamps had been lit, filling everywhere with a cosy light that cast deep snug shadows all over. There was magic in the air and a warmth, comradeship, belonging. The walls of the pub had, it seemed, taken hold of life and embraced them all with its affection.

Then Scrumps, who was by now slurring his words, gestured to Harry.

"What about the story of *Old Dyke Mill?*" he said.

Everyone joined in to enforce the request and wanted him to recount the tale that they had heard times many before. Harry's chest puffed out with pride. He knew the whole thing off by heart. It was his pièce de résistance, his party piece.

"All right, all right. Come on let's have a bit of order then. If you ain't got a drink, get 'em in now. It's a long one this is. I can't have you dying of thirst on me, eh?"

When everyone was ready he began. The place became hushed. The only sound was that of the clock on the wall. Harry looked into everyone's eyes creating the mood for the tale he was about to tell. He motioned a subtle nod to George who placed his fingers on the piano keys ready to make the muted accompaniment. Then he quietly began his monologue.

"There is a stretch of marshland, at the end of Old Dyke Lane,
It's always bleak and lonely, and there's often wind and rain.
And no one ever goes there, save the keeper of the mill,
And he's been dead for twenty years, but people sees him still."

The soft piano music that played alongside this sinister monologue had all the makings of a Stanley Holloway performance. Harry certainly had them in the palm of his hand, so much so, that Stanley

139

as well as the lion and Albert, would have been proud of him. Harry went on in a polished fashion, his wide-eyed gaze fixed in turn on each person present, bent on sending shivers down their spines.

"At times when dusk is fallen and there's not the slightest breeze,
The mill sails start a turning. Least that's what some folk sees.
It goes against all nature that the mill should come to life,
And you can guess that rumours round the village pub are rife."

He went on to tell of the miller who tramps the marshland, carrying a sack containing his soul on his back as he searches for the man who killed him.

"But no one dared to follow in his tracks beyond the lane.
The blacksmith, he turned down a bet, and said, 'You're all insane.
Though I've the biggest muscles hereabouts, and I'm not boasting,
There ain't no way in this wide world you'd get me out there, ghosting'."

At the mention of a blacksmith all eyes turned to Jack Manders.

"You wouldn't get me going out there neither," he said.

The long drawn out story, beloved by all who had heard it time after time, described how a diamond robbery had taken place nearby. The thief's attempts to hide his ill-gotten gains in what he thought was a disused mill ended, instead, with the death of old Tom Carver, the miller, who lived there. Except for Harry's voice and the simple chords of the accompaniment there was quiet. Not a word passed from those listening, so masterly was the spell he cast.

At this point in the tale a schoolboy called Adam Weedon, fascinated by books on crime and criminals, enters the story and sets out to solve the mystery. After many twists and turns he does so. Randall is arrested and confesses to all charges. Virtually every piece of the booty is found, all except for a great diamond called the King of Hearts. The boy even offers an idea as to where the great gem might be.

"The case made every headline as it rumbled through the court,
Which Adam read, bedevilled by the re-occurring thought, that,
The Coppers in the gem search, though each line of thought had followed,
Had not used lateral thinking, and imagined,
Was it swallowed?"

The youngster's hunch, so the story said, was that during the struggle between Randall and Carver, the old miller had secretly

140

gulped the diamond down his throat for safekeeping just before Randall had lynched him. They get permission to exhume Tom's remains from the graveyard and, sure enough, there it is resting in his rotting flesh. It's a happy ending especially for Adam of course, and then, like the true showman he was, Harry slowed down his delivery for the thirty-seventh and final verse.

"The mill became a tourist trap, where folks could hear the story,
Of Carver, Randall and the gem, with details grim and gory.
When Adam tells the tale himself, it gives them all a thrill,
To hear first hand just how he solved the mystery of the mill."

The final chord from the piano had not even begun to fade before the pub was filled with an ovation from the happy band of drinkers. Harry's face, so ghoulish during his rendition, bloomed into a proud, beaming smile. It had been a wonderful moment. More was to come when Herbert proposed a toast.

"What a feast of entertainment we have had this evening chums, wouldn't you declare?"

There was a ripple of agreement.

"I would like to propose that for his singing, joining the choir and his feats of windmillish superlativeness we decorate our Mr Miller here with an honorary membership of The Vikings. How do you say?"

The approval was unanimous judging by the cheers that raised the roof, the happy roof of the old Golden Goose.

Chapter twelve: Songbirds

It was annoying, oversleeping after a Saturday night of heavy drinking. Like old men he had known in another life he was going to have to run all the way to church on a Sunday morning. He arrived at the old arched doorway quite breathless.

Inside the musty interior a congregation of no more than twenty souls were engaged in pockets of discreet conversation, all respectfully conducted at a whisper. Most of the people there were old and female, and they conducted their gossip under the thin sound

141

that emanated from the lean pipes of the organ. It was a high-pitched reedy whine, the stuff of funerals, played with constant errors by the organist who was nursing a hangover - George. With relief the service had not started yet. Thank goodness he thought.

He had only just taken in these first impressions when he was greeted by the frosty attentions of the old lady he bumped into just days ago outside the pub - the lady he had also met in the churchyard when he first arrived. Somehow the pretensions of the high office she now held overshadowed the Christian virtues of love and kindness that ought to have infused her. With apparent self-importance she was giving out the hymnals and orders of service. He let her know that he had come to join the choir.

"Vestry," was all she said, and nodded in the opposite direction of the altar.

Following her gesture he soon reached an antique door and went through into a dank, wood-panelled room inhabited by two old men and three young boys dressed in cassocks and surplices. The smell of this room was a familiar one from long ago – a mixture of damp walls, dust and ageing paper. A cupboard of large, fat hymnbooks and other volumes stood in the corner. One of the men was handing out the hymn sheets and giving the number of the introit, the hymn that they would be singing as they walked down the aisle to their pews. The five faces, interrupted from their lofty labours, rose out of the pages of *Hymns Ancient And Modern* to behold him as he stepped into the old vestry.

"Ah, so you must be Mr Miller," said the taller of the two men, "you're late. You should be here by nine o'clock. You've missed prayers."

"Sorry," was all he could think of to say.

"Well, there isn't much time. You'll find some attire in the closet there."

He grabbed hold of a brass handle in one of the wood panels and it slid open to reveal a deep wardrobe with a motley collection of long cassocks and starched greying surplices. He was soon dressed and took his place beside the shorter of the two men. The taller one reached for a smooth pole made of dark wood that had a shiny silver cross on top of it and headed the front of the procession. A boy stood behind him, then the two others side by side and, finally, he brought up the rear with the shorter man.

The leader pulled on a wooden knob in the wall near the door and, as if by magic, the funeral music stopped and the opening line of the first hymn filled the church. The procession snaked out of the vestry. The vicar was waiting just outside the door and tagged himself onto the end of the line as it crept down the nave. By the time they had sung the first verse of *Hills Of The North Rejoice* they had reached the altar, turned and taken their places in their pews.

He began to wonder just what he had let himself in for. This choir had little if no idea about making music. The shindig at the pub had been more in tune, and if they had entertained any notions about winning the coveted charter for the fayre, then they were going to be sadly mistaken. The entire service, as far as the singing was concerned, was a catalogue of missed entries and failed harmonies. The pissed up state of poor old George made matters no better.

Worst still was the sermon from the vicar. The gist of it was that of man's free will. But the meaning of his message was drowned in fragile academic reasoning and impossible intellectual gymnastics. So much so, that these earthy farm workers may as well have been preached at by a being from a distant star. He watched how the congregation listened with a robotic and pious devotion to the vicar's every word. They were anaesthetised by the drone of his voice to a point of near trance. It was obvious that none of it made any sense to them. They were simply happy to be given an incomprehensible glimpse into the deep mysteries of The Almighty. By virtue of their inability to understand any of it only served to strengthen their sense of mystery and their very need for it.

The service came to a shambolic end with the recessional hymn *Lord Of All Hopefulness*. They walked at an idiotically slow march down the short aisle towards the door of the vestry, enabling the very last line of the very last verse to be sung as they disappeared back through the door. By the time he had disrobed and put away his hymn book he was the last to leave. Both men had been so wrapped up in dissecting what they took to be the finer points of the sermon they had failed to wish him a good morning. The three boys had flung their vestments vigorously onto their hangers, intent on getting out into the land of mischief with as much haste as possible. So he left the vestry alone, only to be met by the vicar at the main door of the church. He had just said good day to the protector of the holy books of song, the strange old woman who was now halfway down the gravel path.

"Ah, yes, many thanks, Mr Miller. And, er, what did you think to our faithful choristers?" he said proudly.

"Well, they're faithful," he quipped hoping the answer would be enough, but unfortunately it was not.

"No, I meant musically? I'd so like to do well when the bishop comes," said the vicar, with an expression of sincere self-preservation.

They had begun to stroll slowly away from the church towards the vicarage. The vicar stared at his feet treading the gravel drive like a detective deep in thought, a perambulating meditation, complete with hands clasped behind his back. He only looked up now and again to acknowledge his new choir member as they spoke. It was not going to be easy telling His Reverence that he thought his faithful choristers sang like shit.

"They're good on volume," he commented, trying to be polite, "but what we need is polish, lots of it. We need to come in together at the same time. Harmonies could be better."

"Oh," said the vicar, his face awash with disappointment. "Bit of an expert, are we?"

"I know good singing when I hear it, that's all," he said, knowing he had overstepped the mark.

"Some of these people have been in my choir for twenty years. Every Sunday, Holy Communion and Evensong," he said with an air of protest, "and I have never felt the need to criticise their contribution, never."

"You've never had the charter for the Harvest Fayre since 1908 either, have you?" he suggested, as their pace quickened.

The vicar had been struck dumb. At length he stopped walking and stood still on the spot. His features were lined and worn, though not through manual labour as Herbert's face was. He seemed in a momentary state of distress, as if his whole being was in the abyss of a dilemma. He pressed his forefinger against his tightened lips and with a full gaze burning across the rims of his spectacles he beheld this impertinent newcomer.

"I'm going to make you choirmaster," he announced, wagging the spindly forefinger towards him.

Then off he strode into the vicarage without a bye or leave.

Back at the pub he walked to the bar in a daze. Harry, who was busying himself there, took one look at him and wondered just what had happened.

"Ain't you had your sins forgiven then?" said Harry.

"Pardon?"

"It don't look to me as if all that praying has done you any good."

"This is all your fault," he huffed to his landlord, "It's down to you that I'm going to be choirmaster."

"Choirmaster!" yelled Harry with an astonished laugh. "You ain't been made the boss already have you?"

"The vicar said so, just now, coming out of church."

"Stroll on. Christ! Oh, I can't wait 'til lunchtime. You're a bloody miracle, you are. Wait 'til I tell the lads."

"That's not the half of it," he said, cupping his hangdog face in his hands, but Harry was not listening. He was yodelling what sounded like the *Hallelujah Chorus* with an air of amused mockery as he went back for clean ashtrays.

By the time the pub had filled up with the lunchtime crowd everyone had heard about Mr Miller's rise to the dizzy heights of choirmaster. Even George had managed to drag himself over for a hair-of-the-dog. The drunken organist had stumbled out of the church first and was more amazed than anyone when he heard the news.

"Go on George," said the new leader of the choir, "you tell 'em what it was like."

"What d'you mean?" he said. "Weren't no different to normal," then he winked at Bill as he nodded his head towards their new star, "except, this one 'ere sang like an angel from heaven, bless 'im."

The pub became a laughing chamber and as his face dropped in embarrassment Herbert slapped him on his back.

"Don't take it to heart lad. They're only taking the piss."

145

"Well I'm telling you it was crap, including the organist," he said sharply, looking across at a half drunken George seated at the piano. "And there aren't enough people in the choir anyway. It needs more voices, sopranos to basses, that's what it needs, richness. I thought the singsong we had last night sounded better than the wailing I heard this morning."

For a second the sentence hung in the air as if it had been frozen in time. Then, as if in slow motion, Herbert came face to face with Scrumps, seated near the window. Harry could see what he was thinking and a smile began to creep across his features too.

"So, you want more people in your choir, ay?" said Herbert, who had now caught the wicked glint settling in Harry's eye.

"Only if they can sing properly," he said unaware of what was going on around him.

"Ah, we can sing properly, can't we boys?" said Harry.

"Oh aye," they chorused, "we can sing all right."

"Well, you couldn't be any worse than that sorry lot," he said, still oblivious to plans being made around him.

"We're going to be a bloody sight better than them you'll see, especially if we can get Jack on board tonight as well. It'll be just like 1908 all over again," said Harry.

His attention suddenly jolted he looked up at the landlord.

"What?" he said.

"You heard," said Herbert. "What you need in your choir are a few Vikings."

"Vikings? But what will the vicar say?"

"Sod the vicar," said Harry. "Is you the choirmaster, or ain't you?"

"So he said."

"Well that's settled then. I'll get hold of Jack, and we'll all walk down to Evensong together, after a stiff brandy."

"And another thing," began Harry, poking his head round the corner to where George was seated, "that don't include you. You're on the wagon, 'til you can play properly. We'll get that fucking fayre into Empton if it's the last thing we do, aye boys?"

There was never much of anything to do in Empton on a Sunday. Harry spent most of the afternoon sleeping in an armchair in the back room, his rhythmic snoring competing with the clock's dependable tick. Ellie lost herself in a game of arguing dolls. One was a rich, nasty sister while the other was a kind, poor one. Her imaginary prince, however, loved the poor one so there were lots of make-believe rows to be heard coming from outside in the yard. He wandered around the pub, bored. For a moment or two he amused himself on the abandoned piano, the random notes displaying his lack of musical skill. He went out to see if Ellie would let him play at being the prince. She pointed out that he would need a man doll if he wanted to play but she did not have any, so that was the end of that.

In two shakes he had dressed an empty beer bottle from behind the bar with a napkin, pushed a potato from the scullery on the neck, and gouged some crude features on it with a knife. Then he popped an upturned eggcup on its head for a prince's crown and went over to the pretend palace grounds, where the fighting siblings were in the middle of another scrap.

"Ladies, ladies. Is this how we behave in the royal court?" said the potato prince with authority.

Ellie looked intently at him as he sat down on the ground to join her. He could see that it was completely alien to her for anyone to be joining in with one of her games - alien but nice. She slowly brought the left-hand doll towards the bottle prince.

"She started it," she made the nasty sister say in an unconvincingly posh voice, "but then, of course, she's poor."

"But she's so kind and helpful," the prince said. "You never give her any of your money."

The game went on like this for no more than ten minutes and it ended with the prince and the poor sister getting married. When they had gone off on their honeymoon he asked Ellie if her face was all right now. He could tell that he had gained her trust. The game had built a fragile bridge.

"It hurts when I lie down in bed," she said. "Just here," and she pointed to the right side of her lower jaw.

"Can I see? Can I touch it?" he asked.

She jutted out her little face. The swelling had gone but there seemed to be a slight lump. He gently laid the tips of his fingers on the skin. The lump could be felt too.

147

"Has the doctor seen this?" he asked.

Her face drew back. Horror filled her eyes.

"No, no, you mustn't. Promise you won't," her voice was a whisper, but it could not hide the panic that his suggestion had created.

"I won't, don't worry. I won't say a word. I promise," he said. "Tell me though, has this happened before?"

"It only happens when I do something bad," she said with a child's sense of philosophy. "He's my dad now. When I'm a naughty girl he gives me a smack," she paused for courage. "I hate him."

"You hate him?"

"When I grow up, I'm running away, all the way to Sozbry, if I can walk that far."

"Sozbry?"

"Charlotte's been to Sozbry. She says that she'll take me to Sozbry one day to see the 'thedral. She used to play with me when I was littler. But now she's married Mr Harper, so I s'pose I'll have to go on my own."

"Ah, you mean Salisbury, Salisbury Cathedral?"

"Sozbry 'thedral, yes. Next time he hurts me I'm packing a bag and going to tell the bishot. The bishot will put him in jail and God won't forgive him when he's in there, will he?"

"You'd best keep out of his way then."

"Ain't you noticed? I already do," she looked behind her at the man and woman dolls. "I think they've had enough honeymoon now, don't you?" she said.

"Oh, the prince. Yes I expect they want to get back to the palace and teach that nasty sister a lesson or two."

She chuckled at the thought of empowering someone with the ability to exact revenge. It was in some way a reflection of her indestructible spirit, one that would never yield to an ill-equipped foster parent who liked to hit.

Somehow or other an afternoon was passed and, when evening drew nigh, it brought with it a strange collection of beings. Never before were Vikings dressed in such fine Sunday best clothes. Herbert had made the most effort with his starched collar and thin tie. His

148

jacket and trousers had been immaculately pressed and his shoes seemed to have been made of jet, they shone so. Scrumps and Splash were clean at least but the only noticeable difference was in their hair. Each of them had applied so much hair oil and combed it in with such precision it looked as if their heads could win a miniature ploughing competition.

"Where's Harry?" the three asked.

"Lord, he's still asleep," he said, having forgotten how late it was. "I'd better wake him."

The minute Harry bounced out of his extended nap and saw them all waiting in the bar, he was horrified to find they had gone to so much trouble to prepare for the evening's service. He rubbed his chin and felt the need for a shave. There was no time. Around his living quarters he began to fly, trying in vain to achieve the same high standard of appearance.

As it got close to six o'clock the unmistakable sound of an American Army jeep punctuated the timeless peace of the village green. Within seconds of its engine being cut there sloped in the most debonair blacksmith one was ever to see. Jack had gone to town. He told everyone that his missus would not believe it when he said he was going to be in the church choir. It was only when he insisted that she could accompany him that she believed his story. She was still sitting in the passenger seat of the jeep, frightened witless by the rocket ride she had just experienced. At home she had insisted they both look their best and she made a meal out of making him look like a real gentleman.

They all had a brandy for good measure then it was off to church. The time had come for The Vikings to invade the domain of the Christians. Just as at Holy Island it was the man of God that caught the first sight of the approaching barbarians. His face showed the same sense of horror as the priests and monks of long ago on Lindisfarne. Mr Miller introduced his friends one by one.

"I thought that my first job as choirmaster ought to be one of recruitment," he said.

"But, but what will the others say? I don't know if this is a good idea?"

He beamed a smile at the vicar confidently aiming to disarm him.

"You made me choirmaster. It's probably best if you explain it to them."

In they strode past the hymn book guardian and into the vestry. The vicar trotted anxiously behind, struggling to think how he was going to deal with this monstrous predicament. Once again, the faithful were there. Their joyless faces beheld them as the invasion moved further in. The vicar burst through the ranks of the Norsemen who were now blocking the entrance to the vestry, his hands clasped, fingers writhing like worms.

"Aha-um, gentlemen," he began with practised politeness.

"Who are these people?" demanded the tall man.

"Ah, yes. I'm coming to that."

He was floundering. There was to be no easy way to put this to them.

"Meet the rest of the choir," Harry said flatly.

"What?" said the shorter man. "But this is preposterous,"

The three boys had stopped getting dressed, each one abruptly distracted by the unfolding drama.

"I demand an explanation, vicar," the carrier-of-the-cross said. "What is going on?"

The vicar's fidgeting hands displayed a heightened state of nervousness.

"Well," he said, "it's at times like this, you understand, when we need to involve the greater community."

He emphasised the last two words, hoping that they would add conviction to his rationale.

"In any case," he went on, "the choir needs to grow. To mature."

"But I've been a member of this choir for over twenty years and, as a senior member, I should have been consulted prior to any major decisions being taken. We all should have been consulted vicar."

The vicar took his courage in each of his wringing hands.

"Never the less," he proclaimed with feeble authority, "it's my duty to swell the flock of this church. These are the new members of the choir," turning to Mr Miller he squeaked, "and this is your new choirmaster."

Both stalwarts inhaled with shock simultaneously.

"Choirmaster?"

"Yes," said the vicar, looking like he was going to faint.

They looked at each other, unable to say a word. The vicar pressed his new choristers.

"Please get ready. The service begins in five minutes," then left to take up his position just outside the vestry door.

Wearing cassock and surplice was something the four old Vikings had not done since their youth. As old men now they found a fond quirkiness in getting dressed up. The two elders of the choir would have no truck with them. A gulf had been driven through each camp - the spiritual and the entrepreneurial - with Mr Miller the choirmaster stuck in between, by the divine will of the vicar.

The church congregation had grown since they had arrived. He could see almost twice as many people. No doubt the word had got out. Mrs Eversage was there near the front to see her Harry. George's music, now perfect, changed from Bach to Wesley as they began the first hymn. The congregation rose to its feet and inhaled. The next second the church was filled with a greater mass of music than it had done for many a long year - what the old stalwarts thought he could only guess, but it pleased him to hear it. It pleased him very greatly.

After the service was over and they were getting ready to leave, the old protector of the hymn books squared up to them. She had her coat on buttoned up to the neck, even though it was a warm summer evening. She took a disapproving look at the new choirmaster.

"One cannot serve two masters," she scolded. "There is God and there is Mammon, but man cannot serve them both."

"What are you on about Mrs C?" said Harry, in a consoling tone.

"I'm not talking to you landlord," she said, moving closer to her target.

"Who do you serve Mr Miller, God or Mammon?"

He looked around at his friends, trying to figure out what to say to her. Was she mad he wondered? There was conviction in her voice but no explanation. Her reason for approaching him had a purpose. Yet it had been delivered with such passionate ambiguity that it left him confused. Serving God or Mammon, how did that apply to him? Harry watched him struggling for a response and came to the rescue.

"I don't know about serving God or Mammon, Mrs Cartwright, but I reckon I'm about to serve a bloody good pint. Who's with me?"

151

To raucous laughter they passed the vicar in the doorway and made their way to the Golden Goose. Taking a backward glance he could see Mrs Cartwright's animated conversation with the vicar. She waved her arms about as if in a tantrum, occasionally pointing at the departing group of men making for the pub. She was not a happy churchgoer.

"So that's Mrs Cartwright," he said.

"Aye, that's her all right," said Harry. "She's off her rocker, poor cow."

"What did she mean, God and Mammon?"

"Oh, you're not going to think about what she said, seriously, are you?" said Harry, chiding him.

He let out a weak laugh.

"Nearly," he said.

Herbert knew more about her than anyone, or so Harry said.

"She's never been the same since Cyril was killed. Cyril, her husband," said Herbert. "He was an engineer. Used to fix up all the machines around here, especially when things were steam-driven. Very good with his hands was Cyril. It was him who divined the water outside their cottage. He sunk the borehole and built the pump himself, very clever but not one of us, if you understand. He was a one off, you might say, eccentric. A genius type but he did put the pump there for the benefit of the community, God bless him. There's a story that he went to Tunby one afternoon to demand payment for repairing a baler. Made a nuisance of himself at Holme Farm by all accounts. The next day he met with what has been described as an accident. Somehow the baler broke again and old Mr Harper called him over to make repairs. Cyril removed the drive-belt from the traction engine to fix it and he delved deep into the guts of the machine. Somehow, quite mysteriously, the belt found its way back on to the wheel again. Accidental death, that's how it was recorded. Mrs C hasn't been the same since that day. Went religious she did after the funeral. She guards that bloody pump constantly. Won't let anyone near it."

They had arrived back home. George was waiting there for them at a table and Ellie had gone to bed. With a yawn Harry slipped behind the bar and pulled a few drinks. He even allowed George off the wagon for a few days, much to his delight.

"Well here's to the songbirds," he said, by way of a toast.

With a click of meeting glasses they drank to their victory - the first victory of the Norsemen since that legendary Viking raid of long, long ago.

Chapter thirteen: Stone Cold

It had been raining in the night. This was the first break in the glorious weather since he had arrived and although the morning was clear and bright as he walked up the lane to work, the ground was damp with puddles spread about. The evening had been full of fun and friendliness. He slept well and, now that he had joined the noble ranks of The Vikings, Harry had gone to the trouble of waking him, feeding him breakfast and setting him on his way, just like a true friend. He would even have had his lunch prepared had he not said that had already been arranged. The prospect of meeting Danno again spoiled his fresh, cheerful memories. Such was the depression that hung over this Monday morning.

He had passed the pump several minutes ago but the old device was still preying on his mind - or rather it was the mental image of Cyril Cartwright who had put it there. Had the poor man been stupid to request payment for services rendered? Would he ever see his own twenty pounds materialise? What would he do if it were not forthcoming when the first prophesied bag of white flour trickled out of the mill? Then again he had been paid for fixing the tractor. Was it possible that these stories were born out of resentment for the ruling dynasty in the area? Could it be that Danno's attitude towards his workers was hewn out of the breeding that formed his upbringing?

The Harpers had been the main landowners around these parts for generations. They had competed with the county farmers for over a hundred years he was told. Naturally, the working classes would see them as just that – them. Was the whole myth about the Harpers

153

simply a matter of them and us syndrome? Still, it was not a pleasant prospect, having to spend time with the latest Harper to throw his weight about.

When he got to the farmyard the lorry was waiting, so were Herbert, Scrumps and the others.

"Where's Splash?" he asked.

"Ill," said Herbert. "His missus said he was down the karzi all through the night playing sit and beg. She blamed it on too much singing. But I reckon it's all that crap she cooks. Whoever heard of kaserolls? Foreign muck I call it. Serves him right for marrying a Frenchy. I bet she's forced bloody frog's legs down his poor little throat before now, you see if I'm not right."

He was just about to say that he did not even realise that Splash was married when he heard the unmistakable voice of the boss. He felt his nerves physically tighten, gripping his stomach.

"Everybody here?" he said, quickly looking at each of them in turn. "Right then, let's piss off and get some work done."

The back of the lorry was lowered and everyone clambered aboard, finding a place to wedge in between the tools and other gear. Besides the usual equipment he had to climb over a wide grey tarpaulin that concealed a large and heavy object. Danno was in such a hurry to get going that they were underway as soon as the last person had been pulled aboard - each man was holding on so tightly, the object ceased to be of any consequence. The journey was an unremarkable one, except that halfway to the mill it came to him that he had not been handed any sandwiches, pickle or otherwise. It made him wonder what might have prevented her from giving him any. Had she been found out he thought? Had he done something wrong? A sense of dread preyed on his mind, further darkening his uneasy mood.

The lorry forged on through half flooded stretches of road, groaning under tremendous strain until it finally arrived at the mill. Nothing had changed - nothing except for the wet that consigned to memory what a warm, dry summer day could bring. Danno jumped out of the cab and moved to the rear of the lorry just as everyone was leaping to the ground. He made straight for Mr Miller.

"Question for you, Caruso," said Danno.

"Go on," he replied.

The boss grinned his sanctimonious smile.

"All right. When you've finished fannying about with the woodwork and drawing your little pictures, just how did you plan to make my mill here produce any flour?"

"I hadn't got to that point yet. We've got to get the sails turning first before we think about making any flour."

"Wrong," he said. "He's wrong, isn't he boys?" he repeated louder to the labourers who had stayed behind on Saturday when he had left with the other three to walk home.

"Aye," they all answered knowingly.

Like a cheap circus performer Danno grabbed hold of the tarpaulin and gave a tug. He could not budge it by himself, it seemed to be trapped under the thing it was covering and he flashed a scowling look at the labourers to come and help. With grunts they ripped it away from the objects that lay beneath. And there they were. Two huge round millstones. The sight amazed everyone looking on, except for the roughnecks.

"I didn't know you were going to buy millstones already," he said.

"Buy?" he laughed. "I ain't fucking bought 'em you pillock. Not that it's any of your sodding business."

"I wasn't trying to pry," he said in an effort to ward off a tongue-lashing.

"Pry away if you want. Go on ask me where I got them from, go on."

He stood rooted, wondering if this was some crazy form of test. He felt completely uncomfortable.

"Go on, ask me," Danno said in a firmer voice.

He had no choice but to ask the question, like a schoolboy who had just been told to.

"Where did you get these millstones from?" he said as an automaton.

"What? These millstones here?" he said, mocking him.

"Yes."

"They were going off for regrinding, weren't they lads?" he said.

"Aye Mr Harper."

"Only they never quite made it to the workshops, did they boys?"

"No Mr Harper."

155

"So where exactly did they come from, if I'm allowed to ask?"

"You know. It's incredible what you can do on a Sunday morning. You can either lay in your fucking bed all day wanking, or get up before the dawn breaks through and pay a little visit to a watermill."

He tried to recall the name of the owner of the watermill, pulling it out of his memory just in time.

"Wagstaff's?" he questioned.

"Who's to say, might have been. The question is, how were you planning to get your hands on the grindstones?" he folded his arms and waited.

He could not say buy them. That had already caused him to be ridiculed. Then Herbert came forwards.

"Begging your pardon, Mr Harper, Sir," said Herbert politely.

Danno observed him and grunted for him to proceed.

"Mr Miller was going to try and find out where the old stones had gone to," he said. "We'd talked about trying to get them back for reconditioning," he looked at the nervous choirmaster at his side, "weren't we, Mr Miller?"

"Yes, we were," he said falteringly, as he thought for a second. "At least then we'd know that they would fit the shaft without any alterations being needed."

It seemed to be the perfect answer. Danno looked slightly aghast at having his attack diluted by one of his workers but how could he argue with such common sense? He chose distraction as a means to distance himself from any sign of weakness.

"Well, enough bloody chit-chatting," he called. "Let's get some fucking work done, shall we?"

Mr Miller went to join the carpenters, feeling slightly shaken. Halfway through the morning Herbert came over to him, ostensibly to get some equipment he wanted on the scaffolding. He slipped over to where the damaged sail was being worked on.

"You all right?" he asked softly.

"I am, thanks to you. He'll be the death of me, that bloke will."

"Listen, he may be a Harper down here, but hardly in the next world, eh?"

"Ha," he laughed quietly. "Mrs Cartwright wouldn't allow him in for a start, harp or no harp."

They both sniggered under their breaths as they parted to get on with their work and repair the huge wooden structure lying in the weeds. After some thought it was decided to carry the damaged sail into the barn where the other sails already lay. The flat floor there would make repairs that much easier - besides if the weather was really on the turn what better place to work. A new boss could be fashioned there. It would increase the precision that such a component required if all the main sections were kept under one roof, but lifting and carrying it was not going to be achieved by human muscle alone. It was several hundred yards to the barn, a long way to move half a ton of timber. The lorry was the obvious answer, or at least part of it. The problem lay in the length of the giant wing, as the carpenters continued to call it. Even if they could hoist it onto the back of the old vehicle, it would still leave an even larger proportion poking over the edge. Somehow they would have to find a way of lifting this section so it did not drag along the road.

"How did they get the other sails into the barn in the first place?" he asked one of the carpenters.

"Search me?" he said, his hands resting on his hips, "This old mill was dismembered not long after the accident. I don't think anyone here's got a clue how they got the bits up to the barn. Mind you, you'd have thought they'd have taken this one with them at the same time, wouldn't you?" he said, staring down at the inert piece of oak.

One of the other carpenters, who hardly ever spoke, piped up like some sleepwalker suddenly awakened.

"What you need is a rig," he said, waiting for a response that never came. "What you need is a rig," he repeated, "made out of scaffolding poles, big enough to carry the wing, with wheels fixed on all four corners, maybe a couple in the middle. We could probably pull it ourselves."

He waited for them to ridicule his plan but surprisingly, the whole bunch of them were thinking it through.

"You know, it's not a bad idea but how about making a kind of dolly out of scaffolding poles and a couple of wheels. Just lash it up to the dangling end of the wing. It would be a cinch for the lorry to pull it along the lane then. What do you think?"

157

"It would be easier to make than a rig," said Mr Miller. "All we need is one pair of wheels."

"We could borrow them from the wheelbarrows," said the first carpenter, "it wouldn't take long."

A smile of agreement passed between them as they went to talk it over with Herbert.

"Sounds all right to me," Herbert said, "but hadn't you better check it out with his nibs first?"

"Who's going to ask him?" put in one of the craftsmen.

They all looked at one another, then all eyes turned to Mr Miller.

"He's not going to take suggestions off me," he said, feeling cornered.

"Well son, it's you he's asked to fix his sodding mill. Reckon you're the bloke what needs to ask him, begging my opinion," said Herbert, scratching his sweaty head.

Danno was in the cab of his lorry, pencil in hand working on a set of figures. The minute he heard the timid tap of the cab door he slammed the book shut and stashed it away. He rapidly wound down the window.

"What is it now?" he said, in an exasperated tone.

Mr Miller had realised that it was going to take a particular approach to get Danno to take their plan seriously so he concocted a half-baked idea that he thought might do the trick. Even so his heart was in his mouth and his confidence was melting away as he got ready to speak.

"I think we've found a way to speed things up a bit," he said.

"You're going to work faster and stop pestering me. Is that it?" said Danno, full of sarcasm.

"Well yes, of course."

The discomfort was palpable yet he carried on with his request.

"We want to repair the broken sail in the barn. The floor's big enough and flat. What with rain on the way, we reckon we could make a better job of it in there and it would be quicker than messing about in all those weeds."

His words were getting faster the more he spoke. His mouth was drying up. He hated the way this man was making him squirm like this.

"So what's all this got to do with me?" said Danno, delighting in the effects of his power.

"Well, we need to use the lorry, your lorry that is, to move the sail. It must weigh a ton."

Danno stared at him for several seconds, as if he were looking into the eyes of an imbecile. His stare stripped away the fragile self-respect of his victim layer by layer. Then a satisfied smile cracked across his heavy features.

"Be my guest. At least you're thinking for your sodding self at long last," he said, opening the door and tossing him the keys as he jumped out. "You've got a week to get the sail fixed, or I'll fucking fix you. How's that for a deal?"

"We'll do it," he said convincingly.

Then he trotted obediently back to his workmates, feeling wretched with himself for being like an animal that had been saved from a beating.

The dolly was a simple affair, a rectangle of poles eight feet by about two. On each of the narrow ends there were two further poles placed strategically to take the wheels of the cannibalised barrows. All the connectors were tightened and the complete device was lashed to the narrow end of the sail. The broken parts of the timber frame were strengthened with more pieces of scaffolding to stop it breaking under the strain of being lifted. Then, as soon as the lorry was reversed into place, the backbreaking job of heaving the widest and heaviest part of the sail began.

At first they tried to pull it onto the flat bed of the lorry with ropes. It was a struggle and, despite a perfect performance of grunting and swearing, could not muster the strength needed to lift it off the ground, let alone raise it to the level of the lorry's rear. The solution, when it finally dawned on them, was simplicity itself - the lorry's diesel engine would do the job. Using two short lengths of scaffolding they constructed an A frame and nudged it in place so that the apex of the frame was underneath the sail with the legs pointing out towards the lorry's back wheels. One end of a rope had been tied to the apex and the other was swiftly knotted to the pull bar of the old vehicle. With some care the poor machine eased forwards, pulling on the tightening rope and lifting the point of the A frame as it moved. The legs of the frame bit into the earth and slowly the sail rose upwards.

It had been an ingenious idea and soon the sail was high enough to be placed on the back of the lorry. Bits of timber were hurriedly packed underneath the resurrected wing to support it whilst the A frame was removed. No one could resist smiling as the lorry was reversed into place, but there was no time to waste. Mr Miller was on board, long pole in hand to lever it an inch or two so that the packing could be knocked away. Then, with some relief, he lowered it down onto the lorry's wooden platform. Everyone heard the rear suspension creak as it took the weight. It was as if the lorry's back wheels had taken their tension away. The sense of achievement ran through all their veins and they so wanted to cheer or slap each other on the back - but Danno, who had taken up position high up on the scaffolding, dampened any notion of celebration. They carried on as if nothing remarkable had happened, determined to hide from him any joy they might have felt. It was a learned condition. This project had not been Danno's idea. Of course, had it been then things would have been different, very different.

The huge white sail, festooned with dangling weeds, was lashed securely on top of the millstones that were still weighing heavily on the lorry. There was some satisfaction when, at last, the entire combination rolled away from the mill towards the barn slightly higher up the hill. By the time the operation had been carried out in reverse inside the draughty old building everyone was starving. He had not stopped to think about food all morning but now that he had, the connection reminded him of Lotty and the ham and pickle. The carpenters had grabbed their tins and were tucking into their sandwiches. He was hungry too. But he did not dare face Danno again to ask him if there was a food parcel for him. He went over to where the broken sail rested and sat and thought about Lotty and why she had not contacted him.

A moment later Danno strode into the barn and headed for his old lorry.

"Keys. You got my keys?" he said.

"They're in the ignition," he replied.

160

"Good. Well don't fart about eating all day. I want these stones putting in place by the end of play," he looked down at the makeshift A frame resting on the ground. "When you've had enough of being a smartarse maybe you could dream up how to get these buggers in place?"

Danno patted one of the millstones to show him what he was on about. He wanted to reply that he had not got anything to eat, but there was still a remnant of pride within him that prevented him from doing so.

"Where there's a will, there's a way," he said, trying to sound unaffected by his attitude.

"Oh yes," Danno said, "my will, and my way. Got it?"

"Got it," he said, hating the words that had just come out of his own mouth.

Herbert caught sight of him without food and gave him a pork pie and one of his apples to eat, saying that Vikings should stick together in a crisis. He told him to sort his own lunch out in future, a view that was heartily agreed upon.

There was faint drizzle in the air when they emerged to begin work again. The sunshine was gone and all would have been grey even if there was colour in the world. Danno had taken the lorry back to the mill. Everyone else walked. They all knew that a difficult job was laying ahead, one that the boss would be having a more direct hand in. The afternoon was going to be purgatory. They could all sense it.

The millstones were destined for the first floor and it was obvious to everyone, as they arrived back at the old tower, that their journey from the back of the lorry to the first floor of the mill was going to be fraught with problems. The major part, lifting them from the ground to their resting place one floor up, was by far the most challenging. By contrast, though with some effort, the two great stones could be rolled along the ground like massive stone-age wheels. Most of the men had voiced this as the best way of getting them from the lorry to the mill - but lifting, now that was an altogether different proposition.

Mr Miller arrived on the scene still hungry. Danno called him over, standing like a cock of the walk on the flat bed. Some of the men around Miller, including Herbert, mumbled curses under their breaths, their weary faces expressing with more eloquence a sympathetic prayer that Danno should leave the poor bugger alone. No one dared say it out loud. Danno had one foot resting on one of the grey round stones as he drew closer. Miller's heart felt just as heavy as one of them, as he looked up at the boss and waited for the show to begin.

"I'll take charge of this bit," ordered Danno through the fine rain. "My millstones, you see. My mill."

"Fine," answered Miller.

"Take two poles, and put 'em here," he said pointing down to the tailgate of the lorry's rear, "and make a ramp."

He nimbly carried out the request. Danno then shoved a spade under one of the stones and heaved it up half an inch.

"Right, get yourself up here sharpish and put a rope under it and through the hole," he barked, sounding out of breath. "Then tie a knot. And hurry the fuck up. This thing weighs a ton."

Once more the request was carried out with speed. Herbert came alongside to help. With the rope secured the large stone was shifted this way and that until it was at the end of the lorry's wooden platform. Danno was exhausted and told one of his labourers to lend a hand. So the burly man took charge of the spade ready to lift it onto the poles. Danno had taken hold of the rope with both hands ready to take any strain. With some effort on the part of the labourer the stone reached the pole ramp and, as it was lowered down onto them, its heavy mass levered the poles off the ground trapping them under its bulk so that they now poked out horizontally.

Danno swore at what he saw as his workmen's incompetence and ordered Herbert to put his weight down on them and force them back to the ground. He grabbed a pole in each hand and pushed down until they touched what had now become mud. The leverage made it easier work than it looked, the fulcrum point being so close to the lorry, but at least the ramp had been restored. Once more the labourer edged the stone further. It was now dangling precariously over the end of the lorry. Danno took the strain. Herbert continued to press down on the poles to keep them in place. The labourer heaved the stone beyond its centre of gravity so that it now rocked and tilted over the edge. Danno had it by the rope. Everywhere was wet through. As Herbert got ready to get out of the way, suddenly Danno slipped, falling flat on his back with a cry. A blur of rope slithered through his grip. The stone hurtled with force down the pole ramp smashing into Herbert's chest like an express train punching him flat on his back. In a second the stone's immense weight had skidded over Herbert's upper body and head and come to rest with half of the huge thing still touching the ramp. The leading edge had bitten into the wet earth. Underneath, trapped and still, lay Herbert.

All that could be heard was the gentle sigh of drizzle and the shallow breathing of everyone present. Though there was now a sense of urgency no one could move. Danno was flat on his back in some pain, not quite understanding what had just happened. Five seconds ago Herbert had been doing his job. Now he was still, his head trapped under the great stone. He was still. All was still.

The sound of the labourer dropping his spade roused them. Its clank on the wooden deck caused him to wake up and jump off the lorry. Miller, his face not able to hide his horror, joined him. It was plain to see that Herbert's head was pushed into the soft, wet ground. They looked to where the stone had ploughed into the mud and rocked back on their heels, taking on faces of disgust. The look in their eyes told everyone present they could see something awful. Scrumps had also shaken himself from the shock and had arrived with the two at the place where the millstone hit the ground. A small mound of mud was driven up by the stone's impact. Poking out of it was the remains of Herbert's nose.

"Oh fucking hell, Herb!" Scrumps cried out to his friend. "Oh God, get that bloody stone off him!"

Soon there were people all over the place. Danno had not joined them. He had sat himself up and was sitting with his back resting on the side of the lorry. He gazed at his hands where friction burns from the rope had scarred his palms. Many of the men shouldered the millstone, lifting it up to the perpendicular and rolling it a couple of yards away. It was dropped unceremoniously into what was now becoming a quagmire as the drizzle turned to rain. The minute they turned from this job to attend Herbert, they were met with the hideous sight of their friend with no face. The stone had scraped it off as if by a plane. Pressed into the mud was a head with no eyes. A random collection of displaced teeth protruded from what looked like a mess of blood and skin. Black blood was flopping out of the remnants of his features as if it were a lava flow. Someone reached for his arm to feel a pulse. There was none. He was dead.

"How the hell did this happen?" said Scrumps unable to fight his tears. "Did anyone see what happened?"

"The boss fell. He was holding on to the rope," said Miller. "He fell and lost his grip on the rope."

"And who had the bright idea of sliding that bastard stone down a couple of poles anyway. Yours?"

"Not me, his," said Miller nodding his head in the direction of Danno on the back of the lorry.

"I'll kill him," sobbed Scrumps quietly. "Kill my best mate would he? I'll bloody kill him so help me," he looked back at the dead body of his friend. "All through the Somme we went. The poor sod survived all those years in the shit of the trenches. All them Jerry bombs and bullets and a Harper bastard does this to him."

He knelt into the grey mud close to his dead companion and hid his head in his hands. No one knew if he was praying or crying but it looked like he was doing both.

A gathering had now collected round the scene. Miller took off his sodden jacket and placed it over the head of the man he felt had been his friend. As if by instinct they all bowed their heads. There was a familiarity with the many Armistice Days he had known, standing in the rain proffering a meaningful two minutes of silence, only the silence was shattered by the slamming of a door and eruption of the lorry's engine. As the acrid belch of the exhaust polluted the air everyone was surprised to see that Danno had crept into the cab and was driving away. The poles that had made the ramp clanged on each other like tubular bells, as the back end of the old vehicle moved forwards. Scrumps's wet face looked up. He had stood to his feet by the time the lorry reached the entrance to the lane.

"That's it, you fucking bastard, piss off home, why don't you?"

He was waving his fist as spit ran down from the corner of his mouth. He filled his lungs to bursting and then yelled with full ferocity.

"Bastaaaaard!"

The shock and depth of loss rendered everyone else unable to talk. Miller put his hand on Scrumps's shoulder. He shrugged it off with venom and went over to the mill tower, yearning for solitude now that his friend was gone. What grey the sky had possessed earlier had become darker and with it a heavier rain. It was decided to lift Herbert's body into the mill. Some of the older ones talked of their time in the Great War, lifting the partly rigid shape off the ground and recalling fallen comrades. It was a grisly task. Even in death there was a moment of macabre oddity, as one of the labourers picked up Herbert's nose and brought it into the dry interior of the mill. The lifeless figure was draped with the tarpaulin that had been retrieved and Miller's blood stained jacket was returned to him.

Work on the mill never resumed that day. By home time, as the sky cleared and long, horizontal strips of cloud draped the evening like trailing dragons lit beneath by the setting sun, they heard the sound of an engine. It was a car and as Miller stepped out of the door to look he saw an Austin 7 make its way along the rutted track that led to the mill. It stopped near the spot where Herbert had been killed. He immediately recognised it as the doctor's car. As if by instinct the doctor took out his black bag. For a second he stood and thought, then put it back. Tossing it into the back of the old heap of tin he made his way to the door, hands in pockets and looking very sober.

"I hear there's been an accident," said the doctor to Mr Miller.

"It's Herbert, Doc," he said. "He's dead."

"You're certain?" he asked. "Did anyone see how the accident happened?"

A voice came from the first floor.

"Accident my arse," blurted out Scrumps. "It was no accident. Harper killed him."

"Please," urged the doctor as he lifted a corner of the tarpaulin. "Let's not jump to conclusions, shall we?"

He lifted Herbert's arm and placed three fingers across the rigid wrist. Slowly he replaced the grey covering, staring at it for the briefest moment.

"So, what did happen?" he said, his tone more serious now.

Scrumps had descended the steps to the ground floor and strode towards the doctor.

"He got Herbert just where he wanted him, then he let that drop on him," he said, gesturing at the great round stone lying in the rain outside. "What else could you possibly need to know?"

Miller piped up and was about to explain in more detail just how it had happened, when Scrumps, his face full of rage, turned his venom against him.

"This is all your fault, this is," Miller was stunned at the outburst. "If he hadn't gone and stuck up for you this morning he would still be here."

Miller was almost unable to speak. He had classed Herbert as a friend. Given time, he was certain that they would have been close friends.

"Stuck up for me?" he said, trying to remember when Herbert had come to his rescue. "When?"

"You never tried to let it drop with the boss, did you?" before Miller could speak, he was off again. "This morning, when the boss was asking you how you planned to get the flour made, he jumped in and said you were trying to find the old millstones. That was not your idea. That was his. He said that to get you out of a tight spot and it made Danno look a fool. That was the first time in his life he had answered a boss back. He may as well have jumped in front of a bullet. When I think of all the bullets that missed him in the Somme. When will you bloody well learn your place?"

Scrumps was close to tears. He looked at each face gathered there. All except for Miller's, each one had been impregnated with this truth. It was as real as the seasons and as solid a fact as day and night. Miller knew of it but he did not know it. This simple fact had been running through his brain over the past weeks. Their souls by contrast had been marinated in it and, until it had become a part of him like it was with them an outsider he would remain. At that moment, surrounded by people, he felt more alone than he had ever felt by himself. How he wished he could say the word sorry. With every second of silence his shame grew.

In the end the doctor, sensing his aching heart, offered to take him back to the village. Danno was on his way back to fetch them and the body he said and he thought it best that Miller was not there when he arrived. It was a long walk back to the doctor's car and an equally long drive back home. Not a word was spoken. It was too loud in his head to hear himself think, let alone talk.

Chapter fourteen: Life And Death

It was a barrage. Attack after attack of misery and anguish, sadness and confusion, even fear mixed with guilt. The concoction bombarded him with no less ferocity than a line of artillery would have done. Scrumps's words rained down on his mind like hammer blows, filling the space in his head with their deafening repetition. There was to be no sleep that night and, in the morning, there was nothing but exhaustion.

Not knowing what reception he would get, he stepped with trepidation down the wooden stairs to the bar. Harry, who was already up and about, noticed him and gave him a quizzical glance. He felt wretched and hated and, he knew that like Herbert, part of him had died under that lump of stone. It was all he could do to sit at one of the tables and be lost in torment. Perhaps it was the thought of losing a friend, or the notion that he had somehow been responsible for his death, either way his throat became choked and he began to experience himself weeping. He tried to hold it back, as he had been taught, but his efforts were futile. Even the futility itself made the tears flow faster and the cry grow louder. He buried his head in his folded arms that were resting on the table and let it all burst away.

The heavy sound of a mug landing on the table top and a large warm hand resting on his shoulder made him stop and look up. Harry's face could not hide his concern looking down onto Miller's drenched face. The tear-streaked eyes looked back as if they would never see a friend again, but maybe Harry did not know about what

167

Scrumps had said. Before he knew what had happened he blurted it all out, as if confessing all his sins.

"The Doc told me what old Scrumps said to yer," said Harry, with a reassuring half-smile. "I happen to know that Danno had it in for Herbert Ashcroft for some time."

Miller's eyes showed surprise.

"Oh aye," Harry went on. "Trouble with the rent, his age even, and one or two other little problems. When Janet, Lady Ashtray as we called her secretly, died from cancer of the lung two years past, Herbert changed. He never stopped being a likeable bloke but I think he stopped caring. Caring what the boss thought of him anyhow, I reckon. That's why he was the only one to speak up for you. You did well to keep your gob shut and you just mind you keep it that way."

"But what about Scrumps?" said Miller.

"Ah, well, he knew the score too. Herb was his best friend. More than that, Scrumps, he had been best man at his wedding. They went through the First War together, joined up at the same time and all that. It's a bitter pill for him, but he knew that Herb was lost without his chain-smoking missus. He'll come round. It'll just take time. You just remember, this is Danno's doing, not yours. I'll talk to old Scrumpy."

A millstone had been removed from Miller's neck. He let out a deep breath, smiled at his good friend and drank his tea. Harry talked him into going back to work, saying that to hide away would only make matters worse. He managed to make him eat some toast and sent him out into the rain.

The rural landscape by now had changed almost beyond recognition. The village streets had become transformed from their previously light grey dust into dispiriting stretches of dark mud. The warmth had gone. Only the derelict house remained the same. It had looked miserable from the first and now it seemed at home in its saturated surroundings.

Out along the lane and all the way up to Bofindle the countryside stood and accepted the dead day. The dark sky spilled out its burden, like a water tank bursting at the seams. It was a constant deluge. Leaves on trees would be knocked violently by the endless bombardment of raindrops. Nothing was dry, so clothing became heavy and walking turned into a foot slog, with a head bent keenly before the pelting drops of misery.

As he squelched his way into the farmyard he could see the lorry loaded up with a tarpaulin that appeared to be moving about. Getting nearer he could see that there were men beneath it trying to keep dry. He was allowed in without acknowledgement and took his place nearest the tailgate that he helped to pull up and pin into place. Less than five minutes later he heard the boss shout an indistinguishable command to his wife, then climbed into the cab, yell to ask if all were present and set off, after he heard a voice shout back a cold, hungry reply.

He now inhabited a world of mud. It came in an endless variety of drab types, but all grey. The roads were covered in a film of it, spread by horses' hooves and vehicle tyres. Grass in the verges poked out of slime, whilst the fields that were being used for pasture, now boasted deep ruts and gouged out water-filled depressions where cattle feet had distorted the dark sludge on their parcel of land. It got everywhere too. Wet hands, once dry, were left gritty and seemingly made of clay.

Even as they arrived at the mill they were met with mud. Near the tower its almost black presence had been spread over the ground as if by a manure sprayer. And like some living thing, the mud gave the impression that it was trying to scale the walls of the old structure. It reflected the weak light of the morning, giving the appearance here and there of mud holes, where a subterranean sky of equal greyness to the one above shone through. In fact it was the sky that had changed everything. The oppressive thickness of the clouds scudding by darkened their entire world.

The lack of light only made the mud blacker, as if it was oil, crude and viscous. Walking on it was a contest of balance too, for the oil-like character of the mud ensured that feet would slip and slide, as the earth beneath gave up its solidity, treating those who trod upon it with the same contempt as they would have received from polished ice. Wet, filthy and soul-destroying, little wonder then that the death of Herbert seemed an event from which none of them would recover.

Even Danno was changed, at least for the foreseeable future. He avoided eye contact with his workforce and got on with organising the men quietly. It was almost like he was trying to avoid a riot, or that he did have a heart and guilt was at work. In fact every man carried the burden of seeing Herbert die in their minds and it crushed them with no less a force than the millstone that had taken their friends face away. Their whole lives had become loathsome like the mud.

The lack of warmth made him hunger for it, not just physical warmth but another sort. Losing Herbert had triggered off more losses. He wanted to feel Lotty's warmth. He knew that she would drive away his sadness, but then he imagined their hideaway in the woods, drenched and spoiled and unfit for them. Her lack of contact had shoved him further out into the cold, the cold world of rejection and his memories of her clawed away at his heart as surely as the pangs of starvation. Starve he did, for the summer days past, Herbert's company and the love of Lotty.

At Maltoft he headed to the barn with the carpenters. He was always one step away from bursting forth into a fit of crying, for it seemed to him that even the sky was mourning for all that he had lost. The splattering of raindrops on the ground was akin to millions of tears being shed, and he held as many in his swollen heart that at any moment would over-spill like a broken river. By the time they reached the dry interior of the old barn it looked as if they had all been weeping, their dour faces drenched from the downpour going on outside.

There they set to work immediately, almost without a word passing between them. No one wanted to be anything other than sombre that day. The only distraction came when someone from the mill gang arrived to say that Herbert's funeral would be on Friday afternoon at one o'clock and that everyone was expected to make an effort to be there as soon as morning work was over. They all grunted that they had heard him, then the dreary day proceeded on as before silently, cold and damp.

There was no sense of accomplishment as the sail benefited from its repair. By midweek the slats had been dutifully installed into the refashioned superstructure and by Thursday evening the long steel connecting rod was fixed to the pivot of each one. Even as they pulled on it for testing and the slats moved up and down in unison, there was no joy felt, no celebration held. It was a meaningless achievement. Without Herbert to share it with the whole project was now hollow.

One measurement of the mood could be seen in the workers' journey to and from the mill. Arriving or departing at the bus stop, as the dirt track had come to be called, they beheld at least twice daily the two discarded millstones - the one that had been lifted off Herbert's body, and the other that had been rolled from the truck near to a hedge. For the time being no one wanted anything to do with them and it only seemed right and proper that all efforts to retrieve them should be left until after the funeral. Before the accident there had been the wild and animated chatter of men making the best of having to work hard for a living. Now all that had become subdued. Only here, when they caught sight of the stones, especially the one lying in the mud near the mill tower, near 'Herbert's stone', the talking stopped completely and each man's thoughts turned to their dead friend and the crushing power of the Harpers.

On Thursday night, at the Golden Goose, a meeting had been arranged to discuss Herbert's funeral service. The remaining Vikings were there, including Jack Manders and his wife, along with Doreen Eversage and the ever-timid Ms Campbell. The vicar had been asked to come the day before but mentioned that he might be late. It was into this gathering that Miller, now cleaned up, made his entrance from his room. He knew that all eyes would be upon him as he rounded the door into the bar. Inwardly he was quivering like a leaf, though he tried hard to hide his trepidation. He anticipated that Scrumps would fly into a rage at him, which was why he had kept out of his way all week. Now there was to be no question of avoidance.

With nerves stretched he scanned the room and saw Scrumps at the bar. There was an awkward moment as the two men's eyes met and neither knew what to say. Finally Scrumps spread his fingers over the top of a full pint glass, grabbed it crane-like and placed it on the bar in the direction of Miller.

"Sorry lad," was all he mumbled, looking at him square on.

The two words were voiced with honest sincerity but it was enough, more than enough. Miller strode over, took a swig and extended his arm. The blessing of forgiveness cleansed him as he felt the rough grip of his friend grasp his hand. Miller's face said all that needed to be said in reply. Everyone could see that he felt accepted again. By degrees the tension evaporated allowing conversation to resume.

Time passed and the night became nostalgic. Stories of Herbert's life abounded - long forgotten stories, some hilarious. The respectful laughter helped them to heal. It was to be a cathartic night and, despite an ever-present sadness, there was a joyfulness that they had known Herbert - even though for some, that knowing had been so short lived.

It was the ladies who brought their attention back to the matter in hand. They each had a list of hymns they thought would be appropriate. Ena Campbell broke her silence and quietly suggested that a line from one of Siegfried Sassoon's poems should be read out.

"*If I should die, think only this of me*," she courageously managed to squeak past her own wall of shyness.

When Harry asked her if she would like to perform it, the poor brittle personality of Ena Campbell withdrew into her half-pint of stout and kept herself to herself for the rest of the evening. They were in the middle of writing ideas down onto a scrap of paper when a bedraggled Reverend Spriggins came in out of the night rain.

"Great news, great news," he said, taking out a cloth from his Gabardine coat pocket to wipe his spectacles.

He seemed unable to say anymore until he had replaced them and could see everyone again.

"Ah, yes, splendid," he said.

No one knew if he was referring to his improved vision or the great news that so far only he was privy to.

"Great news, vicar?" enquired Harry, bursting to find out what had caused the old duffer to get so excited.

"Oh it is Harry, yes, great news indeed. I've just come back from Salisbury, through all this rain. It's been a frightful journey. The road is under flood down by the river. Wagstaff's men have had to abandon the mill, God protect them."

172

"And that's your great news is it Reverend?" said Mrs Eversage, looking mystified. "That's only good news for Daniel Harper, is that."

"No, my dear. No, the great news is that the bishop is coming to officiate at Herbert's funeral. He's on his way to London for the weekend. I happened to mention that one of our much-loved parishioners had met with an awful accident," a suggestion of a wink came into the vicar's eye, barely the slightest trace of a crooked grin as he continued. "I also mentioned that we have the most melodious choir. I knew he would not be able to resist, so he's arriving by motor car at lunch time tomorrow," and as if it needed asking he said to them, "for Herbert's sake, you will all be there in the choir tomorrow, won't you?"

"Well, bugger me, you old reverend you, course we will," said Harry apologising for swearing.

The vicar forgave him with a mildly disapproving smile and took out some papers and a couple of books from his black case. The papers in fact turned out to be thin pamphlets, orders of service for funerals, stapled to a card cover. And the thick volumes were doorstep versions of *Hymns Ancient And Modern* and *The Bible,* a beautiful, but very worn *King James Version.*

With these tools the vicar guided them through the kind of funeral that he thought befitting to a much-loved member of his flock. He thought that *Abide With Me* would have been Herbert's own choice had he been able to choose. The vicar said that Herbert often commented on the effect the tune had on him on Remembrance Sunday. Scrumps agreed, saying that he used to hum it in the trenches when they were getting ready to march into oblivion. Then the vicar opened his bible, having said something about a reading. All present assumed that he was about to show them a piece of scripture, a suitable couple of verses from the good book but instead the elderly dog-collared gentleman removed a sheet of paper that had been folded away in the *Old Testament.* With great tenderness he opened it out and looked at the words then he put it back. Slowly, he raised his head to speak to them. He knew instinctively how to hold their attention.

"I too was in the war to end all wars you know," he said, though no one actually did know. "Oh yes. I was at Passchendaele in the

173

same regiment as my brother. He had been a teacher before the war, very clever he was, a lovely man. I was the chaplain and Richard was a captain."

The old man appeared to shrink in his chair, as if the past was dragging him down and his eyes looked forwards, not at their faces, but at a muddy stretcher from long ago.

"He'd been hit in the neck. Awful mess it was. He'd only managed to get ten yards with his men. There were doctors waiting to treat the wounded, in readiness for after the battle and two of them risked their own necks to bring him back," a tear had by now released itself from his eye and was making its way down to the corner of his mouth. "I read the last rites to him as he lay in my arms and when he'd gone and I embraced his dead body and, with all the noise going on above me, I composed in my mind the words that I finally committed to that tatty piece of paper," his moistened eyes were now fixed back to theirs. "I can never read that out loud without making a fool out of myself you know, but I should like it to be read," he looked directly at Miller. "Choirmaster, would you read it, please?"

"Yes, vicar" he said simply, without hesitation, "of course I will."

Little Ena Campbell smiled to herself, gloating that her idea about a reading from the Great War had been taken up after all despite the bullying she received from the landlord.

The following morning was foggy and wet. One of the labourers drove them to the mill. Danno was nowhere to be found. It was just as well. The few hours that were spent at Maltoft were a waste of time. No one could get organised, or wanted to. Miller half-heartedly took measurements of the sail's spars and drew sketches of the boss they planned to make. He tried to work out what kind of mechanism would be able to operate the slats whilst the sail was revolving. It was a problem that so far had not been matched with a solution. His brain was crowded with thoughts of the service to come, thoughts that flashed film footage of Herbert's mangled face, thoughts that spilled into areas normally set aside for design and innovation. There was nothing normal about the inside of his head this Friday morning. In the end he gave up and helped the carpenters clear away the accumulation of junk from the last few days.

Danno's absence accounted for everyone's peace and quiet, their wanton wasting of time and their indulgence in lethargy. In the prevailing spirit of indolence, work ceased altogether around mid-morning and it was decided by consensus that they would head back home and get cleaned up ready to give Herbert a good send off. The silent band of men took the lorry back to Empton having achieved nothing whatsoever.

He dropped his things in his room and, through the thin mist, trudged through the muddy lane up to the old church. The drizzle had slowed down and the faintest haze of water droplets clung to his face and hands. Suddenly something caught his eye between the church and the wall of the vicarage garden. His curiosity pricked, he tramped through the long, saturated grass to get a closer look. It was just a hole in the ground, earth piled up on either side, parallel to an existing grave. He bent down and carefully parted the prickly brambles that had begun to choke the headstone. He felt stupid that the penny had not dropped sooner. The stone read:

Sacred to the memory of
Janet Ashcroft
Departed this life 18th August 1953, aged 54
My Father has prepared a place for you

He craned his neck to peer down the hole into this freshly dug grave. It had wet and slimy walls from the incessant rain, and he did not envy the poor bastards who had been given the job of digging it. The bottom of what was little more than a rough pit was awash with an accumulation of the drizzle. There was nothing noble about it. No holy resting place was this. Here, someone he had known in life would lay there in a lifeless state and inexorably rot away and decay. If life was a one-way street to the grave then death surely was a scrap yard at the end of it. He had pondered death before, like everyone else had from time to time but it came to him like a home truth, this notion of the very permanence of it and how Herbert's remains would be here for all time to come. Long after he had died too Herbert and his wife would still be in this place, on this hill, next to this old church. It seemed like a macabre reuniting and an awful thought, this image of them buried in their pits, side by side, forever and ever.

The wet was permeating his clothing, so he prepared to head back to the pub. Instead though, he entered the church and sat down at a dark oak pew, crudely carved. There were prayers he knew by heart, prayers he had said thousands of times before. Their mechanical repetition seemed pointless now and so too did the leaning forwards and the bowed head. Defying all the traditions that had been pumped into his brain he sat up, opened his eyes and stared straight ahead. A power was at work within him - a strange power gaining dominance over his sight. Another eye was planting pictures over those that his physical eyes could see. Visions of past events were taking place right in front of him, put there by his mind's eye, rolling his thoughts backwards.

'*At first, they walked along in a shambolic heap. It was amazing how eventually they began to form into a group. By the time they had reached the lower part of the hill, they had become a squad of marching men. It was no one's decision, it merely happened, each person kept step. The sound of their unified march on the road set up a perfect rhythm. It was a while before anyone spoke and it was Mr Miller who eventually broke the silence.*

"*Why Scrumps?*" *he said, as they reached the level road.* "*Come to mention it, why Splash?*"

"*Go on Herbert,*" *said Scrumps,* "*you tell it best. You tell him all about it.*"

"*Oh my word. That's going back a bit, ain't it?*" *said Herbert chuckling.*'

Herbert chuckling. He could hear his infectious laugh clearly, as if a gramophone record of it was being played inside his head. Without concentration he heard Herbert telling one of his dirty jokes and, as if he was standing there before him, he could observe his leathery skin wrinkle round his laughing eyes. He smiled. It was as if these images and snatches of sound were being rewarded like a prayer answered. He did not realise it at first but, as he sat in the cold and watched his breath curl away in the damp air, he had begun the act of saying goodbye.

How long he sat there, he could not say. There was no measure of time except for the mechanism of the dilapidated clock in the bell tower. Its clanking workings muffled through the thick walls of stone.

176

All his ears could pick up was the low frequency clonk and clunk of the old timepiece as the slow pendulum regulated its iron escapement. He had not been paying much attention but he guessed that half an hour must have gone by. His body grew cold, very cold and he was just about to get up and leave when the vicar strode into his church and came over to him.

"Ah, found you at last. Might have known you'd be here somehow," he said.

He had been running.

"It seemed the right place to be," said Miller.

"Quite so," the reverend replied, out of breath, shaking the rain off. "Look, the bishop's here. We need you at the vicarage, now."

He looked quizzical.

"To carry the coffin, remember?" said the vicar widening his eyes in reproach.

Without waiting for a reply the Reverend Spriggins reached into his cassock and pulled out a neatly folded piece of paper.

"Look, I've copied this out for you. It's that reading I mentioned. Don't read it now please, I'd rather you read it fresh, in church, later on, if it's all the same to you."

He took it from the vicar's wrinkled hand like he was receiving a precious piece of his battered heart. Then he popped it into his trouser pocket and nodded his agreement.

"Cut along then, there's a good chap, we're ready to begin. Harry will show you what to do when you get there."

So he left and darted through the rain down the path to the front door, knocked and went in like a sprinter hitting the ribbon. Harry must have heard him bursting in. He was the first person he saw as he closed the door behind him and shook off the rain.

"Where the bloody hell have you been?" Harry whispered, toning down his language in the puritan atmosphere of the vicarage. "Everyone else is in the back parlour with the box. Follow me. Where's the vicar?"

"I left him at the church. I expect he won't be long."

"Christ, I hope not," said Harry still keeping his voice down. "The bloody bishop's in there," he said nodding towards a door as they sped past.

177

Then there it was. The coffin. It had been placed on a table. Someone had even laid a tablecloth on it, making the table appear like an altar. He was relieved to see that the lid was in place and glad that he was not going to be forced to see the stuff that nightmares could so easily have been made of.

The room smelled of wet clothes and wet hair. These were new smells to the house. The ancient smell of beeswax and furniture polish was playing host to these rude, unwelcome aromas. The quiet voices that normally occupied the vicarage knew little of the forced whispering of men who would usually be giving free reign to their loudness. As he looked away from the coffin he could see that Scrumps was there, standing next to old Tom. So too was Splash, looking so much like death warmed up it seemed likely that he was destined for the coffin next. In the corner standing beside a chair were Jack Manders and his wife who was seated in it. Next to her on the opposite side he was shocked to see Lotty. The front door opened and slammed shut again. There were lowered voices coming from the room they had passed. Presently two sets of footsteps approached and entered the room. As if presenting royalty to them the vicar introduced the bishop to everyone present.

The bishop beheld the gathering as if he were an angel looking down on them. Here was a man who knew little of the lives of ordinary people it seemed. Miller looked back at him, or rather examined him. He examined him closely. His hands were as smooth as a girl's and his large, almost overgrown features were as clean as marble. The most impressive things about him were his stature, he was well over six feet tall and, when he finally spoke, a giant's voice emerged. Although he borrowed his vocabulary from a different world to theirs, the way he put those words together, his delivery of them had people like Harry and Jack Manders spellbound. His voice was deep and capable of projecting to the next county but it was a slow deliberate voice that never hurried. Miller thought it was beautiful. It was full of the kind of tone that was hard to tire of.

"I know that your hearts grieve now as we meet in this holy house. But our dear departed friend and brother here resides with our Lord today. Remember that truth throughout the *Slough of Despond* that verily you must at this very moment be passing through."

178

"Thank you, Your Holiness," replied Harry, who had been briefed by the vicar on how to address the bishop.

Then, with only half an understanding of what the bishop had said, Harry replied while looking at his perplexed companions.

"We will, that is we will try to remember that, won't we everyone?"

There was a mumble of voices that sounded like, we will. Lotty moved closer to Miller as the bishop was speaking to them. She tugged at his wet jacket and whispered.

"We have to talk when this is over."

Her face was a harbinger of dread and he felt a change overtake him, as if being infected by the toxin of her expression.

"Not now," she said before he could reply. "Stay behind after the service."

"Where?"

"The vestry. Stay there afterwards."

The briefest hint of a smile flickered at the corners of her mouth.

"I've got to go now," she said, and she left, wrapping her coat over her head as she darted out of the front door.

"I told her to tell everybody when the time's come," said Harry, aiming his explanation at the bishop, "There's a crowd at the pub, keeping dry there."

"Very well," sighed the bishop. "It's the Lord's rain, so we may as well begin."

The six men lifted the coffin off the table. It was eventually perched precariously on their shoulders at an ungainly angle. Jack Manders and Harry took up the rear. Jack, who was by far the tallest man in the group, was unable to stoop low enough to keep it level. Harry was bearing the load next to him. He reached over to place his hand on Jack's shoulder and interlock arms but could hardly reach. Miller and Scrumps took up the middle. In front of them they could see the oldest and sickest pair of individuals stagger under the weight of the front. Miller knew that it would be a miracle if they ever got through the rain to the muddy hole without spilling their friend on the sodden ground. Their collective effort had the appearance of a huge, bungling, twelve-legged beetle. As they emerged into the downpour, and the bleeding clouds soaked the top of the coffin, that image intensified. It was a giant rain beetle with the coffin as its shiny back. The beast waddled towards the church as a crowd of black umbrellas made their way up the lane from the pub.

The vicar led the bishop and the pallbearers into the damp air of the old building. By the time the coffin had been laid down onto a couple of trestles the procession from the Golden Goose arrived. Some of them sat down in the pews and leaned forwards to pray. A number of women as well as men were shown where the vestry was by Mrs Cartwright, who had arrived directly from her house with the pump. Miller, Scrumps, Splash and Jack made haste there too, to change into their choir robes. They were met with a vestry packed with people, all trying to find cassocks that would fit them. Some had not been worn for years and were torn and moth-eaten. The smell that they gave off was stagnant, almost like a cry of protest at having been abandoned for so long. Presently the vicar arrived with the bishop in tow.

"Please, pay attention everyone. Here is a copy of the order of service and a hymn sheet that I have typed out. If there aren't enough, then you'll have to share," he looked across the room towards Miller, "Mr Miller here is the choirmaster, please follow his lead. I am also pleased to introduce you all to His Holiness, The Bishop of Salisbury. He has come here on this saddest of days to hear our little choir at Empton. Let's give Herbert Ashcroft a good send off shall we and show the bishop how we do things in this neck of the woods?"

Little choir, thought Miller. This had to be the biggest turnout for this church since well, probably since 1908. The Reverend Spriggins would have made a very good salesman indeed, he thought to himself as he looked at the hymn sheet. There was to be two hymns. He flicked through the pages of his copy of *A&M* to find that the first one was *Abide With Me*, just as they had arranged, the choice of a second hymn a mystery. His fingers flipped through the pages and in no time he saw the words of an old favourite. Its appropriateness sent goose bumps running down his arms. He remembered them reminiscing about Herbert's days in the trenches, *Onward Christian soldiers, marching as to war, With the cross of Jesus, going on before*. He took out the soggy piece of paper from his trouser pocket and used it as a bookmark. Then he made his way through those present to wait for the signal to begin.

When the time had come they all proceeded down the aisle to take their places. The church was well attended, a testimony to Herbert's capacity for making friends. Not far from the front he spotted Lotty sitting alone. He wanted to ask where Danno was. There was so much he wanted to ask her - things that he was desperate to find out, but it would all have to wait. With the sound of rain hammering on the lead roof the vicar rose to his pulpit to speak. Like many people in the congregation the vicar knew Herbert well. He spoke about him from the heart. This was not a rehearsed collection of notes passed to him by family members whom he had never met. All the notes he needed for his friend inside the coffin poured from the box of memories now opened inside his head.

Then for the benefit of the bishop, as well as Herbert and the future well being of the village, they sang the first hymn. Miller conducting used his hands to soften and raise their voices at just the right moment. Never before in this church had the words been released with such beauty and passion. The bass singers provided the bedrock to the music and all the other voices created chords that massaged the souls of those listening, or trying to join in. Miller stole a glance at Lotty whose head was buried in her hymn book. He flashed a fleeting look at the bishop too who seemed to be in rapture.

After the prayers it was time for the reading. Miller made his way to the pulpit and removed the piece of paper and carefully unfolded it. He turned his head to see the vicar looking back at him. He could see that the poor man was holding back an ocean of tears. His voice began to echo within the walls and around the pillars, bouncing the words of the vicar's writing into the hearts of all who listened.

I do not know the reason why,
Your life was ripped asunder.
I cannot say why did you die,
Except by mankind's blunder.

Like every soul to walk the earth,
Born to an earthly mother.
You've touched our lives by your own worth,
None more than mine, your brother.

But will you ever fully go?
Your lessons taught may find us,
Learning that whate'er we sow,
Such things we reap shall bind us.

I wept to see your life escape,
I cry that now you're leaving.
Run swift the race past heaven's tape,
As we on earth stand grieving.

The bishop could see that the vicar was incapable of speaking so, placing a caring hand on his shoulder he rose to his feet and invited everyone to pray. He took over the service from that moment on, his large, deep, booming voice making the funeral service a much grander affair.

As the last hymn resounded into the cold air with its mock militaristic beat, Miller paid attention to the still coffin resting as if in centre stage. Herbert would have enjoyed belting out the words to this one he thought. It was not as if he was there, it was his mind playing tricks again, but he felt that he could almost hear his voice, his powerful lungs forcing the glory march out at full volume, *Forward into battle.*

By the time the service was over and they had carried the coffin out into the churchyard the rain had stopped. Grey clouds promised more. Then after more prayers Herbert was lowered into the slimy pit. The heaps of soil either side would later be poured in, the material was so waterlogged. He was gone. The crowd parted. Miller stayed for a moment. Then he turned his back and went to face his own future.

He arrived back in the church to see Mrs Cartwright collecting the books that everyone had left. She was grumbling about it. Grumbling seemed to be her hobby he thought. The vestry was almost vacated as he went in. All except for the stalwart choir men - none of the new recruits had hung their vestments where they belonged. He grinned to see that Scrumps, Splash and Jack had neatly folded theirs up and left them on the table.

"Where do these go?" asked one of the two ladies who were about to leave.

"I'll see to them," said Miller.

So off they went, rather hurriedly, somewhat glad to be getting away from a strange man in a place where they had just removed clothing. Out in the church he could hear the warbling sound of Mrs Cartwright humming the tune of the last hymn whilst she sorted out the books and he joined in quietly as he picked up the robes and hung them where they belonged.

He did not even notice the vestry door open and almost jumped out of his skin with fright, as he turned round to see Lotty standing behind him. She was clasping a pair of gloves, fiddling with them. She looked mesmerised with anxiety. He could see that she was bursting to tell him something but was unable to find the words or where to begin. Mrs Cartwright had stopped singing.

"What on earth's the matter with you?" he said, finding her anxiety transferring over to him.

"I've not been ill," she said.

"Not been ill, what do you mean you've not been ill?"

"I've not had my time," she repeated in an agitated tone, "you know, my illness."

"You're not making sense Lotty. Why are you getting worked up because you haven't been ill?"

"Do I have to spell it out to you then?" she said in a raised voice.

"Go on then."

"I'm having our baby. Is that clear enough?"

The room was frozen with silence, all except for a loud crash of books falling to the floor of the church and footsteps making haste.

Chapter fifteen: New Arrival

The messy conception from a host of sentences began to mutate in his head. His mind aborted each one. He could not think of anything sensible to say or ask, let alone do. At the same time a torrent of random thoughts jostled for attention in the space within his head, deafening and demanding. His mouth tried to form words, the first words of questions that he was unable to pose. He looked and felt stupid. Before he knew what was happening he had wrapped his arms around her and allowed his body to comfort her.

It was she who pulled away first. Her eyes were wild and frightened. They bore into him like a drill. He took a long, deep breath and held it a few seconds before releasing it with a sigh. For a brief moment it helped, but the eyes would not leave him be.

"Our baby," he said, thinking that the words would not be taken the wrong way; he was careful not to voice it like a question but it was taken no other way.

"Of course it's our bloody baby. You don't think it's his, do you?"

"I just thought. You know?"

"Huh! He got the farm. He's not interested in me. I told you there was no love between us. Didn't you listen?"

"I don't know what kind of hold he has on you, do I?" he said. "He might be forcing you to do all kinds of things as far as I know. I know you're not happy to be with him up on that farm, anything could happen up there."

"Well, nothing ever does happen, as you put it. This baby's yours. Yours and mine."

A black silence followed, blaring with inaudible noise. He was finding it hard to think of something to say until, by chance, a sensible thought finally flickered inside his head

"Have you seen a doctor? I think you ought to see a doctor."

"Oh aye, brilliantly stupid idea. Once Doc Fletcher knows about this, we might as well put up posters around the village."

"Well, ought we not make certain?"

"I am bloody certain. I've never been more than a day late since I began. It's been four days now. I know my own bloody body, or not bloody in this case."

Her witticism had a touch of humour about it and a spontaneous but unwanted smile animated his face. It was a fleeting smile but she saw it.

"Oh, big joke is it? You'd better start taking this seriously. You got me into this mess."

Mess. She was right. This was a mess he thought. His mind was racing. His heart had adopted a similar strategy. He knew that the distress and despair had only just begun. Instinctively he knew that this was shock and that it would pass, to be replaced by the day-to-day dealings of living in hell. It made repairing a windmill seem like child's play. He scratched his head. It did no good. He did not expect it to. Then an altogether unrelated question sprang up.

"Where was Danno today? Everyone else was at the funeral."

"The great Daniel Harper," she began, "is presently in a drunken stupor."

"Oh," was all he could say.

"He came home the day after Herbert died. I asked him what was wrong. He bit my head off. I said that maybe it was the shock of the accident, and he said that I was never to mention the accident or Herbert Ashcroft's name again."

"Did that strike you as odd?" he said

"Look, forget him. You've got enough to worry about without paying any mind to him."

Her rebuke tossed him back into the fiery furnace and he tried to be creative once more.

"Have you got any relatives?" he asked. "Anybody you could visit, away from here, 'til it's over."

"And what about the farm?"

"Look, if this was Danno's baby, then they'd have to get along without you."

"What are you suggesting?" she said, a fresh rage percolating beneath her pale skin.

"Keep your hair on. Have you got a sick aunt who needs you?"

"Is that the best you can do?" she said.

This was not what she wanted from him. He was supposed to take control. She knew he did not know how. With every sentence he uttered she realised she was more alone than ever.

"Haven't you and Danno ever, you know, even on your wedding night?"

"He got three-sheets-to-the-wind at the wedding. He said he had a French letter in his pocket. It was there the next morning when he woke up in the armchair. It's never happened. It's not that kind of

185

marriage. It's a business arrangement, pure and simple. If he found out I was pregnant he'd kill me. I think he'd actually kill me, or see to it that I was killed. You've no idea what a heap of shit you're in, do you?"

The silent scream in his soul intensified. She was right. He had no idea. He threw the last cassock back on the table. Trapped like a caged beast, that is how he felt. It was all he could do to slam an old garment onto a table. He knew it was pathetic.

"I can't stay here. I can't breathe in this room, let's get some air," he said.

His jacket needed cleaning. He noticed as he put it on. Everything he wore needed cleaning, but it was inside where he felt truly grubby. His life had become a grubby mess and he knew not how to get it clean again. As they passed through the church from the vestry they saw the pile of hymn books scattered across the stone floor. He had been oblivious to Mrs Cartwright's sudden departure until now. By the time he comprehended what she might have heard, the thought of where she might have gone sounded the alarm. He would normally have picked up the books. It was the kind of thing Lotty would have done too. Instead they left the heap where it was and escaped into the breeze and gulped in the cool, fresh air.

"Come on," he said, "let's go for a walk."

"Huh, and what good will that do?"

"Better than going mad in that church. We'll find a way round this Lotty, so long as we face it together."

It was the first time he had sounded positive. She liked it, even though she did not quite believe it. They headed for the brow of the hill near the old oak. The wind was delicious, almost as good as a drink of clear water. The cold air fanned their brows and cooled their heads and promised salvation with its therapy. Then, as if mirroring the hand of fate, the rain began to fall. It was only spots carried on the wind, but the sky threatened a deluge - dramatic clouds advancing like the heavenly host, full of foreboding.

They decided not to go back to the church but to head for the pub. Herbert's wake would be well underway. They had talked enough to know that each would support the other. It was enough for her to know that Miller was not going to abandon her and, though they possessed no clear plan, they each felt that one would eventually materialise. The main thing was that they were united. There was no talk of love. It was almost as if that could be taken for granted. A weary tiredness was gradually creeping over them. The day had been exhausting all in all and this news only served to sap Miller's energy yet further. For the sake of propriety they decided that Lotty should enter the pub first. Miller would follow her five minutes later.

It was not to be. As they approached the front door Ellie shot out crying, wailing hysterically and, oblivious to where she was going, collided with Lotty. She looked up to see whom she had rammed into and on seeing Lotty buried her head in her coat.

"There, there. What's up El?" Lotty said softly, hiding her surprise.

"Look," the child managed to say, tilting her face sideways.

There was the slash of a grey mark on her left cheek in the middle of which ran a cut some four inches long. Blood was oozing out of it down towards her lips.

"I hate him," she sobbed, "I wish he was dead," then she summoned up her tiny spirit and declared with maturity beyond her years. "He's a bastard, that's what he is."

The minute the defiant words had escaped from her mouth, her heart lost its temporary resolve and she resumed her anguish. Miller burst through the doors to have it out with Harry once and for all. If anyone needed teaching a lesson it was Harry. The pub was full of confusion, raised voices and pandemonium. This was not what he expected at all and his rage was consumed by curiosity, especially when he saw heads crouched behind the bar as if hiding from someone. Getting closer he could hear a moaning sound emerging from the cluster of crouching heads and he peeped over the bar when he got there. Scrumps's face looked up as Miller peered down.

"Oh, it's you. Where've you been?" he said. "Never mind," he carried on without waiting for an answer, "get the doctor, quick, he's broken his leg."

Miller could see a shape poking out from under Harry's trouser leg as he lay there in agony. Lying close by, propped up against the worn out skirting board, was something else that was broken. It was a doll. Harry's prophecy had come true. Miller flashed a glance back at Scrumps.

"Where's he live, the doctor?"

"Up near the war memorial, you'll see, his place has a sign outside. Get your skates on, quick."

He raced out of the pub with his admonishment still undelivered. Lotty was dabbing Ellie's wound with a hanky. He gave her a brief explanation then dashed round the corner and up the lane to the old stone monument. The housekeeper opened the door. He had hoped the doctor would greet him, but instead he asked to see him and was shown in.

"You're just in time, he's only this minute returned from a funeral, you know," said the frail old lady wearing a pinafore. She had a Scottish accent.

"I know," he said. "Please, it's an emergency."

"Wait here one moment," and she scurried off like a mouse-woman.

After hearing some faint voices coming from deep inside the house he picked up the sound of approaching footsteps.

"Ah, the new choirmaster," said the doctor as he entered the room. "Emergency you say, not bumped our head again, have we?"

"No Doctor, it's Harry. He's gone and broken his leg."

"You're sure?" Miller nodded. "I'll get my bag. Where did this happen, in the pub?"

"He's flat out, behind the bar."

Within seconds the doctor was there too. He cleared everyone out of the way and thrust a needle into Harry's leg.

"Very nasty, very nasty," was all he kept saying, but it was easy to tell he was a gifted man by the way he treated his helpless patient. "Well, you've done it this time, landlord. Good job it's a clean break."

"Good job? Good job?" Harry was almost crying in agony. "Shitting hell, you're a heartless bastard when you want to be."

"You can save the insults for when I send the bill," said the doctor, taking the curses in good part. "We've got to get you back to the surgery. I'll have to reset that leg in plaster. You're lucky the bone didn't penetrate the skin. Otherwise it would be off to hospital for you. And how long do you think it would take an ambulance to get here from Salisbury, eh?"

"So I'm supposed to feel lucky, am I?" groaned Harry. "Bad lucky, that's what I call it. Her and her fucking dolls."

The doctor sent Scrumps to get a stretcher from the surgery round the corner. Lotty had now come in to see if she could help. Ellie hid behind her. She felt safest there. It seemed to take ages for Scrumps to get back. The doctor said that he should have gone himself. He knew where the stretchers were - there were three of them and Mrs McKintire would never remember.

Minutes dragged by. Harry reached down and touched the bulge in his leg. His trousers had been cut open, and feeling the bone protruding out beneath the skin turned his face as white as death. Everyone listened for the sound of Scrumps's running feet heralding his return with the stretcher. Instead, all they could hear was the approach of a vehicle in the distance. It was a lorry, Danno's lorry.

Miller stood up and caught sight of Lotty. The blaze of a white-hot spark seemed to arc like a lightening bolt between their eyes. A complete conversation flashed by in a millionth of a second. Each could only guess what questions the other was asking yet the answers that passed between them were being distorted by blind panic. Outside the engine grew louder, the brakes squealed, tyres slid on mud, the motor rattled and died. A cab door opened and then slammed shut. There were footsteps. The eyes of Miller and Lotty screamed at each other. The guilt was doing its job perfectly.

Until, that is, it dawned on Miller that maybe it was not Danno driving the lorry. Danno was pissed up at Bofindle Farm, after all. Who was to say that the lorry was not being driven by a farm hand dropping off for an illicit pint? In any case, how could he possibly know their secret? She had kept it to herself up until now, had she not? Miller's eyes darted to the door, then over to Lotty and back to the door again. He could feel the beat of his heart with the back of his tongue hammering blood round his body like it was a race.

Then the door crashed open framing the shattered form of Danno. He held on to the doorjamb in a posture that made him lean forwards. His great head rocked twice from side to side - the huge, heavy brow overhanging the eyes that were even now scanning the bar. Tears were running down his face, fresh ones following the tracks of their predecessors.

"Is it true?" he bawled out like a giant child. "Is it true what that old bitch says?"

No one dared speak. He swallowed a chest full of air and cried out like a dying dragon.

"Is it true what she says Lotty? Has he been fucking you behind my back? She says you're having his baby!" he yelled with spit flying everywhere, and he took another breath. "Well, answer me, damn you. Answer me."

Ellie began to cry as she gripped Lotty's hem. Nobody could leave. The broken body of Danno still blocked the door, then he stumbled over to where there were some chairs and grabbed hold of the back of one. Mrs Eversage and Ena bolted out seeing a chance to escape, slowing down only to tip a backward glance at the drastic scene inside. Ellie took a half step forwards and pushed out her bleeding face. The child had lost her control. Petrified, she lost her temper and screamed back at the drunken mess before her.

"Don't you shout at Charlotte. You're just..." she wondered whether to say it, as she took another defiant step forwards, but the word had to be said.

"You're just a bastard!" Ellie shouted at the top of her voice.

Danno's eyes filled with black blood and staggering forwards, he flung his hand across Ellie's head sending her reeling like a tossed rag towards the tables. Lotty went to pick up the dazed little body that lay limply on the stone floor. Seeing her chance she lifted the little girl into her arms and fled into the drizzle, not even waiting to catch the eye of Miller who was holding on to the bar, his face white, crippled with anxiety.

Danno flung away the chair he was holding onto and stood on his own two feet. He wiped the wet from his face and moved towards the shaking body of Miller. His face was misshapen by anger. The mouth was open but the teeth were clenched. His whole face was a weapon and it seemed to have the power to destroy just by looking. It was pointed directly at Miller who could feel the onslaught of his gaze dismember him limb from limb.

"I'm waiting, Caruso," he said, his spit flying out of his mouth like venom.

190

Miller was cornered. He was so terrified it did not occur to him to lie. He felt trapped. Trapped by the limitations of his character.

"At least it wasn't a business arrangement," he said weakly.

Everyone in the pub was stunned to silence as Danno's features darkened with deeper rage. His body lurched forwards like a mechanical being, stiff and powerful. He tried to voice profanities but he could not think of a vile enough response to the answer he had just received. When the answer eventually came Miller did not see it arrive. The fist that Danno had unleashed hurled Miller back into the optics that held the spirits. Two bottles fell to the stone floor, smashing far too close to the landlord and the doctor who were crouching behind the bar. For a while Miller had no clue what day it was and Danno was able to grab hold of his jacket and drag him outside as good as if he were drugged.

It was the cool rain that brought him to his senses, even though it took a moment for him to realise what was happening. Danno had by now gripped both of his lapels and was screaming abuse. His voice was a mixture of heartbreak and fury. His tirade scented by a random mixture of bad breath and hard liquor. Miller felt his body being yanked backwards and forwards as Danno flung him around. Then as he released one lapel to make a fist once more Miller saw his opportunity. Before his chin could receive another blow he freed himself from his jacket and was fleeing across the green leaving it behind in Danno's grip. Danno flung the filthy garment into the mud and took up the chase.

Miller ran aimlessly at the chestnut tree. Why, he could not say. It was the same lack of plan that made him dart into what he thought might be the safety of the old derelict cottage. He was dirty and messy now. The bird shit did not bother him as much as it had. He looked around in the gloomy grey for a place to hide and it was then that he noticed the staircase. It was wet from the leaky roof and appeared to be unsafe but he was scrambling up it before he had a chance to think. Thinking was for men. He felt like an animal - one being hunted.

He could scarcely believe this was happening to him. The stairs creaked and groaned as he made his way up. Some of the timbers gave way and as he reached the top step his foot burst through the

191

wood with a loud crack, just as Danno skidded into the sludge in the hallway. The hunter looked up to where the sound had emerged and caught sight of Miller's disbelieving eyes. Miller stepped back from the landing. He could see Danno catch his breath as he clung onto the remains of the banister. Then he began to climb.

Miller frantically searched for a hiding place. The rotting wooden stairs had already been weakened by Miller's careful ascent. Danno's attempt was in a different league. He was a brute and using the force only his kind knew. The fragile timbers gave way under the impact of his boots. Several times his foot went through these worthless planks, lacerating his calves and shins in the process. He was like a demon possessed. Each time he crashed through a step he clung to the swaying banister and hauled himself out and continued the assault.

Miller was in another room, dark and layered in the same way as the ground floor with the slime of bird shit. He could only listen to the grunts of effort and the splintering of wood getting closer. Then, the noise stopped. A brief respite as Miller held his breath. He was aware of blood dripping down his face for the first time but he was too busy trying to fathom what was going on in the silence to do anything about it. The quiet was short-lived however. Miller could hear him checking each room. There were only four rooms upstairs, Danno struck lucky on his second try. Like a vision from a nightmare, the outline of his body stood in silhouette, back lit by the dim light from the landing and framed by the doorway.

"No, way, out," groaned Danno, trying to catch his breath.

Miller stepped backwards knowing there was nowhere to go. It was a bad move. In the darkness he stumbled on an object behind his heels and fell, hitting his spine on the floor. He now looked pitiful. The fall had hurt him. Instinctively his fingers searched through the excrement to feel what it was he had tripped on. He touched wires, firm and taut, attached to a metal rim. A further grope confirmed that it was a wheel - a bicycle wheel.

Danno came over and stood above him looking down. Miller thought he could hear the snap but the pain was too great. Then the boot came again and bludgeoned another rib. He was unable to breathe. He had never had a beating like this before. He tried to get up. It was no use. Another rib was splintered with a crashing blow. He was drowning in agonies.

"How many kicks do you reckon you can stand, eh, singer man?" Danno said with mock kindness. "Made you welcome didn't I? Ate at my table, didn't you? Did I not give you a job? No, I gave you two fucking jobs."

Then he hammered his boot into his genitals. Miller could not help it. He vomited into the bird shit on which he was laying.

"So how many times did you do it? How many times did you fuck her, Caruso?"

Miller tried to haul a breath into his lungs, passing by the vomit, through the sheer, piercing pain.

"How many times?" Danno screamed.

He sent another kick that smashed into Miller's face. Even as he sank through the quicksand of his torture he was aware that his jaw had become dislodged. His mouth was unable to fit back together as it hung down, strangely.

"How many times? I wonder how many times it will take to sort you out once and for all, five, ten, twenty. Let's see, shall we?"

Danno drew his leg back like a catapult for another kick.

"One!"

Miller felt his body shudder under the impact. The agony was beyond bearing.

"Two!"

There came another blow that crushed the bones in his chest. He could hear the number three but his head had been hit and the sound of Danno's voice had become distorted. The pain was numbing. It was almost as if his body was anaesthetising itself.

"Four."

The word was quiet, mumbled, as if coming from a distance. The pain was going. He was going. He never imagined that it was going to be like this, with no goodbyes, no departure from a deathbed. His last deliberate thought created by his brain was of Lotty and what would become of her but the quiet, soft sound of the number five floated into his dying senses. His ears were barely working. The voice that breathed the word six sounded lighter. It came to him an octave higher, almost as if it was the voice of a female. The pain had gone and he was free. The counting continued. It had become a whisper. Its tone came from another world, kind and gentle, not unlike Lotty. But it was not Lotty's voice. The accent was different. Its intonation was much more measured, easy, but with a velvet authority. He knew that it was the voice of an angel. He knew where he was going and he wondered. All his life he had imagined this moment. What kind of reception waited beyond the passage through which he was passing? He seemed to carry the rags of his life. There they were draped on him, each stain depicting some misdeed, and what kind of place would he have to stand in, or on, and show the kind of life he had lived? He wished more than anything else that he could have presented himself in clean garments. He yearned for clothes without sin. He knew how he would look. Thinking had ceased. He now knew things. Thinking had been for his brain. Now he had been granted knowing. God was all knowing and he realised that God's knowing and his knowing would merge and each would know the other. Except God would see his dirty remnants and judge him by them and he became terrified. For as he moved towards the place where the angel was taking him, he knew also that he would be sent by the spirit of God to a place fit for him, as decreed by the judgement that The Lord of Hosts would decide, and he knew how he would look, and he knew where he would be sent. The Lord God would judge him. He would see the stains left by the things that he had done and the things that he had left undone. He would see the stain left by his time with Lotty. The knowing intensified. He had dreaded this moment. It was something to believe that millions of souls had passed this way. It was a road to heaven or hell. His heart cried out for forgiveness. From the depths of his spirit a wailing began, charged with sorrow and remorse, and he knew that by itself it would do no good but he cried all the more. He knew that he was trying to sell his supplication to God. He was trying to sell his miserable worth to God. It was absurd. God was God. Why should God forgive him? He had broken His commandments. His garments showed it.

Then, as if a light had been created, a warm spirit washed through him and, without being told, he knew it was love. Never before had love descended upon him in such a way and his heart gave away its secrets. All of his secrets were poured out as if from a cup and in amongst the secrets was something that he had kept, and it was this. He had believed that Jesus was the Son of God. He had held on to the belief that Jesus had died to take away his sins. He had decided to believe in this one thing as a boy, as a choirboy, long ago and, though it had been buried deeply, he had not cast it away. Quietly and fervently he found his new being rejoicing, *Oh Lamb of God, that taketh away the sins of the world.* The spirit of the *Agnus Dei*, a prayer that his heart had learned to love long ago, began to wash around him. He reached out to touch the sensation and the angel took hold of his hand.

She spoke softly once more, lulling him like a child with her numbers and, when the angel had reached twelve, she said:

"You can open your eyes now."

As far as he knew his eyes were open but she said it again. He prepared himself to see God's glory, as he felt his eyelids separate. He was aware of a great light as the angel cradled his hand in both of hers. The light was golden and warmth came from it. He saw the light and it was good.

"David," said the angel. "Take your time, David."

He took his time, getting used to the light. Beside it he could see a face. The face was of his angel, beautiful and clear and wearing glasses. Glasses? He sat bolt upright in the armchair. His body was soaked with sweat. The face next to the light, he knew it. He knew the armchair. He knew the room, the closed curtains. He even knew the smell. The reality rushed in like air filling a broken vacuum.

"Helen," he said.

He spoke like a man brought back from the dead, staring straight at her or rather through her, as the playback of what he had just experienced ran like a DVD in his head.

"Helen, it is you, isn't it? Please tell me it's you? I'm back, aren't I?" she could tell that he dare not believe it. "It worked that time," he said excitedly. "Tell me I'm back. For God's sake tell me I really am back."

"I had to bring you back, Dave," she said lighting a cigarette and taking a well-earned drag. "You were having convulsions. You've been thrashing about for the last thirty seconds. I've been scared sick."

He took in her words, even as the images of Empton and Lotty continued to overlay themselves upon the reality that was before him. Her instructions returned to his memory, that she would bring him out of the hypnosis by counting slowly up to twelve. He had been sceptical about the hypnosis, especially after the army of counsellors he had seen on his long road to understanding, but it had worked it seemed and, after a few moments of letting it sink, in he felt a tempered sense of elation.

"I've been there you know, Helen. I've really been there."

"I know you have, Dave," she said, offering him a smoke, "I know."

For a while he sat. There were no words between the two of them in that moment. Something remarkable had happened. His thoughts were not so much for the long road he had travelled to get here, but of Lotty. He could not get her out of his mind. Then he began to retrace his life. He wondered if this was, at last, his long awaited turning point and the means of his salvation.

The Curse of Beckett's Wood

Part Two

Chapter one: A Beginning

I had to turn the car radio off. It was Radio Four, *Woman's Hour*. Middle-class women were talking about their silly, infinitesimal problems. Did anyone really care about how to break the biscuit habit, or what went into making a successful coffee morning? It all seemed sickeningly cosy, in an out of reach kind of way. The idea of the BBC putting aside an hour a day especially to rally the cause of the neglected sex seemed so out of date, not to mention patronising. The underlying sub-text was that they were all downtrodden and it was all because of the male sex, the bad sex. It made me sick. Even their lush elocution seemed wasted on such banality. Pathetic, that's what I really thought, pathetic.

Maybe they should try interviewing me on the show - now there was an idea. I could tell them a few things about their sex. The notion of it caused the sneer of a smile to prick one corner of my mouth. How that would have shocked the delicate sensibilities of the biscuit ladies. As usual sarcasm was my medium and habitual bitterness my inspiration, but then you would have been the same if you had been me all your life.

Life, now there is a word. Actually it is not just a word, it can be a sentence too, a life sentence. One step away from the hangman's noose that is life. Then there are the trials of life - the struggle through time to stay alive. To the women on the radio it meant fighting against the tempting lure of the sinister biscuit made, as we had been reminded time and again by the evil empires of men. To me life has been a painful mystery that I have never unravelled, at least never fully unravelled until today.

As I had been flicking through the channels, I heard a snatch of an old song, '*I can see clearly now the rain has gone*', on Radio Two. That is how I had felt that day, a year ago last August, when I was here before. I could see the ruined landscape of my life clearly and, just as now, it was a bright, bright, sunshiny day as I drove the car into this same cemetery car park. I could indeed see all obstacles in my way, real and daunting. The achievement, I suppose, was that I could actually comprehend that they were there, standing in my way - but now the rain had gone, gone for good. Ever since I can remember the rain had completely obscured the things blocking the road out. Metaphoric rain that had been pouring down since the day I was born. Now I knew why life's rain fell like it did for so many years.

Of course, back then when I was growing up, I was like any child I suppose. I accepted unquestioningly everything that made up my developing life, until everything got too much and I got too big to have to take it anymore. They were all bad days, some worse than others, but all bad. They have scarred me deeply. The scars are still there but on that day, here in this graveyard, I began to know the difference between a scar and a wound and I could see how to move forward. I could see what needed to be done to start to set things right, or at least begin to see. That day, that glorious day, I found the road to freedom. I began to feel freer than I had ever done and it was a sense of freedom that I had never experienced before. By an awful paradox it became the wellspring of my angry bitterness. It is, after all, possible to feel free and bitter at the same time, believe me.

I left my coat on the back seat of the car. The day was now warmer than when I set off in the early morning. The stroll was like walking through a gallery of sculptures. As far as the eye could see there were examples of the mason's craft, from simple slabs, to elegant tombs adorned with cherubs and elaborate crosses. I followed a green moss-covered tarmac path that led from the central avenue and counted thirteen stones after the praying angel monument. Three places in and there it was, mum's grave. The inscription was simple. No, I am sorry, that is a cop out. The inscription was heartless, purposely heartless. They were my words. I had decided them. It just said:

Charlotte Harper
Died 12th November 1971
Aged 36

There she was six feet beneath the path, and now it was different. I now had all the facts and I wanted to wrench the stone out of the earth and plant a new one in its place with new, kinder words on it. I no longer felt guilty to be David Harper, just saddened and pining to be given all my wasted opportunities back. I was not the only victim as I had long thought, we both had been. I began to think of those far distant days, the days in the beginning, when things were new. So I looked down at the dark brown soil, at the lush green grass and I could see her. I could see her face. Her young, tired, care-worn face, returning the gaze of my six-year-old features that stared back, trying in vain to understand the way she behaved.

We would go on anxious shopping trips, food shopping that is, or else to buy clothes for me. Rarely did she buy anything for herself.

Times were hard for her. Not that I realised it when I was so young. I was just a boy, Davy boy. That is what they used to call me then, aye up, Davy boy. I can hear it now.

"Aye up, Davy boy," said Mr Grant. He owned the greengrocer's shop. "He's growing up, isn't he Mrs Harper?"

"So he is," mum said, as if she was mad at the shopkeeper for talking to her. "Too damn big, if you ask me. Half a pound of taters please."

"It's me birthday on Sunday," I said to Mr Grunt.

I called him that in my head, on account of the strange nervous cough that he had. Mum cuffed the top of my head with her bony fingers and told me to talk only when I was spoken to. I rubbed the shaved hairs that shaped my short-back-and-sides and longed to be seven.

"What did you have to tell him about your birthday for?" snapped mum as we walked back outside. "Think you're so special that the whole world needs to know when you were born? Is that it?"

"I was just excited that's all Mum," I said, a little afraid.

"Aye, well mind you don't swell up with your own self-importance, mark me."

"No Mum," I said as we headed home.

Home. I hated and loved the place at the same time. Home was where I felt protected and despised in equal measure. Even with the limitations of my childish mind I was aware of the parallel tracks of my mother's neurotic love and inexplicable resentment. Even whilst she hugged and kissed me, something she often did to be fair when I was very little, I always had the feeling that I was in trouble. In fact it was more than that. I always had the sense that I was made to feel that way on purpose, like I was in the way at home. Home was where I created a magical world of my own that was full of pretend adventure. Home was a warm refuge where I came in out of the rain, only to get a whack on the back of the head for getting wet. Home was a grimly furnished flat in the arse end of town. It was a place where people ended up. People like us. We lived in a land of dreary bricks and grey slate. The nearest things to wildlife were the weeds that grew out of the cracks in the pavement, or the pigeons that shitted on our windowpanes. The place was like any other you would find in any one of the market towns in the East Midlands.

The pace of our days was regulated by the haunting moan of the factory siren. It wailed its melancholy call to the workers at seven in the morning. It echoed across the rooftops at twelve and again at one in the afternoon – but the best bit of it was at five-thirty. Sounding like a beast that had dropped a boulder on its foot, the siren filled each and every evening with its declaration that the working day was over and marking the time for those souls whose fate it was to work through the dark night. Within five minutes hundreds of bicycles poured out through the factory gates of Ansons Limited like a river. They seemed unstoppable. They were unstoppable. Some stood up on their pedals to race out faster. The older ones remained seated on their saddles and rocked from side to side to keep going. There were dozens of riding styles. It was a spectacle that I loved to see - like watching a mighty army charging into battle. I used to wonder what kind of homes the men were going to. I used to imagine what it was like on top of one of those huge black bicycles. I tried to guess what it might be like to have a daddy ride his bicycle back to our flat. Guess was all I could do. I never had a daddy that came home to me. My daddy was in a book, a book of pictures.

The book was kept in a sideboard in a section that had a brass lock. Whenever it was freed from its confines I would always get a rush of pleasure, as if I was being permitted to gaze upon secrets, real secrets. Mum would sit close to me and lay the dark brown album on her knee and she would fill my head with tales about everyone who smiled back at me in those black and white images. With calmness normally lacking in her nature, she would paint a picture of my father. By the time she had finished I yearned to meet him. I imagined that he would come home from his journey and lift me off the floor and pour all his love over me. He looked so big and strong as he stood to attention next to my mum. I thought that they both looked beautiful. My favourite one was of them standing beside a severe-looking couple.

We played a memory game to see if I could remember who everyone was. I knew this old couple off by heart. They were my mum's Auntie Emily and Uncle Gerald. At the front, with her back to the photographer but turning her head to face the camera, was Ellie proffering a horseshoe that she had in her hand. Little Ellie's smile was picture perfect. The reason I liked the image so much was because Ellie lived with us and I loved her. To me she was my Auntie El.

Although she went to the Secondary Modern school Ellie's main job was helping mum, and my mum needed a lot of help. She seemed to be in need of it all the time as I recall and Ellie had to work and work hard. I never questioned why she lived with us. She had always been there. I knew that she was not my sister, even at a very early age. As far as I could tell I was the only person who had an auntie living with them. We were unique in that respect, except for the Martins - they looked after a sickly grandad at their house down the road - but it was nice to have her around. I loved my Auntie El.

Mum called her Ellie but, because my infant mouth could only pronounce the El part of her name when I was learning to talk, El she remained. On my mother's insistence I was encouraged to refer to her as if she was my auntie. That was about the time I began to go to school. It was not until later that I understood why.

Why? I seem to have spent my whole life trying to understand a legion of whys. I could never understand for instance why my mum and Auntie El spoke in a different voice to everyone else around. The bare bones that I was able to piece together was that mum had moved from somewhere else to this part of the world looking for a better life. I readily accepted the tale that my dad had gone away before I was born and I had to be content with that. At least I had got pictures of him though. Some kids I knew did not even have that little comfort.

By the time I came into the world during the spring of 1956 my mum had secured a poky flat somewhere. I was too young to remember the day we moved out of there, but I must have been between two or three when we left and came to the flat that, in my primary school days, I called home. The days of Mr Grunt the grocer, hugs and kisses and smacks around the head.

Then there was school. Here was where I felt I had become the loneliest little boy in the whole wide world. My mum scrimped and saved for me to have a uniform. I was trussed up in a grey blazer and matching short trousers, a grey shirt and bottle green jumper. She would show me how to put on my red and grey striped tie and how to fasten my uncooperative shoelaces. Then it was on with a peaked cap that matched my tie and it was out of the door holding her hand. When we got to the black gates on that first day she knelt down to my height and took a good, long look at me. Then she tenderly kissed me on my lips and smiled at me. We were in a world of our own in that moment, a moment that was shattered by the ringing of a hand-bell. It shook her out of her daydream, whereupon she stood up, pushed me through the cast-iron gate and turned her back on me. I cannot remember ever feeling more abandoned than I did that day, and that is saying something.

I remember nothing of that first day at school itself except for that feeling of isolation. It must have made an impression on me because every time I looked at that building when I was older I was able to invoke that same sensation with complete clarity.

Soon after my starting school mum began a part-time job at Ansons. I loved to watch her get ready for work. I used to peek round the door and look at her drawing on her face with a pencil and dusting white powder all over it. By the time she had put on the two-piece suit, which she had made from a pattern, she looked like a vision from the pictures - the kind of woman that the cowboy kissed at the end of the film.

Some of the other women walked to the school gate with her to drop their kids off too. Many of them wore heavy clothes and tied their hair in scarves. They had grubby hands and grubby voices, consequences of their filthy jobs and habitual smoking. They were loud and intimidating, frightening in fact. I had them branded as witches in my simple mind, filthy witches. Then one day by chance I saw my mum smoking a cigarette as she waited for me outside the school. I remember being afraid of her as she breathed out the grey wisps that were carried off by the wind. I hated seeing what she was capable of becoming. How long before she would be wearing a headscarf and talking in the same gruff voice as did the other women?

"You're not going to be a filthy woman are you?" I plucked up the courage to ask, threatened by her impending metamorphosis.

She craned her neck down to behold me. With a mystic's powers her eyes penetrated into mine. Their gaze twisted and turned like a dagger far beyond my own eyes to the very depths of the little me. It was a moment that terrified me. That look did more damage than the belt on the back of my head that followed and we hurried all of the way home in forced silence.

Then one evening, when I was about nine years old, I peeped round mum's bedroom door to see her painting on her face as she did when she was going out to work. I asked her if she was working nights. She told me to go back to bed. Auntie El, she said, was going to be looking after me and just before she went out she came into my bedroom and stroked my head. Mum's body was evaporating with scent and her eyes were more beautiful than ever. I flung my arms round her neck and told her that I loved her. She did not say a word in reply but simply kissed my forehead and left my room, dabbing her eyes with a white handkerchief as she disappeared.

The next morning she was different. I could not explain how or why. She seemed happier but less affectionate. She teased me in a way that was consumed with joviality but left no place for tenderness. It was impossible to explain then, and even now I can only express my feelings by saying that it seemed as if she had traded what little warmth she had in exchange for a sense of the pleasurable. Following each and every nocturnal excursion this inner light seemed to posses her - but it was a dark light. Her smile was dark and not one of her own. It was a mask, untrustworthy.

One night, quite late, I heard her return. From my state of half sleep I picked up her voice. She was talking to herself, whispering. Her bedroom door clicked shut and I heard a key flip in a lock. All of the doors in our old flat had locks in them I remember. Mine was the only one without a key. As I drifted back into unconsciousness I became aware of a tapping sound coming from her room. Being just a young boy I strained to hear. Sitting up I tried to make sense of the creaking of bedsprings and the repetitious knocking of the headboard on the wall. My mum was grunting as if she was trying to move the furniture by herself. I imagined too that she was jumping up and down on the bed, just as I did when I thought no one was looking. After about five minutes of this it stopped. The house became quiet.

For the next couple of minutes all I could hear was the sound of my breathing. Then my nose picked up the exotic aroma of cigarette smoke wafting into my room. I sank down into my bedclothes terrified that my mum had turned into a witch woman. In the morning she was once more the strange happy person that I did not recognise. Like the shift of a subterranean tremor the foundations of my life had been shaken. I felt excluded from her, realising there were things about her that I was not permitted to know. I loved her and feared her with every second that passed. I was desperate for her to love me back.

I got my chance to make her do just that on her birthday in February. I decided to make her a card. I would be about nine or ten by this time. I had kept a piece of white card that my new shirt had been wrapped up in. It was secretly stashed underneath my bed. Every night I worked on its design, building it up bit by bit. In the centre there was a heart, crayoned red, with the word LOVE in blue at its centre. Then in bubble letters coloured orange was the word HAPPY and in green, below the heart, was BIRTHDAY. The best bit though was inside. I had drawn a picture of me, all coloured-in, and had carefully cut out a heart shape where my own heart would have been. The words inside said simply *I'll give you my heart for your birthday*. Then I signed it with my newly formed signature and put it in a brown paper bag that her present had come in. It was an apple bought especially at Mr Grunt's.

I could not wait for the big day. Auntie El said it was the best card she had ever seen. I lovingly slid it under the bed the night before and tried to sleep. I was wakened as usual by the rattling sound of Ellie making the fire up in the kitchen boiler. After a few minutes mum stirred and made her way downstairs. This was it. I got up, dressed and ran downstairs apple in one hand and card in the other.

"Happy Birthday Mum," I said even before I got into the kitchen.

Then I saw her. Tears had decimated her make up. She looked like she had been destroyed from the inside. I could not bear to see her this way, but it was impossible to know what to do. In the end, cheering her up seemed to be the only option.

"I've made this for you," I said, handing over the brown paper bag and the card that was supposed to make her love me. "It's for your birthday."

Without looking at me she said, "I hate birthdays."

The card was dragged out of its bag and, holding it in her right hand, she glanced at it for a second. There was no transformation in her stony face as I expected there to be. As she looked at the colourful design I was sure her heart would melt. I had at least hoped for a smile. There was nothing. Finally, with a derisory laugh she muttered the word I had crayoned in the centre.

"Love. Aye, well you can keep it," she muttered.

Then, opening the top of the boiler she coldly tossed in my little card. Even as the iron lid clanged shut I could hear all my hard work being devoured by the flames. The image of her ravaged face was soon blurred over by the tears that flooded my own eyes.

"You never even looked inside it," I managed to blurt out before I slammed the apple on the table.

The sound made her aim her witches stare at me.

"Don't even think about crying. You've no idea how many heartaches I've had bringing you into the world. So don't ever let me catch you crying again. Do you mark me? I had enough of listening to that bloody noise when you were a baby. Now bugger off to school and leave me alone."

The clang of that boiler lid remained with me all that day, all my childhood, all my life.

When I got back from school she was still mad. The minute I walked in she began to bash the pots and pans on to the cooker as she made the tea, making her point, whatever that was. How she had managed to remain angry all day long was a mystery, but mad at me she was, there was no getting away from it. Ellie was out, and I was alone with her. Before me was her back, slender and strong. Even the peeling of the potatoes was an act of violence, performed with acute jabs of her knife. With anxious knots clawing at my stomach I knew I was going to find it difficult to eat this meal, made as it was with such rage. It would soon be slammed on the table before me. She would expect me to consume it. There had to be a way to set things right. So

I approached her knowing how timid I looked. Even though I was terrified, I just wanted her to stop being angry and love me.

"I'm sorry," my ten-year-old voice said. "I'm sorry about the apple," then it waited for a few breathless moments before having to speak again. "I didn't want to make you unhappy Mum."

I could feel myself welling up ready to cry again. I fought the urge with such bravery. She slowly put the knife down and wiped her hands on the towel, turning to fix me with those eyes, now less possessed.

"Go and get ready for your tea," she commanded sternly, warmed with just a thimbleful of tenderness. It was enough for me, that thimbleful, and I smiled back at her. Despite everything I loved her.

During that night I was haunted by bad dreams. Nightmare visions overran my mind like an occupying marauder so that I awoke in a state of blind fear. Even as I stared into the darkness with my eyes wide open the dreams continued to play on. The long night was spent being afraid, afraid to scream or cry. I was petrified of waking my mum, so I let the demons continue to scare me, projecting the dancing, horrifying pictures, in the blackness of my little room, weird pictures, haunting and bizarre. I longed for daylight to come and release me, so I turned my eyes to the curtains and watched for the first glimmers of a February morning to appear, holding the covers to my chin. I was exhausted by the time I heard the first bird announce the dawn. Only then did I know that I was safe and I allowed myself to drift off to sleep for the few hours until breakfast.

I recall little of the dreams themselves, only the awfulness of that bad night and the nights that followed. The only recurring theme in most of them involved a house, a house that was capable of changing its character from one of benevolence and comfort to a place of dread. The house would alter as if it was alive, like watching a smile morph into a grotesque scream.

Then, to add to the grimness of my life, mum and Ellie had a row. Not the normal arguments that were part of everyday life. This was no skirmish. This was all out war. It was the summer holidays, that glorious time in 1966 when England could not fail. A great many years had to pass before I learned what the row was about but I heard the tail end of it as I was prised from sleep one hot, sultry night. Two voices, one more mature than the other were each locked in combat with primal screams as their weapons. The fever of it made discerning words impossible. No one gave ground. Both mum and Ellie were like two galleons firing broadsides into each other. Then came the noise of smashing crockery, or maybe it was glass, I was not sure until I wandered down the stairs to see what was going on, and there they were. The two of them were ugly and terrifying. I had never seen Ellie like it before. She stood with her face only an inch away from mum's, with her coat on and a case in her hand screaming out words that were drowned out by mum's bellowing voice. None of it made sense. I was even unaware that lines of tears had begun to run down my face as I watched them slug it out. Ellie caught sight of me in the doorway.

"And you wonder why I hate you," she said to mother. "Look what you're doing to that little chap."

She looked at me, her face red as rage, and she smiled, just for me. It was the smile I knew and loved. Mum looked to where I was. Her eyes were bloodshot and filled with exhaustion and madness.

"Get back to your room. This is all your bloody fault."

"Don't listen to her Davy," said Ellie. "You take care."

"If you're not back in your room in five seconds," began mum.

I did not wait for her to finish the sentence. As I flew back up the stairs, I heard the back door slam. Another item of crockery shattered against the door as it shut. Then all was quiet, all except for the sound of my muted sobs and the voice of a demented woman ranting away to herself in the kitchen below.

Chapter two: Lost And Found

I have learned to compartmentalise my life. It is the only way my mind can deal with the experiences it has lived through. Only this part of my life, this secret compartment, the part that began with Ellie leaving home has been dropped down the deepest mine shaft, buried under tons of denial and declared out of bounds. Only occasionally, under the most extreme pressure have I had cause to dig up the hidden box, open it up and dare myself to peer into the hideous memories that lie within. If I were to put a label on it, I would call this time of my life the dark ages, hard ages, hard to come to terms with, best forgotten. Best forgotten and never understood, until now.

I turned my back on the grave of my dead mother and walked back along the path to my dark blue Astra. Visions of the past still flitted through my head as I strolled soberly through the freshly painted gates to the crunch of the cinder-covered car park. I looked down at my brogues making the sound. It is a timeless sound. Cinder paths made that noise back in my boyhood, as they do now, and always will I guess. I think of soldiers marching when I hear it. No, that is a lie. I think of the soul-destroying, gut wrenching footslog back home from school, back home down the cinder track to mother.

I ran the gauntlet of the cinder track twice each school day. It ran alongside a large municipal playing field and linked the estate where my new senior school was situated, to the back end of beyond where we lived. Ellie had not come back. Instead she had written me a letter and addressed it to my headmaster Mr West. It arrived one Friday morning and was handed to me after morning assembly. She told me that she had got a job in Nottingham and that she shared a small flat with five girlfriends. There was going to be no room for me but she thought about me very often. All she said about the night she left was that she and mum had stopped seeing eye-to-eye and that none of it was my fault. After telling me that she loved me she wrote something very odd: *'and don't forget, you've got looks on your side and handsome people go a long way in life. I think you're a very handsome chap Davy, the spitting image of your dad, so keep your chin up'.*

I thought it odd because though I was familiar with my dad's face, I failed to see how Ellie imagined that I had any likeness with him at all. Anyway, she finished off by wishing me good luck and signed it Auntie El. I stuffed the letter back in its white envelope and popped it in the inside pocket of my blazer alongside a pen, pencil, rubber and half-sucked humbug rewrapped in its cellophane. It remained close to my heart all day like a good luck charm. I could not help reading it again at dinnertime, and then I stopped to look at it again on the way home - on the way home to the sound of the crunching cinder track.

208

My plan was to hide the letter cunningly in my bedroom. Some of the wallpaper behind my set of drawers was peeling away at the join. To tell the truth it was me who saw to it that it was peeled away in the first place. My treasure map was already hidden there, only now there would be some real treasure to join it.

"And what time do you call this? Where've you been?" she snapped as I walked in, her arms folded tightly over her bosom.

"I've just been walking down the cinder track Mum," I said.

"No you haven't. I can tell you've been up to something."

Her lips were now drawn together, sealed in an inverted pout. Up to something, she said. I flashed a glance down towards my treasure then back up to her face, a face lined with the burdens of staying alive and the effort of dragging me along with her.

"I've just been walking slow, that's all."

"The hand was faster than the eye and my head flinched sideways with the slap that caught me across the ear. Her voice bore down on me slowly delivering one deliberate word at a time so that I would get the message.

"Don't you, ever, give, cheek. Do, you, mark me?"

"Sorry Mum," I said, what else could I say?

"Aye, well mind you are. Now get those things off. It's Friday. I'm off to the launderette. You can peel and chop some carrots while I'm gone."

I thought of the letter.

"I'll just go up and get changed then," I said.

"You can get your things off here and now. I haven't got all day to wait for you."

So I stripped off in the kitchen and handed her the clothes I had worn all week. The blazer was flung quietly over the back of a chair so I could hide the letter when she had gone.

"Right, well make sure those carrots are ready for when I get back."

As she turned to leave with a bulging sack of dirty linen in her grip, it hit the chair, the chair with the blazer over it. The lino floor clattered to the sound of falling pens. The rubber bounced under the table. The letter fluttered down, landing address side up. She saw it. She bent down to pick it up. She read the name and address. Down went the sack of washing. She picked it up, stood straight and gripped me with her stare.

"Not up to anything, aye? What's this then?" she growled as her fingers delved into my treasure. "Well, let's see what sort of trouble you're really in, shall we?"

She slid out the precious contents and took in the words. I swallowed hard as I watched her face betray the rage that was building up steam inside her. I was petrified. Her eyes bulged inside a face burning with hatred that I could not understand as she reached the end of Ellie's note. The letter was slammed onto the table. The next minute she reached into the cutlery draw and fetched out the wooden spoon.

"What are you going to do Mum?" I said, knowing what was likely to happen.

"Up on the chair," she commanded. "Up on the chair!"

"Please, no Mummy. Please no," I begged, placing my hands in front of my hairless genitals.

"Up on the chair!" she screamed, yelling with so much force that I jumped with the shock of it.

I could see the wooden spoon being slapped against her palm. I could hear the sound of its impact on the inside of her hand. There was no choice. I hauled my bare body up on to the chair and waited for it to happen. I did not have to wait for long.

The first one was a stinger, almost numbing. The second only a moment later was bang on the same target. I can feel it now, like a white-hot poker, burning and savage. Each time I winced, as my soft buttocks were made red-raw in this way. There was no time for the pain to dissipate before the next whack slammed into my wobbling bottom. It made me want to puke. I tried not to cry but in the end I had to. I cried out from the sheer pain. My punishment ended on the sixth lashing. I felt as if a monster wasp had stung me. I was just a boy, embarrassed and humiliated, standing naked on a chair in agony. The dark ages had begun.

There was to be no tea that night. In her rage she swept her arm across the cooker, sending pots and pans that she had got ready to cook with hurtling across the room. The noise of them crashing to the floor was violent and ugly and I was terrified. The letter was flung into the boiler, to be incinerated like my card. I was sent to bed where I cried and felt worthless while mum went to the launderette. I dreaded her coming home and it was ages before she did so. When the sound of the door finally announced her arrival I trembled in my bed like a whipped dog. The terror of her feet climbing the stairs traumatised me that first night and, as she got nearer to my door, I knew that my heart was going to pound itself to destruction and that my brain would follow suit. I prepared myself to see her burst into my room, ready to dish out more of the same. Instead the door opened slowly, softly, and the face of my mother crying looked down on me through the crack. She smiled through an expression contorted by anguish and without any effort I smiled back. She knew at that moment that I still loved her. She came in, wrapped her arms around me and told me that she was sorry. She smelled of cigarettes and a new scent, beer – but she had found the ideal method of executing her wrath and, over time, she perfected it and developed it so that, at its zenith, the mere mention of a wooden spoon would cause me almost to faint.

Then again something good came out of those days. I met a boy at school, Ian Crabtree. Our school was divided into houses and Ian was in a different house to mine. I cannot remember how we first became friends but we both had a love of bicycles. Neither one of us had one but we loved them never the less. Sturmey Archer for girls and Derailleurs for boys. Ian had very set opinions when it came to the pushbike. He also sang in the local parish church choir. One Thursday evening, on the way home, he asked would I like to go with him to choir practice to see if I liked it.

"You get paid," he said, "sixpence for each service and half a crown for weddings. Sometimes you get invited to the reception. Well, once I did, anyway are you up for it or not?"

He could see it in my face why I thought the idea was preposterous.

"Look, I'll come home with you and ask your mam for you if you like, she don't mind me?"

"Okay," I said with misgivings, imagining the scene at home after Ian had said his goodbyes. "Just don't make her mad, that's all."

"A choir, a church choir?" said mum. "Are you sure you want to be a chorister?" she asked with a meagre hint of enthusiasm.

"It's choir practice tonight Mrs Harper," piped up Ian. "It's just to see if he likes it."

"Oh, but I think he is going to like it, aren't you Davy boy?"

"I hope so," I said, hedging my bets.

Then, somewhat surprised, I caught the look she gave me urging me to modify the answer.

"I mean, I'm sure I will," I said.

Ian arranged to call for me at seven. We would walk up to St. Peter's together for seven thirty practice. Even when Ian had gone home there was no interrogation. I held my breath for all hell to break loose but it did not. It had all been easier than I expected. Perhaps it was my first miracle. I can remember thinking that. Mum made me put on my best going out clothes, saying that I was not to go to the house of God dressed as a tramp. I did as I was told, even though I felt awkward about it. It was a small price to pay for a little freedom.

Bang on time after tea there was a knock at the door and there was Ian togged-up in his jeans and baggy green pullover. He tried to stifle a grin as he saw me kitted out in my Sunday best. I forced a knowing smile back, kissed mum cheerio on the cheek and off we went to wonderland.

The grey spire of St. Peter's dominated the skyline of our town like it was a great thorn rising out of the rooftops jabbing towards an Anglican heaven. No one paid any attention to it in our town, except to give directions - head towards the church, you can't miss it, then turn left, that sort of thing - but here I was walking up to the great stone monster with my head tilted back. The golden weathervane at the very tip of the spire seemed halfway to the moon, I had never realised how tall the building was and it had been made to appear even taller. It was the style of its construction. Everything was made to rise ever upwards. Window columns, arches, even the four pinnacles on the corners of the tower groped the sky to reach up to God. We passed the main door an impenetrable slab of heavy dark-brown oak laced with ornate ironwork, then made for the side entrance entering into a world of echoes.

The sound of our footsteps filled the great interior, mingling with the noise of excited boys that were congregated in a group at the end of the church. Its inside was big enough to accommodate our flat many times over. Slender stone pillars rose majestically upward, supporting the most ornate ceiling I had ever seen high above my head. I could not take it all in and in any case my attention was interrupted by three rapid handclaps made by a thin man who appeared from nowhere. The sound of this call to order was still rebounding around the walls as we approached the wooden screen that separated the main body of the church from the smaller area where the boys were.

"Ah, Mr Crabtree, I see you have a guest," said the thin man's nasal voice.

"This is David Harper, sir. He's wondering about joining the choir," Ian said, as if he was talking to a teacher.

"And can you sing, Mr Harper?" said the man eyeing me up over the rim of his spectacles.

"I don't know," I said, aware of Ian's faint frown glaring at me. "I mean I've sung at school sir."

There was a repressed wave of giggles.

"Well, if you want to be a chorister, you must be sure that you can sing, mustn't you?"

"Yes, sir. I suppose I must."

I had a nasty feeling where this line of questioning was heading. The thin man reached over and grabbed hold of a book. He flipped it open looked approving at the page it had settled on and handed it to me.

"You can read music, I presume?"

"Well, I can read words, sir."

"Are you familiar with this hymn?" he said pointing to the title on the left-hand side.

It read: *There is a Green Hill Far Away*. I knew this one.

"We sing this at Easter, sir. I know how the tune goes."

"Then please sing the first verse, would you?"

"What, now, sir. I'm not even in the choir yet, sir."

"And you're not likely to be in it if I don't hear you sing. You're not the first to do this. Everyone has to. Now, the first verse please."

So I took a deep breath, swallowed hard and began.

My treble voice broke the quiet of the holy air. It bounced off the pillars and off the decorated roof. I could hear my notes hang within the great walls for long seconds as the words came out shrill and strong.

"There is a green hill far away, without a city wall,
Where the Dear Lord was crucified, who died to save us all."

I listened to the final word *all* echo itself into silence and then I looked up from my book to see what the thin man would say. The other boys had stopped messing about acting stupid and even Ian was waiting.

"Would you mind singing the second verse, please. When you're ready."

So, I filled my lungs once more and sang.

"I did not know, or could not tell what pains He had to bear,
But that I believed it was for us He hung and suffered there."

I knew the words almost off by heart. They had made an impression on me. I had never understood how one man dying could save everybody but it was a nice feeling to be saved anyway. Saved from what I could not say either, though I must have been saved from something pretty bad for the dear Lord to get nailed to a cross to save me from it. The thin man took off his glasses and cleaned them with a cloth taken from the pocket in his gown.

"Have you ever been in a choir before, Mr Harper?"

"No sir."

"And you've never had singing tuition?"

"Twoishon?"

"Singing classes."

"No, sir."

"Very interesting. See me after practice and we'll get you a probationer's robe."

I looked puzzled. I had no clue what he meant. Ian was smiling at my mystified face.

"You're in, stupid," he said almost laughing, "you're in."

The hollow sound of a far away door latch shot through the church like a prison lock being opened, followed moments later by the voices of men and women. Most of them were clutching books and papers and each made their way to their seats knowing exactly where they were meant to go. One elderly gentleman made his way to a long seat halfway between two rows of men and unlocked what seemed to be a cabinet. A sliding wooden cover was pushed open, revealing what to me looked like three pianos arranged on top of each other. He flicked a switch and I could hear the hum of an engine and the hiss of air. So far this evening had been full of fascination, but I had not had the half of it.

"Right," began the thin man, "I think we're all present. *Magnificat* to warm up please."

With that the old chap at the long bench placed his fingers on the piano keyboards and pressed down. A tidal wave of pristine sound boomed out from pipes above his position. I was awe struck. I wanted to fall to my knees in submission to its might. I was in the midst of a musical beast. And then there came the accompanying host of voices - boys, ladies and men, all singing different tunes overlaid on each other. I had no understanding of harmony. Chords to me had meant rope, but here was beauty entering my ears, powerful beauty that took my heart and flung it to the ceiling to fly on the rapture of this glorious music.

"*My soul doth magnify the Lord,*" they sang, like a host of angels. They certainly magnified Him all right.

I spent the next hour transfixed in serene bewilderment. A new language flowed from the assembled as if it had come down from heaven. Words like doxology and descant, or crescendo and creed pricked my ears for the first time. The alienation I felt only served to fuel my thirst for what it all meant. Then there was the practice of an anthem. Bit by bit each section of the choir tried out varying parts of the music. When the men with their deeper voices tried out their part, it seemed so unmusical, the same was true of the ladies as they reached for the highest notes their mature voices could reach. Ian joined in with the other boys, singing more of a proper tune. I watched him concentrate on the booklet he held in both hands, glancing up at the thin man frequently to follow the ballet of his arms.

The pianist sat round watching it all, his arms folded. He caught me looking at him and he smiled back. I wondered how he had ever learned to play two pianos at the same time.

With a brief pep talk the thin man raised his arms and all the voices joined in together. Like some harmonic tapestry all the parts blended together. How had someone dreamed this all up I thought? The music acted like a cool breeze inside my mind. Then it stopped and they had to sing some of it again as one boy was going wrong. He was given a telling off. The thin man sang it for him and they were off again. Finally, it was time for the older man to turn round and add the booming sound of his pipes. Oh, what wonder! Majestic, there was no other word for it.

"What you going to tell your mam" Ian said, as we walked home in the evening dusk.

"I know what I want to tell her, I just don't know how to," I said, "but we'd better get a move on, or I'll be for the spoon again."

"She don't hurt you, does she?"

"Only when I'm evil, then she does. She says it's to drive the devil out of me."

"Evil? What do you do that's evil?"

"I come home late, so let's get a crack on, shall we?"

She was there, waiting when I got home and shut the door. She was standing next to the drawer, the drawer where the WS lived. She looked me up and down searching for signs of misdemeanour. I turned around to show her that I was clean from top to bottom. She moved and sat at the table.

"Well, tell me what it was like then," she snapped.

My mouth went into ecstatic overdrive describing it all. I had learned on the way home that the piano was called an organ and I told her all about that, and the men, and the ladies and how they all sang weird tunes that all fitted together, and the thin man, the choirmaster, and the church and oh how wonderful it all was. I left the best bit until last. I told her that I was a probationer and that I had got a robe and could be in the choir on Sunday morning if I was allowed to go. She looked me up and down, wondering what to make of me. After a moment's thought she stood up and stepped towards me. I stepped back, afraid. I braced myself for my daily dose, but

216

instead she wrapped her arms around me and kissed the hair on the top of my head.

"Good lad. Now, off you go to bed."

Friday morning was bedlam. There was no milk on the doorstep. We had not paid our bill. Worse still the rent man had said he would be making trouble for us if we did not sort out something to do with our ears. Mum was rushing her getting ready routine and had made a mess of her face, or so she said. She shouted downstairs for me to come up and find her black shoes. The air was blue with swearing as I hunted her bedroom for a pair of shoes in black. There they were. I ran up to the bathroom door and knocked.

"Get in here in and drop them down there," she fumed, pointing towards the side of the bath.

So I did. I saw her dressed in nothing but her underwear as she faced the mirror, sculpting her hair with a brush.

"You stupid boy," she yelled, "not those!"

"They're black," I dared to say.

"You got the wrong ones on purpose, didn't you?"

"I'll get another black pair," I said.

But I had missed the point. Black shoes, red shoes, it did not matter now. I had crossed the line. She threw down the brush and picked up one of the shoes, one of the wrong shoes.

"What are you trying to do to me you idiot child, send me to the nut house. You know what shoes I go to work in," she screamed. "Don't you?"

I could not answer. I had never paid attention to her shoes before.

"Don't you?" she screeched only inches from my face.

"Yes, Mum," was the only answer I could give.

"Then why get me these?"

"I don't know Mum. I didn't think."

"I'll tell you why, shall I?" she said slapping the shoe against her palm, "Because you hate me."

"I don't Mum. I don't?"

"Oh yes you do, you hate me. Well, shall I give you something to hate me for, shall I?"

217

Down it came on top of my head, the top of my head that she had kissed only the night before. Again and again it crashed down on me. She was holding the heel so it could have been worse. Nevertheless it hurt. I put my hands on my head and crouched into the corner of the room. In this position it was the backs of my hands that took most of the beating, twenty or so whippings of unleashed temper raining down. When it was over I peered through the gaps in my fingers. There she was towering before me, like some goddess of Greek literature, dressed only in bra and panties, holding the shoe like it was a sword. She was breathing heavily from the exertion of it. Her breasts heaving up and down. How beautiful she looked, how awful.

"Get out of my sight," she whispered, fighting for breath. "Bugger off to school. I don't want to see your stupid face 'til tonight, and then it'll be too soon."

I got up, went out and walked the cinder track with her words beating me as painfully as had her shoe. I felt worthless. I had no worth. I was the unloved and was unlovable, and it mattered not how much I tried to give my love to her it would never be enough. My love was bad love, I thought. I prayed for Sunday to arrive, so that I could escape and fill my ears with the music I had just discovered. The day arrived at its own speed, two beatings later.

Leaving the house on Sunday morning was easier than I had expected. I was prepared for some kind of conflict. There was none. I presumed that my mum was feeling glad to be getting rid of me for an hour or two. I was glad to be out, striding down through town with Ian to the great spire. This time it seemed as if the church was primed. It seemed alive. Thursday had been a practice. Today it was for real. Then I realised what the difference was. It had been part of my Sundays for most of my life. Only today I was paying attention to it and noticing it for the first time. It was the bells. They pealed up and down the scale by unseen hands, changing their order, but singing, singing the chimes of a Sunday, an English Sunday.

The main doors were now open and a queue of people was filing through. I followed Ian to the side door, avoiding the line of Christ's followers and entered a church now three-quarters full of the faithful. Wide-eyed I tagged along with Ian and made for the vestry. The room was full of people slipping into robes, hanging ribbons round their necks and reaching for hymn books perched high on shelves in a cupboard. The thin man was there, the choirmaster, helping to organise. I put my blue robe on and did up the buttons right down to my feet. Ian showed me how to fit a ruff round my collar. Then he got ready adding a white smock, a surplice he called it, to his red robe, a cassock.

The choirmaster looked at his watch as if he was a football referee and asked us all to bow our heads in prayer. Then another man came in dressed in the most ornate robes I had ever seen and said a blessing. Before I knew it we were walking out of the vestry into the lofty heart of the church. The mighty organ belched out its chords and the choir filled everywhere with choral delight, leading the congregation in song, so that the vast interior was alive with music - music that rose up the pillars, out through the roof and up to God himself. Somewhere in the middle of the line of singers making their way slowly down the central aisle was little me trying to join in. It seemed as if a family that I did not as yet know had taken me in and, even as my tiny voice added its meagre contribution to the juggernaut of sound, I knew I had found a place to belong.

Chapter three: Mother's Love

The one thing I can say I loved as a child with unsullied affection was Saturdays. I could escape on Saturdays and take myself off, alone. Our town lay snuggled in the cradle of a shallow valley, a valley with a dirty river at its lowest point and rolling fields on the higher flanks to the east and west. There was a road that led eastward towards the morning sun, and beyond the road, a lane, or dirt track, that emptied out into fields rising ever upwards.

On many Saturdays I ventured up there, past grazing cows to the highest spot near to a farmhouse smothered in a copse of dense trees. The only frightening part was a terrifying dog I had to pass. It was always tied up and shielded from me by a thick hedge and an old five-bar gate that had chicken wire stapled to it. I hated that dog. It made me hate all dogs and I prayed that it would never find a way out of its enclosure. I was always glad when I had passed that part.

From the farmhouse I could see the spread of the municipal borough below punctuated by the elegant spire of St Peter's. Up there I felt free, the wind stoking my hair and kissing my face. Up there I could look down on the whole damn lot of them. I could see Ansons' five chimneys like black smoking fingers. They seemed to be biding their time knowing that, one day in the not too distant future, they would beckon my soul to be sold as a slave to their industry. Looking down on it was like looking into a grave, my grave, and climbing back downhill was always depressing.

But a shining Saturday could be made to gleam brighter with a golden promise in it. A golden Saturday was one that included a wedding and, just as Ian Crabtree had said, that meant money. My mum would often sleep a great deal on Saturday. Often I would hear her crash through the front door on a Friday night and fall headlong into the toilet. I would feel ill myself listening to the retching sound of her vomiting into the loo. Then she would crawl moaning into her bed and pass out.

On several occasions I was able to sing at a wedding and be back before she came round. Her temper had a shorter fuse when she was in this state, though her condition rendered her less effective. It was when she was sober that I had no option but to tread carefully. I was just glad to be away on Saturday, away from home and away from school. I had found a better home and a more exciting school in the shape of the church where, on those blessed mornings and afternoons, I was able to get my hands on silver. That is what they called it in those days, silver.

There was something very distinguished about a half-crown coin. Not only did it look like silver, it was similarly heavy too. Just describing it as two-and-six denigrated it. Reducing it to figures took away some of its personality, its dignity. Giving something a name always seemed more pleasant than giving it a number. Tanners, bobs, florins, thrupenny bits as we pronounced them, they could all rest in your pocket like a bunch of friends - but a half-crown, now there was a coin, big and bulky, elegant in design. It was more like a piece of jewellery than an item of currency. In your pocket it was the most welcome of friends you could ever possess at thirteen-years-old. Not bad for just singing *Crimond* at a wedding.

A marriage service was a window into a different world for Ian and me, especially me. It was about my only chance to see proper happy families with perfect mums and dads and grandparents all happy to be together with their children. My mum seemed to be at war with the world around her. She fought hard looking for scraps of happiness and never found any. These people seemed to have had it handed to them on a plate. Maybe it was the effect of the special day they were enjoying, but rarely was there anything dysfunctional about them.

Normally eight boys turned up to sing. Eight boys for a quid would be enough to make a decent sound and with the organ on the reeds we were still loud enough to be heard. Quite often during the signing of the register we would sing an anthem that we had practised on Thursday night. In effect it was nothing more than a final run-through before Holy Communion on the following day. Without the men and ladies it lacked power. Somehow though it fitted the delicacy of the happy event taking place before us as we performed like cherubs sent down from heaven. Maybe the people watching imagined that we had perfect lives too, I often thought, but if they had taken the trouble to look closer they would have seen the marks of a wooden spoon on the backs of my hand, or that one of my ears was redder than the other one.

I cannot say wooden spoon or think of one without my pulse quickening. I sometimes see them in shops hanging next to egg whisks and tin openers. The egg whisks look functional enough but the wooden spoon always seems out of place. Being wooden they belong to another age when wood was the one trusted material. Anyway it is not a utensil to me, it is an implement of punishment, even torture. When I see them on display I want to snap them all in two, to save all the other kids huddled in corners wondering when the pain will stop.

I think my mum felt powerless most of the time. I reckon that Ansons put unbearable strains on her. The rent man wanted to screw her and used to play with the hem of her skirt every time he called round for his firm's money. I wonder if she ever went down that road now and again to help the finances. Then with Ellie gone there was no one else for her to lord it over. As long as I lived she knew that she was not at the utmost bottom of the heap. She told me often enough that I was to blame for her predicament as she called it. Hurting me made her feel better for a while. I doubt she even thought about me as a person. I was just a problem who was getting bigger and needed feeding more - but that was the paradox, I was eating less and less.

After school I would wait for mum to come home. I would help to get parts of the tea ready. Then, when she crashed in exhausted, everything was set for trouble. I felt like I was a lamb in an abattoir. I used to think of what to say after trying to lend my cheery hello. Whatever I said it was wrong and the shouting would start. Sometimes she would put her mouth right up against my nose and yell at me through clenched teeth. My face took all the moisture flung at it and my ears took in the noise - but it was always my heart that broke from the words.

Then all would be quiet - quiet, except for the slamming of plates and cooking pots. I would try to help but I would get in the way and that only served to make her madder still. When finally the meal was ready to eat my stomach was knotted so tightly that I could hardly force the food down. I would balk every so often. Mum took this as adolescent defiance. I was reminded of all the hard work that had gone into making the meal and, just to make sure that I eat it all, out came the WS strategically placed next to the salt and pepper.

Once I was sick all over the table. It splashed everywhere. After a ten minute thrashing, I was made to clear it all up. Even now I can recall the vile job, made even worse by my hands that refused to stop shaking and a shoulder that felt like it was broken. Yet I loved her. I tried to imagine what it must have felt like to have nails hammered through my hands and feet. At church there was a huge wooden sculpture of Christ on the cross. The only things that were not made of wood were the nails themselves. If you stood in exactly the right spot you could make the figure of Christ look down into your own eyes. I used to think that if he could still love people after all that, then surely I could still love my mum after a whipping from the thing in the drawer. I was wrong. Me loving her was the easy bit. I wanted her to love me back. It was the one thing that I prayed for the hardest. I longed for peace to descend upon the house. Peace. Just to eat a meal in peace. That would do for starters.

Then one day during a games lesson I collapsed. I was told later that I was carried on a stretcher to the Headmaster's office. Funnily enough it was the first time I ever had Ovaltine. I lay there for fifteen minutes next to a warm radiator and, after being examined by the school nurse, I was taken to the hospital for a check up in Mr West's huge black Rover. The school telephoned mum at the factory. She was at my bedside within the hour, still dressed in her overalls. I looked at her with a shock that she picked up on. I had expected to see her in her smart suit, yet here she was dressed like the filthy women I hated.

"When can I take him home?" mum asked the doctor.

"We're keeping him in overnight, just for observation," said the doctor with a voice that sounded like a robot.

"What's wrong with him?" she wanted to know.

"Well, Mrs Harper, his blood sugar levels are low and he's extremely underweight, almost malnourished. Has he had a fall lately, we suspect a fractured shoulder?"

Mum's face seemed to drain of colour as her eyes darted to mine. At the hospital, she was powerless to use her evil eyes on me to make me be quiet. At any moment I could have blurted out the truth. For the first time I had one over on her. Of course I did not capitalise on it. I loved her still. All at once, as she stood there in her grubby overalls, I caught a glimpse of her secret life at Ansons. The oil stains and frayed cuffs of this working garment told a story of the effort she had to put in to keeping me alive, but I was glad to be spending a night in the ward, believe me.

Like the weddings the hospital was an eye into a different world. Unlike home it was well ordered. All around there existed what I can only describe as regimental kindness. There was a nurse there, nurse Dring I think her name was, who broke with the emotional detachment and became my friend for the twelve hours I was to spend on the ward. In that small amount of time she showed me more kindness than I had ever known in the whole of my brief life. I loved her and at the same time wished I did not. Life at home was bearable, only if I did not know any better - but there she was pouring out cheerfulness and warmth and there I was wishing that my mum could be like that. She sat and talked to me about my mum and what it was like at home. She had a clever way of making me talk about things. Without giving anything away she made me give things away, things about what my mum was like as a person.

"I suppose your mum gets tired working all day in that factory David?"

"Yes, she does."

"But you help her out at home don't you?"

"I try."

"Well you're only learning. You can't be expected to do things right at first, can you?"

"I try my best. I really do."

"I know you do. She must love you a great deal David."

"Well, I love her."

Whether she was taking mental notes or not I have no idea, but when mum came to pick me up, this nurse and one of the white-coated doctors took her into a separate room for a chat. By the time I left I had learned the awful truth about goodness and compassion, and that I was a thirteen-year-old boy who weighed just four stone.

We took the bus home. Mum held my hand very tightly all the way. Now and then she repeated this expression at me. She would look down on me with this exhausted face then flick the corners of her mouth up to make a smile, then let it go and look away with her tired face restored. I did not know what to make of it. Mum smiling, it did not seem real. It was Saturday afternoon as we arrived back at our soot-stained dwelling. It was like taking a fresh look at the place. After the super clean hospital I realised that I lived like a pig in shit. We entered and closed the door behind us. There we were, me, mum and old WS all alone and together again, but things had changed.

Looking back, I think that she must have been given a warning at the hospital, a warning that I needed feeding up or she would be given special help by the authorities. The time of peace that followed was welcome, although eventually I would come to learn that it was nothing but an interregnum - a period during which she would modify her tactics. For the time being though, I was lulled into being happy.

My grotty little bedroom was cleaned up to the state of a well-ordered garden shed. I was propped up in bed and brought Heinz tomato soup on a tray. I was kissed on the head and stroked on the face. Out came the photograph album and we talked about her wedding day and about a far away farm. It had a curious name she said, promising to tell me what it was called when I was grown up. She described it in great detail, how it was nestled near a wood and about its great barns and fields of golden wheat. She would gaze at the ones taken in a garden. Like me, the one with Ellie in the picture was also her favourite I learned. She said that it was taken in the village. We both wondered what had become of Ellie and mum cried and laid her head on my shoulder and I brushed her hair with my hand as she sobbed. She let me love her. It was bliss. I wanted more than anything to ask her why she left the farm and the village, but I felt that the precious beauty of the moment would have been broken if I had. So I held my tongue as I stroked her hair and rejoiced that she was letting me love her.

My mother had the most beautiful eyes in the world. It was a rare thing to look into them. Most of the time she was working herself to death. Or else she was at home feeding us both, or trying to keep the flat in order. With me having just gone through a naughty patch and getting into so much trouble with her, they had been locked behind frowns of rage, but now, as she wiped the tears away from them with the hem of her dress, I could see how perfectly exquisite they were. If her face had been a well-worn picture frame, then her eyes were the masterpieces painted on the canvas within. As her eyelashes blinked I was drawn ever deeper into them, and the kiss she gave on my lips to say goodnight, filled my heart with more contentment than it could ever have held. In that moment I knew that loving her had been right. I knew it had.

Having survived on such mere scraps of love from her, I felt as if I had been given a banquet. It had been a just reward for all my years of keeping faith with her. The event was almost as historic to me as the landing on the moon that same year. All my barriers of self-protection came tumbling down. Even walking the cinder track lost its power to intimidate. She drew me close with her touch and I allowed her to overpower my mind by hers. I knew that I was giving in to her. I was like someone in a flickering wartime newsreel, cheering the invading troops as they marched past, but surely it was all in aid of a better life?

A few nights later, I was in the grip of another bad dream. It had got to the point where I dreaded going to bed, knowing what things would visit my head as I slept. At church I heard stories read out in the lesson of prophets who had been warned about things in dreams. Even Joseph had been given the wink by God to move his family to Egypt so that he could escape the pogrom of children planned by King Herod. So what did my dreams mean? Why did they herald the same message if indeed a message it was? In the dream I was wandering around on a hill beyond a farmhouse. I had left the town below far behind and had reached a hamlet far higher up. There was always a strange church set apart on a rise and a lonely house that had once known love and happiness. The church spoke to me that this was a warning from God and the house, I believed, represented my mother who must have known happiness as a child.

Usually, the house drew me in and once inside it would transform into an abode where evil dwelt, whereupon I would wake up and beg the morning to arrive. Only on this particular night the dream had mutated. Somehow or other I had reached the small village and had been to the church where a witch had chased me away. As I ran, I looked behind me to see a monster thundering after me. The monster was in the form of a huge caveman, growling and intent on killing me. With no clear plan, I hid in the evil house. I huddled in the dirt, for the house had been abandoned for so long, and as I did so I could hear the caveman sniffing the air outside. With the instinct one is granted in a dream, I knew that he could smell me and he burst into the house and chased me up the stairs.

I woke up screaming. Mum burst into the room and switched on the light. Nothing had changed. With the light hurting my eyes I could see that all was well and that my room was just the same - but I had awakened my mother. Was she going to become the monster in my dream? Was this the house that had once known happiness? Was

226

she going to kill me for waking her? She was bleary-eyed as she sat on the edge of my bed and placed a cold hand on my forehead.

"You've had a bad dream, that's all. It's over now," she said, stifling a yawn.

As if to exorcise the spirit of the nightmare, I hurriedly emptied its details to mum. A strange expression of knowing came over her face as I described the village and the church and when I had finished she was lost in thought. She looked at my face as if she was looking at someone else as she ran her fingers through my hair. She rested the palm of her hand on the side of my face and caressed my cheekbone with her thumb.

The dream had shaken me, or was it the cold night air? I was trembling at any rate, and she picked up on it.

"You're cold," she said. "Here, I'll get in bed with you, turn over you fat lump."

So the light clicked off and the room was lost in the darkness once more. I heard a garment fall to the carpet. As I rolled over onto my left side to face the curtains I felt her warm body press up to mine. Even through my pyjamas I could sense the curves of her body, her breasts I could feel nestled between my shoulder blades. She was melting the bad dream away with every stroke of my hair and I was drifting back to sleep.

The movement of that hand however halted my descent into somnolence. It had left my hair alone and was now undoing the buttons on my pyjama jacket. I was aware of the change as she lovingly traced her fingers over my chest, rubbing my nipples from time to time with her forefinger. I had awoken slightly, wondering what she was doing. Then the chord on my pyjama bottoms was untied, and her hand slipped down below. I was fully awake now, staring wide-eyed into the blackness of my room.

"Mum?"

It was a scared whisper.

"Be quiet," she said, quietly.

"Don't do that."

It was a feeble plea, as she coiled her hand around it and slid it up and down, making me grow there.

"If you know what's good for you, you'll shut up."

227

I knew what that meant. It was either this or the WS I thought. So I lay there unable to do anything about it.

"This will stop the bad dreams," she added, the menace in her voice hidden once more.

I could hear her breathing quicken. The movements of her hand were becoming more rapid and she was getting tired. She was hurting me, my soft skin felt torn and painful, and suddenly from that place I wet the bed with a strange, gushing liquid that felt as if it had burst from the pit of my stomach. It covered my mother's hand and made it easier for her to slither it up and down me. It was not long after that she stopped and kissed my face lying on the pillow.

"There, you can sleep now," she said as she wiped her fingers on my bedclothes. "All the bad dreams are gone for tonight," and she slipped out of bed, picked up her clothes on the floor and returned to her own room.

She was right. There were no more bad dreams that night. Sleep was impossible. I touched myself to make certain that I had not imagined it all. I was stinging and wet, and wondering if all mothers did this to their children after a bad dream.

All that was said the next day was that I was not to tell anyone about my nightmare. There was an awkward atmosphere pervading the entire house, as if it knew I was to keep mother's special love a secret too. She cocked an eye towards the drawer to make certain that I knew she meant me to do what she said. I will never forget the confidence she displayed in the knowledge that I would do exactly as I had been told.

I walked the cinder track in an altered state, mesmerised by the memory of the night passed. I felt dirty. Dirty because I had let her do it, but what could I have done? Was I a coward for succumbing to her to avoid a beating? The event prayed on my mind all day, as surely as if I had committed a murder. By giving in to her I had sold some of myself away. My sense of worthlessness grew like a disease. To add insult to injury I was singled-out in class for daydreaming and given the slipper across the palm of the hand. So one way or another I got my beating in the end. I looked at my red hands during break time and felt wretched.

My schoolwork was falling behind during these days. Home was not a place for homework and that was falling behind the most. As time went on, I got into more and more trouble with my teachers. Just before my fourteenth birthday the school wrote to my mum and asked to see her. I had to wait outside the headmaster's office as I heard the muffled exchange of words coming from Mr West and mother. Then I was called in and invited to sit next to my mum. It was like being in the hospital once more. I wondered what would happen if I told the Headmaster the reason why I was so constantly tired. How could I explain the terrible dreams, let alone mother's love, which by now had taken on a more physical meaning? The chance passed by. I sat in silence, crushed by the weight of my mother as surely as if she was lying on top of me.

God knows I had laid in silence often enough with her weight bearing down on me in the dead of night. It was not just my bones that she had crushed. It was my heart and soul. So I sat and shrugged my shoulders when Mr West asked me a question. Even mother tried to encourage me to speak, safe in the knowledge that I would keep mum for her. For my reward, I was given some special mother's love that night. Love? I had nothing but hatred for myself as well as for her as she lowered her body on top of me and made the headboard bang against the wall.

My world began to dissolve around me during this time. Ian, my only friend, had to move away with his parents. Without him the choir seemed empty. Not that Ian was the best singer in the world but his company and the sharing of the choral music that we loved was wrenched away from me. When during a practice of a Hubert Parry anthem my voice flew to touch a high note and cracked, I knew that my days as a boy treble were over too. I was devastated and left the church in tears, running all the way to the top of the hill above the town near to the farmhouse.

There I looked down, cursing that smear of humanity down below. I knew where my house was and I cursed that. I could see the school playing field and I cursed that too and the school buildings adjacent to it. Ansons got the most potent curse of all. The town was out to kill me, to drag me down as good as quicksand.

"Fuck the whole fucking lot of you!" I yelled at full bore, astonished at the release of my feelings.

"I fucking hate the whole fucking lot of you. You fucking bastards!"

The words were carried on the wind, as the town, like some deaf animal carried on regardless.

Chapter four: The Stone

There is a disadvantage to the porous quality of a child's mind. Mine was no less absorbent. It soaked up all the awful experiences it endured. It stored all the derogatory remarks thrown at it by teachers, bullies and mother and became saturated by them. It got to a point where I believed them completely - I was stupid, I was a weakling, I was ugly, I was hopeless.

I did not realise it then but my mother was all of these things too, but her power over me was total. She owned my mind. Once when she was mad at me, she was so tired that she told me to hit myself. I slapped my own face until she told me to stop. I was fourteen years old, taller than she was. Yet here was this physically and mentally sick woman making me hurt myself just by telling me to do it. People talk about the wonders of the human spirit. Take a look at the soul of a person when it has been dragged through shit so often that it loses its sovereign will. It becomes an automaton. It changes. It goes through a grizzly metamorphosis. Like the inmates of the Nazi concentration camps it becomes a Muselmann gradually casting off its humanity. I had not gone that far, yet, but I was aware that I had begun to tread the path to that destiny and, with every week that passed, there was an ever-depleting supply of my own inner strength to turn the tide. I think my outburst up on the hill was the beginning of a yearned for revolution. It was a bridgehead on the enemy shore as I began my own war, a war of independence.

Things took a turn for the worse one Wednesday afternoon. Mr Charterhouse, our geography teacher, announced that we were going on a trip. I conjured up a bus with a journey to some far-off town, the whole day spent away from school. Then I imagined how I was going to ask mother for the money for such a trip. Mr Charterhouse continued:

"We're amalgamating this field trip with a careers development opportunity," he waffled.

My mind immediately ran thoughts of an RAF station and a chance to see fighter jets take off and a tour round a radar installation.

"We've nearly finished our joint project of the effects of industry on the environment and the economy so, to help with the conclusion of this, I have been lucky enough to arrange a guided tour round PW Anson and Sons Limited. I am sure that you will all get a valuable insight into the work of this, the main manufacturing company in the town, nay the area. You can bring notebooks and of course I shall be bringing my Pentax camera so that we can take photographs of interesting aspects of the firm's work. I will make copies of them in my darkroom for you to stick into your project books. The tour will be a week today, and will take up the whole of the afternoon."

Career opportunities, I thought, what bollocks. Then the thought struck me that I may catch a sight of my mum at work. Or rather that she would catch sight of me catching sight of her and I knew just how badly that would go down. I began to dread the trip. Of course I did not say a word about it to my mother. There was this other more sinister thought. This would be the first step. It would be the first part of a terrible journey. The five black fingers of the Ansons' chimneys had been patient. I was now on the road to the place where lives were devoured. It was a place where youth was steadily ground down and turned into tired worn out heaps. It was a place where time crawled at a snail's pace towards that promise of retirement a few years before death came to make a mockery of the whole damn thing.

The factory was like a great city within the town where frighteningly loud men commanded deafening machinery to do their bidding. It was blackened with decades of soot. Soot that poured out from the tall brick fingers in a constant breath of grey smoke. What monstrous machinery they were connected to I could only guess. Well soon it was Wednesday and I was about to find out.

There was something eerie about the march out of school after we had our dinner. We processed in double file with Farterhouse

(Charterhouse's first nickname) leading us from behind. He did this so that no one could mess about as we wove through the streets. I felt as if I was being pushed rather than led. Led into the gates of Ansons - the gates of hell it seemed to me.

We slid past a car park and a massive covered area completely crammed with thousands and thousands of bicycles. There was not a new one in sight. They all leaned against one another, each and every one blackened with a sweaty film of grease or oil overlaid with black dust. How anyone knew which bike belonged to whom I could not imagine. This single thought alone only served to compound the fact that I knew little if nothing about the adult world. To be honest I was inwardly terrified.

More terrifying still was the size of the buildings. I joined with each member of my class raising my face upward to see where the sheer brick cliffs rose to dwarf us. Then higher still, far higher, were the five fingers. Being slightly tapered they appeared taller when viewed from beneath where we were. They were alive. The billowing clouds that poured out from them possessed life. Life that was being sucked from the army of workers trapped inside the factory's belly. It was as good as a mass crematorium.

A surly fat man at a security kiosk met Shithouse (that was his other nickname) and telephoned for someone to come. After five minutes a lady dressed in a smart suit walked up rapidly to lead us to the main foyer of the admin block. For one dreadful second I thought it was my mum. It was not. After being told to be quiet we went through two spring-loaded doors into a large room packed with row upon row of desks, each one clattering to the tiny hammers of typewriters. This sound was punctuated with the occasional ting of a bell, or the zipping sound of paper being pulled out of the machine's rollers. No one spoke. You could tell it was more than their job was worth to do so. There they sat, all day, for endless hours, wearing out their spider-like fingers so that Ansons could communicate with the world beyond. No one looked at us as we filed down the central aisle. I felt embarrassed to look at them in turn. It was like being forced to watch slaves. It seemed inhuman. Charterhouse gathered us round and addressed us aiming his words mainly at the girls.

"Some of you, especially the young ladies among you, may like to consider a career as a typist, or better still, a secretary. As you can see, it's exciting work and not badly paid either. Right double-file once more and follow Mrs Draper again."

That was it. That was all the career advice I ever heard the girls receive, the poor bitches. Then again what else was there in this bloody town? Mrs Draper shook Mr Charterhouse's hand.

"Oooh, sir!" said one boy, and received a stare of white-hot disdain in return. He turned back to face Mrs Draper and thanked her for her cooperation. She then handed over to a tired-looking fellow dressed in a shiny black suit who had a pencil tucked behind his ear. He took us all in with one glance.

"Right you lot," boomed a voice marinated in the military, "keep close to me and don't mess about. Follow the yellow line once you're inside. You may want to put your hands over your ears at first. Don't touch anything."

He had more command in his being than old Shithouse would ever have and we followed him obediently through a great metal sliding door, wide-eyed, into the cavernous bowels of the monster.

The place was dark, like a filthy cathedral built to the gods of industry. Instead of an organ there was the endless anthem of production, great clangs of hammers against steel echoing from one end of the building to the other. The smell of oil and ferrous metals was as apt here as incense would have been in a church and, here and there in the dim light, showers of golden yellow sparks would burst in arcs that disappeared as they hit the soiled floor. High above we could see grubby windows made of wire mesh glass fitted into the saw-tooth roof. The jib of a great crane slid along up there carrying a great grey slab of metal - steel perhaps. Colossal machines pounded other metal sheets into shape with an explosive energy that was felt almost more than it was heard. I had not entered into this place as much as I felt it had devoured me. Here was the army of workers that I had seen racing through the gates on their bicycles when the hooter sounded. This then was where they sold their lives.

We passed along the remains of the yellow line to the other end of the building and took our guide's lead through a hatch cut into a pair of huge steel doors. This next section was just as big, but not half as noisy. The machinery in this part was electrically operated, so the banging and clanging was subdued and replaced with high-pitched, reverberating whines. Rows and rows of men and women stood at lathes and drills, fine tuning castings, or cutting into sheets of iron. Everyone here wore overalls, albeit cleaner ones than those in the previous workshop, so the only way you could tell the males from the females was in their headgear. Men either wore caps, or else nothing, but every women bar none wore a headscarf tied in a knot at the front – and there, wearing one made of green cotton, drilling holes into the blades of a plough was my mum.

I could not help but stare at her. I stared at her as the notion of time evaporated. I hated to see it. With an industrial force I realised, more than ever, just how I had been given clothes to wear and food to eat. Day after day, year after year she had done this. She had done this to keep me alive. I wanted to cry for her. Yet I was glad that this dark place was able to overpower her. I wanted them to work her harder, to crack the whip and make her squirm for a change. So I was annoyed that, despite the things she had done to me, I wanted to go over and hug her. How strange. All the hate that had been developing inside me became tainted by an unwanted love. The only thing I can really remember is the confusion that came from seeing her. How right Mr Charterhouse had been about it being an educational visit. I learned that there was so much yet to learn.

Knowing that she would despise me for invading her other life I chose to hide from her. I made sure that she could not see me by moving to the other side of my class. She would have felt I was ridiculing her, I knew it, and no one ridiculed my mother, least of all me. She would not have lived down the humiliation at all, but it would be nothing compared to the humiliation she would have meted out to me later. So from behind the shoulders of the other kids I watched her pull her lever down and make the drill bite the metal. I knew nothing about engineering, but I could discern that my mum used a skill that I had never been aware of until that moment. How is it possible to fear and be proud of someone simultaneously? I understood that I did not understand my mother at all and I felt very tiny and stupid.

Back outside we crossed a large square of concrete, glad to smell the fresh air, tainted though it was with the heavy scent of coal smoke. On the other side of this quadrangle was a double-storey building, blackened with years of pollution but enlightened with metal-rimmed windows. We were herded in through the main doors and up via a cast iron staircase to some offices on the first floor. We were all told to be very quiet and not to touch anything by the army-type chap. The doors were opened for us and we went in.

We entered a wonderland. There were rows of giant drawing boards, tilted, almost vertically. Standing in front of them were men with sleeves rolled up drafting out designs for indistinguishable components. On one of them, as we filed past, I could see the design of a bridge drawn perfectly to scale so that it appeared like a model on paper. I wanted to talk to the man doing the drawing. He had a pipe in his mouth, unlit, and he was half-perched on a tall stool. How had he learned such a talent? Could I be taught? Before I had managed to brew up enough confidence to speak to him we were moved on. Even as we left to go back outside, I knew something had happened. Something had happened that I knew in my heart of hearts had significance. Not since joining the choir had I felt such a pull. I knew I had discovered something for me.

It is funny how the heart's desire can become the soul's curse. Walking home I realised that I was at the bottom of a deep pit, a pit of ignorance, staring up at the stars, reaching out with no hope of touching them. The dream became my torment. I longed to have a pipe and design bridges on the drawing boards at Ansons. I let my imagination project a film of me driving over a new bridge and saying to my imaginary passenger I designed this. The vision taunted me. It measured itself against my academic failure. The pit seemed to deepen and the stars fell further away from my grip.

Reaching home one evening I had to stop. I just stopped and looked at the place. The shit hole called home. It was a shit hole outside and full of shit inside. Shit happened there. It was all fucking shit. Shit, shit, shit, shit, shit, all bloody shit. Before I knew what I had done a stone had left the whip of my hand and was hurtling through space. The aim had been true. No longer under my control it made impact with the kitchen window. The dull, ice breaking thud was followed instantly by the tinkling, crashing sound of shards shattering on to the hard kitchen floor.

I picked up another stone as a flicker of remorse tempered the urge to do it again. It dropped from my fingers and fell at my feet. Looking around to see if I had been spotted, I sneaked back part of the way I had come. I was keen to delay my arrival home by five minutes to make certain of my innocence preserved, but soon I was back, thrusting my key into the door. It was not until I went inside that I found the true extent of the damage and felt sick.

Glass was strewn everywhere. Worse still the stone had continued on its trajectory past the window and hit the mirror on the far wall. The scene horrified me. Instead of pride in my rebellion I cowered in the corner of the room. Fear electrified the inside of my head short-circuiting straight thinking. How I wished I had not done it. What should I do, clean it up and try to explain the hole in the window, or leave it for her to see? In the end I decided to half clean it up and I concocted a fib that I had found it just like this when I had come in. At least that would be true. So I began clearing up a few of the larger pieces, placed them in an empty cereal box and waited. I did not have to wait for long.

I could hear the, "Oh my God," halfway up the street. Her pace quickened on the pavement and soon she was through the door.

"Who did this? Was it you?" she said, flinging off her coat.

"It was a boy. He was outside," I said truthfully. "He ran down towards the cinder track when he'd done it."

"What boy?" she said, thundering across the room to where I was resuming the clean up.

"Just a boy, like me. He threw a stone, it's just there look."

"Do you know who he is? I'll have it out with his Mum, just see if I don't, mark me."

"I couldn't see his face, but he was the same height as me," I said, taking pride in my skill at adapting the truth.

She came closer and told me to stand up. I did. She grabbed me by my arm and looked into my brain.

"You know who it was, don't you?"

"I couldn't see him," I repeated unnerved.

"A boy in your school?"

236

"Yes," I replied without thinking.

"Your class?"

"Yes, I mean no. I'm not sure,"

"So how come you know it's a boy in your school?"

"His uniform."

"You'd know every boy in your class from the back, wouldn't you?"

"Yes, I suppose."

"Then you'd know if he was in your class or not, wouldn't you?"

"Maybe."

"Did he run like someone in your class?"

"Yes."

"Like you?"

I did not answer.

"Like you?" her voice was louder.

She widened her gaze into my trembling eyes that poured out the answer back into hers.

"It was you, wasn't it?"

I lowered my face to the lino and turned my eyes away from her. It looked almost like a nod. She grabbed hold of my ear and yanked my face back round.

"I'm going to make you wish you hadn't been born."

She dragged me stumbling over the broken glass to the drawer near the sink. I knew what was coming. She reached inside the drawer, rummaging like a mad thing, searching with her free hand for the WS as I felt my ear seemingly being ripped off.

That is when I caught sight of the stone on the floor. Her thumbnail dug into my right lobe. As I looked down on this little, angry ball of a woman hurting me I felt a kinship with the stone and the act of rebellion we had shared. Before I knew what was happening my foot had rammed the front of the drawer shut, the drawer with her hand in it. The slam was violent, full force and brutish, as good as a mantrap, clamping her wrist as if caught in a vice. She screamed out in agony as I kicked at it again, almost guillotining her hand off and making her let go of my ear. I stepped back horrified at what I had done and watched as she freed her arm, flinging the drawer out of its cabinet and sending cutlery clattering to the floor. She had a fork embedded in the fleshy part of her hand.

Wincing with the pain of it, she wrenched it out and flung it down to where the rest of the knives and spoons were scattered. Her face, now contorted with pain made her look more terrifying than ever and in a flash she bent down to pick up the WS, gripping it in her blooded hand as if it was a dagger.

"You've never wanted me," I began to cry.

"Damn right. You were the biggest mistake I ever made."

"Don't say that."

"Fourteen years of utter waste. I hate you. Do you hear, hate you. I've never loved you."

She ran towards me with the WS held high, rivulets of red covered her forearm. I lifted my arms over my head to protect myself from the first blow. But I was fourteen now and bigger than she was and it was easy to grab the round wooden ladle just before it hit me. I wrenched it from her feeble grasp and smashed it down on the tabletop. Bits of wood splintered everywhere like shrapnel. The symbol of her reign was now five broken pieces of a tree and a jagged shaft that rested in my grip.

"You'll never do that to me again," I said through heavy gasps, "and that's not all. I ought to report you to the authorities. You're sick in the head you are, what with your mummy's special kiss, and mum's secret cuddle. No one will do that to me again. No one, do you hear? You're just filth that's what you are. It's you who should never have been born. You'd have done everyone a favour."

I wagged the wooden spike I held in my fist as if I was going to poke her eyes out. In the space of less than a minute her stature had withered. All her power seemed to have gone. Though she cried and held on to her injured arm and, though she looked frightened of me and did not know how to react, I knew that something was going on in her head. Mine was doing the same. I was wondering where I went from here.

She sat down at the table and began to weep. Hers were deep, uncontrollable sobs. Her tears were dragged up from a well of enormous depth. Or was it just exhaustion and defeat? Either way she looked broken like a ship that had come to grief on the rocks. I never meant this to happen, not like this. To be honest I felt unequal to the situation I had created and had no clear plan of what to do next. I felt the foundations of my life give way to complete uncertainty. There was to be no turning back from this and that thought alone caused waves of despair to drown me. The kitchen too was littered with despair. Glass and cutlery covered the floor. The drawer was broken where it had crashed, as was the mirror-frame. In the middle of the debris was the dark brown stone.

It was just a stone, a pebble. Millions of years ago it had been a round cobble as big as a potato. In a distant past it had been broken in half and aeons of erosion had worn it down to a smooth finish, a round body with a flat side. To me it was a full stop at the end of a very long paragraph. What the capital letter for the next chapter would be I could only guess but I knew that it would be my job to write it. The stone had changed everything. I went over to pick it up and let it nestle in between my thumb and forefinger as I had done when I had thrown it. This ordinary stone had been ordained to alter the course of my life.

Chapter five: The Invitation

"An apprenticeship?" I said, laughingly. "Who told you about apprenticeships?"

"You remember Donald Campion?" said All Legs. "The one who got done for setting fire to the bogs. He did."

I remembered Donald Campion and the toilet fire fiasco.

"So how come you were talking to him?"

"Oh, it was yesterday. He saw me getting thrown out of Masons, trying to buy fags. He went in and bought me a packet. We just got talking about leaving school while he was waiting for his bird."

"So what did you think?" I asked.

"Lovely," he said, "Nice knockers, nice face and a nice arse."

"No, I meant the apprenticeship. What do you think about doing that?"

"What the fuck else is there?" All Legs said, "You learn a trade, get paid so you can get laid."

"You're a poet now, bloody hell."

"It was just something Campion said," he eyed me with a friendly frown. "You know, you ought to think about it. You never know, you might end up behind one of those drawing boards like you're always banging on about."

I did not answer. Annoyingly he had made me think. All Legs it seemed had got a plan. More than I bloody well had.

"Fancy a fag Harpo?"

"Yeah, but not here. Let's go under the bridge," I suggested.

Under the bridge was a place where you were told not to go. It had the interior design of a doss hole and a perfume to match. Special features were broken bottles, urine-soaked mattresses, and a wide variety of used condoms. What better place to enter into manhood than by smoking a fag. To real men, though, the bridge was the main trunk road over the river. We could hear the sound of the lorries they drove thunder overhead, as they earned their livings like real men did. Deep down we knew that we were still boys.

Why we tapped our ciggies on the back of the packet I never really understood. It looked grown up and, when the match blazed into life and ignited the paper tube, I knew that I was finally mature. My cheeks indented as I drew in the smoke from the burning leaves, then I held the fag awkwardly by my side so that I could blow the stream of grey vapour away like a film star.

All Legs did the whole business with much less self-consciousness. Breathing in the smoke and pumping it out again through his nostrils or out of his mouth whilst he was talking were skills he had perfected. He was an odd character though. Nature had seen fit to create him with a fantastic lack of proportion. His head, arms and feet were as unremarkable as anyone else's, but his body was short and squat by several ribs it seemed, whilst his legs were stretched to fill the gap, gifting him with an astonishing height. You could always spot him a mile off. In Victorian times he would have been a freak: SEE THE AMAZING STILT MAN, ALL LEGS AND NO BODY

That is how he would have been billed in one of those dingy sideshows. Like me, he was a loner and, up until the trip around Ansons, I had never really had much to do with him. At school I had survived by having little to do with anybody, truth be told. All except Ian Crabtree, who had promised to write and never had.

"What's your mam like?" All Legs asked.

"My mother? What do you want to know about her for?"

"I want to know what it's like to have one parent, that's what I mean?"

"Now, why the bloody hell do you want to know that for?"

All Legs chucked his half-smoked fag in the river, lobbing a stone in after it. The light was fading. He was agitated. I could tell he was trying to form a question.

"What's it like without your dad?"

"How the hell should I know? I've only seen him in pictures."

"So what's it like to be with just your mam?"

I grew suspicious. What if tales were going around?

"Why all the questions?"

I wanted mummy's secret cuddle to remain just that, a secret. Just as she had done it to me in the dark, so it should remain, forever hidden in the blackness of my bedroom. All Legs fidgeted with his box of matches as he gobbed into the murky water flowing past.

"Mine are getting a divorce," he said, finding it hard to admit it to anyone.

"It's rows morning noon and night. I can't stand it. I expect I'll be left with me bloody mam. I'm fed up with 'em both. They're like a couple of kids picking fault and scrapping all the time. So I wanted to know what it's like, you know, to be just with your mam. I think it'll be bloody 'orrible. I'm planning on moving out to a place of me own once I get me apprenticeship. We could share. What do you think, eh, Harpo?"

"What's your mum like?" I said, side stepping the invite.

"Huh, she's been in a bad mood so long, I've forgotten now. What's yours like?"

"Mine?" I said.

I wondered what to answer. Broken, I wanted to say. My mother seemed to have been broken ever since I could remember. Somehow she did not work properly. Underneath her fatigued exterior there was still the remains of a beauty, deep in her eyes especially, but inside her head, I think that she was shot to pieces. She had to be, to treat me the way she did.

"She's tired all the time," I confessed. "Bad tempered, you know."

"Yeah, I bloody well do."

We walked home. All Legs talked. I listened. He was going to join the system and create a life for himself. Only it seemed so clear to me that his life would turn out like everyone else's. His ideas were not so much a plan as it was a game of follow-my-leader. As much as the money and the flat that he was planning to rent held credibility and a common sense down-to-earth practicality, it lacked - I still cannot think of the word to describe how I felt - it just lacked. But I could see him in fifty years' time, in my imagination. All his youth poured away in making parts for agricultural machinery and pieces of bridges and no one would know that he had been a part of it, save himself and a few work mates. His whole scheme sounded so laudable and ghastly. I wanted no part of it. The more he enthused about his own pad, and the girls he would take back there, and the screwing he would do to them, and the trade he would learn, the more abhorrent it became.

In the distance I could see the spire of St Peter's church. Slowly, our steps took us closer. By the time I could make out the shape of the arched windows I had stopped paying attention to my friend's noise. Far down in a hidden recess of my heart, somewhere between my mind and my soul, I heard a cry. No, it was not a cry, it was a bloody scream, like hearing a scream from the far side of a lake, loud but dissipated. When I said goodnight to All Legs I stopped outside the main door of the church. I knew it was no accident that I was there. The place held me like a magnet, resting me. Lovingly, the exterior of the holy place had a sense of sanctuary. The sandstone walls seemed to quieten the rush of the traffic and the hum of the town. My head could hear the scream more clearly, and as I sat down with my back against the wooden door, I knew that it was a little piece of me that was crying out. No one had told me that praying could be like this, but I knew that is what it was. I was praying. I was praying with an inner yell get me out of this. Even as I began to sob onto my upturned knees I knew that my body had linked with the old building and like a lightning conductor in reverse, my plea was

242

shooting up the flying buttresses, past the tower and spire and onwards, onwards to God, and I knew that God was there.

So, what was it like? Well, there was no vision of glory. There was no great man with a beard, dressed in white robes looking down upon me from above. The eyes in my head simply saw the cake shop across the road. The scene was earthly and mundane. The shop belonged to the confusion of the here and now. I did not even know who ran it. To the owner it was his or her livelihood, merely a means to an end. Clearly the picture of the shop was just that a picture, a report to my brain from two organic cameras stuck into my skull. No I was seeing other things with an eye never used until now, not a mind's eye, but an eye nevertheless. How can I explain? All I can say is that if I had seen two people walking past, lovers for instance, I would have seen the love. Even if I had never seen them share a kiss, or touch, or the manifold things that lovers do, I would have beheld their love as good as if my real eyes had seen it. That does not do the feeling justice. Even the word feeling fails. I was seeing beyond anything visible so to speak. Not infrared or ultraviolet but images made from something other than light. How they came to be I suppose I will never know but believe me they were real and for a long time afterwards I longed for them to come back.

"Been out with our silly friends have we?" said my little mother as I got home. Her arm was now out of its sling and she was readying herself for Ansons once more.

"I've been for a walk," I said, forcing an explanation I felt was unnecessary.

"Well, I suppose a clever lad like you doesn't need to revise for exams, does he?"

"I've been swotting, see," I lied.

"Have you indeed. So when's your first exam? Next week, isn't it?"

Next week, I thought. My whole future was to be mapped out from the passage through the ordeal of the O Levels. Swotting? I was as unprepared as it was possible to be. How could I study at home with a mother who had ranted and raved half the time I was a schoolboy and raped and abused me on and off for the other half?

"Next Monday," I said.

"You'll get a rude awakening if you go into the big, wide world without good qualifications, mark me."

I left her pontificating on my future and went to my room. As usual it was a mess. Scrappily written exercise books with adverse red notes from teachers on most pages were littered across the floor. Dog-eared textbooks were piled up, unread in the corner.

"Peel some taters, Davy," I heard her shout from the kitchen, "my arm's still a bit bad."

Oh yes, the arm. The fault was all mine, her arm. Well it was, was it not? We never talked about what I did that evening, the evening of the stone. She had changed since that incident, becoming a performer of invalid caricatures. She had downsized her spirit and buried her power-base under the rubble of her former self. She gave the impression that I intimidated her. I knew it was an act but there was no way to fight against it. It was her version of mustard gas, light as air but full of harm. I had begun to realise that the days of physical punishment were most probably behind me now. Ever since I almost broke her wrist in the drawer, she stopped coming into my bed at night. Instead she projected an image of a failed future in my mind, my failed future void of achievements, barren and worthless. It even made sense the way that she put it to me. Everything she said carried with it a high degree of logic, reinforced concrete logic and, even though it was wrapped up in fake concern, her words burrowed deep into my head, making them take on their own fulfilment, their own prophecy.

I peeled the vegetables and went back to my room. There, sitting on the edge of my bed, I heard pots clatter downstairs as the making of the tea was finished off with one-armed martyrdom. I picked up the maths book and tried to unravel the mysteries of algebra. Like the bullies they were, the Xs and Ys taunted me. They were on my mother's side.

"You're hopeless," they said. "You'll never understand us, stupid," giggled the equilateral equations.

It was no good. There was no way I could get my head round any of it. The exams would be a disaster and, just as my mother kept repeating, so too would the rest of my life.

Two days later at school I was called to the Headmaster's office.

"So, who do you know in Nottinghamshire, Harper? And why are they writing to you here, at school?"

I could see the white envelope on the desk as Westy motioned for me to be seated.

"Auntie Ellie," I said guessing and trying to hide the thrill I felt.

"Be that as it may. I find it irregular that your correspondence should be forwarded here, to my office," he slid his spectacles to the tip of his nose and beheld me over the top of them. "I'm not your private postman, Harper."

"No Sir. Sorry Sir."

"Harper. Is there any trouble at home?"

"Trouble Sir, no, no trouble. It's just that my mum and Auntie Ellie don't get along anymore. Mum threw her last letter to me in the boiler. That was years ago. I expect she wondered why I didn't write back, Sir. She knows she can't write to me at home, so she must reckon that this is the only way to get hold of me."

"Mmm, indeed," said Westy.

Then, quite out of the blue his voice lost its headmaster's tone. He leaned towards me and spoke to me as if I had been his friend all through my miserable days at his school.

"David, if you ever need to talk to someone, you know, in private, you're always welcome here in my office to talk to me. You'll soon be leaving us for Ansons I expect, so if you have any worries, you know where to come."

With a flick of his wrist he handed me the letter, reburied his head in papers and without a second look told me that was all.

"Good luck," he said as I closed his door and that was the last time I ever saw the creep.

As for the letter, oh my word, what a letter. Ellie had married a vicar. A vicar! He was in charge of three parish churches close to each other in an area near a place called Southwell in Nottinghamshire. He was a lovely man, she said, and they wanted me to go and live with them in their vicarage, not a holiday mark you, she said I was to live there, properly.

I read and re-read the invitation. An image of the sun breaking from behind a cloud to warm my skin formed like a picture in my head. That was how my heart felt, warm - how odd that after a lifetime of existing in the cold I found the opposite sensation hard to trust. Good things were never meant for Davy Harper, surely?

The letter continued with a set of instructions. I was to copy down the address and phone number and keep it safe. Then I was to show the letter to mum, so that she could agree to me going. Fat chance of that, I thought. Let me go away and be happy, and me about to become an earner - yeah, dream on. There was no way I was going to show this to mum. It was going to be hidden before she could get her nasty little hands on it. I took no time deciding that I would find my own way there and turn up on the doorstep. How pleased to see me she would be.

I wrote the address and phone number in biro on the lining of my blazer inside pocket. I kept the letter itself in my locker at school. This time, there was to be no hysterics at finding an envelope. My dumb mother would be oblivious to my going until it was too late. It would serve her right. *Vengeance is mine, sayeth the Lord.* I had heard that read out often enough at church. Well I was going to borrow a bit of vengeance from Him. I deserved it.

Leaving was going to be easy. I pinpointed Ellie's village in an old *AA Manual* I once found and worked out a route. All I had to do was wait until mum got paid, nick a few quid out of her purse while she was otherwise occupied, grab some food and skedaddle on foot. Saturday morning was the best time. She had stopped getting pissed on a Friday night and used her Saturdays to go shopping instead, usually ending up with her cronies in the pub after. I would be out of the way as normal and she would be in town. It would be the middle of the day or later before she even had inkling that I was gone at all. Perfect!

The day arrived, grey and damp after a night's rain. Hardly being able to sleep, I rose early and waited in my room for sounds of life to materialise. All was quiet, save for the clink of milk bottles on the doorstep. In the hush of the morning I could hear St Peter's bell strike six o'clock. It would be another hour or so before mother rose from her pit so, to make use of the time, I emptied Friday's schoolbooks out of my duffel bag and rammed my coat deep into the bottom. Trying hard to be quiet, I tiptoed downstairs to search for the black handbag and, even though I knew it was theft, I delved into its forbidden interior to feel for the purse inside. There it was bulging with coins and paper. I was delicately closing my fingers around it to lift it out, when I heard a sound coming from upstairs. I stopped dead, impersonating a statue of *The Thief*. My ears pricked. The handbag was returned unmolested where it had rested all night and, like a spooked burglar, I left the scene of the crime and headed for the kitchen. By some instinct I grabbed a glass and filled it at the tap, creating my cover story for why I was down here. Then I heard the toilet flush and her bedroom door click shut. My shaky hand poured the water away down the sink, as I held my breath a few moments longer. Still no sound, she had gone back to bed, surely?

With more trepidation than before I thrust my fingers back inside the handbag. At least I knew where the purse was and I was soon trespassing into its contents. Mum was still paid with a wage packet on a Thursday. There was talk of her being paid straight into a bank, but she was going to have none of it. Much of the money in the brown purse had been kept for today's shopping. The rest she had hidden somewhere safe for bills and such. It was her tried and trusted approach to finance and it was fool proof. I never found out where Fort Knox was in that house. I whipped out a fiver, leaving her with twenty odd pounds in assorted notes. She would probably curse that it was gone and blame me without question but, even if she planned to give me grief about it, I would be gone as usual. She would have to wait until teatime before she could let rip with her accusations and by then I would be miles away. With that thought in mind I availed myself of a further tenner, replaced the purse in the handbag, and crept without noise back to my room.

A watched pot never boils they say. Neither does a watched house. I slipped back into bed, fully clothed, just in case she came in to see me. I would, of course, pretend to be asleep. Outside the rattle of the day was beginning. I could hear more cars on the road outside. A man shouted abuse at someone, his wife perhaps. Everything was normal. Then, as the Saturday shift was declared by the howl of Ansons' siren, she got up, coughing, and went down to put the kettle on. I knew every sound off by heart from the clatter of cups, the slam of the cupboard where the cereal was kept and the unlocking of the door as she retrieved the morning milk. It took her ten minutes to eat her breakfast and drink her tea. Cigarette smoke trailed up the stairwell and under my door. It was a long ten minutes.

If all went according to normality she would drag herself up the stairs and get dressed. I waited. It happened. As she passed my room, she banged on my door with her fist.

"Up!" she said loudly.

The radio went on in her room. Gilbert O'Sullivan sang an essay on matrimony. I lay on my side impatiently, ears pricked as boring song followed song. Time was being stretched like elastic. I went over the route I would have to walk repeatedly in my head to ease the waiting. Then the music stopped dead and I heard footsteps.

"I'm off, do you hear?"

There was no question of answering. I continued with the sleeping act, a performance that I usually managed with ease, but not today. I heard her mumble her disapproval at my laziness as she made for the door. It opened, it closed, a key turned in the lock and all became quiet.

I bolted for the landing window and peeped out of the corner. There she was, going - going out of my life, for good. Now anxiety had fermented into excitement. It was an intoxicating sensation and one that held a slight aftertaste of sadness but only the slightest hint. It was time to go. It was time to scribble out Ellie's address and phone number in the pocket of my blazer, after first copying it into the front cover of my *AA Manual*. In it went, along with the money and the stone, into my duffel bag. I also managed to get in two jumpers before I went down to the kitchen and loaded myself up with food, a noggin of cheese and a bottle of milk. In a most supreme state of alert, I forced down some cornflakes, and that was it. As I rose to my feet, I realised that I would never stand in this wretched kitchen again. I wanted to trash the place but the plan had to be carried out as conceived. So, with one last look, I turned my key in the door, stepped out into what was becoming a pleasant day and relocked it. I was free. I was free and I made for the main road.

It was hard to believe that the adventure was actually underway. Familiar scenes seemed just that, familiar, yet the world was a different place. All I had to do to keep it that way was maintain a sharp eye out for mother. To minimise that happening, I made for the main road by back alleys and side streets. It was also hard to remove the grin that had planted itself on my face. Anyone looking would have thought that Davy Harper had made it with a girl the night before. How little they knew about my Friday nights.

After a good march I saw the trunk road out of town. I was coming out of a side road, on the corner of which was an unattractive, terraced-house pub and it was there that I saw it, leaning by its pedal against the kerb. The pub was closed so I could not understand why it was there. Nor could I see who owned it. My eyes darted around looking at windows to see if anyone was looking. The whole area was deserted and still there was no sign of its owner until, that is, my hand grabbed it by its handlebars and I realised that I had taken ownership of it. I ran all the way to the junction. No one shouted for me to stop. I kept going, running with my duffel bag slamming against my back. No one followed. Soon I was out, trotting along the pavement that belonged to the main road. Five minutes later I was a mile away and the proud owner of a grubby bicycle, complete with saddlebag and Sturmey Archer gears. How Ian Crabtree would have laughed. To him this would have been a girls' bike, even if it did have a crossbar.

Chapter six: A Cyclist

There's no rule that says you have to feel bad about stealing, but I did, as far as the bike was concerned. It was not guilt or anything obvious like that, I just felt a bit of an idiot. Who in their right mind would steal a bicycle when they could not ride one? I had never been on a bike. I dreamed about it often enough, especially when I was a child, but I had never tried it for real. I never had the chance. What possessed me to nick the bloody thing in the first place is a mystery. I was drunk on freedom I expect. I was in a mood. I believed that I could do what I liked. I was invincible. Seeing thousands of Anson workers break free on their dilapidated boneshakers during their evening break-out would have made anyone deduce that riding one was a piece of cake. I was about to put my theory to the test.

As the road gradually began to incline I took advantage of a lane to my left. Where it led I had no idea, it was of no consequence, but it was flat and secluded by trees. Here I would be able to try out bike riding away from prying eyes. My duffel bag was leaned against the trunk of a tree and the bicycle walked into the middle of the lane. It felt odd to cock my leg over the saddle to the other side and even odder to allow my scrotum to come to rest on the seat. But here I was one foot on the pedal, the other one on the road propping me up, as my hands gripped the handlebars. All I had to do was push on the pedal and I would be off.

The presumption proved true. I pushed hard and in a second I was off in a heap in the centre of the road. For the minuscule amount of time I was on the damn thing I was aware of an alien sensation. My position on the saddle seemed so high. It seemed impossible to keep upright. As for steering, well I never got as far as steering. Suddenly the idea of dumping the bike in a hedge and resorting to walking had a degree of merit. Except for a little voice telling me that here was the means to save me a lot of toil I would have done so. With a mix of curiosity and fun I picked it up and had another go, and another, and another.

Somewhere in my head, quite unknowingly, I was building up an accumulation of experience with every failure. By commands that came to me as if by a spirit I turned my handlebars towards the direction I felt I was falling. This corrected my fall, only to be replaced by a sensation of falling the other way. Another adjustment kept me on the straight and narrow. It was maddening. Staying upright on two wheels seemed impossible. Did all the cyclists coming out of the factory really have to concentrate so hard? I could see them all now in my mind, thousands of them, bunched in threes and fours, chatting away to each other, without staring wide-eyed at the road for stability like I was. Thank goodness for the avenue of trees and bushes that hid these embarrassing attempts, but they were my first steps and, thinking that it was wise to learn to run before I could walk, I pedalled slowly along, handlebars flaying wildly to regain that elusive balance. Being unable to do this one little thing only emphasised my ingrained belief that I was stupid. Oh, how ready I was to dump the bloody thing in a ditch.

Then it came to me like a revelation. No, that is not strictly true. It came to me purely by anger if I am honest. In utter frustration I had driven down on the crank like a madman and built up speed. Speed had been the answer all along. The faster I pedalled the bike the easier it was to control. Getting going was the hard bit but once I had generated momentum I passed through to an almost supernatural world of motion, fast motion cutting through the morning air like an arrow. It was an emotional thing to make myself fly along with such swiftness. I even laughed out loud like a lunatic at the absurdity of it all. How incredible it was that my legs were making me travel faster than they were able to make me run. The air rushing past my ears sounded like rocket thrust, as I became a booster powering down the road. I must have spent half an hour on the lane doing this before I got on with my journey. Only now I had acquired a new skill. I was a cyclist.

Out on the main road the upward gradient made it impossible to ride quickly. I had no chance of speeding rocket-like up a hill like this. So holding on to my steed I tramped ever upwards on foot, leaving home behind. It was hard work. Higher up, just before the road flattened out, I took a glance over my shoulder. It was a last glance beholding the shit-hole of a town in one view. I seemed to know every rooftop, every landmark. I stuck two fingers up at the Anson five and felt sad at leaving St Peter's behind. St Peter's, the only place in that dreadful dump where I had known anything resembling happiness - but it was not enough. There could be no more. A snatch of contentment on Thursday night and twice on a Sunday singing in a cassock was never going to be enough. I took a good long look at the slender spire, burning it onto my retina and recording it into my memory. Then turning round once more to face forward the road ahead beckoned. Eventually, as it became flat and I had fully climbed out of the valley, I plonked myself on the saddle, got up speed and I was on my way, whistling.

I wish that I could tell you everything about that bicycle journey but, apart from the lesson on the lane, I can only recall big lorries passing by too closely and white clouds on a blue-sky background.

251

Oh yes, and country lanes bordered with high hedges and grass verges swollen with wild flowers that I began to pass through once I left the main road. I must have eaten the cheese and drank the milk, though I have no memory of it. There is a vague recollection of a town with a tall church and a ruined castle near a bridge over a river that I would one day come to know, and a rather elegant building bordering the same river further on near another bridge. One thing that does stick in my mind though was the constant stopping and checking of my progress in the *AA Manual*. I can relive that sense of adventure quite easily. Stopping at a signpost was a thrilling experience to me. Out in the middle of nowhere I would come across a concrete stake with two or sometimes three signs poking out of it. I knew in advance where I was to ride to next and I can remember the tickle of relief to see it written on the sign and how far away it was. I loved the villages. I felt at home as I passed through them. How different they were to towns, compact and close to nature, full of old habitations set in grassy lawns with huge trees for backdrops.

Along with the sense of exploration I also felt giddy in the knowledge that I was free. So I only have memories of feelings and sensations to call upon and tiredness, aching, wearisome tiredness because, by the time I rolled into Southwell, I had travelled over twenty-five miles.

Let me describe Southwell. My first impressions of that place have proved to be lasting ones. I had cycled through Upton, a small village that boasted not only a stately hall and a pub, but a shop with a thatched roof as well, the first one I had ever seen. A few miles further on, as I pedalled round a double bend in the road, I saw two tall pyramids far off in the distance. They were poking over the brow of a hill that was green with early wheat. How strange I thought, straining to make them out as I powered along. But there was no doubt about it they were pyramids, tall, extruded ones, impossible to miss. Then they disappeared from view as the rolling countryside closed in around me and I descended into a dip.

Pushing on into the town proper I passed over a railway crossing and turned right onto the main street. There they were again. It was impossible to miss the pair of pointed spires now. That is what they were, spires, each built upon two colossal stone towers belonging to a majestic church. The spires were grey, the grey of lead. The stonework was heavy, having a design unlike anything I had ever seen. Worn out as I was, and eager to get to Ellie, I had to stop and take a look. I propped my bike against the perimeter wall, and passed stiffly through one of its arched entrances. It was hard to put one foot in front of the other after the hours I had spent riding, and difficult to trade the circular motion of pedalling for the linear gait of walking. The main door was easy to find at the front of the church, positioned exactly between the two towers that held the pyramid spires. Looking up my eyes beheld a massive window of breathtaking elegance. Slender pillars interlacing high up above formed a criss-cross of smaller geometrically perfect arches filled with a life's work of stained glass. Without shame I had fallen in love with Southwell Minster.

A service was taking place inside. Immediately I recognised the tune of *Crimond* and taking a peek inside I knew straight away that a wedding was going on. I felt a pang of envy of the choristers at the centre of it all and the thought of the half crown they would be getting. That was until I thought in modern terms and wondered just how far twelve-and-a-half new pence would go. New pence. Just as on the road, my life was passing through signposts, and decimalisation would be just one of the signposts that I would measure my life's journey with.

I left the sound of the shrill descant and went back to the bike. It was still there to my amazement. No one had nicked it, except me. I rode towards the old Saracen's Head, a half-timbered inn steeped in antiquity, then turned left to pedal past the pointed conifers that graced a weathered stone arch. A line of flagstones led from the arched gateway to the main door at the Minster's west wall. It was a fleeting glimpse as I cycled past, but beautiful and somehow comforting.

Before I knew it I was almost there. The final dash to Ellie's home is but a blur in my memory. The brief three miles of the last leg are little more than a collection of pale images. Images of lush trees dressed in full summer greenery, set amongst the lighter greens of passing hedges. I meandered through one more village, Halby, not shown on the map, before rolling down the lane to my final destination, the picturesque community of Edlington. Walking would have taken days I realised. It was the bicycle that had done the job for me. My bicycle.

The map at the front of the yellow manual had also done its job, so too had the signposts, but I had done the navigating and cycling. This was the furthest I had ever ventured from home by myself. To have come this far without mishap or getting lost was to me an achievement. All I had to do now was find the address that I knew as intimately as my own name.

Passing by the village sign my eyes looked hawk-like for The Croft. I was in an exhausted state of excitement. Each turn of the pedals took me by a procession of dwellings. It was like searching through a set of keys to the lock of a great door. So far none fitted. Most houses had a name. None were called The Croft. I grew anxious. Even as I ticked off the parade of properties, I fretted that the letter had been a joke, a practical joke of the worst kind. The implications of such a trick did not bear thought. Worry spread through me like a plague. Before I knew it I was heading out of the village back into open country again on the Mansfield Road.

There was not much to Edlington. It was just a place you passed through on the way to somewhere else. I stopped, turned around and decided to take a more detailed look. I had to have missed it. There was no other possible explanation. A kind of roasting warmth had taken hold of my face, which seemed to be a manifestation of the jitters I was feeling. It was the veins in my face, boiling hot veins, brought on by hours of exertion. The return to the village brought a passage through the afternoon air that immediately cooled and calmed and the thought that I had come all this way for nothing vaporised.

The search for The Croft was carried out diligently this time. Ahead I could see the church, a poor excuse for one, resembling a medieval shack with a simple slab of stones pointed at the top like a gable end creating a pauper's spire. Two little arches within it housed a bell apiece. With images of the Minster still fresh in my mind I felt sorry for this tiny house of God. Yet despite its crudity there was a forlorn attractiveness about it, set as it was within a small but pretty plot of holy ground. Across the road there was a school and a Wesleyan chapel, along with a telephone box, a sizeable pub and a long line of red brick houses quaintly roofed with terracotta pantiles, many sagging through centuries of gravitation. Everywhere there were trees, huge spreading monsters that seemed to hold the village together. I finally reached the other end as the road began to climb back up the rise to Halby. Panic was banging away in my head by now. I was tired out.

Once more I retraced my tracks. What else could I do? I would have asked someone for directions had there been anyone around but the place was a ghost village. As far as I could tell I was the only one there, a demented cyclist who had bitten off more than he could chew. By chance I noticed two lanes leading off the main thoroughfare. Graves Lane and Station Street they were named. How I managed to miss them is hard to say. The result of a weary mind and the obsession with house names I put it down to. Suppose The Croft was down one of these lanes. With renewed hope I rode my bike down Graves Lane past the side of the church grounds. I finally ended up at a farm, a dirty place containing dilapidated buildings that seemed more in need of demolition than restoration.

I turned round to go back when out of the filth of the farmyard a mad dog shot towards me with the speed of a torpedo. I stood up on my pedals to accelerate as the bounding black shape closed in on me. Gripping the handlebars for dear life I did my best to pick up speed. My legs had little left to give and the dog was lithe and fit. The eyes in my head must have become wild. My mind threw up the image of the dog I once passed at home - the one that had been tied up safely behind a hedge. Safe as I had been then, it had always scared me. Now the snapping teeth of a free animal were barely two feet away from my thrashing thighs. Then I felt it bite into my trouser leg, my left leg, as it growled fiercely like a leopard throwing its head wildly about and ripping the material of my trousers. I kicked and tried in vain to pedal. It hung on. I must have yelled at it. The two of us must have made a racket because at that moment someone way behind me at the farm threw out a high-pitched whistle and the miserable bastard let go and trotted back to its master.

I was in the process of looking down at the damage when I heard the whistler shout at me. The voice ordered the dog to go home as his running footsteps paced up the lane towards me. I had the feeling I was in trouble.

"This is private property," said the runner. "You're trespassing."

I was right. I was in trouble. He shouted again in a rough Nottinghamshire accent.

"What business you got cumin' down 'ere?"

I could see him now. He was a fit looking youth with scruffy, black hair and filthy dungarees that unfortunately I was able to smell as he drew level.

"I'm lost," I said, telling the truth. "I'm looking for The Croft."

"Vicar's in Suthull," said the young man, eyeing me suspiciously.

"I've come to see my Auntie Ellie," I explained. "She's married to the vicar."

"Oh, Mrs Crampton you mean. We didn't know she had relatives."

At hearing this a wave of happiness washed through my tired body. Ellie had said her name was now Mrs Crampton in her letter. I was sure of it.

"I'm Davy, Davy Harper. She's invited me over," I said with contained ecstasy, unable to prevent my tongue going into such detail.

"Turn left towards Mansfield at end of't lane and keep an eye out for Ivy Cottage. The Croft's set back frum't road a bit behind it."

"Right," I said, feeling all doubts melt away.

The dog barked from the inside of a shitted up barn and I was on my way. So it was back along the main street once more until I saw Ivy Cottage. I remembered seeing it before half hidden by a thick, tall laurel hedge and the marks of ivy that had once covered its walls were quite evident. I cycled down the drive and there was my prize. An old, red-bricked house two storeys high with three windows in the pantile roof. A cast iron plate was screwed to the wall near the door. It was painted shiny black with the letters highlighted in white gloss. The Croft it said. I had made it.

Oh, what a stupid time it was to be afraid. I should have raced up to the door, hammered on it and thrown myself into Ellie's embrace, but now I realised that it was possible for things not to turn out that way. Considering the effort it had taken me to get to this house, any outcome other than the one I wanted was too awful to contemplate. I hitched the bike up against the wall throwing my duffel bag down next to it and stood facing the red door nervous and full of foreboding. Before me was a knocker shaped like a fox's head and placing my hand around it I drew it back. There I stood, reluctant and unsure. I wanted the world to stop here and now. I wanted to keep the imaginary visions of this moment safe in my head where they had lived for so many days. It seemed wrong to sully them with reality, but I was aware that the afternoon sun was becoming an early evening one, declaring time's constant march and I knew that I had to act. Almost against my better judgement I brought the fox down heavily on the door three deliberate times. Contact. In time there were footsteps. Then the handle moved down but the door remained closed.

"Hang on a moment, please," spoke a voice from the other side.

It was a voice I knew. I dare not answer as I listened to the steps walk away and return to the accompaniment of jangling keys. The sound of locks unlocking, the sight of a door handle levering down, the seeing of a door opening, my pulse reverberated through my whole body, making it shudder with every surge. I had never known anticipation like it.

Then, there she was, a grown-up version of the beautiful Ellie I remembered from when I was a boy, looking at me with horrified disbelief.

"Miller? It can't be," she blurted out, unable to stop herself.

I had no idea what she meant.

"It's me, Davy," I said, wondering what had come over her, "David."

She appeared to re-examine me for the briefest fraction of a second, as she attempted to regain her slipped composure. Her face, so shocked, tried in vain to muster an expression of delight.

"My goodness, it is you," she said, staring at me, "you look just like…" but she never finished the sentence, quickly burying it. "My word Davy, you're… you're a man now."

Never before had I been made aware of the passage of huge chunks of time. How we had both changed. Ellie was fully a woman, dressed in a smart white blouse and a beige skirt. She wore sandals. By comparison I felt grubby in my torn cords and Oxfam shirt. My shoes were ones that let water in when it rained. I was hot with sweat.

I could smell myself, pungent with adolescence. All these things made me feel as if the gulf between us had grown too wide and that by making my own way here I had made a terrible mistake. My distress must have shown because she looked at me and smiled. It was the smile I knew, whereupon she stepped out from the doorway and held me in a way that I once took for granted. I felt rescued and, although I did not let myself, I wanted to cry for the sheer joy of it.

She led me into the house, past a room full of books on shelves opposite a staircase. After the heat of the summer day outside the house was pleasantly cool and gently welcoming, calm and well ordered. We came to a white glossy door on the other side of which was a large kitchen. In I went and sat on a stool offered to me. Ellie put the kettle on and sat down with me at the table.

"You got my letters then?"

"I got two," I replied.

"Only two? And who brought you?" she asked. "I thought you'd have written back for us to come and fetch you."

"I cycled here. By myself."

"Cycled?" she said with honest disbelief.

"Cycled," I repeated proudly, "all the way. My bike's outside."

"And what did your mum say when you said you were coming over here," said Ellie, hating to mention mother at all.

"Huh, she said she was glad to get rid of me."

"I bet she did," she sneered, and instantly apologised. "Sorry Davy, I shouldn't have said that."

"Don't be, I'm glad to get away from the bitch."

I could see in her eyes that she understood. So mother became a topic best forgotten. We talked for ages. A seamless flow of effortless chat and just like the two old friends that we were we fell into conversation as if the long years apart counted for nought. We left the kitchen and Ellie showed me to an upstairs room that was in the throes of refurbishment. She said that it had once belonged to an old lady who had died there and, as if to offset this grisly tale, she opened the window and cast before me a glorious view of the countryside. The scene before me of rolling hills and enclosed fields, framed between two large horse-chestnut trees, dispelled any morbid thoughts of death. It was a calm room, peaceful. I could smell the

258

love that hung in the air. It emanated from Ellie and, like a pomander, she filled the house with goodness. Ever since she had moved to The Croft she had intended this would one day be my room she told me, but for a modicum of finishing touches I was to make it my own as soon as I wished. Then our ears pricked.

"We appear to have a visitor, darling," came a man's voice from below stairs.

"John's home," said Ellie. "You'll like him, come on."

I let Ellie hurry to the landing and peeping from behind the bedroom door I could see in the half-light a man in his fifties. He was a vicar, balding, with a rim of soft, dark grey hair ringing the back of his head. He was smiling up at Ellie as he put his briefcase on a dark wooden table in the hall.

"You managed to get away a little earlier then?" she said as she went to greet him.

With obvious tenderness he wrapped his arms around her and pressed a gentle kiss on her head.

"They invited me to the reception. But it's in Newark, so I made my excuses. Whose is the bike?"

"Ask and ye shall receive, you said. So I did and I have."

He looked vacantly away until he gathered an inkling of what she might mean.

"Really?" he said, his face widening with astonishment. "I thought we were planning to fetch him. The room's not ready yet," then he remembered the bike. "He didn't come all the way on that, did he?" he said gesturing towards the bicycle.

Ellie nodded back, grinning.

"Well where is he, darling?"

Ellie looked up the stairs.

"Davy, you can come down now."

I emerged, making my way down in mild trepidation, as if I was being asked to meet God. The thing I remember most were his eyes, brimming with compassion and, although I knew that I looked a mess, I knew that he was looking at me the person rather than the person I appeared to be.

Instead of being calmed to the warmth of his gaze, I felt uncomfortable, stripped bare, as if my inner fortress was no match for this new kind of technology. Cruelty I could understand yet, but for knowing the goodness of Ellie, this was new to me. This did not try to bludgeon down my defences. It dissolved them and they had served me well these fortress walls, battered and knocked about as they were. Over time I had reinforced them, thickened them, outer walls had been built layer by layer until the delicate little me was able to keep some of my self safe. How his eyes were able to penetrate through such defences I was at a loss to understand. In my mind's eye it was as if all the cannonballs hurled at me by life were of no consequence, the walls would stand up to them - but here was something different and, like a mist it permeated every stone, every stockade until I was completely surrounded, completely defenceless. I do not mind admitting I was terrified at being so unnerved.

"Well I'm very pleased to make your acquaintance Davy," he said and held out his hand.

I thought he was going to give me something for a moment but there was nothing in his upturned palm. I glanced at Ellie who made a shaking motion with a gripping fist. I then realised and, extending my own arm, we shook hands. People did not do that very much where I came from, at least not in my part of town. This one tiny gesture made me feel ill at ease yet further, as if I had come into a world that, with something as simple as an act of politeness, had made me feel altogether inept.

"Sturmey Archer gears, aren't they?" he asked.

"Yes Sir," I replied, through years of indoctrination and impressed by his knowledge.

"I've got a racer in the garage. Care to see it?" he added with an air of boyish enthusiasm.

"Yes please."

I caught Ellie smiling at me. I could tell that she knew that all would be well.

"Come on then, you can have a go on it if you like, then we'll make you feel at home and we can have a chat over supper. How's that?"

I wondered what he meant by a chat but it was hard to say no to him. So I followed him outside as he opened the garage doors and wheeled out an elegant shiny racing bicycle, black frame with Derailleur gears and taped-up drop handlebars.

"There you go. See what you make of that. Take it up the lane if you wish. Just watch the brakes, they've recently had new blocks fitted."

I walked it to the main road and hitched myself up onto the saddle. It was higher than mine and strange to be gripping onto handlebars that curved downwards like a pair of ram's horns. The balancing came back easy once I pushed off, but soon I was pedalling like mad and making no headway. From a distance I could hear the vicar yell something about gears. All I knew about gears was that Sturmey Archers were meant for girls whilst Derailleurs were meant for boys. Why they were fitted to bicycles I had not the foggiest idea. I never even touched mine on my journey. So I managed to turn round further up the lane and pedal back, just being able to reach down to squeeze the brake lever in time to stop.

"Well done, well done. What do you think? Don't worry about the gears. You'll soon get the hang of them. I'll show you how they work tomorrow after Communion if you like?"

With that we put the bike away and went inside for something to eat. How strange. I had failed to ride his bicycle properly and yet he had not called me stupid, or got angry, or made sarcastic remarks. He actually said well done, twice. I felt good deep inside where the mist still hung behind my great, useless walls.

Chapter seven: The Shop

Can you ever remember your very first taste of something that was exceptionally good? Chocolate? Now can you recall eating chocolate for the absolute first time, or shepherd's pie, or chewing gum? I do not mean can you conjure up the actual taste of any of these or whatever it was you liked. No, I want you to think about how you yourself felt the very first time. The very first mind you, when you enjoyed whatever it was. There is a first time for everything, so they say and, for me, at The Croft that summer it was happiness. If anyone tells you there is no such thing as delicious happiness then I doubt if they have fully experienced it. With Ellie and John I was truly happy for the first time in my life.

After two weeks in Edlington I realised that my escape had been completely successful and I absorbed myself in my new home. Village life was quieter than the town but filled with enough difference as to make it enthralling. In the town most of the people I knew rushed around trying to look as busy as could be, but making sure to do as little as possible in the process. In the country it all seemed the opposite way around. Their kind of industry forced them to put in long hours on the farms or in the fields. Yet it was all done at a steady pace - a pace regulated by the seasons and the vagaries of the weather. Everything ran to a different clock. Work still got done but there was never any need for the wail of a siren to start the day.

I was allowed to wander at will around the village. I took my bicycle to neighbouring communities and even paid another visit to Southwell. I had found my own paradise where I could put the past behind me, and get on with being as normal as it was possible for me to be. Then one day, straight out of the blue, John asked me to step into his study. He said he had some news for me, and that I should sit down to listen to him. Ellie stood by his side emotionless, as he leaned back in the leather chair behind his desk. I tried to look into their faces for clues. What could this be about? I grew uneasy.

"Davy," he began, smiling at me as he fiddled with his fountain pen, "I've been discussing your arrival with a great friend of mine Mr Saltby of Newark. He has recently informed me that there is a position of stock handler within his company on Barngate. I have taken the liberty of acting as your referee and therefore the post has been offered to you," he leaned back further in his chair, grinning contentedly. "So, my boy, you have a job and you start on Monday morning at eight thirty. You'll receive ten pounds a week after stoppages, which will be divided up in the following way. Five pounds will go to Ellie for your board and lodgings and one pound a week on a pension plan that I will set up for you with the Prudential. Two pounds will to go into a savings account, which will leave you with two pounds spending money for yourself. You'll be a man of means dear chap, a man with a future. What do you say to that?"

He was beaming as if he had just played the part of Father Christmas.

"Thank you, thank you very much."

What else could I say? The thought of going to work had not occurred to me. I suppose I had begun the think of my stay in the village as an extended summer holiday. At least the job would not be at the dreaded factory Ansons - but suppose this Mr Saltby was the owner of a factory just as bad? A Newark version of Ansons now that would be too cruel to bear.

"This Mr Saltby, does he own a factory then?" I asked outright.

"No, no, no. Saltbys are agricultural merchants. Very well known around here. You'll find them a good company to work for. They'll show you what to do, so you've no need to worry. I'll write you a letter of introduction. How about that?"

"Thank you," I said again. "But how will I get there, how will I get to Newark every day?"

"Easy," he said getting to his feet. "Up with the lark at six, get a good breakfast down you and catch the Mansfield to Newark bus outside the church at seven. You'll be at work in plenty of time."

"You can work your way up, Davy," said Ellie, trying to sound supportive. "Make sure that you do a good job and Mr Saltby will see to your advancement. You'll be all right. I know you will."

I was finding all this hard to face up to. The real world of work was inescapable. Even out here in this beautifully rural spot my life was for sale. It was all so ugly, even somewhat vulgar. Seeing my bewildered face John came over and placed a fatherly hand on my shoulder.

"Don't worry my boy. We'll iron out all these minor details. The main thing is that you've got a job, which means you can stay here with us and pay your way. And besides there's always the risk that you might enjoy it," then he laughed a little chuckle and I felt safe again.

Before I knew it I was standing in the wooden bus shelter at six forty-five in the morning with Ellie by my side. It was cold and damp, though the day had all the promise of being a beautiful one as the early sun began to bathe the village in its light. My duffel bag had been commandeered to carry my sandwich box and Ellie had made up a bottle of squash. My jacket pocket held the all-important letter of introduction. So the stage was set. Ellie kissed my cheek just before I climbed aboard the green bus. Then I was on my way through the villages into Southwell, finally arriving at Newark passing the castle before reaching the terminus at the bus station. Following John's scribbled instructions I retraced part of the bus journey to the damaged remains of the castle, strode past a cafe and stopped at the printing works.

Over on the other side of the road was Saltbys, a ramshackle business that looked as if it needed a coat of paint at the very least. I crossed the road to the curious little place only to discover that the entrance was locked. In a mood of resignation I leaned my back against the wall and watched the traffic go by as I waited for them to open. As Newark's parish church struck half past eight, three people turned up from around the corner. One was a well-fed rotund gentleman in a black suit that was accompanied by a woman with the most feather-light stature. They had in tow a young man who, I learned later, was nursing a hangover. The man in the suit pulled out a set of keys and unlocked the door. This was done in total disregard for me. Perhaps they thought I was a vagrant, or else I had become invisible.

"Get the kettle on Maisey," shouted the man in the suit, then yawning he added, "can't start the week without a brew."

Maisey picked up the morning mail and went to do as she was told as four other people came in, two men and two women, who quietly got on with getting the place ready for the start of business. What a place Saltbys was. I followed the last four people inside and entered a huge junk hole. I got the feeling I had walked into a farmer's scrap yard. A narrow gangway cut diagonally across what passed for a showroom, on either side of which was strewn an untidy collection of ploughs and harrows. Scythes hung on the walls along with shovels and spades, rakes, forks and combine augers, sieves, jerry cans and hoes. Great piles of bagged-up fertiliser were stashed away in one corner, whilst heavy looking bits of machinery bearing the Massey

Ferguson name were leaned against the wall at the other end. How I was going to make head or tail of the world of Saltbys I had no idea.

I went up to the sickly-looking chap, the one who was the worse for drink, and asked to see Mr Saltby. His watery, glazed-over eyes flipped up to meet my own rather nervous expression and he nodded his head in the direction of the far corner of the haphazard shop. Looking where he had directed me I could see a corner room made of so much glass that it looked like a greenhouse. Within I could see the man in a suit waiting for the lady to deliver his morning tea. He was busily reading the morning mail. So pulling my own letter out of my pocket, I made for the fragile glass door marked OFFICE. Even though the two knocks I made on it were timid and light, each pane of glass rattled alarmingly. Without even looking up the man called out.

"Thanks Maisey. I'll get it," and rising to let her in he was surprised to find that not only had his tea failed to arrive, but that a scrawny adolescent was waiting there before him.

"Now then youth, what can I do for you?"

"I'm David Harper," I said shoving the white envelope under his nose.

"Are you now? And what's this?" he said taking the letter and opening the flap with his little finger.

"It's a letter of introduction, from John, I mean the Reverend Crampton."

"Ah, so you're him, eh? Oh well, come in and sit down," so I did. "Right then, what do you know about agriculture?"

"More than I did two weeks ago," I said.

"Oh aye? So if I said I wanted you to fetch a customer a hand-held excavator, you'd know what I meant, would you?"

I thought for longer than was necessary and with some reluctance shook my head.

"Didn't think you would. Well I don't go in for all this modern lingo, I call a spade a spade, and you'll do well to remember that."

He called over to Joe, the hangover victim, and told him to get me a pair of overalls and a brush, with further instructions that I should be tasked with sweeping the pavement outside the front of the premises. This was duly arranged and so my first day began.

Next I swept the aisle, as the gangway was called. During this job, I could hear Mr Saltby gradually losing his temper on the phone. The argument seemed to be something to do with times. Something had been promised by mid-afternoon. I heard him shout down the mouthpiece that ten thirty was no good, it was too soon and that he was not ready. He said he did not care if it was inconvenient for them. There was more talk and then the receiver was slammed down. Mr Saltby stormed out of his office like a bull, shaking in the process his little conservatory of an office to the verge of destruction.

"Joe! Joe! Where the bloody-hell are you?"

"Here Mr Saltby."

"Joe, go out and find Eric and Alan, quickly."

"Yes, Mr Saltby."

I was riveted to the spot by all this as he looked at me.

"Right my lad, put down your broom and go with Joe. It seems we have a tractor arriving earlier than we thought. These three ploughs have got to go to make room. You just do as Eric tells you. Off you go."

Off I went and ran into Joe and his two colleagues heading back to the office. They were the gents I had followed in that morning. Eric, the elder of the two men was in full grumble like his boss about not having enough time to clear the place. He was a round man with a round face. Beneath his grease-stained flat cap he was almost bald. A burning fag hung out of the corner of his mouth and he wore dirty blue overalls. Alan, who I later learned was his son, was slimmer and had the kind of face that, with his thick black moustache and hooked nose, made him look like a Mexican Comanchero. Eric scared me. He was a powerhouse of a man with a gruff personality and a foul mouth to match. One choice expletive ran like a thread through his language that took on the mantle of an adjective. It was not enough for him that the tractor was coming too early. To him it was coming too fuckin' early. He stormed into the showroom, lifted his cap and scratched his hairless head.

"Right you fuckin' lot, I want these moving out to the fuckin' back," he pointed at three large ploughs, brand new shiny ones, light blue and pristine, "but don't fuckin' scratch 'em or we'll be really up the fuckin' creek."

I was given the job of moving a mass of supplies out of the way to make a path through. It was made clear to me that I was not to touch the blessed ploughs. I got the impression that that was an honour bestowed on a select few only. So as not to get ideas above my station, I was set to work removing massive rolls of barbed wire, galvanised cattle troughs and lawn mowers. A large display of yard brushes that had been thoughtlessly positioned in front of a set of shabby double doors had to be moved, along with a jumbled heap of sacks. Once the doors were opened I could see into an Aladdin's cave of disorganised merchandise. The idea of untidiness was evident in the shop but here the chaos was out of control. It made me want to scream at someone for letting it get so bad. Eric and Alan waded in with a purpose and began tossing wooden boxes about with complete disregard for the rattling contents inside them. Chaos being chaos it multiplied. I was told to make myself useful and join in, an order delivered to me in Eric's inimitable fashion.

After half an hour or so, there was room enough for three ploughs to fit in. I stood breathlessly with pissed-up Joe, as father and son wheeled the ploughs into their new home. For a brief moment I looked around at the utter mess everywhere and wondered just how such a business could ever survive. More to the point I wondered just how I would ever fit in and understand it all.

"Right then, young man," boomed Eric as he closed the double doors, "you can make tea I hope?" I replied that I could. "Get on wi' it then, and don't forget 'is nibs," he said cocking an eye towards the office.

I was given a verbal list of preferences, milk and sugar levels, none of which I could possibly remember, whereupon Joe led me to a grubby back room in the middle of which was a pine table covered in old teacups and newspapers. A dog-eared *Playboy* magazine was hidden amongst them strategically opened up to show off the top page of the centre fold, massive tits and all. Beneath a window was a stone sink, draining board on one side, worktop on the other. A dented steel kettle and a badly stained teapot stood on it surrounded by soggy invoices and bits of wire. There was a dishcloth and tea towel so dirty I elected not to use them. Joe opened a cupboard on the wall and pointed to the mugs, the tea and sugar, turned round to show me where the fridge was, then flopped down in a chair, burying his thumping head in his arms on the table.

"God, I feel like shit," he said. "You'd think by now I'd have learned, wouldn't you?"

"What? Not to drink?" I asked.

"No, stupid, not to mix 'em."

At the word stupid I slammed a cup on to the worktop, just holding back from smashing the damn thing into the wall. How had he worked out that I was stupid so fast?

"And have you learned now?" I asked.

"Oh aye, 'til next time," and he managed to make a laughing groan.

I made the tea and went to say that it was ready. Without a word of thanks it was consumed. Eric motioned to Piss Head, as Joe had come to be called, and explained that the front wanted opening. Everyone was needed to do this it seemed, save for the ladies, and soon we were all outside in the mid-morning sunshine making ready to open it.

Eric went into the office and came back with a large steel pin. When he had inserted it into the bottom of the front door I realised at once that it was in fact a key of sorts. The lock was stiff but not resistant to Eric's muscle power and foul mouth. Then, like some highly trained team, they each took up their positions. It turned out that the front of the shop was made of a concertina of wooden panels, split in the middle where the built-in front door was located. Eric urged us to push. I realised that one obeyed Eric's urges without question. As we pushed and grunted the panels zigzagged open, rumbling in their runners set in the concrete floor, occasionally squealing through lack of lubrication. The front had seldom been opened I was told, and my orders were to push like I was trying to get the coalman off my mother. No one realised how uncomfortable this remark made me feel. So far I had done a good job of keeping my feelings locked away. With some exertion the opposite side was opened and a breeze of fresh summer air brought the fusty old shop to life. As we caught our breaths, St Mary's church clock struck the half hour chimes.

"He's fuckin late. I might have fuckin' known, the lying, fuckin' sod,"

It was just gone eleven when a large, red, articulated, flat bed lorry pulled up noisily outside where the entire workforce of Saltbys was waiting. Out jumped the driver and ran straight into Eric's tongue. The driver's tongue was in no mood for effing and blinding and fired back in a similar vein. Mr Saltby, disgusted at the row, intervened and said that enough was enough and could we please get on with the job in hand. So the driver hopped up onto the trailer and began to undo the straps holding the prize that everyone had been waiting for, a bright orange-bodied tractor. It looked too clean to be destined for fields of mud, too perfect for being thrashed over the years into a dented, paint-scratched, worn out, patched-up old plough-puller. The driver, aware of its pristine condition reversed it down ramps hooked to the lorry's rear with a delicate touch. Then with no apparent difficulty and understated skill, the bright, gleaming workhorse was parked in exactly the right spot on the shop floor, its fat, heavily treaded tyres squeaking on the painted concrete. The doors were closed, the lorry went away, the promotional poster was attached to the window and lunch was declared.

After my sandwiches, I went to have a closer look at the new arrival. I had never been this close to a tractor before and I was not prepared for just how big this one was. I was struck by the exactness of its manufacture. To me a tractor was just a dirty four-wheeled monster that pulled equally dirty things behind it. Agricultural machinery had always looked badly built and shitted up to me. Here was one that had yet to be baptised in this way. The steering pinions were precision made, covered as they were with a thick layer of orange paint. The engine gleamed in its cowling, each nut and bolt fresh and bright. It was like touching elephant skin to feel the tyres, solid and massive. I went to the front where a grille protected the radiator. A silver plate with the name Nuffield announced the origin of its manufacture.

"I expect a young lad like you wouldn't mind having a sit in the driver's seat. Am I right?"

"Mr Saltby," I said, shaken out of my reverie. "It's a nice tractor, isn't it?"

"It ought to be for the dosh I paid for it," he said. "Well, up you go. Tell me what you think."

I climbed up onto the seat behind the wide metal rim that was the steering wheel and looked down upon the top of Mr Saltby's balding head.

"It's high up here. It must take some controlling," I said, trying to sound grown up.

"Do you like it up there then?" he asked.

"I feel quite important," I said, enjoying the sensation.

"Can you drive? Have you ever driven a car?" he asked.

A car, I thought. I had only just learned to ride a bloody bike for heaven's sake.

"No never."

"Well, you keep this beauty clean every day, and we'll see about taking you out onto Winthorpe aerodrome and get you started. If you like it you can save up for lessons, can't you?"

"Yes I can. That would be great. Thank you Mr Saltby."

It was decided to attach a plough to the tractor so as to make an interesting display. Good marketing Mr Saltby called it. So with permission Joe and I carefully brought a heavy one out of the back where we had hidden them earlier. Eric and Alan fastened the two together while I watched and tried to learn. Then I was given the job of making the plough as clean as possible. It was a bucket of soapy water with a cloth sort of a job and promised to take me the rest of the afternoon. The blades of the plough were grubby and grey. I turned them into gleaming mirrors of silver that reflected my eager face. I next went to work on the light blue framework scrubbing every particle of grime I could find. Then my hand detected a roughness in the cast metal like there was some soil that I could not remove. I recharged my rag with more soapy water to have another go. It would not budge. I looked closer at what had attached itself to the metal body of this plough, only to find it was a word moulded into the face of the beam I was cleaning. I looked. I looked closer. I dropped my rag and stepped back. I think I held my breath. There was a single word, one word only – Anson.

Here, even here, I could not escape the tentacles from that dreaded factory and looking at the polished steel blades that I had cleaned earlier there was a further thought. Each blade was fastened onto the frame with three heavy-duty bolts - bolts that passed

270

through holes in both frame and plough. I had seen holes being drilled into the blades of ploughs on my visit to the factory. I had seen who was doing the drilling of them. Was it possible that she had drilled the holes in these very blades? Of course it was possible and so the tentacle went deeper, further. My mother's influence had even penetrated into this shop. There was to be no real escape from her, was there? She would always find a way into my mind no matter how hard I worked to keep her out.

'You stupid boy', I could hear her calling out from the blades that she had drilled, 'reduced to scrubbing for a living, is that it? And just think Davy boy you could have had an apprenticeship at Ansons. Well you can run all you like, cycle away as far as you can, but you are still soft in the head. You still need to be looked after. You are no good on your own. You need me Davy, me, your own mummy. You need a bit of tender loving care. Remember our special cuddle? It was our little secret, wasn't it? Wasn't it, wasn't it, answer me you little shit? Answer me you stupid little bastard. Answer me, answer me, answer me or I'll get out mummy's little helper. Not the one you broke, a new one, harder. Here it is. Now let me give you a cuddle. We don't like the spoon, do we? You like mummy's love, don't you Davy boy? Don't you? Don't you? Don't you. DON'T YOU?'

"No! Piss off and leave me alone. Fuck off!" I screamed it out as loud as I could so she would go. I was gasping for breath.

"Oi! Who shouted that on the shop floor?" It was Mr Saltby and I felt my face colour up with embarrassment as I heard his rapid footsteps head towards me. "Was that you?"

"Sorry," I replied, unable to think up a lie quickly enough.

"Who were you shouting at? There could have been customers in the shop. Even Eric doesn't swear on the floor when there are customers present. So what's your excuse?"

The cobweb I could see cluttering up the corner made me see a spider.

"A spider?"

"I hate them."

"Well hate them or not, no more swearing. Understand?"

"Yes."

271

"Good. Anyway you've done a grand day's work today, so it seems a pity to spoil it. Tell you what, tidy up then go and catch your bus. We'll see you tomorrow. Say hello to the Reverend and Mrs Crampton for me. You won't forget, will you?"

"Thanks, yes, I will. I mean I won't forget. Thank you."

I caught an earlier bus home and spent the journey back to Edlington running the day's events through my head and cursing the plough that had made me cry out loud. It was only a plough. It was only a piece of metal and so what if she had drilled a few holes in it? Big deal. She could not really get to me, could she? So, I just sat back, head flopping against the corner of the bus window and watched the countryside flip past. Trees and hedges flashed by hypnotically as, with practised skill, my mind drew a veil over her.

It was bliss. An evening of calm and warmth back at The Croft dispelled the power of the goblins in my head. The television in the living room silenced them further with layer upon layer of rubbish. John and Ellie were delighted when I mentioned the driving lessons. I tried to describe everyone who I met, particularly Eric. With a vicar's sensibilities in mind, I outlined his character as being a bit on the rude side. This hit John's funny bone and he burst out laughing, saying he knew of Eric and that he thought I was a complete master of understatement. We all laughed together. The happiness had come back. I felt safe again. Ellie looked at me with eyes that failed to hide her sense of pride in me. As I headed off to bed that night I realised that cycling here had been the most intelligent thing I had ever done. No one would call me stupid again.

The next day Eric burst into the showroom swearing about the mess everywhere. All around was a blanket of straw littering the place underfoot. I could not hide my annoyance, especially after all my hard work the day before. The place was a tip. I tramped across to where the tractor was and saw that someone had tampered with that too. The beautiful paintwork had been scratched and it looked as if the perpetrator had taken a hammer to what was now a dented body. Dried-on manure was plastered over the rest of it. Eric came closer. It was, as he drew level in full fucking flow, that I noticed there were

272

engine parts covering the floor. I picked up what to me looked like an oil filter.

"Haven't you got that fucker finished yet?" he said staring at me with his deep-set eyes.

I apologised, wondering just where this part was meant to go. Looking into the guts of the engine I could see a metal orifice with a screw thread on the outside edge of it. Obviously something was meant to go there. Using my initiative I tried to fit the oil filter where I thought it should go but the opening was too small. So I looked back onto the straw and picked up a fan belt. No matter how hard I tried this would not fit either. Eric became madder and said that if I did not get it fixed there would be no five quid for me.

Eric's gaze had become menacing. He no longer resembled himself. He had almost become a Neanderthal. Even the showroom had changed. Given that it was a shambles at the best of times it could never be described as a barn and yet that is exactly what it appeared to be, a barn, a dirty old barn, with someone whom had once been Eric losing his temper. The angrier he became the less I understood about the tractor. In a state of panic I ran out into a farmyard, past a pretty girl and down into a lane that led to a church. The running feet of the man were never very far away so I ran past the church and down towards a village. All I could see was a house that had once known happiness, so I ran inside there for cover, but the caveman had seen me and gave chase. It was dark and in the fading light I climbed fearfully up the stairs to the filthy remains of a bedroom and closed the door. My heart was in my mouth. With the power of a demolition ball the door was flung open and there he stood. I screamed out loud but he came closer. I screamed again, trying not to make the sound emerge from my mouth. Breathing heavily I managed to make the faintest squeak break away from my throat. It did not stop him, not even as my scream got louder. His hands were huge. Hands that grabbed hold of my shoulders and began to shake the life out of me. Breathing rapidly I let out a series of panting yells. He shook me more. I cried out again like a torture victim. Then I opened my eyes only to see her holding onto my shoulders like she often did. I knew straightaway that it had been a bad dream but the nightmare would continue. It would never end if I had been stupid enough to cry out in the night. The special cuddle would have to begin. Off would come my pyjama bottoms and away would fall her nightdress. Down would go her hand and she would make me ready. Only this time I did not have to take it anymore.

"Get out!" I yelled at her. "Get the fuck out of here. Do you hear? Get out!"

"Shush, calm yourself," she said. "You've had a bad dream."

"You'll never do that to me again, do you hear me. I wish you were dead."

In that instant the light clicked on. John was standing in the doorway. I could see now that it was Ellie who was holding me. Sweat was clinging to my forehead and half of my mind was still in the old house. There was silence for several seconds and then I spoke.

"I'm sorry," I said, trying to hold back the sobs. "I'm ever so sorry."

Chapter eight: The Pit

Joe Witherspoon the stockman at Saltbys was a strange person. He had a jaundiced view on life - views that he expounded with a crude wit, like sarcasm with accessories. I once asked him why he did not change his life if he hated it so much.

"My life changes without my help", he would say. "It keeps getting worse all by itself."

He would tell me that he was planning to immigrate to America. His scheme was to go on a tour of Paramount Studios and halfway round fake a heart attack. This would be done just as the tour had reached a part of the studio where a scene was in the process of being filmed.

"The filming would have to stop, naturally."

"Naturally," I urged.

"Well the director would come over to see what all the commotion was about, and then I would stand up and say, there now wasn't that convincing? I'd be a star before you could say Kirk Douglas."

He lived in a dream world did Joe. That is why he drank so much, to bury the crushing disappointment he felt for himself. I wonder now if he was a homosexual. He behaved in a faintly camp manner, like a sort of bridled extroversion but he knew his way around Saltbys all right. He knew where every kind of nut and bolt was, every type of nail and pin. He could lay his hands on one-inch galvanised fencing staples with as much ease as if he had got them in his hands all along. He taught me the ropes and more to the point he showed me how to deal with customers and how to sell to them. Watching him in action, especially with dyed-in-the-wool farmers, was a treat. Taken that he had slightly effeminate ways, it was incredible how he interacted with men of more robust natures. I am sure they left with more items under their arm than they ever intended to buy when they first walked in. Somehow he would convince them that they needed it all.

He showed me what to do when an order came in. How to keep records of the stock and where it all went. He taught me what everything did, what it was for and why customers needed them. He passed on to me his knowledge of the seasons and where in that cycle of the year each implement was employed. Ploughs for after the harvest, harrows to break up the top layer of a field and make it ready for the seed drill. He was from Nottingham originally, at home in the city and, like me, was out of place here where the soil formed the basis of working life. His arrival at Saltbys had been as unplanned as the rest of his career but he had made a success of it, and the company had grown to the point where he needed an assistant. Me.

One Wednesday afternoon, as a summer downpour greyed the sky, I watched him stitch up a farmer from Muskham. The farmer strode into the place as if the rain was of no consequence, being evidently at one with the elements and the wide environment of the great outdoors. Joe, recognising him, leaned against his side of the counter and pretended to study a pile of invoices.

"Barbed wire," said the farmer.

"With you in a minute," said Joe without glancing up.

The farmer looked at me impatiently and repeated his request.

"How much would you like?" I asked.

"Four hundred feet," put in Joe, shoving the invoices to one side.

"I want a hundred feet and no more," said the farmer indignantly.

"Yes, I grant you do," said Joe, "and you'll get back to Muskham, in this weather and find you need it to patch up another hole where the sheep are getting out and you'll have to come back and buy some more. Only you'll have to use up more diesel in that clapped out Land Rover, waste more time, risk more of your stock and blame me for not selling you a more sensible amount."

"So how do you know there are more holes to be fixed?" said the farmer.

"It's raining. You can't do anything on your north field so you decided to take a look at your pasture. You've found a break in the fence and you've come straight here."

"How'd you know that?"

Joe tapped the side of his nose at the farmer.

"And what's your wife going to say if you don't get the field secure by nightfall?" Joe warned. "Mrs Holby, she'll demand you do it right this time I fancy."

Mr Holby rubbed his chin with a weathered hand, thinking.

"I'll take two hundred feet then," he said.

"Bet you've not thought about staples to pin the stuff to the posts, have you?"

"Staples?"

"You'll need five hundred, galvanised."

"Oh aye, s'pose I will."

"Have you got a decent hammer? Don't want to have to come back on account of an old hammer breaking, do you?"

The old farmer thought again and decided there was a shred of sense in what he was hearing.

"Aye. Well go on then," he said.

Joe priced it all up and got me to fetch it over to him. The barbed wire pricked my fingers as I dragged each bundle over to the counter. My hands were bleeding when I had done.

"And there's another thing," said Joe, "you can't be too careful with barbed wire. I'll throw in a pair of gloves in at ten per cent off. There you go."

"Aye, well thanks, and good day."

When he had gone Joe looked at me with those wicked eyes of his and we both giggled ourselves silly.

It was halfway into my second week when Joe introduced me to what would eventually become a good companion. It was lunchtime and I had forgotten to bring my sandwiches. I made them the night before in a bid to be organised but had left them in the larder. Forgetting them had bothered me all morning and I grumbled to Joe about it, to the point where he had become bored to death by such constant triviality. Unable to listen to more he offered to buy me my lunch.

At twelve-thirty on the dot we left the shop and walked down to a pub in the corner of the town's large cobbled market square, bustling and busy with traders in full cry. The pub was an elegant three-storey building, very old, Tudor in style and displaying its black wooden skeleton on the outside, as houses of that period were designed. Up we went to the first floor and I was introduced to Yvonne, a woman of thirty or so who had an enormous bosom that almost flopped out of her blouse. It was hard not to stare at them as they protruded towards me over the bar. Joe ordered two pints and we sat down near the window to enjoy them. From here we could watch the bustling market do its trade down below. Each striped tarpaulin roof waved in the breeze as a horde of shoppers mingled between them, and untold money changed hands. Joe bought me pie and mashed potatoes that I washed down with the beer. By the time we were strolling back to work I felt drugged. It was a feeling that I liked and I had a hankering to feel it again soon. Beer. Now what a fascinating liquid that was. It was the start of a long and intermittent relationship.

As the days passed by and I learned my new trade I got to like Joe. He could be a miserable bastard at times but he knew people and how to have a good time with them. Most of these so-called friends were less well off than him, financially as well as mentally. One of Joe's particularly unattractive features was that he enjoyed mixing with people who were lesser creatures than he was - that is why he had taken to me I suppose. These people held him in some sort of esteem and he lapped it up. Joe was cunning and crafty but not completely intelligent. He was a good judge of character, given a limited criterion to measure them against. This valuable ability only served to help him determine how he could get the best out of them.

I am certain he found it impossible to judge them in any deeper sense. I believe he allowed me to tag along for one reason and one reason only. It was simply to show his world that Joe Witherspoon was a mentor of some stature. Well to me, at that time of my life, he was.

It became commonplace to go to The Elizabethan, the pub in the market square, at lunchtime. I watched him chat up Yvonne the barmaid there. He used to delight in popping his paper money into her cleavage when he paid for the drinks. She never seemed to mind. On the contrary, she liked him putting his money there, removing it from her bra in a most seductive way especially when the bar was empty, save for us two. She would catch me watching her do this and pick up on my embarrassment and she would flash a smile that was supposed to give me a thrill, except I hated it. I hated anything to do with it. So I drank my beer and allowed myself to fall into bad ways. Bad ways and, if I had known just how bad, I would have stopped right there.

I do not think Ellie or John knew anything about my trips to the pub. I would take my sandwiches and bottle of squash and eat the food on the way back to work after my lunchtime pint. On the bus back home I would drink all my orange juice from the bottle so as to remove any smell of booze from my breath. It was a perfect disguise, camouflaging my newly acquired vice. I was pouring the dregs of one such bottle of juice down my throat while the bus pulled into the village one evening. As I twisted the screw cap back on I noticed a car outside The Croft. It was a police car. I was intrigued.

I was always intrigued when I saw that we had visitors. Professional people of all types were part of the traffic of The Croft. John knew lots of people. As my stay there lengthened I too became acquainted with other vicars, even the Bishop of Southwell. John also knew the Chairs of both the Mansfield Chamber of Commerce and the WRVS. He knew people on the General Synod. So it did not seem strange that someone from the police had called round.

Normally I would come home, hang up my bag, wash out my sandwich container and squash bottle, make myself a drink and flop in front of the telly before laying the table for tea. It was very seldom that I actually saw any visitors if there were any. So it came as a bit of a surprise when, upon hearing my cheery hello as I came through the door, I heard John call me from his study to see him.

Honest people find it hard to lie. They are good at making up tall tales, fabrications and altered versions of the truth. The trouble is that they can never get the face right. They can never marshal their eyes to fall into line and get in on the act. Behind Ellie's smile something was wrong. Even as John asked me to take a seat, I knew from his body language that things were not right.

It was only as I took my seat that I noticed the two other people in the room. Two uniformed police officers, a man and a woman, stepped closer to Ellie and John. They hid nothing. I had a bad feeling about all this. I knew straightaway that it was the theft of the bicycle. I even readied myself to prove all my theories about lying, preparing a web of deceitful concoctions in my head, and my own eyes especially, for when the questions would start.

"Davy," began Ellie, carefully picking her words, as if choosing the wrong one would have wrought a catastrophe. "The police are here because they have some news," she looked for reassurance from the coppers beside her, "news about your mum."

At the sound of that name, my head filled with hot, rushing blood. Was there to be no getting away from the bitch? Then I could see it all. I could see the whole miserable picture. She had put in a missing persons report and somehow they had tracked me down. Mr and Mrs Plod here had been given the job of taking me back. Well, I was not going to go, not back there. Not back to her.

"I'm not going back. They can't make me, can they John?"

John always kept his cool. In typical style he just asked me to sit quietly and listen to what the police lady had to say. So I did, and she spoke. Almost in a whisper she said that my mother was dead.

The hot, rushing blood felt odd. I looked up at her. She looked sad. I did not know how to feel. I was not glad about it, as I ought to have been. Over the next few seconds I became light-headed. Only Ellie seemed to have grasped my reaction. We had both elected to leave this person who had once been part of our lives. Now she had left us, permanently, but how? I turned back to the policewoman.

"How? When?"

"The rent man found her, near the stairs."

279

"When?"

"Five days ago."

I looked for the meaning of this in John's face. He came over, crouched down near my chair and placed his hand on my shoulder.

"Old chap, this isn't going to be easy. Not when you've heard the whole story. You see your mother was very upset when you left. We thought she'd told you to get out of the house. You told Ellie that she was glad to see the back of you, but that wasn't quite the truth, was it?"

I shook my head. There was no point lying now.

"We know that she was upset by your departure, because she left a note."

"A note? What sort of note?" I said, knowing what they were actually driving at.

All the faces staring back at me could see that the penny had dropped.

"The bitch killed herself, killed herself! You know she did that just to spite me, don't you?"

I became outraged. John tried to calm me. But it was no good. She had proved that she had overall power over me. She was no longer a living person, placed away from me at a safe geographical distance. She was a dead person who would be able to live on in my head. She had cursed me.

"The selfish fucking cow," I yelled out at everyone.

John's face filled with pity. He was a man of the world. He had heard more swearing than I would ever know.

"Go on then. How did the stupid sod do it, go on, tell me that?"

"The rent man cut her down. That's all you need to know," said the policeman who had been quiet until now.

He got a deadly flash of the policewoman's eyes for his insensitivity.

Ellie went to the cabinet and poured me a tiny measure of brandy. She stroked my head. I drank it down in one. At least I smelled of alcohol legitimately now.

For a while, a long while it seemed, the room vanished. I was no longer in the study. I was in a black world like some eerie cinema that smelled of blood. Pictures flashed in front of my eyes, the same eyes that I had seen God with outside the church, that night I was with All

280

Legs. Only now there was a parade of images taken by my heart during my life with her.

There was the birthday card tossed in the boiler. A hundred wooden spoons thrashed me mercilessly. The pain was unbearable and I cried out for it all to stop and then I could see my mother's face coming towards me and going away again. Over and over this image taunted me. Her hands were gripping my shoulders as I lay there on a bed, my bed. Her tits flapped about as she writhed on top of my little body, making it do things that it was not ready to do. Then she laughed and kissed me. She kissed the top of my head. Her face was beautiful and I began to cry at her loveliness. Seeing my tears she changed. The serenity vanished and her face became contorted with rage. Down came her shoe on top of my head, over and over. My guts could stand no more. Shaking all over I could hold back the vomit no more. It gushed out. I felt hands all over me, groping my shoulders. I shrugged them away as more sick pumped out of me. I could hear it splashing on to the floor. Through watery eyes I could see it in a mess on the carpet, the study carpet in The Croft. John and Ellie's hands were comforting me. John was saying not to worry.

The trembling had overtaken me completely. I was cold. I was frightened. Everything that made me who I was began to crack as good as if an earthquake was ripping a city apart. My world was falling to pieces and I felt like I was dying with it. Through the blur of my moistened eyes I looked up to see Ellie bringing me a bowl to be sick into. She said that it would be all right and she stroked my head. My heart that had become ripped apart could contain the tears inside no longer. My voice let out an agonising shriek of self-pity and the tears rode out of me on the back of it. All I could do was cry. Ellie held me tight. I could feel her love embracing me, pulling whatever it was out of me like a magnet.

I cannot remember the police leaving. Somehow I ended up in bed. John and Ellie were there too.

"What happened to you back at home, Davy?" said John.

He spoke very slowly, softly. He had a lovely voice and I wanted to tell him. I wanted to get everything out in the open. The trouble was that if I talked about it I would have to relive it and I had already made the strong box to put all those bad memories in. In my mind the mineshaft was about to be sunk. I was going to make damned sure that they would stay there. Even the demons that I knew would surely come would not be able to reach them and release their terrible contents. So I just stared at the wall, digging a hole in my being. No one was ever going to know what had happened to me. Besides, would anyone ever believe me? Somewhere I still held on to the belief, slight though it was, that my love had been bad love. I suppose I was too ashamed to confess that what had happened was partly my fault. That thought was also put into the strong box destined for the deep pit. So I answered John's question with a question.

"How did the police find me?"

"That's their job old boy. They asked the right people the right questions and there you go. Eventually, they talked to your school. A search of your locker revealed Ellie's letter. Simple really."

"Oh," I said, and went on digging, and staring.

An hour or so later, during which I was aware of talking going on outside my room, another question sprang up in my head.

"What did she write in the note?" I shouted, wanting to know.

The talking stopped. Footsteps could be heard on the carpet. John and Ellie in the room. They looked. Their faces were afraid.

"The note she left. What did it say?"

"Not now old chap, you've been though quite enough for one day. We'll talk tomorrow when you've rested a bit."

"Rest?" I yelled at him. "You expect me to fucking rest?"

"There's no need to swear. You've got to calm down, or you'll be ill."

"What did she write?" my voice was nasty, sounding evil.

"I don't know," he said, his eyes darting around the room, unable to comply with the mouth's performance.

"I know you're lying. It's in this house, isn't it? I know."

His eyes betrayed him once more, as Ellie delved into her dress pocket and pulled out two sheets of notepaper ripped out of a spiral bound pad. She handed them to me.

"He's a right to know John darling," she said to her husband.

I held the shopping list paper. I knew exactly from where the sheets had been torn. My Mum's handwriting was there, clear but shaky, as if the hand that held the pen knew what kind of deed it was next about to perform. The words went in, sick words, full of self-pity. They even made sense in a twisted sort of way. Such was her hold over my mind still.

Dear Davy,

I have come to the end of my tether. I can't bear to live anymore all by myself now that everyone has left me. I know now that you've left me too. I can forgive you for stealing most of my money, but I can't forgive you for running away and abandoning me to this life of loneliness.

You have no idea how bad my life has been. Ever since your grandad passed away I've had to struggle to carry on. Everyone who I ever loved has deserted me. But I've tried to go on by myself and be a good mum to you. I've made sure that you were always fed and clothed. Why did you have to leave me too? I'll never know.

By the time you read this it will be over. It breaks my heart to think about it but what else can I do? There's no point in being alive now you're gone. You don't want me anymore. You're just like the rest of them. If you knew what I had given up to have you, you would have stayed with me. But you're as selfish as all the rest.

Just you wait until you're twenty-one. You'll receive something of great value. I pray it curses you as it has cursed me.

Goodbye Davy,

Mother xxxx

Even as I screwed up and shredded the leaves, the words remained. They burned themselves into my brain with the hiss of a branding iron. Even without the letter in my hand I can recite some of her note word for word. Hateful words, typical words of my mother designed to make me feel at fault, always passing on the blame for everything that went wrong in her miserable life. The paper pieces fell to the floor. John picked them up mentioning something about evidence for a coroner. Inside myself I pushed open the lid to the strong box and dumped the words inside it. I imagined myself slamming the top down with a clang and fixing a huge padlock to it with chains all around the catch. I became quiet once more as I watched the Davy within, dig deeper and deeper into the dark depths of my mind, down past the earliest memories, down where I never wanted to venture again.

Outside on the surface I was only aware of people in a vague sense. I responded to breakfast the next day. I understood when I was told that I did not have to go to work and that John had explained everything to Mr Saltby. I did not give a damn what was going on. I even went out and lost myself in the landscape, forever digging my mineshaft.

Then came the day I learned about the funeral. They asked me if I wanted to go. It was a stupid question. I ached to see her put out of the way for good. I would go and rejoice. In my mind I would prepare a glorious fanfare. I was told that she was to be buried in the town's cemetery. I had a week to wait. So I decided to dig my shaft for a week and toss my strong box down it when I watched her coffin being lowered.

A week went silently by, save for the boring of a great hole and the vague noise from the outside world. I was asked what I wanted on the gravestone. I gave the bare facts. That would have to do. What else had she deserved?

Presently I found myself sitting on the front seat of John's car and was conveyed back to the town where I grew up. Even as I came down the hill I could smell the despair. All Legs was somewhere down there close to the five fingers, cheerfully selling his life away, bonking everything in a skirt to give meaning to his pathetic existence. The car descended ever lower, down into the streets I knew so well. Nothing had changed. There had not been time for it to do so of course.

John pulled up outside the church. My church. Here at least was a haven. Here I had once found an oasis of peace and beauty in a world turned ugly. I was glad to go in here. We were early but the organist was there, playing a quiet piece and filling the belly of the church with a whisper of reedy calmness. I bowed my head as I sat in a pew near to the front. I vaguely recall John and Ellie sitting beside me. Anyone looking would have assumed I was praying. Instead I just wanted go to sleep. The week had tired me beyond belief and sensing this John and Ellie wrapped me in their love. A noise at the back made me sit up quickly and take notice. Craning my neck round I could see six men in black walking two abreast with a large black box resting on their shoulders. It was she.

Slowly the cortege passed by me on its way to the top of the aisle near the steps that led into the choir stalls. How ironic that this would be the only time we would be in this hallowed place together. The service began. A meaningless talk commenced, followed by a hymn. Then there flowed more talk, hypnotic. It was all nonsense, words created by people who had not a clue about the corpse in the coffin. Words that tried to justify her time on earth as a time spent in worthwhile pursuits.

"... and a loving mother to Daniel, her only son."

They could not even get my name right.

I tried to imagine what she looked like now. I fancied that there was a deep laceration round her neck. God knows I had often wanted to get my hands round that neck in my latter days at home and to squeeze just as tightly as the thing that she had used to kill herself.

There were readings. John did one on my behalf. He had written it especially for the day. I think it was his way of supporting me in what he saw as my hour of need. I am sorry to say that I did not listen to a word of it. Afterwards he gave me the typed-out piece of paper. I read the first line and folded it up again. I often find myself wondering how the rest of it went. All I can recall is the first line:

"A man finally reached the end of his life and looked back along the road he had travelled."

The rest of the service caused me to feel increasingly upset. I found myself crying - crying softly so as not to be noticed. I could not understand myself. After all I hated her and here I was crying. It did not make sense. Maybe it was something to do with the trouble John had taken writing my piece. How long he had spent typing it I could not say, but he had done it just for me, only for me. That he should have been so giving was more than I was used to. No one ever did things for Davy boy as a rule. Or was it nerves. My heart was full of a deeper sadness than the death of a mother whom I was glad never to see again. Perhaps it was that by hating her with such a passion some of the good had died in me. Somewhere in a recess of my own soul I was grieving for a special part of myself. There was also a bit of me in that coffin, part of my kindness. I had heard often enough that it was right to forgive. I could not let myself do it. I could see that forgiveness was as good for the forgiver as it was for the person forgiven, but it would not come and the hate remained, growing like a cancer. Something of heaven had been lost and something of hell had replaced it.

Outside in the cemetery it was warm. The coffin sank into the hole. I was the first to lob a muck-bomb down there. It fragmented noisily in all directions as it impacted against the wooden lid. I wanted to follow it with a gob of spit but thought better of it, there being some of her work-mates present, dehumanised individuals who did not give me the time of day. I pictured in my mind my strong box being lowered into the great hole that I too had prepared within myself. A new life would emerge I felt from this point onwards but it was not as easy as I would have liked breaking away from the past. So I just took in the final images of the coffin at the bottom of the grave and wondered just what kind of David Harper would walk away.

After what seemed like a lifetime I wandered off to be by myself for a moment. As John's typed out sheet of paper dropped from my grasp onto the spreading plants at my feet in the garden of remembrance I cried my heart out at what I was going to become.

Chapter nine: Driven

"It's very flat," I said to Alan sitting beside me.

"Needed to be," said Alan, "for the bombers, during the war you know."

I could see the remains of a runway, great slabs of uneven concrete strewn with stones and broken rocks. They went a long way did these slabs, the edges of each one outlined by tall, healthy-looking weeds and grasses that waved knowingly in the wind.

"Must have been a sight to see them come in to land here and listen to the wheels screech on the runway."

"You just put your mind to that bloody wheel," he said nodding towards the steering column.

It was my first day back at work after the funeral. A week had passed. There was nothing to be gained by moping about all day. I was bored. I had decided that my dark ages were behind me. I had even managed to put the bad times into a compartment, a life compartment. A compartment that was over, gone, vanished all except for the dreams - but maybe they would go one day. So I looked down at the gear stick on my left and rocked it from side to side to check.

"Neutral," I said, smiling at a mildly apprehensive Mexican-looking face.

Mr Saltby had been kind to me. It was he who had given Alan and me permission to leave work early so that I could have a go at driving. We both left the shop at four in the afternoon and Alan drove me down to Winthorpe aerodrome in his red Volkswagen Beetle. For the first ten minutes he demonstrated how to move forwards. Up and down the bumpy runway we went, with me under strict instruction to keep an eye on his master's feet.

Now it was my turn. I was grinning like a demented imbecile. I had no idea why. I must have looked a complete fool.

"Right. Clutch pedal down."

Down it went.

"Remember how to get first gear?" Alan reminded.

I did. That bit was easy.

"Now, here's the idea. Slight bit of pressure with the right foot."

Just as commanded I made the engine rev into a scream.

"No, no, no! Not so much! Not so much! Just a slight pressure," screamed my instructor in unison with the thrashing pistons.

I yanked my foot off and tried again. This time I pushed gently. The engine's hum increased slightly.

"Okay, good. Now this is the moment," said Alan looking worried. "Look ahead, and very slowly, lift your left foot off the pedal. Very slowly, don't rush it."

With the reflexes of a sloth, I lifted the pedal upwards. Nothing happened, so I lifted further and further and then, I felt it. Something was connecting. The engine was labouring slightly. I could feel myself moving forwards.

"Good, good, keep it up, slightly more on the accelerator. Take your time."

I did take my time. With a sense of fulfilment I had become a driver. I was rolling along the runway, in first gear, travelling at twelve miles per hour with the engine in the back protesting that I shift to second. We had gone about fifty yards and I was feeling great. The engine was not. The four-stroke was having one - a stroke I mean. I could feel Alan's concern for his car as if I had been given the gift of telepathy.

"Right foot off the pedal, lift it off, that's right," he urged, trying to hide his agitation.

The engine calmed. So did Alan. With reduced nervousness he got me to depress the clutch and return the gear stick to neutral. There was a quiet sigh from my instructor as we continued to roll forwards out of gear.

"Good. Now feel for the middle pedal, the brake. Move your right foot onto the brake."

So I lifted my foot as he said and pushed the pedal right down. A human being travelling at twelve miles per hour collects quite a momentum. My instantaneous stop caused us both to shoot forwards at that very speed. My forehead smacked into the steering wheel. Alan's nose hit the dashboard. It took no time for the blood to flow. His eyes were screwed up ready for the pain to come. It soon arrived and he let out a yell.

"Fucking hell, you stupid fart. I didn't mean that fast. I said take your time. God, how stupid can you get?"

It is amazing how I managed to do things so calmly. I got out of the car, its engine still ticking over and walked a short few steps along the old runway. The disused airstrip was littered with bits of concrete and debris. I chose a lump about the size of a coconut. The windscreen turned into a mass of white particles as it struck. I could hear the incredulous voice of protest emanating from within the car as another chunk blasted the passenger window as I stalked round to that side. This time a gaping hole was created, revealing the bloodied face of a shocked Alan Dixon. I bent down and took hold of a third missile and cocked my arm ready to fling it at his face.

"Don't ever call me stupid," I said.

Alan's face tried to form a word. I raised my voice a notch.

"Don't ever call me stupid. Do you understand?"

The shock in Alan's eyes glazed over into a rage. My heartbeat quickened. He flung the door open and rushed me. The lump of concrete was released. It hit his shoulder. I picked up another. There was plenty about.

"You're fucking barmy," said Alan. "You're a complete nutter. Look at my car. I was doing you a favour today. You want locking up."

"Never call me stupid," I repeated.

"No, you're worse than stupid," and he turned about, got back into his car, punched a hole in the windscreen so he could see where he was going and sped off like a demon.

As the sound of the Beetle's engine merged into the hum of the traffic on the A46, I found myself standing alone holding onto the rock, abandoned to the unfettered wind that flew alongside the ghosts of the old air base. The rock fell beside me and I began to walk towards the gate, along the lane to the roundabout and followed the signs for Newark.

"Never call me stupid," I kept on repeating to myself.

There were spits of rain in the air by the time I reached the town. I passed Saltbys without calling in to collect my sandwich box and continued on past the library and the castle towards the bus station. I felt tired. It had been a long walk along the monotonous, straight-as-a-die stretch of the Old Fosse Way from the aerodrome. I could easily have gone to sleep on the bus as it wended its way back through a darkening landscape to Edlington. By the time I reached Southwell the rain had become heavier. The water droplets that rushed diagonally down the windows of the bus distorted the view of the passing Minster. I was not interested in the brooding shape of the building. It was all I could do to lay my tired head on the cold glass to try and ease my headache.

Ellie could sense that I was out of sorts the minute she saw me but she was ahead of the game and her concern stemmed from a phone call that had passed between Mr Saltby and her earlier. Alan had arrived back at work in a blind rage. Everyone had seen the damage to his car. Old man Saltby had even driven up to Winthorpe to take me back only to find me gone. He probably passed me going the other way into town. Even the police had been called though they had done nothing definite about it as yet.

John had immediately left for Newark on hearing Ellie's news, having only just arrived home from there himself. It was all a mess. A mess that I just wanted to walk away from. Talking only made me stare at the trouble I had caused. I had caused? What was I thinking? It was Alan who called me stupid. I had not been the cause. No one was going to do that to me again. He only had himself to blame. So I satisfied myself that here was the only way to view things. There was no need to verbalise it any further. Even as Ellie pressed me for an explanation I sat quietly at the table wishing her kindly voiced words would stop. I was too tired anyhow to move my mouth to speak. So I got up and went silently to bed, hungry and exhausted. It was time for the dreams to torment me instead.

As it happened my night was torment free. I was woken by the sound of talking coming from the next room. The hands of the clock on my bedside table stood opposite each other. It was six in the morning. The voices were those of John and Ellie. No one was shouting but I could tell that an argument was taking place. I tried to listen for words, but all I could make out was a man's voice, calm but forceful, and Ellie's higher tone, returning replies charged with feeling. I came away from the wall and sat back on my bed. I felt as if I was in the way. Not in the same fashion as I had done with mother, but in a way, a burden.

Breakfast was a quiet, atmospheric meal. John patted my shoulder like someone pats a dog before it is put down. Ellie tried to smile but could not. I set off for Saltbys knowing that there were forces at work that I did not understand and it unnerved me. Even as I strolled down Castlegate from the terminus towards the shop I knew that I was in for some sort of trouble. I knew that I had to face up to it - but I had been given a hard time by a past master - or should that be a mistress? There was nothing any of them could do to me that was capable of outclassing mother's reprimanding skills. No one could ever hurt me like she had done. Even if they gave me the sack, it would mean nothing. They could stick their poxy job. Joe was the first to see me. His normal smile was gone and his face reflected the mood of the entire staff and his air of concern he felt for me.

"Boss wants you," was all he said as I walked past him on my way to the rickety office.

It was a long walk to the glass room, like the walk to the gallows. Heart pounding, knees weak, adrenaline racing, I felt pathetic for it to have got to me like it had. I prepared myself for the abuse, the barrage of tongue-lashing. I knocked. I was invited in. His voice, Saltby's, betrayed nothing of anger or harshness. That surprised me. I walked in ready for whatever was about to be meted out to me.

"Sit down Davy lad. I think we ought to have a little talk, don't you?"

I sat down. Mother had done this before, been nice so she could attack me while I was nudged off balance. I braced myself.

"I don't think you're a bad lad, Davy, old son. You've just been through a bad time lately, haven't you?"

I nodded agreement.

"But we can't have you damaging other people's property can we?"

Like a puppet I shook my head this time, gulped and said no we could not.

"Mr Dixon's having to get new glass put in his car. It's going to cost a few quid, is that," I looked old man Saltby in the face. "Aye lad, it'll be a tidy sum. And I'm afraid it'll have to come out of your wages."

"How much?" I asked.

"Don't know yet. He's down the scrap yard now. He's not happy, Alan isn't and I can't have unpleasantness here at work. You're going to have to get along with him if you're to stay here. I want you to apologise. I want to see you two shake hands."

I was being shamed into this, belittled. I stared at the floor unable to speak. He wanted me to say sorry - sorry to a man who had called me stupid.

"Don't worry lad. I've spoken to Alan. I've explained about your recent family upset, and he's going to let bygones be bygones. But listen my lad," his voice put on its office of authority, "I don't want a repeat of this to happen in work's time ever again, never in fact, anywhere else either come to that. You've got to have respect for other people's things," the friendly voice returned. "You know what I mean, don't you David?"

I nodded again.

"Well then, off you go. I'll give you a shout when Alan gets back. We'll sort things out then, okay?"

"I said okay and shut the office door behind me. Joe was still there with a questioning look on his face. He drew a dagger-like index finger, slashing it across his throat, making his question more defined. I shook my head in reply. He stuck a thumb up and broke into a smile. I felt a little better.

In the mess room a brew was underway. Helen, one of the two office girls was there with Maisey Dilley making the tea. Helen was a couple of years older than I was. She had never been nosy but she always made me believe that she took an interest in me. Maisey took the tray containing the tea and biscuits for Mr S, leaving Helen and I alone to pour out our morning drinks.

"Will you miss me then?" she said.

Her voice was small, yet refined and certainly not local. It was a voice that had an honest ring to it, imitating how she was in person. Her apparent fragility seemed strangely at odds with her natural vigour, giving the impression of an inner strength and not fragile at all.

"Miss you?" I replied, "I didn't know you were leaving?"

"I thought everyone knew," she said, surprised. "I'm off to Uni, to Bristol."

"Uni, you mean university?"

"Of course, university," she laughed. "Sorry, I thought you'd been told."

"No one said anything about you and university. I hated school," I said, casting my mind back a few weeks and the years that preceded them. "Hated it."

"Uni will be nothing like school."

"So what are you doing here?"

"Saltbys? Oh this is just to get a bit of money together. Pad out my grant, you know?"

I did not know but nodded as if I did all the same.

"What are you going to learn there then? How to be a professor or something?"

"Psychiatric medicine. One of my A levels was psychology."

"Oh," I said, feeling out of my depth, "like a doctor then?"

"Something like that," she said.

I could tell she knew I was unable to talk to her on her level. I even detected a hint of embarrassment coming from her because of it. She took a slurp of tea and then looked directly at me.

"My mum died six months ago. She had cancer. So you see, you're not alone you know. You're getting on with your life as best you can," she said. "That's the best you can hope for, isn't it?"

She took another sip and left for her office. I think I heard an invitation to talk if I wanted to. I even wondered if I should take her up on it. I decided not to and went to sweep up outside and clean up the shop front instead, ready for the day to begin.

That's how every day began at Saltbys over the next two years, sweeping down the front. A whole host of Helens came and went, too many for me to remember their names. Most of them arrived from school. They usually left to go on to bigger and better things whilst I carried on sweeping the front and learning from Joe how to screw the customers.

Joe and I made a great team. I would listen to him in full flight with his sales chatter and I would go out and find as many items connected with whatever he was talking about, bring it out front and pretend to create a display out of it. Joe would pick up on the shop's latest exhibits and use his talents to link into these items. It usually worked and the farmers would have us loading their vehicles thinking that they had decided to buy all these extra purchases without prompting.

His greatest attribute, if you can call it that, was one of tolerance, almost indifference. He never judged me. Then again he never advised me. He neither hindered nor helped. A lot of the time he was just a plain miserable bastard who, without fanfare, could sell sand to the Arabs and who drank to cloud the view of his life. I liked the idea of making a mist obscure the view of my own pointless existence. The lunchtime drinking sessions began to flourish. They flourished to such a point that even at three in the afternoon I was still partly pissed. Worst of all people were beginning to notice.

The only benefit to this state of inebriation was that I too began to try out Joe's tricks. Selling, as I learned, was a theatrical process on the one hand and controlled on the other by an acute listening ear. I slowly developed my own selling style as I became more and more educated in the field of agriculture, if I can use such a pun. My way of selling was more conversational. I must have sounded naive at first, I certainly looked it, but my knowledge of farm machinery and the business of farming grew by degrees. I would read everything I could get my hands on. Ransomes had a wide range of sales literature with particulars on tillorators, subsoilers, sprayers and drills. When it was quiet I would leave Joe and his mood swings and read up on disc harrows and cultivators.

Ploughs were a different matter. To me they seemed full of evil and menace. To be honest a great deal of farm equipment had that effect on me. Much of it had the appearance of being built for torture. Great claws emerged from them to rip open the earth, razor like wheels arranged in rows to slice it.

Mr Saltby noticed my keen interest. He even took time away from his own work to explain how things operated. He took me to the yard at the back and showed me flail cutters and forage harvesters. He knew all about what a hydra ditcher did. He had grown up with agriculture. Saltbys was a family firm and, even though he was the top man, he had decided to take me under his wing and help me flourish. Little by little I became a bit of an authority in my chosen subject, able to quote from the simple brochures of companies like Barfords of Belton, and Bamfords of Uttoxeter. I remembered the lot. There was the Derbyshire firm of Ogle and Sons renowned for their manure distributors. Mr S introduced me to Howard Janes the spares manager at Martin-Markham of Stamford. I even met one of the directors of Ransomes, Sims & Jefferies Limited. So I knew people. I felt as if I was going up in the world and, for the first time, took a sip from the cup of pride.

All this helped me become better than Joe. Joe with his little tricks of the trade. I took the trouble to learn the trade itself and slowly left his conjuring stunts behind. I would appeal to my customers' sense of pride and impress them with my understanding of their requirements. I found my way into their egos. It was not done in a sycophantic kind

294

of way, nor was I overtly lavish in big-headedness. The whole thing was carried out like a friendly chat. I would explore how they conducted their business and pick out what I considered to be their particular forte. I sold a new flexible harrow that way.

White Farm, near Southwell always had fields finished to perfection after the ploughing was done. I would see them all nice and flat, but achieved with antiquated equipment. It took the farmhands ages to do it. Old man Wells' chest puffed out with delight as I waxed lyrical about how perfect they looked in the early morn, as I bussed it to work. Of course the new harrow would cost but it was wider and more efficient than his old one, made as it was of harder steel. So no breakdowns and fewer trips up and down those twelve fields he had. Think of the savings in diesel I told him, drivers' wages and not to mention the billiard-table finish the fields would have. Best fields in the county they would be, the envy of all Nottinghamshire. A week later he sought me out and bought one, a Bamford model. It had 81 tines, came in three sections and folded up hydraulically. His bank had agreed to stump up the cash required, £503.00. Mr Saltby gave me a rise on the strength of it. It was the first time I felt that I was becoming good at something.

I found a perverse pleasure in watching Joe Witherspoon wither away too. His chancer-like sales had seemed like a kind of magic when I first arrived. I suppose I even looked up to him in the early days like a kind of mentor. The cockiness that emerged from his sullen character became lame with time and his clever tactics, once uncovered, were not that clever in the end. It was just good old-fashioned ripping customers off, that is what it was. What had at first seemed an art form slowly took on the performance of a cheap sideshow. I was even able to put more drink away than he could at lunchtime and who cared if I went back somewhat inebriate? Who could reprimand me for reading up on fertiliser broadcasters? What better disguise could there be than to use an hour's research as my cover story for sobering up, especially when it was having such devastating results on Joe's reputation as the master salesman?

I had never appreciated the value of studying before. In my other life my schoolbooks always had a tenuous grip on reality. Kings and queens of England had had their life and whatever they had done with their time on earth made no sense to me in mine - but here, in the pages of these price lists and product information booklets, there was power. Being knowledgeable about the things that mattered to our farmer customers not only made me look good, it was good for Saltbys too. Joe began to lose heart. He stopped keeping up with me. Maybe he hated the competition. Our once shared drinking at dinnertime became individual to each of us too. He would take his midday break earlier or later than me and, as friends, if such a term can be used in connection with our relationship, we followed separate paths, the gap between us getting wider all the time.

The idea that I could beat him like this had a slow gestation period. Being proficient at anything was a novelty to me and its existence, as a concept, kept my attention focussed at the beginning. Very gradually I came to see that I could use this gift to crush someone else's spirit. After years and years of being the victim, I woke up to the idea that I could wield power over another soul instead. After each large sale I had engineered, I would find ways to make Joe feel inferior with innocent remarks that were anything other than that. I could tell that it was working just by his eyes. No matter how pleased he said he was for me, I could tell it was shrivelling him up inside. I knew that feeling so well in myself and I could detect it a mile off in someone else. Even as I knew very deep down that I should have felt a sense of pity for him, it was rewarding to watch another human being suffer from it, as I had, and even better, because I had brought it about myself. In my mind I had God-like powers. God-like. I was unstoppable. Joe had to be destroyed. He would be my trophy that would stand as a testimony that I was not stupid after all.

Like the pile driver that I had become Joe was hammered deeper and deeper into his inner despair. Not that I went out to make an exhibition of my domination over him, no, it was done much more subtly than that. An opportunity arrived one morning that fitted the bill perfectly. I cannot remember what it was that I sold. I think it was a request for spares for a seed drill. Whatever the customer wanted we did not have it in stock. So I priced up two quotes from different suppliers, asked Mr Saltby to check my sums and wrote a letter describing the benefits, as I saw them, of each manufacturer's product. I popped in some sales particulars and said that I would be glad to get a lift out to Temple Farm to be of further help. Once you have convinced yourself that you are important, that is it, you are, even if you are a young chap at the bottom of the ladder. Self-delusion is almost undetectable in the self-deluded and even dangerous when it becomes self-fulfilling.

Well, my correspondence must have made an impression on the customer. In addition to giving us an order, he wrote a letter that glorified my care and attention to his enquiry. It was a letter of praise like I had never known before, and Mr S, after patting me on the back, made a Xerox copy of it on his new machine. I asked for two copies so that I could give one to John and Ellie, but one copy was strategically placed on Joe's counter. I waited and eventually he read it. I rejoiced as I watched him heave out a tired sigh. Nothing personal Joe but who looks stupid now, I thought? It was another puncture in his self-esteem. It was perfect.

Joe's place in the hierarchy had been a comfortable one, if perhaps not completely fulfilling. Now that had become a thing of the past. He hated coming into work. He even lost interest in himself, forgetting to shave and paying little if no attention to how he looked, hair a mess and all that. People at The Elizabethan who knew both of us said that in the evenings he would drink past the point of excess. There had been times when he had to be escorted outside. There was talk of banning him altogether. He would eff and blind about his job, but his most severe expletives would be reserved for me. I looked shocked, even upset as I was told all this, but it was music to my ears. It was proof positive that I was really getting to him.

The final blow came one Wednesday afternoon. It was more of an anti-climax actually than a finale. I had just put the phone down. I cannot even recall to whom I was speaking, but I must have had a smile on my face. The next thing I can remember is Joe racing towards me with a shovel in his grip, shouting that he was going to wipe my grin to the back of my head. Then there was a great shriek from his screwed-up features as he let fly with the shovel like an axe murderer. I had a fraction of a second to duck. I ducked. The shovel sliced over my head and across the desk where the phone stood. With a crash and the clattering ring from the phone's bell, papers, pens and files exploded in all directions around the showroom. He lifted his weapon above his head to bring it down upon my head as I crouched on the floor. A fat fist grabbed hold of it from behind before it had chance to make its fatal strike, then Eric's other fist hit Joe in the chin and knocked him out.

Maisey went to fetch some smelling salts from the Red Cross cabinet and brought him round after he was propped in a chair. Mr Saltby had heard the commotion and was now waiting for his demented worker to cough himself fully into consciousness. As he began to get a grip on reality, I was tenderly asked what had happened. All I could say that was that for no apparent reason Mr Witherspoon had charged at me with a spade. I said I thought I could smell drink on his breath. I could not, of course, but it was a safe bet that it was there.

As soon as he confirmed his name and proved that he could understand what was being said to him, Joe was fired on the spot, dismissed with a broadside from Mr Saltby who had taken on the character of Winston Churchill. Eric, taking his cue from the boss saw to it that he was driven forcibly from the building.

"You all right lad?" asked the Mr S.

"Shaken, that's all," I said, then after a momentary flashback, I murmured. "I thought he was going to kill me."

"Aye, well I wouldn't dwell on that youth. Can you stand up?"

"I should report him for that," I said, not listening, but feeling mad.

"Report him?"

"Aye, report him. I'll tell the bloody police about this. Attempted murder that was. He could have killed me. I could be dead now."

"No, no, no. I wouldn't bother. No, it needn't come to that," he said as he helped me to his office, closing the door behind him. "We don't want to start feeding the gossipmongers, do we? What would be the point of all that unpleasantness?"

"Publicity," I said, quoting the obvious. "What you're on about is publicity, aren't you? The bad sort."

"Well, quite," he replied.

"I'm within my rights, you know. I'm within my rights to get compensation for this if I go to the police."

"I'm within my rights to give you a rise and a promotion. So it's either that or see Mr Witherspoon get off with a fine from the magistrate and you come off the worse for it. The choice is yours but I know what I'd do?"

"Double my wages you mean?"

"How about Chief Stockman and an extra fiver in your wage packet?"

"Make it a tenner and driving lessons?"

"Seven pounds fifty pence, and ten free lessons, but we'll keep today's unpleasantness to ourselves. What do you say?"

"Agreed," I said, smiling.

"Good lad," said Saltby.

Good lad, I thought to myself?

So why did I not feel happy about it like I should have done? I just felt bad. Something was missing, something in me. Something gone.

Chapter ten: She

He was a painfully frail man. His glasses came from a National Health spectacle museum of the fifties, so it seemed. His dark blue suit was old and displayed a shine that betrayed its constant employment. For the past forty minutes he had spoken to me in the same monotone voice, void of excitement or interest. He was a boring old fart. Only now did he allow any feeling to emanate from whatever soul existed within him.

"Well done, Mr Harper. You have passed the test as laid out by the Ministry of Transport. Please sign here."

I signed on the line. I had a licence. Ten lessons, that is all it took. See, I was not stupid. Anyway, John was waiting outside the test centre as I left. I prepared a little game for him if I had managed to pass. I would walk up to him with a grave expression and he would say, never mind, there's always next time. Then I would grin from ear to ear and surprise him. Only the smile on my face would not go away. I tried to pull the corners of my mouth down which only made me look deformed so I gave up. It was a cliché anyway.

I waved the piece of paper and John leapt out of the car and shook my hand. From a long way down inside me I could hear a faint whisper that wished it could have been my mum. The whisper wanted her to see this, the mum I knew before she went funny. John's invitation for me to drive us both home boomed over the niggling whisper. Like a national anthem drowning out one dissenting voice it became lost once more. I was excited this time. I was going to drive in a real car, not the rickety old Mini I had my lessons in. No, I was to drive a man's car.

Here was an altogether new experience. John had a Rover. Only now could I appreciate the luxuriousness of it. The steering wheel was wrapped in leather, laced up around the inner rim. The dashboard was made of polished wood. Walnut, I think John said. The seats were plush, the kind you sank into. It even had an exotic aroma of leather that filled the interior and set your state of mind. What I remember most is the clear distinction between this vehicle and the one I had learned to drive in. It was bigger, better, more sophisticated and, as I turned the key, I could tell that it was more powerful. The engine had a deep throaty growl to it. The pedals were not stiff like the ones I had become used to. I was aware that I would have to treat the controls much more gently, and I did, more easily than expected. I managed to drive home to Edlington without mishap.

Ellie was standing at the end of the drive when we arrived, waiting expectantly. I could make her out in her white apron even at the far end of the lane. The moment she saw the person at the wheel she raised her hands to her face as if she was struck dumb. Slowing down as we drew closer I could see her wiping away tears with the corner of her apron. We stopped and I clicked the handbrake through its ratchet.

I could see something was wrong. John jumped out to go over to her after mumbling well done to me. I turned off the engine and raced over, following John to see what the matter was. Women do this and I need not have worried. Ellie was just overcome at seeing me doing the driving. She understood the significance of her husband being the passenger. We held one another tightly, each knowing what we had had to live through to enjoy this moment. I cried too, quietly, buried deep in her safe embrace.

After tea, I helped put the Rover away and there, at the far end of the garage, were the two bikes that belonged to John and me. In a quiet moment, by myself, I took a good long look at the bicycle I had stolen. Each of its two spoke-laced wheels had carried me on that day when I propelled myself the long, long way to this house. It sounds idiotic I know, but I found myself blessing those wheels and the saddle that I sat upon - the saddle that had cut off the blood to my genitals. I cocked my leg over the crossbar, sat down, and gripped the handlebars. The feeling came over me again just as it had that day. The sensation had been so slight all those weeks ago that I ignored it. I was too busy not getting lost to pay it much attention, except for noting it at the back of my mind. But here, in this dusty garage, in the peace and quiet, in the dark, I could feel it, a resonance. Just holding my body in this position was enough to release it like a faint catch of a fragrance. It was something about being a cyclist. I recalled the scream I could hear across the lake, the night I sat against St. Peter's church and the prayer that had risen up the walls. It was a similar kind of thing. There was no noise, no scream but this feeling came from the same place. I was convinced that God was talking to me. Was he telling me to return the bicycle? I jumped off, afraid of the emotion, if that is what it was and I went outside into the evening air. The feeling went, leaving only its memory.

That memory, the feeling's spirit, tagged along with me all evening like a lost dog might follow a stranger intent on securing a home. As I drifted off to sleep it trickled into my dreams. Dreams of hard work, cycling up hill, up hill to an odd place, a far away place, miles from anywhere. It was a collection of dwellings, not unlike Edlington, but more compacted. The dream wanted me to look around. It wanted me to see a church on a hill. I was transported there, where I met a terrifying elderly woman. Her face became distorted as she pointed to the way I had arrived and commanded me to leave. So I tried. I tried but my bicycle was nowhere to be seen. Other women gathered around her. All of them were old. One was my mother, her face deformed by rage and bitterness. I was terrified. They chased me to an old house. A house that was deformed like their faces. The first old woman dared me to enter and, as the door creaked open by itself, I awoke and sat bolt upright.

Damn these dreams. They were like the harpies that tormented Phineus. Like the blind man that he was I was unable to see the meaning of these pernicious visions, consistent visions. I tried to unravel the significance of the old house. How I knew that it had once known happiness, I have no idea. The dream carried this knowledge within it. That is the only explanation I can offer, but I never had peaceful dreams. Not like the ones other people recounted. Mine were recurrent, or at least the theme was. There was always a village with a church on a hill and this bloody house. I was getting tired of it. It was bad enough being deprived of sleep every other night. I understood what it meant to be haunted. To be hounded by something terrible. This was a haunting of a kind, a haunting of the head. Like ghosts tormenting my mind.

Now four years have passed. Blink your eye. It seems that fast. It seems that fast to me. I have met someone, or rather she has met me. Of course, I am looking back reminiscing about a long, hot summer and Gwen. Her name was Gwen. She was from Colwyn Bay originally, North Wales, lovely accent. I could listen to it forever. She said that she wanted to get to know me. Why she wanted to do that had more to do with her than anything particularly interesting about me. From the outset she had given herself an uphill task because by now I had created the empire. There was no way she was going to find a way through the defences that had been meticulously contrived in the empire.

My initial defensive walls were crude affairs. They had served to protect me against mother and the things she had said and done to me. Inside those walls there was but a spartan place for me to hide. It had unnerved me how easily John had been able to gain access to the inner me. I knew that I needed a place to dwell. A place within me where I would be able to relax, in comfort, to be able to grow, safe in the knowledge that no one could storm my protective shield.

To ensure that I could develop and grow I had now fashioned something that, in my mind's eye, looked like Hitler's Atlantic wall. Great imaginary guns looked out towards any advancing enemy who dared to approach. Inside the empire, as I called it, I had created a kind of government, complete with laws and a congress for the meeting of various areas of my mind. Finance featured quite heavily as did career advancement, even personal matters. At home under my bed I had a red, hard-backed exercise book. I kept a record of all the major decisions and how they had been made. My empire was not just defensive. On the contrary, it was capable of attacking too. I would give no quarter. My troops were ruthless in assaulting anyone who was stupid enough to get in my way - the empire's way. It was a secret, the empire. No one would have understood it. Since something so crucial to the health of my mind was not to be ridiculed, I laid down laws akin to the *Official Secrets Act*. Gwen was keen to delve into the inner me only to be thwarted at every turn. I was invincible.

Gwen Jones was a born-again Christian, a term she tried to explain to me. Her religion filled her whole being. There was something scary about it. I disliked the jamboree-style of worship she took part in. I saw it once on an invitation to her church, the Pentecostal something or other. I was unable to find any beauty in it, no beauty at all. My heart once soared to God on the wings of anthems and choral psalms. How could masses of hand clappers compare with that? It seemed cheap and I never went again.

Gwen persisted though. She was very persistent, with a mind full of theological theories. I just thought she had a luxurious way of speaking and a slim figure. Her body was sculpted to perfection, especially her upper body. I was twenty years old by now. Not far off twenty-one in fact. She was nineteen. We met outside The Elizabethan after I had my lunch one baking hot day. She was with a group of the churchies as I used to call them. They wanted to get to know me too. It was only on account of Gwen's looks that I stopped to talk to them at all. I was in a hurry to get back to work so I promised to see her the following lunchtime if she wanted to. Surprisingly, the next day, she was waiting for me. We went inside and I fell for the soft Welsh lilt.

Whenever she finished speaking and stopped to listen to me I would behold her. She had a wonderful way of holding her mouth. Her lips were like advertisements, tempting me with pleasures -

pleasures that I could never enjoy. Any urges I felt were confused by a stronger sense of revulsion. So anything like that seemed forbidden to me. I was repulsed by the thought of kissing. Mother had put paid to that. I knew that I was supposed to like it. The whole world was supposed to like kissing and what came after. The best analogy I have is, if you can imagine a car engine where most of the parts are bent or twisted, broken even. Only these parts are hidden inside the machine, so from the outside all looks well. So whether you want the engine to start or not, even if you feel the urge to switch on the ignition, you know that nothing will happen. The likelihood is that more damage will occur if by some miracle it did start. That is what it would be like for me to kiss a girl. Even if I wanted to and there was a voice telling me it would be right, the voice of revulsion would crash in like a dictator and I would be paralysed. I knew what it would be like all too well. I knew it would be just like it was when she had done it to me. None of that was to be resurrected. No, I was content just to listen to the girl from Colwyn Bay and let her mesmerise me with her Welsh voice, no matter what rubbish she was talking about.

"You 'ave to open your heart to God see, and let Jesus in," she would insist.

"And how do you know that he's not already there?" I would say.

"Well you don't seem very 'appy. Is it sin you're worried about?"

The guns were loaded and ready - ready to fire if she so much as suggested that I might have sins buried away, or probe into what they might be.

"How can you tell that I'm unhappy then? Where's your proof?"

"Your face looks sad. It is the burden of sin, isn't it? Look, Jesus will take away all your sins."

"I already believe in God. I might not understand it all, but I know that *the dear Lord was crucified, who died to save us all,*" I countered, quoting part of my favourite hymn.

"So why do you seem so 'ard, like. You have an 'ard streak you. That's why I want to help, see?"

"Stop talking crap then and I might just give you a smile," I said, knowing it would bring her up sharp.

The beautiful mouth sank at the rebuke. Target hit.

"Would that make you 'appy?" I said, imitating her accent, making another strike.

"I just want to get to know you. What's the 'arm in that? Why do you keep me at a distance with your nasty little remarks?"

"What you see, is what you get," I said, showing off a great concrete defensive wall.

It went on like this for weeks. I became tired of it and yet I liked it. I liked the attention. I enjoyed proving that my defences worked. But God knows I was lonely, isolated and lonely. It was the bitter cost of such impregnable protection.

Why then did I accept Gwen's invite to a prayer meeting? It was to be held in a house of one of the churchies where there would be fellowship. Was it curiosity? Was it Gwen's voice? Was it that I actually liked her? To be honest she was bloody irritating and yet in a controlled manner I was allowing her to build her precious relationship. John was not terribly keen that I should go. He said that God's word could be misinterpreted. How could he know that his version of the Holy word was not already corrupted? Why was the Church of England right every time? Could it be that the churchies were any the wiser? Why did I care? I almost made up my mind to stand her up. Yet here I was, waiting uneasily at the door of number sixty-four for it to open. I did not really want it to. Why I was drawn here I could not say.

Before I had the sense to change my mind I saw someone through the textured glass of the front door. The locks clicked and it opened up to lure me into a house full of the scent of joss sticks. I was introduced to the group, a set of seven sickly individuals who looked as if a good plate of roast beef and Yorkshire pudding would not come amiss. Each of them, including dear old Gwen, had in their possession a *Bible* bound in black leather, a King James' version I assumed them to be. The owners of the house were in their fifties, thin and unfashionably dressed, not that I knew much of fashion, but I knew that they did not fit into the nineteen seventies. He was balding, wore glasses and had a stammer. She was nervous of me, a stranger in their midst. The other five were polite, very gushy, selling their friendliness as if I was a valued customer. Again there were two couples, married I presumed, each one almost emaciated. One gust of

305

wind and they would all have blown away - like health food fanatics who live on tablets and never get raw meat into their bodies. Their smiles were like masks. Only the seventh one seemed different. He was a large man, young and a slow talker. It did not take long for me to deduce that he had some kind of mental problem. He did not say much but it was plain to see that the brain of a five-year-old controlled his twenty-year-old stature. He was a boy in a man's body. That being said he seemed the most sincere of them all.

We entered a room lit by two standard lamps each of which stood in opposing corners. The room had bookshelves along the narrow wall. Volume upon volumes of Christian books stacked there. What did these people do, read about life instead of living it? We all sat on chairs that had been arranged in a circle around a coffee table in the centre of the room. No one spoke. I could only hear a clock ticking in the next room and the odd car passing by, their wheels hissing on the rain-soaked road outside. Every head was bowed. I felt like an impostor. I felt like I had made a bad decision to put myself here. I ought to have got to my feet and fled there and then. I should have fled like mad, but I was curious. So I stayed. Stayed in this strange place, gently forced, so it seemed, by the peculiar smell of incense massaging my mind with its exotic perfume. An alarm klaxon rang out in the empire. Every soldier was put on standby. Thank God that the empire was awake and doing its job. I felt ill at ease that some kind of mind takeover was being planned. Planned? It was already underway. We were under attack.

So I stole myself for what was to come, in the silence, as all nine of us sat quietly in the circle and did bugger all, with our heads bowed low. I raised my eyes to peek at them all. What idiots they all looked including Gwen. How had she been persuaded to do this? Why was she not doing what normal nineteen-year-olds were doing? How had she got caught up in this? Was I next? Never, said a voice within. We shall fight them in the prayer rooms. We shall fight them in the *Bible* classes. We shall never surrender. I was safe in the empire's stronghold.

Then a warm palm reached out to me. It was Gwen's tender hand, intertwining her fingers in mine, squeezing with a butterfly's grip. No one else saw. I tilted my head sideways to behold her face, that mouth, that provocative mouth. I liked the sensation of her hand in mine. I liked the way she looked at me. I hated how hordes of unwanted emotions were storming the outer defences of the empire. It was time for the first counter attack. I gripped her hand tightly, very tightly, our knuckles crashing together. I felt the pain myself, in the joints of my hand, so I knew she must have felt it too. It was the pain of battle. I relaxed the grip. She withdrew. My counter attack had been successful. Her face showed the pain of defeat, an expression of misunderstanding painted all over it.

Somewhere, from deep within, I missed the hand on mine, yet I had to be strong. There was no place for emotion in the empire.

"I would like Gwen to open the prayers tonight," said the owner of the house in his mouse-like voice. "Gwen?"

Gwen, still rubbing her bruised hand, coughed to clear her throat. For a moment she dwelt on what to say. Then she talked, not to us, nor to me, but to a God she loved. You could tell that the being she was in communion with, was someone she adored. Nor were her words formed in the *Book of Common Prayer*. Her words were her own, not ideas from some anonymous prayer writer from the nineteenth century. They had a simple beauty.

"Lord," she said. "Father. Help me to forgive those who have wronged me. Teach me to love the ones that would seek out to hurt me. By your example on the cross, show me that love is the way, your love, so that my persecutors may, too, learn your ways and come into your kingdom. I ask this in the name of Jesus Christ, Amen."

There was no guessing why she had prayed for that. I was the one who had hurt her. She was forgiving me. How dare she. She was supposed to have withdrawn. Now she was saying that she had been unaffected by how I pushed her away. No, it was more than that. She had ended up bigger than me, better. I began to seethe. The prayers went round in the circle, until I was the only one who had not said anything. The owner of the house invited me to offer my prayer if I wanted to, then we would adjourn to the back room for coffee and biscuits before hearing a bible reading from Adrian.

I was now in a spot. I had never learned to say prayers like they had. How could I pray like them without seeing the words written down on a page? I felt ill at ease. I felt silly to be uncomfortable in this way. I was being tested. My troops concentrated their forces on this front. How could I possibly send up a supplication to find forgiveness feeling like this, feeling under threat? I brought a battery of field guns to the ridge where this battle was being played out. Twenty, thirty, nay fifty of them, each one loaded and pointing at the forgivers down the slope, as they advanced towards my first wall of defence. My soldiers stood behind this artillery and waited for the order to open fire. The volley that rang out was in a voice louder than I would normally speak. They would all hear this.

"God, show me how to defeat my enemies," I said, sincerely hoping that God would really hear me. "Show me how to trample them underfoot."

Images of God smiting the enemies of Israel came flashing to mind. Stories from the *Old Testament* that I had once heard inspired me to continue.

"Give me the strength of David over Goliath. Give me the power to drown my foes as you did for Moses at the Red Sea. Make me invincible. Give me the power to destroy. Clothe me for battle so that I may kill those that would stand in my way. Amen."

When I had finished, I bored my gaze into each upturned face. Their looks of horror were works of art. What a victory! What an empire! Gwen's face was the best. She was open-mouthed. Overcome with embarrassment. Her eyes darted around the room, seeking absolution for bringing the leader of an alien empire into their midst. There was no sound of absolution. There was just silence. The owner of the house sighed as he searched for what to say. He had to say something and I thought he was going to pray again until he returned to my reloaded eyes and spoke to me through his stutter.

"We talk of Christ here, David. We don't talk of beating our enemies, we talk of loving them."

I had not defeated them all. One of them was still alive - this man before me. From a clear vantage point high up on my rampart walls I slung a sniper's rifle to my shoulder and took a careful aim with my finger round the trigger. Squeeze. Aim at his heart. Fire!

"I have seen love destroy people," cracked the sound of my first bullet. "I have seen what happens when the finest love is thrown into the fire. Power is what keeps this world spinning, Mr Christian, not the power of love. Just power. It had always been so. It will always be so. It is the way of things. Look around you. The evidence is everywhere. Love is an illusion. Civilisation allows this illusion to exist, man-made civilisation. Take away civilisation and we all revert to the rule of self-preservation. In the end it is the one with the greatest power who survives. David had power over Goliath, God-given power. King David went on to become a great man in God's eyes. God helped him to kill his enemies. He will help me to kill mine too," I drew my head closer to his. "You don't want to be my enemy, do you?"

"Well, no," he said.

"Then I reckon it's coffee time," I declared, as I heard my troops jumping up and down in celebration over this great event.

The empire had scored a victory. What a great feeling. Even as I felt it, I knew that it was hollow, but the music of the victor was loud and pleasing and I allowed it to take me over. I was not aware what forces in my mind were at work. Why should I have? I really thought I had been in control of everything at the battle of prayer time. There was no sign of a coup being planned as I sipped my coffee and enjoyed watching Gwen's cup come to rest against her luscious lips. I was too busy chastising myself for wanting to press my own lips against them. It was forbidden that such a thing should happen, no matter how I wanted to. The strong box at the bottom of the shaft had to remain there. Kissing Gwen would raise it up again as if by a crane, a thought too terrible to contemplate. So I stayed strong – strong, hard and very lonely.

The meeting ended at ten and I managed to reach the bus station only just in time to catch the last ride home. Even though I could drive now, John had explained that the insurance would be well beyond his means to include me on the Rover's policy. So I sat on the bus and relived the evening in my mind as we trundled through the darkness. Gwen said nothing to me as I left the house. I remembered asking how she was getting home. Someone said they were going to give her a lift. I knew a euphemism when I heard one, realising they meant to interrogate her about me. It was clear they were keen to investigate how she had misjudged her guest so badly. I imagined she would be chastised for bringing the prayer meeting into question, and I began to wonder why I was bothering about her at all.

Ellie had waited up for me when I came through the door. She asked how it had gone. I told her it was boring. She smiled almost through relief and anxious to go up to bed to tell John I would not be joining a cult. I watched a bit of television before going up to bed myself, trying to delay the run of the gauntlet the old house had in store for me. It did not disappoint. It seldom did.

As I awoke into the black space that was my bedroom and once I had calmed down, I lay staring up through the inky void and wondered how the empire could deal with this. Dreams were enemies too, pernicious, abusive. They were the one last remnant of what had been allowed to remain of the old life. There had to be a way of removing them. There had to be a solution to the problem of being haunted like this. I was tired, and I could not think. Besides, it was Tuesday tomorrow, a workday. So I turned over and tried to drift off again. There were no more dreams that night and I greeted the dawn with only a memory of it and a recollection of the need for a solution to stop them all.

The answer came a week or so later. I had given Gwen a wide berth for a while. She called me on the telephone twice in that time from a call box - once to see if I was all right and again to see if she could catch the bus over to see me. I put her off. She sounded depressed about it. I did not care. Emotions. They were as much of a nuisance as the damned dreams. A solution would have to be found for them too, and a solution was not far away, minutes in fact. I made myself a cup of hot chocolate and sat down to watch some late night telly. A series on World War 2 had been screened over the past few weeks. I watched The Battle of Britain episode. It had given me a great moral boost for my own troops. I was open to any kind of propaganda that would help strengthen my powers, and watching Spitties going head-to-head against the Luftwaffe, clothed me in a kind of invincibility. Why I missed the other programmes I cannot recall. I missed the fight through France and Germany thanks to my own battle at the prayer meeting. So I was glad to be by myself to rearm. Seeing visions of war helped my own generals become more focussed, more inspired, so the entire military of the empire was keen to learn as much as possible from part six. There was no indication as to what the theme of the episode would be, except that it was entitled *The Final Solution*. I was open to solutions, any solutions. I watched the hour-long episode unfold with growing disbelief. The whole thing was beyond comprehension.

What branded my memory the most was not so much the terrible facts but the harsh and grainy black and white moving images. Somehow, as these horrifying events actually took place, someone had managed to secrete a movie camera to the scene and point it at the naked women I saw shot in the head. I knew the flickering and badly deteriorated pictures would haunt me. It seemed as if all the evil that entered the lens of that hidden camera had splattered onto the film. Each frame of celluloid was stained with a grimy film dirtied by the atrocity before it. I knew it was down to age alone that it looked like it did, but the images were dirty nevertheless. It created the atmosphere in which the pictures had been preserved - a poisoned atmosphere. I also heard the testimonies of Eastern European people talk about what they had lived through. Photographs of massive piles of skeletons covered with thin, stretched skin seemed unbelievable. Soiled bodies left to rot. Naked. The programme revealed the inside of a gas chamber that remained intact after the war.

Looking at the television screen I was gripped by claustrophobia. I breathed the free air that I normally took for granted and felt for the millions that had once passed this way, but it was the shadows on the flickering screen that bored into my soul. Dancing images of men running to the edges of pits, the silent puff from the muzzles of rifles and the drop of limp bodies tumbling into their graves - graves that minutes before they had been made to dig themselves. I saw the remains of pieces of film showing ghastly experiments carried out in Auschwitz by Dr Mengele. There was barbed wire, railway tracks, huge crowds being selected, cattle wagons, German guards, dogs, and broken people dressed in stripes. The programme makers told the story just as it had been. There was no need to use shock tactics to grab the viewer's attention. The calm narration only served to heighten the overwhelming awfulness of what they were presenting. At the age of nearly twenty-one I learned for the first time in my life the reality of what was the Holocaust. When the programme was over and I switched off the television, I felt afraid. It seemed as if six million or more ghosts had latched on to me and would not let go.

I had never met a Jew in my life. There could not be many left to meet after what I just witnessed. I knew about Jews being the butt of jokes usually in connection with money. There were always jokes about them at school - but I could not understand this. We covered very little about the twentieth century in our history classes. We had been preoccupied with the dead and dusty past, Tudor times and beheaded queens. What I saw on the television had taken place a little over ten years before I came into the world. Much of what was screened still thrived in living memory. Somewhere there were survivors who had experienced such atrocities first hand and were still alive today. As my heart beat out its life so too did theirs. Somewhere, in this same instant, there were the perpetrators of these crimes still living. Why had one done, what I had just seen, to the other? To say that they were Jews or Gypsies was not enough. It was absurd. How could they be so unwanted? This to me did not seem like a solution at all. A solution suggests some kind of repair. This was demolition plain and simple. The questions hung in the air. They floated around in my head. For days I found myself contemplating the images of mass graves and bulldozers shovelling corpses into pits, wondering about it all, fearful of it all.

The programme had been well made. Provocative. It was made in such a way that I was able to appreciate the human heartbreak, the millions of personal stories of suffering - stories that in almost every case had been cut short. Of course I was always searching for how to use what I had seen about war to put to good use in my own life. How I was supposed to find a way of using what I just watched was beyond even me, at first, but there were forces in the empire now at work. It was they who over the next few weeks gradually made suggestions to congress and the idea of a final solution for unwanted thoughts, emotions, and dreams began to emerge in one of the backrooms of my brain.

Life passed by as usual. At work I continued to forge ahead. I was given the job of training a new stockman who had joined us to replace Witherspoon. I was no longer at the bottom of the pile and it

312

was soon to be my big day. April the tenth, nineteen seventy-seven, was going to be my twenty-first birthday. I knew that a party was being planned, but I was not supposed to have cottoned on. I played along protecting John and Ellie's feelings with my practised air of ignorance. I was good at making it look sincere.

I also let slip it was soon to be my twenty-first to Gwen. She phoned The Croft and spoke to John and Ellie whilst I was out. I later learned that she had convinced them she was not part of any cult, and that she was just a good friend who wanted to be with me on my big day. It was unfortunate that I had mentioned her name to Ellie. Without me knowing it Gwen got herself accepted as a nice girl and was added to the small list of people invited to the party.

The day dawned like any other. I had by now been conditioned into the habit of waking at six. Normally I was the first one to rise. It was usually me who went down, opened the curtains and put the kettle on. Not today. On this day, this big day, I could hear movement downstairs. The house was uncharacteristically alive already. As I crept down each stair, I became aware of humming. It was Ellie's voice. She was up to something and, guessing that it had something to do with the date, I turned quietly and headed back to bed. Whatever was going on I was not about to ruin any surprises. Surprises should be as important for the giver as they should be to the receiver, so how could I hurt her feelings? She was the only person in the whole wide world whom I loved with all my heart.

I waited, I heard clattering, then footsteps. I closed my eyes and snuggled into the sheets, trying to hide my grin. Softly the door opened. There was a quiet word, one word, couched as a question.

"Morning?" she said.

I pretended to wake. I rubbed my eyes for effect and yawned for real.

"Happy Birthday Davy," she said, smiling.

She had a tray in her arms, a tray full of proper breakfast - bacon, eggs, mushrooms and fried bread. There was even toast, hot and buttered beside a cup of tea. John had heard her voice and he followed her into my room in his pyjamas.

"Happy twenty-first," he grinned.

I drank in the love and breathed in the happiness. I had never before been granted a breakfast in bed. I sat up and tucked into it, smiling at the two lovely people who had seated themselves at the end of the bed. They chatted. It was a Sunday morning, John's busy day. He would have to fit in three Holy Communions in the three churches that he cared for. I could tell that today, his heart was not in it as much as usual. He wanted to stay with me but eventually, after his own breakfast he was off, saying that he would be a little late for lunch. A tiny spark passed between them. I just picked up on it. It was fleeting but I had noticed a minute hesitation in her reply. Something was going on, something I was not to know about. Or was it I? Was I not able to read people like books? I could spot a liar at twenty paces and I could spot a scam going on purely by the chemistry in the air. Yep, something was going on all right.

Presently we followed John to the village church to the first of his services and, although I was not yet confirmed, I joined Ellie in receiving the Holy sacraments. The church had no choir. The singing was bland and roughly hewn out of the ragged throats of the locals. John's sermon was a ragged piece of work too, designed more for the benefit of insomniacs than as instruction for the soul. My mind began to wander. It began to wander inwards. It was the planned order of the Eucharist however that I picked up on. Its order made my thoughts come together. The Sunday Service had survived the years by having order. I came to see that the empire growing within me needed order too. It needed discipline. It needed a leader. A Fuhrer. Surely Nazi Germany had been able to create a great order by having a highly disciplined framework. Even though it had succumbed to the allies and allowed history to crush it, the ideas of strength over weakness still held true. Of all the blueprints to use to advance the empire, the one of Hitler's Nazi Party was by far the most elegant. Whatever was against it would be trampled underfoot. The empire would have a focus. It would be unbeatable. This would be the perfect day to allow it to be born - my twenty-first birthday. Today would be the birth of a new nation, a new empire. There would even be ways to exterminate emotions, weaknesses. Under this new regime

I would be able to rearm to Herculean proportions. I would be a force to be reckoned with.

Soon the service was over and I came out of my head. It was time to go home and help prepare the lunch. Apparently we were having visitors. Quite a few it seemed, judging by the amount of food there was to peel and chop. I was all right with it. This was no chore. Any amount of time spent with Ellie was time never wasted and we set to work on the vegetables and chatted as we always had about this and that and nothing at all.

The house had warmed itself through with the aromatic scents of roast beef and steamed greens by the time we heard John's car tyres crunch down the gravel drive. Two more cars followed. I heard voices, laughter. As I made for the front door I could pick out John's infectious chuckle. Another man with a deeper voice was with him joining in the joke. Even before I opened the door I recognised Mr Saltby's accent. He was talking to a female voice. It was a Welsh voice.

I flung the door open letting in the fresh April air and beheld John with a tall stocky man in a large black overcoat standing at his side. He wore steel-rimmed spectacles and carried a brown briefcase and from his face there beamed the most unappealing smile. Behind these two were, of course, Mr Saltby and Gwen. Gwen had a parcel under her arm. Mr S seemed to be empty-handed. Ellie had caught me up by now. She placed her hands, damp from cleaning, on my shoulders as she stood behind me. I could tell that she was anticipating something.

"Davy, old chap," said John, still standing on the drive with the other three, "happy twenty-first birthday. Now, we don't propose to give you the key of the door today. You've already got one. But keys do come into it, don't they Ted?"

John directed the question to my boss. It was the first time I had heard him called by his first name. I had not even known it until now.

"Yes vicar," said Mr S, "not just keys though. A bit more to it than that wouldn't you say?"

The stocky man and Gwen were seemingly electrified with some kind of expectation. Ellie tightened her grip on my shoulders. I was becoming strangely energised.

"Would you do the honours, Ted?" said John.

315

"Delighted to Your Reverence."

Mr Saltby stepped forward and told me to hold out my hand. I did. He extended his own and dropped two keys fastened to a key ring in my palm. Then he turned and pointed to a grey Morris Minor parked beside John's Rover.

"She's all yours my lad. Happy birthday."

I could hear Ellie trying to hold back sobs - sobs of joy. Feeling the keys in my grip I searched for expression. My mouth tried to form words of appreciation. None seemed adequate.

"I don't know what to say."

It was all the pathetic thanks that I could give.

"Well," said John, discerning how my heart was leaping about inside, "she's all taxed and MOTed for a year and at the moment you're on my insurance."

"I can't... I don't know... you've been..."

I felt like one of those fellows who try to begin a letter and end up with balls of screwed up paper about their feet. How could I express my wonderment, the loyalty, the affection I felt for these people? Only one word fitted.

"Wow!" I breathed softly.

Yelling it would have been vulgar. I could not do that. It was not possible to shout. I had never been allowed to. Instead I flung my body round to kiss Ellie. She was warm, alive with something akin to a mother's love, as it should have been. I felt John's hand on my shoulder, and turned to face his jovial grin. I was about to shake him by the hand when I thought better of it and flung my arms around him too. He held me like a father would have. Happy birthday. These two most appropriate words summed it up perfectly. Distant echoes of other birthdays shouted across the void of time like the voices of spirits or the chants of far away singing borne on the wind, but the past was safely locked away, surely?

"Well, how about a spin round the village before lunch, aye?" said John.

So wiping the moisture from my eyes everyone, except the stocky man, piled into the car and I drove up to Southwell and back. I was brimming with the most incredible sense of joy by the time we returned down the driveway. I got out and looked at her. I slid my hand along her curvaceous body. She may only have been a Moggy 1000 but she was mine. She was mine.

Chapter eleven: The New Testament

Mr Littlebody, the stocky man with the briefcase, turned out to be a very old friend of the family. He did not say much on account of his rather introverted personality, which considering I learned he was a solicitor seemed to me a rather surprising fact. He ate his lunch at our table as if he was performing a surgical operation, using his knife and fork with precision and chewing the food with the small teeth at the front of his mouth. Never before or since have I witnessed a person resemble a rodent as much as he did. In fact, given his size he reminded me of a giant rat. I chose to dislike him on the spot.

The meal before us on the other hand was one of Ellie's best. Roast joint of beef with attendant vegetables and a mountain of creamy mashed potatoes emerging like a newly formed island in a sea of gravy. Ellie knew this was my favourite, Sunday lunch, and she made it with love, making use also of my peeling and chopping skills along the way. There followed rhubarb pie awash with custard. I was toasted with sherry before we began. The alcohol continued with red wine, three bottles of it, something rarely seen on our table. Neither Ellie nor John had any idea how much booze I could put away and I felt slightly guilty at having to feign caution. Any showing off on this subject would have belittled their gesture. It would have taken away that something special they were trying to convey. They wanted this to be a moment. I let it be so.

Conversation flowed like a lubricant. John's past life in the East End of London was a fascinating insight into the life of a parish priest. I learned how he was given a parish in Beeston in Nottingham. After being there about ten years he was given three small parishes in rural Nottinghamshire. It was during his last year in Beeston that he met Ellie who was working in a factory there. Despite their age gap a love story unfolded and the rest was history. It was a romantic tale that became the building blocks of my salvation. I found it spellbinding to think that as I was enduring what I had, there were things happening many miles away that would have a direct and positive influence on my life. John heard about me early on in their relationship. It was he who suggested the idea of adoption, an early blueprint for the life I was leading now.

Gwen was shy in front of these new people. I liked her to be shy. I found her politeness quite becoming. I did not like loud women like the hags who worked in Ansons. What battleaxes, what witches they were - unlovely, rough and crude. Not like Gwen who behaved with an impeccably virginal air. It was that side of her that attracted me. Now and again she would slide her gaze towards me. For a while she would simply look. I looked back, not knowing what to make of it, only to find my heart rate climbing and my swallowing reflex quickening. Then she would allow a smile to be released and that mouth of hers would come alive. How could I not smile back? She had a way about her. I liked and mistrusted it with equal measure.

At some point during the meal she reached out from under her chair and passed me her parcel. All eyes were on me as I took it from her. Ripping open the paper I could see it was a leather-bound book. The sides of the pages were edged in gold. Each page was made of the lightest paper. It was a *Bible*, a King James' version, the authorised version, where holy words sounded holy. Words printed within its chapters and verses were crafted to make you stop and think about their meanings. Such a delivery of the spirit of God became lost to me when in modern versions the holy book took on the vernacular. I turned to the start. Such beauty poured out. *In the beginning, God created the heaven and the earth. And the earth was without form and void, and darkness was upon the face of the deep. And the Spirit of God moved upon the face of the waters. And God said, Let there be light. And there was light, and God saw the light, and it was good.*

She had chosen her gift with skilled premeditation. Divine intervention perhaps. John and Ellie naturally approved, John especially. Littlebody, alias Ratty, and Mr Saltby watched and smiled at the innocence of it all. I liked it instantly, knowing too that she had given me a road map into her world. It was almost like an invitation for me to share the path she trod alone, at present - but it was a step towards me too. It was a step towards my new nation, my fatherland, my empire. My mind accepted the gift with the trepidation that should have been exercised by the Trojans when the ancient Greeks offered them their gift of a giant wooden horse. She reached over to kiss me on the cheek much to the delight of those present. It must have taken such an effort on her part to do that. She must have been steeling herself for that moment to overcome her shyness. A kiss on the cheek another one of her steps closer to me, a soft invasion, an attack by stealth. I put the empire on standby. The alarm had been raised - raised just in time.

I hurriedly flicked through the pages of the bible. There was a passage in the New Testament in the gospel according to Saint John. I knew it to be the cornerstone of Christian belief. I knew it would be there but I searched it out anyway. My fingers turned the pages through to chapter three, counting the lines down to find verse sixteen. *God so loved the world that He gave his only begotten Son, that whosoever believeth in Him should not die, but have life everlasting.* It comforted me that it was there. Even in the empire there was some room for a spiritual belief. I was glad that it had not all been lost in the rebuilding. I thought about the words as we chatted over the table. *He gave his only begotten Son*, the same Son in the green hill far away, *who died to save us all.* A fragment of faith had survived.

John brought out a bottle of Cointreau and we were all treated to a small measure in a small glass. The group of us adjourned to the living room sipping the sweet, thick liqueur as we went. Ratty brought his briefcase with him. He seemed to have the thing welded to his side. Why had he been invited? There were so many other friends John and Ellie could have asked to come. It never occurred to me to question anyone they chose to invite into The Croft before, but his presence on this date had by now made me wonder.

Satisfied and full we sank into armchairs and settees. Mr S began to recount the days of his childhood. We younger ones, apparently, had never led a hard life like people in his time were forced to live through. In his day water was fetched from a well and, being in farming circles, his day would begin at three-thirty in the morning. His own father wanted him to have a true grounding in country life. He painted a picture of a slow but exhausting world, milking cows from four in the morning to bedding them down for the night at ten, locking up the cowshed to the glow of a hurricane light. He was fond of his memories now that the years had edited out the pains of his labours. As he spoke, I could understand how his character had been shaped. The kind but hardworking Mr Saltby had been made into the man he was, by the education his father before him had handed down. I enjoyed listening. I enjoyed being told stories.

Gwen sat beside me and listened too. She listened with as much interest as I did, I felt. I could sense the warmth of her body next to mine. She never did anything other than sit next to me. It was the warmth of her body that was carrying out her work for her. I glanced down to the hem of her skirt where her knees emerged, lovely knees and slender calves below. I was not allowed to want her like this. I wanted her. It was not permitted. I would have to be strong. The empire would not permit it. I dug the nail of my index finger into the top of my thumb's knuckle. I wanted the pain to take the ache away. The empire had decided I was to be punished for allowing these evil emotions to find their way up from the deep. Somehow these emotions would have to be rounded up and like the Jews they would have to be exterminated. John's announcement interrupted my thoughts.

"Well, Clive," said John to Ratty, "it's time for you to perform your little task."

John was smiling. Ellie was not. Mr Littlebody became nervous like an inexperienced soloist. He put the briefcase on his lap and took out some papers. He spent some time putting them in order whilst he mumbled to himself. Then, keeping the papers on his knee, he placed the case next to him and looked me in the eye.

"You can confirm that you are David Harper, can't you?"

I looked at John and Ellie for a clue as to what he meant by this question. John nodded as if it would be all right for me to answer.

"Yes, that's me."

"And you can confirm that your mother is," he coughed at his error, "sorry, was Charlotte Harper?"

I could not believe I had heard him right. The question hung as if a giant gong had been struck. I brought my stare to bear on the dark pupils of his eyes, his rat's eyes. With the blue cornea and dark pupil

320

they resembled targets. I took aim and fired a volley into them hoping something would impact with his soul. He swallowed hard. I was making him feel ill at ease. That name. I had never wanted to hear that name mentioned to me as long as I lived. By now my head was filling with my blood's boiling rush. I had to speak through this. Somehow, I was going to have to let some words escape before I exploded.

"Don't ever, ever mention that name again. It's cursed. Do you hear?"

"I'm sorry Mr Harper, but I must carry out my duties, or else I…"

Gwen's body was now taut. There was a transfer of anxiety from me to her. John had lost his smile. Ellie was bracing herself. Even Mr S was ready. They all knew something. I wanted to know nothing.

"You mention her name to me again, and I'll shove those papers up your fucking arse so fast they'll stick out of your mouth. Mark me. Do you understand?"

By now a panzer division had arrived at the battleground. Other reinforcements were on their way. The tanks swung their cannons towards the target, took aim and let rip.

"Do you understand?"

"What's up lad?" said Mr S. "You ain't given him a chance yet."

"No chances, not where that fucking bitch is concerned. I don't want to know what he's got to say about her."

"It's important that you listen to him Davy," said John, in his best soothing tone.

He looked shocked and taken aback. John got up and laid his hand on Ratty's shoulder. He looked as if he was in on the act. Come to think of it they all looked in on it. This was a pincer movement of the best kind but the pincer had not closed yet. There would have to be a withdrawal.

"Take that evil shit away from me. I don't want those papers to be anywhere near me, ever," I was shouting now. "Do I make myself clear?"

"Look Da…" implored John.

"No John, you look. She's dead. I'm glad. Life's better now she's not in it. I don't want to know. I don't want to know anything about her."

321

"It's to your advantage, sweetheart," said Ellie.

"It's the curse she wrote about in her suicide note. I want nothing of it."

I was standing and flinging my arms about like Hitler at a great rally.

"We will not dwell on those days," came the mighty speech, "we will rid ourselves of anything that stunts our growth. I will not tolerate anything that seeks to destroy the empire. You can wave those bits of paper around all you like but you will never talk about them, or divulge their contents," I moved towards Mr Littlebody. "Now, get out. Take your bits of scrap paper and your little bag and go," I was yelling at full bore as I showed him the door. Spit was flying out of my mouth like real bullets. My hand was raised in the door's direction with the palm face down and realising it was a true Nazi salute I screamed. "Get out! Get out! Get out!"

John showed the shell-shocked solicitor to the door, glancing back at me with a cocktail of expressions. There was subdued talking and I heard the front door close and eventually a car engine start up. Mr Saltby came to me with fear in his eyes. I glared at him and asked to be left alone. He said nothing. He did not dare to. In any case what could he have said? I headed for the kitchen leaving a tearful Ellie being comforted by Gwen. No words came out of her beautiful open mouth - she did not even know what questions to ask.

I made for the garden and tried to hold the tears back by biting on my lower lip. Any tears would be classed as deserters. The pain in my lip was military discipline, Nazi discipline the best sort. My mind regrouped. A strategy had to be decided. There was bound to be more hand-to-hand combat when I went back in. I would have to see the full picture in order to win a victory. Herr Hitler would want it no other way. I re-evaluated matters, what the fight had been about and what outcome I wanted. I visualised the man, Littlebody, and his evil documents. Was I right or wrong to object to listening to more vile messages from beyond my mother's grave? There was no question of wrong. Had I overreacted? I wondered how the solicitor would have reacted if his mother had wanked him stiff, and more - but of course, that information was buried. The fact was that he would have resisted any attempt to revisit matters that were strictly out of bounds. If he had been part of a mighty empire, of course he would bring all he had to bear, to prevent them doing it.

I took command, slid down the side of the house and went for a route march down the Mansfield Road. It was dark when, after about an hour, I got back sweaty and invigorated.

It is strange when you see people out of context. I had never seen John angry before. I thought it was my eyes that could only fire salvos. His were Howitzers. They were aimed directly at me, firing at will. I could see great fragments of my concrete fortress blasting away from the explosive impacts of his shells. What his words would do, I could not imagine. Either way, this was going to be a great battle.

"Don't you dare look at me like that vicar," getting the first audible shot in.

I looked around the hall. There was no one there save him and me. We were alone it seemed.

"I don't want you under my roof if you plan to behave like this again," he threatened.

"Is that the best you can do, oh forgiver of souls?"

The missile hit him close to his heart. His face changed as the words ran from ear to brain in a split second.

"There is forgiveness, and there is repentance. They come as a package," he said, pulling a cliché out of his repertoire. He was clever.

"And there are things you ought not meddle with and things you should keep your nose out of. That's a package too," I was amazed at my own answer, quick as it was.

"What things?" he said.

"You'll never know. No one will. But don't let me ever have to see that rat-faced bastard again, or I'll really unleash my forces."

"What forces?" he said, quietly. "The empire?"

The face of the John I knew had returned.

"You'll see, if I lay eyes on him again," I replied, trying to hide my inner disgust for blurting out secrets about my new nation.

"We put a lot of thought into your birthday and this is how you repay us," he said with a low, exasperated sigh.

The guilt weapon hit home but I had endured years of that. I was only taken by surprise because it had come from John this time.

"It was that man I was attacking, not you, not Auntie Ellie. I didn't mean for you to get hurt, only him. He was meddling in things that are long forgotten, buried things, never to be mentioned again."

"Your mother, you mean?"

"There you go, now you're at it. Won't any of you ever learn?"

"I think I understand," he said in his best vicar's voice.

"I very much doubt it," I said.

"It's all right to talk about these things," he said.

"And how many words will it take to wipe out all that is past?" I asked.

"The past is the past."

"If I broke your back today, you'd live with it for the rest of your life," I said.

I could hear my troops give a rousing cheer at that reply.

"Look, Davy. You can keep these things bottled up like this all you like. Sooner or later it's going to make you ill."

"Never. Never! You have no idea how my past has made me invincible. My mind is stronger now that it's ever been."

"Is that why you lose your temper?"

"That's not a lost temper," I said, "that is self defence. There's a difference."

"And what are you defending yourself against?"

"Nosy buggers just like you're becoming. Keep out of matters that don't concern you."

"You look tired," he said.

"So what?"

"I don't want us to fall out son. I'm not a nosy whatnot, you know. I'm your friend. You're a big part of Eleanor's life too."

It was the first time I had heard Ellie referred to by her real name. It brought home to me the special place she had in my heart and John was my friend. He had proved it.

"I'm sorry I spoiled the big day you had for me. There are just things I never want to talk about. Okay?"

"We're all tired. Things will seem different in the morning."

He wrapped his arms around me, and I felt safe. Faith, hope and love and the greatest of these is love. I had heard it said a hundred times or more at wedding services. Now I could feel its truth. I went to bed exhausted, with my emotions in disarray and my thoughts in a muddle. It was like the aftermath of a great conflict with dead bodies strewn all over the place. It was hard to see who had won. I pondered on it before sleep took me. I had not let anything slip about mother but I had divulged the name of the empire. Mistake. I looked upon the quiet, smoking theatre of battle and surmised that there had been a victory of sorts – but, as I knew, in war there are no real winners.

The morning came. I felt the same. Ellie held me at arm's length, with a suspicious look, as if my face was the epitome of betrayal. If anyone could make me feel bad about myself it was Ellie. She was the only person who had the right to be this close to me. I took her disdain seriously, seriously enough that I took the bus to work that Monday morning, unable to face the new, shiny, grey Moggy in the drive. I had forfeited the right to enjoy my first drive to work.

What of work? Saltbys was its usual self, busy and chaotic but the word had got around somehow, or at least I felt it had. Could it have been Mr Saltby's attitude towards me? He was trying very hard to be polite but gone was his usual geniality. He was the boss, pulling rank and acting it out. Putting distance between us. I was out in the cold.

Days passed by like this. Soon the week was gone. Home had regained some of its warmth, but not all. I was being treated in a certain way. It brought a faint chill to the place that had welcomed me with open arms so many weeks earlier. Did I feel in the way? Yes. I have to say yes. I was twenty-one after all, old enough to know better. I contemplated these matters, as I lay awake in bed on the Saturday morning. The phone was ringing in the hall. I was about to go down to answer it when I heard Ellie's voice pick it up. Whoever was on the other end of the line, Ellie's tone suggested that she was glad they had called. I heard the goodbyes, three of them. Then the phone's bell tinkled as the receiver dropped back into its cradle.

"Davy? Davy? Are you awake?"

"Yes Ellie. I'm awake," I shouted back.

"That was Gwen. She's just called from phone box at the bus station. She'll be here in about half an hour. She wants to see you."

"I wish you'd put her off," I said as I came downstairs in a dressing gown.

325

"Well, I didn't. You want to be glad you've got a friend like her. Anybody else would have…" she stopped what she was about to say. "What I meant was, good friends are hard to come by."

I had a bowl of cereal and a cup of tea. By the time I had washed and dressed Gwen was knocking on the door.

"You get it Davy. I'm busy," Ellie lied from the kitchen.

So I went and opened the door and was greeted by a vision. Gwen had put on her blue denim jeans. A white, very loose top hung on her body, allowing her breasts to move freely about inside. The jeans clung to her legs. I could see the shape of her womanhood where the material gathered tightly around it. All those things, taken together with her free flowing hair and that wonderful mouth, gave her an unworldly appearance. She had taken me by surprise.

"I hear you've not christened that car yet," she said teasingly.

"No, not yet."

"Well where are you taking me then?" she said with a laugh in her words.

I did not know how to reply. Had she forgotten the day of the party so quickly? Everyone else had been affected in some way by my outburst. I could not make her out. She was either putting on the most incredible act of forgetfulness, or she actually understood my point of view and was on my side. I regained my concentration.

"Where would you like to go," I asked.

"The seaside. I'd like to go to the seaside, Skeggy or Mablethorpe. Come on, what do you say?"

What could I say? Was I being persuaded against my will? Ellie shouted from the kitchen where she was tactfully keeping out of the way.

"Go on Davy. You know you're dying to take her out for a spin. The car I mean."

I was, and this was the first hint of the permission I needed, the first hint that I was back in the good books again. I went to the key rack and grabbed hold of my independence.

Two hours later we arrived safely in Skegness. Considering I was only just a beginner, I skilfully managed to back into a parking space on one of the side streets. I could not hide my satisfaction that I had driven all the way there in my own car. That event seemed like a huge achievement. It was as big an event as the cycle ride years before and that day spent by the sea was all the more special because of having got there under our own steam.

We walked past guesthouses and on towards the shopping area. There were outlets for everything. Plastic buckets, spades and sandcastle moulds in every primary colour. We were tempted by sugary candyfloss and toffee apple stalls and pervading throughout the resort was the aroma of fish and chips, cigarette smoke, cheap perfume and masculine body odours. On we marched to glimpse our prize. This would be a first for me. On we strode past the lifeboat station, festooned with the bunting of an Open Day. Then, as we turned to where the donkeys were, there it was. I had not been prepared for its size, its greyness or its power. I was looking at a whole county, no, not a county, much bigger than that, a whole continent, completely made of water as far as the eye could see. The North Sea.

I could smell it. It was a scent like you get from an electric arc fused with the faint smell of rotting vegetation that created an age-old aroma, older than mankind, and demanding of respect. So we left the donkeys behind and powered across the sands to meet her. The tide was out and it was a long way. She was going to make us work hard to effect an introduction. But eventually, a little out of puff we arrived. As if we were both telepathic we bared our feet in order to paddle. Gwen cast me a look offering her hand to hold. I took it out of a sense of history and together we made our one small step. Bloody hell it was cold.

I do not remember the events of that day in terms of a list of things we did, apart from the paddle. I recall it more as an impression of a day. There was something of the Freak Show about Skegness back then. Here was a place that had once known the patronage of the masses. Loyal armies from a thousand Anson factories around the industrial Midlands had journeyed by train, and later by motor car, to raise their tired heads away from the mighty machines that held them in bondage the rest of the year. For two glorious weeks they would descend into what then must have been a wonderland. They had left their ghosts behind, happily enjoying all the attractions, before being

327

plunged back into the behemoth. Back in those days it must have been a well-preserved place. The ironwork would have been brightly painted, like benches and railings. The gardens would have been immaculate - but the glory days were now gone and the paint was peeling away. Spain was the new wonderland. Poor old Skeggy would have to make do with her memories, memories I could almost hear as Gwen and I made use of what was left of the old place. Money went into slots. We pulled levers and shot at targets in the amusement arcade. We visited a fairground on the front and became intoxicated on the rides. I think I had fun but it all had to end and, before we knew it, we were driving towards a tired sun in the west, heading home.

Gwen asked me to stop near an escarpment. There was a fabulous view of the fens from there, with Boston Stump showing like a thin, vertical pencil mark in the distance. On the horizon was the sun, orange and blazing with its fire. One of nature's paintings cast with perfection across the dying blue of the day's sky. I was lost in its wonder as Gwen's head blotted out the scene. She was reaching over the gear stick, her left hand cradling the side of my face. The beautiful mouth hovered an inch from mine for a brief moment, before closing the gap, pressing her lips to mine. Soft and luxurious they were, soft and nubile. I was lost in the sensation they provided. She was kissing me, kissing me like I had once been kissed before, long ago. Gwen's lips were moist like hers, were smooth like hers, were too much like hers. I pulled away.

I pulled away from the sheer loveliness of it. I could hear protests in my head. I was sitting bolt upright with my back against the inside of the car door, my lips continuing to tingle with the afterglow of her kiss, like they had when mother had done it to me as a boy.

"Don't do that," I said. "You mustn't do that."

My words came out as a host of subhuman desires yelled at me to shut up and smother her with my own lips.

"I thought you liked me, Davy," she said, shocked and upset.

I looked back at eyes now clouded with disappointment as the dissenting voices urged me to wrap her in my arms and love her back.

"We mustn't do that Gwen," I ranted on, in a calm undertone put out by the empire. "I just can't, that's all."

328

I could tell that she was trying to understand, trying to understand me.

"It was only a kiss, nothing more," she said, trying not to make too big a deal out of it.

I could not take my eyes off the lips that spoke to me. Just looking at them, their fullness, their shape, they glistened, moist, she was doing it on purpose.

The car now felt very claustrophobic. The two of us seemed crammed together. She was still leaning slightly forwards and I could see her neck blend into her chest where it formed into the breasts that lay inside the white top. It would have taken no effort to reach in and hold one in my hand - but they were like those that I had to watch flapping about above me on those nights the bad dreams had forced a comfort session.

Gwen was digging down the shaft. She seemed perilously close to the strong box. I was terrified. My fingers grabbed the door handle and I burst out into the open air, and there outside, panting for breath, I steadied myself on the front wing sucking in the cool of the evening. I felt embarrassed, foolish, but right. She had got out too, looking at me with an uncertain gaze. I wondered what she was thinking.

"What's wrong?" she asked. I could tell her concern was real. "What's wrong with you? Have you got someone else? Is that it?"

Someone else she said. In a way she was right. I had, but she was dead now. Not that that helped, she was all too alive in me. I wanted to rip my brain out, find the memory of her and throw it away, burn it, reduce it to a pile of ash.

"It's not you Gwen. Just don't ask me what's wrong, because I can never tell you."

I watched her eyes take in the faint hint of a secret. I could see her mind at work, as if she was on to something and that she would be able to save me after all.

"You've got to tell someone, sometime. You'll be ill if you don't. Why not tell me?

"No, be told."

"Oh, come on Davy. We've had a lovely day. We're friends, aren't we? You can tell me anything. It'll be our little secret."

"What's that you said?" I rounded on her, flashing my eyes at hers. How I hated that term our little secret. Little secrets were never little in my experience.

"I won't tell anyone," she persisted. "You can confide in me."

"Don't you ever listen? I said no."

"Oh come on Davy. Come on, you can tell me."

She had to be repelled. It was no good.

"No! No! No! Fucking no! Got that now?"

Undeterred, brave even, she came over to me, ready to hold me like a child who had been hurt. How I hated myself for what I did. I pushed her away. I pushed her over the bonnet of the car. She fell, breaking off the wing mirror as she went, ending up in a heap on the lay-by. From her undignified position she stared back at me as if I was a lost cause. She got up and went back inside the car. I picked up my wing mirror. We drove home. It was an awful journey.

The empire had won again I told myself. The war on emotions had taken on a new development. It was the beginning of the end for my emotions and all the needless feelings that got in the way of an all-powerful empire. This might have been the end of the celestial day but it was a new dawn for me, a New Testament in the writing.

Chapter twelve: Exhausted

"I'll pay for the petrol if that's what you're worried about," said Mr Saltby.

"I'm not worried," I replied, knowing he had picked up on my bad mood.

"Well, you know the way, don't you?"

"Course I do," I said, but sounding uncertain.

It was a week after the Skegness trip and I was being persuaded to travel on the same road I had used to get to the coast. I was reluctant to relive any part of that day, even to the point of loathing the idea of hitting a section of the same route as I had that weekend. Gwen aroused things in me that would not go away. Even now, days later, I was in turmoil. Riots in the empire, a riot of emotions that threatened to overthrow it. Taken as a whole it was nothing short of an insurrection that festered within what would otherwise be a clean and strong empire. They would have to go.

The boss got out a road map from a filing cabinet, opened it at a well-thumbed page and pointed out the village of Stapleford just on the outskirts of a large area of trees.

"Just follow the signs for Sleaford, then come off this here road. You'll pass through this wood," he said pointing to a rectangle of green, "and the farm is just after that. If you reach Stapleford village, then you've gone too far."

"And what if he's too busy and he refuses to see me?" I wanted to know, but trying to get out of going.

"Oh, bloody hell Davy. It's all arranged. Ten-thirty outside the barn, he'll be there."

So I grabbed my brochures and drove out of town on the A17 towards Coddington village and the woods beyond. What a wood it was, too huge for me to miss, and yet that is exactly what I did. I had passed it a week before and never bothered to take any notice of it.

As instructed I took the side road and delved down the wood's main artery. Soon the trees had swallowed my little grey car into their depths. Deeper and deeper I drove into its interior. The tarmac road, three main sections of it, each long and straight, cut through the middle of Stapleford Wood like a dog's hind leg. Either side of me there grew tall, dark pines some sixty feet high or more and going back further than I could tell. Bordering the road just in front of the firs were swathes of rhododendron bushes, masses of them, bursting out in bright green foliage, cascading over the ditches that ran the length of the grass verges either side of me. Now and again small side lanes cut off, delving deep into the trees, disappearing God knows where. I was intrigued. I was also late and I ought to have pressed on out of the wood to reach the farm, but the car slowed and the steering wheel turned. The lure of the little side lane was too compelling. It took me on a mystery tour through dense vegetation.

After a while the path took a turn and on its shoulder there was a track leading away. I found a place to park and decided to wander down the dirt track into the depths of the wood. There were thousands of trees all around. Thousands, all huge, tall, perpendicular pines swaying high up in the wind that scurried across the tips high above. I could hear gunshots, far off, muffled. Alone, with the cracks of shooting reaching my ears, I could imagine how the Germans would have brought the Jews to places like this, forced them to undress and machine-gunned them down. In woods like this it would have happened. If they had reached England this is where British Jews would have been murdered. Down these very tracks gassing vans would have set up operations, processing hundreds of people in the experiment that would ultimately lead to the building of permanent gas chambers. I could see it all in my mind's eye, just as the books I had been reading outlined. The final solution was tried out in places like this, isolated, away from prying eyes. Perfect for obliterating the unwanted. The images were too powerful. Everywhere felt creepy. I got the sense that ghosts were watching me.

So I returned to my car, spun it round and made for the main road out of the woods, ready to watch out for the farm. In the end it stood out like a sore thumb. The tyres crunched down the gravel drive that led to a concrete yard, on one side of which was a barn. Sure enough Mr Harrison was waiting there for me and in one exaggerated movement he checked his watch. Damn it, I thought. It was not a good start.

"Sorry I'm late," I apologised.

"If you think I've got time to waste on folks who can't be bothered to be punctual, you can think again my lad," he said.

"I had a devil of a time getting out of Newark," I lied.

"I ain't in the mood for excuses. You got them brochures on you?"

"Yes," I said, feeling I was on a hiding to nothing.

"In the barn then. You've got five minutes. I've a feller coming from Chanders this afto, and he's always on time, he is."

The presentation if you can call it that was hopeless. In my rush, I had forgotten two important price lists. I was like a fish out of water. Somehow being on my own, out of the familiar surroundings of the shop, here at this farm, the whole selling process seemed alien. I was surprised at this. It should have been a doddle. Each time I made a mistake old man Harrison just sighed and mumbled.

"Fuckin' stroll on," he said to himself.

In the end, disgusted he walked out of the barn halfway through my hopeless spiel. Hurriedly I packed up my things and followed him out into the morning sun. By now he had reached his car, got in and off he went. I was left miserable and dismayed as he drove away down his gravel drive, leaving me in a cloud of dust. I felt like shit. How was I going to explain this to the boss?

Arriving back I could see Mr Saltby on the phone. He caught sight of me as I walked in and gave me a look like thunder. I resigned myself to a bollocking with every step towards the gallows inside his office.

"Look, I'll have a word with him. Yes John, I know but come on. It was only his first day. Remember when I came to see your dad just after the war? He told me I couldn't organise a piss up in a brewery that harvest time."

There was a pause as Saltby listened to the caller's voice squawking out of the receiver.

"Okay, John, leave him to me. See you tomorrow, bye."

The phone was thrown down on its cradle.

"Right lad, shut the door," said Mr S, his kindly voice energised with authority.

He picked up a pile of papers from his desk. They were the price lists I had left behind.

"You forgot these," he said, and I knew that I had, "and you were late. Half an hour late. You had time to be there ten minutes early."

Had I really been in the woods for forty minutes? He continued with his dressing down.

"This can't go on Davy lad. Can't go on like this. Nip it in the bud and all that. If you don't pull your ideas up, you'll follow Witherspoon out to the dole queue, you see if you don't. I've given you a chance to make something of yourself here. I didn't give you driving lessons for fun so you could go swanning off round the countryside. I need a reliable rep, one who gets to his appointments on time. So what have you got to say for yourself?" he said, shaking his head in dismay.

"It was like I told Mr Harrison," I said as rehearsed, "it took me ages to get out of town and then I drove straight past the farm and spent ages looking for the damn place. At least I know where it is now."

"Good, 'cos you and me are going to see him tomorrow to smooth things over," slamming the papers into my chest he barked, "and don't forget these next time."

Without calling me stupid he made me brand myself so. Somehow it was worse because I gave myself the label, but it was all Gwen's fault really - she and her lips, her perfume, her body. These insidious, lecherous wants were a vile scourge on the grand plan. They attacked the very fibre of the empire. Nothing could be permitted to allow memories of that dead woman to rise up and overthrow it and Gwen had the power to do that. She and others like her had to be repelled. Even now unwanted masses lived and roamed in the streets of the empire, weaving their evil dissent, gnawing away at its very foundations. It would surely fall unless they were taken care of. Like a plague of rats they would have to be rounded up and dealt with. They would have to be treated like the Jews - special treatment, a final solution. They would have to go, all of them, until there was no one left. Only then would there be a pure and noble nation. Only then would it be fit to take on the world. Every last remnant of them would have to be rounded up, taken away and shot, or herded together and gassed. A way would have to be found, but what rewards we could bathe in. I was determined that a day like today would not happen again - only glorious days glowing with the splendours of success upon success. I was fired up. All emotions would have to be exterminated, taken into the woods and shot, or gassed in vans. Like an unstoppable juggernaut subconscious plans began to be made, as the David Harper on the surface got on with his work.

I think Ellie had left it on the table. Or was it resting on the mantelpiece? Perhaps it was on the mantelpiece. I got it down and read it at the table. However it happened I found myself reading a letter saturated with power. It was from Gwen. Even as I drew a knife through the envelope I had the sensation I was being watched and, finding no one around as I looked furtively about me, only intensified that feeling. According to Gwen I was in need of love and help, her kind of love and help, the kind that was channelled through her from God. She had loved me the moment she met me, it appeared, and my outburst, on what was otherwise a perfect day, had after much prayer, made her want to find a way into my heart and bring about healing. On and on it went, layer after layer of devotion, intermingled with Christian reasoning.

In the same instant I found myself embracing and repelling it. The discomfort this brought about was sickening. I should have stopped soaking up its contents but I was mesmerised. Something inside me wanted to be told these things. So the words went in unchecked. Even as I read passages about finding the cause of my hurting soul, I could not stop. Perhaps at my very core I wanted someone to find the hurting soul. By the time I had read the last line, there was a full-scale revolt going on in the empire. It was utter confusion. Order had to be restored.

The letter was hidden. I have often wondered why I did not destroy it. All night it preyed on my mind, this plague. The inner me was overrun with feelings that were decreed unlawful by the new nation. In a supreme effort, a grotesque marshalling of thoughts began to emerge. This part of my thinking did not try to understand Gwen's attempts to infiltrate the hidden world of the empire. It simply stopped them. I had to be hard. Letting her in was not an option. I would have to write back, to exorcise the feelings that were running amok and, if that did not work, then more drastic measures would have to be found.

After tea I went up to my room and penned a diatribe I hoped would deal with her once and for all. I was cruel. Each nasty comment pushed the beautiful lips further away. I called her weird, a misfit like all Christians. If I needed a girlfriend then she would be the last person I would choose. I found her dull and boring. On and on I scrawled. I said that she had spoiled my life and that she had made it impossible for me to live it anymore. When it was done I felt empty, empty and alone, with only an empire for company and a mass of emotions that decimated my chances for any peace of mind whatsoever. I wished that I had never met her. Such was the aggravation, the agony and the debilitating confusion. The feelings would have to be killed. Just writing a letter alone would not do it. The feelings would have to be singled out and killed.

It was a bad night's sleep, fitful, drifting in and out of slumber. Once more it was the dreams and always the house. Gwen featured in them now though, or someone similar to her. In my dream I had given in to her and loved it. By the time the alarm clock declared another working day ahead, I was exhausted.

Mr Saltby was absent from his office when I arrived. Normally he was behind his desk going through the mail but today his chair was empty. Maisey broke the news that Mrs Saltby had been rushed into the General Hospital. My mood darkened. The boss was the only one to smooth things out with old man Harrison. Without him I was on a sticky wicket. In any case I was in no fit state to think about any of it. I was not interested in work. I wanted nothing more than to get rid of the crap going on in my mind. That was all that mattered.

Yawning continually, the morning's tasks got completed. I had never been so tired. Sleep was what I wanted, just to kip down somewhere even in the car. Even in the car. The idea hit its mark and made me decide to find the same spot in the woods where I could take a nap on the way back from old man Harrison.

"Are you going to Stapleford later youth?" shouted Eric across an empty showroom.

I said I was.

"Nip over to Norton Disney village with this then afterwards, Vale Farm. It's the one just after the railway bridge. There's a sign. Won't get fuckin' lost this time, will we?"

"What have I got to take?" I asked.

"Not much. I'll pop 'em into the back of yer car. Make sure old man Trickett gets 'em. You won't forget, will you?"

Bastard, I thought, not wanting any more jobs.

"Leave it to me," I said.

The drive to Stapleford was a dour trip. I had to push myself on, knowing what was ahead. Harrison was going to be pissed off. Pissed off that the boss was not with me and pissed off that the incompetent buffoon was back. I hated the way it made me feel. This situation had come at the worst possible time. It was like going off to war. Harrison was in charge of the machine gun. The farm was the beach I was about to land on. I was tired through lack of sleep and I could not get Gwen out of my mind. I wished I had never been born to feel emotions like these – confusion, utter confusion. Shit.

The car trundled once more down the drive to Harrison's farm. I was exactly on time. No one was there. For a few moments I sat and waited until I became bored. Walking over to the barn I found it empty. A farm void of human souls is a bleak place. The wind gallops across it unchecked. The buildings seem embarrassed at being redundant. I felt idiotic just being there, wondering if I had got the right farm, but no one had said anything about the meeting being at another farm. So I stayed for a while as a sense of isolation crept over me.

Then I saw a Land Rover slow down on the lane and pull into the track. It drew level with my car and a bald fellow in dirty blue overalls jumped out. He was a big man and sounded out of breath.

"You from Saltbys?" he asked.

"Yes."

"Boss says he won't be needing you after all. He's happy with Chanders quotes. He said you'd know what he meant," he said, speaking as if he was reciting a spy's message that he had just had to swallow, "and he can't wait around. He said you'd know why."

"But I've got a new price list," I protested. "Are you sure he won't see me?"

"I'm just delivering a message," said the bald man. "Any road I've got to get on, boss is in a mood. Bye."

Then he was gone, leaving me in another cloud of dust. I stood there for some time feeling like a total failure, dejected, useless, blaming the feelings that caused me to have messed up in the first place. Mr Saltby was going to have a fit.

A few miles from Stapleford was the village of Norton Disney. As Eric had said there was a railway bridge, the Newark to Lincoln line. Passing beneath its shady expanse I came upon the sign for Vale Farm. Again the farm was deserted. Once more I got out of the car to look around. Three fields away I could see a tractor. It was stationary and straining to see in the far off distance, I thought I could see its driver, sitting motionless, like he was dead. Shouting as loud as I could the word hello rang across the countryside. I heard my echo bounce off some trees half a mile or so away. It made no effect. At least I thought not. Until, that is, a frail old lady, dressed in what looked like Victorian costume waddled out of the shed on the far side of the yard and demanded.

"Was that you yawping?"

I looked around sarcastically to see whoever else it could have been.

"We don't buy from hawkers, so push off," she barked, getting closer.

"I'm from Saltbys," I explained, terrified. "Eric sent me. I've got something in the boot for Mr Trickett."

"Ah, 'bout time. Well, let's hope they're better than the last load of rubbish we got off you," she said abruptly.

Opening the boot, I happened upon a coiled mass of green hose. In fact there were two of them. I learned that they were destined for the two, hundred gallon gas-oil tanks, used for filling up the tractors. The old biddy lectured me about how useless the last ones were and, as if to prove it, she deposited the old lot where I got the new ones from, messing up my boot. It did not take a genius to see that they were the wrong size. The woman, who I took to be old Mrs Trickett went into great depths about how they would not fit the tanks no matter what they did. Diesel was spilling everywhere she went on and rounded off by saying that we could have the buggers back, sniping that we ought to count ourselves lucky that they were not suing us for lost fuel. I strained to remain polite, shut the boot and drove away.

If I began the day feeling down, I had by now reached new depths. Things became worse as I passed back through Stapleford village, where outside a phone box a romantic couple of teenagers were passionately ramming their tongues down each other's throats. I tried to suppress the envy I felt. It was obvious that they were both lost in the pleasure of it. I had somehow got to kill these thoughts in my head, murder the desire. Nothing like that could ever be part of the empire. They seemed to be able to permeate everywhere. For this reason the entrance to the pit where the strong box lay had to be guarded day and night, and what of the thoughts and desires that

Gwen had already unleashed into the back streets of the empire? They were enemies of the state. Like the Jews in Nazi Germany they would have to be rounded up and given the special treatment - a treatment that I had not yet decided upon.

Soon Stapleford Wood enveloped me once more as I sped homeward. Almost as if by an unseen hand I drove down the little track, managing to find the spot I had reached the day before. I was exhausted. Half of me wanted to sleep. The other half was grappling with the enemies within. Pictures of Jews being rounded up and put on cattle wagons flashed before me. In my mind's eye I put many of them up against a wall and shot them. The ones in the cattle wagon rolled through dense woodland to the great extermination camps of the Third Reich. They were overpowering images, compelling. They were my inspiration. All my sexual desires, thoughts of wanting to be loved and held, visions of kissing and caressing, unwanted erections brought on by thoughts of Gwen were all lined up to march into the gas chambers - chambers that were almost ready. With my help, the killing squads of the SS connected the hose to the exhaust pipe of the car and, as if to prove the empire was doing the right thing, the hose fitted perfectly. Here in the woods, just as the Germans had done during the pogroms of the nineteen-forties, my car was becoming a gassing van. I gave the order to the rounded-up feelings to march into it as the other end of the hose was pushed through the small, triangular draught window that I had poked open in the front passenger door. The Jewish thoughts were herded into the chamber as I sealed the driver's door behind them. They did not want to go - of course they did not. They wanted to bring down the empire and all it stood for. They were determined to live to purvey their disgusting lies. It just remained to start the engine and let the gas do its work and wait for all the unwanted ideas, demands and lusts to die. The empire would soon be free. With a turn of the key the engine began its glorious task, the Holocaust of emotion, the annihilation of a vile and dissident state of mind. The gas did not hurt and I was very, very tired. It was a sweet gas, hinting only slightly of petrol mixed with the whiff of diesel. Shouting and screaming the thoughts began to die, one by one they fell on top of one another and I too slowly began to fall into a deep, deep sleep, glad in the knowledge that by the time I awoke, a new empire, strong and pure would emerge. I sat behind the wheel closing my eyes to the tall pines emerging from their carpet of brambles, smiling, victorious.

What had been achieved was heroic. I felt like a hero. I could tell that I was held in the highest esteem. With the rest of the Einsatzgruppen we were paraded through the empire like gods, showered with glory and affection. It was like being at the birth of a new age with all the pristine future that it promised. I can remember walking up a long, wide flight of stone steps. Steps built before a great monument that led to a set of mighty marble Corinthian pillars that graced the front of an imposing mausoleum. The atmosphere was filled with deafening chants, the cheering of millions of souls, adoration - but not all of it was for us, for as we climbed up the steps we could see a podium. The face of the man who stood behind it looked upon us as we drew near with a proud, unsmiling face. His uniform was immaculate. The hair that swept at an angle down his forehead was well groomed, as was his small tuft of a moustache. We stood to attention as we reached the top step, looking for the first time on the majestic face of our Fuhrer. What a moment! He personally placed garlands of laurels about our necks and pinned medals on our chests. Then he smiled at each one of us and shook our hands. Herr Hitler's hand touched mine. Can you believe it? It was a moment I knew that I would never forget.

Following the parade, I was given a period of leave. I thought of taking the train somewhere but instead decided to take myself off on a cycling holiday. So, on one hot summer morning I set off to God knows where. I set the road before me and off I went in search of adventure. The countryside was in full bloom, rich in the vapours and scents of wild flowers and fanned by a hot breeze. On and on I rode, hours passing by. I became lost in the ride as the road began to rise up before me. It became warmer as time marched on and the miles passed beneath my rubber tyres. By gradual increments the road became steeper. For a long time it was like this and that blistering day it seemed as if the hill would never end. The clumps of trees that bordered the road obscured the view and gave me no indication where the upward gradient would level out and I would be able to relax. The last seven miles were like this all the way, a persistent incline - not a steep slope, but a gradual, energy-sapping ascent. I contemplated getting off the bicycle and walking. I knew from experience such a move would lead to yet more exhaustion but I was too tired. Realising how similar a bike ride could be to life, I knew that I needed rest. So I got off the saddle, let my bike drop against a gatepost and lay gasping for breath on the soft, grassy verge. I drifted away into a sleep - a sleep blacker than I had ever known. It was a sleep without dreams, the first sleep without dreams I had had for years, decades even. It was wonderful and I decided that once I got my strength back I would continue. Yes. Up the hill. The hill. Up. Hill. The hill. Back. Hill, hill. Heil Hitler. Heil empire. Rest, sleep, sleep, slip. Slip away, slip, sl… s… ss… ssss… sssssssssssssssssss*ssssssssss*

Chapter thirteen: Hymn

Quiet.
Quiet.
All quiet.
   What?
Gone again, just a snatch, far away.
Taken away, no sense, nothing.
Leaving.
   Wait.
Quiet, all is quiet.
Time, immeasurable. No hours or days, just silence.
But sometimes. There again, just a snatch, far away.
Pulled away, gone.
Leaving.
   Patience.
Quiet, all is quiet.
Great stretches of time.
   Listen.
From a deep hole, muffled. Male.
Gone again, no, it's back, he's back.

What are the words? Too muffled.

Tiredness, Heavy and dragging.

Falling again. Lost it, sorry.

Bones moving, pushed about, face being covered again. Millions of tons of exhaustion. Can't fight it, give in. Wait, just wait. That's all there's left to do. The quiet has a dark light, like a sea, a sea with a swell. Submerged, sinking and rising. Sometimes rising to the surface where sounds break in. Muffled sounds, distorted. Speech but undefined, a male voice, before the swell of the sea drowns again. Sinking into the darkness. Wait, just wait.

Condition!

A full word possible to make out. He said condition, just detectable, before it went again. And there's a smell, severe, precise, a strict smell. It's the smell of absolute cleanliness. Muffled bangs and a clatter and a heat of sorts, burning me somewhere. It's the clean air, hurting with each breath.

I heard her.

"Yes Doctor, right away," she said,

He replied to her.

"Thank you."

Oh to be able to swallow. I do. It burns, hurts like hell in fact. The pain creates a shock. The shock makes me aware that my eyes are closed. It hurts to open them. My eyeballs seem covered in a film. Crusty eyelids blink it away. There's something on my face. People are moving. It's exhausting to watch anymore. Sorry. I want to sleep just a bit more.

The sea finally spilled me out onto the shore, a shore of pains. The pains were in my head, and throat, lungs, and joints. I became aware of awareness. I could hear a world around me, a world of the senses. I was lying down on cloth, and in it. Something was strapped to my face. I reached out to take it away. It was a mask with a pipe attached, delivering air. I opened my eyes to look at it, only to find a room full of beds, beds with people in them. Then the avalanche began. It was like a vacuum seal breaking, allowing memories to flood back in, back into my brain. Hospital, why? Hurt, how? It hurt to breathe. Why did it hurt to breathe? What had I breathed in? Then my memory slammed me back in the car. The gas chamber, the gas chamber in the wood, but I had been on a cycle ride, I had met Hitler, but I had been tired. Disappointingly I knew that it was only a warped vision. The car in the woods, had I really done that, had I, and if so, how come I was here? How come I was alive?

A nurse came over and replaced my mask. She was very kind but distant. I felt upset, frightened, like a lost child. With no more ado I wept my heart out. Another nurse came over and pulled the curtains around me. She injected me in my left arm. Being afraid became less of a worry and sleep took me away again.

When I awoke once more I opened my eyes to see John and Ellie sitting in chairs beside the bed. John placed a warm hand on my ruffled hair. Ellie wrapped her arms over my chest and kissed my face.

"You're going to be all right," she said.

I felt reassured. John said that I was to be in hospital for a week. Under observation he explained, then I would be allowed home. I could see it in their eyes, that questioning look. It took all their self-control to resist the urge to ask why. I could also see how hard it was for them to love me. Ellie especially was showing the signs of strain. I could see that I had scared them. I had scared myself. Even as I came to see how I had done this, I could not accept that I actually had. That was the part that scared me most of all.

All these defences, these walls, the empire, they were all to blame for the pain I was in. Yet I had needed them, still did. How else was I to protect myself from the things that might get to the box of secrets? Yet I could have killed myself? There was another question. How come I had not?

Through a larynx ravaged by carbon monoxide fumes, I forced out a string of grotesque sounds that were meant to sound like how did I get here? Ellie put her ear to my mouth and I tried again. John though had unravelled it before her.

"A woodsman from The Forestry Commission found you and dragged you out of your car," he said, unable to hide the fact that he was annoyed.

He opened all your windows, took the hose out, got in and drove it to the nearest house for help. He saved your stup… he saved your life."

"Why have things got so bad?" asked Ellie, unable to skirt the issue anymore.

She was crying. She held me again. I cried too. John watched us both, not knowing what to make of it. How could I tell her? I could never tell her. I could never tell anyone. It was a curse. I felt cold, and despite these two lovely people beside me, I felt very alone.

"You've got a visitor," said one of the nurses about three days later.

I was sitting up, having just read about myself in the Newark Advertiser. I insisted on reading it and, against their better judgement, they gave me a copy. They were right. I should not have read it. Wrong, wrong, wrong, all wrong. The stupid fools. How could it have been attempted suicide - but I had nearly died and, had it not been for the fluke of a passing forestry worker going about his business, I would have done? What protocols had the empire in hand to save me? The lack of answers made me feel low, abandoned. Now the idea of a visitor cheered me up, until I saw who it was. She walked in like she was entering a church, smiling at me with that beautiful mouth. She had a couple of small books in her hand. This was the last person I wanted to see. If it had not been for her none of this would have happened.

I was told later that I went berserk at her. Getting to my feet I threw the newspaper across the ward, screaming for her to get out, smashing the books she brought me out of her hand, sending them hurtling from her grasp. They said she looked terrified and fled down the corridor away from me. I had to be restrained as I smashed my fists on the glass of the swing doors. I split the lip of one of one of the male nurses with my flailing arms. I kicked chairs in all directions and frightened the other patients. They had to overpower me. I was given a sedative and I was referred. Referred to whom? I did not know what was going on anymore.

So I sat and focussed on a scratch in the wall opposite. There was nothing but despair. I had not woken up to a new dawn. There was no glorious empire. In my head I walked through ruins. The dead were everywhere. Dead feelings for Gwen lay with the thoughts that were to rebuild the empire. It was not the way forward as hoped, but it had been the only way for me. So now, without it, I had nothing. Worse still, how could I protect the shaft I had made for the strongbox? On and on went this thinking, on and on. It deafened me, louder and louder it got. Putting my hands over my ears did no good, the shouting was coming from inside. I made a noise to battle with it.

"Arrrrrrrrrrrrrr," I would chant until my breath ran out.

Then I would chant it again, over and over. They moved me into a room of my own shortly after this. The questions kept coming relentless. What are you going to do now Davy? Mother can get out now, how are you going to stop it Davy?

"Arrrrrrrrrrrrrr," I replied out loud, trying to drown it out.

I rocked back and forth in my chair to help me fight it. The empire was gone, and it was hard to fight this torment by myself. I rocked harder, back and forth, back and forth, a rhythmic motion one two, one two.

"Arrrrrrrrrrrrrr*bide with me, fast falls the eventide*," I began to sing with the rocking beat of my body. "*The darkness deepens, Lord with me abide*," I sang louder, this hymn from a world I once lived in. Long ago it seemed. "*When other helpers fail and comforts flee, help of the helpless, O abide with me.*"

I remembered the night I sat against the church door and my prayer rose up the walls, up the spire and into heaven. I sang again. I offered my singing prayer out of the top of my head, out of my mouth. Tears were in my eyes, tears of joyfulness as I sang with a full heart.

"*Lord with me abide*," The words were charged with a holy beauty, "*Ills have no weight, and tears no bitterness.*"

Tears no bitterness. I sang myself to sleep. I was so tired. Tired.

Some days later, I was taken to a room. It was a bright room, with white walls. Constable's *The Hay Wain* was on one of them and there was a desk, bookshelves and an armchair. I stood and waited after being shown in by a male nurse, not the one I hit. Then a fat man in a doctor's coat came in and sat behind the desk. His hair was thinning and he wore wire-rimmed spectacles. The voice that asked me to sit down was educated and pervaded a sense of high intellect. I sat down.

He looked at me for a couple of minutes, saying nothing. It seemed longer, protracted by the discomfort of his gaze, which I tried not to return. Then he got up and went to stare out of the window, his hands clasped behind his back. It was a miserable day outside.

"Do you like rain?" he asked politely after a long silence.

I said nothing.

"Rain. It always reminds me of my father's funeral. Does the rain remind you of anything, David?"

"Being at school," I said without a second thought, wishing I had not in the same instant.

I thought he was going to develop this line of questioning. Instead, he returned to his desk and took out a three-inch thick pile of papers, removed the pen from the breast pocket of his white coat and began to mark ticks on them. At first I was curious, his ignoring me like this. It passed, the curiosity, and I fell into myself, content just to stare. My gaze reached the bookshelves. I deduced that he was a meticulous man on account of the alphabetical arrangement of the titles printed on the spines, and there side by side was an odd juxtaposition of books. Cocking my head sideways to read, I made out *Hitler, The People's Leader* and next to it was a black bound copy of *Hymns Ancient and Modern*. He caught me looking at them over the rim of his glasses. His eyes bore into mine. The silence was awkward, he almost commanded it so. Like a poultice he was drawing the words out of me.

"Were you in a choir?" I asked him.

"I still am, he said. "Are you?"

"Used to be."

"Why not now?"

"There isn't one in our village," I said.

"Do you miss it?"

Miss it, I thought? Yes, I did. More than I had realised.

"Yes, a bit."

"I'm a baritone," he confessed. "One of my favourites is *Guide Me O Thou Great Redeemer*. I rather like that bit near the end of the verse where we repeat that line over the other parts, you know?" and from the pit of his deep voice he sang. "*Lead me now and evermore, evermore, lead me now and evermore,*" He looked satisfied that he had split the room in half with such unashamed exhibitionism. He smiled and beheld me again. "Do you have a favourite hymn David?"

I did, two favourites I recalled. They were, *There Is A Green Hill Far Away* and *Abide With Me*. The latter had the edge at that precise moment.

"*Abide With Me*," I said pointing to the book on the shelf, "hymn number thirteen in that volume there I think."

He took it out and flipped through to where I had said. He smiled down at the opened page.

"Very good. I'm impressed. When was the last time you picked up a hymn book?"

"I was fourteen," I said doing the subtraction. "Seven years ago."

"And you still remembered the hymn number after all this time. It must be a special hymn?"

"It is, I suppose."

"And why's that do you expect?"

"It makes me feel looked after," I said, with clear honesty.

"And do you feel you need looking after?" he said.

I wanted to say yes but he was getting too close. I said nothing, waiting for the next question. I thought he would look back at my lack of reply with disappointment but he did not, he just went back to marking his papers.

My breathing, his scratching pen and the timpani of the rain on the window became the only sounds to be heard. The hymn book lay on the desk. I was about to reach for it, when he picked it up and put it back on the shelf. By now, I was out of my seat. What was I supposed to do? I would look silly just sitting down again. With one sliding motion, I stepped towards the window and looked through the beads of clear water wriggling like transparent beetles in a race to the bottom of the pane. Beyond was the car park looking like a playground, the school playground, the yard where all the bullying had taken place. It had always seemed to happen on rainy days, the bullying.

I sat back down after a respectable time. Minutes passed. Then he put the papers back in the drawer and told me he would see me tomorrow. I was back in the day room before I knew it, humming

Abide With Me and wondering at the purpose of the strange meeting and what that had all been about.

Afternoon, evening, night, morning, dragged out in bewilderment, and always tired. Mid-afternoon and I was escorted back. I took my seat straightaway this time and waited. Once more he came in, only this time he wore jeans and a T-shirt. He also had a cassette recorder with him, which he placed on the desk. Out came the papers again, then the pen, then the ticking. I got bored with watching and began to nibble at my thumbnail as I watched an elderly bloke trying to park his car outside. I did not even hear the click of the play button being pressed. There was a hiss coming from the tape recorder, only for a second. It was instantly overpowered by the booming of a chord. Four beautiful notes joined in harmony coming from a cathedral organ. The last line of the hymn was being played in introduction. I had heard it countless times. My heart latched on to it as the choir came in on the first verse. It was a sound I once made.

"Abide with me, fast falls the eventide."

The bass line was solid, the tenors clear. There were the altos wholesome and feminine, but there at the top, it could have been me along with Ian Crabtree sounding like angels.

"The darkness deepens, Lord with me abide."

Down it went, the music, down the shaft it went. I could not stop it. I did not want to. It had seduced me. I let it go, swallowing down the tears that were trying to escape. I tried to stop the corners of my mouth dropping.

"When other helpers fail, and comforts flee."

Was that all the happiness I had been allowed to have, an hour on Thursday night and two hours on Sunday? Why had my happy ration been so small?

"Help of the helpless."

My breathing had become a series of trembled gasps. My eyes were leaking. I really tried to stop it. I really did, honestly.

"O abide with me."

I let go of it all. I leaned forwards so that my head lay in the palm of my hands and shook almost to the point of convulsions. It was a flood, a great outpouring, sob upon sob. My hands could not hold them, tears spilled out onto the carpet. The music was turned down, not off, but down. I felt a tissue against my hand. I stopped, blew my nose and sucked in the air as if it was my first breath.

Anyone else would have asked me if I was all right. Not him. He went and brought his chair from behind his desk and sat at right angles to me. He waited. I looked at him. He looked at me. I had to say something.

"Sorry about that," I said.

"Why should you feel sorry?" he asked.

"You know. For crying like that."

"Do you feel that's wrong, then?"

"Yes," I replied.

"Why?"

"It's weak. It shows that you're weak."

"Is that what you think, or what other people have told you?"

"I don't know. But everyone has weaknesses, even you I expect. I bet you have weaknesses, don't you?" I said.

"I do," he said, "I'm fat, overweight, and I've had two heart attacks in as many years. I have to watch what I eat, how much I drink and I have to keep fit, which I hate doing. I'm ashamed to be fat, but I am and I have to make the best of it," I was taken aback by his direct honesty. "And what's your weakness, David?"

Bastard, I thought, a direct hit. How could I say nothing after just crying like a baby? What excuse did I have? After a few moments to think about it I answered his question, or rather I did not.

"I don't want to talk about it," I said.

"So, you admit that there's an it something?" he said.

I could not bring myself to agree. I felt cornered. I had to free myself.

"Where did you get the recording?" I asked.

"Oh that. It's a copy of a record I have. I taped it especially for you. You can borrow it if you like. I won't be here tomorrow or the day after. Bring it back on Friday," he stood up and replaced his chair. "That's about it for today," he said, and then as if an afterthought had just struck him he asked. "How are your lungs now?"

"Getting better," I said, catching a sense of compassion in his look that made me add the word, "thanks."

I left with the tape recorder under my arm, determined to learn how to keep him out of my head. The strong box had to be protected from his sort, whatever it took. I wanted to go home. I wanted love not interrogation.

Ellie and John visited later. A strange meeting, with no real connection, distanced somehow. I said goodbye feeling parted from them by more than just geography. Perhaps it had something to do with the feeling of being trapped in the hospital. Or maybe it was because I was still tired. I do not know. At length, with nothing worthwhile to do, I played the tape recorder in the day room. There were two people there as I arrived and switched it on, but the hymns drove them away and I was left on my own.

Abide With Me ended, *Praise My Soul, The King Of Heaven* followed. Each opening line was like a time machine hurtling me back to a life that I never meant to relive. How strange the effect this music had. It made the past so real and gave things gone by a kind of reliving. This effect was felt the strongest as I heard *There Is A Green Hill Far Away* pour out of the little speaker, flooding my mind with memories of that first choir practice all those years ago and, like a flood, other memories spilled out. My mind was wandering. Wandering to places best left alone - but the music would have its own way and, to be honest, I was powerless to stop it. It was too seductive. It was like the stone was rocketing backwards off the window towards me and back into my whip hand. Back, back, back, back there.

'Up on the chair, she screamed, yelling with so much force that I jumped with the shock of it. I could see the wooden spoon being slapped against her palm. I could hear the sound of its impact on the inside of her hand. There was no choice. I hauled my bare body up on to the chair and waited for it to happen. I did not have to wait for long. The first one was a stinger, almost numbing. The second only a moment later was bang on the same target. I can feel it now, like a white-hot poker, burning and savage. Each time I winced as my soft buttocks were made red-raw in this way. There was no time for the pain to dissipate before the next whack slammed into my wobbling bottom. It made me want to puke. I tried not to cry, but in the end I had to. I cried out from the sheer pain. My punishment ended on the

350

sixth lashing. I felt as if a monster wasp had stung me. I was just a boy, embarrassed and humiliated, standing naked on a chair in agony.'

Lead Us Heavenly Father, Lead Us had led me down to the bottom of the mineshaft and the box had been unlocked. How had this happened? How come I was here? Why was I allowing these memories to violate me like this?

'The movement of her hand however halted my descent into somnolence. It had left my hair alone and was now undoing the buttons on my pyjama jacket. I was aware of the change as she lovingly traced her fingers over my chest, rubbing my nipples from time to time with her forefinger. I had awoken slightly, wondering what she was doing. Then the chord on my pyjama bottoms was untied, and her hand slipped down below. I was fully awake now, staring wide-eyed into the blackness of my room'.

The music suddenly stopped. The play button snapped up automatically. The tape had ended, stopped abruptly, and there was now silence. Like the ghosts that they were, the visions hung in the air around me, like so much smoke. It had not been a cathartic experience as I am sure it was intended to be. It was more a journey into an abyss, a descent into hell.

All that time, listening to the tape, my head had been still, as if in a trance, staring at the corner of a curtain while the hymns had played. I moved my neck and brought my eyes down onto the tape recorder. I could not take in what this little machine had just done.

"Clever little bastard, aren't we," I said to it, as if it was a living thing, respecting and detesting it at the same time. It had been a key, a key to locks that should never have been undone. Before I knew what I was doing I picked up the little box of tricks and cranked my arm back ready to propel the damn thing at the wall. I was going to bring it smashing against the wallpaper. Springs and circuit boards were going to explode in all directions. Its destruction would be complete and then I was going to crush the cassette under my heel and make sure that those secrets remained hidden away, reburied, resealed.

Then I thought better of it. Questions would be asked. They would want to know why I did it. More interrogation would follow. So I put it down on the easy chair and decided to be clever instead of reactive. Come Friday I would have to deal with the doctor, make him feel as if his work was done. Then I would be able to get out of here and rebuild a new me, so that no one would be able to reach into the dark recesses of my being again.

Friday arrived as quickly and as slowly as it could and I was soon back with him. I carefully placed the tape recorder on his desk and thanked him for letting me listen to it. My smiling face gave no indication to him that I knew of its power. He smiled back. Then, with no warning, he just came out with it. It was the questions of questions, the mother of all questions, and my smile vanished.

"David, will you tell me about your mother?"

"She's dead," came my answer, as I gathered my wits.

He said he already knew that. He persisted and asked me to tell him about her. Tell him? How was I supposed to do that calmly? My job was to make him feel as if he had finished his work. If I made a scene now there would be no escape.

"You don't want to talk about her, do you?" he went on.

I thought about what he was asking. If I said no, he would think that he was on to something. If I ran for the door like I wanted to, then I may as well chain myself to the wall. So I would have to say that I did not mind talking about her. After all, it did not have to be the truth, did it?

"I'll talk about her if you like," I said.

"But it's if you like," he said, correcting me, attaching me to the question, as good as if I were dangling from a meat hook.

"Go on then, ask me something about her, go on."

"No, you tell me something about her. I don't know anything about her, do I?"

"Her name was Charlotte," I said as if I was resurrecting the dead.

"And what was she like, was she fat, or slim?"

"She wasn't tall, but she was strong, strong, at first."

"What do you mean, at first?"

"She became more and more tired. You know, as the years went by."

"Why was that, do you think?"

"Work, she had to work to keep the three of us, and then when Ellie left, my Auntie Ellie, she had no one to help her, and she got tired."

"And you couldn't help her much, could you?"

"I tried," I said, remembering all the times I had peeled potatoes and cut up carrots.

"She must have been glad to have you around?"

The lie slipped out effortlessly.

"Oh she was," I said.

"In your own words, Davy," he went on, almost as if he had ignored my reply, "could you explain something to me?"

I nodded.

"Why did you run away to Auntie Ellie? You don't have to answer that but I will only imagine the worst if you don't tell me."

I had to think of a small reason, quickly, a small unimportant reason, a good reason. A reason that would not shed light on the past. Then it hit me.

"Ellie invited me and besides, the flat at mother's was too small. She seemed pleased for me to go, she really did."

"Mmm," he said, unfastening his briefcase.

He took out a clear plastic wallet that had a savagely creased piece of paper within it.

"Then forgive me Davy, but can you explain the meaning of this. I've tried to fathom it, but I need your help."

He handed it to me, slowly, watching my face as he did so, waiting for the moment that I recognised it. It was mother's note, the one that they had found next to her body. I had begun to tremble. I could not touch it. I was afraid. It was almost as if the paper was possessed by the devil.

Dear Davy,
I have come to the end of my tether. I can't bear to live anymore all by myself now that everyone has left me. I know now that you've left me too. I can forgive you for stealing most of my money, but I can't forgive you for running away and abandoning me to this life of loneliness.

I could not read anymore. I was biting my lip, heaving back a reservoir of emotions. I raised my head to meet his gaze. The bastard. He had got his fucking reaction. What more did he want? I felt panicked. But then, anyone would have been upset being forced to see their mother's suicide note, and I said the only thing that anyone who did not know the facts would have said. I told him that I did not understand it either. None of it was true I said. I told him that I thought she must have been ill.

"She seemed happy enough when we said goodbye," I said.

"So why didn't you leave a suicide note?" he asked on the heel of my reply.

"Suicide? I wasn't trying to…" I slammed on the brakes. I had already said too much, too much to the wrong man.

He clasped his hands and brought his index fingers up to form the spire of a church, which he placed meditatively to his lips while he thought.

"I don't believe you were trying to end your life either," he said.

What kind of game was he playing? He was calm and his voice was drenched in intellect, an intellect that was outsmarting me. He pushed the old question once more, but from a different angle.

"Would I have liked your mother, do you think?"

My mind was racing, trying to weave and bob. What a question.

"That depends on what kind of people you like?" I asked, playing for time.

"I think I might have liked her if you did," he answered. "What did you think of her?"

"She did her best for me," I began, resenting having to talk about her.

I hated him having to make me do this. He was clever. It was not so much the answers he was after but rather the way my answers came, the way he was forcing their delivery. He was taking in every inflection of my voice, the angle of my head, my breathing, my eyes, the multi-lingual facets of body language. I was tempted to blurt out the truth, to get it over with. After all, she was dead. What could she do to me? Plenty, that is what. Plenty when she was still alive in here. At least she was buried in here. Letting her out of the box was too frightening to contemplate. I was going to have to tell him lies.

354

"We didn't have much, but she always made sure that there was plenty of love around."

I loathed the words. I loathed him for making me say them. My mouth had been bent into a smile as I spoke, but behind my eyes I was loading up a super gun. I was going to use my empire to fire a shot across his bow. No, I was going to hit him. Sink him.

"She must have loved you very much," he said.

"Oh yes," I said with my happy voice, "very much indeed."

"And how did she show you that love?" he said.

The breach was open. In went a huge shell, three feet in diameter.

"Did she hold your hand?"

The breach closed. The smile was cracking.

"Did she put her arms around you? Did she hold you in her arms?"

I took aim, bringing my sights to bear dead centre between his eyes. The smile was gone.

"Did she kiss you a lot David?"

I widened my stare. I could almost feel the recoil as the blast let rip and the shell vomited forth from the barrel. I said nothing, just stared.

"What did she do to you David?"

With that I was out of my seat. I threw my body at him. In half a second we were nose to nose. I felt exultant as I saw him jump out of his skin with fright. I was growling like a dog, no, more like a leopard. His eyes began to screw up tightly and he tried to climb to his feet, but he was too fat and too ill and his intellect could not save him. The last thing he did was to clutch the white coat near to his heart. Now it was he who was wondering what was going on. His stare was gazing at a deep, black unknown. He was petrified by fear. His mouth gaped open just like a fish taken out of water. Then he slumped, falling heavily back into his seat. The sound of a snap came from the bones inside his neck as it whip-lashed over the back of the chair.

I stepped back to my own chair and spent a second or two taking in the event that had just occurred. Had the gun really worked? Had I just performed something supernatural? Then I thought of my own survival. It took only a moment to run out into the corridor and yell for help. People were soon on their way, as I took a backward glance into the room where a head hung upside down over the back of a

355

chair, looking at me. The eyes were open but the life was gone out of them.

Chapter fourteen: Push

The questions the police asked over the days following the doctor's death were crude and matter-of-fact, the antithesis of the kind the poor doctor had used on me. With their straightforwardness I was able to answer them truthfully and without fear that they would bore into my being. The two plain clothes officers wanted to know where I was seated when the doctor had passed away, what I had done during our session, what I had witnessed. They talked to me as if I was a small child, seemingly walking on eggshells, as they probed the inmate about the last moments of the doctor's life. I just said that we were talking, that he put his hand to his chest and had fallen into his chair. They took my fingerprints, made me write a hand-written statement and took my photograph. After all that I never saw them again.

I kept the image of the doctor's dying face in my mind for some time. It did not haunt me as I worried it might. I felt sorry for him of course. I knew that my giant gun was an imaginary one and yet it had empowered me, empowered me to resist him. Had I terrified him so much? Had I caused his heart attack? Would it have happened anyway? He had mentioned his condition to me. Maybe I should have thought about that before I lunged at him, but I told myself, his time had come, it was not my fault. I told myself that over and over, many, many times. I do not think I ever fully believed it deep down. I often wondered what would have happened if I had just remained seated.

Ellie came over to see me on her own later in the week. She had arrived by taxi, she said. She looked tired, careworn and not her usual self. I said I felt as if I had let her down. She smiled weakly and told me not to be so silly. I asked her what was wrong. She half-smiled again and said that nothing was. I knew she was lying. I had lived with unhappiness long enough to know. I told her how I yearned to come home. She said that I was better off in here. Better off for whom I wondered? It was beautiful when she put her arms around me as we said goodbye - beautiful and miserably heartbreaking. I watched her walk to the taxi outside. Only it was not a taxi, it was a Rover, a black one. I could see John at the wheel. He did not even turn to look at me. He had abandoned me. I shuffled back to my prison feeling destroyed, alone, broken and heavy.

Over the next few weeks I was seen by a variety of other doctors. They were all different and yet all the same. Firstly, there was the frail woman with mousy hair, Mrs Bryce, who insisted that I closed my eyes whenever we spoke. She was infuriating, droning a meditative umm when I answered a particularly relevant point, nodding her head as if to emphasise it. I peeked occasionally to see her doing it. I liked Jack Bentley best of all. He brought me fags and we talked about all sorts of things. He was a cockney, well an East Ender at any rate. For days we chatted about this and that, what he had done with his life, how he had been a Physics teacher for twelve years and how he had been divorced twice. Like me he had an overbearing mother. A lot of what he said sounded like he was talking about my life. Too like mine in fact. I began to suspect him. One day, when he went out for a pee, I rushed his drawer and found a copy of my notes stuffed in there. In the margins he had written suggestions for gaining my confidence. Assimilate that you once had a domineering mother to explore the mother-son relationship. I was not quite sure what assimilate meant but from that moment on I held him at arm's length and used him just for fags.

I had five trick cyclists altogether, all conmen as far as I could tell. I got quite good at peddling a story about a happy childhood and a balanced upbringing. I even made up a tale about the car and the hosepipe, that the heating had packed up and I was using the exhaust to warm the car up. It made me look idiotic but not suicidal. More to the point I was able to keep my secrets safe. They tried to make me cry with emotional ambushes. They tried to catch me out with open-ended questions and metaphors. They talked about the incident with Alan Dixon and the driving lesson up on the aerodrome. They wanted to know what motivated me to lash out at Gwen. I admitted

357

that the days after the funeral had put a strain on me but that I was over that now. All the time I kept up the act. It was particularly difficult to keep up when mother was brought into play but, as time went on, I managed to clothe her in a disguise. In my head I imagined we were discussing a fictional character, Mrs Peggotty from *David Copperfield* for example, or Auntie Em from *The Wizard of Oz*. With these visions before me I could pass through the minefield that they made me traverse. I made myself take part in life at the hospital too, learning to play chess and taking lessons from eighty-five year old Mary Tomkiss on the upright piano in the corner of the hall. I even sang at the concert given that Christmas.

By the end of nine months in there I was told that they felt I was no longer a danger to myself or to others. How strange, I thought. How strange. I had always yearned to get out of the place and, now that I had the chance I did not want to. They allowed me to phone Ellie from the office. I had got my confidence back and as I heard the ring-out tone stop and a voice pick up and say hello, I was in a buoyant state of mind.

The Ellie I knew and loved had changed. Our conversation was one of logistics and pick up times. She was pragmatic with me. I sensed trouble. There was a leak in my buoyancy and I began to dread the future again. One look around the day room, the hall and the garden made me realise that this had not been a prison. It had been my refuge. I was frightened to leave it. Never mind that the nights had been punctuated by the sounds of people crying or that at unpredicted times of the day a primal scream could be heard in a far-off room. In here there had been an order. Meal times began and finished with such precision that you could set your watch by them. It had never been possible to find total privacy, but then there had never been a time when I did not feel looked after. It was almost as if I had once been a high-wire performer who had fallen and come to harm. Only now I was on the verge of being placed back on the wire to continue the act. Ignorance is bliss, so they say, and knowledge is power. The knowledge that it was possible to fall from the wire was unnerving and I felt no empowerment, only a lurking sense of dread.

My suspicions were well founded. One early January morning, as the crisp, freezing air pricked the back of my throat I stepped out into the unknown. The New Year's party was a faint memory and the year nineteen seventy-eight had ceased to be brand new. Already it was time to leave. With leaden reluctance I moved my things onto the back seat of the Rover and peered pensively through its rear window. My heart's grip held on to the mock Tudor frontage of Saxenby Hospital, unable to prevent the view receding as the car pulled away. I waved back at the building as much as to the few people who had turned out to see me off. In seconds we reached the main Nottingham road and made speed towards the A46. John and Ellie were in the front. Their togetherness was gone. A sickness had infected their relationship and I could see very clearly that I had something to do with it.

Taking the Lowdham Road we arrived back at The Croft in no time at all. It was bleak inside, dark, forbidding even and, like the relationship of the people whose home it was, the warmth had gone from the place too. I could sense the echoes of a hundred arguments, clinging to the walls as I took my bags to my room. I knew that I no longer belonged. I could hear John and Ellie moving around downstairs but there was no conversation between them. Even my room did not want me anymore. Old Rose who had died there seemed to want to prise it back. I relived the last time I sat on the end of the bed putting my tie on ready to go to work, fearful of seeing Mr Harrison again, unaware of what kind of day it would eventually turn out to be. The future. It was impossible to plan. How was I supposed to move on? I had forgotten how to tread the high wire.

Ellie knocked on the bedroom door after a while and entered without invitation. She looked drained, her eyes especially had suffered and, although she was not crying, her eyes looked well practised in it. She said it was about time that we had a proper talk. Not just a chat mind, a proper talk. I followed her down to the study where a tension lingered like a bad odour. John, sitting in his usual chair had changed beyond his old self. He appeared irritable, I would say pissed off if he had not been a vicar - but it was more than that. He was burdened with something, something that made him feel uneasy. It was impossible not to pick up on it. I looked round to Ellie

359

for some kind of reassurance, only to find a carbon copy of John's expression planted upon her face. I began to feel a tightening of my gut and a dry feeling in my throat.

"There are things you ought to know, David," he said as I stood there like a corporal on a charge, "things we have to talk about, unpleasant things."

I could sense the faint vibrations of a tremble running through my legs as I nodded my receipt of the words.

"Firstly, Eleanor and I want you to find a place of your own. The last few months have put a great strain on her and it is my decision that she should be spared any more. Of course, we will help you do this, but at twenty one years of age now David, it's time that you began to stand on your own two feet."

My knees struggled to keep me upright and I asked to sit down. John pointed to the arm of the easy chair where Ellie was sitting and I lowered myself without dignity as his words continued.

"You will also need to find a new job, I'm afraid. Mr Saltby's wife died last September. His loss has affected him deeply and he has been unable to work since. A manager has been put in place until he's well enough to return and this manager has hired a new representative to do your job. Fortunately he has penned me a useful reference for you to present to future employers. Talking of which, I have taken the liberty of cutting out a few job vacancies from the *Newark Advertiser*. You're good at approaching firms, so it should be no trouble for you to secure an interview," he looked closer at me and removed his spectacles. "David, whatever was the matter with you, you're over it now. You've got to put it behind you and get on with your life. I don't mean to sound hard, but it's the only way for a grown man to follow. We'll do all we can to help you of course, but I'm afraid you cannot remain here."

I swallowed past the hard lump jammed in my throat and felt the resurrection of the lost emotions that had gripped me on that first day at school. Ellie took a deep sigh but said nothing as she stared at the carpet. It eloquently declared her agreement with John, who by now had got up from behind his desk and handed me the newspaper cuttings. Then he took Ellie's hand and they left me in the study to be alone to read them.

Instead, once they shut the door on their way out, I sat there by myself and came to grips with my isolation. These little pieces of paper were all I had to call a future. What was I to make of them? All hope was contained in the words printed on the snipped out paper rectangles, but it was the removal of happiness that was the worst to bear. The excommunication, the denial of love that had once flowed so freely that cut the deepest. In this room I faced true loneliness because I had now known true affection. Taking that away pained me to the heart. It drugged me with its misery. Davy boy all washed up, alone. The thought hit me repeatedly, like bullets from a machine gun, hurting my soul, bruising it until it wept. In my hands the little pieces of paper began to absorb the drops of moisture dripping on them. There, in private, I held them to my face and sobbed quietly into them so that no one would be able to hear me, not even mother.

I heard the mail arrive a few days later and ran downstairs to pick it up. The envelope was coloured cream and had a logo printed on it in red. Carridges it said in a paintbrush style, with the word Printers Ltd set underneath in a more formal type. I slit the envelope with a knife and unfolded the letter within. If things went to form it would be another rejection like the other three - but it was not. It was an invitation for an interview, an interview for the post of sales representative. I was to report to Alan Carridge no less. Rejection had been easy to deal with. It created emotions that went inward. Rejection required no response except self-pity. A reply like this though was something altogether different. This created nerves that went outwards and demanded I do something about it.

I had known about Carridges for years. Their premises were on the other side of the street from Saltbys, on the corner of Barngate and the street that led to St Mary's church, called Kirkgate, unsurprisingly. Nothing ever seemed to happen there, except for the regular deliveries of paper through the Kirkgate entrance and the loading of the Carridges' van with finished jobs. Saltbys had all their forms printed there but I had never been inside to see how it was done. Maybe now I would get my chance. The date was set for Monday 15th February at 3pm, two whole weeks away.

Ellie, meanwhile, tried to repair bridges by coming with me on flat hunting expeditions. She was doing her best to help me grow up and took an interest in the places we looked at, giving her honest opinion about the various aspects of each one. I would then take her shopping around Newark and gradually we found our old selves again. Poor old Ellie was ill I could tell. Now in her mid-thirties, she should have been in the prime of life. Instead she tired easily. Yet she pushed on, pushing me on, until one afternoon we found a place reached by a side door in a little enclosed alleyway of shops known as The Arcade that led from the large cobbled Market Square. Upstairs through the side door was a well-maintained living room, kitchen and bedroom with a toilet and shower leading directly off it. The interior decor was a little old fashioned but there was no damp and the heating worked, so long as the meter was fed with its diet of coins. Ellie and I went to the landlord's office later on and she managed to get a six-month reduction in the rent. She was marvellous to watch in action, using all her feminine charm to appeal to the middle-aged man to get what she wanted. She was polite yet forceful, a real role model when it came to assertiveness.

When we made our way outside once more her colour drained away and we had to go and find a cafe so that she could sit down. I was worried about her and demanded that she tell me what was wrong. She absorbed my concern and reached over to take my hands that had been lying on the table as we waited for our teas. She smiled the smile I knew and said that nothing was wrong. There was a pregnant pause as she steadied herself to let loose with the words. Her voice was calm just like it always was. She was not poorly she explained, she was just having a baby that was all. From that moment on everything fell into place. I now knew why it was so important for me to find a place of my own. John and Ellie were to become a family, a real family and, although I was close to Ellie, even though I once called her Auntie, there was never a blood link, I would never reach that high status of being true family. Somehow I managed to congratulate her, knowing full well that the foetus growing in her belly was pushing me out into the big wide world, where it was cold and lonely and a little frightening.

362

Everything rested on the interview, everything, particularly the shimmering land in the distance called the future. My future. I worried about it constantly, mainly because of my feelings of not being up to it. What they would ask? How much would they expect me to know about their line of work? Selling was easy, as long as you knew what you were talking about. At Saltbys I had soaked up mountains of information about agricultural equipment. It was a key that worked and it would have to be the same with Carridges. Just a little research and I would be able to impress them with a choice selection of jargon. It could not be that complicated, could it, pressing ink onto paper?

John, who was taking an accelerated interest in my progress, suggested that I visit the library near the castle. He even offered to drop in on Carridges' office and pick me up a company brochure if they had one. Meanwhile I badgered the young female librarian to help me find books on my chosen topic. There was not much of a choice. I had the pick of *Printing Through The Ages*, more of a history volume with more reference to Caxton than modern day methods. Then there was one called *The Story Of The Press* but it focussed maddeningly on newspapers. The young lady said she would go out to the back room and look in there and would I please wait? I waited. She emerged after three or four minutes trying to hold back a victorious smile.

"I hope this will do?" she said, presenting me with a large coloured book.

Taking it from her our hands brushed. She looked at me for the briefest moment, then darted her lowered eyes away like a frightened animal. The book was heavy as I brought it to rest on the table. The cover showed a set of metal printing letters on a flat steel device. The letters were upside down and back to front but I could see straightaway that they spelled out the title, set in larger type at the top, *A World In Print*. Inside, were black and white, and colour photographs, with pages crammed full of terms and processes. There was a chapter on printing history of course, but beyond that an unknown world opened up. I was enthralled by it all. Even the story of how the particular book I was reading had been made was told as if it had been created by magic. Printing. There was a beauty to it, a simple sophistication. I was going to enjoy this.

The brochure John got for me was not so helpful, except for learning how long the firm had been in business. They were established in nineteen twenty-seven. They boasted a wide range of presses, one of which was a Heidelberg. I read about them in the book and made a mental note.

Before I knew it I was being shown into a room littered with folders, files and mountainous piles of paper. Behind a desk that was in the throes of a war against administration, was a young man smart and alert. His mind seemed to be elsewhere as he asked me to move some boxes off a chair and sit down. I handed him my reference from Saltbys, which he took without reading, dropping it onto the desk, where it joined in the war against tidiness. The walls were festooned with graphs, maps and notice boards crammed with letters and other companies' business cards. The same management of chaos reigned here in much the same way as it had at Saltbys. This was a world I was familiar with and immediately I began to feel less intimidated.

"So, why do you want this job?" he asked, and sat back to see my reaction.

"I'm good at selling things," I started. "I like to excel at the things I'm good at, and I'd like yours to be the company to benefit from it."

It was sick-making, old charm and bluster, pouring forth from a wellspring somewhere in the centre of me.

"But I don't like selling rubbish. Oh, no. I want to work for a company that can turn out a quality product like this."

I pulled out of my suit pocket a handful of samples that had been resting in a leaflet dispenser on the coffee table in the front office. He smiled. A spark arced between us, just as it had done with countless customers at the old place across the road. I knew I was reeling him in. Bit by bit with manufactured sincerity I built up our rapport. I even asked to look round and to see his Heidelberg. He was taken by surprise, but excited that someone should be so interested.

It was like delving into the engine room of a tramp steamer. How on earth clean printed matter emerged from such filthy conditions seemed an impossibility, and the clattering, rhythmic noise of the presses was enough to send you deaf. We shouted our conversation over the din, over the sound of a million sewing machines rattling their levers back and forth. He pointed, spinning his index finger around where rollers were doing likewise. His hand flowed downwards where I could see paper performing the same charade as him. He tapped one of the operators, an old man, nearing retirement, wearing a light brown overall. Mr Carridge asked him to step aside and from the end of the booming machine, pulled out a sheet of paper still wet with ink. It was an invitation to the Mayor's Ball, with gold edging and flowing, elegant writing on it. All across the workshop other machines were doing similar jobs. He then took me to another area where two smaller machines stood idle. It was a little quieter in here but he still had to shout.

"We need to generate more business to keep these beauties fed with work. Think you're up to it?" he said.

"Try and stop me," I said, throwing as much positive energy into the reply as I could.

We concluded the interview back in his office and I left unsure of how I had done. I would be notified within a week. That is all I was told. Doubtless there would be more like me, eager to pour their various brands of dynamism onto him. One week, that was all I could guarantee. I drove back to Edlington running the meeting over and over, again and again, sifting for errors or missed opportunities. I felt tired. How could I face a future with my mind in such a mess - a future on my own at that? Just thinking about it made me want to sleep for the rest of my life.

I went for two more interviews, one at a glue factory and another at a motor dealer. Both were awful, dingy places with matching people. I strolled into town after the last attempt to get a cup of tea. I forced myself to The Arcade afterwards and stood for a few seconds looking resentfully at the black door that led to the flat. Anyone else would have found the prospect exciting. All Legs certainly would have. I just felt the overwhelming desire to have a proper mum look after me. My body sighed all by itself, a long outpouring of breath that did no good at all.

A week passed during which I wrote off for more jobs. It all seemed so futile, sitting at the kitchen table, using my best handwriting and best phrases trying to make a good impression. Then the second cream envelope arrived with the Carridges' logo on it. The letter was wrenched out. Would it be we regret to inform you, or we are glad to say? It was neither. It said that I was to attend a second interview. Ellie said that it was a positive sign. John was encouraging and, had it not been for his hitherto hidden agenda, I might have found his encouragement genuine.

Anyway I went for the interview. I gave them my ideas on how I could improve their sales. It was a development on the Saltby days. A combination of mailshots and aggressive canvassing that is how I was going to do it, with accurate record keeping of how each campaign had performed so we would know what had worked best. I was full of bullshit but it was good bullshit and he loved it. He told me that I was the best candidate and that today's meeting only served to confirm it. Salary and commission discussions followed. Holiday entitlement and the company pension scheme were ironed out. I would have use of the company van for appointments and to make deliveries and I was to start a week on Monday. That was it. We shook hands and bid each other good day. Stepping into a grey afternoon I left wondering what I had let myself in for.

Ordinarily I would have expected some sense of celebration at home but the mood there was strained. My past behaviour did not help of course and my low mood only made matters worse. All our faces reflected it and it was a wonder we were not at each other's throats. To be fair Ellie and John had agreed that I could stay at The Croft until my first salary cheque had cleared the bank. So a date created by Carridges' pay office was set for a life cut off from them. In one month's time I would finish the day's work in a strange empty place and wake to the same ghastly situation. I kept it all to myself though. They had no idea how much heartache I was keeping a lid on. If there was one thing that my life with mother had taught me it was to hide hurt away. Back then it had been a matter of survival, but I could never fully fool myself then and not now.

So the world spun on its smooth axis and rolled along its invisible track around father sun. One twelfth of an orbit it travelled, by the end of which I was opening my morning eyes to another world. Only this world was a lonely, cheerless place. From the low position of my bed I saw the outline of daylight breaking through the edges of two curtains. The projected light fanned upwards onto a high ceiling like sunlight does from behind a cloud, illuminating flaking wallpaper and stains created heaven knows how. The bed was just about all the furniture there was in the room. Everything else was spread over the floorboards, clothes, shaving things, alarm clock and shoes. Cartergate, the road that ran at right angles to The Arcade, was getting busy. I heard a whistling man walk by down at pavement level. All the sounds of life rose up to the first floor, but up here there was no indigenous sound save my own breathing. There was no sound of Ellie coming downstairs humming as she used to. No John to impart advice to us both.

I got out of my pit and felt immediately cold. The low temperature rammed home that I was on my own. The cold world that I was going to have to make my own way in was exerting its power to crush me. Just by making me cold it was proving that it could flatten my tiny spirit whenever it wanted. The thought of getting a breakfast of sorts seemed too much to handle, but a person will do anything if they are hungry. So I got dressed and went out, through The Arcade towards the Market Place. Just past there was a Wimpy restaurant. I bought a Bender something-or-other, strange by name and strange by taste. It seemed such an extraordinary thing to do, to just go out and buy a breakfast. The whole thing made me feel extraordinary too. It was eight o'clock and I would have to be at work in half an hour, so I returned to my queer little flat to have a shave and get ready.

Going to work was the best thing I could have done. Having already completed a month there I was beginning to feel at home. Mr Carridge was supportive but did not suffer fools. He wanted results and he was not backward at coming forward in demanding them. Whilst he showed a keen interest in the systems I had set up, he never let me forget that they were there only to assist the outcome, that being an increase in orders. We worked well together but were by no means friends.

367

That honour went to Colin in accounts. He made me laugh and being a great practical joker there was always some kind of mayhem happening around him. His immediate boss was a tin goddess. Busty Brenda she was known as, and her attributes were so enormous that they sat contentedly on her desk, sometimes for hours, as she went through her ledgers. Colin had planned to place two areas of binding glue on her desk having first ascertained where exactly these wondrous shapes would settle themselves. Thursday was set aside as the best day, when she prepared the figures for the weekly meeting on Friday. Colin had waited for her customary trip to the loo then, with split second timing he had done the deed with the glue before she got back. Colin explained all this with a deadpan expression. I found it hard to keep a straight face as he went on to describe the shrieks of horror from poor old Busty as she tried to leave for lunch two hours later. I heard about it on the grapevine, so to be taken into his confidence like this helped to forge a bond between Colin and I. However, he was newly married, a fact that precluded any social life we might have shared. Instead, when home time arrived I would slink back to my empty flat and wish the empty night away.

The months passed by in a whirl of sleeping and working interspersed with buying food, cooking, washing up, clothes washing, ironing and cleaning. I never had all this to do for myself before. By the time I rolled into bed I was in the last stages of extreme fatigue. But what could I do? I had to put up with it and, even though I yearned to have Ellie cook a meal for me again, I knew that those days were gone. They were gone for good. In the early days I used to drive the firm's van to Edlington to see the baby, little Matthew, hoping for a little free grub too. I was made welcome in a don't-stay-too-long kind of way. Things had changed there. The baby was all consuming. My bicycle was still there but the car had gone. The Morris Minor was sold during my time in hospital and it was with a little uncertainty that Ellie waved me off, as I said goodbye and headed back to Newark to begin another week at Carridges.

Work was monotonous and uninspiring. It seemed as if I had managed to fool myself too during the interview. Now and again I would secure a large printing order, usually bulk orders for business forms, triplicate NCR pads for invoicing, or delivery notes, goods receipts and the like, and that feeling of achievement kept me going. These orders though were what kept the presses going, that was the main thing, and my follow up strategy made sure that they would come back for more. I was hardly ever disappointed with how obsessed with their own companies most businessmen were. They would entertain me with details of immense triviality, going microscopic on me when giving me their printing requirements. All the time I picked up the lingo - point size, leading, fan apart sets, interleaving, crash numbering, Bodoni, Palace Script, Helvetica, spot colour, registration. After six months I was an expert or so I thought. At least I was an expert in knowing what most customers craved from us. It was speed and reliability. That is what they wanted.

So part of the job was working closely with old man Cooke the shop-floor gaffer, to make these promises come true. Cookey was an old hand. He had been in printing all his life, except for a brief spell in the army and an even longer spell building a railway for the Japs. He went over to Burma in nineteen forty-three young and fit with a crop of auburn hair. He returned with pneumonia, malaria and thinning wisps of snowy white crowning his old head. He hated anything Japanese and would have no war talk within earshot, but he had been blessed by the military discipline received in his youth. It had served him in the jungles of Asia and it enabled him to come up with the goods in a sickeningly reliable fashion. I never enjoyed bringing him a job for this reason. He would stare through me as I gave him the job specifications, almost as if I was a child, which, I suppose, is just what I must have seemed to him. Then, somehow, he would go away and do it, organising his team as if they were a platoon.

In this way years passed by. Layers of identical days laid like the pages of a book on top of one another. I never got used to being lonely, tolerating it like one does a bad back. By the mid-eighties I had become Marketing Manager for the firm, and Carridges were going into full colour printing. There was talk of moving to bigger premises. I felt valued but it was never quite enough somehow.

Chapter fifteen: The Widow

"You're kidding? Widow Twankey?" grinned Colin.

"Don't let her catch you calling her that," I said.

"Yeah, but half past seven. That's way out of office hours, isn't it? Above and beyond the call, and all that," he said winking at me with that impish face of his.

"It's just a business meeting and no more. We'll be talking about letterheads, comp slips, a new company brochure perhaps."

"And she can't see you between nine and five?"

"She's a busy woman, is Mrs Tindale," I said, feeling needled.

"Not too busy to book a table at the Olde England Hotel though. I expect you'll be going in your new company car then?"

"She's picking me up, in her Merc."

"Ooooh," said Colin, pretending to sound camp, "Trapped, that's what you'll be. Come into my parlour you poor old fly."

"It's all in your filthy mind Colin. This is business," I replied, beginning to feel more nervous than I had been.

I stopped off at the launderette on the way home and shared a couple of jokes with Sheila who worked there. Bless her heart, she had picked up a couple of pints of milk and a loaf of bread for me with her shopping. I told her about the meeting later on, but all she could comment was that she had never been in a Mercedes before.

I headed for home. The flat was a tip as usual. Even though there was more furniture in it now, including a wardrobe, I never had the time to keep things in shape. It was enough just to cook a meal and wash up after a day's work. Sometimes I simply left the dishes to rot, though a day of reckoning could never be avoided for long. I hated living by myself.

Nights were the worst. Nights possessed by dreams - not every night but often. Perhaps they had something to do with cycling to Edlington but I was usually on a bike, riding to a village and never being able to get out. The frustration of it always made me wake up. In some way I was glad because it seemed to me that I was spared the worst of it and had escaped the terror of a nightmare. I remembered those dreams when I was in the old house and was always relieved when I had woken up.

I glanced round at the clothes strewn everywhere and the library books scattered where they had been dropped, and chose to leave them there. Instead I groomed myself for the evening to come. Tonight I was going to pick up enough business so that I could lie back on my laurels for the rest of the month.

I emerged into the evening air looking pretty good and feeling confident with that sense of youth being on my side, cocky almost and full of life. She was bang on time, perfectly punctual, a true pro. Even through the windscreen I could tell that she was worldly-wise. Leaning across the passenger seat she flipped the door handle and swung it open. It was impossible to miss the view as I stepped in. Both breasts hung like ripe fruit inside a lace-topped blouse. The top three buttons were undone, framing the scene. She had seen me look. She saw that fraction of a second flick of my darting eye and she fashioned a wicked smile, a small smile, controlled but very provocative.

Mrs Tindale had been married to a local tycoon of sorts. Not a big tycoon in the great scheme of things but big in these parts. He had been known as The Chemical King, supplying many well-known companies with industrial chemicals and gases. His picture was often in *The Advertiser* doing great deeds like donating money to worthy causes and such like, but in every picture he looked like a tired old bastard. Now being close to his widow I could not help wondering if his demise was completely down to hard work. I mean Mrs Tindale was a handsome woman, late twenties perhaps. Everything about her exuded a wealthy knowledge of life. Her legs, slim and shapely, knew how to aim her in the right direction, usually towards money, lots of it. Her face was elegant with high cheekbones beautifully made up but the kind of face that was dismissive of idiots. Not a hair was out of place. When she said the single word hello, I knew that I was out of my depth.

With the flick of her wrist on the selector, the Merc, an automatic, heaved quietly forwards through the streets and aimed for the A1. She was a slick, no nonsense, got-what-she-wanted type of woman. I sat like a lap dog in the passenger seat and tried to make small talk. I felt small, but she liked it and laughed at what pathetic wit I was able to muster. Now and again I turned my face from the dual carriageway passing beneath us and looked at her. She was like a Bond girl, full bodied and submerged in scent. Even before we got to the hotel my head was in a spin.

The Olde England Hotel was aptly named, set as it was in a wreath of trees. It even had a cockeyed roof made of pantiles that gave it character. We passed by the bar to the restaurant, running the gauntlet of admiring stares all aimed at her. Inside oak beams supporting a low ceiling created an atmosphere of cosiness. I was anything but cosy. Just holding on to my nerve put relaxing out of reach. I tried to concentrate on making sure I did not foul up any deal that may be coming my way. I moved my briefcase so that I could reach it easily. She saw me make the preparation and leaned an inch or so towards me.

"Look," she said, with a disarming smile, "you've got the printing and whatever you do as far as I'm concerned. So put your case away and relax. We're not at work now."

I do not mind admitting I was outclassed. I moved the case out of sight as requested and watched her order a bottle of wine.

"You do like wine, don't you?" Not waiting for an answer she said, "I hope they hurry up with the menu, I'm ravenous."

"What sort of business are you starting up?" I asked.

"Oh, come on Mr Harper no shop talk please. I've left all that back at the office and I suggest you do too. Why don't you tell me about yourself instead, no let me guess. You're an Aries, aren't you? Got a girlfriend?"

"Aries yes, girlfriend no."

"Mmm, I'll have to see if I can fix you up with someone then, won't I?"

"And who do you suggest?" I asked, daring to return her gaze.

"I know just the person," she said knowingly. "You just leave her to me."

As the evening drifted by I sank increasingly under her strange medicine. It was a combination of seduction and a misty unknown. She tantalised me from the beginning with her eyes and body. It came naturally to her, angling her figure like a living sculpture, and performing eyelash art at me. She drew me out of myself to speak as if to a confessor, often gabbling about things I had never let slip to another soul. Like the time I pedalled to Edlington. How she was able to do this without my defences going up I cannot explain. She was able to put me at my ease and in the next moment she would flick strands of her golden hair back over her shoulders and trade one of those breathtaking smiles of hers.

A waiter proffered leather-bound menus, took our orders and left, leaving us both in a state of anticipation. His move had punctuated the conversation and upset its fragile momentum, until she kick-started our talk towards the future and how I saw my own. I answered vaguely, having only a hazy idea myself. I thought Carridges a good firm to work for and that I thought I was getting on there. Her eyes stared into mine as if making sure that I was telling the truth. Then she asked about the flat and how I felt living there. Did I mind being on my own? A picture of the desolate place came into my head and I confessed that I hated being by myself. I did not mention the dreams of course, but I admitted to her that the night was the worst time of all. I could see her mind going down the same track as mine. She saw me pick up on it and she apologised.

Our meals finally arrived, leaving the strange moment hanging in the air just above our heads. Hers was a beautifully presented dish of duck, hidden beneath a veil of sauce, the tang of orange from it just detectable. The waiter served our vegetables, arranging mine beside a medallion of steak, an inch-thick slab of tender meat bathed in a pepper sauce that ran over the plateau of beef like molten lava.

The conversation moved on to the safe topic of food for a while. She ordered more wine. Even in doing this simple thing I could see her command of life. We had wine at The Croft on several occasions but this was something different. She had a way of doing things. It was her courtesy coupled with an enormous assertiveness.

We both drank and ate and she began to tell me about Mr Tindale. He had been a powerful man, she explained, not just powerful in a local politics kind of way. His whole being was a powerhouse. He wanted and expected the best, the best out of his investments, the best out of his businesses, of which he had quite a few, but mostly, he demanded the best out of his people. He searched out the best experts in their field and fashioned teams that way - teams that would profit their employment on the one hand, and him to prosperity on the other. He was very good at that, but he wanted an attractive wife to wear like a badge she told me. She said that she had been too young to realise that he was using her when they first met at a dance. All the money he lavished on her blinded her to it. She was often left alone in that great house of theirs and, when he was there, they lived almost separate lives, even sleeping apart.

I sat there astounded that this elegant woman was telling me all this. She was a stranger up until a couple of hours ago. I was drawn into those exquisite eyes. Eyes that possessed a gravitational pull, eyes that in the dim light of the restaurant appeared larger than ever. Even now, as they looked sadly down towards the table, I could not fight them. I watched, unable to move as they flicked up and caught me looking. Electricity flashed through every organ of my body as she hooked me in. Then the waiter came, took our sweet order and removed the empty plates. Another moment evaporated and hung like a mist over and around us.

I cannot recall what sweet we had, a Grand Marnier Supreme or something like it. What I do remember is the way she ate it, playing with it as the little girl hidden inside her might have. She let the spoon rest on her lower lip, closed her mouth around it and slid it empty from a glossy pout. I did the same just for fun. It made her smile. She could see me relaxing. Maybe that is what made her smile.

We left the table and went into another, quieter room away from the restaurant to sit on a couple of armchairs arranged close to a log fire burning in a large grate. Once more she bade the waiter bring coffee and liqueurs, which duly arrived on the small table that rested near to us. Once more she felt the need to talk about life with the late Eric Tindale.

"You understand loneliness don't you?" she asked.

Before I could reply she said she did too. I poured us both a Cointreau from the small bottle she had ordered and it warmed us both from the inside, and inside my head my mind was giving in. I told her that being on my own was crushing me as if a weight was bearing down on me. If it had not been for the job, I said, I would have gone crazy. At night, all alone, I could almost cry myself to sleep.

Her warm hand reached across and placed it over mine. She knew where my words were coming from. It felt it as if our minds had become connected. Her whole demeanour was full of compassion. I could feel a tremble coursing through my body. I tried to stop it. It would not.

"You don't have to be lonely anymore, you know?"

I looked at her for further clarification, realising straight away what she might mean.

"I often watched you when I came to pick up Eric's printing. I've seen you in the back office, on the phone, or saying goodbye to a customer. I love your smile. I love the way you are with people. You're a very attractive man Mr Harper."

My trembling intensified.

"And you are a beautiful woman," I replied, unable to hold it back.

"Then why do two good people have to put up with being lonely?" she said, and with that she got up and pulled me out of my chair.

"I've got a room booked, if that's all right with you?"

The Cointreau, the wine, the perfume, her ways, all had laid bare any resistance I might have mounted. I had fought this for years, tooth and nail and yet I followed her upstairs to a room halfway down a corridor, a room that was warm and smelled of jasmine.

As soon as the door clicked shut the white blouse fell away. The dim wall lights were on and she had no inhibitions. Except on posters and the odd magazine in Saltby's restroom I had never seen a young woman's breasts in the flesh before. They were perfectly elegant three-dimensional liquidity and they quivered as she came up to me, removed my shirt and tie and pressed their warmth against my chest. I buried my mouth around her neck, because this time it was me who wanted this to happen. Or was it the effect of the drink? Whatever was going on the desires seemed all my own. Every taboo about what I was about to do had been silenced - silenced by this woman who had somehow crossed the dark abyss to reach me. Her musk filled my nostrils, intoxicating, luxuriously tempting. In a strange backward dance, we staggered towards the bed. She fell backwards onto it and I fell on top of her. For one brief age, we shared a gaze, a gaze of screaming want before our mouths mingled together and our tongues intertwined.

How could the tables have been turned so swiftly? This woman, a person above me, high and mighty, a pillar of society, was letting me be an animal with her. I have no recollection of becoming nude. I remember ripping off her skirt to discover no underwear there. All night she had worn nothing but a blouse and a skirt, all through the drive when I had been drawn to her legs, and then at the dinner table she had been virtually naked.

She opened her legs wide, threw her head back on the bed and let me in. I rammed myself deep into her like it was a wet, bloody wound. I pierced her with the force of a spear. I drove myself in repeatedly, grunting like a madman. Stabbing her. Stabbing her. This was not love or lovemaking. It was like an act of war - vengeance against womankind. I was too drunk to think more deeply about the things that had once happened to me in a bed, as a child. I was too far gone to let the past overlap the present. To recall those dark nights in that awful flat, but I was aware I was getting my own back for something.

In went my dagger, the pubic hairs around it now drenched wet with her moisture. I could feel the wetness cooling as I withdrew to thrust my hips upon her again. She arched her back so that I took in a tiny lip of her flesh with me. I could feel it being drawn in with every violent shove. On and on went the attack, relentless, frenzied. I was up on my arms eventually, supporting my upper body, looking down on her from a dominant position. She moaned with a kind of music I had never heard before, all the while adjusting her back to take full advantage of what I was doing to her. I wanted my erection to split her wide open such was the force of my pelvis. Her body shuddered upon the bedclothes with each ramming, the now flattened breasts rippling to the hammer blows.

Now she was almost screaming, saying words I could not comprehend through her panting breath, words that emerged from the depths of her throat. By now she was gripping the sheets, thrashing her head from side to side, little squeals, high pitched, coming in between short breaths. My loins exploded at this sound. I could not keep it in. I flooded her womb so that she was even more lubricated than before. I cried out loud, as if I had been shot. Then gasping like an exhausted athlete I fell upon her naked body and curved my arms around the soft, supple skin of her slender waist. We

376

lay there in our own private world of recovery, lost in the experience, still connected.

Chapter sixteen: Boxes

Power. That's what matters in this world. It has always been so. A year or so on from that first meeting with Rebecca Tindale, I discovered what it meant to wield power over another soul. Despite all her money and apparent command of life, I saw that she was as insecure as the rest of us. Understanding the mess inside her head was the key. Such a person was open to manipulation and she was a willing victim. She had been one all her life. The cars, and the house, and all the trappings were a disguise. So too was all the bossiness and assertive behaviour. Behind it all was a tiny person, terrified of being alone, who lived in mortal fear of being rejected. She put me in mind of the wizard who appears at the end of the film *The Wizard Of Oz*. Behind the terrifying facade of the great Oz was nothing more than a little man pulling at levers who made the trick of maintaining his omnipotence a reality. My trick was to keep her on the edge of her own security abyss. How hard she worked at keeping me in her affections. All I had to do was go cold on her every now and again and the neuroses would kick in - for this she got a tit-bit, a reward with my own brand of special cuddle.

I was gloriously devious, spying on her at times. Gone was the crudity of the simplistic world of the empire. I had learned from its limitations. A new order had arisen. I had grown up, become more intelligent in my approach, less aggressive. I knew how guilt worked and I could use it to tinker about in her head to make her think all manner of things, just as had once been done to me. Her defences were useless, in fact I believe that in those days she had none except for the aura of wealth. Beyond her undeniable beauty and learned sophistication I found a life in turmoil. How easy it is to set oneself up as a saviour. People will believe anything if the message is packaged to suit a particular need. I was a salesman. I could sell her anything. So instead of being at war with the world around me, I realised that it was better to exploit it. It worked.

Long gone was the crappy flat. I now found my mornings began with a view across a billiard table lawn and a beautiful woman in my bed, her bed. She had moved me into Eric Tindale's great house, The Old Rectory in the village of Winthorpe, a rambling Victorian abode with five bedrooms. There I lived with her. It seemed almost like love - I knew it was not, well not towards her anyway. If there was any love at all then it was the love of domination.

It is easy to run away with the idea that Rebecca was stupid. Nothing could have been further from the truth. She was smart, very smart. Streetwise we say these days. Nor was this an easy relationship. I found I had to vet whatever I was going to say before it fell headlong out of my mouth. Once in a while I came close to upsetting the balance. It would only take one display of treachery to lose my place in her temple. The mechanism of our alliance depended in part on spontaneity. I would organise surprises. Like the time I serenaded her one night outside the bedroom on the lawn. One of Colin's mates was a guitarist, so as I strummed a dummy instrument without strings, he played the chords to the song from behind the stone built wall. The song was the classic from Casablanca, *As Time Goes By*. She came to the window and looked down upon me playing the fool on the grass. She loved stuff like that and I knew it. So when I pulled my affection away she would do anything to get it back. It was not so much a case of stick and carrot, more like give carrot then hide carrot, much more effective.

It was also easy for me to fall into the trap of beholding her with awe, an awe that emanated from the remnants of the schoolboy that I had once been. She could be beguiling with other men. I raged inside when she did this, only to find my jealousy unwarranted when I realised it was a means to her own ends that she behaved this way. I found it odd to appreciate how I had ended up with someone like her, but as the months passed I found that we were not all that different after all.

She, Rebecca, had been born into a well-off family in Lincoln. Both her parents had been killed outright in a road accident one awful New Year's Eve. That was all the only family she had and, at ten years old, there was no one to look after the family home. Who would look after the pool and the ponies? There was certainly no money. The Breckons had nothing more than a tenuous grip on the wealthy lifestyle they had paraded around. It was all a facade. What had seemed like the high life to the young Rebecca was just an illusion. Creditors and the taxman carved her world away around her and left her to the tender mercies of the social services and the care homes. This is where she discovered the disadvantages of a well-heeled upbringing. Her polished pronunciation was ridiculed and the dainty way she ate her meals was imitated with derision. Once in a fit of reprehension towards her tormentors she mentioned the ponies she once had. It backfired on her and she rued the day she let it slip. Then it was foster parents, one after another until, like me, she left to seek her fortune. By the time she was eighteen she had met Eric Tindale and the rest became history.

Eric did not just want a beauty. He was on the lookout for someone he could mould. Even so, he had to have the right raw materials and Rebecca suited his requirements perfectly. She could carry herself in public and betrayed nothing of her unfortunate upbringing - but Eric knew all about it. Her past was the reins around her neck with which he controlled her and he never missed a chance, in private of course, to yank at them and tighten his grip. This was the currency with which she paid for the splendour of her open prison. Now, as memories of the funeral faded from sight, she could look around and know that her account was paid in full. It was time to play and I was her toy.

Learning all this made my own attempts at controlling her all the more difficult. Eric's tactics had been clumsy, brutal in fact. I had to avoid taking a sledgehammer to her mind. It was more a case of crawling into it with a screwdriver and monkeying about with the wiring. Analysing what it was in me that she found so interesting was a question that also rolled around in my head all the time we were together. I had not much money and, compared to the world she inhabited at the first time of meeting, I classed myself far beneath her. It is possible that she never felt comfortable with the kinds of people in Eric's world. Maybe ours was a fling that simply caught on. I never dared to ask lest the spell be broken. I only knew that for a great swathe of her life she had not known, nor been given, much love. It is possible that she believed I provided it. It is true that whenever I took it away she craved it back, like a child begging for its doll to be returned. Now and again when the remnants of bad dreams wrenched me from my sleep, she was glad to be there to assure me that all was well. It was as if she welcomed these nightmares of mine in order to show how affectionate she could be, at least in those early days, when things were new.

Our relationship was good for Carridges too. I had inroads into businesses that had once been beyond my grasp. So much so that the firm had to speed up plans already in existence to move lock, stock and printing press to new purpose-built premises on the industrial estate. I had become the blue-eyed boy. The dark ages were well and truly behind me.

The only smudge on this picture of apparent perfection was the health of John back at Edlington. Debilitating headaches and nausea brought on by giddiness threw him off his well-regimented routine. He battled through it as best he could, but with the result that the sermons got shorter and less meaningful. The curate from Southwell was forced to step in with an unwelcome regularity, though granted willingly. Poor Ellie had called me on the phone to say John had not been feeling well and was going off to Nottingham for tests. She wanted to know if I would mind looking after Matthew for the day, a child who was by now nearly eleven years old. It was to be a Friday. I agreed. Rebecca was uncharacteristically keen to come along too on this occasion. I could hear the hesitation in Ellie's voice the minute I mooted the idea, but there was no stopping Rebecca, so that was that.

We arrived quite early, early enough to see the changes that had consumed John Crampton. A quiet fear seeped from mildly sunken eyes, searching my face like those of a frightened child. Even his body held itself awkwardly. These were only subtle manifestations but they were real and detectable. He tried to put over his old self as cheerful as ever, even mustering up goodwill towards Rebecca, but there was a gulf between her and Ellie and, though she sided with John to portray an illusion of acceptance, it was clear to me that she hated the woman I lived with. I felt uncomfortable. Ellie was the only woman I ever really loved, but I was trying to make a life with Rebecca, so I had hoped for a sense of blessing. All I could pick up on was the silent curse.

The day with Matthew passed. That is all I can say about it. The boy was a bore. The poor little fart had had it easy throughout the duration of his safe little life. He detested the outdoors, preferring books instead. Rebecca seemed to warm to him more than I could. So now and again, urged on by restlessness, I left them to it, using the opportunity to have a look around the once familiar place.

Why nostalgia did not pour forth like a spring I cannot explain - it should have done. My mind worked hard to feel the touch of a long lost emotion as though it was trying to move a rock. No matter how much concentration I brought to bear the rock remained motionless, the good old days stuck fast, lifeless like the dead events printed in a history volume. Disappointing, that is what it was. It was only when I wandered into the old garage that something of the past finally came to light. It was the chance sighting of my old bicycle, or at least the frame, hung as it was at the end of the garage from two large nails hammered into the brick. I could not see where the wheels were. Maybe the bike had been cannibalised, but the diamond shape of its tubular steel set my mind racing back to that day long ago when I was a boy, that day of freedom. I stopped myself from rewinding back further to another time long ago and a peculiar age long before that, deciding reactively that nostalgia was a drug best left in its bottle, I returned to the house to pass the day away with the little old man of eleven.

John and Ellie returned late in the afternoon evidently tired, bringing their world of doom with them. The results of the day's tests would not be available for a few days but enough had been said at Nottingham to extinguish all hope. Ellie's face, once so youthful, looked old and ravaged by a burden that could almost be measured in tons. John looked lost, his mind hanging onto its faith by a thread, trying to pick its way through a path of resignation and an end that was wreathed in mystery.

We left them after an hour or so, having shared a very English remedy to trouble, a pot of tea. Going was like leaving a bombed city, like seeing palls of black smoke rising from the ghosts of its shattered buildings. They clung together as we waved goodbye. Ellie and I had hugged each other outside on the doorstep. I could feel the helplessness inside her as I held her limp body. It was all she could do to hug me back. Rebecca, wanting to prove herself the dominant character over Ellie went to kiss her as we left, only to be given a curt handshake, a limp one, at the very tips of her fingers. Not a word passed between us as we drove home, although I could hear the scorned workings of Rebecca's mind grinding away over the constant drone of the car engine.

So it was that the good times began to slip from my grasp. A time of slipping away began. There is a time when a ship is launched, a great ocean liner let's say, when she's been released from her shackles. For a moment she remains still, rooted to the slipway. It is obvious that there is nothing holding her, preventing her from sliding down the ramp, and yet gravity has not yet done enough to shift her. That is where I was the day after the visit. I knew inexorably that Rebecca and I had begun sliding away. She was the ship and I was the slipway. She would sail gracefully away and I would be dismantled.

The dreams did not help. I began to wake up in the dead of night trying to scream, only to behold Rebecca's face looking at me in horror as she turned on the bedroom light. Then I would realise who it was, or rather who it was not, and I would feel ashamed. She would look at me with a mixture of despair, revulsion and irritation. She never wasted pity on herself despite all she had lived through. None was wasted on me. The game of compassion had become a bore to her. I was condemned to the same fate. How could I exercise any power over her whilst I was waking her in the night like a child? Whatever respect she had for me began to fade and shrink. It was like the first tiny jolt of the ship's downward passage and I could not hold her back.

A week or so later Ellie phoned. Her burdened voice explained what the tests had revealed. How hard she tried to restrain her desire to weep. They had found a brain tumour she told me. Inoperable the doctors said. It was late summer, nearly September. He was not expected to see Christmas. They were right. On October the fifth, nineteen eighty-eight, John died in his bed at The Croft. It had been that swift.

John had been a steadying force in my life, significantly pivotal. He had not always got it right, but he tried to make a man out of me. He was the nearest thing to a father I ever had and, even though I had not had much to do with him or even Ellie come to that, over recent years, the fact that he was no longer around unsettled me. I felt a sense of vulnerability, as if someone had taken my parachute away.

That was nothing compared to the landslide of grief that enveloped poor Ellie. John Crampton had taken hold of her life and imbued it with the finest love she had ever known. He had polished her good nature until it shone like burnished gold. The age gap between them had never seemed to matter. They adored each other. It was that simple. Now she just stood and stared out of the window of that empty house knowing that, despite all the ladders she had ever climbed with him, she had just slipped down the longest snake, back to square one, all on her own.

The plain funeral two weeks later at St. Giles in Edlington was preceded by a much larger service of remembrance at Southwell Minster. Strange. There were so many people there I felt envious of the affection held for him. He had touched so many lives, more than I had realised. There were hearts and minds, like my own which had been the better for the existence of John Crampton, as many of them said in words of recollection. John would have been embarrassed if he had been there. Then again he was there in his box, a beautiful shiny oak coffin, lying on two ornate trestles, just in front of the great screen. The bishops of Lincoln, Nottingham and a host of other members of the clergy spoke lovingly about the man they referred to simply by his initials JC. How cleverly apt, I thought.

When the funeral at Edlington was all over and the guests had said their pitiful but heartfelt goodbyes, Ellie and I were left alone in the empty heart of The Croft. Rebecca had stayed away, declaring that she was not one for funerals and, besides she had hardly known John like I had. So, I came alone with her blessing - not quite knowing if she meant that sarcastically. All at once Ellie turned to face me and took my hand. I was dragged into John's study, over to his writing desk and invited to sit behind it in John's chair. Then, over-riding her emotions, she reached into the sliding doors of the cabinets under the bookshelves and removed a large brown cardboard box. It looked old, as if it had been there for years. Its lid was secured by a black ribbon, which Ellie proceeded to untie before placing it in front of me on John's desk.

"Before you open this box," she began in a voice charged with a quiet, unfathomable energy, "there's something I have to tell you."

I looked away from the box and into her eyes, those same eyes that beheld me from a mask that had once been her youthful face. I waited for the rest to unfold.

"I have to go from here, Davy, and I wanted you to have this. Think of it as a going away present."

"Have to go?"

"Yes," she said, pausing a moment, "but it'll be a new start I expect. No better time I suppose."

"But where will you go?"

"I've got a few ideas. I'm not sure yet."

"But why? Why can't you stay here?"

"It's this place. It belongs to the church. It was only my home whilst John was the vicar here. It was part of his job, part of his stipend. The new vicar will make it his home, and I've got to find a new one. That's the way it is."

"You can stay with us. I'll see what Becky says."

"You and I know what she'll say. There's no love lost between us, let's be honest. And she's not for you Davy either. Let's both be honest about that too, you mark me."

"We're fine," I protested weakly.

"Fine is it? That won't get you to the end of the road, Davy. You must have more than fine. You must have the best, like I had with John. You can do better than her, you really can."

"So, when will you go?" I said, side-stepping the issue.

"I haven't a clue right now. I've been given two months. That should be long enough to find somewhere I think," she said.

More sadness enveloped me at the thought of her going, and my head drooped down to the desk and the box.

"So what's in this, then?" I asked.

"Open it," she said.

So I pulled away the ribbon and took off the lid. I could not believe my eyes. It seemed alive, lying there, rejoicing in its paralysing effect over me. I could not speak or even look away. It had me once more in its awful power. The album.

"It's yours Davy," she said. "I want you to have it now. It's more yours than mine anyhow."

It had found me. By sheer patience it had tracked me down. Like a living entity it had borne witness to my past. It had heard things that belonged to a distant time, best forgotten. Its brown cover scratched and marked over the years were a record of all those times it had been dragged out of the sideboard. Dragged out by her, by the hands that were capable of such mistreatment.

Ellie took it out and, not noticing my wide-eyed reluctance, she opened it to the page she liked best, the one with her in it as a young girl, the one that had been my favourite too.

"Look, there's me," she said.

But I could not see. My eyes were blind from moisture, impossible to hold back. My throat, swollen up found it hard to swallow. I was in free-fall, out of control. In five seconds, my adult identity had been stripped away. Next to the picture on the opposite page, obscuring the photograph beneath it, was a brown envelope. There was a rubber-stamped post-mark on it that read, Sturman and Kleaps Solicitors. I paid little attention to it, mesmerised as I was by the black and white image on the right. This book of pictures had reduced me to Davy boy again. There she was, with her new husband, the father I had never got to know, the dad who had not come back. I could see little Ellie smiling into the lens. It was a perfect picture, beautifully and painstakingly composed. Some of my scraps of boyhood happiness had been spent looking at this picture. Yet all I could think of were the most awful times. They all made their way back into my mind, one after the other. Wooden spoons mingled with ejaculating into her rubbing hand, her controlling ways, her ranting and raving, her weight thrusting up and down on top of me in the dark and, when the memory of the burned birthday card arrived from this sickening mass of visions, I could not help myself.

"You fucking shit," I managed to say through the heartbreak and snot hanging out of my nose, "look what you've done to me," I could not miss Ellie's shock. "I don't mean you," I wept to her, and pointing to the picture I blurted out, "her!"

I slammed the album closed, shoved it back in the box, and pushed it towards Ellie.

"You have it, it's too much to bear. It's cursed. I'm sorry I shouted, but you've no idea Auntie El."

"You haven't called me that for years," she said calmly, and came over to me and drew me close to her in her arms. "Do you want to tell me all about it?" she asked softly.

I was safe here and yet she would soon be gone. I would be left to my own fate, my own mess. With my head buried into her shoulders, I said the only thing I could.

"No one must ever know, no one, not even you Auntie El."

Chapter seventeen: Crash

I have never seen a train crash, well, never in real life that is. Oh, I have seen the aftermath of one on the TV before, the tangle of wreckage scattered across a twisted track. In some very old pictures it is the poor old steam engine that has come off worse having taken the brunt of it all, but at what point in the train's journey do these things actually begin to go wrong? There must come a point in the actual journey when the wheels start to leave the track. When there is nothing neither man nor beast can do to alter the dreadful outcome of the derailment. From then on it can be guaranteed that the colossal momentum of the mighty machine will impact with the solid ground, slice open the earth with its cataclysmic force and tear itself to pieces before it comes to rest.

The night I came home from John's funeral and wept in front of Becky was, to me, the point at which our wheels jumped loose. I was an idiot to have expected any sympathy or understanding. The act she had put on at our first meeting was just that, an act. Ellie was right all along. Over the next few weeks I watched and listened as our engine hit the ground, followed by the carriages of our relationship. It tore me to pieces to watch something that I took as being a good thing, disintegrate before my eyes. I had lost control. I was helpless, tumbling through life, wondering what the eventual wreckage would look like.

I dreaded sleeping with her and as the nightmares became worse I was pushed out into the spare room so that her sleep was not disrupted. Mornings brought shouting and rows. I think she was scared of me. There was no need for her to be so. If only she had just tried to understand, but she was having none of it. She was not that sort and we continued to crash and crumple in the dirt of our times.

There have been times when I wished I could be like other men. Men who attract and keep their women with a kind of animal brutality - their females seem to like it. In fact they seem to need a man like that. There must be a trick to it but it is lost on me. When the relationships of these brutish males fall apart they go down the pub and laugh it off, or so it seems. I could not laugh at any of it. There was no humour in John's death, nothing to laugh about at Ellie's impending departure. Becky was avoiding me, spending her evenings at meetings or seeing friends. Sometimes she would not return until the next afternoon while I was at work. She had broken away. Steam needs to be contained to have any power and any that I generated was now at the mercy of the wind, powerless to achieve anything.

One afternoon I came home to collect a proof that I had left behind on the table. The house was quiet, much too quiet. Going up to have a pee I could not help taking a look at the bedroom that I had once been welcome in. Oddly the bedclothes were in disarray, unusual for the normally methodical Rebecca Tindale, and lingering in the air, like a ghost, the aroma of bodies, recent smells of a recent event. So I searched the house like a madman. I went through the big old place from top to bottom but no one was there. What I would have done if there had been I do not know. So I halted the search in the living room and sat down feeling like an impostor. No, it was more than that, I felt unwanted, pushed away, sensing that I was irrelevant, history.

I paid no attention to the man at AC Systems during my 3.00pm appointment. I know this because we cocked up the job. Half of the things he wanted changing on his proof were ignored because I failed to mark them up. Ten thousand full-colour, eight page brochures, printed onto 200gsm matt art, varnished, spot laminated, creased and stitched had to be redone. Two grand's worth of business had gone down the drain. Carridge called me in and went berserk. I sounded contrite, I think I was to some extent, but that job going tits up was nothing to the mess my life was in. In fact AC Systems was but one in a long line of jobs that I ballsed up. Every one that failed to make the grade pushed me further towards a dark place in my head - a dark region where the vigour of the world about me faded away. It was like falling asleep at the wheel, knowing somewhere in the world of consciousness that the car was careering all over the road but finding the desire for sleep all too powerful.

Colin took me to one side the afternoon we broke up for Christmas. He sounded genuinely concerned, even though he said I looked like shit. Some part of me could tell he wanted to help. I will never forget the pain in his eyes when I just shrugged at him and told him to piss off.

The main impact of my life's derailment took place on December the twenty-eighth nineteen eighty-eight. Ellie called me on the phone to say that she had found a new home and would be leaving early in the New Year. She wanted to meet so that we could say goodbye. I was at home, alone, watching the film *It's A Wonderful Life*, a black and white Christmas classic starring James Stewart. The film had grabbed hold of me like a pair of concrete wellingtons and I was sinking into a quagmire of self-pity.

"Go then," I had said, "it's your life, do what you like."

It was cruel and even as I uttered the words I regretted it. The words had been said and I lacked the strength to make things right with an apology. So I put the receiver down and sank back into the movie.

I cried a lot in those days. For no reason I just cried. I cried in the car, cried in bed. After a meeting I would find a private place, as an animal does when searching out a place to die, and just cried. I could not understand what was happening to me. Something awful was going on inside me like a disease, invisible, unstoppable and bad.

Then on the night before New Year's Eve I dreamed I was screaming at my mother who was crawling out of her grave, a rope still around her neck and a wooden spoon in her hand. Becky burst in to see a freak of nature gripping the sheets to his face, screaming at the wall. She was half asleep, which was half the reason she was able to overcome her fear and slap me across my face. There she was again, that bitch of a mother, hurting me just because I had a bad dream. No more. No more slaps, no more playing with me. How much more of that old house was I expected to take? There she was, the all-powerful Charlotte Harper ready to hit me again. Well, no more Lady Jane, I said to myself. I hurled myself at her, grabbing at her thin little throat. My hands went almost all the way around, each thumb cradled her knobbly little windpipe and I pressed them in, crushing her neck to the music of muted screams and gurgling.

"I hate you mother," I yelled. "I should have done this years ago."

As I dug my thumbs in to squeeze the life out of her the room went dark and I was nowhere.

I cannot recall what I felt next. I think it was the freezing cold, followed by a severe pain near my right temple. As I opened my eyes I could feel dried blood covering my right eyelid, and there was grass everywhere. Shivers began, nature's way of warming me up. Nature was not very good at it. Above my head was a row of bare twigs and, as I sat up I could see it was a hawthorn hedge. The grass, covered in frost, was the floor of a ditch, quite a deep one. I could see a solitary bare tree in front of me. Sitting up hurt. In my ribs there was a terrible pain as if I had been kicked. Even so I managed to pull myself upright and peer over the ditch to where I could see the gravelly tar of a country road. The pain in my head was agonising, worse than the ribs and, touching the area around my temple, my fingers felt a large indent encrusted with the makings of a massive scab. Some of it had matted up my hair.

How long had I been there? Who had put me here and why? Was this a dream? No, the cold and pains were too real even for a dream. Looking at myself I was wearing my long raincoat. A pair of training shoes covered my feet, the laces undone, but except for that, I was naked, cold, shivering, and naked. Fighting the agony in my side I

389

tried to stand upright on the lane, just to get my bearings. It was hard to stay on my feet. I was so cold and dizzy. The lane led up a hill away from a village. It was such an overcast morning that everything seemed to be in black and white, pretty similar to the film I was watching the day before, supposing this was the day after. I decided to head for civilisation to get help, staggering forward a foot at a time. The small cottages seemed so far away and I made no progress at all, fighting all the while this swimming sensation in my head that made me swagger from side to side. Then I spotted a car emerging from the village and turn into the lane in my direction. As I raised my hand to gesture him to stop I felt myself lose control and I hit the road. In and out of my lungs went the cold, crisp air. I was exhausted, tired beyond imagination. Oh, thank God for sleep.

There were people around me when I woke up. My body was slumped in a leather easy chair and a blanket had been draped over me. I could even feel the warmth of a hot water bottle close to my abdomen and the faint smell of brandy on my lips. I struggled to say something but the man holding the brandy glass put his finger to his mouth. With him was a young girl aged about eight-years-old and another man wearing an overcoat fiddling with his car keys.

"Do you reckon he'll be all right to leave now?" he said to the man with the glass.

"Don't know what to do with him, New Year's Day and all. He's badly done in."

"It's just that I'm supposed to be at Jenny's for lunch, that's all."

"Give her a ring. Tell her what's happened. I'm wondering about getting him to the hospital and I'll need you to give me an 'and."

The man with the car keys went off, whilst the chap with the glass gave me another sip. I could hear a one way telephone conversation going on in another room as the car keys man made his call. With him out of the way I could see beyond the large brandy glass man and the girl that I was in a pub. A vague recollection of the ditch and the smell of the spirit heaved at my guts and I threw up all over the blanket. The man put his glass down, lifted the cover from me, put it on the floor and went to snatch the phone off his friend to call for an ambulance. Two hours later I was in a hospital bed.

There is something tangible about physical injuries. It was fairly obvious that I had not done this to myself. In that I mean that the outward signs of why I was here were not the result of something odd going on in my head. It was for that reason alone I think, that I received a great deal of sympathy and care from the nursing staff as they X-rayed me. It was easier for them to accept and approach an injury that they could see with their own eyes.

I learned that a disc shaped object had struck my head, I had sustained two broken ribs, and that I was crawling out of a hypothermic state. What the doctors wanted to know was how I got there, how I ended up in a ditch on New Year's Day? They were not alone in that regard. How had I? They asked me where I lived. I told them The Old Rectory in Winthorpe. Did I live alone? No, I said, a vague, floating nucleus of images swirling around in my mind. No, I said. I live with my girlfriend, Rebecca, Rebecca Tindale. I said I thought she ought to know I was here. They said they would call her. They wondered if I had been to a fancy dress party? They asked if I could remember being in a fight. All I could remember, I told them, was that I had gone to bed alone. Becky had gone to a party. I had not heard her come home.

It was like trying to recall a song that rests on the tip of your tongue. The fragments tantalise, evading capture, but then I had it. I recalled having the awful dream. I kept it to myself, but it was the last thing going on in my mind before finding myself in the ditch. How had I gone from my bed into a ditch and broken my ribs and smashed my head open? Maybe the bang on the head had fouled up my memory. My brain rolled it over and over, again and again. It was a fruitless and disconcerting exercise.

They patched me up and kept me overnight under observation. I was told they had called home but that no one was there. I began to wonder if all this was a bad dream too but the pain was too real. Everything was equally balanced between reality and illusion. The day wore on. By mid-afternoon the pain was unbearable, mostly in my head, so they sedated me and I slept without dreams throughout the night.

After lunch the next day I they said I could leave. An appointment was made for a week's time. Some clothes were found for me. Where from I never thought to ask. I received socks, jeans, a white shirt and a bright green sweater. I promised to give them back when I returned for my check up, along with the bus fare that they kindly proffered me.

Just before three in the afternoon I put my raincoat on over my new clothes and walked a little unsteadily to the bus stop. It was a cold day, January at its worst, with freezing drizzle cascading out of the greyness that did not seem like a sky at all but a drab dome instead. Getting onto the bus was painful, so too was the rickety journey to the bus station, where I had to change for a bus to the village. It was dark by the time I made it home. The place was uninhabited and I did not have a key. My car was still there but Becky's Mercedes was gone. So I walked round to the back expecting to see a light on in the kitchen, but it was dark there too. Before I had chance to think about it rationally I began to shout up to the bedroom. A dog a few houses down heard me and joined in the noise, but it was no use. The house remained dead.

It was while I was sitting on the drive trying to ease the ache in my side, that I felt the lump of rock cradled in my fingers. Here I was, yet again, with a stone in my whip hand. Only this time, I would wrap it in my sleeve and carefully crack a back windowpane. I would have done it had it not been for a shout coming from across the road.

"Can I help you dear boy?"

The voice was that of a man warbling with age and well pronounced with a southern accent. I turned to see a stooping figure dressed in black. On closer inspection I could see a dog collar. On the opposite side of the road was a large house, newer than the Tindale's Old Rectory and, as if in perfect counterbalance, bore the title The Rectory. I let the stone fall into the shadows and limped towards the old chap. He came towards me his hands clasped and his head cocked very slightly to one side in a poise of concern.

"I'm locked out," I said, as we converged.

"Great Scott," he said when he caught a better glimpse of me, "whatever's happened to you my dear fellow?"

"I'm not sure," I mumbled, "but I've two broken ribs and a bad gash on my head."

He stole a glance at my clothes, which stopped him asking whatever it was he was just about to ask. Instead he took my arm and led me back to his home. It was warm inside. The house was still full of Christmas paraphernalia, a lovely tree and cards pinned everywhere. There were even old-fashioned, handmade paper chains hanging in a criss-cross from each corner of the living room into which I was escorted and given a large comfy chair to sit in.

"I say, would you like a sherry?" he asked, over the quiet beauty of a Bach cantata playing on the hi-fi in the corner of the room. I said yes please.

So, down we sat in the dimly lit room and drank a sherry each in a state of sublime civility. It seemed ridiculous considering the state I was in, but the man was one of God's best. All he did was care for me, never probing too deeply. It was morning when I next opened my eyes to find myself in a cosy chair with a thick blanket tucked under my chin.

Having not moved all night my first attempt at motion was excruciating. I must have called out in pain because a moment later the vicar was there. He enquired after my health, touching his own ribs to demonstrate that it was not just a casual enquiry. I said that it hurt. He offered me a cup of tea, as if that was the perfect remedy. After an effort I got to my feet and went over to the curtains. Peeping through the crack I could see the Old Rectory over the road. Her car was back. I shouted out that I had to go and bolted as best I could for the door. Before the vicar had a chance to stop me I was halfway across the road. I heard him call something out as I limped towards the house intent on ripping the door off. I was there in short order and without hesitation I slammed my fist against it like a madman.

I shouted so that the entire length of Rectory Lane could hear me. I do not know why I was so mad. I felt out of my mind. Maybe Becky had been out searching for me, I thought, trying to justify her absence during the night. I was confused. I expected her to be sick with worry. At the very least I knew she would be glad that I had turned up safe and well. A sign of life inside stopped my voice in mid-yell. My breathing was erratic and laboured in the cold of the morning air. The locks clicked, a bolt snapped undone and the door opened to reveal a young man dressed only in boxer shorts, his well formed biceps bulging as he folded his arms over his muscular chest.

"Back for more, are we?" he said, with manly confidence.

"I beg your pardon?" I said.

He turned his head up toward the stairs and shouted, "He's very polite Becks. I thought you said he was a monster."

I heard the words coming from the main bedroom.

"Get rid of him," Becky's words, Becky's voice.

The man turned to me, still smiling with an ego as fit as his body.

"I should have finished you off when I had the chance."

With that he grabbed hold of a black bin liner from behind the door and tossed it onto the drive.

"Your sort should be locked up. If I hear of you trying to strangle any more women, I'll come after you and throttle you m'self. That'll be the last bad dream you ever have."

I held my hand up to my head where the wound was.

"Coming back to you now is it, you stupid weirdo?" he said. "I'd have knocked you out with more than an bloody ashtray. I'd have ripped your sodding head off," the smile had gone as he reached over to the small windowsill and grabbed something. They were car keys, my car keys. He lobbed them over to where the bin liner had landed. "Now fuck off, and don't let me catch you hanging around here anymore."

The door slammed in my face. My eyes were wide and my mind was trapped in a swirling vortex. I did not know what to do next. After a while I picked up the black bag and looked inside. All my clothes and shoes were in it, as well as a few books and an assortment of personal belongings. Submerged in a trance, I shoved the whole lot in the boot of the car, got in and drove away. I just drove, over the hill and far away. I felt that if I stopped, reality would catch up with me and I would die. I was nearing the Derbyshire border by the time I looked at my fuel gauge and realised I had only a quarter of a tank left. I was on the road to Matlock. There came into view a lay-by. I stopped. Reality caught up with me and I cried my heart out.

It was as if my life's road had been washed away in a flood. I was in a wilderness, as wild and rocky as the Derbyshire countryside around me. Had I really tried to strangle her in my sleep? Did the dreams possess me to that extent? Where would I live now? What should I do next? I was tired, just tired of life and everything that went with it. It would have been easier for me if I had just taken a job at Ansons like everyone else.

I locked the car and went to trek over the fields. I half expected some divine guidance. The half that did not expect it was not disappointed. How had I lost control of her so utterly? I could not understand why things had been good between us for so long, only to disintegrate so swiftly. I only saw it coming when it was too late. It had begun with the dreams. The dreams had worried her, like I was worrying the sheep through which I was passing. The line between respect and fear had been narrower than I thought. What the hell, I said to myself. Analyse it how you will, it was over. However could I live on, having known what it was like to wake up with her next to me? The dreams had robbed me of her and what was the wellspring of those dreams? It was she, the evil one. Her badness was haunting me like a phantom. Wherever I went. Whether it was Saltbys, Ellie, Gwen, Becky, she would always find me and destroy me. I could hear her laughing. I could really hear it in both ears at the same time as if she was there. I shouted for her to stop, but she would not, it got louder. Somehow she had climbed out of the strongbox and made her way up to the surface. Now she was in my head, taking over, and the pain in my heart was ever as great as the whips of her wooden spoon. I thought that I had escaped all that, but no, here she was again, as large as life, telling me that I was a stupid fool to have tried it on with a woman like Mrs Tindale. What did I know of real women? I was never going to amount to anything, her voice jeered, now get the tea ready and make sure it's all done by the time I get back, or it's a taste of my little helper in the drawer for you, mark me.

I ran back to the car and drove back to Newark at crazy speeds trying to get away from her, but there was to be no running away. Mother had found her way home in the mind of a homeless man.

I have no idea how I lost control of the car so easily. It hit something, a kerb probably. I was suddenly aware that the vehicle was sliding over the road at the will of fate. I whipped the wheel instinctively trying to regain command of it. Outside blurred visions hurtled around me as the sound of screeching wheels filled my ears. I was helplessly terrified. My face became hot with fear. It seemed to go on for hours until there was a massive jolt, accompanied by the sound of crunching metal on the passenger side of the car. I even saw the door bend in towards me, as my head was thrown at both it and the tree that the car had impacted. The life within me was only saved by the seat belt that I had decided to wear on a whim. It is incredible how quiet it became after that - nothing but the sound of my heavy breathing. Thank God I was alive to hear it. I could not move. I just sat and shook. At least the voice of mother had stopped, for now.

Chapter eighteen: Gone

My body mended but that was no recovery. They could not put my mind in a splint. They could not bandage up my inner me. They had no clue how, and nor did I. As for the car, it was declared a write-off, unsurprisingly. That about summed me up too, written off. I managed to summon up the strength to find somewhere to live, a bed and breakfast place. It was somewhat expensive, meant only as a short-term measure whilst I found more permanent lodgings.

Alan Carridge was matter-of-fact about the company vehicle but not compassionate. All I had to do was fill in the accident forms and draw a diagram of what had happened. Purely for commercial motives I was given a new car within the first week back after the Christmas break. It was an ex-demonstration Metro, deep red. He paid little attention to me, Alan Carridge. He was like that more now, becoming less human as the years passed. Everyone else said all the right things to me though. Even Colin, who had held me at arm's length ever since our minor fracas, popped his head round my office door on the first day back and said, in a roundabout way, he had let bygones be bygones, life was too short and all that.

So there it was. David Harper, the magician-salesman, returned to the treadmill where it was decreed he belonged. After all, he was so good at it, was he not? He was back doing the job he loved. I am sure that is how they saw me, judging by their narrow remarks and ill-fitting compliments. Now the world that I once held so gladly in the palm of my hand had become heavy and the palm of my hand despised it.

Every project I went to quote on, every visit to a client, every bit of irritating paperwork pushed me further towards a life without purpose. Like the barren silence of a ghost town where only the sound of the wind brings animation to the dead objects therein. In my head there was always a wind, a zephyr, a moaning, lonely sound of isolation. Sometimes it was like being submerged, as if the world was going about its business above me. From this sunken place I picked up snatches of what people said until they made an effort to ask me if I was listening. Then I would emerge from below, apologise and become involved once more in their idiotic business plans and where the great firm of Carridges fitted into them. It was hard to give a shit quite frankly.

The disinterest deepened. Jobs were printed without the scrupulous attention to detail that once I had lavished upon them. By a safety net of flukes and the dedication of others they turned out flawless, at first. Then some got through to livid clients who ranted and raved at me, then took it out on Mr C, or worse still wrote to him. I would be called into his office to see him lift his face from a client's letterhead and give me that burning look of his. Then I would get the rants and raves from him. I used to stare at something nearby, a stapler or the map on the wall. The map was the best thing to look at. I used to go on imaginary journeys, following the blue and green lines of roads as they snaked towards Cornwall or Snowdonia, hardly aware of his venting spleen. Then I would be brought up sharp with the question.

"So what have you got to say for yourself?"

To which I repeated that it was probably the effects of the accident. The same thing happened when someone on the shop floor just happened to notice the misspelling of an address on a client's brochure. I was supposed to have arranged its alteration, but how could I find the impetus to be bothered? My heart was tired and, if all the print jobs in the whole bloody world were to go wrong, so bloody what? I could not give a flying fig.

Eventually I moved out of the bed and breakfast and into a poky little flat, a bed-sit, above a fish and chip shop, one of four that had been converted there on the first floor. It was all I could afford now that my commission was non-existent. I hated the smell of the place and the noise. Every night except Fridays there was the cacophony of people being served, drunks looking for something to help them vomit up their beer, or lonely old folks buying a bag of scraps as an excuse to find company. Then the clatter of clearing up that took place until midnight would deprive me of the sleep that I dreaded anyway. In the morning the stale stench of haddock would lace my hair and nostrils as I lay there gazing up at wallpaper peeling away from the walls and paint flaking off the door and the skirting boards.

No one came to see me. I never sought out anyone either. I just got up, went to work, cocked things up and came back to my hovel. It could not go on like this for long and it did not. One morning, as I shuffled downstairs to the mail shelf, I saw a letter with the Carridges logo on it. It was a warning letter. I read the words explaining that if my performance and attitude failed to meet the level expected of the company, my services would no longer be required. Like an automaton I went to work anyway and performed the tired old act.

How can you go on when the life within you is cursed? Days of drudge, followed by evenings of noise and nights of terror. How do people crawl out of such lives? All I can remember is being constantly tired and down. Pulling myself together would take energy. Mine was all gone. So I sank deeper and cared less.

How she laughed at it all. Although I never saw her, except in dreams, I could always hear her, laughing. She told me I was no good. She said I had proved it by how things had turned out. How could I disagree? She was right. She had been right all along, but would she shut up? She kept on, nagging and nagging.

'Sorry mum, I didn't mean to say that. Yes, you're right, I should have tried harder at school and got a good job with All Legs at Ansons. You'd have liked that, me at the factory sharing a nice flat with someone like All Legs and perhaps a nice girlfriend who'd do what you told her. And you could have us come round for tea when we were married. Oh, Sunday dinner, sorry. She'd make us all a Sunday roast, wouldn't she? What's that? No, I don't suppose they would have me back now. Yes, I know, I'm too old for an apprenticeship.'

It was a training booklet for the local TEC. I only have a vague memory of them asking for page numbers to be added. It seemed such a small point but it was also the last straw. Even as the job was reprinted, laminated front cover and all, along with all the stitching and trimming, I was fired. I walked back to the flat feeling a strange sense of relief. It was short lived. As soon as I got back mother was there. On and on she went, shouting so that my ears were ringing from the mocking jibes that she yelled at me. I put my hand over my ears to shut out her voice but if anything her ranting became louder.

I went outside to get away, but she was still there. I found myself near the river, where the bridge crosses the fast-flowing Trent near the castle. I wondered if anyone else could hear her too. People were looking at me very strangely. I apologised to them.

"It's my mother, I told them. I didn't mean to be a bad boy."

Many quickened their steps to move away from me. The voice carried on as I walked along the towpath close to where the old oil depot used to be. I had to yell out loud. Leave me alone. My words rang out across the river, bouncing off the old warehouses on the other side in a mocking echo. It was getting cold. I went back to the flat and tried to sleep as the life of the chip shop went on below.

What started me muttering to myself, I cannot say. I know that I was pissed off with the constant noise from downstairs and I even think I shouted through the floorboards for them to put a sock in it. I mumbled to myself about what a bloody racket they made.

"You noisy bastards," I said to myself, "clattering around all hours of the day and night. Fish and chips. Pie and chips. Chicken and fucking chips."

I realised after a while that as long as I was talking she could not say a word. So I kept on. My own language was my secret weapon. Thinking up things to talk about was the hard part and, if I stopped for more than half an hour, she would be back, coming into my head

399

as if she had a key. Ever since I had seen that blasted album she had made her way back into my head - all that digging, sinking that mineshaft, well that had been a waste of time.

"So what would send her back into oblivion? What would happen if the album were to be destroyed, say in a fire? Would She be unable to exist without it?" I was saying all this to myself, talking in a low voice, one up from a whisper. "If I could get to Edlington, seek out Ellie and get the album, I could lob the sodding thing in the Trent. Good idea Davy lad."

I went for my car keys only to realise that I no longer had a car. Down into despair I fell. So I scratched up a few quid and trudged up to Lombard Street to the bus station and caught the Mansfield bus.

It was almost dark by the time I made it to The Croft. There was the glory of a summer evening, balmy, with a breeze that held on to the day's warmth and a sunset that made nature seem wonderful. I knocked on the door, ready with my apology for my remarks over the phone all those weeks ago. One of Ellie's friends opened the door. At least that is what I presumed.

"Hello," I said, "I'm Davy, is Ellie in?"

On seeing her confused expression, revised my enquiry.

"I mean Mrs Crampton, the vicar's wife."

"Sorry," she said in a soft West Country accent, "I'm Mrs Branbourne. My husband's the new vicar here. Mrs Crampton's left, I'm afraid."

"Oh," was all that came out of my mouth.

"She's been gone a fortnight," she added.

"Any idea where she's gone?" I asked.

"Sorry, I can't help you there."

"She didn't..." I knew it was going to be a stupid question even as I asked it, "she didn't leave a box behind, did she, a box with a photograph album in it?"

"No. No definitely not. The house was totally empty when we moved in, that's how I'm so sure."

"Oh," I said as my heart broke. I could not stop my voice from becoming shaky, "sorry to have bothered you."

I turned my back on the old place as I heard the door close behind me, close for the last time. I had lost her. Surely though, she would have left a forwarding address with the new people, I thought. It seemed impossible that Ellie would have failed to let me know where she was going. She would have got word to me somehow, even if it were just a phone call, or a change of address card to… to where? She had no idea where I was. As far as she knew I was still with Becky. Becky. Maybe she had received a call or a card, I said out loud to myself. I decided to call her from the village phone box. Surely she would help me with something as harmless as this? So why was I so nervous? I climbed into the telephone box, put in my money and called her number. I think I knew that just hearing her voice would destroy yet more of me, that part of me which was too fragile to take anymore. I was right. That voice of hers, all it had to do was say good evening and I could taste her lips against mine and recall in clear pictures our nights of delight.

"Hello?"

"It's me, Davy. Please don't hang up."

"Oh fuck off, weirdo."

"Just one thing, then I'll go."

"You make a habit of this and…."

I interrupted her.

"Has my Ellie been in touch? She's left home, and I don't know where she's moved to."

"To get away from you, I expect. No, she hasn't," she said.

The reply made my heart crack.

"Oh, wait a sec', she did," said Rebecca. "A card came in the post, something about a new address. It was junk mail as far as I was concerned. It went out with all the rubbish on Tuesday. So that's that. You can sod off now. Don't call again."

The phone made the click of a terminated call, terminating my contact with Ellie for good. I wanted to cry an ocean, but no tears would come. Instead, I left the stuffy confines of the phone box and emerged into the cool, night air. I had to get out of the village in case I met anyone. So I walked into the pitch-black void down a dark country lane that led nowhere in particular.

I felt wrung out. It was as if I had gone backwards, no longer a man, but in reverse through infancy to become a foetus. The nocturnal world around me seemed like a metaphor for my life, empty darkness with no clear path and lacking any signposts to guide my way. I spun around in my head like a drunk, feeling drugged by the despair, as if the misery was a poison. The cool night became cold. It was a clear black sky. Looking up I could make out Orion and The Plough. I did the trick with the last two stars on the end of The Plough and followed them up to The Pole Star behind me. I could tell that I was walking south. Big deal, I thought. All I have left are the bloody twinkling stars. It all suddenly seemed pointless, this carving a career, relationships, finding a place to live, money, even love. Whatever I did on this crazy planet, or whatever I did not do on it, the stars above me would still be there, millions of years after I have disappeared, they would still be twinkling as they were in that moment. I could feel the engine within me slow to a crawl. The revs decreased until they stopped. So, here I was on the earth, with the stars above me, and none of it mattered. My knees buckled and down I went. The rest of me rolled sideways and I came to rest on the grass verge near a field gate, flat on my back. There were thousands of stars now to see, with the ribbon of the Milky Way threading its way through them. I could well have been set free in outer space since I was unaware of the world behind me. The last thing I saw before I closed my exhausted eyes was the cold, endless universe.

It was a perfect way to die; only I did not. A cool breeze and the flicker of early morning sunbeams poking through the hedge awakened me. I was sprinkled with dew and chilled throughout. I did not want this. I would have been glad to go. I wanted God to take me home but he had not. The beautiful night had gone and a new day was here. I did not want it. The days before had served to crush me. Why would this one be any different? I rolled into the undergrowth. Hawthorn does not make a comfortable shelter. So dying this way was not going to be pleasant. Never mind. This is where I was going to die. I would lie here all day, all night. I would lie here for as long as it took until I passed away. Someone would find my body. The story would make the news briefly and then I would be as unimportant as the stars. Even the feeling of hunger gave me hope that the end was not far away. The misery anaesthetised my mind so that I never felt bored curled up under the hedge. There was no need to plan. I did not have to create an empire for protection - no need to think of anything really. The overwhelming sadness and hopelessness were enough to cradle my mind between life and death.

I was only aware of the passing day in a vague sense. The sun moved across the sky. That is about all I can tell you. Deep misery is exhausting. This was a concentrated tiredness that came from carrying a heart as heavy as lead. It was all consuming. I think that this is how dying cats feel when they search out a place to die. Here was mine. The day was warm. Coldness returned with the blackness. Light revolved around me and later, warmth again. It was a cycle. I was a cyclist in the universe, a universe that I would soon be at one with. My belly began to hurt, as did my head. Most painful were my eyes. When I thought of mother, Ellie, even Gwen, and Becky, when the vision of John came into my mind, and the picture of the dad who I had never known, I began to hurt in the pit of my being. This was a real pain, not just a sense of upset, but pain so severe that it dominated the other discomforts. It was enough to dismember my mind, so that I began to float away, to disengage, rather like a computer being shut down. The heartache was shutting me down, which made the dying easier to bear. There was darkness and light, cold and warmth. Several times this happened. Days were passing. I had no idea what was going on or where the hell I was.

Nothing anymore, a void, shutting down, have I said that already? This is a quiet draining away of life, mingled with birdsong and the occasional sound of a passing car, each unaware that I was here.

I believe this to be good. I would go in peace if… I will go from Ellie so that one of these days she can… can what?

What was I saying?

Sorry. I'm tired, so tired, beyond tired. I'm losing. Will John be…? I can't think amy nore, amy nore. Anymore, I meant, I mean. What's happening dear God? Is it apernin? Listen. Nothing. Am I deaf? I wondered what it would, sorry.

Where was I? I wondered.

What was. I wonder. Wonderful, I can't feel a thing. All is well. Is this serenity? It's silence. It's all going. Time's going. I'm going. Going. Going. Go... ing. Go. Let it be, let be, oh I can't find. And the light shone through the stained glass so that. So that it. It. And a choir of the heavenly host. I'm in an anthem, is it? What is this? Just a peaceful sense of going and then I'd be able to fly. I'll be able. Fly up to ev'n, heaven. Prayers, hands together. Davy boy. Our Father. Can't breathe, don't want to now. Mayther peacof God. Peace. Which passes. Wch pas sall underst, understanding. Understanding keep yur arts, can't breathe, breathe. Tired, so tir. Where was? Anmin in the ledge lovef God. God, Oh God, God thefath. Father, Ftherson and lysprit, Jesus, Amen. Amen, amen, amen men. Was happenin? Hapenin, haperrid al dslrh the ankls pshksh? I'm, let it, dy peace last time, time to, is it the don't know... Can't hold on any mo got in every thought letter... Let lit lother lotanar tad aashs prl gha mmmm... All dgdhd... Df... gg... h...

Chapter nineteen: Reunited

Swallowing. I think this to be the first sensation. I swallow the spit that has built up in my mouth. It hurts because I have something in my throat. By a reflex I lift a heavy arm to feel what is there. I seem to be pulling something with me. This is all done with the dregs of consciousness, so cognitive thought is out of the question. The world around me is the world of only six inches away. That is my universe. My mouth is clear of any objects, but a flexible tube has entered my nose and runs down the back of my throat. That is why it is hard to swallow. This is primitive thinking. I have no knowing, no understanding. The objects that I pull against are tubes also. They run under a piece of tape lashed round my left arm and seem to penetrate my skin there. I let it be.

When time has been obliterated there can be no measure of it. I cannot say how long it is before I begin to grasp what might be happening, or what has happened. My memory rebuilds painfully. I am not experiencing what I expected to. I begin to feel the disappointment that I have not gone. I will not be in heaven when I open my eyes will I? I am right. I am not. Some bastard has saved me. I am back in my own hell, back in my life, back in a hospital.

In marked contrast to my acceptance of leaving my life behind, I became furious that someone had interfered. There was nothing I could have done about it during this period, as I was so weak. But it bubbled like a poison in a witch's cauldron with more vigour than any feeling I had ever known. This was evolution turned on its head, designed, as we are to survive at whatever cost. I had been prepared to die no matter how cold it became or how many pains my body could withstand. In the ditch I had faced them all until Mother Nature took me in her arms and carried me beyond my own mind. Now, I had been stolen away from her grasp. I bided my time. Like a neap tide my knowledge trickled gradually back into my brain and refloated the curse.

It never occurred to me to pull out the tubes that connected me to life. Why not? I can only assume that I had nearly made it and that it had affected my reasoning. We just found him in the nick of time. I bet that is how they see it, but not me. I am not thinking straight. The nutrition that flows through the clear tubes did its job. I improved. The time came for the doctors to try me on some real food, tomato soup. A nurse brought it and placed it on a wheeled tray that straddled my bed. The bed was adjusted so that my body sat upright. She went about this task oblivious to the rage in my head. I did not want sustenance. I wanted to be left to die. The spoon in the nurse's hand took a small amount of soup, red like blood, and brought its life-giving promise to my mouth. Where I got the strength from I will never know but I managed to knock the spoon away, sending stains all over the bedclothes. I managed to grunt a few words that were supposed to have said leave me alone. She tried again, bringing the spoon to touch my lips. I was beside myself with anger, red, furious anger. From a pit of reserve I pulled myself from the pillow and grabbed the nurse by the throat. My grip was feeble and she pulled away easily as the soup splashed all over the floor. Exhausted, I flopped back into the pillows and lay there gasping for breath as an army of staff arrived to see what the nurse's screams were all about.

405

Days passed after that. No more attempts at food. Against all my desires I began to recover. I did everything to show my displeasure at the fact. I spat at doctors, urinated in the bed and, as my voice grew stronger, I began to shout at them to let me die. It was not until I grabbed a plastic knife that had a serrated edge to it and commenced to drag it over my jugular vein that they accepted I was not playing games. My powerless arms caused nothing more than a scratch but, as a demonstration, it had eloquence.

Everyone employed in the business of keeping my body and soul together became figures of hate. Mother too hated them. After all, she wanted me to join her. She told me that everything would be different when we got back together again. Things would go back to how they had been when I was a baby and a little boy. She said that she would love me and that she was really sorry about the card. I adored her when she spoke to me like this. It was like the times when she got out the album and we shared those few beautiful moments together. We had to be reunited. All those in the hospital were against it. They had to be stopped. So, when one morning a doctor came over to see how I was getting on, I was ready for him.

His visit was a well-worn routine that included amongst other things a blood-pressure examination. My fake whispery voice was almost inaudible as I tried to catch his attention. He looked at my lips for a clue to what I was saying. I tried again, just a little quieter, pushing my face slightly towards him. He understood my gesture and placed his ear near to my mouth. That curved knobbly structure was between my teeth in no time. How he yelled for me to let go, but my bite was good. Part of his ear was between my back molars. I crushed the cartilage with them so that I could hear the grinding crunch and taste his iron-rich blood in my mouth. I could hear his terrifying squeals as I tortured him. He was in agony as he writhed about on the bed thrashing away. Pieces of his ear remained in my jaws as he finally yanked himself free. Other members of staff had by now arrived. Some went to his assistance as he yelled in pain. They looked at me with misunderstanding. Three of them restrained me as another went to a room and came back with a syringe. I could feel the bee sting in my arm. All went calm.

There is an aching sadness in a ruined city. Death hangs over it like a lamentation, a final, calm, but hard-to-bear sense that its days are over. Its good days wander through the rubble like ghosts, already dead, waiting for the few stragglers to follow. It has gone beyond heartbreak. There is no heart to break anymore. This is the great goodbye.

This was how I was. If I looked up, all I could see were a mass of fists, all with their thumbs pointed down. Each breath was a farewell to life. Dying, like living is a process, and gradually the things that had made me who I was collapsed, like the blackened walls of bombed buildings into a heap of dust. Possibly because I was in this state of mind, I never noticed that I had been moved to another hospital. It was not until much later when I realised that I was once more back in Saxenby.

The wheelchair wheels had crunched down the gravel drive that reached a path of flagstones. The motion had stopped and I could see a tree, an apple tree full of fruit. The air had been cold on my face and it was this that had made me pay attention to the tree. It matched one in my memory and I understood at that point where I was. Far from being angry, I felt as if I had been caught by a safety net. I knew that here, there might well be people who would understand why I wanted to leave this life behind. It was almost as if I had spotted something like a wild flower growing out of the rubble that surrounded me.

It was a shock to discover from a newspaper that the year was nineteen ninety-two. I have no recollection of the four years between biting the ear of the doctor to the time I saw the tree. It was as if I had been dead after all - but my body had hung on, doing all the work until my mind had come back to join it.

The doctors there were patient. There seemed to be a different atmosphere about the place, a change in attitude. How are you today, Mr Harper? This was about as interrogatory as the questions got, at least in the first weeks that I began speaking again. A thin chap called Norman who wore sandals over his socks visited me often. He always wore a tie and a blazer or a jacket and his brownish hair was always parted down the side, as was done in the sixties. He must have been about my age but he looked older. He was good to talk to. We only

407

had chats about meaningless things really. We discussed what would happen to the rotation of the earth if a rope were fastened between the world and the moon. How much weight could a bumblebee lift? Does God eat? Silly stuff like that.

I found these discussions completely amusing and gently stimulating. I do not know why? It was just idle chatter, but it made me feel good in a way I had forgotten, or have possibly never known. One day he pondered why it was that siblings, who were made of the same ingredients, often ended up being so different. It was like hearing a piece of music sink into a minor chord. I became uneasy about him. I told him that I did not want to talk about that. I had a feeling that we were gradually edging towards the topic of families. There could only be one destination for that conversation to end up at. So I changed the topic. I asked him how was it that people drowned under water, despite an atom of oxygen being in it. Quick as a flash, he began to explore why that would be so. We were back on safe ground again. Secrets kept so long are hard to give up. Believe me, I would sometimes have been glad to pour them out, to get rid of them altogether, but it had become a habit, a compulsion to hold on to them. To expose them after all these years would hurt. I could not do it. Even drug addicts know that the drugs are bad for them. Can they stop? No, they cannot, and neither could I. So, my life remained locked away.

It was in this way that we ended up talking about anaesthesia. Who knows how we got onto it. One notion led to another. Here we were, Norman trying to hold me up as I took my first steps out of the wheelchair, whilst chatting about putting people to sleep.

"So even though your abdomen's cut right open, you don't feel one little thing, not the slightest, most minute pain?" I asked.

"Well, it wouldn't be worth doing if you could, now would it?"

"So, what do you think about while you're out then? Do you dream?"

"I was put out at the dentists once," said Norman with a little laugh, "and I dreamed about the demolition of a power station."

"A power station? Why a power station?"

"There was something about a power station in a magazine in the waiting room," he said, "that must have triggered it."

"I never want to be put out," I said.

"No? Why not?"

"I wouldn't be able to stop the dreams."

A damning silence followed. What had I said? I looked at Norman's face as he tried to hide the fact that he had struck gold.

"You wouldn't want to stop it if it was a nice dream," he said.

I did not know what to say back. My lack of response answered his non-question. He had unlocked a tiny part of me.

"Anyway, let's hope you never have to have an operation," he said, withdrawing to safe ground, his prize nugget hidden in his professional pocket.

A day or two later he asked me quite directly if I minded telling him what my dreams were about. His voice was polite and charged with sincere interest. This was no trick. I said that I would tell him one day and we left it at that. I think that his approach toward me helped me to trust him. All the others had been manipulators. The last time I was here I had felt betrayed almost. At least Norman had the decency to ask me this in a straightforward way.

So it was that evening I began to tell him of the cycle ride into the village and the church and the old woman. Bit by bit I divulged how the caveman would run after me and we would end up in the dead house that had once known happiness and I would wake up in a sweat. Instead of analysing it he went on to tell me some of his bad dreams. It seemed refreshing to talk this way and I found that I could tell him almost anything and we became good friends.

Squinting in the long lost light of day, on the doorstep of my mind, were the things that had happened when the bad dreams had dragged me screaming out of sleep. The things that had happened when, as a boy, someone would come into the room with a voice as soft as silk and as hard as iron. Even after all these years they were shameful things. I could not understand how the guilt of them had infected me. These things had been done against me yet, even as the victim of it, there was a paralysis in my head that stopped them coming out, a guilt paralysis, a shame paralysis. Ah, but the dreams. Now they had come out into the open.

Was it possible to have nights free of them? Was there an anaesthetic under which the dreams could be removed, amputated out of my mind? The idea was too idiotic and I thought no more about it. No, that is not true. I began to think about it a great deal, not in realistic terms, not in terms of a scalpel and gas, but in an abstract way. Maybe a physical removal of part of my brain was the only way but even that had an abstract quality to it. The fact was that I did not know how it could be done, only that I wished it could be. Never having thought about it like this before, I found myself thinking about it to the point of obsession. So much so that I mentioned it to the only person who would listen properly, Norman.

"Are the dreams that bad?" he asked. "Enough to want you to contemplate surgery?"

"They begin beautifully," I said, "but I know it's a beauty that can't last. Even as I fall into the dream I know that it'll terrify me at the end. It's not like I know what will happen. In the dream it's like I'm dreaming it for the first time. All I can feel when it starts are the fingers of its doomed ending pulling me in."

Norman nodded that he understood what I had meant and sat back in his chair staring vacantly into space. Then his face came once more into sharp focus, the trace of a smile quivering with the brightness of an idea shining.

"I might just have the very thing for you," he said. "You leave it to me. She might just be able to do us both a bit of good."

With that off he went back into the hospital saying something about having to make a phone call. I began to wonder what I had let myself in for and questioned the wisdom of spilling out the dreams - but it had been done and the prospect of their removal, gave me hope for peace, peace of mind, long overdue.

By now I was able to walk unaided. The muscles in my legs were growing with the diet and the exercise. Out of nowhere, Norman appeared one morning, out of breath and excited.

"Your dreams," he blurted out, and before I had chance to reply he said, "well I've got a surprise for you. Come with me."

With that he took me by the arm and urged me back to the rear steps and into the hospital. On we went down the corridor of the

410

East Wing until we came to the day room. No one was there, except for a small, solitary person sitting with her back to us. I would have asked what was going on had not events unfolded so hurriedly. In we went. Round she turned. Up she stood. Before me was a face I knew, a young, attractive face, with clever eyes that beheld me from behind a pair of designer specs. A thousand images of people raced through the library of snapshots in my head. Her voice added sound to the pictures of people I had come into contact with over the years.

"Hello David. Remember me?"

I shook my head.

"It's me, Helen. Helen Knight?"

So now I had the face, the voice and the name. She could tell by my expression that I had nearly got it.

"You used to work at Saltbys, didn't you?" she said. "I'm Helen, remember? The one who went off to Bristol, to university?"

"My God," I said, "you're a grown woman."

She was dressed in a knee-length denim skirt with what looked like a man's white shirt tucked into it. Her brown hair was shorter than it had been at Saltbys, all the better to show off her natural beauty. I could not believe it actually was her.

"So, what brings you here?" I said.

"I did," said Norman. "She's your dreams doctor. She's the anaesthetic you were talking about."

I looked bewildered. They both could see I was.

"I'm a trained hypnotherapist now," she explained. "I'm here to help you, like you helped me once."

I sat down, not knowing whether to laugh or cry.

"I helped you?" I asked.

"More than you'll ever know," she said.

"I don't follow," I said, finding all this odd in an interesting sort of way.

"I hated it at Saltbys," she said. "You were the only one who was kind to me. My mum had recently died and I was thinking about giving up the idea of university. We had a chat one day. Remember? You seemed to be battling against something yourself. I could not fathom it but, despite all that, you were trying to make your way in the world. I resolved to stop feeling sorry for myself that day and go

411

for it. Sometimes a straw can break a camel's back. But there are other times when the right straw in just the right place can hold it up. You were my straw that day. I owe you one," she took a deep breath and smiled into my eyes. "There, I've been waiting years to say that to you."

Her eyes had all but misted over, beautiful eyes with dark brown corneas magnified behind her wire-rimmed glasses. Glasses. For a moment I allowed myself to be caught up in her appreciation, the sincerity of which overshadowed her true intent. I felt a little embarrassed receiving such gratitude, especially considering that I had nothing but a vague recollection of what to her had been such a life-changing conversation. Norman looked nervous, the same way a bad salesman does when he is on the verge of a belter. Both of them seemed to be waiting, and they were. They were waiting for me to say something. I began to collect my thoughts.

"A hypnotist?" I said to her. "Is this a wind up Norman?"

"I'm not a hypnotist," said Helen before he could answer. "I'm a hypnotherapist. There's a difference."

"I'm not having people play tricks on me. Enough people have done that."

Helen motioned to Norman. He took this rehearsed cue and said that he had some paperwork to do.

"I'll catch up with you in a while David," he said almost mechanically as he strode off.

"Tell you what. Let's go for a stroll in the sunshine and I'll tell you everything you want to know. No one, least of all me, is going to play tricks on you. In fact I want you to tell me what to do. That's the way it works."

So we found ourselves in the clear outdoors, walking leisurely through the hospital gardens. She was very calming and friendly, even offering me a smoke. Everything she said was interesting to listen to. It was not so much a conversation since she did most of the talking. In those first few minutes she captivated me. I could not help but pay attention to her, like a child sinks into a bedtime story. Without knowing it I was becoming mesmerised by the tone of her voice. She spoke with an essence that drew a person in like a magnet. She was like balm to my mind.

With great enthusiasm she went on to explain that she had used her skills to stop people smoking, which considering we were both cheerfully puffing away I thought rather funny. One woman, terrified of stairs had overcome her fear through her hypnotherapy work. I found it hard to believe. It was disbelief that I was happy to suspend, sure in the hope that I would soon be benefitting from it.

We finally stopped our walk and sat on a bench. From here, beyond the fence was the village of Saxenby cradled in a dip of rolling fields on either side. I took control of my tongue and made it liberate the words in my head.

"I have bad dreams, you know," I said, staring dead ahead at the church spire and feeling like a lost soul stepping into a bright unknown. "That's what terrifies me. I have voices of people in my head, as real as yours. I don't want them there. Do you think you can make them go away?"

"You may not realise it David," she said, "but you've just taken the first step towards getting your wish."

A lump swelled up in my throat at her words, and spontaneously, tears built up ready to spill.

"Do you think so?" I managed to say.

Chapter twenty: Hope

Helen and Norman had met at Bristol. He was a year older than her and a year further on in his degree course than she. They became good friends. Good mates as Norman put it. He told me that she was a gifted individual and that she had helped countless people in so many ways. I said that she told me that already. I asked if they were in love. Norman just laughed. I do not think so was all he would say on the matter. But he was right about her being gifted. She was. There was a light hidden inside her, powerful and bright. I imagined that if she ever cut herself, a shimmering brightness would burst forth from the wound like a sunbeam. She was kind and considerate, yet there was always the touch of the professional about her.

Over the following weeks I found her to be great fun. Once when we were discussing hypnosis she remembered a daft comment I made on our previous session. She took a watch out of her pocket. It was only a plastic toy tied to a piece of cotton but she let it swing before my eyes and kept repeating you are feeling sleepy, your eyes are feeling heavy. Nothing happened. She had made her point though. Any notions that I was going to enter into any state of hypnotism by such a cliché parlour game were swept aside. I was going to have to learn to be hypnotised, she told me. It was going to be a combination of effort between her and me. I did not care how it would be done to be honest, so long as the dreams were exorcised.

Sometimes she could not make it over from Clifton and, on those few occasions, I experienced an aching disappointment. Clifton, on the outskirts of Nottingham, was not far away but I could tell on the times when she arrived late for our meetings that she was under a lot of pressure. It was then that I felt sorry for her and not a little guilty for the trouble I was causing. It was on one of these occasions that she rushed into the room where I was waiting. She apologised for being late, threw her bags down, and closed the curtains to our room.

The room. It was a box room. The broom cupboard she called it, but it was an intimate place with one window and one door. The carpet was quite new and gave off a luxurious, freshly manufactured aroma. On a small table in the corner stood a standard lamp, complete with a floral shade that, along with its fifty-watt bulb, generated a cosy glow everywhere. A made-up bed lay along one wall, leaving room for two comfortable armchairs in the limited space that remained. Mine was a recliner made of cream fabric. Helen plonked herself in the light blue one opposite mine after switching on the light, putting her fags and lighter on the table saying that they were for afterwards. I watched her body relax, listened to her breathing slow down and observed her eyes close as if she was falling asleep. Then suddenly she was ready. Her eyes sprang open and she leaned forward to talk to me, all her cares momentarily removed.

We began where we had left off, talking about relaxation. We practised breathing properly, something that I found a little silly at first. Had I not managed to breathe for thirty-seven years without instruction I used to joke? Anyway, I got over my self-consciousness and learned to do it the way she wanted. It was going to be worth it to put an end to my haunting visions. Normally, after the breathing, she would talk about the different ways that she could induce the hypnosis. Usually we would do a few minutes of listening. It was possible to let silence create a trance. Self-hypnosis was possible. Other times I would imagine the scenes that she was describing, allowing her voice to relax me to a point of no return. I never wanted to fight it but there was always a part of my mind that stopped it working. We had done this every day so far. But, on this day, she did not do any of that. Instead she asked me about the nightmares, very specific questions. She wanted me to describe the people, the places and especially the events. I had to say that there was no story to them as in a book or a film - it was the theme that was recurrent and the ending. She persisted, probing me with a calm determination. I became uneasy. I looked round for the door. My breathing quickened. All the relaxation boiled away.

"Let's stop there," she said, "I need a smoke. You coming for one?"

It was like taking a break at work, I thought. This was her job and, in a way, it was mine too. Going out for a fag break took away the feeling that she was my interrogator and that rather we were working towards the same end. An autumn wind played with the doomed leaves on the trees and spoke of winter's advance.

"Doesn't time go fast," I said. "The summer's nearly gone."

"There are never enough hours in the day," she said, glancing at her watch.

"I meant life," I said.

"Life!" she said. "Now there's a word." she took a deep sigh. "It can be more like a sentence sometimes, I think."

"You don't have to tell me. My life's been a pile of shit so far."

"In what way, a pile of shit?" she asked with well-practised nonchalance.

"Huh! How long have you got?" I said, unaware of her opportunism. "You'd have to go back to the beginning."

"Then start there. I'm listening."

I would have, but I could not. My past wrapped its fingers around my throat ready to strangle me if ever I uttered one thing about my growing up. She gave me that look of hers, the one that was packed with patience, the one that said you'll tell me when you're ready. Only I could never see myself being ready. I could not even face the future, let alone the past. Then she said something that at first meant nothing but came to mean everything.

"It's a pity we can't start our lives again sometimes, isn't it?" she said, although I felt that the words were turned inward on herself and not so much to me.

I agreed.

By now I had settled into the institutional way of the hospital. It was safe here, if not peculiar sometimes. Some of the other patients wore their mental afflictions on their sleeves, throwing tantrums and yelling abuse at the drop of a hat. I felt quite normal, except for the fact that I knew I could not take care of myself. I kept busy. I even helped produce a newsletter called *The Saxenby Times*. My rehab included supervised trips to Newark College, where I studied computer publishing and graphics. Eight of us went along. I was by far the sanest one amongst us. A girl who came with us would burst into tears if the slightest little thing went wrong. Another chap refused to have anything to do with the machine. He said that Satan could see him on the other side of the screen. He was encouraged to carry on but no one could shake him from his beliefs so he dropped out. By far the worst person was Nick. His wife and only daughter had burned to death in a fire at their home. He had tried to get them out by running headlong into the flames. I understood that he had emerged empty handed from the burning building with the sleeves and back of his sweater on fire. Day after day he could be found in the hospital grounds, imagining he was standing in front of the remains of his charred house shouting for his family to come out. Sometimes, I watched him at the computer. He would just stare straight ahead with silent tears pouring from his eyes onto the keyboard. He was very ill.

My sickness on the other hand was different. I just felt that the thing required to enable me to survive out in the world had been smashed to pieces. Like a snapped femur would prevent someone from walking properly, I could not live properly. All I needed was

416

healing. I knew it, but I could not see how. So I put my faith in Helen and Norman. My hopes were wrapped up in the pair of them.

"You do trust me, don't you?" said Helen after the breathing part of our session had ended.

"That sounds ominous," I said, still smiling.

"I'm going to ask you to do something and I need you to trust me."

A frown settled on my brow overshadowing the smile.

"Go on."

"Your dreams David. We are agreed that we're trying to deal with your nightmares, aren't we?"

"That's what all this is about, isn't it?" I said, concerned at her serious tone.

"So you do trust me then?"

"I suppose I do. Yes," I said.

I could see that she had come to some sort of critical moment. She wavered over her bag that had come to rest next to her chair. Then she took out a black object. It was a tape recorder, a small one, and she placed it near her on the bed. My face alone asked all the questions that my voice failed to utter.

"This isn't going to be easy," she said after some time. "I want you to try and recount all the things that have ever happened in your dreams. This is to help me. It's to help me help you. I need to know what we're up against. I know you don't like it, but there it is. There's no other way."

She looked at me like someone who had just admitted they had run over the family dog. I felt cornered but could see that here was someone taking a risk - a risk on my behalf. So I stayed put.

"Why the tape recorder?" I asked, knowing really why it was there.

She smiled for the first time and told me not to ask silly questions.

"We're going to make this a conversation, not an inquisition," she assured me.

"Hadn't you better turn it on then?" I said nodding towards the little black box on the bed.

"Not just yet," she said. "I want this to be a private moment before we start."

"Private?" I asked.

She was looking concerned again.

417

"I don't want this going on tape," she said. "Some things are best just between ourselves."

"What sort of things?"

"The things we are about to talk about," she said.

"I've got a bad feeling about this," I said.

"Okay," she began, "let's make a pact. If I venture on to things that you don't like, you tell me you don't want to talk about it. You're in control in other words. Do we have a deal?"

I could find no fault in that, so I said yes we did have a deal.

"Right then, let me start with this one. When did you first have these dreams?"

"When I was a boy," I said.

"How old?"

"Nine or ten, I think."

Do you recognise anyone from that time in your dreams?" she asked.

"No."

"What was happening in your life at the time, say moving schools or being bullied?"

"I was still at junior school. I'd got used to being singled out for bullying by then," I said.

"How were things at home?"

So, we had arrived. She had brought me here. Like so many before her she wanted to probe into that awful chasm that had been my life with mother. But she had put me in control. I did not have to answer.

"I don't want to discuss that part," I said.

"Good," she said without showing any signs of irritation and carried on. "How was your school work at that time?"

"Poor, I'd say."

"Did that bother you?"

"I was fed up with being told off by the teachers. But I didn't care about being called a duffer Miss. Sorry, I mean Helen. God, what made me say Miss?"

"Just a slip of the tongue, that's all," she said. "Right, are you all right if I switch this thing on and we can begin on the dreams themselves?"

"Does the deal still stand?" I said.

She grinned, and pushed her glasses further onto the bridge of her nose.

"Of course," she said.

For half an hour, until the record button snapped up at the tape's end, I tried to divulge everything I could remember about the dreams that I had. I told her about the bike ride, the village, the farm, the old lady, the church, the young girl and the man who became a caveman. I went into as much detail as I could about the house that changed, how I knew that it had once been a happy house and how it altered into a dreadful place, even the way I was chased into it. I tried to paint a picture of the people in the dreams, their faces, their clothes and their voices. I even tried to give her an idea of what the village looked like. That was the hardest job of all. It was nothing more than a place to me, a stage on which the dream was performed. A collection of old houses was all I could say about it, except that I did remember the church was on a hill a little distance away from the main village. In that regard it was unlike most of the villages I had ever known where the church snuggles cosily in amongst the houses, like a family of dwellings where the faithful dwelt.

I found myself trembling as I talked about what happened in the dead house. I was not even aware of Helen changing the tape over and setting it to record again. This was always the worst part. My wide eyes were staring into a dark corner as I told it all. I was almost having the dream there and then. Almost as if I had woken up for real, I told her how I would open my eyes to find myself in a state of panic, praying for the first glint of morning light. The damn things were blighting my life. Three or four times a week I had to endure them, these unwelcome, unrelenting visitors to my brain. It was more than I could bear anymore.

We stopped then. I became quiet. She turned the machine off and we had a fag. I was surprised at just how weary I had become. The topic of the dreams was dropped, for a while, though I knew we would have to delve into them again. I began to wonder if all this was worth the trouble. So far the whole process had been slow and unrewarding. A sense of guilt and a feeling of wasting everyone's time on what must have seemed like my personal, self-indulgent trivia began to grow inside me. Feeling like this I wondered if it was a sign that I was getting better, but I kept it to myself. Just how far off being well became apparent during one of Helen's sessions, some three weeks after I had taped the nightmare diary as we dubbed it.

"Do you believe in courage?" she asked in the calm after our minutes of slow breathing.

"It exists," I said.

"Does it exist in you?" she said manoeuvring me to a fulcrum point over which she would lever me in line with her thinking.

"It ought to exist in everybody," I replied, trying to get off the hook.

"What about cowards?" she said. "What's happened to their courage?"

"Sometimes being a coward is a smart move."

"Okay then. Suppose you were in a burning building and you had a fire phobia," she began. "The smart coward would find a temporary hiding place away from the flames until it consumed the building he was hiding in," she contemplated me taking this in. "Not so smart, ay?"

"Why don't you just come out and say what's on your mind?" I said growing tired of games like this.

"Okay, then," she moved her body closer so that she could observe my reaction. "I want to hypnotise you into your dream. I want you to confront it. You can either hide in the corner where the flames will consume you, or you can take your courage in both hands and fight your way out. I'm here to help, but the decision is yours."

"You must be fucking joking. Never."

The panic was rising over me like a tidal wave.

"I can't do that," I said gripping the arms of the chair, hanging on as if I was at the dentist. "What good would that do? I'd be terrified. No, sorry I can't do that."

I got up to leave. She got up in the same instant and tried to touch my shoulder. I shrugged her off.

"I need a fag. This mumbo jumbo is getting me nowhere. I think you're making all this up as you go along. I don't think you have the faintest idea of what you're doing!" I was shouting now, a hair's breadth from losing my temper. "You're like all the others. You're a phoney, a fake. I'm pissed off with this frigging prison!" I yelled at her full bore, almost crying. "And I'm fucking pissed off with you."

Outside, there was a fine dampness in the air like micro drizzle. It had a cooling effect on my face. Only then did I realise how much blood had rushed to my cheeks. Only then did I come face to face with myself - the scared little boy, the coward. I sat down on the bench, numbed. Helen sat next to me.

"It'll get tiring, running away all your life. This is your chance to do something for yourself, you know. None of this is for me, is it? I mean do I benefit anything if your bad dreams disappear?"

I did not want her to be right but deep within me I knew that she was. I drew the smoke in from the cigarette, deep into my lungs and pumped its cool vapour back out into the cold air, like a dragon's sigh. There followed some time, akin to a two-minute silence. Then I looked at her.

"I'm sorry I said those things. You must hate me?" I said feeling scared stiff.

"I wouldn't be here if I hated you, would I?" she said.

"All this scares me you see," I confessed.

"I'd say living with this for the rest of your life is the scary bit. How can you cope with that?"

"I don't want to. I've had enough. You're right. I'm tired of running. I've run out of road, haven't I?" I said.

"I know that you're afraid of these dreams?" she said.

"They terrify me," I admitted.

"Courage can only grow where there's fear," she said to me. "Listen, if we changed places, what would you say to me?"

"This isn't going to be easy, is it?" I said, moving on from her question.

"Nothing worthwhile ever is."

"How do you know this will work?" I put to her.

"Just trust me. It will."

"Trust and courage you say?" I took another long drag. "Oh shit, come on then."

Back in our broom cupboard we sat in our chairs, in our darkness, trying to find that calm place in our minds, beyond the smell of our wet clothes and hair. She told me to listen to her voice, to be aware of the sound it made at the back of my mind. She said that if she counted up from one to twelve I was to open my eyes and everything would be over. I was petrified and held on to my bravery as if it was a life belt, trying against my better judgement to relax. How could I? How could I voluntarily jump into the horror of dreams that had plagued me for years? I fought my own will for the hypnosis to take hold but my frayed nerves prevented it.

In the end we stopped the session. Helen said that even having a go at it was a giant stride forward. She said that we had made great progress today. It did not feel as if we had but then she said something that put it all in perspective.

"At least your days of being a victim are over David. For the first time in your life you know you've got hope, don't you?"

I did and it felt good.

I met Norman the next day at breakfast. He had spoken to Helen on the phone and asked how we had got on. She told him he would have to ask me, confidentiality being something she swore by.

"Tell me to mind my own bloody business, but how's it all going?" he said, open faced about it all.

I explained how far we had got, happy to be honest with him.

"But that's fantastic. You've worked a miracle you two. You're a bloody hero David, a bloody hero."

"You think so?"

"What, face up to something that scares the shit out of you? I'd bloody say so. I'm petrified of heights. I can't even climb a flippin' ladder. You've done more than I could."

It seemed that I had come a long way from being a stupid bastard.

The weekend came and went. It seemed as if the brief summer had run its course and that autumn was firmly upon us, dragging our weary souls down with it towards the bleakness of winter. As a counter balance to this feeling, I held on to the words Norman had said. They made an impression on me. Encouragement was always a rare commodity to me, so to be called a hero, well that was something special.

Helen arrived at ten past eleven, dashing apologetically in to the day room where I usually waited for her. She said hello with a tone that was more of a question than a mere greeting. I knew what she was asking. I just smiled back at her and let it go at that. I could see a smile creep across her flushed face. She understood. She knew from just one observation that I was prepared. Never would there be such a quiet celebration within a person's heart as there was inside Helen's that morning.

Without any grand gesture, we left the day room, walked side by side to our room and went in. There, like dozens of times before, we sat ourselves down, darkened the place except for the lamp and went through our relaxation routine. I could feel the hero inside join with Helen's mind. I knew that I would be all right this time. There was nothing for it but to let the calmness take over. I had had enough of fighting this the old way. Now I had support. Helen had never given up on me. I owed her my cooperation and so it was willingly that I let her voice float into my mind as she told me about how she would bring me back by counting from one to twelve.

I was going to tell her everything I saw. That is what she was saying. Everything I saw. Everything I saw. I had to listen to her voice. It was telling me to let go. She told me to fall back into the arms of her words. She would catch me. I was to fall backwards and tell her what I could see. Then came the bliss, like a waft of air, warm and soothing. The air ran through my hair as I moved forwards. I said that I was moving forwards. At least I think I said that. It is hard to remember. I was too interested in the warmth of the air rushing through my hair. It had warmed up quite a bit. Even the handlebars were warm, not only from the blistering air but also from my hot, sweaty hands.

There before me was a road, rising upwards, a gentle yet long hill, slowing my forward progress. It seemed as if it would never end. Clumps of trees that bordered the road obscured the view, giving me no indication of where the upward gradient would level out and I would be able to relax. I knew that the last seven miles had been like this all the way, a persistent incline, not a steep slope, but a gradual, energy-sapping ascent. I thought about getting off the bicycle and walking but then I knew from experience such a move would lead to

423

yet more exhaustion, so I pushed on. In my idling mind I thought how similar a bike ride could be to life. There had been times in my own existence where I had to struggle forwards with no end in sight. Recent times. But now I was free, locked in my own micro world, a simple world, where the only problem to overcome was the arrival at the top of this hill and the glimpse of a brand new horizon.

Chapter twenty-one: Out

So the angel took hold of my hand. She spoke softly once more, lulling me like a child with her numbers. When the angel had reached twelve she spoke.

"You can open your eyes now."

As far as I knew my eyes were open, but she said it again. I prepared myself to see God's glory as I felt my eyelids separate. Before me I was aware of a great light, as the angel cradled my hand in both of hers. The light was golden and warmth came from it. I saw the light and it was good.

"David," said the angel. "Take your time, David."

I took my time, getting used to the light. Beside it there was a face. The face was of my angel, beautiful and clear and wearing glasses. Glasses?

I sat bolt upright in the armchair. My body was soaked with sweat. The face next to the light, I knew it. I knew the armchair, the room, and the closed curtains. I even knew the smell. The reality rushed in like air filling a broken vacuum.

"Helen," I said.

I spoke like a man brought back from the dead, staring straight at her, or rather, through her, as the playback of what I had just experienced ran like a DVD in my head.

"Helen, it is you, isn't it. Please tell me it's you? I'm back, aren't I?" she could tell that I did not dare believe it. "It worked that time," I said excitedly. "Tell me I'm back for God's sake tell me I really am back."

"I had to bring you back, Dave," she said lighting a cigarette, and taking a well-earned drag, "you were having convulsions. You've been thrashing about for the last thirty seconds. I've been scared sick."

I took in her words, even as the images of Empton and Lotty continued to overlay themselves upon the reality that was before me. Her instructions returned to my memory, that she would bring me out of the hypnosis by counting slowly up to twelve. I was sceptical about the hypnosis, especially after the army of counsellors that I had seen on this long road to understanding, but it had worked it seemed and, after a few moments of letting it sink in, I felt a tempered sense of elation.

"I've been there you know, Helen. I've really been there."

"I know you have, Dave," she said, offering me a smoke, "I know."

"No, you don't understand. It was a real place, absolutely real," I said, still cartwheeling from the terrors of being killed and the shock of being alive. "It wasn't a dream."

My whole demeanour must have seemed electrified. I was staring ahead like a nervous wreck that had just been refloated.

"You sure you're all right?" she asked, seeing my right hand shaking, trying to hold onto the little white cigarette.

"Never mind me. What about you?"

"Me?" she said. "What about me?"

"You must have taken it in shifts?"

"Shifts?"

"You and Norman," I said. "You can't have been here the whole time, can you?"

"We've only been here half an hour. Just you and I."

She showed me her watch just to prove it. My mouth gaped at the incredulity of it.

"Half an hour? But I've been gone a month."

"There possibly," said Helen, "but not here, not in this room David."

"I'm not making this up, you know," I said, feeling patronised. "I've been away for four weeks. Four weeks, or was it five, a month anyway all in the same place."

"And where's that. Do you know?"

I could not make up my mind if she was taking the Mick.

425

"My God, it's like I've just stepped off a train from far away. I still feel like I'm there."

"So tell me, where is there? Do you know?" she asked.

"Empton, a village, a village called Empton. You're never going to believe it, any of it. Never in a million years."

Without waiting to be interrupted I began telling her everything, from the bike ride up the hill to Empton, to the wedding. I recounted every detail about seeing my mother and the life she lived, how I got to know her as just a woman, just Lotty, how I had fallen for her. My mouth ran away on its own, babbling on about the tractor, the windmill, the time with Lotty in The Beckett, Herbert Ashcroft's death, Lotty's announcement that she was pregnant, all the way up to Danno's attack outside the Golden Goose and the terrible events in the derelict house. She taped it all. It took a couple of hours, possibly more to get it all out, sometimes going back to recount things I had forgotten. I was able to remember every detail, down to the boot scraper outside the church and Mrs Cartwright's pump. Never had my dreams been this detailed.

After all I had seen, after all the apparent reality of it, there remained the sense that this had been just a trick, an inducement created by Helen, that fed off the dreams that had tormented me most of my life. Could it be a possibility that all I had was a mega-dream, a hypno-dream, built up of amplified elements of nightmares? After all, the story ran along the same lines. The best I could expect to get out of it would be a lifetime's freedom from the terrors of the night, assuming this had managed to exorcise them. Was that what all this had been about anyway?

Even as I waved Helen goodbye and watched her car head for the main road out of the gate, I could not prevent myself fiddling with the idiotic notion that what I had just lived through had, in fact, been a real event, a historical happening. God knows it felt like a real experience. Just suppose it had been real. The tangle of implications was too mind-boggling to contemplate, especially those concerning Lotty. That I could have visited a previous life alone seemed too crazy to take in. There was probably not even a place called Empton, was there? Was there? Now there was a question. That was something that could be found out, could it not?

426

I became a man on a mission, an obsessive. Out of nowhere I discovered a new lease on life. It was more than just the intrigue of it. It was like being in a totally dark room, where no light could get in - a room where I had just seen a faint outline of a door. Finding a village called Empton represented a key. Where the door might lead was anyone's guess.

I eventually found a road atlas in the back of one of the kitchen staff's cars. The truth is I badgered everyone until Sue from the catering company agreed to lend me her route-planner. This was it. This was the moment of truth. Already my fingers had flipped through the book to the index as my eyes ran down the list of Es. I ran through them again, over and over, and repeated the process almost frantically again. Where the hell was the place? I lifted my head from the page and sat back in my chair, casting out a huge sigh. I suppose it had been too much to expect? A dream it would have to remain.

As if to pass the time I flipped the book to the page where Southwell was. I knew all of these roads like the back of my hand. It was easy to find Edlington, albeit a little dot on a white country road. I traced my finger on an imaginary bike ride from Edlington through to Farnby and the villages beyond, on towards Mansfield. Back again I recounted the day I had gone to Southwell, through the pretty village of Halby. The atlas was not a very precise one. The village did not appear anywhere on the page, being nothing but a small hamlet I concluded - but then Empton was a small hamlet and that had not been shown either. I even recalled that Halby had not been printed in the little AA booklet I had used on my bike ride to Edlington all those years ago. A new wave of hopefulness built up in my heart. All might not be lost. I just needed something better than a road atlas.

What I really wanted was an *Ordnance Survey map* - a good one, maybe one from the fifties or sixties. I was going to need a trip to the library in Newark or better still the one in Nottingham. All I had to go on was a place fifty odd miles from Salisbury, but it meant that the search was not over. It meant that there still might be a chance, that there was still hope. Interestingly, it was not the chance of finding Empton that intrigued me in all this. It was that I began to feel more alive than I had done for, well as long as I could remember. If Helen had achieved nothing else she had achieved that.

A dreamless sleep did follow that night, a fact that I was eager to report to Norman. I saw him at breakfast, staring into his coffee cup, fiddling with its handle. Ignoring the signs of his mood I burst onto the scene with my great news. A half-hearted smile and a polite acknowledgement threw my enthusiasm into an unexpected anti-climax. I sat opposite him for a while and then asked if I had done something wrong. At this his good nature resurfaced and he became animated once more, telling me no, no, of course not. He said it was nothing really and that I should ignore him. I said that maybe it was I who could help him this time, at which he grinned, recognising a turned table when he sensed one. It transpired that he had asked Helen out and she refused him. It had taken him weeks to pluck up the courage to ask her, only to be thwarted when the time had come.

"Anyway, it's good news about your dreams," he said.

I think he was about to say that he hoped it would stay that way, but changed his mind, avoiding any hint of negativity.

I went on to tell him about the session, ranting on about what had happened in my self-absorbed fashion, about the life I had lived in Empton. Norman shoved his coffee cup out of reach and sat back in his chair, adopting his professional face, which after a while filled with the eyes of someone absorbing a tall tale, told with passion.

"But I've tried to find the village on a map," I said, "No luck though. I need to take look at an old *Ordnance Survey map* I reckon, an archive one."

I knew I was asking too much, but I had to ask it anyway.

"Norman, I don't suppose you could take me to Nottingham Library, could you?"

"I can't drive, Davy. Sorry."

I watched his expression as my face dropped.

"Look, I'll get you a permit to go out, and I'll arrange it with Helen to see if she can take us. We can all go. You'd be doing me a favour too that way, wouldn't you. How's that?"

"Just the job, old boy," I said, with that feeling of being enlivened warming me once more.

So Friday morning arrived and Norman had arranged for an accompanied pass and organised a chauffeur. I let him sit in the front with his beloved Helen who had been delighted to take us both out, after Norman had explained the reason for the trip. I was content just to be out of the place for a while. It was different from the minibus that usually took us to college. This car was our own private world as we sped down the A52 to Nottingham. We chatted like people who had bonded in some way. Helen was keen to discover just how my nights had been. It was a delight to tell her, seeing her beam with pride as her eyes crunched into a smile from behind her specs. I watched her look of satisfaction reflect through the rear-view mirror. It made me feel good that I was one of her success stories.

After parking somewhere in the city, we walked like detectives hunting for forensic evidence into the great library. This was my first trip to a city and I felt like an ant lost in an anthill. The interior of the great building was lofty and hushed. As if acting out a cliché we whispered to one another as we stepped towards the information counter. Norman said to the lady there that he was the person who had phoned ahead, with reference to the old *Ordnance Survey maps* in the Wiltshire area. It staggered me that he had the foresight and consideration to do this, for me.

Minutes later we were led away to a smaller room, where the atmosphere was altogether more close range and less formal. The slim, polite librarian asked us to wait a while, leaving us to seat ourselves round a long table in the centre of the room. At length she returned with an armful of tatty maps, worn at the edges, maps that had evidently been opened and closed thousands of times. She asked us to let her know when we had done with them and were ready to leave. Informing us that it would cost twenty pence if we wished to photocopy them, but that only one A4 copy per map would be permitted. She announced these regulations like a female Gestapo Officer and then left us to it.

So here they were. The maps, the earliest of which was nineteen-fifty, the most recent one being printed in nineteen seventy-two. We each took one, opened it out and began to stare. No one said a word and yet it was possible to hear three brains saying nothing but Empton, Empton, Empton, over and over. Scanning systematically, I took in each and every village around Salisbury. The tedium caused me to feel drowsy. I had to shake my head to fling the sleepiness away, admonishing myself for feeling heavy-eyed at this moment of all moments. Back and forth went my head, village after village, but nothing. Then.

"Oh, my God," it was Helen's voice. "Oh my God, it's here. I've found your Empton."

We all left our seats and peered over her shoulder. Her finger was pressed against the yellowing paper. Just above it was a collection of square dots set around a T-junction, with the symbol for a tower church set to the east. But it was the six letters that made the hairs on the back of my neck stand on end. Empton. Unmistakable. Norman looked at me as if I had just performed a miracle in front of his eyes. The only one who did not look overly surprised was Helen.

"Now we know where your dreams came from David," she said quite calmly, "here."

I fell back into a chair as my brain filled with a million questions. Helen pushed the map nearer to me so that I could take a second look. It was still there, Empton. I still could not believe it. I traced the black lines of lanes to Rembleton and Tunby. I could see the great swathe of green, over which was printed Beckett's Wood. It was all there. Not a dream. Not a dream.

Then it hit me properly for the first time. My head filled with the sound of rushing blood as the thought took hold. I began to wonder about whatever had happened to Lotty after Danno had murdered me in that house. What had happened to her baby? Then it was clear, clear as flesh and blood. I looked at my sweating hands, living hands. Here was her baby. I had created me.

"I've got to go there," I said to my two friends, feeling like the chain reaction of an atomic device was going on inside me.

"Don't worry," they said in unison, "you are going. We're all going."

There was to be no stopping us, no stopping us. The twisted finger of fate had beckoned and we were on our way.

The Curse of Beckett's Wood

Part Three

Chapter one: Pilgrimage

The thin slender line of a road cuts through the emptiness of Salisbury Plain like the silvery track left behind by a snail. That is what it looks like from the air - a strand, nothing like the thick, red jugular as it appears on road maps. On it slithers overland, reaching out to the Mendip Hills, rising above the plain by degrees with every mile. A small red object moves swiftly along it travelling in a north westerly direction. It is an Austin Metro. The road has been there for hundreds of years, thousands perhaps. Quite recently in its history, almost fifty years previously, a smaller object was being propelled over its shiny surface. It was a bicycle. It is fair to say that the car's journey is something of a reconstruction, a re-travelling - but for one of the travellers in the car, it is a pilgrimage.

David Harper's tired body lay slumped in the passenger seat of the small, red Metro. He was lost in a pensive mood. The trundle of the car's wheels on the rough road created the perfect world for idle contemplation. There was a large colourful route planner on his knee, with a photocopy of part of an old *Ordnance Survey map* set within the front pages, acting as a bookmark. For the past half an hour there had been no conversation between the three occupants. He only had to dart his eye to his right to see a young woman concentrating at the wheel. She too looked tired. Her name was Helen. It was her car. The poor machine was not accustomed to the demands of the long haul. It was a town and city car, only its hometown was well over a hundred miles away as it sped along. Almost spiritually they could hear the engine protesting at being called upon to perform such a task. Behind the driver, slouching on the back seat half asleep, was Norman Hart, his arms folded and his head uneasily at rest against

431

the continually shuddering window. He looked bored, and yet he had been as excited about this trip as each of them, not only because it was a culmination of sorts, but also because he was painfully in love with the woman driver.

David sighed, abandoning his reverie and opened the atlas. The bookmark revealed Wiltshire. It rekindled the conversation between them.

"How far now?" Helen said, as she yawned a new breath.

"Fifteen, twenty miles, I'd say. Not far now," David guessed. "I can see the hills up ahead, look."

They were back out in the countryside now. The town of Andover was well behind them and soon they would be coming off the main road and hitting the country lanes. So far the map had been true. There was a wondrous unfathomable quality that it was actually making any sense at all. By rights none of this should have been real, but it was.

The gradient increased. Without her saying a word it was possible to hear the worry niggling Helen's mind. She was doing her best, choosing a lower gear almost in an act of compassion for her beloved vehicle. For miles they climbed. It was only by the lines on the atlas that they knew how much further they would have to ascend up hill. There were trees on each side of the road obscuring the view. Without a map it would have been impossible to say where the hill ended, where a brand new horizon would be. Then the trees thinned, to be replaced by houses, new properties, bungalows some of them set back from the road, so as to display the rolling gardens laid out before them. Suddenly, as if a clearing had been carved into the wood, it was possible to see the top of the hill.

Resembling an advancing army ranged for battle along the brow of the hill, a mass of dwellings had invaded the countryside. They were expensive homes, it appeared, standing elegantly on the rim of the escarpment, each one blessed with a commanding view of the plain spread out beneath them. David could hardly hide his disapproval, even a breathtaking sense of disappointment. There should have been a tree tunnel here, where the road had begun to bend and curve. There should have been, but mankind had been busy and things had changed. All of a sudden the idea of coming to this place took on an unhealthy aspect, as if a feast held in great anticipation had been poisoned - but how could they stop now? How could they turn back and go home after all that had happened? How could they? How could he? So on they went, up the steep hill, past a crossroads and into the village. Only it was not a village anymore, not as it had once been. Time had marched on and had trampled over the past.

The Metro was now labouring up the hill in first gear. Its speed had slowed to a crawl. It was almost as if the hill deadened their pace so that they could behold the fact that the long years had caused things to alter, to make an exhibition of all the changing scenes of life. Somehow, even though the modern road map showed it to be as it was, David felt a gnawing sense of discontent that it had been right. He hated the book's arrogance, its correctness. With high revs the car dragged them higher.

Then, set in the clipped grass verge, a clean white sign with black letters stood. GREAT REMBLETON it read, along with a customary announcement that the place welcomes careful drivers. Where was the place they were looking for? What had happened to it? How could a place vanish? He slid the photocopy out of the atlas and brought it closer to his eyes. Here, the place had once existed. Printer's ink had once declared it real. Beyond it the mapmakers had recorded the existence of another village, Rembleton. He began to wonder if they had already passed by the place they were looking for but he knew this was not so. They were all tired. It was as if the car's engine thrashing away under the bonnet had transferred its exhaustion to the cargo of people.

A collective sigh of relief seemed to escape from all of them as the gradient levelled out and Great Rembleton welcomed them in. They had arrived into a wide expanse, a broad junction where the road carried on straight ahead from which a lane ran away to the right. The road fanned out in a large triangle at this junction, forming a central car parking area. Great Rembleton appeared busy but nothing like the kind of place he had expected. Where there was now a large expanse for cars to park he knew there should have been a village green. There should have been a large, spreading chestnut tree on it. Even the villageness of it was gone. The houses and cottages were trim and neat. What had been anticipated was a collection of old, slightly run

433

down dwellings, snuggled within trees, bushes and wild flowers, even weeds. They should have been dusty and dirty in an earthy kind of way. They should have been relaxed in their rural grime, but they were not.

Each property was clean and repaired. Instead of being set within a wilderness of foliage, there were tidy gardens with carefully tended bushes or trees. Nothing was left to chance. Even the road was pristine, as if nothing was ever allowed to drive upon it. The place had matured. Masses of people were busily going about their business. There were mothers with pushchairs, old couples, and young men on their mobiles laughing. They were just people living their noisy lives - lives that belonged to the twenty-first century. In front of them, as they looked for a free space to park, they could see a pub. At least that looked promising and then, wonder of wonders, a sign. Almost like a sign from heaven there it stood, a real sign, a street name set in place on a cottage wall. It was a simple acclamation. It read Old Empton Road.

As the realisation sunk in that they had arrived at the right place, another surprise jumped out. Helen had just drawn the car in between a blue van and a motorbike. The engine stopped. Everyone sighed and stretched. For a moment they just sat, listening to the ticking of the motor cooling down after its exertion. Directly in front of them was a line of shops. Actually it was a line of shops with another building made of stone set in the centre of the row. Still visible were the words EMPTON VILLAGE HALL 1957 carved in the masonry above the door. Only a wooden sign screwed on to the wall underneath declared it to be the Rembleton Community Centre.

David could not take his eyes off the place. He knew that some fifty years previously a derelict house had once stood on the spot, the same spot now occupied by this structure. Only then did he know that he had arrived. His mind knew how the broken house once looked, as if a photograph had superimposed itself over the building that stood there now, but it was in the centre of his bones that he felt the chill. Looking at the Community Centre he knew that he had once died there. No, been killed there. Killed. The date above the door, it was a year after he was born, a year after he was kicked to death. At the heart of the matter he realised it was here that a

434

thousand nightmares had met their screaming end. This place was a part of him, it was all wrapped up in the person he had once been and ended up becoming. The house that once knew happiness was not there anymore. It had gone. The derelict old place must have been torn down and the village hall put up in its stead. None of it would sink in. It was akin to seeing the *Mona Lisa*, the original painting, for the first time. Likewise, he could not believe he was looking at a piece of ground similarly unique - unique to him.

The others were outside now. The cold air had drawn the warmth from the metal womb that had protected them from the autumn day. When they set off at ten that morning it had been very cold. The car's heater lulled them into thinking that the sunshine had held on to its summer power. Now, standing in the car park, they could all feel the tentacles of winter coil around them. Helen locked up her Metro and they walked towards the pub, the Golden Goose. Of course, where there is time there is change and the pub was no exception to the rule. The basic structure remained as it had been, only seeing it now in colour as he had done on that first day here, seemed at odds with his memory of it, just as with the other buildings. It was too neat and too well presented. There above the door was another twist. It was not so much that the pub's name had been meddled with. It was what it had been meddled to that caused him to catch his breath. The large black sign above the door had rendered the trip more foolhardy than he had bargained for. Why had they changed its name, and why to this? Why call it The Miller's Drop as if he did not already know?

He took a backward glance before going inside, turning his head over his shoulder. The view out of this door had, in that previous time, been a cherished one. He could only see ghosts of the past there now. The chestnut tree had been a beautiful sight. Even the green had been a better focal point than the bland car park filling that space today. His Empton did not exist anymore. How was he to reconcile the fact that he had been here, fifty years back, only a fortnight ago? Norman saw him lost in his own private fog. He slapped a hand on his arm and asked if he was all right. What could he say? That this was all too much for him and that he wanted to go home and waste this peculiar opportunity of finding things out?

David turned his face from the outdoors and followed his friends inside. He half expected to see Harry and little Ellie going about their chores, 'Well now, here's someone who can sing. Come on George, strike up a tune', but there was no Harry there. No one was there. The place was deserted just as it was on that first day he cycled here. As with everything he had seen so far, change had been at work. He had wanted to see a museum piece, or at least a timeless quality that he would be able to recognise. Even the bar was new. Mock brasses hung on the walls where old and real worn out implements had once been nailed. The only thing that felt right was the shape of the pub's interior. He could see where the piano had stood all those years ago. A jukebox was in its place. A modern piece of industrialised popular music thumped a beat out of its speakers like a steam hammer, hindering any attempt at reminiscence. Over on the right he could see the area where the wedding cake had stood, the same place where Danno had pushed Ellie down. The door at the far end led to the yard outside. He knew it. Stretching his eyes across the bar he could even make out what had once been the scullery and beyond it, out of sight, the door that had led to his room upstairs. This was the Golden Goose all right.

It was impossible not to wonder what had become of Harry. He had grown to like him in a qualified kind of way, despite his rough treatment of Ellie. With Harry's face floating through his memory he imagined him behind the bar. The story of Old Dyke Mill seemed to have hung onto the oak beams that straddled the low ceiling. What else was there to hang on to? The grandmother clock was gone but there were old pictures on the wall. He went to have a look but felt self-conscious about it. All the time he was aware that his two friends were watching him, keeping an eye on him. They could not fully let him forget that he was still a patient. This trip after all was part of the treatment and it was with eyes in the back of his head that he watched them watching him as he examined the sepia-toned old photographs. By the time he had seen a quarter of them he was too disappointed to look any further. Most were just copies of old postcards showing views of nineteenth century Salisbury. He had expected something else, something tangible. Norman's voice interrupted him.

"Do you want to stop for a drink, or shall we go for a look around?" he said.

"A drink would be nice," he said turning back to them, trying to smile. "I'll have an orange juice, please."

Norman asked his wannabe girlfriend what she wanted and then in his most polite voice attempted to shout for help. Norman was not built for assertiveness.

"Is there anyone there?" commanded Helen's more direct voice, and suddenly footsteps could be heard approaching.

"Sorry about that," said a young, slim man, friendliness pouring out of him like a fountain.

His diction was decidedly effeminate. Even the way he allowed his left hand to hang on the end of its wrist had a feminine quality. He had the most infectious smile, a smile that was perfectly at home with folk, precision made for magnetising people to his personality. Just as well considering his profession, thought David, beholding him for the first time. There was something of the Joe Witherspoon about him, a younger more concentrated version.

"Oh, you're all together are you?" he asked. "Right then, what'll it be?" he continued, as they were all drawn in by the beacon smile.

Norman placed the order as Helen and David grabbed a table. She could not help but ask the question.

"So, is this the place, the Golden Goose you mentioned on the tape?"

"Everything's changed," he said, "but this is the place all right. It all fits," he pointed to a door. "Beyond there, is a yard surrounded by an old crumbling wall. There's an elderberry bush near to it. That's where the photograph in the album was taken."

Norman arrived with the drinks and for a while there was nothing but the sound of throats at work. Helen finished first, intent on seeing if he was right. She got up and walked over to the door. The chap behind the bar eyed her suspiciously, what with her getting up and going without her friends.

"That's to the beer garden," he said. "Bit nippy for that today though."

"I just wanted to have a look," said Helen, sounding as if she was caught spying.

437

"Be my guest, dear."

He put down the glass he was cleaning and left the bar to where the scullery had once been, leaving Helen to pass through the magic portal. Moments later she was back, smiling. She beckoned them to follow as she disappeared through the door once again. Quickly emptying their glasses they followed and there she was, looking out at a garden, a smart beer garden, surrounded on three sides by a neat brick wall. An equally neat and well-tended elderberry tree grew at the far end of it. It was just as he had said. The far wall belonged to the cottage next door, the same cottage that once belonged to Mrs Cartwright. He made a mental note to take a look and see if the old pump was still in situ when the time came to leave. Anyway the wall had been repaired, repointed. Its mortar looked clean and gave the bricks a fresh and youthful exuberance. There had once been a patch of grass, divided by a flagstone path, above which ran a clothesline. None of it remained. Block paving had now sanitised the entire yard. Wooden picnic style benches were all that alluded to the title of beer garden. No one else was out there. The chill in the air had seen to that.

It was the sight of the far wall that most accurately matched his memories, if it was possible to call them that, now much more orderly. He was able to appreciate a small window in what had been Mrs Cartwright's home. Its four tiny, clear panes of glass suggested that it was likely to be the window to a larder or pantry. He could see Norman, who was standing just in front of him to his left, reflected in it. He realised that this was a bit of a fluke, an accident of the relationship of their positions. Norman was staring straight at Helen who had gone over to the far wall to see how old the elderberry tree might be. David realised he was witnessing a private, secret moment, even to the point of feeling Norman's longing, as if it were a song emanating from his heart. He was about to move over to catch up with her, when he stopped dead, seemingly rooted to the spot. Norman noticed David looking around in a state of frantic observation.

"Don't move," David shouted to him.

Helen heard him and came over to see what was up.

"What's the matter?" she said.

"I'll tell you in a moment. Just, no one move. Stay exactly where you are."

He caught the look that flashed between Helen and Norman, and it was not romance.

"This might be important," he said pointing to a place near a picnic table. "Helen, stand there."

She moved to where she had been told and he looked back towards the pub's back door as if checking something like distances, locations.

"Can you see me in that window over there Norman?"

He looked and raised his hand, waving at the reflection of himself that he could see.

"Yes."

"You know who you are, don't you?"

"What kind of question is that?" Norman asked.

"You're a photographer," said David.

"A photographer?"

"You're standing exactly where the photographer stood when he took the picture for the wedding album."

"I don't follow?"

"I'm standing as close as I can guess to where I was when I saw the picture being taken."

Helen then understood immediately.

"How long has that window been there?" she wanted to know.

"You'd think I'd remember seeing it, the number of times I've looked at that album, wouldn't you?" said David.

Norman had caught on by now.

"I see. So, if you're right, you think the reflection of who you were will be found in this window on the old photos in your mother's wedding album?"

David shrugged his shoulders, his excitement dying away.

"I suppose it's all a bit academic now, don't you think? Ellie had the album last. And who knows where she is? I don't even know if she still has the bloody thing."

Helen could see the delicate recovery of her patient in jeopardy of relapsing.

439

"Are you feeling all right?" she said, a caring tone in her voice coming through.

"Aye," he said in a resigned tone. "Come on, let's get out of here."

The faint smell of cooking began to fill the inside of the pub as they passed through. The place was starting to fill up with lunch timers. It would have been sensible to stay, but they left, awkwardly standing outside on the pavement and wondering where to go next.

So far, except for the name Empton agreeing with the old *Ordnance Survey map*, there had been nothing to support the story that David had imparted to them after his hypnosis. Even the reflections in Mrs Cartwright's window had proved nothing. The thought hung in David's mind until a connection clicked like a shutter. The pump. Mrs Cartwright's pump. That would be a fairly conclusive piece of evidence, surely? He looked left up the lane to where he knew it to be. Only it was gone. A chilling uncertainty began to take hold, insecurity, and a crimson fear that he was being dragged back into insanity. He was glad that Helen and Norman were there. He understood why he still needed them. He was being reminded of what a mentally crippled man he really was. Where was the pump? It should have been there. He went over to the spot where he knew it ought to be. He told his two companions what ought to have been on the spot he was pointing to. He heard them believe him but he felt they were laughing. The pavement showed no signs of a structure ever having been there. It was like it had never existed and he began to wonder if any of what he had experienced in the trance had been real, or just a huge dream - but then he had spoken the name of the village on the tape and that had proved right. How could he possibly have known, unless someone had planted it in his subconscious? Had someone done that? There ought to be something else that would set his account in concrete and help to shore up his fragile mind.

He voiced his thoughts aloud, ostensibly to himself. Norman and Helen heard him mumbling and took a professional interest. Mrs Cartwright was playing on his mind. It was she who had betrayed him to Danno on that rainy evening. What a witch's persona she had. That tragic combination of piety and bitterness mixed in with grief and the ravages of old age. Even her self-proclaimed godliness was twisted by the life she had lived. The death of her husband must have

440

pushed her over the edge. It was her grand office of hymnbook protector that had kept her going all the years following her introduction to widowhood. He knew how easy it was to go mad. She had been saved from total insanity by one thing and one thing only, the church. The church.

"The church," he said clearly, as the linking strands of a brainwave hit him. "We need to go to the church. Follow me."

Off he strode, knowing exactly where to find it, leaving Norman and Helen trotting behind, trying their best to catch up with him.

The old building stood on its hill, now hidden behind the small copse of birch trees that stood between where the village hall was and the spot on which the vicarage had once been. Back in the nineteen-fifties the trees allowed a clear view of the church from the village green. He realised that was why he had not noticed its crooked tower as they drove in, the trees were now so much taller.

Now he was at the gate to the driveway that led to the place he knew. The gates had gone and all that remained were the stone pillars that once held them. Fresh, muddy tyre tracks left behind by a small lorry had soiled the wide tarmac path that led up to the church. His two friends soon caught up with him and together they marched up the rising path. There it was. A poor, squat, little stone building held up by scaffolding. It was either being dismantled or else it was undergoing repair, it was hard to tell. It almost seemed as if it was greeting him, like an ageing relative would have done from a hospital bed. Their pace slowed at the sight. David knew this place. The arches and the windows were just as he had seen them two weeks before, in a time long ago.

The scaffolding workers had made room for entry through the main door, and there, still fastened to the ground, was something he had seen over and over. He had seen it in the pictures of the wedding. He had seen it for himself. It was the boot scraper, now in a state of decay and rust. Even still, he knew that it proved nothing. Proof, he needed proof. That is what he had come for. This is where the brainwave had led him. Soon he was striding across the long grass in the churchyard and there, beneath a tangle of weeds, he found what he was looking for. Sorrow filled his eyes as he read the words, now eroded by time:

Sacred to the memory of Herbert Ashcroft
husband of Jane Ashcroft
Departed this life 17th July 1955

The stone lay next to an older one that belonged to his wife. David craned his neck to behold his two companions.

"See," he managed to say through his tears, "I told you I'd been here before."

Norman took hold of the weeds that obscured the stone and read the words out loud. David did not know whether his emotions were the result of his vindication, or at seeing the resting place of his friend. Perhaps it was both. Either way it was enough for Helen to attempt to comprehend David's tortured life.

Their eyes met, the hypnotherapist and the patient, only now she too found it hard to hold back the tears that were welling up behind her glasses. She removed them, wiped her eyes with the back of her hand, and flung her arms around the lost soul who stood before her. Norman stood up from the grave and beheld the two in embrace. By some instinct he joined them. Whether he did this so as not to be left out, or because he too felt for the one who had proved his incredible story, or so that he could take his beloved up in one arm at least, he could not say. Maybe it was all of these things and many more besides. For in the bundle of the three of them, the three that had so spontaneously and yet so unpredictably come together, there existed the hot magma of silent feelings, as if a red-hot core of emotional energy was about to burst from them. It did not. Instead they just stood there in the cold air that seems to belong in a churchyard, each one thinking their own thoughts and wondering where they would go from here.

Chapter two: Dropping In

There was no direct way through to the fields where the oak tree had once stood, besides which the fields had gone too. A housing development, mature, as if it had been a product of the seventies or eighties, occupied the spot where the tree had lived its long, uneventful life and where he had once seen its gnarled bark appear to gaze, like an old man over the valley below. For convenience a latch gate punctuated the stone built wall that surrounded the church. They passed through it and emerged onto a residential road. A street decorated on each side by well tended lawns and swollen gardens, full of the hues of late autumn colours, that spread away from the roadside up to neatly kept detached houses, all uniform. At odds with such perfection, sounds of laughter and squeals of play rang out as children corralled in isolated areas. The planners had used the space, where the open fields had once laid, to stamp upon them a man-made aesthetic, curving the roads to create a seemingly jumbled layout of dwellings. Pennine Close and Snowdonia Walk gave a minuscule splash of dull inspiration to the names of the streets through which they passed. As they walked to the end of Chiltern Way the road stopped abruptly at a dangerously untamed barbed wire fence. It was here that human order gave way to a place governed by nature. Beyond the rusty wire, from this lofty position, they could see a spectacular view of Salisbury Plain beneath them. These were the houses they had first seen as they ascended the rise and to the right was the road they had driven up. Clever to name the streets after hills he thought with sad sarcasm.

He was over the fence in no time. The desire to stand on the edge of the escarpment and feel the freedom of the hill was impossible to ignore. Now, with the rudeness of the housing estate at his back, he could behold his hill just as he had recalled it. The trance did not seem dreamlike anymore. As he looked out towards Salisbury it was almost as if he had returned to it - had it not been for the rich colours signifying the time of year that flew in the face of the monochrome memory. He even found himself wondering about his bicycle wheel,

443

only to remember where it had actually turned up. It was here that he had chatted to the visitor, the beauty that so transfixed him that hot, sultry summer night. It was here where he had come to think and gaze at the golden spire in the far off distance. Apart from the houses to his right that had been built along the road up the hill, nothing had changed. Then he turned round to rejoin his companions and realised, with a heavy certainty that nothing stayed the same forever, nor ever could.

Great Rembleton had become busier by the time they got back to the pub. Helen suggested lunch there. So it was agreed. They entered a place heaving with customers. A place drumming with an overture of shouted conversations, punctuated with raucous laughter every now and again. They regretted not buying sandwiches from one of the shops, but they were here now and soon a path was carved through the tight mass of bodies. The odd chap pulling the pints alongside his male colleague was trying to serve all those pressed up against the bar. He saw the three of them find a niche in between a pair of shoulders and take up position ready to order.

"With you in a mo!" he called out, with his polite soft voice.

He squeezed behind his opposite number to serve two ladies at the far end of the bar. His colleague, sensing the bodily contact turned momentarily and tried unsuccessfully to stifle a grin. Their eyes met, fleetingly, before their owners returned to matters in hand. Norman pulled out ten quid and held it out, attempting nonchalant assertiveness. David knew how to attract people without such means. He stared at the back of the head of the first bartender and, without so much as a spark of concentration, saw his face turn from the women he was serving and nod in David's direction. In a trice they were being served. They ordered things with chips together with a pint apiece. Then, with the most amazing good fortune, found themselves an empty table to wait for their lunch.

The food arrived twenty minutes later and was only half bearable, with what seemed like cardboard chips and tasteless things that were supposed to be chicken. Hoping it was at least nutritious and as they were famished they quietly devoured it all. By the time their plates were clean the pub had half emptied, so that when they swigged the last drop of beer the old place was virtually abandoned. Then, with in-built courtesy, they took their plates back to the bar, where the two barmen were in a disagreement.

The argument was carried out at a whisper - the kind of whisper that emanates from the back of the throat and ought to be a shout. Sensing customers at the bar their row was bundled away and faces of strained friendliness smiled back at them. The three thanked them for the meal then turned to leave. As they reached the door the argument resumed. They would have gone out of the door except David pulled away from his friends and darted back to the bickering barmen.

"Tell me," he said, startling the two men. "Why The Miller's Drop?"

In a moment Helen and Norman had arrived by his side, cajoling him to leave. The barmen could see that there was an air of imbalance lurking behind their questioner's eyes. They too could pick up on a mild hint of what seemed like patronising mock altruism that the questioner's two companions appeared to display. Only it was not that. They were concerned for the health of someone whom they had come to know, to like, and even to find the beginnings of an understanding. They did not want him to make a fool of himself, nor did they want him to put at risk his fragile recovery.

"The name of the pub", he persisted. "Why The Miller's Drop?"

The barmen looked to the questioner's two friends for a sense of permission to answer. They gave a resigned shrug, as if to say why not?

"Well, we learned of it five years ago when we first came here," said the first one.

"No, Neal," his friend disagreed. "We came here six years ago, remember?"

"Well, it was called The Miller's Drop when we arrived. We thought nothing of it 'til the locals began filling us in with the legend."

David's eyes began to widen. A legend?

"The miller in question wasn't a miller at all, or so the story goes," began the first barman.

"There isn't even a mill hereabouts," put in his friend. "He was found miles away up the rise at some village or other. God, the times I've heard this tale, and I still can't remember."

445

David was about to say the name of the place when friend Neal proudly demonstrated his superior memory.

"Maltoft," he declared. "It was up at Maltoft mill. God you can be so dim sometimes, Len."

Len looked hurt momentarily then carried on.

"Well, the chap in question wasn't from round these parts, but it seems that he got roped into fixing the damaged windmill up at Maltoft-on-the-Hill."

"Aye," interrupted Neal. But he never finished it, did he? No, poor sod. He was found dead at the bottom of the tower, having fallen to his death. All mangled up he was."

David had by now turned pale, listening to an account of the past that had been twisted out of shape by time. He had not fallen. He wanted to say he had his life kicked out of him, but he knew that if he said anything he would be viewed as an oddity. So he let the two effeminates continue with their ridiculous story.

"Yes, ribcage all smashed up, and the head. The mill tower was all fixed up with scaffolding like the church here, you see. He must have hit every steel bar on the plunge down. Who knows if it's true or not, but either way, it makes for a good, local, gruesome tale doesn't it, the tale of the Miller's drop?"

David pushed out his next question, knowing full well what the answer would be.

"But, if this all happened miles away, why give that name to this pub here?"

"Because," continued Len, "the Miller, as he was known around here, stayed in this very pub during the renovation of the mill. It was called the Golden Egg in those days, or something like that, and he stayed in what is our office room, or so the previous owners told us."

An awkward silence hovered over all of them like a strange spell. Norman and Helen, who had taken all of this in without saying a word, seemed to be absorbing the implications of what they had just heard. The two barmen had run their story out and had nothing else to add. What else was there to say?

It was David who wanted to say everything. He ached to tell them what had really happened. As he looked to his left, he would have liked the chance to tell them that a burly farmhand called George once played the piano there on Friday afternoons and how he had witnessed his parents' wedding reception in their beer garden. He wanted to tell them how he drank Daniel Harper under the table here, and how that very same man had dragged him out and chased him into an old house that once stood where the village hall now rests. He would have explained the story of how he had been brutally murdered there. Only he resisted the urge to do so, to scream out how grisly it had been. Oh, there were a thousand recollections that he could have imparted but he kept them locked away inside his head.

"Thank you," was all he said in the end.

"Pleasure," replied the first one. "Now you will excuse us, won't you? We've got the brewery coming to see us later."

He pulled a face of disdain, evidently not relishing the prospect.

Back outside in the cool chill David stopped to look back at the pub. He looked up at the dormer window to see where his bedroom had been. New roof tiles took away the purity of the way he had known it, but it was his room all right. Almost everything had proved one way or another that what he had seen under hypnosis was correct. Had time not bulldozed the past away he would have been able to stand with surety in the cradle of his dreams. Even so it was a comfort to see that the passage of the decades had moved things along, as if to show that he too could do the same and leave the past behind. Helen broke the quietness in the end.

"Where to now?" she said, taking the tinkling car keys from her handbag.

"Don't know," said David, thinking. Then as if a flash of light had burst brightly inside his head he woke from his dream-like state and smiled. "Bofindle Farm. Come on, I know the way."

The car's central locking clunked open at Helen's command and they all piled in.

"Weird," said Norman, unable to think of anything more intelligent to say.

It was somewhat gratifying that the road out of Great Rembleton spilled them into the countryside. David had walked this road so many times and nothing about it had changed. Now, sitting in the back seat, he turned to see the dense woodland passing by. It was The

447

Beckett. There within, hidden from view, completely hidden, were secrets. As he caught the sound of his breathing coming back to him against the car's window, he contemplated that his own conception had taken place there. The life he had lived and still lived. That is where it had sparked into life. The emotion would have overwhelmed him had it not been for Helen's voice interrupting.

"Well, I'll be buggered," she said with uncharacteristic crudity.

He turned his attention away from the wood to see what she was looking at. It was a sign, quite new, white background with green letters. He did not have to read it to know what it said and, as predicted, a rough lane ran away from the road towards a collection of buildings some quarter of a mile away. It was Bofindle Farm.

He had once loved and loathed this lane. It would have led either to Lotty or Danno - heaven or hell. He squinted his eyes to try and see the buildings in the distance, as the sound of the car's engine, quietly ticking over, created a sense of mild apprehension - but it was more than that. Lotty was now in her grave and therefore the things down the lane would be new and unknown, just as they had been that day when he saw the farm for the first time, that time he emerged from the wood's end.

Before he had chance to stop thinking like this he was thrown back in his seat. The car had lurched forward and was rumbling down the pot-holed track. He pulled himself upright, gripping the headrest in the front seats and staring ahead between them, watching the farm come closer. The weak sun had by now begun to lose its grip on the day. Already it had fallen back to the tops of the far trees that formed part of Beckett's Wood. It would not be long before darkness would fade away the scene they were now viewing.

Helen and Norman beheld a set of grimy buildings. A farmhouse stood square on to them revealing its front elevation, a door and five windows, two on the ground floor and three upstairs, the middle one directly above the front door beneath. It was a simple house and grubby. To the left, at right angles forming an L shape, were two old barns. A solid, brick built affair, complete with two huge, heavy wooden doors, hinged to fit a massive arched opening in the longer wall, and painted with a deep blue, now faded with age and dust. Behind it, in parallel, was another barn - a Dutch barn in need of repair, waiting for gravity to demolish it. Surprisingly it was still in use. Silage, for the coming winter's feed, in bales stacked high beneath its decaying curved roof. In the space before the house and barns there was a rough yard, void of concrete or gravel, ready for the autumn rain to turn it all to mud.

David saw things in a different way now. He had become slightly accustomed to time's eroding hand. So far there had only been whispers of a past he knew. Save for Herbert's grave, his recollections had been supplanted by the evolution that had taken place into the modern world - but here, on the fringe of the yard, his eyes took in a sight that had hardly changed at all. He clambered out of the car following Norman. Helen had caught the detective bug and even now was striding toward the farmhouse door, intent on knocking on its weather beaten exterior. David could do nothing to stop her as her knuckles rapped on the thick wooden door. Who would answer thought David?

Helen looked back at the two men standing beside the car grinning in anticipation. Nothing moved. She stared back at the door, formed a fist and struck the door with the fleshy part of the side of her hand. The knock was duller but louder like this. Still nothing. Norman and David watched her sidestep from the door and peer in through the dirty window to her left. Shielding her eyes from the daylight with her hand she pressed her head to the filthy glass and took a peek inside. After looking this way and that she gave up and strode back to the car.

"It's too dark to see anything," she said. "The place looks deserted."

"The sun's gone down, maybe we should come back tomorrow," suggested Norman.

"And stay where?" said Helen, as if talking to an imbecile.

"It was just an idea," he said.

"I fixed a tractor here once, you know," said David, "right here. I had to ram it against one of those old conifers over there."

He pointed to some trees on the far side of a field, now ploughed and harrowed. David was lost in thought, remembering Lotty and unable to divorce the fact that she was someone he would come to despise in time. In the dimness of dusk he began to march over the clumps of soil that formed the field. Norman and Helen, now silent, followed him.

At the other side they came to a wall of conifer trees. Thick brambles and some nettles barred the way through but, by treading down the prickly stems with the soles of his shoes, he was able to make a path through and reach the tall dark trunks of the old trees. The day had beaten them though. Now in the shade of the dense firs there was almost no light to see by. There was little chance that they were going to see any marks left by a fifty-year old impact from a tractor on the trunks of one of these aged, majestic specimens.

So they trampled back through the brambles, stumbling, and made the awkward return over the field back to the car. It was time to go. Time to go back and leave the past behind. It was Helen who spoke first, as she slid the key into the ignition. She turned to David who was seated behind Norman's seat.

"How do you feel?"

Norman turned in his chair to face him. His eyes asked the same question.

"I don't really know what's going on," he said. "This all makes sense one minute and then the next it all seems too barmy."

"I'd find it crazy," put in Norman, empathising as usual.

"In what way barmy?" asked the hypnotherapist.

"I spent a month here," said David. "I fixed up an old Fordson tractor just where this car now stands fifty odd years in the past. It was as real to me as, well, as real as I know you two. Only it was not fifty years ago, it was only a couple of weeks ago, in our broom cupboard back at the hospital. Yet in my life I must have been here, because everything fits. I've never been here before. And yet, in some other life, here, I made the person who sits here with you now. How barmy is that? I bet none of you have ever had anything so crackpot happen to you?" he thought for a moment and sighed. "Only I'm glad that you were here to see it happen. Who would ever have believed me? I can hardly believe it myself really."

David let out another long breath, as if he was trying to put a full stop at the end of his thoughts.

"Come on, let's go. We found what we came for, didn't we?"

450

He felt tired. It had been a long day, a strange day that only bordered on satisfying. Helen and Norman smiled back. It was going to be a long drive home, but at least they were returning as changed people from the ones who had arrived that morning. Maybe this is the best any of them could hope for - except Norman was no further ahead with his own private mission. Even as the car rolled back down the hill to the plain below Norman was contemplating what his next move would be, little knowing how hard his patient was thinking about his own future and just how that was going to pan out from this moment.

There was very little conversation as the car plunged into the night, its headlamps lighting up little more than two hundred yards of the advancing road ahead. Salisbury Plain was a dark place and looking through the back window the pitch black made it impossible to see anything. The metaphor was not lost on David Harper. Looking back did no good, only the light ahead held any hope of finding a way home, but then the past did hold a key to his future. Finding out more about who he had been would illuminate how he became the person he is now. It held the key to other people in his life, those who had a hand in shaping him. There was only one other person alive who was present at all those events in Empton those long years ago, but where she was remained a mystery. She had known Danno and Herbert Ashcroft and, as a little girl, she would have known all about the Friday afternoon singsongs. Most of all, she would have known about Mr Miller. She would know what he looked like. She would be able to piece together the gap between Danno dragging Miller out of the pub and him leaving the village with Lotty. Where was she? David knew not where but he would have to find her. He would have to find his Ellie.

Then other questions began to invade his brain. Questions that made him feel a fool for not considering them sooner. If he had fathered himself, so to speak, why did his mother insist that Danno had been his father all along? Why go through the charade of showing him the album over and over and pointing at Danno and telling him with pride that he was his Dad? Why did he never come and find them? Why was she so keen on maintaining that Danno was such a wonderful man, when she had fled the village never to return?

451

He had often thought as a boy that one day his father would come and create this magical family reunion and that he would have a dad like all the other kids. It was a notion perpetuated in his childhood by his mother. Why did she peddle such a story if she was afraid of him? Why tell him that, when all the time she was making sure that she could never be found? Come to that, why did Ellie never tell him the truth, when she had been present at all these pivotal moments?

Gradually, he began to feel a sense of betrayal. The one person he had always leaned on and trusted, in whose integrity he had always believed, that very person had strung him along. She had lied to him with a silence as big as a string of lies. Why had she done that, when almost all of the time she loved him like no one else ever had, or possibly ever would? Somehow Ellie would have to be found. The car delved on into the blackness.

It was still dark when he was shaken from his sleep and was told they had arrived. Arrived. The geographical ending of the journey was of no consequence to him. He had arrived in a world that was permanently changed to the one he had left. Even as they had embarked on the trip to Wiltshire he knew that things might never be the same again. Now that he had walked around the place where his dreams where born, a real place, he was able to come face to face with some elements of what made him the oddity that he was. At the same moment the trip had explained everything and confused him to hell.

Tired and weary he went to bed. Thoughts of the place from where his dreams had sprung filled his head as he drifted off, but only thoughts. As tiredness dragged him into his pillow he entered the state that he always dreaded. Only now there were no more dreams and he slept well. A rocky road of recovery lay before him, but at least he was on it now. The journey to wellbeing had begun.

Chapter three: Incas

Saxenby Hospital was undergoing a refurbishment. Great chunks of money had been allocated to the old Victorian building, where in places it was in much need of repair. The announcement of this good fortune had been plastered across the local press and had even made enough of a ripple to hit the regional evening news on the television. The effects of this on staff morale was noticeable, as some of the money formed part of a much overdue adjustment to the pay spine and this meant that, in Saxenby at least, there was a settled mood, optimistic one could say, and it had put a spring in everyone's step. The mood was not just a preserve of the people who worked there. The patients had picked up on it too. Even the ones whose condition was severe seemed to have been drawn up on a thermal of collective good humour. It was a good time to be there.

With a sense of irony David Harper was preparing to leave. He felt sure that the gusto with which his friends delivered their well-wishing was partly a symptom of this artificial atmosphere - but then he too was dragged along with it, although he knew it to be a synthetic aberration, like the phenomenon of mass grief that at certain times was gradually becoming an element of the nation's psyche.

It had been six months since his trip to Wiltshire. Christmas had come and gone, and now it was springtime. As luck had it his date of discharge was set as the day after his birthday. By far and away the person who had carried out most of David's own refurbishment, the one who had rebuilt him from the inside, was his friend Norman Hart. It was he who had arranged the hypnotherapy in the first place. Enlightening therapy that then led on to the trip to find a place called Empton - but he had done more than that. Norman had politely asked for entry into David's inner world. Except for discovering the things that his mother had done to him in adolescence, Norman knew as much about David Harper as there was to know. He had been instrumental in stopping the dreams. In short, in David's eyes, Norman was a miracle worker. He had even secured him a modest little flat, a kind of sheltered accommodation, a halfway house to the real world and total independence. He even found him a job, a job at the local supermarket, stacking shelves and patrolling the car park for wayward trolleys. Along with the allowances that were to come his way he would be able, with Norman's help, to find his feet once more.

So it was, as his modest birthday party wound down and the last of the happy guests began to leave, David sat down with Norman and Helen and began to tell them the story of mother's special cuddle. Only now could he find the reserve to do it. It was a combination of the events that had unfolded and that were unfolding even still. He wanted to begin his new life cleansed of it all. He wanted to pull from the depth of his twisted heart this blackest of boxes, the one thing that he knew if unexposed could harm his recovery when he was finally on his own again. Only now did he feel strong enough to let it all out. Only now did he have the two people before him who were worthy enough to receive it. So he began not really knowing where to start, awkwardly attempting a sentence only to abandon it in favour of a different approach. It was like a stammer in slow motion but finally the words formed a perfect beginning.

"There are things about my mother that I've never told you, never told anyone."

The initial words had escaped. This first full sentence led onto the next. There was nothing to be gained by keeping it a secret anymore. The sad thing was that it should never have been a secret in the first place. All those wasted years, he thought, as he unravelled the story. Helen held his hand, as his trusted Norman sat square in front of him, listening, saying nothing never judging. The tears began to spill as the box was hauled from the shaft. Without any verbal encouragement the story of his childhood made its way to the surface. He felt safe to do it. All of the past came out of the darkness and into the open. It was the most cathartic thing he had ever done. He brought his account up to the point where he had wanted to die in the hedge. Then he stopped talking and soaked up the first few seconds of life without secrets.

The three of them sat amongst the debris left by the party, mentally linked in silence. David had hated his mother. He had spent a great many years fuelling the hate that he felt within him, but now the fuel had run out. As if with a great hiss of steam all the pressure had been lost and he realised that he was strangely free. With the sharing of a few words, the past had been rendered impotent. The monster that had haunted him relentlessly both in life and from beyond the grave was reduced to nothing more than a sick woman who had needed help but never got it. Like an infectious disease her sickness had passed over to him. He had even played a part in her illness himself. Had they not met and fallen for each other in the little hamlet of Empton all those years ago, who was to say how things might have turned out for her? She might even have learned to tolerate her role in village life - but then Lotty was Lotty. She would never have been satisfied. If it had not been him it would have been someone else - but it was him, a different him, Mr Miller as he was then. The name Miller hung like the curl of cigarette smoke does in still air. Miller. Where had he heard that name prior to the hypnosis? Like a line from some long forgotten poetry, it evaded capture. Miller? Miller? There was something about that name that meant something else, but he could not put his finger on it.

"That was a very brave thing to do," put in Norman, finally daring to break the quietness of the room.

"Yes, Norman's right, very brave," agreed Helen.

"I've wanted to say that to someone for ages. It feels good to have got rid of it at last," David said, trying to overcome the tremble in his voice as he stared down at his shoes and contemplated a life of freedom.

*

Connie Brown was a woman in her late eighties. She had white hair that was always done by the visiting hairdresser on Thursdays. Of all the things she was proud of, one of them was that she had never, ever needed specs. A consummate chatterbox, David learned from her that she had been married in nineteen forty to a man she thought was the spitting image of Clark Gable. Unfortunately his good looks did not match his manners. She described him as a brute, often adding with a whisper, in the bedroom. After four years of mistreatment he left for the south coast with his regiment and was killed north of Caen a few days after D-Day. Connie vowed never to marry again and she was true to her word. She never fully recognised that she lived in sheltered accommodation, being a fiercely independent woman. As a flirt she had been an expert, still was, and she made a beeline for David Harper the day he moved in. She was good fun to be with and none of the eyelash fluttering or suggestive remarks were ever meant seriously. She was just lonely, as was David.

On his first day back from working at the supermarket Connie was there, waiting at his front door, walking stick in one hand and a freshly baked cake in the other. He could not resist her smile, her cake, her simple gesture. With a twist of the Yale key they both entered his new home, a place full of strange smells that would in time become the aromas of familiarity and contentment. David put the kettle on as Connie cut the cake. She made no bones about being nosy, straight in at the deep end that was her way. Not that it came over as an interrogation. Connie was too practised to make it look that way. She knew all about how to have a chat. To her, finding out about other people's lives was a piece of cake, literally and figuratively. In an odd sort of way, they complemented and needed each other. It was and became a good friendship.

He found it refreshing to confess the trivial concerns of his days, those endless days at work. She would love to listen to the problems of another soul, problems that she would consider and attempt to advise on, anything but look at the abyss of emptiness in her own life. He never told her of his past, though she itched to know about it, and with carefully selected questions would try to prise a snippet of juicy detail from the terra incognita that she knew lurked behind his placid and polite countenance. Above all she wanted to know if he had met anyone, at work perhaps or anywhere. Her longing for true love, denied to her by her own rule, had transferred to her desire to see David find someone, anyone, in order that she could experience, if only vicariously, the raptures of falling in love. She craved romance so much that it did not even have to be her own, so long as she had a grandstand seat to witness it in someone else.

For all that Connie Brown was harmless and never crossed the line of respectability. When she took ill, it was David who called for help and accompanied her to the hospital. She insisted that David be present when the diagnosis was announced, news that she was prepared to wait all day for until he had finished his shift. It turned out that she had experienced a mild heart attack. Connie laughed it off as nothing more than an irritation. David was not convinced by her bravado. Attention seeking, she insisted, pressing her knobbly fingers against her chest where the troublesome heart had dared to have an attack. They both laughed. What else was there to do but laugh? Underneath it all she was glad that she had someone to care about her and in return he was glad to have someone to show him just what the human spirit was capable of. In this way they fed off one another.

By the autumn they had become an odd kind of couple. By some binding chemistry their beings had coalesced. Sometimes they would get together in either one's flat, share a meal and quietly watch television together. Being at one with each other was easy. Had it not been for the acres of time that separated their ages, things might have been deeper still - but without the complications of that kind of relationship to develop, they were both happy just to be at ease as they were.

Norman became less of a frequent visitor. His weekly drop-ins became fortnightly, monthly and then erratic. Helen had got engaged, Norman explained one evening when he called round. She had not chosen him. How strange things had turned out. On the odd occasions he popped over, Norman spilled his heartbreak out to David, going over and over about the hurt he felt inside. It was a time to give back, to return a bit of life's sticking plaster to someone who had once stuck his neck out for him. The former patient listened. He let him empty it all out, seeing how beneficial it was to leave nothing inside to fester away. He had learned that, if nothing else. Through occasions such as this he realised that his strength was returning. He had matured and gained a little humility along the way. So much so that one teatime, after Norman had emptied his cup and said goodnight, he decided to nip over to Connie and do something he had never thought possible.

"Hello dear," she said with affection. "I'll get the kettle on. You've had a visitor, I see. He's the chap who calls to see you now and again isn't he? Good friend of yours, I expect?"

457

"Norman, oh, he's more than a friend."

Connie misunderstood the phrase and eyed him quizzically.

"Oh, good God, not like that," he said, realising what had gone through her mind. "Norman, that's his name. He saved my life once you see."

"Saved your life, dear?" Connie said, the excitement of having unearthed a priceless artefact all but giving her palpitations again.

The kettle and teapot were abandoned as she rapidly ushered her friend into the living room. In a moment a sherry bottle and two glasses had graced her occasional table, the golden liquid poured and the stage set to delve into the hidden secrets of another person's life.

"Saved your life, darling, how exciting."

"Hardly exciting Connie," said David. "I'd been quite ill you see, well, very ill to be honest. He put me back on my feet you see. I couldn't have got better without him, I really couldn't have. He's a super bloke."

"So what was wrong with you, cancer or something?"

"Oh no, Connie, nothing that bad. You see I was in a mess. A real messed up kind of mess. Still am a bit to tell the truth."

"You weren't one of those drug thingies, were you?"

"Druggy?" David laughed at her suggestion. "No, no, Connie nothing like that."

"Like what then, dear?"

"You wouldn't believe me if I told you," he said sipping his drink. "I wouldn't even know where to start."

"Would you like to tell me about it?" she asked quietly, desperate to know.

"How long have you got?" said David.

"All the time in the world," she said, replenishing his glass and sitting upright in her high-backed chair. "If you want to do the telling dear, then I'll do the listening," she said in her slow, dependable voice.

So David rewound his life to when he was a boy and played out the story of what happened to him as he was growing up, right up until the time he met Helen Knight at the hospital. There were times when the frail old lady had to wipe tears from her eyes. She pressed her gnarled hand on his knee when he struggled to express certain events. Then he went on to describe the strange experiences he had experienced under hypnosis, as the hours and minutes melted into a meaningless lump. For ages he went on so that, by the time he astounded her with what he had discovered during the visit to Great Rembleton, Connie had been rendered speechless, the sherry bottle had been emptied and the clock showed two in the morning.

Once more he had got the story out to another living soul. Again he was able to do it. It had seemed easier that time. A sense of extreme elation infused him with a sense of pride. The past was a corpse, harmless and impotent. There was therapy in turning days gone by into words and sharing them with another person.

Connie looked tired. He too felt that somewhere beneath his veneer of wellbeing a hidden sleepiness was tapping him on his shoulder. They said goodnight, a touching hug and a kiss on the cheek and soon he made it home, slipped into his bed and left the waking world behind.

The days that passed became processed in a mechanical rhythm. It was a relatively easy existence, void of pressures, unchallenging and repetitively boring. Maybe it was a sign that he was mending, becoming something that he should have been all along, a normal person. It all seemed artificial though, as if an invisible hand of kindness had ordained that not much be asked of him. Increasingly the impression that all he was doing was getting through each identical day preyed on him. With every passing week he felt more and more that it simply was not enough.

One evening Connie came over for tea. It had become the custom that he would do the shopping at the store where he worked and she would come over when he arrived home and cook whilst he got washed and changed. She loved the job of mothering him properly and he loved the warmth of being properly mothered. After the meal, they would divide the local midweek newspaper in half and have a quiet read before deciding what to watch on the box. Normally, they would join forces to attempt the crossword on the TV page, but on this night Connie noticed an advert in the sits-vac section.

"You know all about printing, don't you David?" she said thinking out loud.

"Printing?" he said, only half listening.

459

Connie passed the page to him, pointing to where the job was with her pen.

"There, see, that job there. Inca Marketing. They want someone who knows about printing, and computers and all that stuff. And you've been a salesman, haven't you dear?"

"Mmm," said David, plainly unsure at the reality of it.

"Well there's no use telling me that you're bored at the supermarket, is there? You've got to get off your..." she wondered whether to say it or not, then decided she would. "You've got to get off your arse."

After a moment's pause, David fell about laughing at hearing her speak so. In the end they were both laughing like a couple of kids. Connie Brown saying arse, whatever next, but she did have a point. Why not try for it, he thought? So he told her that he would apply. Nothing further was said about it that evening. Instead they pitted their brains against the challenge of one across, house of God six letters.

What trouble he had gone to. Even as he held the envelope in his hands a week later, he was afraid of its contents. Failure, that is what he feared, failure. The local library had been a great support with time on their computer to perfect his CV and, even though he was a little out of practice, the accompanying letter sounded rather confident, boastful almost. He wanted Connie to be there to see the end result of her encouragement but it was early morning. She would still be asleep. The rest of the mail was deposited in the bin. It was all junk, all except for a postcard from Norman who had decided to wander across Europe for two weeks. The card was from Krakow in Poland. A fridge magnet secured it in pride of place in the kitchen. All that remained was the letter, still unopened, its franking mark clearly showing the Inca logo. After an agonising few minutes, he decided to go to work and open it when Connie was there. It seemed, after all, the right thing to do. Not knowing was easier to deal with than knowing, somehow.

There was a kind of safety in the monotonously familiar. That day, the normality he had begun to despise now mesmerised him by its simple routine, the people, the usualness of their comings and goings,

460

even the place itself and the way he fitted into it. In some strange way that day was desperately seducing him, like a lover clinging on at the end. The letter at home would change things, had changed things, however the message therein would be read. Just by being a reply, it stood as a testimony that he wanted to escape the life he had, to move on. Rejection or success, it did not matter. It was a sign pointing to a future now yearned for.

He brought smoked haddock home that evening as a treat. They would have boiled new potatoes, minted peas, and a treacle tart with custard to follow. Connie was there in her slippers waiting with the paper. Dressed in her pink blouse and black skirt, wrapped up in a thin cardigan made of dark blue wool, she looked unwell. David's eyes asked the question, but all she would say was she had a funny turn and would be all right after a bite to eat. He told her about the letter inside. She put on an act of excitement to paper over the cracks in her health. After getting out of his work clothes there was nothing for it but to slice open the envelope. The fish was cooking in the pan. It was time. They both sat at the table now set for tea and David took a knife, slit the edge and pulled out the single piece of folded paper. It expanded like a concertina, revealing four paragraphs of text and the flourish of a signature at the end.

Inca Marketing. It was a good logo with a progressive corporate style crafted from elements of ancient Peruvian symbolism, simple but effective, very confident, now seen in colour for the first time. He flashed through the jumble of words looking for the phrase we regret to say, but it was not there. Connie's eyes were on stalks, it seemed as if she was holding her breath. Finally David dropped a glance at the name at the bottom. Even now he had not read any of the contents, being nothing more than intent at searching for the thumbs up or the thumbs down. One name only sat at the foot of the letter. Not a forename and surname joined, not a Mr or Mrs, but a Christian name only. The name was Ian. David looked up at Connie's anxious face. She could see he did not know what to make of it.

In a flash his eyes had darted back to the beginning, to read it properly, back to the Dear David that he thought had come over as far too familiar. Then it all made sense to him. Inca, there at the foot of the letterhead in small blue type, Inca was the trading name of Ian

461

Nigel Crabtree Associates. Ian Crabtree what a bloody fluke. So, his old friend had made good it seemed and moreover was offering him an interview. An interview, dressed up in the letter as a friendly get together to explore a few options. It took some taking in, these words. The chances of this happening had to be a million to one. David read it over once more to see if he was not dreaming it all. With a lifetime's supply of ill fortune to rely on, something good was coming straight out of the blue and, like anything good, he had an unhealthy mistrust of it. There was no mistake. Here was a brief potted history of Ian's hard work and opportunities grasped. Their lives had gone their separate ways. Ian's had led to the motorway of life, David's had taken the country lane to the swamp at the end of the meadow. It had been a long time since their time in St. Peter's church choir and Ian Crabtree had finally written to him as promised all those years ago.

Chapter four: Expectations

A nervous palm attached to a damaged life reached out for a hand that was powered by a healthy dynamism, a dynamism that David found hard not to envy. Ian Crabtree oozed charisma. His smile shone with a brilliance that was further enhanced by two energetic, intelligent, deep blue eyes. David had done his best with his own image, even to the point of buying a new jacket and trousers and polishing his shoes until he could see his face in them. Ian looked expensively casual, demonstrating wealth without even trying. The handshake, when it happened, was like two worlds colliding. It was Ian's voice that widened the gulf between them still further. Gone was his old accent, except for a mild trace. His tone had undergone a marvellous transformation, an airline pilot's voice, friendly but glittering, as if his larynx was diamond encrusted. So there they were. Each saying how pleased they were to see each other again after all these years, weighing each other up, studying each others changes, looking for any remaining strands with which to make a connection.

This meeting took place in a large, first floor office that looked as if it had once been a factory of sorts. They were in what had been the heart of Nottingham's old textile empire, an area known as The Lace Market. The office, or Concept Suite, as Ian preferred to call it, was a converted loom room where today brilliant ideas were spun instead. The well-hackneyed line rolled off his tongue with a zeal that seemed to be part of the company creed. This huge room was tastefully furnished with modern, ergonomically shaped desks, each equipped with large, flat-screened computers - mission control for the world of marketing it seemed. The whole place was alive like the inside of an anthill. The work was evidently fluid, people sharing ideas with colleagues, leaning over their co-worker's computers, pointing at their screens, resolving issues, creating.

A girl caught Ian's eye. A girl with long, slender legs, dressed in a short black skirt and a high-necked white top, a large A3 proof in her hand, rolled up. She obviously wanted to discuss this piece of work with her boss. With the most consummate demonstration of people management he charmingly put her off until later and asked her if she would not mind getting him and his guest a coffee each. We will be in my office, he told her, rewarding her with a special touch on the arm and one of his smiles. The interviewee felt like a caveman who had stumbled upon an advanced civilisation.

David followed Ian along a short corridor and into a smaller office. There were no windows here. Spotlights mounted on the ceiling pointed at a curved desk where a laptop purred quietly, whilst other lights shed their beams upon large framed pictures on the wall. On closer inspection these turned out to be advertising and marketing campaigns. There were a dozen of them - each apart from one, having a paragraph of explanation, above which was the name and year of an exhibition or competition, and the all-important word Winner.

They sat down either side of the desk, and for the first time saw each other, as they had once been, boys, pals. It was as if the two of them wanted to regroup in the choir stalls, to find that common ground on which to build a conversation. David could almost sense what he was thinking but chose to break away from delving into the

463

past. As he was about to say what a fabulous place he had got, Ian leaned forwards and said:

"Do you still sing?"

"In a choir, you mean?" said David, surprised that his hunch had been right. "No, not anymore. I left St Peter's not long after you left. My voice broke you see. I didn't enjoy it after that."

"That was the worst part about leaving town. The choir was my only bit of fun," said Ian.

"Mine too," said David, allowing his guard to drop, reflecting. "It all seems a million years ago now though."

"Seeing you again, it only seems like yesterday," said Ian.

"The choir didn't seem the same when you went. It felt empty," said David. "I couldn't see the point going there by myself. But, it was good while it lasted though, wasn't it?"

"Best days of your life childhood, isn't that what they say?" said Ian with transparent irony.

"So, where did you end up when you left?" asked David.

"Oh you know, all over the place. Dad couldn't wait to get out of Ansons. First it was Berlin, then we moved back to the UK for a year before heading off to Milwaukee in the States. Surely you must remember the letters I sent?"

"You wrote to me?"

"Well, I gave up in the end. You never replied to any."

"None ever got to me," said David, detecting a latent, silent anger towards the person who had obviously prevented him from seeing them. "I thought you'd gone on to better things and forgotten about me."

"Better things? What, with a dad like mine, come on?"

"But all those places Germany, America, and now this business."

"My dad was a bastard," said Ian. "A bully who would not accept second best from anyone, least of all me. I lost count of the times he whacked me round the head or took his belt to me because I didn't come up to scratch. My life was a misery. I resolved to do better than him, just for spite. At least you had your mother. She might have seemed strange, but she was always there for you."

There was nothing for it but to drag out his own sorry tale, editing and abridging as he went. Although their stories were different in

464

their own separate ways, they bore a common theme, a black ribbon of abuse. Whereas David had been wrong footed into the darkness, Ian's experiences had propelled him into the light, but one thing remained the same after the long decades that had passed since their childhood. It was something that could be seen in the way they were with each other. It was a shared sense of friendship, reforged through the sharing of their individual histories of suffering.

The interview, such as it was, touched on technical matters but briefly. The coffee duly arrived and David, surprised at his powers of recall, spoke with authority about his experiences at Carridges. Without it appearing to be a question and answer session, Ian Crabtree worked out just how much his friend knew about things like repro, printing, post-press, and software developments. From Quark Express to Photoshop, EPS to ISDN, Ian grew satisfied with everything he was hearing. Thankfully, those trips to Newark College had kept David sufficiently up to date with technology to sound convincing. Finally Ian explained the kind of person he was looking for, someone who could liaise between the business, the client and the production companies, printers and the like. He continued to say that he was looking for a reliable Project Manager. He paused for a moment and then, with a broad smile that hid nothing, he reached out his hand to his old pal and declared with satisfaction that now, at last, he had found him.

"It'll be just like old times again," said David.

"Sod the old times," replied Ian. "It's the future we're going to make. We won't have time to look back to the past. It's onwards and upwards for us, my friend."

David smiled. It felt good to be strong and positive like this. He felt as if he had reached the motorway at last.

The following weeks passed in a blur. He had hit the ground running but it was exhilarating work and vastly varied. The trick was to be organised. Ian had warned him of the dangers in not having a clean approach to managing the assignments that were to come his way. So, as a stopgap, until he learned the finer points of his new laptop he adopted a manual system that never let him down. He found the creative guys, as they liked to be called, oddly thrilling to be around. Sometimes he would be in on the initial meeting with a client. He would quietly watch how they tossed an idea around in their heads, joking occasionally with the customer, some of whom would feel the discomfort of having their product abused with such childlike levity. A mass of stupid ideas would pour out of them, until at an uncertain point, a crazy run-away notion would come out of the blue. Then they would all go silent, look at each other as if one of them had farted and with some kind of telepathy knew that they had hit on something. Then there was no stopping them. The creative process would go into overdrive and the client would beam a smile and wonder why they had not thought of it themselves. David found this stimulating beyond belief.

It was with an inner joy that he went about his job of finding out the practicalities of making these off-the-wall ideas come to fruition. Often it was just a matter of finding the right printer or packaging manufacturer and briefing them on what was needed to make the client's dreams come true. It was the television ads that were the best, especially if they were going to be animated ones. That's when the creative team buzzed with an invisible energy that was capable of anything. David often found himself sounding like a moaning old codger, as he tempered their ideas with the cautions imposed by reality. It was his job to find what it would take to breathe life into these wild ideas and, though it often took a lot of head scratching to come up with the solutions, he loved every minute of it.

As with many good things in life, this one came at a price. The little sheltered flat that he had spent a happy time in was evacuated now that he had made good. Leaving the flat did have a sad side to it, particularly having to say goodbye to Connie. How she cried when she learned that he was leaving. For half an hour she tried to bottle it up, telling him that he must make his way in the world. It was she who had shown him the advertisement for the job in the first place she told him. She took his hand in hers telling him how pleased she was that he had managed to find his long-lost friend. The bravado began to crumble as he got up to go. She put her fragile, arthritic arms around him and held him as if he was her child. Of course there was the usual lines that people say at times like this, lines that promise to keep in touch, lines that say that they will come and visit as often as possible. The thing was that David believed it, but Connie knew what would really happen. As he turned to wave to her when he left, it was he who had real tears misting up the view of her, the view of her standing like a tiny statue framed by her own lonely doorway.

A month of life lived at a hectic pace followed. He had become a new person. There was health within him where once there had been disease. A new flat became part of his life, as did his new car, a dark blue Vauxhall Astra. The gregarious designers, the men and women who formed the creative team, the boffins as he dubbed them, had by now taken kindly to their quiet and diligent Project Manager. He in turn enjoyed the acceptance. The place was a perfect health farm for the soul, a place to drink in a feeling of goodness. A deluge of positive energy poured out of the indefatigable Ian. David watched him throw himself into seducing new clients and setting up deals. There was never any question of failure and it all seemed so effortless. Then again David could never recall him leaving the office before anyone else, unless he was out on business, and he was usually there before the rest of the team had arrived. Even then he had fitted in a half-hour workout at the gym. In between that time he had busied himself with finding out all about the client he was hunting. Doing his homework was performed with a passion that somehow seemed more like a well-played game than hard work. David bathed in the inspiration that emanated from him.

In the middle of this glorious mayhem David received a phone call, a phone call from the hospital. Connie had taken ill, very ill, and she was asking for him. The work was piling up. There were important clients to serve. There was no time, was there? Was there? Ian told him to go. There was always time for people he told him. Go and see her, just go. So he did.

The ward where Connie was had a smell, a disinfectant mask that somehow never managed to disguise the pungency of urine. There were two rooms just before the main ward opened out and in the one on the right Connie lay slightly propped up on pillows. The patient and the visitor were tugged towards each other like two magnetic hearts brought into close proximity. Connie was very weak, too weak to appreciate the flowers he brought. He sat and took her hand in his.

She heaved it up to her lips to kiss it and beheld him with eyes that knew the time had come. With a voice as quiet as a sigh she spoke his name. He heard her clearly in the noiseless room.

"David," she whispered.

"I'm here, Connie," he whispered back.

"Will you miss me when I'm gone?"

"Don't talk like that," he said, "you'll be out of here in a week."

"We both know that's not true don't we?"

"I'll never forget you Connie. How could I?"

"You might," she said. "Now, what are you going to do about your Auntie Ellie?"

"Ellie?"

"You must find her and make things right between you," she said, a stamp of insistence ringing out from her tone.

He looked at her wondering why she had brought him here, only to bring this up.

"You must promise me," she pushed on.

What else was there to say but to promise and agree with her?

"Life doesn't last that long, you know David. Just think how things might have turned out if you'd managed to talk to her the night you went to find her. Think how many years of illness it could have saved you. You'll be a fool if you don't find her. You listen to your old Connie. I haven't lived this long without learning a thing or two about people. Money isn't everything, you know."

Behind her eyes he could see a lifetime's experience, an accumulated wisdom greater than his, kept alive by the organs within her that even now were closing down. He leaned forwards to press his cheek against hers.

"I'll find her Connie," he promised.

"Good boy," she said.

He kissed her smooth cheek, as in the same instant her hand in his went limp. By the time he had brought himself upright, her eyes were closed and her body was still. David's heart broke in half and grief poured out of it like a flood.

On the day Connie was laid to rest David realised just how lonely she must have been. She once mentioned a daughter whom she had

468

resigned and consigned to a long, distant past, as if she was referring to the Jurassic Age. Apart from a number of health workers, the warden who managed the sheltered flats and David, no one else was present at the crematorium. All that was left when the coffin had disappeared behind a red curtain was the promise he made. It was as if some of Connie's spirit had made its home within him, a gentle, watchful haunting that felt more like a warm solace than a sense of being possessed.

Two weeks after the funeral David received a letter. The words within required him to be present at the reading of the last will and testament of Constance Eleanor Brown. The firm of Carpenter, Lock and Hardwicke had given him a month's notice of the meeting at their Nottingham offices. David made a deadline with himself that he would do all he could to find Ellie by then. He had learned the value of a deadline. Without them his world was aimless. Now he provided himself with a month of disciplined searching.

Life became busy once more and in amongst its chaos, David began to tease out the fine strands of Ellie's trail. He emailed a request for information on the late Reverend John Crampton to the website of the Southwell diocese. Did anyone know what had become of his widow? Later that day a reply dropped into his inbox, with regrets that such personal information could not be given openly. The respondent obviously had a heart, as there was a contact in the shape of the Bishop of Southwell's secretary. The suggestion that David should write an old-fashioned letter to her was concluded with the words, good luck.

What an ignominious letter it was, sycophantic to the point of being sickly sweet. It was all crammed onto the page faith, hope and Evensong the wondrous works of John Crampton and his dutiful wife, his Aunt Ellie, and how he wanted to trace her whereabouts. Politeness had never been more over exaggerated in a written piece, concentrated courteousness underpinning this one-chance-only opportunity. When it was posted off, and David had the time to read his copy again, he was appalled at its blatant shamefulness.

A week later a reply arrived in the mail. It seemed as if the ever-so-humble approach, favoured by the acquisitive Uriah Heap, had paid off, at least in as much as soliciting the acquisition of a few out of date facts. Ellie had moved from The Croft to a town house in Rye, East Sussex. It mentioned a son, Matthew who had gone with her. She had worked as secretary to the vicar there, a woman priest with whom she had experienced some difficulties, as the letter put it. The bishop's secretary was unsure where on earth she had gone on from there. The only hearsay that she felt able to convey was that Mrs Crampton had mentioned Cornwall prior to her departure. The letter ended with the words, *God bless you in your search*. David read the letter again. Cornwall?

She was now further out of reach than at first he had believed. Surely it was possible to hide oneself in Cornwall and never be found? It took a week, trawling the web sites of several parishes in Cornwall, to make him realise that he was on a hiding to nothing. The deadline was fast approaching and he was letting himself down. There had to be an avenue of enquiry that he had not tried yet, but what?

On Ian's advice, he phoned up three Cornish newspapers, the local rags of Bodmin, Truro, and Penzance respectively, placing an advert in each, David Harper seeks Eleanor Crampton. He supplied his address and telephone number and paid for the ads by credit card. One advert even bore a box number, a measure suggested by the telesales girl, in case the missing person held a reluctance to reply directly. Nothing came of them. The box number took not a single deposit. It was like looking for a needle in a haystack, a haystack at the end of a road going nowhere.

One weekend he even drove to Edlington, to ask one or two of the villagers whom he knew if they had any information as to where his Ellie had gone. He was treated with suspicion, disdain even. No one felt free to talk. It seemed to him as if he had left a legacy, a bad smell in the village, the sort of thing that folks there would whisper about for years afterwards, about the odd cyclist who had gone berserk. The place was unhealthy, and had it not been for his promise to Connie, he would have given up looking for his beloved Ellie there and then. Besides, less than a week remained before his appointment with Connie's solicitors. His options were running out. Apart from driving down to Cornwall and roaming around the county like a madman, what else was there to do? Even whilst he racked his brains for another thread of exploration, the day of the will reading arrived. He felt like a failure.

It was Saturday morning and he was in Beeston, a district of Nottingham. The directions given by the firm Carpenter, Lock and Hardwicke had worked out perfectly. With uncertain expectation he crunched across the gravelled car park towards a well-kept Victorian lodge, wondering who else would be present and how they would regard him, an outsider to Connie's family. Inside, the atmosphere had been aged in oak. Old timber panelling and heavy wooden furniture infused the air with an aroma that was to the place more of a biography than a mere smell.

A frail receptionist, who looked as if she survived on nothing more than a meagre diet of pulses and lettuce, directed him to a waiting room, a one-time front parlour that appeared steeped in austerity. The law magazines on the small table were evidently there not to be read by people waiting, but more to reinforce the fact that the firm took a very grave and conceited view of their legal prowess. As it turned out there was no time even to pick one up. A well-dressed man in a dark blue suit, introduced himself as Mr Lock, asked to see his letter of invitation and, on seeing it, bade him follow on to a larger room that contained a long and highly polished oak table. Two other gentlemen of a similar age and appearance were already there at the table's head as he was invited to sit down at the opposite end. They were duly introduced as Mr Hardwicke and Mr Carpenter's secretary. So far everything about this visit had been decidedly Dickensian. The three portly souls who had arranged themselves like an interview panel were not going to disappoint.

"Very good," began Mr Lock. "Now that Mr Harper is present, I put the case that we should commence our discourse."

"Am I the only one here?" asked David.

Mr Hardwicke looked purposefully about the room, making it obvious that he was searching for another person whom he knew not to be there.

"The evidence does seem to point to such a conclusion Mr Harper. But pray, allow my colleague to continue."

David sat back in his chair, annoyed at being chastened like a child, waiting uncomfortably to hear what next would be said. Then, from a file Mr Lock produced a letter. The secretary walked it to the other end of the long table and placed it on the blotting pad that marked out David's place. He could distinguish Connie's handwriting. He had seen her slender, shaky style on many a crossword. Against the limitations of her arthritis, and with obvious care, she had written: *To my dearest David*. Mr Lock invited him to open it, but later. The odd meeting continued.

"I will not trouble you with the legal anatomy of this will, Mr Harper, save to say that Mrs Brown was soundly compos mentis at the time of its creation," said Mr Lock, pleased at the sound of his own voice.

Mr Hardwicke took the lead from his partner, much to Lock's irritation.

"You are to be a beneficiary," Hardwicke said. "A sole beneficiary no less."

David did not know what to think, much less what to expect. Hardwicke delved into the folder that Lock was guarding and from his grasp retrieved a parchment-coloured paper. Even from the far end of the table he could clearly see the word *WILL* written on the front of it, as Hardwicke opened it out to read the words within.

"Upon selling her house near Newark, a house that she owned outright, Mrs Brown put all the proceeds of that house into a building society, drawing off the interest and occasional capital for her day-to-day expenses during her time at the sheltered flat where she placed herself when ill health made it impossible for her to look after herself."

Hardwicke inhaled a desperate breath. It had been one of his longest sentences so far. He cast a glance at his two colleagues and turned to behold a wide-eyed David Harper staring back at them. Lock seized his chance.

"You are to inherit thirty thousand pounds," he blurted out.

Hardwicke could hardly contain his fury at having had the punch line stolen from him.

"Yes," he said loudly, "thirty thousand, one hundred and twenty six pounds, ninety two pence, to be precise," Hardwicke put in, stealing back the limelight.

David sat in a daze. The long table seemed to grow longer. The three men appeared to drift further away as it did so. Thirty grand. He could not take it in.

"We now come to the matter of the letter," said Hardwicke, shaking David out of his stupor. "Please feel free to read it now."

Like a robot he did as commanded, taking out the white sheet of paper and trying to decipher the wobbly hand in blue biro.

My dearest David,

By now you will be getting used to being a much richer man. I'm glad about that. There's no one better to receive my worldly wealth than you. I have no family left now with whom to leave my money and you are therefore the nearest person to a son to me, so have it with my blessing.

The evening you told me of your life I was very moved. I couldn't sleep that night thinking about you and your Auntie Ellie, and what she meant to you. I believe that a great deal of good can come your way if you and she could be reunited. I have taken the trouble of passing on the calling card of an old friend of mine, a Mr Tulip (strange name, but very good at his job). He has been a private investigator for over fifty years. I would like you to get in touch with him should you find that locating your Auntie proves difficult (as I imagine it will). He will be of great help to you I'm sure.

I have always known that I was on borrowed time you know. I'm not worried about dying. I've had a fulfilling, daft, exciting, boring and sometimes peculiar life. I'm just glad I got to know you before it was too late. Don't waste the money, use it sensibly and you're bound to enjoy its benefits. God, I sound like a wise old sod, don't I?

Miss me a little,
God bless
Connie XX

A lump formed in David's throat. It almost strangled him. With every fibre of resistance he withheld the urge to weep. Connie. How he missed watching the telly with her. He remembered how she found it impossible to follow a film on the box. She would never be sure if the man in the white suit was the killer. David could see her trying to figure out the plot, as he explained for the umpteenth time that he was in fact the detective. She would call herself silly me and then stare at the screen determined to stay focussed and to solve the murder. David smiled. She had been a batty old thing but he learned to love her. He tipped up the envelope that the letter had come in and a white card flipped out on to the table. The name Percy Tulip, Private Eye was printed on it, along with an address in West Bridgford and a phone number, mobile and email. Only Connie Brown could know someone who went by the odd name of Percy Tulip. He wished, for a moment, that he could have met her fifty years earlier.

Chapter five: Reflections

So here was the voice he heard on the phone, finally matched with its physical manifestation. Percy Tulip was nothing like he had imagined. He was short, stocky, balding and irritable.

"You've given me nothing to go on, nothing whatsoever Mr Harper."

This was the greeting that David received even before entering the room, and what a room it was. Mr Tulip had filed his paperwork by gravity it appeared. Letters and notes had built up like sediments, creating paper lines of strata everywhere. There were four chairs in what Tulip called his office and, save for the one he sat on, the other three were employed as filing cabinets.

"You'll have to stand," he barked, shutting the door behind them both and shuffling past the mess to a chair behind a similarly littered desk. "Who else knows your auntie?"

"As I said on the phone, she was well liked in Edlington," he said, going on to reiterate how he had already followed that line but got nowhere.

"You mentioned Rye?"

"She's left there, now."

"Quite so. Any friends there?"

"Don't know."

"Don't know much, do you, Mr Harper?"

"No, not much."

"Where does she come from, this auntie of yours?" asked Tulip.

"Oh, a village in Wiltshire. It's not there nowadays."

"What do you mean, not there?"

"A neighbouring village has sort of swallowed it up. Empton it was called. It's part of a place called Great Rembleton these days."

"Any family there?"

"I doubt it. I don't know really."

"And why do you want to find her, if I may be so bold?"

"We lost contact. I miss her," was all he would say.

The questions went on for half an hour, questions asked in a direct, often brutal kind of way. Percy Tulip it seemed was a man of no emotion. He would not smile. He did not raise his voice. All he seemed capable of was digging out facts and setting out his terms and conditions. His was no psychoanalyst's approach. He was like an ageing fist fighter, too old to get back into the ring, but brimming with a wisdom that knew how to win the round. After the thirty minutes were up, he said to David that he thought it was time he left.

"Is that it, then?"

"It is."

"Are you going to take me on?"

"You think I'd waste half an hour of my time on the likes of you if I thought I couldn't find your Ellie?"

"But where will you start. I've tried no end of places in Cornwall."

"She's not in Cornwall."

"How do you know that?"

"I'm a private detective. I detect things. And in Cornwall, she ain't."

"You will let me know when you've found her, won't you."

"I'll do the finding, Mr Harper. You do the paying."

"Well, call me if I can be of any help."

"Please shut the door behind you Mr Harper on your way out."

Tulip bent his head towards a pile of papers on his desk, making it seem as if he was about to drop off to sleep.

"Very well," said David, taken aback by this stark dismissal. "Goodbye."

"Bye," was the final word grunted from the barren head now hidden in a mess of paperwork.

As instructed he closed the door with a click as he went. By the time he was back to his car he began to wonder if he had done the right thing. He started to panic and chide himself for paying the old codger five hundred pounds. Five hundred pounds on deposit, to cover expenses he was told. How daft was that? He just hoped that Connie knew what she was doing when she paired him up with this geriatric Sherlock Holmes.

Four weeks of mistrust passed. Twenty-eight days of cursing his bad judgement. A month of regretting the day he had taken Connie's advice seriously. Then one Saturday, like some insignificant postscript to the epistle of his life, a letter arrived in the morning mail. The words had been bashed out on an unpredictable typewriter that seemed to have long forgotten the concept of creating words in straight lines. After the pleasantries of addresses and dates there was a single paragraph.

Dear
   Mr Harper,
   I have located Eleanor Crampton, wife of the late Reverend John Crampton, formerly vicar of the parish of Edlington. Contact me at your earliest in order to meet and conclude matters. Your final settlement of one thousand pounds will be due on completion of our business.
      Yours truly,
P. Tulip.

How had he done it? Was it true? He had written yours truly but could he be trusted. By now, of course, David had built in his mind a picture of a complete conman in the shape of Percy Tulip. All he could imagine was that he would be given a fictitious address, then part with a cool grand and wander blindly up the garden path. What else was there to do? After reading the letter once more he picked up the phone and rang the number printed at the top of the page. An answerphone message recorded by the grumpy voice of the bald, little fart, declared the office hours and invited the caller to do the necessary after the long beep. He put the receiver down and prepared for the long wait until Monday morning.

The weekend was an empty one, like all other weekends. He loved his job but by Friday night he was drained. Besides there was shopping to do and shirts to iron for the week ahead. For the most part he came face to face with the knowledge that he was plain lonely. He could say with complete honesty that he had carried out Connie's request that he should miss her a little. Only he took it a step further and missed her a lot. It was almost a relief, he found, to get to bed on Sunday evening and look forward to contact with his new family at Inca Marketing.

Back at his office the next day he made the call. Tulip answered and David's hackles went up at the sound of the pinched Nottingham accent, which seemed intent on ripping him off.

"So where did you find her?" said David.

"Cash on delivery, Mr Harper," said the whiny voice. "Cash on delivery."

"I'll call round tonight if that's convenient."

"Quite so. Six-thirty?" Tulip said.

David could detect a repressed sense of glee coming from the private investigator at the prospect of a one thousand pounds pay out. He felt the whole thing had been an altogether grubby business but he was dutifully there at half past six on the dot. Tulip seemed agitated. David sensed that something was wrong, as if he were soon to hear bad news. Tulip cleared a chair and motioned for his client to be seated. He then pulled a drawer open and retrieved a brown envelope, checked its contents and passed it to David.

"Take them out," said Tulip, pointing to the envelope, and trying to suppress a tension in his manner.

David took out five or six colour photographs. They were in order, and as David looked through them, a notion of movement unfolded, as if he were looking at individual frames from a strip of movie film. Evidently the snaps had been taken in quick succession and showed a woman walking arm in arm with a young man. There was no mistake. The woman was Ellie striding down a high street in some undisclosed town accompanied by a fresh-faced escort.

"It's her all right," said David, as Tulip tried to hide a feeling of relaxation.

"Splendid," he said calmly.

Then a silence followed. David knew any further questions would cost him a thousand quid. Tulip knew that too, but allowed the silence to continue, playing games with his client, just wondering how long it would be before he had to speak. After an eternal minute, David reached into his trouser pocket, drew out his chequebook and stared at the empty blank cheque behind the front cover. Tulip came close to salivating. The client was playing the master at his own game. Mr Tulip, with a reflex now long inbred, offered a pen. David took it and began to make the sound of nib on paper. The noise of a perforation ripping followed, as David handed over the torn-out cheque. Tulip allowed a smile to escape his poker face, a smile that vanished as he read the words written thereon.

"Perhaps I did not make myself clear," began Tulip. "I said..."

David interrupted.

"I know what you said Mr Tulip. Don't worry. You'll get your cool grand, five hundred now and the other five hundred when I see her for myself. Now the address please."

Tulip's face was a thunderstorm. Words were forming behind his foxy eyes but none found their liberation from his mouth. He delved into the drawer he had taken the pictures from and took out a small white card, holding it just out of his client's reach.

"How do I know I can trust you to pay the remainder?" he asked.

"How do I know you'll give me the right address?"

"This is the right address."

"Then you'll have a further five hundred pounds within the week if you're right."

Tulip realised that this could go on forever and he was in no mood to wait that long. With a gasp of exasperation he handed over the card. David read the address typed on it by Tulip's antiquated typewriter. Ellie, it seemed, was in Salisbury.

He was glad to leave Tulip's dishevelled workplace, yet there was a tinge of admiration for the man. Whatever his own prejudices, there was no denying, he had done as asked, he had delivered. Just how had he tracked down his beloved Ellie? Now there was a question that would have to remain forever unanswerable. Tulip would never disclose to him his methods, especially now he had riled him about

478

the money. Doubtless he would never divulge his professional tricks of the trade anyway. He began to wonder how on earth Connie had got to know him in the first place.

He reached his car where he had left it, down a back street, away from the double yellow lines, close to the Trent Bridge cricket ground. As soon as he sealed himself within the car's quiet interior he brought out the photographs from the envelope. There she was, his Ellie, looking fit and well and in love, it appeared, with her young man. He wished he could have been more like her. Even seeing her on the flat sheets of Kodak paper, he was fuelled with all the positive energy he required. There in the bottom of the envelope was the address. Friday night seemed a lifetime away, but he resolved that come the end of the working week he would hit the motorway and head south.

As the days crawled by he wondered at the rashness of his plan. Maybe he should write, tell her he was fine and ask after her. He could put the seed of an idea that he might come and see her, possibly. The plan morphed one stage further. He could ask Directory Enquiries for her phone number, even look it up in the complete range of UK phone books at the library. He could search for a Crampton E that matched the address. He would call her and begin from there. How would he start such a conversation? How would he begin such a letter? What would he say on the doorstep if he went? Suddenly the week speeded up as the plan fell apart. By the time Friday evening arrived he was completely unsure of what to do. Ian advised him to send her some flowers by InterBloom and break the ice that way. One way or another the time had come to jump across the great chasm that the long years past had created.

With no clear idea of what he was doing anymore he left town and soon reached the M1, an overnight bag stashed in the boot and a bouquet of flowers on the back seat. Every mile seemed to take him deeper and deeper into the lake of foolish ideas. Even as he reached the M25 the voices in his head were screaming at him to turn back. The dusk began to fall. The sky's light diminished and that alone seemed to make a difference. Somehow the simple act of flicking on the headlights brought a hush to the protesters. As the miles slithered beneath him the gentle balm flowing from BBC Radio Three silenced them altogether; Max Bruch's *Scottish Fantasy* had managed to give meaning to the trip, its dark, funereal beginning changing, like the journey, into pleasantness. By the time the car had slipped onto the M3 heading west, he knew that he had his own destiny in his hands once more.

It was dark by the time he entered Salisbury, though less dark as the ride had been on the motorway. There were streetlights illuminating the way now, banishing the blackness he had become used to. He stopped at a filling station to get petrol and bought a street map there. He had learned the address on Tulip's card off by heart, knowing it as well as his own, and it did not take long, once he pulled up in a pub car park, for him to find the road he wanted. His finger followed the roundabouts to the final destination, his target. He could see that the A36 curved like a sickle hooking its blade around the eastern and northern edge of the old town. Somewhere in the oddly named Paul's Dene, north of Salisbury he would find his beloved, his auntie, his Ellie.

He was a bundle of nerves as he moved out of the car park. In this feverish state, he stared with a heightened awareness on every road sign that came into view, lest he should loose the delicate, unfamiliar thread, and find himself lost. He was unaware that his breathing had quickened and his pulse had likewise joined in. It was like the trip to Edlington all over again.

In the end it took no finding. Lit by a street lamp he could plainly read Chadwick Avenue on a wall-mounted sign. On either side of the kerb, lime trees grew out of the grass verges that lay between the road and the pavement. Each garden had its own wall as a territorial symbol of ownership, from where shallow gates declared the beginning of a short drive that led to its own garage. The houses were semi-detached, all of them, each a perfect mirror image of its neighbour. He pulled up and parked outside number ten, picked the flowers from the back seat and prepared for the walk to number twelve.

It was now nine-thirty, almost too late to burst in on someone, but then it was late already, years late, and the time of day seemed irrelevant now. So here he was, finger poised on the little white button that he hoped would connect to a bell. All he had to do now was to press it. He knew that as soon as the door chimes had rung an unknown chain of events would unravel. One little push, that is all it would take, and lives would be changed, forever.

So they rang out, mellow and resonant. There was time to flee but his feet were planted firmly on the doorstep. Then, through a half-moon window set in the door, an image appeared to move behind its stained glass design. The person was quick and nimble and drew the upper bolt down and turned the Yale latch. There before him stood a young man whom David recognised from the pictures that Tulip had taken. There was an awkward silence. He had not expected this. Ellie was supposed to have answered the door. He was going to have said long time no see. In the end he had to say something.

"I hope I've come to the right place. Is Ellie here, I mean Mrs Crampton, is she here?"

The man regarded the stranger with a searching eye that seemed to register something unclear.

"And you are?" he said with a confidence bordering on arrogance.

"An old friend," he said making sure that the flowers would be seen. "It's supposed to be a surprise."

"Wait here a mo then," said the man, who turned and filled the house with his voice. "Mum, there's someone here to see you."

Mum, thought David, then this was Matthew. He was a man now. Suddenly he could remember the day he found out that Ellie was expecting him and suddenly the chasm of years seemed wider than ever. Then came a voice he knew.

"Who is it?"

His knees almost buckled with what was happening. Even as the man, Matthew, was replying that it was an old friend on a surprise visit, David was not quite with it. He seemed to be rapidly rewriting his assumptions, whilst preparing himself for the meeting that was frighteningly imminent.

From a back room he could see a small figure emerge carrying a book, an index finger inserted in the interrupted page as a mark. Matthew stood aside. David looked. Ellie saw. Their eyes met. What passed between them belonged to the infinite. Emotions, questions formed the basis of an unspoken exchange that seemed to last hours but was barely a second. The book dropped to the carpet, her colour

481

drained from her face. It was Matthew who caught her as she fell. Awkwardly, David helped him get her to a chair and there she regained her consciousness.

"Mum," he panicked, "speak to me for Christ's sake."

Ellie did not say a word, but threw a reassuring smile at her son. David saw it too. It was the smile he knew. The smile faded and an uncertain face beheld the visitor.

"Is it you?" she said attempting calm.

"Yes it's me," he faltered. "These are for you," he said searching for the right words, and picking up the flowers that had fallen to the floor. "This has been a mistake. I shouldn't have come."

"You took me a bit by surprise that's all. I'll be all right in a minute."

"I should have let you know I was coming. I'm sorry."

"No matter, you're here now," she turned to her son. "Darling, this is…"

Matthew had already pieced the jigsaw together.

"This is David Harper, isn't it mother?" he said, with grave undertones.

"Yes, this is my Davy boy," she said by way of confirmation, but really it was to ensure that her son remained there as protection.

Matthew knew all about David Harper and he was not about to leave his mother alone with him. Even David had begun to understand the body language and coded conversation and he felt like his arrival had been the mother of all mistakes.

"I've been ill," David blurted out, feeling an explanation would help, "but I'm fine now. There's no need to be afraid."

He could see far away in the back of her eyes that she was afraid. Matthew could not hide it at all. The man in him wanted to kick him out of the house but the youth that he was could not find the nerve.

So David told his life's tale once more, this time to someone who was qualified to listen. He told of life with mother, much of which she had witnessed herself. He described in as much detail as he could just what it had been like at home when she left and the mental and physical nightmares at bedtime, couching the details in euphemisms on account of Matthew being there. The sad story unfolded right up until the last time he was admitted to hospital. Carefully he omitted the hypnotherapy sessions, the trance he had undergone and his trip to Great Rembleton. He held it all back. He wanted to see if his wonderful Ellie would come clean about why his mother behaved as she did. He was ready to give his absolution to her if she broke the secret and told him about those days long ago in Empton, when his life's sorry tale had truly begun, but she did not.

He asked outright why it was that she thought his mum had changed into the woman she ended up becoming. Her answer was that she was poorly. She remembered her being exhausted most of the time and that her mind was sick. He probed further, trying to stay polite lest Matthew should break the delicate bond. He wondered if she knew any reason why she had become so ill. Ellie shook her head, adding that life had been hard to her, bringing a baby up on her own as she had. If he had not known otherwise he would have believed her words and yet how could he? He knew things, things that she was keeping from him. Why? Why the betrayal? He never expected her to let him down like this but here she was doing just that. There was nothing for it but to open her eyes.

"Have you still got the old wedding album?" he asked.

"Good Lord, the album? Well, yes. It's in the sideboard," she said, a quizzical look flashing across her eyes, "I couldn't bring myself to throw it away, why do you ask? I thought you couldn't stand to see it anymore?"

"I just wanted to have a little look," he said getting ready to pounce, "I've forgotten how pretty the picture outside the church is."

Overcoming her reluctance to comply, Ellie motioned to Matthew to look in the sideboard and bring out the old relic. After a shuffle in amongst the clutter, there it was, the album. He never imagined that he would ever have to set eyes on it again, but there it was being placed nervously on his lap. He opened it up at random, to reveal the one taken outside the church. There she was Lotty, as he knew her back then, before she became that other woman, his mother. His heart lurched as if a starter motor had turned it over. He could still feel the need for her, coming from a fountain deep inside, a wellspring of love. After a moment he steadied himself and looked directly at Ellie.

"Nice church at Empton in those days wasn't it?" he said, watching her face contort in surprise.

He could see her wondering how he knew about Empton, so he dropped a few more surprises. Searching through the pages he arrived at his favourite picture, the one of Ellie the child presenting the horseshoes. The one he had seen being taken in the far off past.

"It seems a long time ago, doesn't it Ellie?"

"Yes."

Her answer was charged with questioning.

"A long time since you played princes and princesses with Mr Miller in this very garden?"

Ellie's mouth opened, trying to form the words.

"How, how did you know that?" she was trying to say.

"They're not happy memories for you either, are they, these pictures?" he said. "I bet you lost count of the times you sat in that old yard nursing the bruises that Harry inflicted on you?"

Ellie swallowed hard and looked directly at David. He could see it in her eyes, that feeling as if a ghost had come calling. Matthew could plainly see her getting upset but did not know how to intervene.

"And then there's my dad there, look," he pointed to the picture of him. "Only we know differently, don't we? Don't we?"

Then he was stopped in his tracks and saw something in the print as if with new eyes. Every time he had looked at this picture, it had been the people who had dominated the scene. Now something else had caught his attention, behind the left shoulder of Danno, the man he had grown up thinking had been his father. In the background set into an old crumbling brick wall, Mrs Cartwright's wall, he could see a section of a window frame. The connection then connected as he brought his face closer to the old print. This time it was David who was dumbfounded. It was there, a reflection, a face, head and shoulders, very faint, hard to make out, just as he supposed it might have happened on that day he and Norman had positioned themselves in the beer garden of The Miller's Drop.

This revelation had been so overwhelming that he had not noticed Ellie gently weeping. Matthew had his arm around her. He plucked up his courage and asked David to leave them alone.

"Why didn't you tell me any of this Ellie?" David asked her pointedly when he had gathered his thoughts.

Ellie did not know not what to say, her mind was in disarray. Her son repeated his request that he leave. So David reached into his back pocket and took out his wallet, flipped it open and drew out a business card. Holding it at arm's length she took it from him. He asked her to call him and through a broken voice she said she might. He asked if he could take the album.

"Take it," she insisted, adding that she never wanted to see it again.

He thought to kiss her, kiss her cheek, or hold her as he had once taken for granted. He did not. He could not. His apology for upsetting her was futile, infantile, and he walked out of the door back to his car, carrying the album under his arm, with dissatisfaction in his spirit.

Chapter six: Revelations

The irony hit hard like a body blow. By finding Ellie he had lost her - lost her for good. She had finally had enough of him. She had reached breaking point and wanted to be left alone. In severing that slender link she had abandoned him forever in his cold, lonely world. His mind staggered from anger to self-pity and back to anger again. He hit his hand hard on the centre of the steering wheel in frustration, mindless to the airbag that was coiled there ready. He had blown it, he kept thinking. When his memory went back to the Ellie he knew and loved, a vast reservoir of sorrow threatened to engulf him. In this way he drove back home, while the album, temporarily forgotten, jostled lifelessly on the back seat.

Tired and low, he slept most of Saturday and spent the majority of the next day agonising whether or not to call Ellie on the phone. Even if she did pick up the receiver, what would he say? The call was never made. During Sunday afternoon, he sank in front of the television lost in thought and oblivious to the programmes delivered to him by the tube. Like a debriefing, he ran and re-ran the visit to

Salisbury. Would he have found out more if he had not been so hard on her? Why, having known about the events in Empton, had she maintained her silence all those years? Should he have been more forgiving? Mostly he felt mad at not having thought things through before ringing her doorbell, even before he stepped into his car. Connie Brown and Mr Tulip had given him a golden opportunity and he had gone and chucked it in the mud. He was a complete fool he kept thinking.

He was glad to get back to work on Monday morning. His mind was weary of contemplating it all. He got in to the office early to start the day alone, only he was not the first there, the alarm had been disabled and the lights were on. Ian had obviously beaten him to it. Or so he thought. In fact, it was the girl he had first seen at his so-called interview. Victoria was her name, but everyone called her Queenie.

"Couldn't sleep?" he asked, as he walked in.

"I've been dreading this all weekend," she said, staring at her computer screen. Her slender feminine fingers fiddled nervously with the mouse. He could see in her eyes that she was in trouble and that this was a make-or-break moment, he could sense it in her body.

"Oh fuck," she said.

"What's up?" David enquired, looking into the monitor.

A picture of a roll-on deodorant bottle appeared. It was one of several for a set of posters for a fragrance company.

"Can't you see?" she said, clicking the mouse.

The picture grew bigger. Almost immediately the photograph was a mass of coloured squares, leaving the object unidentifiable.

"I've scanned them all in at the wrong resolution, all fifty of them. I ought to be able to zoom in closer before it pixilates like this. I wish the bloody photographer had gone digital. This is like working in the Stone Age."

She checked the resolution on another window, just to prove how stupid she had been.

"Sorry Dave," she said, "you'll have to cancel the print, and I'll have to e-mail all these again. It'll take hours. Oh God, what if they've started printing."

"Can't you put them on a CD? I'll run over and drop it off. It'll be quicker in the long run compared to downloading them all."

"Oh that would be a lifesaver. You're a darling, you are," she said, a whole weekend of worry melting away.

"So what's the maximum resolution this thing will do then?" he asked.

"I can scan at two thousand four hundred, that's the number of dots per inch that make up the image. Take up a lot of memory though, but you'd see everything. Three hundred is fine for most print jobs though, not seventy-two like I've cocked-up here."

"So, how good would the picture be at maximum?"

"Oh God, you'd be able to pick out the pimple on a bare bum at a hundred yards," she said with a laugh.

"So, what if the image was too dim, what then?" he probed further.

In a moment, at the touch of her mouse, another box had appeared on her screen. Something like a graph appeared there, which she adjusted by dragging little arrows at its base. In an instant, the deodorant bottle was lightened and it was possible to see more detail despite it being a crude scan.

"There," she said, "it's as easy as that."

"As easy as that," he said thoughtfully. "Then would you do me a favour when I get back from taking your disc?" he said, snapping his attention back to Queenie.

"Hey, you're doing me one, course I will."

"It's just that I've got an old photograph I'd like you to take a look at. It needs enlarging, and lightening. Sure you don't mind?"

"No prob Dave," she said as she got on with her loathsome task.

That night, in the stillness of his empty flat, he prised the old rectangular picture out of its four stick-on corners and took it away from the black page where it had lived. It was the first time in fifty years it had been liberated from its album. Now resting in his hand it seemed impossible that this picture had been part of his deformed upbringing, and even stranger that he had watched the picture being made in the first place. There they were, mum and dad, the lie. Even as he looked into the face of the person he knew better as Lotty, he could not prevent his feelings for her washing over him. How

487

vulnerable she had been in those days. How much he wanted to hold her and to feel her body warming against his. He did not want her to become his mother.

In stark contrast there stood Danno. Memories of the mistreatment he had suffered at his hand at the mill, and again at the end, all rushed at him like a frontal attack. The power of his heavy face charged out beyond the flatness of the picture. It made his stomach turn, so lasting was the bully's legacy. With a storm of such emotions he took his eyes away from these people and peered closer. He was keen to see the face in the reflection, this dark apparition, barely discernible. He had never set eyes on Mr Miller as he was nicknamed, never seen the person he was back then, but who was to say that it would be Miller's reflection. In a state of tiredness he recalled that there was, of course, a crowd of people at the wedding that day. A shift of a few degrees would cause anybody's reflection to bounce off the window. Maybe the image would be of Harry, Mrs Eversage or her dotty companion. His excitement dwindled, along with his strength to stay awake, so he sealed the picture away in a plastic cover and placed it in a file for the morning. Tomorrow, hopefully, if the technology worked as advertised, and his hunch was right, he would get a chance to see what he once looked like in his life before he was born.

David had not told anyone about Victoria's mistake the day before. He asked the studio guys at UPS, the printing company he had taken the disc to, to keep mum and save her from a bollocking. Besides, the schedule had not suffered, so no harm had been done. David was in the process of telling her that she was in the clear as she lowered the picture face down on the scanner. In a moment he could see the whole thing on the screen.

"So which part do you want to see?" she said.

David pointed to the edge of the window, just behind the curve of Danno's shoulder. The mouse on its mat moved. A tiny dotted rectangle was made on the screen just over the part where he could see the ghostly smudge of a face. They waited. The scanner whirred. It took time. The machine was on its maximum setting. But then, there it was a grainy shape of a face, about five millimetres high, much darker than it appeared on the picture itself. He could see hair, eyes, nose and mouth, a shirt and a jacket just going out of frame. But that was all. It was too dim to make anything else out.

"I'll lighten it a bit," she said, making the mouse perform as the picture became more distinct.

"Okay, let's enlarge it to fill the screen," she continued.

She made it happen.

The screen was filled.

Filled with a face.

His face.

Him.

There.

No mistake.

They both looked.

She took her eyes from the screen and looked at him.

He looked at her with eyes that could not withhold the shock. Seen from the outside, as Queenie could, he had suddenly become curiously odd. Inside him there was noise, the din of his brain wanting to know how and why. Despite the graininess of the print it clearly was him. The small part of the photograph was enlarged twenty fold or so, the tiny fragment of the print now made this size, meant that the final magnification percentage was in the thousands. It had been a good quality picture from the start. Had it not been, there would have been be no way he could have seen this face so clearly. Now he wondered whether he should have done it at all. The implications that Miller and he were identical began to explain fragments of the dark part of his life. It shed light on his Dark Ages. To be the spitting image of his mother's vanished lover had significance. He reached out and grabbed a chair, unable to stand up any longer.

"So, how come that's you?" Queenie said, uneasy at the way he staggered backwards into the chair.

"If only Norman Hart could have seen this," he managed to say.

She was about to ask who Norman Hart was, but instead ploughed on with her question.

"Is that really a picture of you then?" she said, becoming worried by the strangeness of it all.

"Would you mind printing me off a few copies?" David said, ignoring her question, lost in a world of implications.

She sent the image to the printer.

"Can't you tell me what's going on? Whose is the face? I'd like to know?" she was asking with all the charm she could muster.

"Him?" he answered, lost in a mist of contemplation. "That's the face of my father. My real father," he said. "It's the only one I have of him."

The day passed in a quiet terror. Uncertainty was building up in his head, as it once had done not too long ago. He knew what it was to go mad. He was prone to it, he believed. All it would take to send him spiralling back, out of control, to that awful life, was something like this. The natural reaction was to build up defences inside against the marauding voices - but he had matured since those days and by lunchtime he managed to get a familiar voice on the end of the phone.

"I've been wondering how you were getting along, Dave," said the voice.

"Sorry I didn't leave a forwarding address. Things got too busy around the time Connie got ill. I never stopped to think," he explained apologetically.

"Oh, well. That's life, isn't it?"

"Yes," he said, thinking, "that's life."

Unable to keep this courteous banter going any longer, he sat bolt upright in his chair.

"Look Norman, I've got to see you. Something's happened."

"What sort of thing?" Norman asked. "Are you in any trouble?"

"Not in the normal sense," he said, "but I think I might be if I don't get to see you."

"Right," said Norman, thinking how he could fit him into his hectic world, "meet me here at seven-thirty."

"What, not at Saxenby?"

There was panic in his tone.

"Okay, not here then," said Norman picking up on the unease in his voice. "I'm meeting someone at nine this evening at Newark. Meet me on the road by the side of the College. There's always parking there. See you at eight. How's that?"

"That's fine. Thanks Norman."

A feeling made up of relief and self-respect, that he had the sense to ask for help, calmed his mind like a balm. In this frame of mind he managed to cope with the afternoon.

By seven-fifteen he was sitting in his car along the leafy Bede House Lane, a tranquil side street between a walled park on the left and the west wing of the old college building on his right. Norman had not made it there yet, but it was still early, so he waited, turning now and again to make sure that the album and the prints of the reflected face were within reach. Banal love songs on the radio wove their stories of lust, heartbreak and devotion until he could stand no more. He put Radio 4 on just so that he could listen to people talking. It lulled him. Suddenly, as if a guided missile had hit his side window, he jumped out of his skin with fright. Norman was tapping on it to say he had arrived. David motioned for his friend to come round to the passenger side. His heart rate had calmed a little by the time Norman joined him, though his face, still affected by the scare, amplified his state of mind. Norman looked back, concerned.

"Don't bother with pleasantries, Dave, just tell me what the matter is."

Glad to get on with it, but surprised at his directness, David explained everything that had happened to him, since they said their last goodbye. Norman knew Connie a little, but as the tale unfolded about Mr Tulip, the trip to Salisbury and how he got the album back, he became quiet and listened as only Norman the professional could, reading everything said between the lines.

"Do you remember The Miller's Drop, that pub in Great Rembleton?"

"How could I forget it? Awful food, as I recall."

"Do you remember the experiment we carried out in the beer garden?" David said, forging ahead with his story.

"Oh, the reflections. Yes, I remember doing that. I was the photographer, or was that you? I can't recall now who was who?"

"Well it hardly matters, the fact is, well see for yourself."

He reached over to the back seat and grabbed the old album, opening it up to the picture of Lotty and Danno with Ellie smiling back.

"See that old window? What do you see?"

"Well, I'll be blowed," he said squinting to make out the blurred shape hidden in the glass. "it looks like a face," then understanding, he said. "So that's Mr Miller."

"Huh, you ain't seen nothing yet," said David. "I've had that reflection digitally enlarged at work. Take a look at that."

He pulled out the copy that Queenie had run off.

"Fuck me!" he shrieked spontaneously. "It's you."

"Now you know why I wanted to see you. You know what this means, don't you?"

Norman began to run along the same path that David had already trodden, catching up. David could see the goose pimples rise up on Norman's arms as he came to the identical conclusion.

"Your mother must have thought a reincarnation had happened," he said piecing it all together.

"Oh, how glad I am to hear you say that," he said. "It explains such a lot, don't you think? She was mentally broken, wasn't she? I know just how much she loved Miller, because I was Miller. For me to look exactly like him, well, it must have been too much for her to bear. What do you reckon?"

"I'm with you," said Norman, trying to go a few more paces ahead. "But I think she knew about the reflection too, I'm sure of it. Why else would she have hung on to her wedding album, and kept all these pictures of a husband she did not love?"

"She did enjoy showing me pictures of my relatives, but this was her favourite photograph, our favourite. We both loved looking at it. For me it was Ellie's smile but I think you are right, she must have noticed the face in the window too. She must have seen a tiny trace of Miller's features every time she looked at this page. I suppose it was the only picture she had of him."

Then something fluttered lightly into his memory, a connection.

"She once kept a picture of a lover hidden in a barn you know, a woodsman, her fiancé. He was called David too. Disappeared he did."

Closing the book gently, Norman was handing the album back to his friend when something brown slipped out of the back cover and flopped onto David's lap.

"Wait a mo, what's that?" Norman said, reaching over and picking it up.

"Good God, I'd completely forgotten all about that," said David, as a memory of Ratty Littlebody brought to mind the awful end to his twenty-first birthday party. "I suppose the time has come to look at that, hasn't it?" he said, trying to hide his surprise and looking for a sense of permission in his friend's face.

"It has, but only if that's what you want?" Norman said, trying in vain to hide his own curiosity.

After being sealed for so long the envelope deserved to have been opened with a letter knife. Instead he used his car keys to do the job, which, despite his care, left a rather jagged rip, and spoiled its pristine antiquity. He removed the bleached white paper inside, and opened it out to reveal its typewritten message.

In the end, there was little to get excited about. It was addressed to him, David Harper, The Croft, Main Street, Edlington, Notts. It was dated May, nineteen seventy-seven. Then in a single sentence it invited him to contact Mr Littlebody's secretary at the above address to discuss the will of the late Mrs Charlotte Harper, and that was it. No mystery, no fearful voice from beyond the grave. It was just a chance to meet with another bunch of solicitors and talk about probate. He gave the letter to Norman who looked back and shrugged his shoulders.

"Is that it?"

David upturned the envelope and gave it a shake, "Yep, that's it."

"And will you go?"

"Why not?" said David, making the answer sound more like a decision.

"Are you sure you're ready to look into this?" Norman said, waving the letter as if it were evidence. "This might be nothing more than a key to a door, but beyond that, there's where mysteries lay."

"What kind of mysteries do you suppose?" David asked.

"Well, they wouldn't be a mysteries if I knew that," Norman said, smiling.

David's face broke into a grin, finding the exchange between them comforting.

"Would you like to find out too?"

"Oh, you must tell me when you find out. Definitely, I'd love to know what happens," his friend replied.

"No, I didn't mean that. How about coming with me? I know you're as intrigued as I am?"

"But the letter, it's addressed to you, only you."

"It doesn't say I can't bring a friend, does it?"

"No, but are you sure? This is private stuff."

"There's nothing private between you and I. It was you who mended me from the inside unless you've forgotten?"

"All right then. You let me know when you've fixed up a date, and I'll come. Just try and make it out of work hours, will you?"

"That suits me too," he said, convinced that now all was well.

Norman got out of the car, said goodbye and walked off to his meeting in town. A date David assumed. With that he drove off, safe in the feeling that his life was not careering towards another Dark Age as he had begun to fear.

Chapter seven: Getting Out

He knew it had taken some nerve to get this far. All that remained was the gravel drive that led to the car park. Little had changed, apart from obvious modernisation features like CCTV and state-of-the-art traffic lights. Fewer trees made everywhere look bare and in keeping with such progress most of the shops had plastered the twenty-first century over the architecture of the eighteenth. Coming down the hill that he had once pushed a bicycle up many years before, he was surprised to find that three of them had gone. Two chimneys, shiny steel ones had replaced the five fingers. In a state of disquiet he realised that he had outlived them all.

What a strange location, he thought to himself as he pulled into the drive. He could see attractive town houses on one side of the road, tombstones on the other. Never more so than here was there such a community of both the quick and the dead. He passed beneath an ornate stone arch on top of which was built a prominent slender spire. Beyond it was the car park, empty, save for an unoccupied blue Volvo. Without waiting for the right time to arrive he was out and walking up the cinder track. He only had a faint, vague notion of where to go. So much wasted time had passed he wondered if it was going to be an impossible task, but he went up and down the rows of stones, reading each one and wondering, albeit briefly, what kind of lives these people had once had.

He had purposely come here on a quiet Saturday morning so as to be assured privacy. Five hundred yards away, possibly more, a lone figure was crouching, making little stabbing movements with a hand tool. The owner of the Volvo he assumed. The figure had brought flowers. He had brought nothing, well nothing physical at any rate. He had brought himself, which was miracle enough. On he went with small steps, sauntering almost, until he was brought to a dead stop. Now he knew nerves, for there she was. He felt sick, as if coming here had been lunacy. Why it also felt right he could not understand, except he knew that standing here was the correct thing to do. He believed it was right ever since he had made his mind up to come, but now he felt unsure about the decision. There she was. Or there the stone was, timeworn and lifeless. Lifeless words carved on its surface sounded more like a docket of contents than a memorial to a person. There was Charlotte Harper.

He did not have to wonder what kind of life she had. He had seen more of it than most offspring ever saw of their parents. He had been part of both sides of her life. He knew he did not know everything, but some understanding had begun to grow out of the mess that her life had been. As he stood there, with the free breeze weaving through the gravestones, he knew that at the very least the hate had gone. What replaced it was chaotic, meaningless and pitiful but now she was dead and the only spark of her life that remained was now standing right above her dead body.

The last time he stood on this spot he was just a boy. He was able to remember willing a heavy box of secrets to lower itself into the ground as the coffin had sunk into the hole. Now the secrets had found their way out. There was no box down there anymore, just a body, just someone who had had enough of life. He was crouching now, kneeling on one leg, as if he were accepting a knighthood. The worn letters carved in the stone were closer. He could see how the years had aged their definition. It was symbolic of how he had aged too. Gone was the boy. It was as if he had died too, the boy. Only David Harper the man was left. Even his childhood memories, evoked by this moment, failed to render the child within him to emerge. They were like films he had once seen. He knew his imagination could make her speak to him again, a product of his creative mind. He could if he wanted make her sing *Yankee Doodle Dandy* if he wanted. It was all a trick.

So, now, how could she have control over him? She was dead. He was alive. It was possible to see things in a clearer light. When he thought of her crying in Beckett's Wood, on the day he found her in the undergrowth, with her wellington boots and pretty dress, he felt so sorry for her lying beneath his feet. Somehow, from being a young carefree girl, she had been systematically destroyed and, though he never regretted running away to find Ellie that Saturday morning, he knew he had played a small part in her destruction too. Had things been different he was sure she would have been a lovely mum - but she had not been. There was no point pretending otherwise. He thought of the birthday card, the wooden spoon, the special cuddle and he sank beneath the sadness of it all. He had spent much of his life thinking he was one of life's victims. With crystal clarity he realised that she had been one too - a victim, a victim of Danno and all the other men who had used her. Now there she lay, her lifeless body crumbling away.

Had he not already known what it was like to experience the end of the world, he would not have possessed the compassion he now felt for her. He got to his feet and looked around him. The Volvo man had gone. They were alone. Everywhere there were ornate monuments to loved ones - fathers, mothers, even children. Some were works of art, beautiful and yet, despite their intricate craftsmanship, they seemed like poor reflections of the human stories of love and grief that had once been directed towards the person now lying beneath their architecture. His mother's was pitiful in comparison. A rectangular slab created so on his instruction. Without a great deal of soul searching he decided to get her a new one. It would be to his Lotty and to the mum who might have been, and that was it. He retraced his steps back to the car, counting the monuments and rows so that he would be able to find it again. A sense of relief greater than he expected told him that more than a visit to a cemetery was behind him now.

Days later, from his office, he called the number on the letter, an act of idiotic curiosity, knowing full well that it was out of date. He tried putting a six and a five in front, and next a six and a seven, the two numbers that had been added to the four digit phone numbers of the seventies, but nothing. There was not even a Sturman and Kleaps in the phone book, neither in the yellow pages. So from the directory he picked a law firm at random, one that looked as if it had been long established and put a call in to them. The young receptionist, clearly disinterested in local history, said that she had never heard of the company he was looking for, sorry. Before he had chance to ask if he could speak to one of the partners he was cut off.

Her indignant attitude forced him to contemplate trying the town library and looking up old newspaper archives in the hope of finding a takeover story, or a bankruptcy, or a merger. It would mean starting from nineteen seventy-seven, a daunting task involving sifting through decades of local news in the forlorn hope of finding a titbit. By comparison his first idea to call up every solicitor in town beckoned irresistibly with simplistic merit. The phone was ringing out before he had chance to consider anything else, ringing out to a firm called Barkers. An older lady's voice answered, professional and gracious, a tone swollen with unabashed femininity.

"Oh, of course I remember them. I started there as a girl," she answered, taking him by surprise with her openness. "Stinkbomb and Creeps, they were known as," she continued.

Her voice was low and husky, well mannered and deeply attractive.

"Ah, well that's a good start," he said, somewhat nervously. "I'm trying to tie up some old family business. I'm looking for a Mr Littlebody. Do you know where I can find him?"

"Not exactly," she said playfully. "I'm not all that familiar with the cemetery," she went on with a wicked chuckle.

"But you knew him though?"

"Who, Ratbody? Everyone in those days knew him. He was one of the creeps in Stinkbomb and Creeps. Big churchgoer, liked choirboys if you understand, got found out and killed himself with a shotgun as the police arrived to arrest him."

David could feel his skin turn to goose flesh on hearing this. In his mind's eye, he could see him chewing his food like a rodent. When he imagined how it might have been for the children, he felt queasy in the pit of his stomach. That kind of thing was all too close to home to be passed off with mere disgust.

"So what happened to the firm?" David pressed on.

"S&K? We're them now. Following Mr Littlebody's funeral, other things came to light. It's all old hat now, save to say that Sturman fell out with Kleaps over it all and we were in the right place at the right time."

"You still have all the old files though," he asked, worried that he had reached a dead end.

"We're obliged to, sir," she said.

There was some relief that, unlike most things in his life, this outcome had been easier than he could ever have expected.

"In that case then, I need to make an appointment to see you," he said feeling as if he had hit the jackpot. "It'll have to be out of office hours. I'm always too busy during the day."

"I'm sure that can be arranged."

He heard the plastic rattling of keys on a computer keyboard being fingered.

"How about a week today, six thirty?"

"Fine," he said, glad that his search had borne fruit.

There was a silence, a pregnant pause, as he waited for her to say something.

"Ought I know who you are, sir?" she said, with an air that passed for quiet sarcasm.

"Sorry. David Harper," and he gave his mobile number, just in case.

"Very well, Mr Harper. We'll see you next week. Perhaps you would wish to bring some form of identification, driving licence for instance. Well, goodbye for now."

"Goodbye," he said, hardly able to hide his Christmas Eve excitement.

He was going to have to endure a whole week's waiting.

There was a need to do something bright and enjoyable when he arrived back at the flat that evening. Alongside his curiosity in the past, his past, there existed a warning, a quiet almost undetectable alarm ringing in his head. He knew not to ignore its message, the Morse code tapping in his head that knew when he was becoming obsessed by something. It was saying that there was more to life and straightaway he knew it was right. There were also dangers in poking his nose into his own history - dangers to his mind that until just recently had been a wreck on the rocks. He knew what was missing. It was Ellie most of all, but that was only part of it. Missing Ellie was just one piece of a jigsaw of a larger picture of loneliness. He needed to get out more, to mix with other people. What was so wrong with wanting to be liked? He sat down in his chair after plugging in his dead mobile and let this feeling run to its final conclusion. He wanted to be loved, that was it. What was wrong with that? Was it too much to ask?

He flicked the TV on and wondered what there was in the fridge to eat. After the news bulletin had bored him he went channel hopping. The Simpsons were an irritation, as was the house makeover show. With a final click of the remote he discovered a war film. Its out of date propagandist message got on his nerves too, so with a directive from his thumb on the plastic box of tricks, the screen went dead. He was bored. It was not until after he had eaten that he noticed his mobile had received a text. Its little beep must have been drowned out by the television. It was from Norman. In his own version of text-speak he wanted to know how David had got on. *Owbout drink 2nite. Givsa call*, it said cryptically at the end. David unplugged the mobile and heard Norman's voice after just one ring. It turned out that Norman was bored too. His date had been a disaster and he wanted some company. After a few suggestions of

499

where to rendezvous it was decided that Southwell was a good place for both of them. With self-imposed fastidiousness, he cleaned up, washed his dishes, had a shower and left. At least he could be bored in like-minded company, he thought as he drove off.

David did not say anything about his trip to the cemetery. Instead, in the smoky and cacophonous cosiness of the Saracen's Head, he brought Norman up to speed on his solicitor soliciting, explaining that he had secured an interview with Barkers. As agreed Norman said he would accompany him, writing the time and place of the arranged meeting on the back of his hand, where a number of other messages in various stages of faded appearance were already written. David could see that his friend was not completely with it, his mind seemed preoccupied. Now and then, during their conversation, he would lose himself in thought, staring straight ahead before realising what he was doing and, without explanation or apology resuming their talk. In the end, something had to be said.

The paradox was not lost on Norman, who grinned at being asked if he was all right by a former patient, but he was glad to be given the chance to get whatever it was off his chest. Helen, it seemed, had become engaged. She had asked to meet him in Newark on the day he met David beside the college. She told him that she had something important to say to him. He naturally took the wrong end of the stick and like a lamb to the slaughter had gone to receive the wonderful news personally. He was magnanimous in his congratulations of course. His ingrained English upbringing forced no other response from him, but when they said their final goodbye, he found he had been dumped in a world where all his hopes had been dashed. It was not until then that he fully realised just how much he had loved her. Now the torch he had long held for her had become a burden and he was left desolate. In typical understatement he told David that he was just plain fed up. His drinking partner expressed condolences, as if there had been a death, telling him how sorry he was for him, going on to say that he felt he understood. He too was citing the loss of his Ellie as the main reason for feeling disconsolate.

"You know, I ought to get out more, meet new people," said Norman, pondering his own situation, "and so should you, come to think of it," he went on. "You can't live in the past, you know."

500

"And the present is such a wonderful place to be," he observed dryly.

"This is all there is," Norman reflected. "There's a future out there somewhere for both of us, no matter what our pasts may be," and he cocked a winking eye at his friend. "Aye, and no matter how many pasts there may be for some of us," he added.

"Ah, maybe you're right. Maybe I should hold a few more soirees on my yacht, don't you know old boy."

"You may laugh," said Norman. "Just make sure you don't become a hermit in that flat of yours. It's bad for you. Promise?"

"I guess so," he said.

The following day as if in answer to an unsaid prayer, a top-of-the-morning meeting in Ian's office was called. Ian welcomed them all in, the whole team. His mood was expansive, his stature magnified. Something had happened and it was not bad, everyone could tell.

"Everybody here?" Ian said, making a quick head count and waiting for quiet to descend. "Well," he announced with a great flourish, "it looks like we're in," he went on, waving a piece of paper in his hand. "This e-mail means the big time folks."

The room began to hum quietly. Sensing the need for more theatrics, he tossed the email on the desk and lifted a large cool box from underneath it. Grinning like an exultant pirate he opened the lid of his treasure chest and handed out big bars, not of gold, but of chocolate. The brand was not lost on those present.

"You all know the company we've been chasing, well now it's truly in our grasp. This is a big day for us. To have pulled this off is a real victory over the London boys," he said, every word infused with honest emotion and unbridled elation. "This has been a team effort all the way down the line and I'm proud of each and everyone of you."

Now the room was in turmoil. Scenes reminiscent of NASA's mission control after a successful event were played out in that small office - hugging, kissing and backslapping, handshakes exchanged, tears of joy. The room was a crucible of delight. David caught a glimpse of Ian from across the heads of people going mad. Their unspoken exchange said it all. They had come a long way since their days in the choir, many twists and turns. It had been a tough road but

501

the camaraderie was no less diminished because of it. A million thoughts passed from eye to eye. It was a good moment to be alive.

"Okay, okay," yelled Ian, reluctantly disrupting the flow of celebration. "We're going out to mark this auspicious occasion," he went on, with a laugh in his voice. "Friday night, we'll finish early, give everyone a chance to get off home to change and be back here by seven. Grace I know has a wedding to go to, which is a shame, but as for the rest of us, it's party time. We're all going clubbing."

Although he smiled, and his face made all the right shapes, inside David felt terrified at the prospect of venturing into this alien world. The worst of it was he had no choice. He was trapped, caught up in everyone's momentum, in the stampede. It would look awful if he were to pull out of going, everyone else was ecstatic at the idea but he knew this was not for him. From that instant he began to dread Friday. What terrible things would happen to him there he could not begin to imagine. He had never been to a club and what he had heard about them through rumours had made him afraid. He would be forced to participate in all kinds of things, but what else could he do? How would he get through it all without being found out? Queenie said that she could not wait to get him on the dance floor. David was not sure if she meant it or whether she was mocking his shyness. Either way, the good news upon which the morning had begun had now been poisoned. He would have to grit his teeth and bear it as best he could. He tried to concentrate on what he would be doing on Saturday morning. Saturday morning, that is what he would hang on to, when the whole ghastly ordeal would finally be behind him.

Without realising it he had begun to withdraw into himself. His normal cheeriness, that had now become a way of life in the work place, could be seen shrinking away, until by Friday morning it had vanished altogether. Unconsciously he had retreated to his own office, avoiding any idle talk with colleagues, lest they should mention the night out to come. It was fortunate for David that the team was too busy to notice his odd behaviour. As the afternoon shadows grew to herald the approach of evening, he held on to his nerve as good as if he were at the top of a white-knuckle ride. With his heart pounding in his ribcage he cursed Norman's suggestion that he should get out more.

As he changed and dressed into his casual gear, the loneliness of his flat beckoned him not to go, seducing him with its TV and cosy warmth, but even the legs of a man walking to the gallows propel him there and soon he was back at work waiting with his colleagues for the mini cab to arrive.

Sitting quietly in the back of the vehicle he tried to square the person he had once been, the person who had once enjoyed the environment of noisy pubs. Memories of his days at Saltbys when he frequented the Elizabethan, those times spent drinking there had never held any fear for him. Perhaps it was the meat market notion of the club scene that terrified him, the rawness of the humanity there, the unbridled goings on.

The trip across town was a short one. As the streets passed by and he listened to his colleagues revving up their spirits, he realised that it was the great unknown that was bothering him. He had changed since his time in Saxenby. He knew it. There was no point pretending otherwise. Any ingrained response that he may once have taken for granted could no longer be guaranteed. Just how would he react to being in a den of wanton gratification, crammed with wall-to-wall lust and depravation? He could no longer predict how things like this would affect him. It was that notion, more than anything else that truly frightened him. It was not the club he feared so much as himself, his post hospital self. All too soon, the cab stopped and they were all making their way down an alley hidden away in the seedy nightlife of Nottingham's city centre.

As the queue for the club came into view he climbed into a submarine of the mind. Inside he felt safe, safe enough to enter these depths without it really touching him personally. Through a periscope he would observe and move within its waters but never allow a leak from it to contaminate his world within. A member of his team, one of the designers, Joseph, a tall man, shouted something about the Inca party to one of the beefcake bouncers at the door. Like an abattoir worker in a black suit, he carved a break in the line of waiting hopefuls, using the weight of his bulky authority, and then, without so much as a hint of a smile, he nodded down the steps to the smoky void below. Down they went, one by one, with David somewhere in the middle, down, down to an engine room where a monstrous sound

503

like the rhythmic, dull boom of giant steam pistons passed for music. Down he went, David, down to periscope depth until he was completely submerged in it. Down in this sea there were creatures he had never imagined.

The underground room, a large cellar, was dimly lit. There seemed to be a bar at the far end. It was hard to tell. Through the darkness, the smoke and the heaving mass of people it was hard to see anything at all. Victoria, Queenie, tried to say something to him, yelling at full bore. She was smiling, having fun. There was no way he could hear her. So she took him by the arm and pulled hard, leading him through the bodies that were constantly bobbing up and down to the naked electronic beat. She behaved like a kind of Livingstone, pressing on through this *Dark Continent*, until she had reached her own Victoria Falls, the bar. He shrugged his shoulders at her inaudible question, so she yelled at the scantily clad barmaid, who managed to lip read her request and pulled two bottles from a glass-fronted cabinet. Queenie took hold of them and passed one to David. It was too dark to read the label. So raising it up to wish good health, and propagate the pretence of hedonism, he put it to his lips and drank the potent brew down in one, just as Queenie had.

Back near the stairs, close to the door, he caught a faint glimpse of some of their friends. They were pointing at someone close to them. Straining his eyes he saw that Ian had arrived. He had mentioned getting there late but he made it in perfect time. His team were now primed. They had been given cause and the means to celebrate and nothing was going to change their mood. Even now he was holding out his arms to them, inviting hugs from all his people. He looked like the Messiah, a small god, almost lost in the darkness.

David's attention to these events had been so complete he had not noticed the small, delicate hand holding his. She mouthed some words but by now his eardrums had become useless. So she began to move about, rhythmically up and down with the jam-packed mass. Bending his knees in like fashion he joined in, knowing how foolish it all looked. He imagined what the scene would look like if the room was suddenly to be emptied - in isolation it would be ridiculous. Even now he felt it. Dancing? This was not dancing, this was knee exercise, but then the scene before him altered his opinion about this. In the dim light, through the smoke, amongst the body heat Queenie was performing. Her body moved in the confined space with a sensual grace that possessed a touch of the exotic. Hers were carnal movements, wonderful swishes of her hips, her hands describing with flowing fingers the shape of her womanly body. She caught him looking and, instead of stopping and taking offence, she playfully bit her bottom lip, smiled and exaggerated what she was already doing. Doing it just for him, it seemed.

How to respond, he thought, gulping with nerves. How to get away from what was happening? He was trapped. Queenie lowered the angle of her head as she danced and lifted her gaze up to him. Even in the dark he could see that she was playing with him. He tried to look elsewhere, tried to be nonchalant, but all around there were couples. Their writhing bodies slithering across each other, their lips rolling around in kissing frenzies. Suddenly the outward pressure on his submarine was beginning to make the sides crack, crushing him. Without warning, Queenie took his hands and placed them around her waist. She drew herself closer to him. The strange musical beat by now had begun to take hold, it was mesmerising, trance inducing. The girl's body was now pressed up against his. Was all this serious? How much of this was fun? How should he respond? She was now sliding up and down him, fingertips tracing the shape of his chest. Everyone else seemed to be doing the same sort of thing, but all he could do was bob up and down and hold on to her waistline for dear life. The smile was wearing thin.

Then the cavalry came over the hill. Ian had managed to cut through the great body barrier, along with the rest of the team and another round of drinks was shouted. Whatever had been going on between him and Queenie had gone. It had become part of the smoky atmosphere and, even though he still felt as if he was in the very heart of an industrial reaction of sexual chemistry, he knew for the time being that the molecules had left him alone.

The night passed by, for David it dragged. He was as bored here as he would have been at home. The drink was beginning to affect him, he knew it, but he did not feel any different. He was trying to make out what the beaming face of Ian was saying to him, when he became aware of a soft hand on his shoulder. Turning round to see who was

505

trying to get his attention he came face to face with a woman of staggering beauty. She was dressed in white, a loose fitting garment that was made to cover as little of her body as possible. Behind her he could make out three or four women looking on, sharing glances with each other. The woman, the beauty, lifted her slender arms and draped them over his shoulders. He was aware of his friends, whooping and shouting in glee and then her mouth met his, soft and warm, moving around his own, alive and charged with energy. If this was kissing then he had never been kissed properly in his life, not in this life anyway. She was a consummate expert and David could hold on to his reserve no longer. He held her soft hair in his hands and smothered her back. He was lost, descending into God knows where, letting go. Whatever happened next would be out of his control, and then, as suddenly as it had begun, she stopped and turned back to her friends behind her. They were laughing, giggling hysterically as she rejoined them. Now back in the bosom of her girlfriends, she managed a backward glance, blew him a kiss and melted onto the dark mass of bodies. He turned to look at Ian who was beaming approval. How could something so intensely personal and wonderful have come and gone so quickly. There was a part of him that had begun to fall in love. He wanted her to come back. Ian pointed to his empty bottle and gestured that it was his round. Even as he yelled his order over the bar, he could not get the woman out of his mind.

The night crossed the divide to morning without anyone noticing, except him. The barrage of sound from the hefty speakers ripped the air asunder, turning drumbeats into endless sonic booms that thumped repeatedly with the power of sledgehammers into his chest. He thought of Saturday's dawning, the day of salvation, willing the time to pass. The night had not been kind to Queenie either. All the worse for drink, her dancing had become a shambles. Only in her own head did she view her movements as graceful. Even the hysterical screeching of her friends' laughter at her antics did nothing to alter her belief that she was a star on the floor.

Leaving her, he carved a way through the compressed mass of shoulders and arrived at the toilets ten minutes later. The air was cooler there, a relief, with room to breathe. His ears were ringing loudly as if a constant tuning fork had been placed inside his brain. It explained why he did not hear it at first, the knocking and groaning coming from the confines of a cubicle. Two voices seemingly linked in pain. It was hard to tell if this was a fight, but then he could distinguish a female voice, making all the breathless noise of childbirth. Only it was not a baby coming out that was making her yell so, but rather something forcing its way in. It was hard to take a pee whilst this was going on, especially when two other men staggered in, becoming vocally amused at the shagging couple in the bogs. How awful he thought, how unbeautiful. His mind ran back to The Beckett, back to a time when he had been picking mushrooms in the quiet of the dense wood. His hunger for Lotty, just his Lotty, ached in him so badly. He felt sorry for the drunken sod ramming his senseless girl in such a squalid place, straddling the cistern of a crappy shithouse, in the depths of a Nottingham cellar.

Following the call of duty he made it back to his party. Queenie had been crying. It was only when she saw David return that she stopped. Her perception of his absence was wrong, as was her notion of why he came back. With uncoordinated exaggeration, she slithered up to him and wrapped her arms about his neck. In an instant, her tear-drenched lips met his, a taste mixed with alcoholic breath, tinged with burned tobacco. The force of her attempt was brutish and rough - nothing like he assumed it would be if she were sober. She was using him, using his lips, his manliness and his nature. It dawned on him that the previous girl had done it for a bet or just for a laugh. This would have been fine, so long as it remained divorced from finer feelings, but he had a sense of what romance should be and this to him was all wrong.

He had had enough, enough of being used. The submarine had gone beyond its critical depth and water was pouring in under high pressure. The klaxon was blaring its warning - surface, surface, surface. Trying not to panic he ripped Queenie's arms away. Her rolling eyes looked outraged. Without giving any reason he pushed away, away from them all, heaved and shoved his way through the throng and emerged into the night air. He stood on the pavement and breathed in the coolness, cursing the mass of urban bricks all around.

Cities he thought, how he hated them, but the fresh air calmed his cheeks and refreshed his lungs. As he took another delicious breath he became aware of a pair of delicate arms coiling round his waist. She had followed him and he cursed again because he had not kept on walking.

"What's wrong?" she cooed, her immaturity magnified by her state of inebriation.

"I'm getting a taxi home. You go back. I'm tired," he said, gently taking her arms from around him. He turned to see a face visibly upset, half-lit by the sodium-yellow street lamp.

"What did I do that was so bad?" she said, holding back a build-up of distress.

"Nothing. You did nothing wrong. It's me, that's all."

She wiped her eyes, though no tears had come.

"Why, what's up?"

"Nothing. Just go back. I'll see you on Monday."

"I think I want to go home too. How about we share a taxi?"

"What about everyone else. You'll be missed."

"Coreen and Dan have left together."

"They did?"

"Yeah. And no one's missed them, have they? So come on sad boy, take me home."

He did not want this but she was determined. In no time she flipped her mobile phone open and was chatting to a taxi firm, who gave her a booking for fifteen minutes. His ears whistled with a high whine like the hiss of escaping gas and he felt uncomfortable - unsure if the reason for this was because she was irritating him, or whether the tiredness was making him feel unwell. Home and bed beckoned like far off sirens luring him to a land of rest.

"You've got something on your mind," she said. "I can tell."

"We've all got things on our minds," he said, trying to out fox her and trying not to lead her to the place his mind had gone.

"Ah, but this isn't normal stuff, is it?" she said.

He did not answer and he knew straightaway from the glint in her eye that his silence had given him away.

"Hey, you've not got someone pregnant, have you?" she said, thinking of the only drastic scenario in her limited itinerary of disasters.

As he listened to her he stopped to think. She had actually got it spot on. Fifty years ago, he had got his Lotty pregnant and the life he was living at this moment was the result of it. What a mess it had all become. Knowing the facts did not really help, it just explained. Had it not been for Danno, the mysterious father figure in this life and the cruellest bastard he had ever known, he would have been able to stay in Empton and look after Lotty and the baby. He was fed up to the back teeth of thinking round and round in circles like this. It was all he could do to stop himself falling over the abyss and back into the darkness - the pain of a mountaineer hanging over a precipice by his fingernails. What was better to suffer the agony and live, or to let go the painful grip and die? It took no time to think all this and, when he turned to look at Queenie's face, she was wide-eyed at her hunch being right. He would have to tell her, tell her the incredible truth.

Chapter eight: Out And About

He picked up on the atmosphere the minute he walked into the office. This was no Monday morning quietness or the malaise from an overindulgent weekend. The silence was tangible, man-made and quite deliberate. Something was wrong. Each avoided contact as he eyed them one by one and, he knew, after just a few had done this, that the hush was directed straight at him. Queenie was conspicuous by her absence. He knew from previous conversations with her that there was another fortnight to go before she jetted off to Greece for ten days. Unable to think why she was not there, he dismissed the question and wondered instead why he was given the ticket to Coventry.

The whole morning passed this way. Several times he thought about saying something, anything to force it out into the open. In the end he did not have to. As Ian arrived he searched David out and, without so much as a smile, he yanked his head in the direction of his office and strode in with a purpose. David dropped what he was doing and followed him in as the sound of the whispering gossip began in his wake.

Ian beheld his friend and tried to figure out how to broach the subject. Unable to find the words he reached into his jacket pocket and took out his mobile phone. In a flash his thumbs had made manifest a message received during Sunday and handed it over to David who was clearly in a state of confusion. It was from Queenie. The gist of it was that David was a weirdo who had scared her to death with awful tales about fucking his mother and getting her pregnant. She explained that she had been in fear of being raped herself when he told her his childhood tales about what his mother got up to. David read on, learning that he had been described as a nutter who had talked about time travel and being hypnotised and being his own dad.

"She's texted everyone, everyone," said Ian, more annoyed than sympathetic. "They all think you're a fucking loony."

David was just about to read the distorted facts again, when Ian took his phone off him and flung it back in his pocket.

"I can't have this kind of aggravation in my company, you know?" Ian continued. "It's not acceptable. That poor girl is scared to come into work because she thinks you are some kind of pervert."

David, reeling from these words, struggled to find words of his own.

"I'm a team member down thanks to you," Ian went on. "What did you have to go and tell her things like that for?"

"I went outside to get some air," explained David. "She thought I looked upset and kept asking me why," he went on, unable to reconcile the events of Friday night and Saturday morning with the chilling details crawling out of this conversation.

"Look, I've told you about my dad, and you've told me about your mum. You had a bad time growing up, but you came through it. We both did. So why in God's name make up all this bullshit about? What did she say, time travel, and having it away with your mother and fathering yourself? What the bloody hell's that all about?"

David's edited and abridged version of his own history, the version that he had peddled during his initial interview, had not touched on the nature of the therapy that was used to help him. Of course Ian knew about his time in hospital but was satisfied with all but the simplest of accounts about the gentle counselling he had received. David failed to mention any hypnotherapy and had blurred the truth with a foggy picture of psychiatric help mingled with rest and recuperation.

Self-preservation, the strongest of conditions, began to ooze through his being as if released by a gland. Rewinding the words that had escaped his mouth, he searched to see if there was anything he had said so far that would incriminate him in any of this. Satisfied that there was not, he began to weave.

"I took her home, that's all. She was out of it. You saw her falling all over the place trying to dance," said David. "She spent most of the way home talking gibberish and trying not to puke."

"And the stuff about you and your mother, all that mumbo-jumbo, where did all that come from?"

"Look, I'll admit to being depressed on Friday night. It ought to have been a night of feeling good but sometimes these things from the past can creep up on me. So I decided to get out for some air. I just wanted to be on my own. Call it self-pity if you like. That's about all I'm guilty of. I blame the drink. It brings out the melancholy in me."

"That still doesn't explain the time travel bit," said Ian.

"Okay, so I should have kept what my mother did to me as a child to myself. I didn't. I told her how she raped me when I was little. You can see how someone completely pissed could interpret that. As for time machines, well, I've known some drunks who think they can fly."

"You didn't try anything on with her, you know, in the cab or when you took her home?"

"Certainly not. I stayed in the cab as she stumbled up to her front door. She probably crawled to the toilet and spent the rest of the day examining the porcelain."

"You've not upset her in any way then? I mean this isn't some kind of revenge, is it?"

"You saw her kissing me in the club. Do you think she'd have done that if she hated me? Come on Ian, it was the bloody drink. People ought to see through that. Do you think I'm a weirdo time traveller?"

Ian's face smiled for the first time.

"You'd make a lousy *Doctor Who*," he said.

Ian called the rest of the team in and tried to explain the origin of Queenie's texts. He outlined David's past. It had not been divulged that he and David had been schoolboy pals for fear of favouritism spoiling the balance of team morale. The time had come to shed light upon David's childhood and, in the most delicate way, David heard him tell them about what his mother had been like and how he had spent time in hospital because of it.

As this was going on David's mind began to wander down the dirt track of his own memory lane. It stopped as it usually did at the feet on his mother. The chain of interlaced thoughts brought him to the photograph and it suddenly occurred to him that here was incriminating evidence. Ian was the only one in this room who could identify his mother by sight. If he was to find the picture of him on Queenie's computer, or worse still, if Queenie was to present it as evidence, what would Ian make of the fact that his own face appeared on his parent's wedding picture? The scan would have to be deleted. As his attention began to drift back to the assembled people the sympathy-ometer had begun to swing in David's favour. The train, it seemed, was pulling out of Coventry and was heading for the city of Welcomeback.

That night, on the pretext of catching up on some work, he stayed behind. Everyone left him to himself. The goodnights were slightly friendlier, in compensation for the frost of the morning. As he heard the last one shut the door he opened up the file on Queenie's machine, the one called wedding pic, and there it was, still there, innocently left for all to see. In a few seconds, he had printed off a final copy of the completed picture. It was an odd thing to do. It was as if he could not destroy the file without salvaging something beforehand. For whatever reason, the image was now on paper and folding it in four he slipped it in his suit pocket.

This small act made him wonder if he should destroy the file at all. He began to contemplate whether or not to use the software to airbrush the part of Miller's face out, but then questions would be asked about why he wanted a picture of his hated mother's wedding photo in the first place. No, it would have to go. In a few minutes all trace of it was gone and he was glad, at least, that he had a copy of it tucked away in his pocket. There was some satisfaction with the thought that only minds that were clever enough would now be able to delve down into its deepest memory. To all intents and purposes it was gone, the file name eradicated. Not the slightest detail that it ever existed on this computer at all. He sat back in Queenie's chair, a smug grin teasing the corner of his mouth, as memories of outwitting Joe Witherspoon ran through his head like an old movie.

As he waited, watching the machine shut down, he berated himself for having told Queenie the things he had. The trouble would begin when she came back to work. Hopefully, she would be discredited, but it would sour their relationship for good, which was a pity as he had enjoyed their friendship. It had all been a severe lesson. Henceforth, he declared to himself he would keep his pasts hidden.

Then suddenly he snapped out of his swirling thoughts. It was Monday evening. Five minutes to six according to the clock on the wall. At six-thirty he was supposed to be at the solicitors in Newark. He was supposed to be meeting Norman there. He had thirty-five minutes to make it. In an instant the computer was switched off and, like an athlete breaking away from the starting blocks, he was out of the building leaving the setting alarm bleeping behind him. He ran like hell to his car and sped out of the city like a maniac, as if a host of time demons were on his tail.

Neither Norman nor the lady with whom he had spoken to a week earlier seemed impressed at David's late arrival. As always Norman's stoicism prevented any show of disdain but the lady's demeanour, though never expressed verbally, was able to yell a torrent of abuse at him by just the angle of her eye and the tightening of her lips. Parking had been difficult so he had to run across town. His out of breath apologies did little to rekindle the warmth in Mrs Fenton's attitude. She was too insistent that matters be moved on quickly and soon both he and Norman were being ushered down corridors and up a flight of stairs to a small room. There she introduced them to a frail man in a midnight-blue pinstriped suit. This turned out to be Mr Barker Snr.

Mr Barker was the epitome of politeness, a graceful manliness, mixed with a conservative confidence and a bright intellect. David took to him in an instant, as the gentleman offered them both seats.

"I hope you'll forgive me," he said, rummaging through a thin cardboard wallet of papers, "but I have another engagement at seven-thirty."

"It's I who should be sorry," said David, explaining the parking problem.

"Well, we're all here now," he said taking out a piece of paper from the wallet, "Right then, I must first verify who you say you are. I take it that you can prove that you are Mr Harper, Mr David Harper, son of the late Charlotte Harper?"

"I've brought my driving licence and my latest gas bill. Will that do?"

"Normally, yes," began the senior Barker, "but in your case, I have to establish a direct link between you and Mrs Harper, formerly a client of Sturman and Kleaps."

"Oh, I can do that," he said, and presented the old letter from the firm of solicitors just mentioned. In doing so he felt the edge of a fresh piece of paper snuggling in his breast pocket, the wedding photograph.

"Would you like to see a picture of my mother?" he said.

Mr Barker did not hear his words. His attention was absorbed in the aged letter, taking in its antique contents, his mind partially lost in the wonder of the old museum piece. David unfolded the printout and pushed it forwards over the dark, polished surface of the desk. The eyes of the old man flicked over the top of Littlebody's letter, whereupon he put it down with deliberate care and picked up David's picture.

"So that's Daniel Harper," Mr Barker said, causing a look of shock to flash across David's features.

The old solicitor took in the face of Lotty.

"You take after your mother it would seem," he added.

"But," said David, taken aback, "how did you know his name, Daniel Harper I mean?"

"Ah well," began Mr Barker, calmly seizing on the surprise, "clairvoyance it isn't if that's what you're thinking," and thrusting his hand into the cardboard wallet he removed a piece of paper, folded in half. "Just a little matter of a birth certificate, yours to be precise."

He handed over the sheet bearing all of the details of how David had been flung into his weary life.

There was something unearthly about this most ordinary item of registration, but there it was, the name of his father, Daniel Harper. He read it several times before he could believe it. Even when he had satisfied himself that its existence in pen and ink was beyond doubt the question remained. Why Daniel Harper? He knew more than anyone who his real father was and he knew that his mother knew this too. He had hoped that here he would at least have learned the actual name of his dad, the name he had once been called back in Empton. He would have discovered, beyond the nickname, Mr Miller's true identity. For reasons best known to Lotty she had cited Danno as his dad. Indeed, she had perpetrated that very story all through his miserable childhood. So why had she done it? What reason had there been to lie to him as she did?

Elsewhere on the old document he saw his place of birth, Salisbury. The place name caused a tinge of sadness to sour his heart. Salisbury, it brought his beloved Ellie back to mind, his lost forever Ellie. It burned in the core of his being, especially when he looked up and caught sight of the wedding picture that Barker now placed on the desk. Even though it was upside down from his position on the other side, to him he could still see her smile, Ellie's smile. It was the smile he knew.

"Your mother made a will of sorts," said Barker, sifting through more papers. "She leaves all her worldly goods to you. They don't amount to much I'm afraid."

Barker stopped his flow of words and peered over his spectacles.

"There's a passage here that I don't quite understand," he went on. "She writes that you have a birthright, but she is frightened to pursue it for you. It appears to be some property reading between the lines. She mentions Arthur Gibson, her own father, and you own something of value that he once owned. It all seems shrouded in mystery. It seems that this Arthur Gibson has the key to it all, but she fails to say where it is."

Barker examined the accompanying letter once more.

"My father arranged things so that all would be well," read Barker verbatim, and continued, *"He gave the name of lawyers in Salisbury that I should contact if I got into trouble,"* Barker looked disappointedly at his new client. "I think she left your father in a hurry. She took great pains to remain anonymous. It would explain how she forgot the name of the law firm in Salisbury. I think it provides the reason why she chose Sturman & Kleaps to make her will," the silence that followed begged more explanation. "Sturman & Kleaps was a small firm, operating from Newark only. They didn't expand to other towns as some companies did. Only someone who didn't want to be found would choose a solicitor some fifteen miles away."

It was an odd sensation, being at an advantage over this well-educated man, thought David. He knew all the reasons why she had left Wiltshire in such a hurry and why anyone should want to steer clear of Danno Harper. Moreover, he already knew about Arthur Gibson, he had mended an old Fordson tractor that once belonged to him. It was obvious what property the Will was alluding to. It was Bofindle Farm, but what had Arthur done that would have arranged things? He remembered Lotty telling him that particular phrase once. He imagined her back then, too fearful of returning to that part of the world, as she allowed her life to sink into the mire and become corrupted into the existence it eventually became.

"It does seem to be incredible that Mr Littlebody was able to track you down at..." Barker looked back at the old letter that had lay hidden in the album for so long. "Ah here it is The Croft in Edlington. Quite remarkable."

"He was a family friend of my Aunt Ellie's husband, the late John Crampton. He was a vicar, vicar of Edlington you know," said David. "Littlebody was connected with him in the church somehow."

"Yes, well, the less said about Mr Littlebody and the church the better," said Barker with just a suggestion of disgust. "Enough about that has already been said."

He took a breath and squared up to David.

"Seems a bit of a coincidence though, this matter connecting up with you. It almost seems as if this letter had a mind of its own and was intent on tracking you down. Strange how all the connections have fitted together so neatly."

516

David thought for a moment before answering, thinking about his illness, Helen's hypnotherapy, Empton, and then Norman, who sat quietly throughout these proceedings. Without that connection he would not have met Connie, Mr Tulip. The album would not have been found, nor would the letter. Something was driving this forward, something invisible but powerful.

"There are times," began David, picking up the copy of the wedding picture, "when I wonder if I have a guardian angel."

Mr Barker sniffed in a way that suggested he thought things were now getting silly.

"Your mother left things in a bit of a muddle, Mr Harper," he said. "I don't want you to take this the wrong way, but I wonder if she was of a completely sound mind, considering…" he trawled through his thesaurus of diplomacy for a way to couch his thoughts, "considering the tragedy of what happened at the end."

"What happens next is the more interesting question," Norman mused, who up until now had been taking all this in with quiet amazement.

"Depends what you want to happen next. I presume you wish to take this further, in which case my firm's services are at your disposal," said Barker, adding that the usual terms would apply.

"We can't leave it like this, can we?" David said. "Not now that we've come this far."

The comment was directed at Mr Barker, but David's face was turned towards Norman, who understood the deep significance of the remark.

"Let's try to find the lawyers who acted for Mr Gibson in Salisbury," said Barker standing up and offering his hand. "With luck, they'll still be in business. Who knows?"

"Just trust in our guardian angel," said David, with the faintest trace of a smile tweaking the corners of his mouth, as he shook hands.

"Facts, Mr Harper," said Barker as he showed them to the door. "Let's put our faith in them first, shall we?"

With that they were down the stairs, past the forced smile of Mrs Fenton and out into the street. David did not know whether to be dispirited or euphoric. He was just glad that Norman had been there to hear it all with him. At least there was still a trail to follow. Where it would lead, well, he allowed it to dwell in the future, happy to be warmed by the anticipation that waiting was able to create.

Tuesday morning ushered itself in like millions of others before it. This one decided to be cold and damp. Nature had chosen a grey canvas on which to spread the sky, allowing drizzle to fall from its laden blanket. The lack of wind made David sense that the weather was exhausted with its task and had given up its dynamic being. The lethargy of the elements transferred to his soul the minute he opened the curtains. Even the radio, the ever-present companion at breakfast, failed to infuse him with brightness. In the end he dismissed the false bonhomie of the DJ and sat before the TV news instead, and even here there was depression, strife, wars and conflict. He could find genuine cheer nowhere. By the time he had washed, shaved, dressed and left for work he was in a low mood, a mood that was deepened by the oscillations of the flapping windscreen wipers. Any other animal would have had the good sense to curl up and sleep through days like this. Not man, oh no, he had to be forced out and made to brave it. By the time he walked into the office he had become morose. Wet through with depression. The last thing he wanted now was a day of troubles.

The presence of Queenie already at her workstation made even this supplication seem unlikely. He said good morning to everyone as he always did. A muffled mumbling of answers emerged from others who had also been brought low by the weather. Only Queenie remained silent. A white-hot stare aimed itself at him like a laser. He did not know how to react. Should he smile back, make a gesture like that? Should he return the scowl? Should he go over and say something, try to smooth things over and explain that he was drunk that night and was talking gibberish? Somehow, he was too tired to think it through, so he walked into the little kitchen area and made himself a cup of tea and took it with him to his office. Here the plod through the day would begin. Here there was peace and quiet, until that is Queenie stomped in and closed the door behind her.

"You're sick, you are," she spat, launching straight into her opinion of him. Her breathing was shallow and rapid.

"Am I indeed?" he replied, too tired to get into a row.

"You're sick in the fucking head, you are. You're a weirdo, that's what you are."

"Yes, so you say," he replied, unmoved.

"Sodding time travel. And all that shit about doing it with your mother. They ought to lock up men like you."

"Should they? Very interesting."

"I'm going to tell everyone that you're a bloody nutcase."

"You already have, haven't you?"

"Yes, and now you've gone to Ian and tried to discredit me. Well, I won't have it. By the time I've finished with you I'll..."

"You'll what?" He had had enough. "Look Victoria, You were pissed. I was pissed. I don't know what you're making such a fuss about. Even if I said all the things you say I did, so what? I'm allowed to talk crap when I've had a skinful aren't I?"

"I know when it's crap talk. You were crying when you talked about your childhood. And when you went on about the rapes in the night by your mother, you scared the shit out of me. So don't come it, your eyes were wild, you looked frightening."

"I didn't mean to put the fear of God into you," he said.

"Ah, so you admit you were saying all those things."

"I don't know what I was talking about. I lost count of how many of those bottles of that stuff I'd put away."

"You can't blame all of that on the drink. You were mentioning places that you were too familiar with, back in the fifties, before you were born."

"I'm familiar with lots of places," he said.

"Yeah, well I could have taken all that as the drink talking, but when you slid your fingers up my skirt, you went too far."

"Now come on Queenie. I did nothing of the sort. You know that."

"You tried to rape me," she began to shout.

"That's a load of bollocks," he said firmly. "You're making all this up. Now fuck off and get out of here."

"Bollocks, is it? Well, I know that you tried to rape me. Wait 'til the police hear about this. Ian will sack you then," she ranted.

"I think you'd better calm down," said David, knowing the minute he said it that he had done the wrong thing.

"Don't you dare patronise me," she yelled, and for good measure again at full bore. "Don't patronise me, you fucking rapist!"

Seemingly out of nowhere her slender palm flicked like a trap released, stinging a slap across his face. She raised her hand to do it again, but this time a startled David grabbed hold of it by an instantaneous reflex. They stood before each other glaring into one another's eyes in a stance of angry stalemate.

The door to David's office flung open suddenly breaking the stand off, and in the doorway stood Ian, his face red with annoyance. Some way off, in the background, stood a stranger dressed smartly in a dark suit, a stranger who David later learned was the bank manager.

"Queenie, get out," said Ian.

The girl searched his face for a sign that he was on her side.

"Get out!" he repeated a little louder.

Jumping at the shock of his barked order she left and Ian closed the door, lowering an angry frown at his old friend.

"I thought all this shit was over," he snapped.

"I've only been here ten minutes," said David quietly, so as not to be overheard. "In she walks, bold as brass and starts shouting rape. I never touched her, for God's sake."

"We'll talk about this later. I'm sending her home. If we can't get you two working together, one of you will have to go, permanently."

Ian closed the door after him, leaving a shaken David Harper trawling through his memory to recall if he really had put his hand up her skirt that night. He regretted bitterly the fact that he had shared his secrets with her. He had not expected this kind of outcome from divulging the contents of his life. It was as if the awful curse that had dogged him over and over was catching up with him once more. If it was true he knew he would not be able to bear it and the more he thought like this the more fearful he grew. In that moment, with the sting of the slap still tingling, there was a real chance that a new Dark Age was about to swallow him up all over again.

It was not until the end of a very long day, as everyone was packing up to head for home that Ian called him over. The morning's events had eaten David up, so that now he was tired. Ian had calmed down but wanted answers.

"Come in to my parlour," said Ian, emphasising the light-hearted approach he was going to use as his opener. "You look as if you need a drink."

From a drawer in his desk there materialised a bottle of brandy along with two small glasses. Without saying another word he poured the drinks and handed one over to a rather nervous looking employee. The liquid sliced the back of his throat, charged his breath with vapours and warmed his belly. In its wonderful way it relaxed him.

"Why is she doing this to you David?"

The question was friendly and direct.

"I don't know," he said.

"Look, we're both men of the world. I'd understand if after a few bevvies you thought that the time had come to try your luck. We've all done it and come a cropper. The oldest mistake in the book."

"I never laid a hand on her. I'm convinced. But you're right. It's been a mistake. I thought I could trust her. That's where I went wrong."

"So why is she shouting rape so everyone can hear?"

"Because I made her out to be a liar over that time travel crap story, I expect," said David, unsure if it really was the reason.

"So, what did you say to her that made her like this. I thought that you'd become mates. She was dancing with you at the club, wasn't she?"

"She snogged me. I didn't want her to. She was drunk. I had to get outside. She followed me and tried to kiss me again. I wasn't in the mood."

"Oh, come off it David. She's a cracker and you turned her down? It's not as if you're married or anything, is it?'

David's mind began to weave. He had to provide a convincing reason why he had looked a gift horse like Queenie in the mouth. She had given him all the signs that night that she wanted him. Instead he went on about Lotty, and Empton, and the awful truth about his mother. Then from his mother, one thought led to another and another.

"I never really wanted to go to the club that night," said David, as he could see Ian wondering why he had said that. "You remember me telling you that my mother died?" Ian nodded that he did. "She

521

committed suicide, you know. She was found hanging from the banister. That night was the anniversary of her death. I tried to put it out of my mind and have a good time with you all. But I couldn't. It got too much. I didn't want kissing. I just wanted to be left alone. Everyone was having fun. The last thing you'd have wanted was a melancholy me spoiling things. So I went out. Queenie followed. I poured my heart out to her. I told her how my mother had treated me as a boy. I wanted a bit of sympathy, not all this crap."

David looked at his old friend.

"I began to cry on her shoulder, I think I put my arms around her. All I wanted was for someone to listen. It's easy to put it to the back of my mind these days, at least when I'm not halfway to being pissed up. The drink and the noise of the club, it seemed to unlock it all. So there you have it chapter and verse. That's all that happened. I reckon I scared her to death. The next minute she's texting everyone saying I'm a sex maniac. I convince you and everyone else that I'm not and she loses face. I wish I'd kept my fucking gob shut then none of this would have happened."

Ian poured another drink.

"The past, hey. Don't you wish it would stay there, where it belongs?"

David swigged his drink back.

"Damned right," he said.

Chapter nine: Letters

It was obvious the minute he pulled out into the street that something was wrong. The car felt as if it were traversing over bricks that had been dumped in the kerbside. He stopped the engine and got out to clear whatever was there. In the fading light of evening, he came upon a sickening sight. Both tyres near the kerb had been slashed. Fuming and, with a sense of disbelief, he went to look at the other side only to find the same thing there. All four tyres had been savaged. David threw his hands up in the air and brought them down with an exasperated slap against his hips. For a while he did not know what to do. In the end he went and sat back in the driver's seat to calm down.

He tried to call Ian but his mobile line was busy. Then he remembered the service booklet in the glove compartment. Within its bound mock leather cover, in amongst the instruction manual and service log, he found the breakdown kit - cards provided by the service organisations to which Ian had subscribed. The young girl from Wheelfixit, the tyre specialists, could not have been more helpful as he put in a call to them. She promised a van would be with him within thirty minutes. David slipped his mobile away and waited. It was an hour and a quarter before his rescuers arrived, by which time David's patience had evaporated. He took his frustrations out on the poor chaps who had come to help. The fitters had seen it all before and David's rants and raves were received with a practised corporate courtesy, only sullied when they happened, on one occasion, to glance at each other and exchange a knowing look. When it was over and the job had been signed off he pulled away, cursing the local kids and the grubby neighbourhood that had spawned them.

Despite the cost he hid his car in the multi-storey the next day. Queenie's desk was empty as he walked in. He felt some relief at this knowing at the same time the trouble that would be generated by the absence of such a valuable team member. Ian too dismissed the damage to his car to be the pranks of vile urchins as he called them, little bastards who had big bastards for parents. Nothing, though, was said of the incident in the office. The bank manager had viewed the matter as nothing more than an internal spat. Even the bank itself had been known to stage such theatrics now and again as the manager had been charitable enough to point out - so no harm done. No harm had been done to his car either as he made his way home after work. He drove away feeling glad that calm had descended on his life once more.

One morning at the office, a few days later, his first cup of coffee was interrupted by the arrival of the mail. There were three letters for him. He knew by the envelopes that two of them were quotes from rival exhibition companies. The third one, clean and white, with his name and work address printed on an attached sticker, caused a slight

523

flicker of curiosity to make a spark. His finger had ripped it open before he had chance to think any deeper. Inside was a flat piece of A4 paper, with a single line of twelve-point text printed slap-bang in the middle of it. The words read:

A bit tyresome having to wait over an hour, wasn't it?

David stormed out of his room, shot into the room next door but one and thrust the note into Ian's hand.

"Urchins? I don't think," snapped David without consideration for manners.

Taken aback momentarily, Ian read the words not quite knowing what to make of them. Then, like some gradual awakening, an understanding crept across his features.

"You're not seriously thinking what I think you're thinking, are you?" he said quietly.

"Well, kids wouldn't send me a note about it, would they?"

"It's someone who knows you, I'd agree with you there," he glanced at his friend. "Any other enemies lurking out there?"

"Only the one you're thinking about."

"She must have been watching you," he said. "She knew how long you waited to get fixed up."

"I'll fucking fix her up," said David.

"You'll do no such thing. We'll keep professional about all this," said Ian.

"Oh, yeah. Just how do we do that?"

"Look, I'm one designer down thanks to," he was going to say you, but decided to be tactful. "Well, I can't afford to risk the schedule. I'm going to get her in here, sort this out properly,"

Nothing more was said. The mettle that ran through Ian's words rendered contradiction useless.

The meeting, when it happened a couple of days later, was a strained affair from the beginning. Ian's powers of persuasion had only succeeded at delivering the physical presence of Victoria. Her body language made it clear that her mind was having no part of it. She was leaning defiantly against Ian's filing cabinet when David was asked to join them. Her arms were folded and she met his arrival with a haughty glare, motionless, her mouth as straight as a knife wound. Her complete lack of fear intimidated David to the point of nausea. He clung on to his cool exterior and calm expression with the same desperation as found between a shipwreck victim and the floating wreckage. How he was expected to be equal to this he did not know. There was no way he could understand her, outwit her. It did not bode well for him.

The usual flurry of business out in the main working area had become a quiet hum. Ears strained to catch what was being said in the room where the three had gathered. They heard nothing. No one was speaking, until Ian had had enough.

"Okay, okay. We can't go on like this," he said, clearly at the end of his tether.

David had missed his chance. He had been wondering what to say. He had to seize the last remnants of an opportunity before it disappeared for good.

"I couldn't agree more," he said, squaring up to Queenie. "Look, I'm sorry if I scared you. I'd had a few too many and it was a bad day, a bad anniversary, you might say. I never meant to frighten you. I needed a bit of comfort, that was all."

He hoped that an apology would dampen things down, but the effects were like water on an oil fire and the whole thing began to spread

"So you admit you tried to rape me, you pervert," she said.

"I said civilised," scolded Ian.

"I didn't rape you," David said, annoyed that his plan had failed.

"No, but you tried to," she said.

"This is getting us nowhere," Ian put in.

"Look, Ian," she said forcibly, "he was crying like a weirdo, one hand hanging onto my tit, his other hand going everywhere. I was terrified."

"My mother committed suicide, you know. The party night was the anniversary of her death," he said, making it all up as he went. "I wasn't feeling myself."

"Too right you little fucker, you were feeling me," she carried on unmoved. "And then there was all this crap about going back in time,

525

and your mother's wedding, and you fucking her, your own sodding mum, for Christ's sake. God, if anyone deserves the title mother-fucking bastard, it's you. You're sick in the bloody head, you are."

"You leave my mother out of it," he said, his teeth clenched.

"The whole story's pure bollocks, if you ask me," she said, then her brain made a sudden connection. He could see her eyes register the spark. "Wedding!" she said. "That photo, the one you asked me to magnify, with you in the reflection. You almost had me believing it. You faked it, right?"

Ian looked at David for answers. He shrugged his shoulders in reply. With that Queenie took her smouldering indignation out of the room and brushed a colleague aside who was using her machine. With erratic movements of the mouse, she searched for the file name she had saved the picture as. It was a frantic search that eventually stopped in an exasperated fruitlessness. Her fingers halted their clicking and she turned to face the two men who had arrived behind her to watch.

"You've got rid of it, you bastards," she said.

"Got rid of what exactly?" asked Ian, trying to keep calm.

"He knows," she said, nodding over her shoulder in David's direction.

"I haven't a clue what you're talking about," said David.

"How can you say that? Don't believe him Ian, he's lying."

"What the hell's going on Dave?" said Ian, confused.

"Beats me," he said. "I think she's lost it."

"He asked me to scan a picture of a couple at their wedding," shouted the woman. "He was in a reflection in a window that I enlarged, only he said it wasn't him, he said it was his dad. Now it's gone, deleted, and he's pretending he knows nothing about it. He's a liar."

"Extraordinary behaviour," said David.

"Is this true?" asked Ian, feeling out of his depth.

"Look, we grew up together, you and me," he said to Ian. "Now you know that I never ever saw my dad. So how would I be able to recognise him in a picture? And why would I want her to blow up a picture just so I could see myself in it? There are easier ways to get

526

into a photograph, you know. None of this bullshit adds up. She's the weirdo, not me."

Queenie's chair crashed to the carpet as she sprang to her feet. In an instant, she picked up the nearest object she could find, a calculator, and flung it full bore at David's face. He ducked only just in time for it to miss the side of his head. It smashed to pieces on impact with a filing cabinet behind him. Like a freeze frame the world around them ground to a halt. Apart from the unanswered shrill of a ringing phone, there was no noise. Everyone was rooted to the spot. David bored into Queenie's eyes, eyes that were so full of rage and hate, the anger within them mildly tempered by what she took as defeat. She knew that her outburst had blown her argument. David could not take his watchful stare from her, observing her in detail. A lioness in a cage would have behaved in a similar way, a lioness with a wound, whose roar was all the more fierce through the pain, her lethal strike made impotent by her wounding. That is how she was as she breathed heavily, looking at everyone in turn, searching for an ally. None came forward. All kept their own counsel. In the end it was Ian who broke the silence.

"Look, I think you'd better go. I'll have your wages sorted out. Your things will be put in a box, you can collect them later."

"What?" she gasped, almost crying from shock of his words. "You're firing me? Me?"

"You leave me no choice," he said. "This is the last straw. I don't really want to discuss this in front of everyone."

"Oh, don't mind me," she said. "I'm sure everyone wants to know how precarious their own positions are, don't you boys and girls?"

"You know what I mean without me having to spell it out."

"Oh fuck this. You can keep your shitty little job and your stupid little clients. I'm glad I made all those mistakes."

"Like the scans you fouled up recently you mean?" said Ian. "Didn't think I knew about them, did you?"

"Oh, weirdo man's been blabbing about all that, has he?"

"He doesn't have a clue that I knew anything," said Ian, his voice remaining calm. "He wasn't going to say a word to me. He was doing you a favour. The printers, they dropped it out by accident that's all. It's the reason why I believe David, and not you."

527

Queenie's face was red with frustrated anger. Words could not burst out of her furious mouth.

"It's either do it this way and I'll give you a decent reference, or I'll see you in court. It's entirely up to you."

After one second, a second where a mangle of thoughts overloaded her mind, she grabbed her coat and stormed out without a backward glance, swearing at the whole fucking lot of them.

Ian's expectation that he would eventually receive a letter from Queenie's solicitor never materialised. In his mind there was never any question of having dispensed an unfair dismissal but, to be on the safe side, he was armed and ready for a fight in a tribunal. It never seemed to bother him either way, but as the weeks passed, everyone could sense that he allowed himself some comfort in the belief that nothing would happen. After all, he had written her a reference worthy of a model employee. As weeks became months nothing was heard from her and she became nothing more than a cautionary tale, a footnote.

Then, one morning, about six months later, quite out of the blue, David found a strangely reminiscent envelope in amongst his mail. It was the sticker bearing his name and address on the front that caused a tremor of disquiet to worry him from half asleep to fully awake. He ripped it open frantically as the connections kicked in. His hunch was right. One line printed with an inkjet in Times New Roman, he read the words:

I'm on to you.

That was it. Just four words, I'm on to you. What did it mean? What did she mean by it? What was she on to? He showed the letter to Ian, who told him to file it and forget it. It may come in handy he later suggested. So David popped it in a filing cabinet and tried to put it out of his mind. But Queenie knew about the workings of people. She knew how they ticked. The little note bothered him, much more than a lengthy diatribe from her could ever have done and he suspected that his tormentor had engineered it so. He would have continued to be affected by its voodoo for days had it not been for a phone call from Barker's the solicitors. They wanted to see him. Mr Barker had sounded mildly excited, an urgency in his tone. Suddenly the silly letter became an insignificance to be replaced by something altogether more incredible.

So David met with old Mr Barker again, one evening - one dark, wet evening, arriving in damp clothes after running from the car park. A single desk lamp lit Barker's tiny office in a hushed light. It gave the dim place an odd cosy atmosphere, a snug quality to contrast with the squally rain that even now was peppering at the old sash windows. The old man motioned towards a chair. They both sat facing each other across the yellow light from the lamp, as Barker pushed a blue wallet file towards him.

"Arthur Gibson's instructions," began Barker, lifting open the cover of the file. "Many of the firms that existed in Salisbury when Mrs Harper left the area have changed beyond recognition, save for one or two."

Barker took out a letter that had been placed for convenience at the top of the file. He slid it out and passed it to David, who read it. The words therein added confusion where he had hoped for clarity. Old Arthur Gibson had indeed made a Will, of sorts. A certain legal mechanism had been established that protected his estate, as well as the way the estate would eventually be inherited. The true nature of the Will could only be made available to Mrs C Harper, or any heirs that had issued from the union between Mr & Mrs D Harper. David did not know quite what to make of it, as Barker could tell from his client's perplexed expression.

"Yes," said Barker, taking the letter back from David. "We would have liked to have read a Last Will & Testament to you, but it seems we are prevented from doing this for some reason."

"And do you know the reason?" David asked.

"No more than you do Mr Harper. But it would appear that the late Mr Gibson, your grandfather, had good reason to fear his estate would fall into the wrong hands."

He knew whose hands he had meant. He pictured Lotty, in The Beckett, afraid of her new husband. Her voice crept out of his memory, Lotty's words about how her father had arranged things. He had no answers as to how or what had been arranged, but he felt a step nearer to finding out. Somehow, Arthur Gibson had arranged it so that Danno's inheritance of Bofindle Farm would not be so easy if indeed possible at all.

"You'll need to arrange a meeting with a certain Mr Tewks, at the firm of Gabbon, Sperry and Butterworth," said Barker. "They are the latest custodians of your grandfather's will. It's changed hands three times since nineteen fifty-six," he added whimsically.

"In Salisbury?" asked David, unable to prevent the mental connection with Ellie.

"Yes," said Barker, "I'll arrange with my secretary a letter of introduction for you, confirming your credentials and such like. I'm sure that they'll explain more to you when you see them."

Old Mr Barker could not stop a shadow of sadness to creep into his eyes.

"I don't think that there's much else we can do to help you now, Mr Harper."

"You've done more than enough already," said David, his mind lost in the possibilities of where this trail might lead.

A week after this meeting a letter arrived at his flat. He recognised the envelope immediately from the embossed *B* in the bottom left-hand corner, *B* for Barkers. The Monday mail always seemed heavier than any other day of the week and, in amongst the bills and junk, he almost missed another letter hidden in the pile. As soon as he laid eyes on it he felt his gut tighten. There was no attempt to disguise the style, always the same sticker, and always the same typeface. He thought of taking it to work and reading it there, but it was open before he had a chance to talk himself out of it. The contents, when he finally looked, made him react as if he had heard a scream fly out of a nightmare. He saw in the first instance that it was just a photocopy, a newspaper cutting. Even when he read the headline, there was no connection.

WOMAN FOUND HANGED

The first line of the story made him retch. *The body of Mrs Charlotte Harper was found by police in her home on Wednesday afternoon.* Apart from

530

the version of events given to him by the police when he was a teenager, this was the first time he had read about it like this. The grisly description of how her dead body was found turned his mind to jelly. *Hanging from the banister rail,* it read, *a note to her son found nearby.* It all came back. The haunting vision that had been part of his road to hell danced again before him on the end of a dangling rope. He knew who had sent him this. There was no proof but he knew. She had even added a line of text at the end of it all. She had promised that this was not all of it. There was more to come.

He had come to terms with his mother's method of death over the years, but being reminded about it in this way was too painful to bear. The assurance of further persecution caused his stomach to turn. He was vomiting into the toilet moments later. Then the tears began. A weak sniffle that eventually burst out of him like a cataclysm. She had got to him and in that instant he would gladly have killed her - but there was a difference this time. Reading about his mother's death, he realised, was also the same as reading about the death of his beloved Lotty. In some peculiar way, it made the mourning of her different. Strange as it seemed to him, he looked upon her death differently than he did towards his mother and, although Lotty and his mother were one and the same person, he knew for whom he was crying the most.

For several days he tried to bear it alone. This pernicious little piece of paper had bored into the deepest flesh of his heart. Inside he felt as if he had been crippled, making his inner self appear to hobble through the days that followed. He could not even raise the energy to contact the solicitors in Salisbury. Every morning, as the mail flapped on the doormat his pulse raced, causing him to search feverishly for the envelope with the sticker on it. Each day began like this. It was wearing him down and each time was the same in as much as there was no such letter. In equal measure there was relief and agitation. It was Russian roulette - relief that the gun had not gone off, but a cold, grim realisation that the trigger would have to be pulled again the next morning. After a week of this, a week of torment, a week in which he lost half a stone through not eating properly, he called Norman.

Any shame that he had felt at not being able to deal with this irritation by himself, faded when Norman arrived. The minute David greeted him at the door his positive vibe re-energised him. His effect, it seemed, was always like this, a warm remedy for life's unhealthiness. When David showed him the letters Norman thought it was an evil trick to pull. His friend suggested it might be a good idea to take a holiday, jet off to the sun for a week, put things back into perspective. Norman could see in David's brightened eyes that he had come up with a good idea. Only he began to toy around with the notion of going back to Wiltshire for a few days. He wanted to see what the Salisbury solicitors had to say, and then follow it up with a trip to some of the small villages he knew from his other time - places like Tunby and Maltoft He could even take a look at what had become of the windmill. Norman was not sure this was a healthy idea for him but the notion was gaining a greater mass than the bland vision of time wasted away on a hot beach somewhere. Norman almost kicked himself for his role as a catalyst in his decision but at least he had halted his friend's slide into the quicksand of depression. Surely that was a good thing?

Mr Tewks, when he finally came to the telephone, was an amiable man, fond of punctuating his conversation with small bursts of explosive laughter. David guessed he was also fond of drink. He imagined him a robust man, overweight, advanced in years, with pen in one hand and glass of brandy in the other. He was hard not to like. The Gibson file had been one of the oldest at Gabbon, Sperry and Butterworth he told David, and that letting the light shine upon it promised to be an interesting exercise. Why he found the remark so funny David was at a loss to tell, but it amused Mr Tewks and that was all that mattered it seemed.

At Inca marketing it had not gone unnoticed that David appeared under strain. Ian watched his friend suffer after the newspaper cutting had arrived in the post. David asked him for a week's holiday and together they looked at the projects in hand and found a way to grant a few initial days off. A two week vacation could be afforded a month or so later. His heart knew the gladness that came from the reunion with his old friend, a friend that even now cared for his best interests.

The bond that was forged long ago in St Peter's church choir had held true between them, and now David felt that the Lord God Almighty himself had brought them together once more to be his saving grace.

Norman Hart's boss on the other hand had been as obstructive as ever. A woman with little or no grace at all, she had objected to one of her team breaking with protocol and requesting a few days' holiday. She had a dogmatic reasoning that believed time away from work should be taken in whole weeks, or multiples of the same. How else can you expect to get the best out of your time off, she had insisted? Norman insisted back that it was a family problem. He only needed the two-day break. Back she came with the notion that surely his domestic crisis could be cleared up over a weekend. Norman tried one last time to convince her, saying that the people concerned could only be seen during that time frame. He hoped the jargon would link with the work-speak part of her brain. Only, with this hanging over him, he persisted, his performance would be jeopardised over such an extended term, adding that the balance of the whole team would then have serious issues. In the end she acquiesced and Norman texted his friend the good news.

They were both going to dig into the dim and distant past like a couple of excited archaeologists.

Chapter ten: The Key

There was a solid consensus between the two travellers. They had both agreed on the joyous sense of freedom that abandoning their everyday lives had given them, short-lived though their escape would be. If David's past ever did manifest itself in their fluid conversation, it was concerned only with what they expected to discover about it. The intrigue was palpable, a palpability that intensified as the city of Salisbury drew nigh. By the time the golden spire of the cathedral had come into view, their urge to uncover the secrets of the past had become all consuming.

The guesthouse David had chosen and booked online was their first disappointment. The proud boast of its website that the place was only five minutes walk from the city centre, failed to point out that one had to be a trained Olympic sprinter to do the distance in that time. Once inside they were surrounded by the nineteen fifties. Linoleum floors met ageing wallpaper bought, it appeared, when Harold Macmillan had been the Prime Minister. Everything from the black Bakelite phone on the occasional table, to the bulbous glass decoration for the hall light, filled them both with woe. Even the smell of cabbage and fish made them wonder if they had come to the right place.

It took the sinewy lady who owned the B&B to match up her own computer printout, for it to become clear that, although their navigation had been perfect, the choice of digs was a flop. The fact that there was a computer at all in such a throwback establishment was a wonder and, that the little terrier of a woman actually knew how to print anything off seemed further beyond belief. She dealt with their arrival with a precise militarism that ended with a forced march to their room, a poky rectangle, clean but infused with a trace of dampness. There were two beds that the woman nodded towards, briefly scowling, hoping that her gesture had been enough to deter them both from any homosexual hanky-panky. David glanced at Norman, knowing that he too felt the self-conscious discomfort.

By now it was lunchtime, so they headed off to the old part of the city on foot, a galling trek of twenty-five minutes slog, punctuated only by a stop at a chip shop. With the flavour of steak pie still fresh on their breath they arrived at the cathedral. Beholding the sight, so close for the first time, there returned a ghostly feeling of the adoration he had once held for such buildings. Here was a gleaming javelin, a golden arrow bathed in God's sunlight pointing up to the maker of the unknown souls who had so skilfully built it. The tiny flapping shapes of birds that wheeled high up around the spire's slender tip only served to emphasise its lofty majesty. The whole scene, along with the blue and white backdrop of clouds and sky, made the glorification of the Lord God Almighty impossible to ignore. David was in raptures and it irked him slightly that Norman's heart was not moved in the same way.

"Nice church," was all he said on seeing it.

The offices of Gabbon, Sperry and Butterworth on the other hand were not so obvious to discover. David had expected something akin to the other law firms he had visited, but not this one. They had to pass through a narrow covered passage between a ladies' dress shop, and a gentlemen's barbers, at which point a flight of stairs at the far end took them to a door furnished with an unkempt brass plate that bore the company name. The passage was dimly lit by a single bulb and it took a second or two for their eyes to grow accustomed to the darkness before Norman spotted a bell button set into the doorframe and pressed his forefinger upon it. It would have been encouraging had a bell or a buzzer sounded from beyond the door but neither of them could hear anything. David wondered if they had come to a back door. Maybe this was a seldom-used entrance, considering the cobwebs and grime that gave the place its character. They were just about to give up and search for another way in, when the old door handle rattled and the passageway was filled with a weak yellow light from the office beyond.

"Good afternoon sirs," greeted an emaciated office clerk.

"Hello," said David, peering beyond the man to the higgledy-piggledy chaos filling what appeared to be a hallway. "I'm David Harper. This is my friend Mr Hart. We have an appointment with Mr Tewks," he said offering the man his letter of introduction.

"Ah, yes," said the spectre-like figure mournfully. "The visitors from Nottinghamshire. We've been expecting you. This way please."

They all filed in, as the door was rammed shut behind them. In the background din, created by typewriters clacking and hushed conversations, they could hear one overriding voice. It was a conversation that seemed to be decidedly one-sided, judging by the lack of responses from a second party, and David concluded that the person doing the talking was on the telephone. He had heard the voice before and, when it broke into a raucous laugh, he knew that it was none other than Mr Tewks himself. The clerk had an ear for when a conversation was in its terminal phase and he had already made his way into Mr Tewks's office as the goodbyes were being said. David and Norman could hear the whispers coming from him as he explained that the visitors were here. There was another hearty laugh, not forced or put on, but one that sounded genuinely excited, almost childlike. The laugh was followed by one word.

"Splendid."

There were footsteps and suddenly the visitors beheld the sight of Mr Tewks. Nothing could have prepared them for it. Mr Tewks was a one-off. The remarkable thing about him was not the fact that he wore a bowler hat or that he sported a bow tie. It was not so much his worn-out suit of black cloth or the boots that were in need of repair. The thing about Mr Tewks was that he was over seven feet tall, a giant, a huge body topped in proportion by a massive head. When he laughed again, as he did when he offered his spade-like hand in greeting, the overall effect was electrifying.

It took time to recognise in Mr Tewks the gentleman that he was. Seen beside the little clerk, he was an awe-inspiring sight, but his manner was deeply polite and warm, if not a little odd. He took to his visitors in an instant, offering them tea and biscuits. From the features set within the large head there beamed the friendliest of eyes bursting with a love of life.

David followed Goliath into a ramshackle office that competed favourably with Mr Tulip's. Only here there seemed to be some attempt at organisation, for each pile of papers was neatly tied up with string and a note bearing the name of CASE and DATE placed beneath the knot where the string was tied. There were hundreds of piles representing the most incredible fire risk. Tewks bulldozed in, cut diagonally across the room and delved deep to retrieve a thin file. Even as he took it out David could see the word *GIBSON* on it and the date *1994*. How the filing system had worked he could not fathom but it was evidently faultless. Norman passed a bewildered glance at David as Tewks bade them into his office. They both felt as if they had stumbled into a strange dream.

Tea and biscuits duly arrived care of the clerk and amidst the clatter of business Tewks took a pair of scissors and cut the string around the file. Dust billowed from its surface as he opened it up. Keen to get on with the matter David presented his birth certificate and Littlebody's ageing note. Tewks was nonplussed but read the documents offered and handed them back with a smile. The moment had arrived. Tewks took out the sparse contents of the file, a few sheets of paper, and absorbed their words with a questioning look that grew increasingly puzzled the more he read it. At length Tewks levelled his stare at his eager visitors and spoke.

"Was your mother ever in any trouble?" he said, his loud voice now devoid of its former impishness.

"I rather think she was," said David, not wanting to give away how he knew so.

"Her father Arthur Gibson, your grandfather seems to have made arrangements that were to help her should she fall foul of Mr D Harper, who according to your birth certificate here is your father," Tewks held up the letter almost as evidence. "There doesn't seem to have been any love lost between Mr Gibson and your father. Was he a violent man?"

"I never knew my father," said David, not daring to tell the whole truth, even though he thought he could sense Norman urging him to blurt it all out.

Behind the letter was a large brown envelope that, even before Tewks opened it, they could tell there was something heavy within. The contents, once ripped asunder by the giant hand, turned out to be a letter and a key. Again the solicitor scanned the words, twiddling the key between his oversized thumb and forefinger.

"Well, there's more to this than meets the eye," declared Tewks. "We've to present this key to your grandfather's bank. It fits a security box. Everything your mother would have needed to help her is in there. That's it. Nothing more," said the great man, trying to fathom it all in his head. "You know, only a man who feared someone would have gone to as much trouble as this. I'm intrigued."

David could hardly hide his frustration.

"You know I'd expected an end to it all here and now. I feel like I'm on a wild goose chase."

Tewks held up the key.

"Then let's go and catch ourselves a wild goose, shall we?"

The monstrous laugh boomed out so that for a second all the typewriters stopped their clatter and the hum of voices went curiously silent. In a moment they were back out in the street and all three of them were crossing the busy road to the bank when the weedy shrill of the office clerk called out from the entrance to the dark passageway.

"Mr Tewks, Mr Tewks, sir," shouted the little man, out of breath, "Telephone call. It's urgent."

The mass of Tewks's body braked and turned to behold the frail creature.

"If that's Armitage again, tell him I'll call him back directly," shouted Tewks across the traffic.

The clerks voice did its best to compete with the vehicles that passed between them.

"It's your mother," Tewks heard him yell, and his face altered in an instant on hearing this.

"Oh Lord," he said, worrying. "Look, I'll have to go."

He looked at the file that had been under his arm and the key held in his hand, weighing up the cost of ignoring his mother against the thrill of discovering what the key would unlock. In the end there was no competition really.

"Alzheimer's, I'm afraid," he said, "Terrible thing you know. Gets worse by the day," the booming voice had gone and the big man seemed drenched with sadness. "Here, take these to that bank there," he said pointing to a grand stone-clad building on the corner, "I'll be over as quick as I can."

David took the file and key from him. Norman said he was trained to deal with his mother's condition and offered his help. Tewks gracefully declined and strode back to the office as if the whole world was weighing on his shoulders. For the first time since they had met him he suddenly did not seem half so big.

David held out his palm and looked in wonderment at the small silvery key. That he should be holding a key, of all things, seemed so apt. Having come so far he had stowed away any ideas that all the secrets of his life would unfold as if by magic. So far the process of discovery had been one of peeling back the skins of an onion, but the key seemed alive with a tantalising energy and the bank was less than a hundred yards away. As hope outshone despair they entered the ornate entrance to the building.

The information desk was like a space-age reception in a modern hotel, quite at odds with its Victorian exterior. One of the two smartly dressed women there greeted them with a practised business-like courtesy. American, with an English accent, thought David and, squirming at the falseness of it all, he handed her his documents, showed her his key and asked for permission to access his security box. The second lady, the other's senior, asked for a closer look at the small silver object in his hand.

"I'm afraid that key is out of date sir," she said.

"Out of date," said David. "I don't follow?"

"We modernised the security boxes ten or so years ago. That key won't work. Sorry."

"So what am I supposed to do now?" David barked, his frustration getting the better of him.

"Surely you envisaged a problem like this when you modernised?" Norman asked, "We've gone to a lot of trouble to get this far," he continued, his tone became determined, "and we aren't going to stop at the final hurdle. Now go and call the manager and let's sort this out."

"Very well sir," she said devoid of any human emotion behind her plastic exterior.

The manager duly arrived at the desk, a smart man, very young and personable. David and Norman explained the problem to him. The manager asked to look at the key.

"Ah, yes. I see," he said. "These were discontinued some ten or so years ago in favour of an electronic system. Would you care to come into my office, I think I know how I can help you."

The two travellers signed the visitors' book, pinned on their badges and followed the manager with renewed hope through the computerised back rooms of the bank and into a separate office. Even with the addition of such high-tech equipment the room could not hide its origins. The Flemish ceiling gave it away most of all, with its ornately embossed plasterwork, but the bank had ensured that the interior design met with its corporate style and blended its own stamp on an older fashion. By the time David had taken all this in the manager had tapped and clicked on his laptop and opened up what he told them was a seldom-used programme. As the manager asked them to gather round David was able to see the heads of six keys on the screen.

"Do any of these match?" he said, offering David the chance to compare his own with those now displayed. "These are pictures of our copy keys you understand," said the manager. "Yours will be in here somewhere. Only thing is there's a hundred and forty-four of the devils to try."

None matched at the first attempt, so with a click of the laptop's silvery mouse pad another six flashed up. It was like this for another seven tries. Then on the eighth there was a match, a perfect match. David felt elated. The manager, smiling at David's sense of relief, phoned a request for a security card to be made, giving the serial number that appeared beneath the picture. Five minutes later David had what looked like a credit card in his hand.

"Right then gentlemen, let me take you through to the dungeon," he said wickedly, and it was a dungeon. The lift had taken them down to what had once been a cellar, a single room with a vaulted ceiling and a large table in the centre.

"This used to be the old vault room before the security boffins decided this was the worst place to have a vault."

The manager could see the questioning look on their faces.

"Tunnellers," he said by way of explanation.

The cellar was clean and painted white, and fluorescent tubes lit it up perfectly - even so there was an air of disturbance about it, a feeling of being trapped. Maybe it was the rows of security boxes that lined both sides of the wall. Stainless steel rectangles mounted six up and twelve across, seventy-two per wall. The card had a number printed across a paper strip on the back of it. It was the number forty-five. The manager led them to the box bearing that same number and asked David for his card. Inserting it into its slot the cover flipped open revealing a thin steel handle attached to a box. Grabbing the handle the manager pulled it out and placed it carefully on the table. He explained how to undo the catches and then left, telling them to call him on the wall-mounted phone when they were done. David thanked him, trying not to yell with delight. He now had the box of secrets in his hands at last.

Here was the Holy Grail, the end of the search. At least he dared to hope. So the catches were sprung and the inside of the shiny box was filled with light. There they were, neatly placed, patiently waiting.

The corruption of atmosphere or mistreatment had never befallen these brown envelopes. They would have looked as good as new, had it not been for the exacting copperplate penmanship that hailed from an earlier age. They seemed to have been placed in order, judging by the flowing script that read *Envelope No. 1*. Even as David's hand reached out to touch it he could not fail to be affected by the historical significance of what he was doing. There was a touch of Carter in *The Valley of the Kings* about it. This cellar somehow echoed the spirit of Tutankhamen's tomb as he pulled the first envelope out. Then he hesitated. It seemed a sacrilege to rip it open but what else was there to do? That is what they were here for and in a moment a jagged tear had almost reluctantly been gashed through its brown card and a paper pulled out.

What a wonderful sight it was, this letter in its ornate writing. How he wished that people still had the capacity to create such beautiful calligraphy - only it was not calligraphy, just the everyday handwriting of someone who had been brought up in Queen Victoria's reign, whose knuckles would have been rapped by the educators of the day to achieve such discipline. It was addressed to no one in particular and had, as its subject matter, details about Daniel Harper that few would have known about.

The epistle according to Arthur Gibson told of how, many years before this letter was penned, a youthful Danno had tricked and raped his daughter Charlotte when she was just thirteen. It went on to explain that when Danno's father heard that he had got a Gibson girl in the family way he went mad at his son. The letter's matter-of-fact description however could not fail to highlight the heartbreak that was to come. Arthur told of how his beloved daughter had lost her own mother when she was very young. Arthur had no choice but to be a pragmatist, a practical farmer, a survivor in a tough hard-working life. What with all the work on the farm to be done, it was decided to give the baby away when it was born. Danno's father owned the Golden Goose and it was he who decided that the master of the pub and his wife should have the baby as their own when it came along, *them being a childless couple, and all*, it said. They were never to say that the child had been a Harper/Gibson conception. *As you can imagine, my daughter was distressed at this decision, but was forced by convention never to*

541

talk about it, the letter explained. Eventually a girl was delivered and, as agreed, the newborn was snatched away and spent her first earthly night at the village pub. Harry and Eliza Tattershall, the couple who ran the pub, did their best to raise the child but it was Eliza who, after a couple of months listening to the baby's constant cries, could stand it no longer. David and Norman's heads were side by side as they read on. It seemed that Eliza had taken all she could stand and ran off with the representative from the brewery one night. Harry was forced to bring up the baby by himself. That infant, the account reported, was christened Eleanor Tattershall.

"Ellie," said David out loud. "My God, I can't believe this, I can't believe what I'm reading."

He turned to Norman who was lost trance-like in the letter too.

"Hold on," said Norman. "How come Charlotte ended up marrying the man who raped her? How could she do that?"

"Your guess is as good as mine," said David. "More to the point, how could any of this have helped her if she'd been in trouble? I don't get it, do you?"

"Weird," said Norman. "You realise, if this is true, you and Ellie are half-brother and sister?"

"My God. No wonder mother ran off with her that night. Ellie, she was her baby too. It seems ironic that I called her Auntie for all those years when all the time she was my sister. I've a feeling that she knew about this all along."

"So, what's next?" said Norman, rudely betraying his hunger to unearth the next nugget of intrigue.

He grabbed *Envelope No. 2* from the box and handed it to David. Once again the envelope was written in the same flourished hand but nothing could have prepared them for the beauty of its contents. It was a folded up indenture, a parchment contract crafted in the most exquisite penmanship. Even before reading it David felt he knew what was at the heart of the old document and, whispering the name aloud so that Norman heard him, they both opened it up and scanned past the legal particulars to behold the name *Bofindle Farm*.

The top of the old contract had been cut away in elegant curves by scissors or a knife. What seemed to be the missing piece was at the bottom of the envelope, but its curves did not fit and the parchment was of a different shade. Neither of them understood the significance of this until they read the document in its entirety. Arthur Gibson had sold the farm to Daniel Harper for the princely sum of twenty-five thousand pounds. Norman suggested that the cut-off pieces had been swapped, so that each party had a section of the other's agreement. David was more astounded that his grandfather managed to do so grand a deal with Danno Harper in the first place. The caveat written at the end only made the deal seem more ridiculous, more incredible. Arthur made two conditions that the whole sale depended on. Daniel had to be married to his only daughter and the farm would have to pass on to any children they produced in wedlock. Astonishingly, in agreement to these terms were the signatures of both men. How had such a deal been forged?

How had Arthur persuaded Lotty to marry the man who once raped her? How had Danno been made to agree to it all? A fresh image of old Mr Gibson began to project itself in David's mind, one of a manipulative father, a bully who was effectively willing to sell his own child to the devil.

The third envelope was less ceremoniously taken from the box. The vision of Lotty weeping in the woods was something that David could now feel. He had wondered why she was so distraught when he first saw her, and the nearest he ever got to an explanation was when she said that there were things she could not tell him and leaving him to speculate. Now he could see her hopeless situation, effectively sold as a slave to keep Bofindle Farm in the genetic line. With a taste of anger in his mouth he ripped the envelope open wondering what other dark things would slither out.

To whom it may concern, the letter inside began. Neatly typed, the pair of tomb raiders came across a record of events leading up to and after the rape of Arthur Gibson's daughter. Like a confession, the words began to shed light on how the vicar of the day, the Reverend Pritchard, had witnessed Lotty being forced quietly against her will by Daniel Harper. The churchman had seen him take her into a recently abandoned cottage in the village, but he was afraid to intervene. The text was full of remorse and self-loathing, as if his hour had come to fight the forces of evil and, in that hour, he had failed his calling. The signature of the vicar alongside Arthur's bore witness not only to the dark deed itself but also to the brutal hold that Daniel and the other Harpers had on Empton at that time.

David reached for the last envelope. It was different from the others. As it was taken from the box David felt the hard cardboard back. His fingers touched something knobbly stuck to the flap at the rear, something irregular in shape that turned out to be a lump of sealing wax. As with the others this too was elegantly scribed with nib and ink, a simple message that read, *A Secret to be revealed; in the event that Daniel Harper causes fear or harm to Charlotte Harper. Take these contents for protection.* David's face was alive with wonderment, astonishment. He could see the same in Norman's eyes, urging him to delve inside.

Once opened things began to drop out onto the table, a collection of black and white photographs, some loose negatives, and a hand-written letter in Arthur's hand. Like a ghostly visitation David knew he had seen the first picture before, only now this one was in a pristine form, not folded in half and dishevelled as the one he knew when he first saw its likeness. He recalled the barn on the day he climbed the stairs and stumbled across Lotty up there. He had gone over to the crack in the floorboards where she had hidden her treasured picture. *To my Happy Lot*, it said on the back. The photograph that David now held was a perfect copy, a picture of David the woodsman.

It was not until they saw the other pictures that the point of it all became apparent. Whoever had taken these pictures had been hiding, crouching down low, judging by the amount of vegetation in the foreground. A figure in the middle distance could be seen striding towards a house, a small cottage surrounded by woodland. He was carrying things, a stubby pole in one hand and a rectangular container in the other. Through the veil of ferns, the next snap revealed the man pouring a liquid from the container, splashing it over the cottage walls. The following images were grainy but in perfect focus, clear enough to show the house engulfed in searing flames. The man was standing back, his face illuminated by the intense fire. There was no mistake. It was Danno. Each picture revealed a new horror. A man could be seen running out of the burning building on fire, flames tearing at the clothes on his back. Now David knew where the house was. He remembered the burned-out cottage in the woods that no one dared mention. David flipped to the next macabre print showing Danno bringing what looked like an iron bar down on the burning man's head. Each shot had been an indictment to Harper brutality, as the last few pictures testified. The final images showed Danno heaving a lifeless body in through a window that was yet to succumb to the flames.

David picked up the letter as Norman held the negatives up to the light. Even as he took in the first few words the macabre visions had depleted his concentration. It was not until Norman put the negatives down and asked what the letter had said, that David read it again properly.

My Dear Charlotte, I can only imagine that you are in grave trouble, otherwise you would not have contacted my solicitor.

The paragraphs unravelled like a coil, exposing a harrowing tale of how the pictures came to be. It was almost possible to hear Arthur Gibson's voice, explaining in the written word how he had once followed Danno into the wood, suspecting that he was up to no good. He had taken a camera in order to photograph him performing some petty crime. Little did he suspect that he would stumble upon the murder of his daughter's fiancé. He even mentioned him by name, David Sawyer. He had written that he knew how much it would break her heart to read this, but the words insisted that she use its contents to convict her abusive husband and send him to the gallows, if she so desired. He explained that Danno was given copies of the pictures and advised by Arthur that these secrets were hidden safely away in the event of him misbehaving.

"My God it's blackmail," said Norman, when he got to the end.

"It's an insurance policy," said David. "But I wonder why my mother never used it? All those wasted years. She could have had Danno put away with this. They'd have hanged him, she'd have got the farm and," David stopped in his tracks, "maybe she couldn't go back because of me. Danno knew he wasn't my father."

"But they'd have hanged him for murder though," said Norman, "then his widow would have owned the farm. She could even have changed her name back to Gibson after, well, you know, the execution."

"So why didn't she?" said David. "I don't see why she didn't use any of this. Her dad had obviously told her where to go and what to do if she needed help. But here it is, untouched, all of it. Arthur Gibson could have spilled the beans anytime he liked," continued David. "He'd got Danno where he wanted him, a fact that few men could have laid claim to. I should know. I'll bet he stalked Danno for weeks. It must have seemed like a godsend, when he got chance to take these pictures."

"Some godsend, photographing the murder of your daughter's fiancé."

"Yeah, but it's incredible what people can do when they're desperate," said David, while thinking. "These photos, the letters, everything on this table, what you see is nothing but a desperate man trying to cling on to his worthless farm through the selling of his daughter."

So there it was, a trap to catch a rapist, a means to an end, a way to get back at him. David's imagination was lost in a time fifty years before, conjuring up a scene of Lotty's wailing protests, as her father pressed her to marry this monstrous man or be made homeless. More clearly than ever, he was able to understand Lotty's claustrophobic life and how she was caught up in circumstances that were out of her control. In his mind's eye a bright light had illuminated his mother's life. It lit up the reasons she was crying her heart out in the woods that day when he had stumbled upon her. Here was a glimpse into his mother's behaviour. Mixed up in the whole ghastly business were the reasons why she had needed Miller's secret love so desperately. Even though she must have known something about her father's arrangements David could only guess that she panicked and escaped the village, ashamed and worried sick when she had committed the ultimate sin. The life that followed broke her up inside and, in a way that he never understood properly until now, he began to see why she treated him the way she did. The fact that he took on the physical resemblance of Miller as he grew older provided him with the clearest insight into his mother's mental state. Above all this, David could see one overriding fact. Everything about his life, his time as a boy, his

546

growing up years, the dark days in hospital, the Genesis of it all lay in the actions of Danno Harper, in fact all the Harpers. They were the very foundation of all that came to pass. There it was. All his woes began with him, Danno. It all went back to him.

Norman stopped fiddling with the contents of the box and began to pack some of it away. The sound of papers rustling was enough to knock David out of his thoughts.

"Where do we go from here then?" said Norman. "Tewks won't be long now. What are you going to tell him?"

"Fifty odd years," said David. "It's a pity they don't still hang people for murder."

"With any luck, he's already dead," said Norman, sympathetically.

"Probably not," said David. "There might still be time."

"Time for what?" said Norman catching on. "Oh, come on David. You're not serious, are you?"

"They still hunt war criminals. A murder is a murder. He's a killer. Tewks will know what to do."

"And then what?" Norman said, his thinking racing faster ahead than David's. "Isn't it time you thought of yourself in all this?"

"I'm thinking of justice," said David.

"Fuck justice," said Norman. "You go ahead pressing charges, and see where your claim to the farm ends up then."

"It won't affect the farm. I'm a legal heir to it."

"So you'd pass a DNA test would you?" Norman teased.

"Would they do that?"

"They might."

David was forced to agree that Norman had a point. Being created by Miller and Lotty, there would be nothing of the Harpers in him. Even his surname was false he seemed to realise for the first time.

"So what do you suggest? We've got to tell Tewks something. We can't just leave."

Norman grinned. It was a slow, wicked grin that simply bent the corners of his mouth. His foxy sparkle brought his eyes to life. With exaggerated theatrics he reached for the old contract that had been taken out of the box.

"This is all he needs to know, surely. This document and your birth certificate should be enough to secure you a grand inheritance," said Norman. "Forget about justice and all that. Take the money. Plan your future. Sod the past."

So they left the bank, handed the parchment to Mr Tewks who was caught up in other complications, and said goodbye. Mr Tewks promised that he would contact them in due course but added that he did not foresee any problems.

It had been a long day. The two friends shared a meal at a small restaurant in the city centre, before heading back to their digs. That night, as the sounds of Norman's sinuses snored themselves to disintegration, David lay awake, running it all through his mind, until the juggernaut of exhaustion finally swept him away towards the morning.

Chapter eleven: Words

Ellie Tattershall. He had never thought of her as having a surname. She had always been just Ellie, Auntie Ellie, the embodiment of his greatest regret. At breakfast the next day, David tried to persuade Norman to come with him back to Paul's Dene, back to Ellie's house on Chadwick Avenue. Norman thought it ill advised. He argued that the disaster of his last visit was due to bad planning. He reminded David that it was he who had suggested mailing flowers to her, but even that simple icebreaker was out of the question now. A melancholy mood had contaminated David's being, the result of the things he had learned, and the fitful night's sleep he had endured. The mild disagreement between them burst out of David intermittently into short spasms of suppressed tantrums that had fellow guests turning their heads.

Calmly Norman persuaded his former patient to put more thought into how he should build such a bridge towards the sister he never knew he had. The mechanics of the persuasion was simple. Norman suggested a trip to the village where the mill had once been. David declared its name out loud, Maltoft. The change of focus did what

Norman expected. It put a spring into his friend's step. The breakfast that was hitherto fiddled with was devoured and over tea and toast they planned their day in a spirit of adventure.

The day was a cold one, the morning damp and still. Soon the snug interior of David's Astra had warmed them through. By the time they made their return to Great Rembleton the figure of just two degrees on the outside temperature display seemed a lie. They agreed to continue past the remains of Empton. With the few trees that remained now bare, the place bore little, if any, resemblance to what it once was. Rembleton itself, on the other hand, was now almost the size of a town. It was always a long village but now it reached out and absorbed the tiny hamlet that had once been his home.

Their journey followed the same roads that old, decrepit lorry had taken, when he went with Danno and the men to the mill. The roads looked different but his memory of those daily journeys served him well and soon the sight of an escarpment could be seen in the distance. He felt like a spirit returning to an old haunt, decrying change and rejoicing in familiarity. Even though the season was late he could see the rise blanketed by trees. Now devoid of their leaves they no longer resembled broccoli and it pleased him that they had not succumbed to the interference of progress.

Just visible, on the top of the ridge where the trees did not reach, was the shape of a monument, a great mound quite distinguishable, like a diminutive church spire on the crest of a hill. As they rose ever higher David glanced across at Norman.

"Maltoft. The windmill. Can you see it?" he said.

"Yes, I think I can," he said, straining ahead.

Unlike the old knackered lorry, David's car managed the steep climb with ease. As they emerged from the forested part of the hill, they came, as predicted, to a fork in the road. A signpost clearly pointed towards the next two villages to come. Maltoft was now only one mile away through tranquil countryside that had barely changed. Cattle still grazed in the fields as if they were the very same creatures that he had come to know all those years before. The dishevelled buildings had gone, either replaced or disposed of forever. Then the slope eased out and the mill came into view.

549

It was a physical feeling real and actual. The crushing disappointment hurt him no less than if he was stabbed. Norman knew something was wrong when he observed David's grip tighten on the steering wheel. He knew instantly that suggesting the trip here had been a mistake. David could do no more than stare at the place he once knew so well. Only now the meddling hand of man had trampled his carefully made plans into the mud, replacing his dreams of a working mill with their own ambitions. There it was, the tower still standing, but now it was a dwelling. A two-storey house made of red brick and a roof of pantiles had been erected beside it. There were curtains at the windows in the black tower, making it look cosy and homely. To David such visions were a sign of occupation. He imagined the occupants knew little, nor cared, of the work that had gone towards the mill's recovery. Once more the past was left behind where it belonged. All around him were the healthy footsteps of progress. He knew that it was he who was chained to the past. As the world moved on he was in some way being left behind.

David edged the car closer. Up ahead about two hundred yards away was Maltoft itself. Little had changed, though it seemed bleaker than he remembered. He looked over Norman's shoulder to what was beyond his window. A neat, pretentious sign made from half a millstone, at the entrance to the brick-paved drive, declared that a visitor had arrived at Maltoft Mill. The drive was well-laid with red block paving, a triangle of herringbone-patterned bricks, that would have been the entire expanse, had it not been for the shallow wall of a small, circular feature in the centre. The last time he saw this place it had been a quagmire of liquid mud. Now that memory was completely sanitised by domestic convention. Only the walled feature having been placed where it was did seem fitting. David knew its plants and shrubs marked the spot where Herbert Ashcroft was killed. A memorial garden, he thought, for his dear old friend.

A great sadness swamped him now. The mill overpowered his mind just as it had done on the day he first saw it. Only now, forever cheated of its rightful existence, it seemed to goad him. It taunted his life, his mother's lost chance, the loss of Ellie, the strange revelations at the bank, a life without Lotty, on and on it went, round and round in his head. He turned to his friend and told him he could not stand being surrounded by ghosts any longer. Even now the tendrils of his previous life were coiling round his ankles. He knew how they could drag him down, cleanse past memories and trap him, so they left, speeding through what had been Empton, heading for home leaving David to think about what to do next.

The journey home was a quiet one. David was think-driving, swerving occasionally on the carriageway as his attention suddenly snapped back to the present. Norman felt a little edgy but said nothing. He could find no way to elicit a conversation, searching as he was for a pathway into David's psyche without causing any further damage.

David tried to deny to himself that the two-day holiday had actually happened at all. The long search had ended at a dead-end place, being neither one thing nor the other. He was probably the proud owner of a set of farm buildings that looked like a pile of crap, or he was at the beginning of a legal battle against an old man who still possessed the power to bring him out in a cold sweat. He knew that eventually, at some time in the future, a DNA test would bring the whole thing crashing down around his ears. So he decided, after being harried by the constant round of nagging thoughts, to be happy with Connie's money and leave the past alone. With this decision made, he booked a couple of weeks off. In just over a month he would be jetting off to God only knew - somewhere hot, somewhere that would make him live again.

During a lull in the work routine one Friday afternoon he made contact with the vicar of St Peter's church in his hometown. In fact it was the vicar who rang him to return his call, his soft, deliberate voice creating calm and authority at one and the same time. David explained who he was and where his mother was buried. He thought there would be a mass of red tape to hack through in order to get a gravestone changed. In the end the vicar said it was simplicity itself. All David had to do was contact the stonemason of his choice, who would then contact the cemetery to make all the arrangements.

Even though time had marched on he could remember the name of Sculleys the memorial masons. He could still picture their poky little premises. So after thanking the vicar he found their number and called them. After expecting a bureaucratic battle, the reality was an anti-climax. They would send him some designs, they said. Then all he had to do was choose the one he liked, suggest some words and they would do the rest. They seemed very helpful and, when he said goodbye and put the phone down, he sat back in his chair and wondered what he should write. It was hard for him to connect Lotty the person, with the one he had come to call mother but they were one and the same and his love for this woman overtook his thinking. Even though she had hurt him in his life he could not completely stop the love for his mother. Although he had often said that he hated her, now he understood many of the reasons why she behaved the way she did. He was able to remember the feelings he had for Lotty and a completely different love bubbled up inside him. What words would be right for both feelings? Even as the last of the design team had said goodbye and gone home he was unable to move from his chair, paralysed as to what he should write.

Somewhere amongst the daily routine of his life David knew he was changed by his trip to Mr Tewks's office, as well as to the mill. The character of Daniel Harper, in particular, occupied his thoughts more and more. Revitalised visions of his own death at Danno's boots, swirled around in his head. Memories of the hypnosis took on a reinvigoration, unlocked in part by the recently seen pictures of David Sawyer's murder. He wondered if the man he was tricked into thinking was his dad would still be alive. He hoped he had met a terrible fate, a lingering illness, or an injury that slowly brought him down to an ignominious end. Was it worth risking his strangely contrived inheritance to find Daniel and involve the police, he thought? A murder conviction would mean a life sentence and for a man most likely in his seventies, that would mean until death. He knew that Norman would tell him to get on with his life and leave any great expectations to Mr Tewks in Salisbury. He knew his mind was prone to obsessions and he tried to blank out the voices in his head, which were urging him to think about it and to seek justice. Meditation failed in this respect, as did his attempts to become a workaholic. Like flies these thoughts buzzed around in his brain, annoying him to distraction morning, noon and night.

It was on one such morning, during breakfast, when he heard the post flop onto the doormat. Immediately, as he went to collect it, he could see the large brown package from Sculleys on the floor, their logo and slogan clearly visible amongst the jumble of other bits of mail. *Rest Assured in Peace* it read in a slender font. He wondered what sickly-minded twit had thought that one up. He picked it all up, took it back to the table and carried on with his Weetabix. The brochure was surprisingly well produced, glossy, with well-printed photographs. A simple letter outlined that, once he had given his consent, all the necessary arrangements would be made. Imperceptibly he became lost in the variety of memorial styles. Crosses, angels, plain slabs and sculpted arches, there was so much choice. Then, for no reason at all, he looked up at the television that had been droning in the background. The clock in the bottom corner of the screen suddenly shocked him back into the real world. He knew instantly that he would now be late for work and in a state of aggravated panic he tossed the brochure onto the table, leaving the breakfast pots where they were. The brochure skidded across the remainder of the correspondence, scattering the lot onto the floor.

Cursing, he grabbed everything together, slapping it back on to the table. That is when he saw it. With a sickening movement, the breakfast lurched in his gut. The envelope lying on top of the rest of the post, the sticker, the printing, he knew from whom it had come. The temptation to shred it was compelling, overpowering, but not quite as powerful as the temptation to peek inside, to see what other sick message she had planned for him. There was nothing about his mother that he did not know already, he thought – or was there?

He handled the white envelope as if it were a toxic substance, taking out the contents like a member of a forensic team at a crime scene. It was another poisoned newspaper cutting. The headline attempted at being sensational.

NEW EVIDENCE – WOMAN'S SUICIDE IN QUESTION

David read on, now oblivious to the time of day, hardly able to believe what was on the page. The date of the cutting was a month after the previous one he had received from the bitch. Someone had come forward with an eyewitness sighting of an elderly man leaving the house on the night Charlotte Harper had supposedly killed herself. The sighting had been at dusk when poor light had prevented an accurate account. The witness, whose identity had not been given, said that the man had run off leaving the front door ajar, adding that the assumption of the man's age had come about by virtue of his slumped back.

A note on the bottom of the paper, printed with an ink-jet simply said:

Gets juicier by the week, doesn't it?

David felt sick. He screwed the piece of paper inside his fist, trying to crush it to nothing. Curses and abominations spat from his mouth, powered by a frustrated rage. The little ball of paper hurtled from his whip hand like a stone, hitting the wall opposite and falling to the carpet. It would have been torn to shreds if he had not been struck by the thought that Queenie was a designer. She could easily have knocked-up a spoof page and made it look like a newspaper cutting. Maybe all of this was made up anyway, he wondered? The chance that it might have been a fabrication put a different slant on it all, but the nausea was still there when he got to work thirty-five minutes late.

All day long plagues of questions like epidemics of bizarre suppositions ravaged his time at the office. People could sense he was not quite with it turning with the passing hours into a spreading whisper. He could not get the man, who had been seen fleeing his mother's flat, out of his mind. Were it true how could the suicide note be explained? A chance burglar caught in the act would have fled. Even if such a person had struck her, he could not rationalise why such a person would have hanged her on the banister. More curious still was the suicide note that she had left. Either the eyewitness had been wrong, David considered, or the little fart had made it all up. Unless, unless?

"Supposing the running man had been real," David was talking to himself, out loud. "What kind of person would make her write such a note before murdering her. Apart from hiding the truth, why make it look like suicide?"

He tried to remember the words she had written. All he could recall was the reference to the Will and the curse on the place he was to inherit. Its details were now lost in the mists of time, but it had been written personally to him, to make him take notice of her. The question as to why she should concoct such a note, such an intimate message, as her murderer forced her to comply, could only be answered by assuming the man was someone she knew. Why else? Then all the sense fell apart. What did the killer gain from pressurising her to put pen to paper as she did? By twists and turns of warped reasoning the fabricated story began to hold water again. Only supposing, his mind convinced him, that this man wanted to create a response? His words became spoken as if to a companion.

"This person meant me to make a move, to flush me out. What kind of person would want to set a trap for me? What kind of murdering bastard would want to find me too?"

In that instant, like a frozen moment, he realised that only one person fitted the bill. David felt a pang of fear chilling his blood. Queenie's letter had broken through. It pierced his nerves. He could not sleep. Every noise in the flat made him jumpy. When the phone rang at work his heart leapt, lest it should be that person. Even when he went out for lunch, or went into Nottingham, he felt as if he was being followed. Occasionally, people found him confiding to thin air, as if another person was by his side. Some joked that he was praying and they may have been partly right. He found it comforting, although he realised with a terror what he understood all too well, that bits of him were falling apart. Amongst all the worry and disorientation that had seeped into his life he became fearful he could no longer hold it all together. The weeks passed in this way and no one came for him in the night. Little by little he began to relax and find his old self again.

One morning, just before lunch, he received a phone call from Sculleys, the stonemasons. The new stone was ready and a provisional date of two weeks hence was booked for the setting. David found he had a new focus. He decided to write to Ellie to tell her what was due to happen. The letter was a strange one, stilted and awkward. He spent an hour on his laptop one evening composing the first paragraph alone. Even then it was a contrivance. Each time he picked up the printout and read it to himself, he clambered through sentences he had bashed and bent into shape but the desire to appeal to her was full of sincerity. Maybe that was the reason for its strangeness. Somehow he felt he had to convince her that he was in earnest. That he did not want to bring disaster upon her but rather to mend bridges. What better place to lay the past to rest than at mother's graveside he wrote, being careful with the genealogical references, not wanting to divulge the truth about her own parentage. It occurred to him that she might never have known about her origins. Telling her by letter, he thought, would be too cruel and would have send his dream of reconciliation with her beyond the brink. He told her the time and place and hoped she would be there. In the end he settled on the best of a bad job and posted it off, praying that she had remained at the same address and leaving the outcome to fate.

Two weeks later he was on his way back to the old town to do the deed. He was nervous. It had been nearly a year since his last trip to his mother's grave and paradoxically, on this occasion it was both easier and more difficult at the same time. None of the CDs in the car seemed to calm him. In the end he ejected his album of choral music and let the BBC provide him with the distraction he craved - but it was no good, he had to turn the car radio off.

It had been Radio Four's *Woman's Hour*, where middle-class women were talking about their silly, infinitesimal problems. Did anyone really care about how to break the biscuit habit, or what went into making a successful coffee morning he thought with a mix of irritation and nervousness? Everything they talked about seemed sickeningly cosy in an out-of-reach kind of a way, and the idea of the BBC putting aside an hour a day especially to rally the cause of the neglected sex seemed so out of date, not to mention patronising. Even their beautiful elocution seemed wasted on such banality. He thought it pathetic. David imagined them interviewing him on the show. He would not mince his words. He would tell them a few things about women. The notion of it caused the sarcastic sneer of a smile to prick one corner of his mouth. Sarcasm carefully blended with bitterness, it had become a habit for him to think in that way. It was the way of his life. As one thought led to another he drifted into his own history, the trials of his own life, his struggle through his own time to stay alive. To the women on the radio it meant fighting against the tempting lure of the sinister biscuit made by the evil empires of men. To David life had been a painful mystery, which he had never unravelled, at least never fully until this auspicious day.

Before he killed the radio he had been flicking through the channels. He heard a snatch of an old song, *I can see clearly now the rain has gone*, on Radio Two. That is how he felt last August, when he was last at his mother's grave. Back then he beheld the ruined landscape of his life clearly for the first time and then, just as now, it was a bright, bright, sunshiny day. The same sun glinted through the windscreen as he drove the car into the same cemetery car park. He could indeed see all obstacles in his way, real and daunting. Getting Ellie back, moving on from the past that was gone for good, even dealing retribution on the man he once thought was his dad - the man who had ultimately forged the awful chain of his life's events. The achievement, he appreciated, was that he could actually comprehend that the obstacles were there, standing in his way - but now the rain had gone, gone forever. From his earliest days the rain had completely obscured the things that blocked the road. Metaphorical rain that had been pouring down since the day he was born. Now he knew why life's rain had fallen like it did for so many years. He had allowed himself to believe that glorious day that he had finally found the road to freedom. He began to feel freer than he ever had done. It was a freedom like no other.

David left his coat on the back seat of the car. It was warmer than when he set off in the early morning. He followed a green moss-covered tarmac path that led from the central avenue and counted thirteen stones after the praying angel monument. Three places in there it was, Lotty's grave. Images of his childhood danced lifelike in the space between the grave and his face. All his growing up milestones seemed to creep out of the earth to haunt him. It was like a set of vivid dreams fast-forwarding through his mind as he stared down at the old heartless slab of stone. It certainly was a long and winding road that had brought him to this point.

Down there, beneath the ground, were the remains of the woman he had loved, still loved. He loved her in life and now beyond it. By some strange goings on, that he could never understand, he had placed the baby in the very womb that even now was decomposing in the ground, the womb that had served to bring him into the world. Poor Lotty never stood a chance. Given the right circumstances she would have been a wonderful person but her mind had been bent and crushed. All he wanted was to go back to The Beckett and take care of her, to love her, not just to make love to her but to love her, protect her. None of it could ever be, he knew it. A chasm of time had ripped their lives open as if a timequake had split the universe apart.

There was no sign of the stonemasons. In any event he was a quarter of an hour early. To defuse his misplaced sense of anxiety he turned away from Lotty's grave and headed back to his car. The dancing replay of his life went with him as he got there. Even the crunch of the cinder-covered car park evoked deep, dark memories. Once the car door had clunked shut he waited, lost in a strange mood.

Bang on time a green van bearing the Sculleys logo in cream pulled in and parked up. Two men emerged smartly dressed in dark suits. Like a music hall double act they proceeded to drape calf-length khaki aprons over their business clothes. It was like seeing into the mystique of their profession, almost as if he had stumbled upon a performance of one of their secret ceremonies. Adorned this way, David could see them looking intently along the row of parked cars. He got out and held his hand aloft to get their attention. They came over.

"Mr Harper, I take it," said the taller one offering his hand, his attempt at a Kensington accent, failing to mask his true origins.

"Yes, David Harper. Pleased to meet you at last," he said. "Would you like me to show you where my mother's grave is?"

"We know," said the rotund, little companion, rudely. "The stone's in the back," he went on, flicking his eyes towards the van, "and we need a signature."

Any feeling of misgiving disappeared when he saw the stone lying on its back, cushioned by layers of rags strewn over the van's floor. The firm had done a beautiful job. He checked it out word for word.

It was perfect. He signed their documents and gave them a cheque for the balance outstanding.

This done, the tall one strode up to the chapel office and came back with two unlikely characters, both dressed in grey clothes, vestments that had been well acquainted with soil and grime over the years. They appeared to be apprentice and mentor - a partnership of tired old bastard and dim powerful youth. With one thin spade apiece David realised that the two suited men were having nothing to do with the manual work but were to be overseers only.

So the work began like the extraction of a tooth. With grunts and whispered curses the old tablet came away and was moved aside, the empty words now discoloured by lichen and moss. David watched it all from a respectful distance. He could see the new mortise being carved out of the earth by the labourers' narrow spades, ready to take the tenon of the stone's base. The sight of these four men encapsulated the remnant of the class divide that even in the present day had been perpetuated in the town. He had known it as a boy in church where little bigots had fooled themselves into importance and had even made lesser people believe in their supposed superiority. That was their power, just like Mrs Cartwright all those years ago.

Then, like a couple of removal men, the stonemasons carried the monolith from the van to the awaiting hole, handing over their charge to the men of muscle. In it went, over a third of it disappearing beneath the ground. The fit was exact, its orientation perfectly erect. With a brief tidy up the workmen said good morning and went back to their lives carrying the old stone away with them. The stonemasons bid him a good day and left him alone in the graveyard.

As the sound of the van's engine faded away, he turned, smiling at the ornate piece of stone, its words now doing justice to the remains of the person who lay beneath it. It was a hard stone, not unlike granite, dark, the words etched deep into its surface being a slightly lighter shade against the surface colour. The top curved arch-like in true Gothic lines to a central point, its grace made even more complete by bevelled edges all round. He was glad he had put so much thought into what was carved upon it, now that it was here in all its permanence. It began in block capitals.

IN LOVING MEMORY

It was easy to recall memories devoid of love, or love misshapen at any rate - but there were memories full of loving to remember. He had Norman and Helen to thank for those. Beneath the first line, smaller, was written.

Of A Mother And A Friend

This line had innocence in it. To anyone passing by it gave nothing away and yet meant everything. In contrast his mother's name was a mass of swirls, evoking a style of times past, judging by the older memorials around him, but that is the way he wanted it. It read.

Charlotte Harper (Lotty)
who left us tragically on 12th November 1971
Aged 36

The space left between the date and the ground was about eighteen inches and here there was a small inscription that read.

Through God, death is but our way to Resurrection

There he stood for what seemed ages just looking, looking at the text wishing that things had been different for them both, but then again, if he had not cycled into Empton on that blistering day, the events that created him would never have happened. They could never have been different. Fate had meant it to be like this, he convinced himself.

The one thing that cut him up inside was knowing that the remains of the woman he loved would never hold him in her arms again, never kiss him, never share the physical and the emotional. Above all else he wanted that, just that. Without it his life was empty, lonely and void of any real meaning. If he were to meet anyone else, they would never be able to outshine the love that existed between he and she, his Lotty. Grieve and protest as much as he liked, he knew that his heart's desire could never be. Accepting the fact that he would yearn for it for the rest of his days would be his lot, his unhappy lot.

Chapter twelve: The Book

After waiting for three quarters of an hour or so, he realised it was never going to happen. Every vehicle that pulled into the car park animated his hopes like a puppet brought to life, only to crumple when unknown occupants emerged clutching either flowers or small gardening tools. He had to face it. He had lost her. In the end he allowed his patience to last for an hour-and-a-half, like a faithful dog waiting for its master to come home, but Ellie never materialised. Something within him began to die. Strangely, turning on the car's ignition was akin to switching off a life-support machine. He had to accept that leaving the car park would sever all chances of a reunion with his beloved Ellie. His letter to her had failed. So he took one look back to where all the dead people lay, managing to glimpse Lotty's stone rising from amongst the ranks of other monuments and drove out slowly onto the road thinking a host of dark laments and sad goodbyes.

In a way he was free, in a strange kind of freedom with no ties or responsibilities to anyone, living or dead and connected to nothing. He could see himself as tumbleweed. In the same way, whether he liked it or not, he was free from his roots, all of his roots, free and alone, tumbling through life to nowhere in particular.

Why he did not just head for the dual carriageway and set a course for home he was at a loss to answer. Dabbling with curiosity he drove to a recently built multi-storey car park and punched out a ticket for a couple of hours. The town was busy and the car park was full. He ended up finding a space on the top level out in the open. He was making for the lift when he stopped dead in his tracks. From up here he could look down on the whole town. There it was unchanged - yet he was mistaken. Looking more closely he could see where progress

561

had once more forced its interfering hand on the familiar scene that lay before him. Ansons looked smaller but cleaner. The yellow sign on its large office block now sported the name Anson Geitz Ltd. The five black brick chimneys had long gone. What looked like two steel missiles standing ready for lift off emerged vertically from the factory spewing nothing but wisps of eco-friendly fumes into the clean air.

He scanned eastward past the hills he had climbed up as a child, until his eye caught the jagged thorn of St Peter's great black spire. Even in its grime its architectural arrogance was without parallel. The view of the old part of town from where the church reigned supreme was virtually devoid of alterations, a timeless vision that fooled his mind into an uncontrollable spiral backwards to his boyhood and the wonderful anthems that rang out beyond the roof of the ancient building. Pricked by a nostalgic sickness and thoughts of his days as a boy, he crossed over to the other side of the car park to see the rows of terraced houses and the railway station area. Somewhere down there was the flat, the dreaded flat. His chest tightened at the prospect of it still being there. Many of the monotonous regiments of dwellings had gone, replaced by modern housing developments. Had his old home been destroyed, he thought? He hoped so and before he had chance to talk himself out of it, he was out of the car park and making his way there.

He would like to have had the chance to see where it stood, but nothing was the same. Great swathes of the old slums were swept away to make way for simple new homes, new slums in the making, where young families could get their feet on the property ladder and be saddled with great mortgage millstones. Where exactly his mother's flat had once stood it was impossible to say. Even the roads were redeveloped. He finally figured out that it had once been where somebody's back garden is now. It was all gone, that world he had once known. Not too far away some of the old world still survived, a broken community cobbled together from damp bricks and filth - but his ancient beginnings had vanished and with it his chance to behold it for one last time.

Even now the graffiti artists had begun to drag the modern day in the same direction as the olden. The same crushed spirit still dwelt among the poor inhabitants, creating the same kind of grotesques that

562

he had grown up with. There was nothing to stay for. If there had been memories here he would not really want to unearth them anyway. There was a part of him that questioned why he came here in the first place. As he turned his back on it all, he felt equally glad and disappointed to be leaving. He emerged onto Canal Street feeling uneasy about his noxious visit. In a moment he left that part of town and idly sauntered towards its commercial heart with no clear aim. Led by something otherworldly in the direction of the place that had given him his only happiness, St Peter's church.

Mother church eyed him reproachfully he sensed. As he came closer to its dirty sandstone walls he seemed to hear the building say, you've come back have you? For a moment he lacked the courage to go inside. His long absence from her altar caused him to seek a kind of peace with her, a forgiveness of sorts. Even the heavy door possessed a cold refusal to allow him to enter. So he stayed outside leaning against the crumbling wall, and there in the hum of the bustle around him he found quietness. Something was happening to him, something slow and delicate, almost as if his body was being absorbed into the stone that had been hewn long ago to build this glory to God.

Over the road a lorry was unloading its supplies to a cake shop. A mother was struggling with a tantrum from her two-year-old. All around life was going on as normal, but he felt as if he was being taken out of it. Deep within him he heard a sound of crying, a shout from far away, a scream coming from a far distance, as if from the other side of a river. He had heard the sound before a long, long time ago, right on this very spot. It was his prayer, the only prayer he knew would be heard and he let it go on. There was a sense that his spine had merged with the weather-beaten walls and sent his screams up through the tower, higher up beyond the lofty spire, past the weather vane and onwards up to the Lord God of Hosts.

The prayer jolted to a stop as he felt the gentle weight of an arthritic hand reaching out to touch his arm. He opened his eyes to see an elderly lady wearing a grey coat, carrying a wicker basket, laden with cleaning items polish, dusters and a pan and brush. With a kind fearlessness she looked him up and down.

"Do you need help, young man?" she asked in a mousey voice, creaking with age.

David looked at her through his blurred vision and wiped the tears from his face.

"I'm sorry. I don't know what came over me," he lied.

"Perhaps you need to come inside, into the church," she said quietly.

"Thank you," he said back, smiling at her meekness, "I'd like that."

It was as if he had been given permission to enter, where his conversation with God could continue in His Holy place. He followed the frail lady in through a slit door cut into the great slabs of oak that made up the ornate main entrance. With a suddenness that took him by surprise, the outside world became muted, supplanted by the subdued white noise of calm and, once the rattrap snap of the heavy latch had finished sending its iron clang echoing in all directions, there remained a holy peace. A timeless smell filled his lungs like a blessing, or a welcome, a homecoming. It was as if the Holy Spirit had washed him from the inside out and all was well. David turned and let his eyes see. Nothing had changed. This beautiful place, where he had once snatched brief moments of comfort, had remained pure to his memory of it. Like the never changing face of the Lord God, so too had His place of worship. In one moment he had become ten years old again.

Not daring to approach the altar at the far end of the nave, he sat at one of the first pews he came to and let that great sight sink in. Apart from the intermittent clattering of the old lady going about her chores, the quietness lulled him like a sleeping drug. Far away he could see the choir stalls. He could even see where he once stood on that far off evening when he sang for the choirmaster. It had been the hand of God, he realised, that had brought Ian Crabtree back into his life, to bless it and give it purpose. He could almost touch that hand as if it were something tangible, like a small child knows the strong and gentle force of an adult's guiding arm.

Then looking up above the dark wooden screen suspended by chains from the lofty roof, he saw the great crucifix. He recalled in an instant the days he used to stand in a certain spot and let Christ crucified look into his own eyes. The temptation overpowered him,

564

so he got up and walked down the aisle to where he remembered the place to be. Searching the worn tiles that made up the floor he tried to find one that had a T shape crack through it, and it was there. How amazing he thought, that through all the twists and turns of his life, the running away, the jobs, Rebecca Tindale, the hospital, Norman and Helen, throughout everything, this cracked marker had changed not one jot. So he stood with his toes touching it, as he often did when a boy, and lifted his head to Jesus that he might behold his gaze - but the eyes of Jesus beheld him not. The gaze now burned into his heart. The eyes of the man on the cross bore into his chest and not into his eyes. He looked down to see if he had chosen the wrong set of cracks, but no, he had not. Then he realised why. It was simple. He had grown from a child to a man. He was taller that was all. The voice in his head was like the voice of God. It told him that he must draw nearer to the cross. His feet shuffled a step or two closer as if obeying a heavenly command. God had been right. Now the eyes of The Son penetrated into his soul through his own eyes. The figure nailed to the wood had seemingly come to life again and for a while David felt afraid. The fear possessed something good. He could not understand it. No audible voice came forth. There were no words of divine advice to be heard. Just the plaintive look from the One who had died to save us all, a look infused with a loving authority.

Then, as he tried to fathom the grandeur of the mystery before him, the moment passed, evaporated away by the sweet pipes of the mighty organ, its great voice now reined in to nothing but a whisper. He lowered his head from Christ and went to sit on his old pew in the choir stalls. He could tell by the false starts and unpredictable halts to the music that the organist was having a practice session. The person at the keyboards might even have been a visitor. It did not matter though. The sound bathed his soul in a balm that only this vast instrument was able to apply. His mind began to wander. It was an idle stroll through the events of his life and the people he had known in both his lives. Particularly he thought about those he had lost, especially Lotty, even the version of her he called mother. He had come to like Herbert Ashcroft in the short time he knew him. Almost imperceptibly the cobweb strands of thinking worked their way back to one central point, to the dark, shadowy figure of Daniel

Harper. It was not a new concept for him to trace all of his woes to Danno. The kicking in the old house was branded on his memory still. Sitting in this church he could almost smell the evil that had lived in this man and still might.

Looking around he grew aware that he was the only visitor in the building. The old woman was there of course and so too was the organist, but no one else had ventured into the place. He was alone. It seemed like a metaphor for his life. All the people who had ever mattered to him had left him in one way or another. Even Ellie did not want anything to do with him and it struck him that even this isolation, this desolation, had its roots in the bad things that Danno Harper had done. He wistfully looked upon the Saviour for help but the figure on the cross was but a carving, a carpenter's interpretation. He knew in his head that the wooden body was not real, that the eyes were only man-made. Oh that He had been real, that He could have spoken. What words of wisdom might have issued forth? The word of the Lord, what he would have given to know that?

The frail lady had reached the pulpit and she smiled back at him as they shared a brief glance. How thin her arms were for such physical work, spraying and polishing. Her twisted fingers could barely hold the duster and yet she was already in paradise, doing a job that she loved beyond words. Beyond words, he thought. Words. There they were, the words, the words he wanted, the word of the Lord. The tiny woman had reached the lectern on the pulpit and began polishing the area around the place where the *Holy Book* now rested. It laid there, open, maybe ready for the next reading, or left untouched from the last. He wondered if he dared climb the stairs reserved for the clergy and read the words that were there on its blessed pages. The very notion of it felt like trespass. Yet had he not asked for words? Had it not almost been a prayer? Had not God used this delicate old woman to invite him into the church in the first place? Surely this was another invitation?

So he waited for her to go and then, after a few minutes, he made his way up to the stone steps that led to the high pulpit. Each stair was climbed with trepidation until he reached the *Bible* sitting serenely in its place. The entire church could be seen from here. From this vantage point he had a bishop's eye view of the masses of pews below and he felt like a thief. It was as he suspected a large King James' Version, the Authorised Version by another name. The great book was bound in leather and appeared heavy. The type was large, perfect for anyone reading the words thereon to a congregation. It had been left open at the book of Isaiah chapter forty-two.

So, now there were to be words as well as the Lord's countenance. Here would be His guidance. The question about David's issue with Danno would be addressed and his mind was open. With his index finger he touched the first words to catch his attention. *Behold my servant, whom I uphold; mine elect.* Each word that issued forth was charged with charisma. Here, in this moment, the Lord Almighty was calling him His servant. He read on captivated. *In whom my soul delighteth; I have put my spirit upon him,* and he did feel it, exposed above the pews below, as if a Great Spirit was close by, even upon him. He felt it the moment he entered the building. He had felt it as a child. *He shall not cry, not lift up, nor cause his voice to be heard in the street.* So, there it was, God himself knew that he had been snivelling outside and now he was telling him that he need not cry any longer.

He skipped a few lines, aware that the old lady was still around and might rebuke him for being where he should not be. More words flowed into him. *Behold, the former things are come to pass, and new things do I declare; before they spring forth I will tell you of them.* The former things it said. Former things. It was incredible. The Spirit of God, even He knew how his lives, this one and the former one, were so intertwined. It was proof that God's voice was coming through to him. He was now at verse thirteen. *The Lord shall go forth as a mighty man, he shall stir up jealousy like a man of war; he shall cry, yea roar; he shall prevail against his enemies.* So here was the word, the word concerning Danno. The Lord would be with him. He would be with him in a war against him, but how was the war to be fought? He searched the two facing pages seeking out the Lord's word, fearful that someone might find him abusing the Holy pulpit. Immediately, he came across a passage that set his mind at rest. *For I the Lord God will hold thy right hand, saying unto thee, Fear not; I will help thee.* So he continued the search, reassured that he had been given the right to stand here on this sacred spot. There he found on the left hand page, towards the end of chapter forty-one, the word from God once more. *Produce your cause saith the Lord, bring*

567

forth your strong reasons, saith the King of Jacob. He knew then, that this concerned Empton. It concerned his claim to what was rightfully his and put forth his reasons for his inheritance, but he did not comprehend how this was to be done. How was he supposed to just go there and say to Danno that the farm was his now? As the questions nagged him the words continued to pour out before his eyes, *Let them shew the former things, what they be.* What former things, thought David? He gazed ahead wondering. Then, in the silver shade of the lamp, he saw the one former thing, his own face in its reflection. He was the former thing. He was as Miller. He would go to the village and show his face and Danno would believe it not, and the Lord would hold his right hand, and lo, He, the Lord God, would do for him what he alone was unable to do, for had not the Lord said unto him that he should fear not?

He read all this in a fragment of time and came to his own conclusions in a briefer span, but the sound of the lady at work was round about him and his welcome in this consecrated pulpit seemed outstayed. Scuttling down the steps back to the choir stalls was a relief of sorts, like an intruder making his escape, unnoticed. As he sat back in his own seat, catching his breath, he knew that he had become infused by this place. He had seen God's face and taken in His words.

Without warning the impromptu organ recital changed tack. He heard the sound of stops being pulled, even from his position in the choir, but thought nothing more of it. The next instant a booming volley exploded from the pipes with a monster's groan, a growling major chord, created it seemed so as to burst the walls asunder and bring the great roof crashing down. It jolted David's calming heart to a shudder, widening his eyes and reawakening his senses. As the deafening notes played on, he knew instantly that it was a chant, a passage of music repeated over and over to accompany the singing of Psalms. By a choirboy's reflex, he reached out in front to retrieve his chant book and Psalter. Even now he found the process of having the music in one book and the words in the other strange and awkward and, in any case, what number chant was being played? What Psalm did it accompany?

He had always liked the Psalms. His namesake had written them and it gave him a kind of ownership of them. Thousands of years before his own birth, another David, a shepherd boy, had played his harp and sang these words to his sheep. Harper being his surname only made the connection more meaningful. The Psalter, the book that contained the words, flopped open at Psalm, number two. His eye fell halfway down it to where was written a decree. *The Lord said unto me, Thou art my Son; Ask of me and I will give thee the heathen for thine inheritance, and the uttermost parts of the earth for thy possession. Thou shalt break them with a rod of iron; thou shalt dash them in pieces like a potter's vessel.*

Inheritance thought David, the heathen, my possession. It could only mean one thing, Bofindle Farm. Whom was he destined to rule over with an iron rod? Who was he to dash to pieces like a potter's vessel? It would be none other than he who was the heathen as the Psalm said. It would be Danno. It would be Danno who would be dashed with an iron rod. He would never have expected that talking to God would be like this, but His word was getting through to him and he felt good, empowered like never before. He sat back and let the music lift him on wings of sound. His heart was strong again and he felt privileged to have been granted this prayer of prayers.

David placed the Psalter and chant book back where he found them. His thoughts flowed to David, the writer of the Psalms, King David as he finally became, and the story of Goliath dropped neatly into his mind. Too neatly, he thought, for by now, he was convinced that God was in communion with him. Goliath the giant warrior, brought down by a simple shepherd's slingshot, fired by the boy David on the battlefield. David and Goliath, David and Danno. It was all the same, the same old story, the bully brought down by the meek.

The music ended abruptly. From the silence came the rattle of the sliding cover being brought down over the keyboard followed by the muffled sound of stops being pressed home. Hardly audible was the precise snip of a tiny key locking it up, as the dying hiss of the great instrument's exhaling breath rendered it dormant until it would be needed again. The organist passed by him as he went out. David thanked him as their eyes met. The musician was painfully shy and fought through his reserve to say thank you back. An indistinct conversation between the organist and the old lady took place briefly. David heard her say to him that she would also be on her way soon. He took her reply as his cue to leave also. He got up and stood square on to the altar and took in the scene shown in the great window behind it.

Outside, beyond the windows, the thickening clouds had dimmed the late afternoon sky, but there was enough light penetrating through the coloured stained glass to see the depiction of the risen Lord. Unlike the tortured man on the cross, this Christ was in glory. Shafts of depicted light beams fanned out from behind Him and, almost floating there, as if he were weightless, he looked out, calmly, from an event that would have been utterly extraordinary should it have happened in the present day. Angels hovered round about Him like helicopters in a sky of azure blue, and set in a swirling ribbon of gold at the foot of the huge design, were words written in a Gothic font that he found hard to read. Then he deciphered it.

Unless a man be born again, he cannot enter the kingdom of heaven

Why the words suddenly made him feel uncomfortable, he could not say. Perhaps it was that he had often heard Gwen push them down his throat. It had made him want to resist the message she used to try and convert him into a born again Christian even then. For a while he stood reading what was on the ribbon. Then, as he had been trained, he bowed before the image, slowly turned and made his way back down the aisle, wondering why the words he had just read suddenly seemed more like an omen than a comfort. He was soon outside, back in the hard world, where God rarely ever spoke, as his mind began to thrash out the meanings of what had just happened to him.

He had grown cold and shivery by the time he got back to the car. It was getting late. He took one last look at the town spread around him. There, above the sprawling buildings, St Peter's church seemed to offer him its farewell. It was the last building he saw through his rear-view mirror as he climbed up out of the valley and left the town behind, to face the future and head for home.

Over the following days he found the words he had read haunting him. Their power had him in their grip. He knew that he was susceptible to it. He could recall how the empire had taken over his life - but this was no empire, this was a Kingdom. The Kingdom of God, the Kingdom of Heaven, call it whatever he liked, it was growing within him with more splendour than any empire could ever have done. He had made the empire himself. This by contrast was God's work and quietly he allowed the Lord God to have His way.

This time, as he had learned from the experience with Queenie, he kept this revelation to himself. No one would know that he had been talking with God. He knew he would be ridiculed. At work he would be the butt of all jokes and discredited. Even Queenie's words would then resound with credibility, but he did believe what had happened. The maker of the universe and all that was therein, He had made His presence felt as if he had shared an afternoon with the man Jesus himself.

One Saturday, as he cleaned the flat, he came upon a box of old things. They were, as if from another life, another person. Of all the things in it, there were two that evoked the deepest of feelings. So much so that he came close to tears. One was a *Bible*, the one that Gwen had given to him on his twenty-first birthday. The other was just a stone, the size of a small potato, the stone that he had kept all these long years to remind him of his liberation. Opening the *Bible* to Psalm number two, he was reminded that something like his stone would be needed to effect his liberation into the next part of his life. The Psalm had said it, a rod of iron.

Chapter thirteen: Mysterious Ways

It said a great deal about the state of things, when Norman called David for a chat one evening no mention was made about the church and what had happened there. The conversation was upbeat and Norman was satisfied that his friend's health was strong, mentally at least. When the talk finally ended and the phone went quiet, David knew what Norman could not know - that a new order was being formed in his head, just as it had happened once before. Only now it was not he who was building it. He allowed himself to believe it was being built for him this time - this time it was different. There was always a kind of emptiness about the empire. Its creation had been the work of one individual, for one individual had rendered it too much a private world, where no one could enter and no one was ever welcome. It was, in fact, the perfect recipe for loneliness.

This new kingdom however, was something altogether different, or so he allowed himself to think. Gone for good were the thick imperial walls of defence. In their place, on the site where structures like Hitler's Atlantic wall had once stood, ecclesiastical pinnacles of imaginary wonder now rose up serenely in his mind. Within him there emerged a Holy City, its splendour kept away from the real world by an imposed vow of silence. The rules had thus been drawn. The universe beyond his mind would see him as if nothing had changed. It was easy for him to do this. Each day was akin to a performance on a stage. The act was a one-man show where he was the star and the scenes were normality. Within the realm where his thoughts could run freely, he permitted whatever was growing there to use him as its host, not as a parasite, but more like an energiser, for he was, he believed, being made powerful.

Often, in between appointments, he would sneak away and enter churches to sit inside them, trying to recapture that touch from the Spirit of God. There was a yearning to sense it, to embrace its uplift. The hunger for this heavenly food became acute and never fully satiated. Nothing would ever be the same as that first time. Instead he came to accept that he would have to be satisfied with what scraps of titbits dropped into his hand from the Lord's Table.

Sometimes he would spend so long in prayer, meditating inwardly, that he would enter into a state of perfect sleep. Once, as he prayed, he nodded off whilst kneeling. He slithered from the pew's edge and fell sideways into the main central aisle of the church, terrifying a group of visiting schoolchildren. Their teacher a young woman, screamed out loudly as he collapsed. She had imagined him to be the victim of a heart attack. The scream and the impact with the stone floor propelled him instantly back to consciousness. The moment he beheld the sight of twenty-five terrified children and their hysterical teacher, he pulled himself off the slabs cringing with embarrassment. Feeling humiliated he mumbled his apologies and made swiftly for the door.

So it was that the world within David Harper began to proliferate in more private ways. The fixation with going into churches never waned but, because of the praying incident, they became less concentrated. He felt an increasing desire to keep secret the way in which he was reordering his mindset. If there were any visits to churches and cathedrals, it took a form compatible with most visitors. He would wander and take in the sights and smells and, if he was lucky, there might be an organist in residence. On those occasions he would sit and listen and nibble on the meagre reward that the Lord sent down to him.

The whole business of going to church had another more worrying aspect beyond his passion of basking in the God's glory. The message that he had received caused him great vexation. He was troubled by it. Was he really being commanded to go and find Danno and to seek revenge on him with a rod of iron? Facing Daniel Harper was going to be bad enough without having to do the deed of killing him with a metal bar.

This is how David Harper's life was, when one gloomy Wednesday afternoon at work Ian knocked on his office door and told him there was a visitor in reception to see him. He looked quizzically at his boss, wondering what appointment he had forgotten.

"It's a lady," said Ian, tipping a naughty wink and grinning with devilment.

"Who is she?" asked David.

"Dunno," said Ian. "She's got one of your business cards though."

David made his way to the reception area where a female figure in a navy overcoat was sitting and reading a magazine. David prepared his mind with all his salesman's charm and began to wonder what sort of assignment it would be.

"Hello," he said, in a warm friendly tone, "I'm David Harper."

"I know," said Ellie, looking up.

David could not have been more stunned if he was punched in the head. His face said it all, disbelief. For what seemed an eternity he stood looking at her, unable to make a single utterance, struck dumb, dumbfounded. Her eyes took in the figure looking back at her. She could see he had done well in life, at least materialistically. In his dark grey suit, cream shirt and red tie, she saw in him the perfect executive-about-town, and his hair, that she had once trimmed herself, was now immaculately groomed. She liked what she saw and she smiled at him. It was the smile he knew, still there, in her old, worn out face. Her smile brought everything that had been between them alive once more in David's heart. But she looked smaller than he had remembered her and, when she placed the magazine back on the coffee table, he could see that her hands were shaking, jerky movements that had an uncontrollable force, which seemed to go beyond mere trembles of nervousness.

"Ellie," he said, wondering whether to smile or not. "Is it really you?"

"The one and only," she said with a faint hint of cold courtesy.

"What brings you here?" he said, immediately regretting the crude question, and re-phrasing his words. "I mean it's great to see you. Oh, what am I saying Auntie El, it's a miracle you're here."

Hearing him call her by the oldest name he knew made her smile again, but she was in control of it and it did not rest long on her face. It was replaced by a pleasant demeanour, a kind of cool benevolence.

"I don't have long, here I mean in Nottingham. Matthew's outside, waiting," Ellie got to her feet. "Do you have anywhere private, where we can talk?"

"Yes, yes of course. Look do you want a coffee or something?"

"Tea, I'd like a cup of tea, please."

So David took her to his office and buzzed for a couple of teas.

"Nice office," she said. "What do you actually do in marketing," she asked.

"I'm Project Manager here," he said, feeling embarrassed at sounding so grand in front of the person who knew him better than he knew himself.

"I find ways to make their crazy ideas happen," he said, lifting his head towards the design team beyond his office.

Her face changed and she held her breath in hesitation, as if a great moment had arrived in her life.

"David," she said, quietly, "I had to come and see you. I'm going away, you see."

"Going away, going where?"

"With Matthew. He's got a new job, and I'm going with him. He's in computers and all that kind of thing, you know."

"Where will you go?" he asked, deflated, having just been reunited with her.

"Vancouver," she said. "It's in Canada."

"Vancouver? But that's the other side of the world. Who do you know out there? Surely all your friends are here?"

"Listen David," she said, her fidgeting hands oscillating on her lap. "There's another thing you must know," she took a decisive breath. "I have Parkinson's Disease."

He beheld her with more attention in that moment than he ever had in all the time he had known her. He tried to think of what to say but nothing appropriate enough would form in his head.

"I've been attending a specialist in Salisbury, but I've been to see a Canadian surgeon in Nottingham this morning. He's developed a new type of surgery for my condition and I'm following him out there when he finishes his lecture tour. I'm pinning my hopes on him. Imagine me, a guinea pig?"

Ellie forced an unconvincing laugh, which highlighted her fear and worry far more than anything she could have put into words.

"Will it be expensive?" David asked with real concern.

"Yes, a bob or two," she replied.

"I'll pay, Ellie. Let me pay. Will you? I have some money put by."

"Don't worry about that. Matthew's taken care of it all."

The tea arrived and she drank half of it. Great care was taken by Ellie not to veer too close to the things that she knew David wanted to talk about. She told him about her life, as it was now, her friends and the trips she had been on, especially her visit to the Holy Land. She enthused about the things she had seen there, in particular Jerusalem where she had visited the Mount of Olives, and the site where Golgotha is reputed to have been. That place had moved her most of all.

575

All too soon she was on her feet. She said it was time for her to go. Matthew was waiting she reminded him. David was in agony trying to hide his heartbreak. Was this really goodbye? It was too heavy to bear. There was too much unfinished business between them. As he reached for the door handle to show her out, she reached into his eyes with hers. He was performing his courtesy like a perfect gentleman but she could see the truth beyond his smile. She knew what was going on inside him. It became impossible for her to keep up the pretence of indifference any longer. She had loved this Davy boy all of her life and she knew that the love would not die. It was Matthew who, with protective intentions, had tried to train her affections from her, but now the tiny remnant that remained was multiplying like a virus, unchecked. Quite slowly they drew closer and wrapped their arms around each other. Tears trickled and hearts melted. Before she left Ellie mentioned that she was having a farewell party at her home.

"It's in just over a week's time," she said. "Is that too little notice for you?"

"Oh, when exactly?" he asked.

"Saturday week," she said. "Most of my friends can only make an evening during the weekend. So a week on Saturday it has to be."

"What about Matthew?" he said, knowing that her son was likely to disapprove of his presence there.

"He'll already be over in Canada," she said. "The place will be a bit empty I'm afraid. A lot of my things are going over with him. I might even have the for sale board up by then."

"I'd love to come," he said, knowing that he had booked a date for the worst goodbye he could imagine.

All eyes were on them as he led Ellie to the door. She recognised the girl who had brought the tea and thanked her. David drew the front door that opened out into the fresh air of the street. Across the road a car was waiting and inside it he could see Matthew tapping the steering wheel with the tips of his fingers in time with music that only he could hear.

"Bye," she said, and smiled her smile.

As she crossed the street, David could see just what the weight of the years had done to her. In his other life he had known her as a small child. Now in her late fifties she seemed much older than that. Her gait was one of an arthritic, though her head remained proudly forward-looking. He found her brave little defiance such a loveable trait. Arriving at the other side of the road she turned and waved. Matthew jolted out of his musical trance as he heard the door of the car open. He looked across at David with deep mistrust, somehow sensing that he was there and, from the safety of his car window, fixed him with a glare. Then she was gone, melting into the traffic, merging into its endless flow. David went back to where he had left off and tried to resume the day's momentum. Now and again he was forced to stop and stare at the wall opposite his desk. A calendar, a clock and bookshelf seemed to vanish before his eyes as he stared them into invisibility, lost in a fog of thoughts.

He began to dread the party. There would be people present whom he did not know. They would no doubt be in a cheery mood, well wishers he imagined who wanted nothing better than to launch their friend towards a new life abroad, happy to see her go. How was he supposed to take part in such a charade? It was like rescuing a man overboard, only to have him slip away again into the deep. So much of Ellie was in him. She was his comfort. There was genuine love between them. Now she was ill and going away and, if she died, how would he know? He questioned the wisdom of going to the party. It would be so easy not to go. It would be the coward's way out. In the final analysis there was never any contest. He knew, even as he held these talks in his head, that the decision to go was irrevocable. The closer the day drew nigh, so did the fear of it all.

Work was the only therapy. It was the only thing that set his mind free of the impending day. Arbiet macht frei, work sets you free. He had once read that during his own dark days and, although it freed his mind temporarily, he knew that the day of dread must surely come. Like a railway line heading out towards a cliff edge he knew that he was on a one-way track towards an ending he found hard to accept.

All too soon he was travelling towards that end. It was that Saturday morning and his car was propelling him towards her, towards Ellie, his beloved Ellie for the last time. He could not believe it was happening. He felt like he was moving through the crowd towards his own execution. Carried along with him in the car were presents he had bought her. Things for her to remember him by, going away gifts, one of which had cost him nothing to make, but one that he knew would resonate deeply with her memories of him far more than the other little gift he bought for her at the bookshop. Thinking about giving her these things, provided him with the only positive part of the visit that otherwise he was dreading.

The journey happened and then it came to an end like journeys do. He was tired and glad to turn the engine off. The leafy lane was just as he remembered it to be, quiet and tranquil. Ellie's house seemed the quietest of all. Not even a For Sale board outside the place, as he recalled her saying there might be, but there were a number of cars already parked closely together on her part of the road. Other people, it seemed, had arrived before him. People he did not know, strangers. Foreboding permeated every step from the car to the front door and with a sense of déjà vu he pushed on the button of the doorbell.

Beyond the door were voices, layers of mumbling, split open now and again by detonations of polite laughter. He pressed the button again and one of the voices called out from the rest. It was a woman's voice. She was shouting softly.

"Eleanor! Eleanor dear, it's the door."

Footsteps on a bare wooden floor grew closer, then halted. He heard the door being unlocked, and then, in a scene reminiscent of his arrival at Edlington, Ellie opened the door and beamed her approval at his arrival welcoming him in. Even as she kissed him on his cheek he could feel her fluttering hand on his shoulder. It would not keep still. It was almost as if she were being possessed by a force unseen. In a way she was being possessed by her condition. Yet, even as the disease advanced within her cell by cell, it had not been completely malevolent. He knew that without the Parkinson's disease the fickle hand of fate would never have had anything to work with. The irony was obvious. As he stood on the doorstep of Ellie's home, it seemed unfair that the very thing that had been responsible for bringing them together again was all too soon about to cleave them apart.

"Let me introduce you to some of my friends," said Ellie, taking David by the arm.

She took him down her hallway to the sitting room. It was occupied by little groups of her friends who were having miniature conversations about infinitesimal matters. They swung their heads round in unison as he appeared through the living room door, still arm-locked to his host. Their chatter stopped abruptly.

"This is David everyone. David, who I was telling you about," she said.

David nodded as if performing a ritual bow and said hello. The nine people present squeaked timid hellos back.

"David's in marketing, aren't you David?" she said poking the embers of a party that refused to relight.

"Yes, that's right," said David, feeling as if he were at a school's careers lesson. "I work for a company called Inca Marketing. You may have seen our Spacebar adverts on television, the one with the cartoon chocolate spaceship perhaps."

No one responded, so he performed the comical, metallic voice of the alien who eats the chocolate rocket at the end of the commercial.

"There's always space for a spacebar."

He may as well have been on another planet too, he thought. Their shocked faces took his friendly icebreaker as an act of frightening extroversion. Ellie saved the situation by introducing him to them all individually in her own delicate way, a manner he always viewed as anything but weak.

Their names dropped into David's brain, and slid straight out again without making any impression. How Ellie had befriended such beings he was at a loss to understand, but they were her friends and that was that. They each in turn shook him by the hand as if they were taking a great risk to do so. Fear, that is what it was, fear. They feared him. He could see it in their eyes. There was astonishment that he had travelled all the way from Nottingham. He felt as if they were meeting an astronaut back from the moon. One guest, a tall gentleman with a slight crop of white hair asked him which roads he had taken to get to Salisbury. Once answered, a discussion into the merits of his chosen route grew swiftly, a discussion that opened up memories of past journeys they had themselves each taken. David imagined if he were able to vanish instantaneously the conversation would have gone on merrily without him, but to honour Ellie, who looked upon the opening of this discourse with some satisfaction, he hummed and nodded in all the right places until he felt like screaming the place down.

Food arrived just in the nick of time. The conversation now became gastronomic. On and on they chattered, smug in their parochial bubble. They were like fishes that had never known the great ocean of life. Their long years, he could see, had been spent paddling in their cosy little stream since the day they were born. All the time David knew that the few remaining minutes with his beloved Ellie were draining away - hours were being wasted on such mind-numbing drivel. He would have to say something even if it was just to bring Ellie back into centre stage. So he spoke. Without waiting for a convenient pause that would never happen, he jumped in, raising his voice over all the others.

"How long have you known my Auntie Ellie?" he said, hoping to strike up a new line of chat.

There was stunned silence, a deathly silence. What had he done, he thought? Even Ellie, he noticed, had been taken aback. Taken aback by whom or what? He was not quite sure. Was it their response, or his question?

"You never said you had a nephew Eleanor," said a woman guest.

Ellie shrank visibly. David, now confused, knew he had to say something, but what? What could he say that would prevent things getting worse?

"Oh, that's just a nickname, isn't it, Eleanor?"

She forced her face to normalise and allow a hastily made and small smile to grace her lips.

"I'd forgotten you used to call me that," she said, lying.

With that the delicate balance was restored. The warped gathering thus progressed in this way throughout the afternoon. David wished it over and done with, knowing that its end meant an even greater ending. With the sandwiches and cocktail sausages eaten, everyone retired to the living room. The house was filled with boxes, boxes that had the content descriptions written on them in black marker pen: ORNAMENTS, BOOKS and KITCHEN THINGS in block capitals. Through such images the end of the road wailed its lament into David's ear, his mind's ear, with a mournful cry it's all over

David, all over, and there was Ellie surrounded by her cronies, enjoying the remaining moments in their company. How could he get her to himself? How could he say the things he was desperate to say to her with such people denying him any intimacy? Then he remembered the presents he had brought with him. They were in the car. He told her that he was just going out to get something. She said that was fine and the door was still unlocked. So he went to grab his two gifts.

It was getting cold. The sky was darkening as if rain was due. He was glad to get back inside only then, to watch with sadness the few flickering moments pass with his beloved Ellie.

"I have a couple of things for you," he said raising his voice. "They're a pair of going away gifts. I hope you like them?"

With this bull-at-a-gate announcement the polite conversation stopped dead. All eyes were on him, on him and Ellie as she looked to see what he had brought her. He offered his first present, a flat, rectangular slab covered in wrapping paper. Taking care to open it, she removed its covering and found to her delight, a book. Bound in a real leather cover it was a *Bible*, smaller than the one he had at home but edged in gold just the same.

"It's a pocket version," he said, enjoying the approval of the recipient and attendant friends.

She leafed through a few pages, deflowering its pristine quality prising the gold edges that had stuck the pages together splitting them open.

"It's lovely," she said, her eyes shining with joy.

"I thought you'd prefer a smaller one for your travels," he said.

She bent forwards and kissed him on the cheek. Appreciative murmurs rippled out from those assembled. Ellie placed her new *Bible* on the table and, like a small girl, glanced at the other box sitting on the chair, its red bow making it all too tantalising. David could feel the anticipation as if he were picking up a radio signal from her. He handed her the present, a box, about a foot high.

"I feel like a child again," she said as she removed the paper.

Inside was a grey, brown cardboard box that was taped shut. Opening the lid Ellie was confronted by pink tissue paper that she carefully removed and placed on the table. Her hand felt inside and gripped something cold and hard. It was glass. She pulled it out. The shriek she gasped on seeing what she had picked up, almost caused her to drop the object on the floor. Staggering backwards, she reached for a chair and brought the bottle down on the coffee table. David watched the effect his gift was having on Ellie with a mixture of fright and satisfaction.

"Something to remember me by" he said, as one or two from the astonished crowd took a step towards their stunned host.

Ellie was now slouching, in stunned silence in the armchair. She managed to lift her eyes to his.

"What is the meaning of this?" she said just ahead of tears that were preparing to well over.

"You remember the prince that I made for you out of a bottle, long ago in the garden of the Golden Goose, don't you?" he said.

She struggled to find the words. A few managed to escape.

"How do you know such things?" she said, straining to speak. "I don't understand."

She turned her head to behold the bottle. It was just as Miller had made it, down to the last detail. It was the prince, dressed with the same crown on a potato head and cape made of a napkin.

"You mustn't cry Ellie. They lived happily ever after, remember?"

Like red-hot pokers, Ellie's searing eyes burned into his.

"How do you know about all this?"

"I know Harry Tattershall used to beat you up when you left your dolls in the cellar and you'd sit in the yard nursing your bruises."

At mention of such deeply buried memories being dug up, Ellie began to weep as if she had never grown up at all. It was all too much for her and she asked everyone to leave. With reluctance her friends began to file out of the house until it was empty, save for her and David. He had got her to himself at last.

"Do you remember the day I arrived at The Croft on my bicycle all those years ago?" he said, not wasting a second.

She nodded, reaching for a box of tissues.

"You said something very odd as you opened the door, something that meant nothing then but has come to mean a great deal since," wiping her eyes she looked back at him, trying to recall what she said to him. "You opened the door and looked surprised at seeing me standing there," David went on. "I thought it was down to your surprise, that I'd cycled all the way there by myself, that made you say it. But it wasn't, was it Ellie?"

"What did I say?" said Ellie, trying to recapture the event.

"You looked astonished at me and cried out a name, does that help you remember?"

All of a sudden the penny dropped. She put a hand to her mouth as her eyes widened like saucers.

"Oh, my God. Miller! I remember now. I thought you were Miller," she managed to speak.

David relaxed a little. The connection had been made.

"You remember the cyclist who came to Empton and stayed at the Golden Goose in the attic room. That's who fathered me, not Daniel Harper. That's not even my real name. God knows what my actual surname is. But of course, you've known that all along, haven't you Ellie?"

She reached out to hold him in her arms. The secret was bursting out of her like tons of water being purged from a reservoir.

"She made me promise not to tell you who your father really was," she said through a cracking voice as David staggered away from her.

"My God, you really did know!" he said, absorbing the truth that she had lied to him through all the long years they had known each other.

"Why did no one tell me all this? Even my mother didn't."

"And how could she?" Ellie said, a hint of authority pricking her tone.

"It would have helped explain all those dreams. But no, instead she would come into my room and… and… Christ, do I have to paint a picture?"

"She was sick. Her mind was ill. It got worse. Month by month she sank deeper. She was in love with Miller."

Ellie squared up to him as he stood in front of the mirror that hung over the fireplace. Protective masking tape was criss-crossed over it ready for removal.

"Take a look in the mirror David. There's Miller. There's not a scrap of difference between you. Your mum was sick in the head. In that state she thought that her long vanished lover had come back. She loved you as a baby, because you were his baby."

"You know about that too?" he said, annoyed that even that secret had been inside her all the time.

"I was in the pub when Danno burst in," she said, her brain rolling back the years. "He'd found out about your mum and Miller from that old church woman," she tried to recall her name.

"Mrs Cartwright," he said, helping her remember.

"Old Mrs Cartwright," she repeated, finding it hard to believe that he knew her name.

"The witch-lady of the pump. She couldn't wait to spoil Danno's life like he'd ruined hers, so she told him her wonderful news, and when Danno burst in, everyone in the pub knew that Lotty was having a baby too. There was a fight. Danno chased Miller out into the rain passed the dead house, out towards the wood we assumed," Ellie's mind had now reversed back fifty years. "Lotty grabbed my arm. I'd been knocked over and hurt myself. We walked and ran back to the farm. She packed a few things, food, clothes and money. She even took her wedding album for some reason. Anyway, that dreadful night we left, tramping down the lane towards Rembleton in the dark. It was awful. She held out her thumb to hitch a ride, leaving Miller to win the fight and come and find us. He never came. He abandoned us. We finally made it to Salisbury. You've no idea how desperate she was. We were always hungry. And all the time she had you growing inside her, getting bigger and ever more immanent. We had to fight for survival, always fearful that Danno would come looking for us. His temper knew no bounds. He was evil."

"Have you ever been back to Empton?" he said, wondering.

"No never. I'll never do that. John used to say it was unhealthy to go backwards in life. I believe he was right about that," with those words she looked again at her potato head prince and suddenly became still. All but her trembling hands were motionless, a strange stare, like a reminiscing gaze crystallised over her face. "How do you really know all this? You weren't even born then. Who's told you all this?"

Instead of answering David toyed with her still further. He began to hum a tune quietly, making the notes of an old song hang in the room. It was the folk song *One Man Went To Mow*. He added the words.

"*One man went to mow, went to mow a meadow. One man and his dog went to mow a meadow.* Good pianist was George," said David. "Friday wouldn't have been Friday without George banging out the tune on the old Joanna."

Ellie was now looking slightly terrified.

"Or how about a rendition of *Danny Boy*?" he said. "Even Danno liked that one."

"Stop scaring me. How do you know all these things?"

"I know about them because I was there. I was Miller. I knew Herbert Ashcroft, Mrs Eversage from across the green, old Joe with his horse and cart. But mostly I remember Lotty. I knew her before she had turned into my mother. In fact it was me who made her my mother, if you follow."

"This is outrageous!" she spat out. "You're mad. I've never heard such rubbish. You may look like Miller, but what you're suggesting, well, it's preposterous."

"So how do I know that you used to leave your dolls in the cellar, and Harry kept on telling you off about them?"

"I don't want to hear another word!" she said reaching a shout. "Get out and leave me alone."

"You sound just like me when I found out. It's quite a shock, isn't it?"

"You're ill David. You need help."

"I've had help. That's how I know all this."

"Rubbish. What sort of help?" she asked.

So David told her his story. He told her how he had reached rock bottom and how Norman and Helen had helped him. He recounted how the hypnosis that was supposed to defy the dreams instead took him back fifty years to Empton. He told her how he found himself in the life of someone else, the cyclist, and what happened as he leaned his bicycle for the first time against the railings of the Golden Goose. He told her everything, right up to the awful night when he ran away from Danno upstairs in the dead house. When he had done that he told the tale of his recovery and how he managed, with a great deal of luck, to discover the other awful truths. He ended at the point when he met the unique personage in the shape of Mr Tewks.

"Now there's a man you ought to meet. He'd introduce you to a few preposterous notions," he said.

"Why is it that you try and spoil everything?" she said with a tired misery.

"Things are often already spoiled," David said. "You should have lived my life, then you'd know."

"I did live your life for a while. That mother of yours, she became a sadist over the years. She'd hit me with whatever she could find. Always on the head she'd beat me. So don't tell me I don't understand. I do."

"I'm sorry. I didn't know," he said tenderly.

"Repeated whacks on the head are thought to have had something to do with the onset of Parkinson's disease. So I may have your mother to thank for being like this."

She held out her thin, ageing arms to proffer the sight of them jerkily moving without control. For a moment there was silence as the conversation jammed into a rut. David wondered if he ought to leave. There was nothing more to say. It seemed best perhaps to draw their lifelong relationship to an end right there, but then Ellie spoke.

"Who was it you said I ought to meet," she said.

"There's a firm called Gabbon, Sperry and Butterworth," he said, dragging the company name from his memory. "They're a firm of solicitors in Salisbury. Mr Tewks, he's the man you ought to meet. He'd tell you things about yourself you'll never believe."

"What kind of things?"

"I'd take you to him if we had the time," he said.

"What things would I not believe? Come on, we've got this far in your ridiculous imaginings."

"None of this is made up Ellie, it's all true. How can you not believe me?"

"You're making all this up just to hurt me. Why do you want to hurt me David?"

"I don't. That's the last thing I want to do," he said. "It's just that it's not easy facing up to all this for the first time."

"I've had to face up to a great many things in my life I'll have you know."

"Have you managed to face up to who your mother is, your real mother that is?"

"She died when I was born," said Ellie.

"Who told you that?" he asked her.

"Harry, well, everyone in the village knew. What are you driving at?"

"Your mother didn't die giving birth to you, Ellie," said David.

"I'm not sure I know you anymore," said Ellie finding it hard to look at him, "you frighten me."

"You've known more about me than I ever knew. Do you have any idea what it's been like peeling away all these secrets? Do you? It would have been a great help if you'd shone a little light on the things you knew," he said.

"I'm sorry," she told him, "but I made a promise to your mother."

"Don't you mean our mother, Ellie?" he said, throwing the line at her.

Ellie did not pick up on the significance of what he said for a second or two, but when the switch went on in her head it was as if she was wired up to the mains. David could see she had heard him.

"Oh yes, I can prove it. I've seen documents that say as much, signed by Arthur Gibson and Daniel Harper."

"What's Daniel Harper got to do with it?" even as the stream of words rolled out of her mouth, she knew the answer. "Oh no!" she almost screamed, "not him?"

So David told her what he had seen in the safety deposit box, the details of the rape and how the baby Ellie had been taken to the Golden Goose to be cared for by the Tattershalls. It was all too much for her to take in. From a face that was a mixture of horror and disbelief, a self-pitying cry broke free. David moved towards her chair and placed his hand on her sobbing frame.

"I was there you know. You'll have to trust me. I lived there for a month in nineteen fifty-four. You were just a little girl then. I can even describe the wedding cake that was made when Lotty and Danno got married. Ask me anything. I was really there."

Ellie wanted to believe him, against all her logical thinking. This seemed like the only explanation, but there remained the doubt that he was tricking her, for what reason she could not imagine. So she thought of something she had done or known as a child, something that only she would know, and if he answered her correctly, then she would have no alternative but to accept his wild tale about the hypnosis. Then she reasoned she would be forced to accept everything else he had told her. Settling for all of that presented her with a giant leap of blind faith. Whatever question she chose, she knew that the rest of her life would pivot on his answer. It would therefore have to be a good question. So she thought and at length it came to her, a fact that few people outside the little hamlet of Empton would ever have known.

"Okay then," she said, wiping her eyes, "tell me about the picture near the clock in the pub."

"You mean the photograph of The Vikings taken at the Charter Fayre in nineteen hundred and eight?" Ellie's face drained away its colour but David continued unperturbed. "There was Harry, Jack Manders, Herbert, Scrumps and, last but not least, young Splash. There was a tent in the background, a beer tent. They had joined the choir to help win the fair for Empton. It was taken the last time they had won, and we would have won again if things hadn't turned out the way they had."

Ellie was lost for words. Her eyes had become windows into the confusion that was boiling away behind them.

"So, you see Ellie," said David, demonstrating how well he had come to terms with all this, "I'm my own father, and you're my half sister."

Ellie breathed a heavy, exhausted sigh and fell back into the cushions of her armchair as if she had died. David held her closely to him. There existed a new bond now, the same golden tie melted down and reforged. He could feel the grinding of thoughts running through her head, thoughts that had run amok through his own mind in his own dark days.

"He was a cruel man," said Ellie as she blended into his embrace. "He was cruel with everyone, Daniel Harper. They were all cruel, that family, cruel with each other even."

"I know," said David, and he told her about what had happened to him in the old dead house the night she and Lotty ran away.

"He killed you?" she said, breaking away from his arms and squaring up to him.

"I lost consciousness. The next minute I was back in Helen Knight's hypnosis chair," but Ellie was not fully listening.

"You're just like him, you know," she said, taking his hand.

"I do know," he said.

He told her about the reflection in Mrs Cartwright's window. He explained how he had suspected it would be there and how he discovered and enlarged its image on a computer.

"The magnifying glass," said Ellie suddenly energised. "That's why she peered at that one photograph with her magnifying glass so many times. That's why she used to keep showing it to us. She used to tell you how wonderful your father was and all the time we were made to think that Danno in the picture was your dad. But it wasn't, was it? She must have known that you were there, her Miller, you, Miller, one and the same. How on earth have you lived with all this?"

"I've just survived it Ellie," he said, "that's all that counts."

"She pined for you, every day. All her life she wanted you to come. Just looking at you here in this house, I can see why she thought you had come back to her. She was sick, sick with love."

"I loved her too. I wanted to save her from the life she had there," said David. "Poor Lotty, she didn't have much of a chance, did she? Between her father and Danno, her life was messed up right from the time Danno... well, you know."

"You can say it David. I had to come into the world somehow."

"Well, he made sure no one else was going to have her. Do you remember the burned out cottage in the woods?"

A deeply buried reflex branded itself across her face. Ignoring her sense of alarm, he told her about the photographs of the burning cottage that had been in the envelope. He explained to her how Arthur Gibson, who had secretly taken them, had brokered a deal with Daniel to maintain his daughter's financial interest in the farm. Ellie's face shone with astonished wonderment.

"Lotty used to say that her father had arranged things for her," she said, coldly. "I never knew what she meant by that, or what it related to. On the day we left Salisbury and took the train north to the Midlands she said that she would never go back. I asked her why not. She never gave me an answer. She just looked back at me, terrified."

"But don't you see Ellie all our troubles, mum's, mine and even yours, they all have their root in Daniel Harper. Mrs Cartwright, Herbert Ashcroft, and David the woodsman, the countless people who fell foul of the dog run. The man was bad all through."

It was getting late into the afternoon. Outside rain could be heard tapping against the window. Ellie reached out and put a table lamp on so as to bathe the room in a warm yellow glow. Kneeling beside her, David rested his head on Ellie's lap, as he had once done as a boy, and she, out of memory for those far away days, rested her troubled hand on the side of his head and stroked his hair. For one brief moment he was at peace.

Chapter fourteen: Rod And Staff

He looked back over his shoulder to see if she was going to wave him off but the door to her house had already been closed. The goodbye in the hall could have been no more painful than if he had driven a bayonet into his heart. Words had forsaken him in those last moments. Instead he ripped himself from her embrace and ran childlike through the rain to his waiting car. In a seeming act of sympathy the leaden sky was weeping on his behalf. Cascades of what appeared to be tears rendered the view out of the windscreen a distortion. It mirrored his emotional state and its relentless sound on the glass was at one with his misery.

In his car strewn on the back seat were ramshackle odds and ends connected with his job and as he had looked over his shoulder in the hopes that Ellie would wave him off he could not ignore the mess there. In a single moment he could see the bleak future stretching ahead. It was all going to be work, eat and sleep from now on. He could see it disappearing into an unknown vanishing point, a drab road to loneliness. He let himself believe that there was to be no more good people in his world, people whom he could love and who would love him in return. The world outside was indeed a cold, wet and unfriendly place. Any peace and happiness had been destroyed bit by bit. Everyone he had felt affection for had gone or had been taken. He had pushed Gwen away, Rebecca had thrown him out, John died, so too had Connie, Lotty had been destroyed from the inside, and now Ellie was to be a part of his life no longer. Feeling dead inside he looked towards the shiny, wet road ahead, started the car and made it pull him away.

After a mile or so David pulled up at the roadside. Even the effort of making the return trip had become a burden of futility. As the car slowed and came to a halt his will did likewise. There was nothing for it but to stare at the carriageway ahead and allow the numbness to take over. The inertia had got to him. With his mind emptied out this way, the life he had lived ran freely around like a taunting projection. The car had failed to become warm since leaving Ellie's. Now, with the engine at rest, the temperature gradually dropped. Outside, as the rain pelted against the car's metal and glass, the sky sank into a deeper darkness. The sun had forsaken the day and the primordial power of the weather was set to continue its timeless task as the night fell. Shivers began to alert him to the chill that now reached through his clothes and into his bones. It pricked him to turn on the engine and use a bit of fuel to get warmth. The hum of the motor reminded him that he had a journey in front of him and a life to rebuild, and it would need rebuilding. Even the holy city within him had suffered terribly as if by an unseen subsidence.

His train of thought on pondering this took his mind back to the conversation with God that he had through the words of Isaiah. The idea of the Lord God holding his right hand had become a powerful symbol. It was the kind of thing that made his fragile little ego sit up and feed from. Would it not be God who would help rebuild his new Jerusalem? He would take his servant by the right hand and create a fresh soul and mend everything that had been destroyed. For there was destruction, he could see it inside him. Beautiful spires made of gold and silver lay fallen into rubble as if some earthquake had shaken them down. *Behold, the former things are come to pass, and new things do I declare*, that is what God had told him. The Lord God, creator of the

591

heaven and the earth, he would reform what others had brought low. The Almighty himself would see that those who had caused his life to crumble as it had done would be swept away with a brush of his hand. In considering those who were the perpetrators of such a crime there was only one real contender and, by the mysterious power of the Lord's will, only a few short miles separated him from the place where he had once lived.

A great wheel had now jolted from its rest. Like the cycle of the earth around the sun it possessed momentum, or like the sails that had once hung to the windmill at Maltoft, a wind of change had loosened them and nudged the giant gears to revolve and turn. In David's mind a chain of thoughts was joining together. Even as he skirted the Haxton Downs on the edge of Salisbury Plain, new ideas were being wrought on what he would do when he finally arrived at his revised destination, Great Rembleton - Empton. Had it not been for the Lord's guiding hand, he would not have been able to face his worst demon this way. Danno still had power over him but, with God at his side, David knew he had become invincible. Although no plan had formed properly in his head as to what he should do once he got there, he knew that he would receive guidance from above as soon as his journey was over.

The windscreen wipers were now swishing frantically across David's blurred view of the snaking road. He found reading the direction signs almost impossible. A voice within him said that the rain had been sent by the devil to prevent him doing the Lord's work. So he began to rejoice at his task, knowing that this was a fight of good over evil. He would avenge the torment that he had received at his mother's hand. He would gain retribution for Ellie's pain. He would get justice for what Danno had done to Lotty and, as the first bright shimmer of distant lightning flickered through the dense blanket of clouds, he knew that God was there with him.

There formed the embryo of a plan. As a tiny organism it could only see beyond Danno being found, tracked and hunted down. What was to happen after that remained inadequately underdeveloped, but tracking the man down, how was this to be done? Where would he be? Recalling the first time he had cycled up the hill to Empton,

David decided to head straight for the pub as soon as he arrived. It was now nine thirty. He estimated that he could make it just before closing time. The elements growled round about, making all efforts to sabotage him at every turn, but he was now warm in the metal shell that conveyed him through the stormy night. He knew that nothing could stop him getting to where the Lord was leading him.

It would be wrong to say that any of this thinking was in any way linear. Like individuals in a frightened flock of birds, each new idea went its own way, moving the mass of the concept about in an unpredictable direction. It was not until he had spent time wondering how Ellie was coping with the facts concerning her birth, that the genesis of his approach began to take shape. If anyone had known both Miller and David Harper well it was Ellie. She had confirmed to him beyond doubt that the identities of each person had been exact, better than any enhanced picture. She had even mistaken them once before. To the many who had known each person in the singular, very few would have known him as both people. In fact Ellie would be the only one still alive. His mother had simply confused each of his separate identities. To anyone else he was either one or the other and that idea began to dance around in the playground of his mind.

Suppose he was to meet Scrumps or Splash in the village. Suppose he found them in the pub when he finally arrived. Of course, they would most likely be dead by now, ten years over their hundredth birthday if they had survived. He imagined them there anyway and an image of their astonishment projected itself before his eyes straining to see the road ahead. It amused him to think of their shock at his appearance. To them Miller would have returned from the dead. What a trick it would be. Then he imagined Danno seeing him and the fear that would be in his eyes on seeing a ghost walk into his old age. From that moment his thinking ceased its scatter mentality and became very linear indeed.

The car's engine laboured slightly under the effort of the uphill road. Through the blinding spread of sheet lightning piercing the darkness he could just make out the distant heights of the escarpment outlined through the pelting rain. When at last he saw a road sign that indicated the turning to Great Rembleton his guts tightened and he was forced to turn down the heat and waft his face by the cool breeze from the air conditioning. It brought his mind back into its deliberations, sharpening his reasoning. Up the hill he would go, ask about Daniel Harper at the pub, find out if he still lived and where, then go to him, assume the mantle of Miller and then what? Suddenly, the plan had no end to it. What kind of end did he want? Did he just want to scare him? Perhaps he would scare him to death. Perhaps not and, if not, how else would he destroy him? The plan was not good enough yet. Up the hill he drove. He was feeling tired. Maybe he should consider coming back another day, but by that time, he had reached the place of the old green and found a parking space outside the dimly lit pub. David switched off the engine and had, by some force of will, arrived.

Ignoring the cars parked close by and other vestiges of the modern world - the pub seemed, through the darkness, to have become once more the Golden Goose. For a moment he even sensed that he had been taken back to those distant days since no colour could be seen in the night, but the light glowing from behind curtained windows was soft with yellow warmth. Their invitation beckoned. So running the gauntlet of the rain he was in the pub in a dash, making an entrance that everyone present noticed as he burst in at speed and shook the water from his arms. Not waiting to be examined in his newly arrived state, he strode purposefully to the bar and calmly ordered a pint. A large cordial man with white hair and white moustache pulled on the bitter pump and drew a pint into the glass. He was thirstier than he had given himself credit and, after paying the man, he sank half the contents without pause.

"Nasty night," said the landlord.

"You don't say?" David replied, vaguely aware of other ears listening in.

"You wouldn't catch me going out on a night like this," said the landlord, almost chiding him.

"On business," said David. "Just passing through. Tiredness can kill and all that stuff. Thought I'd better stop for a break."

"Oh," replied the man behind the bar, looking down at David's beer, and leaving him in no doubt about his disapproval of drink-driving.

Feeling somewhat guilty at having the pint in his hand, he wondered how best to broach the subject of Danno with this man, someone who was likely to know most people thereabouts.

"It's my job's fault," said David, concocting a story just one step ahead of empty thinking. "I'm supposed to be delivering some letters to someone in these parts."

"Can't be posted then, these letters?" the landlord put in.

"They need signing in my presence," David invented on the spot.

"What, at this time of night?" returned a suspicious reply.

David had now shot his bolt and was about to make a hasty retreat when his mouth began to run away with him.

"You try telling my boss that. We don't even know where this person lives exactly, but he's come into some money, and it's fallen to yours truly to do the dirty work. So, whilst my employer sleeps in his warm bed, I've got to drive through this shit and try to find someone who may not even be alive still."

To emphasise the sincerity of this baloney he knocked back the rest of his drink.

"I used to have a boss like that," said the white-haired publican. "Got out of the telecommunications rat race and became master of all I survey," he said patting his hand on the bar.

His wife heard him spouting this way and coughed a mild rebuke.

"So what's the address of this bloke you're after?" he enquired.

"Don't know," said David.

"Sent you on a bit of a wild goose chase then, this boss of yours?"

"Huh! You should have been with me in Scotland last week. Spend four days tracking down a ninety-year-old spinster in the middle of nowhere, up in the highlands."

"I'd change jobs," said the landlord.

"Hunting people becomes addictive," said David. "Kind of gives you a buzz. Do you know what I mean?"

David knew he had got him interested and, moreover, could detect a hint of cooperation.

"So, who are you looking for?" he said, moving three or four glasses aside to make a space between.

David looked shiftily about him so as to indicate secrecy. There were earwiggers that he knew to be there so he leaned fractionally towards his genial host.

"Confidential I'm afraid. I'm sure you understand," he said softly, taking a risk that this would put an end to the conversation, then added for security of its continuum. "I would have to take you into my complete confidence if I were as much as to even tell you his name."

The landlord had seen the visitor's surreptitious glance at his regulars and took the hint and the bait in equal measure.

"If you wrote it down, perhaps I could help? Just an idea mind," he said.

"Good idea. Say, you'd be good at my job, you would," said David. "I could even eat the note afterwards to destroy any trace of its existence."

The landlord's brow rose into his forehead at this cloak and dagger suggestion being proposed, then on seeing the impish grin on David's face knew it to be a joke and chortled back at him in a furtive manner. He then searched out the pad reserved for taking food orders and grabbed the pen nearby. David wrote in very small letters the name of his quarry, the demon that he and the Lord were pursuing. He gestured with just a hint of fingertip to his mouth to refrain from uttering the name he had written. The landlord looked at it for some time, in a way that made David wonder if he had only just learned to read. As the moment passed, he knew that he was taking too long in the task, and it was no surprise to be given the note back with words scribbled upon it, *never heard of him, sorry.*

It was a blow. The landlord explained that he and his wife had only taken ownership of the pub a few months previously, going on to say that Great Rembleton was a big place and he had not got round to knowing everyone yet. Disappointed, there was nothing for it but to leave empty handed, back out into the foul night. The bell rang for last orders as he reached the door and he took one last look inside where, far away in the past, events unfolded that had shaped his present life. He saw the landlord locked in a new conversation with another man. It prompted him before going back to his car to take a swift glance at those present in case he might know any of them but he did not know a soul. Those long ago days were now just too long ago.

In a second his face was being lashed by rain harshly driven, as he ran back to his waiting car, frantically hitting the central locking button on the key fob. Just as he was about to dive into the dry sanctuary of the car's interior, he heard a yell through the pelting noise of the storm. Screwing his face up against the downpour he could see in the pub's doorway a man shouting and beckoning with his arm for him to return. By now David was quite wet as he relocked and sprinted back to the warm, dry cosiness of the Miller's Drop. The man calling him over looked in his sixties. He took David to one side in a disquieting manner, near to where there was a jukebox, an area of the busy pub that was in that moment void of people.

"That person you're looking for. What's he got to do with you?" he said coming straight to the point.

David could now see that the man was the same person the landlord had been having a word with when he left. He was taken aback by this man's abrupt approach.

"I afraid I can't tell you that," said David, unable to think on his feet fast enough, "more than my job's worth," he added as his thoughts caught up with him.

"Bollocks," said the old chap. "You told Stan there," he said nodding his head towards where the landlord was half listening in. "You said he'd come into some money. How much?"

"Do you know the person I'm looking for then?" David asked, trying to turn the interview in his favour.

"Know him, do I?" he said wide-eyed, adding a mocking laugh. "If he's come into money then I want a share. That bastard owes me ten grand or more for renovations carried out on his place. It would have fallen to bits without me, but do I see a penny for my pains? Not a bit."

At this nugget of information there bubbled from under his strained indifference the need to shout and holler that his prey was within reach, but with practised skill and suppressing all emotions he began to close the deal with the stranger.

"Maybe I can help you there," suggested David. "You tell me all you can about this person, and I'll get in touch with head office and

597

see if there's a chance we can divert some of the funds to you. How would that suit?"

The man's widening smile and softening body language indicated that they had an agreement. He moved into the corner of the little room where a table and chairs had just been vacated, the uncollected glasses still wet.

"Your man's a tight git. Very strange he is. Sits alone in an old farmhouse and orders people about. People like me, but not anymore. You get me my money and I'm out of here."

"What else do you know about him? Where's the farmhouse?" he asked.

"Oh some old place up past the old church on the way to a village called Tunby. It's down a dirt track."

"What's the farm called?" he asked, knowing the answer already.

"Bofindle," he said, "I ought to know it. I've written him enough bills. Fobs me off with sob stories, he does. Quite believable at first but then you get wise to him."

"How old is he? Could you hazard a guess do you think?"

"Oh, seventy, eighty. It's hard to tell. Got a short temper mind you. I'd go careful if I were you."

"And you can confirm his name?" asked David, just making absolutely sure.

"Harper. Mr Daniel fucking Harper. Miserable old sod that he is," said the stranger.

So there it was. Like an artillery officer, he now had direction and range but there was a problem. No not a problem exactly, more of a strange inconsistency. He recalled Helen beating her fist on the front door of Bofindle farmhouse and peering in at the windows. Why had no one answered then? Maybe, he thought, by sheer fortune, misplaced or otherwise, Daniel Harper had been out when they called that day. Either way they had missed him, and he laughed inwardly at just how close he came to setting eyes upon the devil himself.

"I'd give you a card, but I've run out," said David beginning the process of extricating himself from this awkward man. "Perhaps I can have your name and address on a piece of paper."

"Perhaps," he said back, reaching into his pocket from where he retrieved a worn out pencil, blunt at the end.

In his other pocket was a packet of cigarettes that he proceeded to tear at, ripping off a flap. Upon this he scribbled in printed capitals his name and phone number. David read the name Robert Manders.

"No relation to Jack Manders, are you?" he said without thinking.

"How do you know that?" he said, totally bewildered that a stranger could make such an enquiry.

David realised that he had said too much, far too much. In his wish to get away he fell foul of his own tongue. He began to think what next to say that would free him from his own trap and release him to pursue the Lord's work.

"I saw the name on a computer file back at the office," David lied frantically. "I'm sure it said Wiltshire. Reckon it was something to do with unpaid taxes, that sort of thing, anyway I can't quite remember."

The ruse seemed to work. He had gauged his opponent well. On hearing of taxes and the like his body language changed. Gone was his assertive manner. He folded his arms defensively and looked back at him with what seemed like different eyes. David suspected that he was on the fiddle too. As he bid this stranger goodnight, venturing out once more into the rain-filled air, he was left thinking just how such a man could have been connected with the blacksmith who once drove an American Jeep.

Before he knew it he had driven halfway to Bofindle Farm when he pulled up and stopped to think. His heart was pounding against the inside of his ribs. It was fear, real fear, sickening and debilitating. Somehow he had to get his mind back on track. The confrontation in the pub had clouded his thinking, whilst the folly of what he was about to do had overwhelmed him. It seemed sheer stupidity to go through with it, whatever it was. He had no clear plan in his head of what was to happen next. Perhaps that is what made the idea so stupid, the fact that there was no plan. So he turned off the engine and allowed his mind to work.

With the storm's torrent bombarding the roof of his car he became distracted and muddled in his thoughts. When the brash burst of lightning flashed its white light all around him he could only think of the power of its creator, especially when like the almighty voice of a deity there came the violent crack of thunder that made him fearful of nature's might. It was as if the Lord was at his right hand, just as he had read in the book of Isaiah. Rather than seeing the storm as malevolence he began to see it as the Lord God speaking to him through the raging of the elements. In this state of mind he was reminded of the Psalms he had read. The second Psalm in particular had resonated with him on the day that the Lord directed him to the pulpit of St Peter's, when he was given God's instruction and promise. *Thou shalt break them with a rod of iron*, the Psalm directed, a rod of iron. Where was he going to find a rod of iron at this time of night? *Thou shalt dash them in pieces like a potter's vessel*. Them. Them. That was the enemy. He was to break his enemy with a rod of iron and smash him to pieces as if he had shattered a piece of pottery. The only metal rod he could think of was the crank for his car's jack. It would mean stepping outside into the stormy night, but the Lord had spoken, so what else was there to do but obey as commanded?

In no time at all his head and back were saturated. Even with the protection of the rear window of the hatchback, now opened and arched above him like an awning, the rain blew onto him directed by frenzied gusts of wind. He was frenzied himself, wild with discomfort, drenched, maddened at having to grope in the dark for the long handle that lay somewhere under the floor of the car's boot. Then his fingers felt its shape, stowed tightly in its polystyrene mould next to the spare wheel. With a sharp grab it was free. He rammed the carpet cover back and slammed the hatch back down, sprinting as he did so, back into the driver's seat, smelling of wet hair and damp clothes and panting out of breath. After a moment, when he had composed himself, he looked across at the passenger seat and there it was, his rod. It was painted blue and shaped in a zigzag like a dog's hind leg, there being a round hook at the end designed to fit into the connecting ring of the jack's hoist.

"What now Lord," he said to himself, whispering the words into the dampness?

In that moment, he found himself hoping for some kind of divine pointer. As the courtesy light in the car dimmed his environment into pitch black, once more he was left alone in the rural darkness, with invisible rain pelting against his metal shelter. It was akin to being dead he thought, where the light of the world is taken away. Upon this lane there was no comfort from light pollution from nearby towns and the night was as it always is in the wilderness.

The comparison to being no longer alive prompted a spontaneous focus of attention on the life he had lived. Long forgotten memories flooded back. They were nearly all of them bad memories of bad times. It made him think anew how much he had hated being David Harper. His time on earth was cursed from the minute he was born and, for a brief interval, he even wondered if he was being punished for having created the reasons for his entry into the world in the first place.

Then he began to imagine what his life could have been like if Danno had been like John Crampton. Had Danno been kind and loving, if he had been strong and supportive, then Lotty would have been the sort of joyful, tender mother he craved so strongly. Had Danno forgiven her infidelity and raised the boy David as his own, who was to say how things might have turned out. Of course it was the useless backward spiral of conjecture that made such hypotheses not worth the consideration he gave them.

The alternative to such thinking was none other than the exact way his life had turned out, and so, not for the first time, hate festered in him towards Danno. Every event that had bent and crushed his fragile soul throughout his life had its origins in the evil that resided in the head of Daniel Harper. Over and over in his mind it went, hate piling upon yet more hate. So, what was he to do? Go to the farm, crash in and beat hell out of the old man who lived there. It seemed too ugly a thing to do, and yet had God not commanded him to smash him to pieces like the destruction of pottery? There had to be a better way.

That way came to him as he remembered his talk with Ellie, the elements of which developed as if they had become infused with life. Gradually, a workable idea began to take shape and the thought of it energised him just as if the hand of God had touched him. The idea was nothing new but it was the development within that held the key. It was beyond all doubt that his appearance was that of Miller. If, as he supposed, Danno had sent him to the next world with his brutal kicks, then what would be Danno's response if he were to see Miller's spirit return from whence it had been dispatched? How would a frail, old man stand up to the spectre of a ghost in his midst, especially the ghost of someone he had once murdered? David knew that Danno had no inkling of how Lotty's child looked let alone how he had developed into a man. All he had to do was strike terror into a man in his final years to help hurry his passage towards its end. He would find him and terrify the very life out of him.

With a twist of the ignition key he began his undertaking, secure in the knowledge that the Lord God Almighty was with him. His recollection of the army of the empire was nothing in comparison to the hordes of angels and the heavenly host charging with him into battle. He was clothed in the armour of invincibility. Onward went the Christian soldier, forward into battle to right a great wrong.

Soon he came to the lane that led to the farm. The farm's sign lit up temporarily by a shimmer of trapped lightning from deep inside the massive clouds above. It illuminated their vast sagging underbellies in a series of random white bursts, precursors to the deafening thunder that split the sky apart almost immediately thereafter. Bofindle Farm the sign read. He recounted the first time he had stumbled upon the place after rambling through the woods one hot summer day many years before. Now the lane that led to it was a quagmire of dark mud made intermittently visible in the short bursts of arced light electrifying the pregnant sky.

As he passed by the barns and drew close to the farmhouse he stopped to look. Amidst its dark outline he could make out the orange glow of light cast from behind a window. Someone was at home. The enemy was within reach. So it was that he turned off the car's engine, grabbed hold of his jack handle and stepped out into the rain to catch his prey by surprise on foot. In less than fifteen seconds he made it to the front door. As quietly as possible he tried the handle. The door opened without resistance, it being neither locked nor bolted and, with a rapidly pounding heart, he stepped inside the devil's lair.

The way into the house gave way to a familiar corridor from which there were doors to various rooms just as he remembered. The house smelled of damp and cat's urine and on the carpet he could feel through his shoes the gritty touch of soil. The house was quiet except for the sound of a well-spoken lady coming from beyond the door of the first room on the right. It was not until the voice of a man with similar pronunciation had spoken that he realised he was listening to the late news emanating from what he assumed was a television. He beheld the door to the room. All David had to do was open it and he would be at the very heart of Danno's attention. It was the worst time of all to be afraid. He began to recite Psalm twenty-three.

"Yea, though I walk through the valley of the shadow of death, I will fear no evil. Thy rod and thy staff will comfort me."

He gripped the jack handle tightly, his own rod and staff, and reached out to grab the door handle. The dank room was dimly lit. A standard lamp in the far corner cast a weak light where it stood. Live images darting from the television screen in the other corner made the subdued chamber flicker as if a hearth fire had released a troupe of dancing shadows to the four walls.

Halfway across the room, facing an unmade fireplace was a threadbare settee. David could just about see the top of a person's head recumbent and still. What was he to do now he thought? For a moment he considered bringing the handle violently down onto the crown of the person's head. He further tightened his grip on the cold metal, ready to smash the head like a potter's vessel. The one and only thing that stopped him was he had to be sure the head belonged to his enemy. The thought of murdering the wrong man destroyed this hasty notion. He would have to be sure the man lying there was the man he sought.

For a moment he stood poised ready to step up between the dead fireplace and the person, to take a look at him at rest, but then, clearing his thoughts he remembered the plan. Trickling through the terror he remembered that he was to play the part of Miller's risen spirit. His entrance back into this man's life therefore was going to have to take on a more theatrical quality. Calling his name would be perfect for the desired effect. So, he took a deep breath and broke the silence.

"Hello, Danno," he said slowly and clearly, trying to hide the nerves that had him by the shakes.

The head jerked awake and was slowly raised up out of its reclining posture by a tired, old body.

603

"I've come back for you Danno," he said, forcing out the words as the figure moved stiffly. "You remember me, don't you?"

Drowsy and disorientated, the elderly frame hauled itself round and David could see the time-ravaged face of a man with a heavy brow. It had been more than fifty years since he had set eyes on Daniel Harper. Fifty years of relentless ageing had carved deep grooves into the leather that clung tightly to his skull, but there was no mistake. It was Daniel Harper.

"It's time to die," said David, soft and kind. "It's time for me to take you away from this earthly life."

"Who the fuck are you?" defied the old man, fumbling for his glasses that were resting on the arm of the threadbare settee.

Finding them, his trembling hands secured them to his face and then, still seated he craned his neck to look at his visitor. The sudden gasp of air into his lungs made its own statement and his horrified face said more than if he had sworn a million oaths. For a brief few seconds the two men's eyes were locked. It would have been stalemate and defeat for David if he remained silent for much longer.

"The Lord God has delivered me from my grave to take you to hell," he said in a low, soft voice.

Danno twisted round yet further and gripped the back of the settee. In the dim light he could see clearly who had come calling and David could tell by his enemy's agitation that he had driven the dagger of fear into him. Faint flashes from the storm outside lit up the curtain and painted the room in nature's electric light and by it Danno was able to see for sure that Miller had indeed come for him.

"The cyclist," coughed the old man getting to his shaky feet. "It is you, ain't it?"

"Yes, it's me," said David, "the singer man, Caruso, Miller. I'll sing you a snatch of *Danny Boy* as I lead you to the flames of hell if you like?" David continued, trying to shift the balance of power.

"This can't be happening," said Danno quietly, clawing at his forehead with his fingertips. "It's a dream, it's a dream," he fumbled, trying to remain standing.

"No dream," said David, "just your life's end. Time to pay for every death that stains your soul. Time to be judged."

Danno sat speechless, trying to understand how all this could be. David watched him, a heap of a man whose natural death was not far away at all. Out of the silence a crack of thunder ripped the night in two. It jolted the old man with more fright than he could bear and, with his knees buckling, dropped back down onto the settee.

"Not much of a deathbed, is it?" David said, unable to hide the laugh in his voice.

"You can't take me Miller," he said, the defiance teetering. "Just leave me. Sod off. I'm an old man now, an old man, do you hear?" he sounded tired.

"You forget Mr Harper, your sins are many," said David sounding biblical, driving home the act.

"You don't have to take me. Why can't you wait?" the old man said, the first catch of upset tugging at his voice.

"Everyone has to die," continued David. "I did once, over fifty years ago, remember?"

"You took my wife," he said back, snarling through his distress.

"You took her long before she was your wife. What was it like watching Ellie grow up knowing she was yours?"

"How do you know such things?" Danno said, shocked by the words.

"Beyond the grave, all is laid bare. You'll soon see. Shall we go?"

At this invitation the frail creature began to believe. Only a spirit could surely know such things, he thought. Living on his own all these years had taken it out of him and twisted his mind and memories into distorted shapes. Now he was about to die alone, taken away to some dreadful eternity by this spectre standing behind him in the dark. He had at last come face to face with the one thing that he could not bully, the great bully itself, death. What a pitiful sight he was, thought David, as he watched his enemy begin to weep.

"It'll do you no good where you're going," said David. "People have been weeping there for thousands and thousands of years. You'll be no different."

"Let me make amends," he said, fighting his tears. "It's not too late, is it?"

How delicious was this power. The hate boiled up from the depths of his life. Every childhood misery, every horrible dream that poisoned his nights, all of it was swelling up, a septic mass of hate. This man who had single-handedly poured evil into every vein of his life, who had pressed fear into the depths of his heart, was now hideously trembling, his tears only moments away.

"Just close your eyes," soothed David, "and we'll be on our way."

"Oh, God no. Don't take me, I beg you," the words were almost inaudible through the sobs that broke free.

"Just stand up, with your back to me, and close your eyes, and we'll go to hell together."

Danno, shaking with disbelief that the end of his life was actually upon him, rose obediently to his feet, awkwardly, horribly, and as he did so, there came from him a shrieking cry. He doubled up in agony clutching just below his collarbone. The shattered body of Daniel Harper collapsed onto one knee. David watched wide-eyed as his heart's desire came true before him.

"Goodbye," said David almost laughing at the spectacle.

Danno, the great Danno was dying, dying right before him, down on the floor. David waited to see how long it would take for the old man to expire, but his agonies passed. Panting for breath and exhausted from pain he looked up at David staring back at him from the gloom. He saw the jack handle in his hand. Cogs began to turn in his mind. It was an uneasy feeling for David to see the change in Danno's face. David knew he had seen the handle by the downward flick of his eyes. It was like watching someone see the shattered pieces of a broken plate rejoin and David knew he was trying to figure out why a spirit would be carrying something so material with him.

"You're no ghost," he croaked, and then with brightening eyes a fresh thought flashed its spark.

He spoke again, sneering, amazed at his conclusion.

"You're hers, that's who you are. You're her bastard. Well, well, well," he almost laughed, "I've been looking all around for you, for years and in you walk as good as gold."

David's shell-shocked face was as good as an admittance of the fact. The Danno he knew and feared was now returned. Damaged, old and frail but restored in spirit.

606

"I've come to take you to hell," David shouted with less conviction than before, his vain attempt at hanging on to his plan melting away.

"You're already here, bastard boy," said Danno, now laughing mildly. "You've not come to take me anywhere Miller man. You and I know it's this place you're after, ain't it? Precious little Bofindle."

David kept silent. The handle weighed heavily in his grip. Should he use it now, he thought?

"You see," continued Danno, "all your legal tricks won't work on me anymore. Oh, I know on paper that I'm supposed to be your dear old daddy, but none of that will profit you a penny."

David wondered what he meant and how he knew. It showed on his expression.

"Public records," Danno went on. "Silly bitch kept her married name. Made her that bit easier to track down. I've even got a copy of your birth certificate somewhere, Mr David fucking Harper," and he forced a snap of laughter to ridicule the fact. "I could never have fathered you even if I'd been stupid enough to try," continued Danno.

"I was fathered by a better man," said David with foolhardy defiance.

"That's why you're a bastard then, isn't it?" Danno retorted.

"She loathed you, Lotty did," said David, "almost as much as I do."

"So what?" said Danno, his breathing labouring under the agony in his heart.

"You raped her for a start. And then there's the murder of the woodsman? Wait 'til the police hear about that one. I have proof."

"So you know about Ellie, do you, and that dim-witted David of hers. Know all about Arthur Gibson's little set up, do we? Seen the little snapshots? I expect she even named you after him come to think of it. Blackmail! It'll do you no good now."

"Why couldn't you just let her be happy?" David snarled at him. "How could she have ever had a proper married life with you? What chance would I have had if you'd been my fucking dad anyway?"

"Ha! Fat chance of that ever happening."

"It might have been, God forbid," said David.

"I was the one forbidden, singer man. My father went berserk when he found out I'd gone and got what he called that Gibson girl

607

in the family way. A violent man he was. Kicked me to kingdom come. He put his boot in, just like I did to your father. Crippled me as I lay on the hall carpet at Holme Farm. Crippled me," he repeated, glancing down to his groin to indicate what he meant. "So, you see, there was never, ever to be an heir. I couldn't father anyone."

David knew not what to do for the best now. Everything was in ruins. He thought of running out, back into the dirty night but how could he? All of his life had spent running away and, besides, he clung on to the Lord God, just as tightly as he clung on to the metal handle. Maybe now was the time to smash his brains in, now whilst he remained kneeling on the floor, but that too changed in short order. Danno hauled himself up holding grimly onto the fireplace, reached up into the gloom above the chimneybreast and grabbed hold of what looked like a black tube. In a flash of movement, Danno swung round and aimed a shotgun at him, cocking it ready to fire.

Suddenly it was David who became terrified. He could see right down the barrels. They were directed at his face, Danno's shaking finger curled gently around the ornate trigger. It was checkmate.

"You had me going there for a bit with that spirit routine," said Danno still in pain. "Very good, I must say."

David was in the middle of his worst fear, as if one of his dreams had cast off its virtual state and become real.

"Not very talkative now, are we? Tell you what, why don't we have that song of yours instead?"

"There are people in the pub who know I've come here," David managed to say.

"Sing," said Danno, not listening to a word of it. "Sing," he repeated, "Sing *Danny Boy* for the last time. Sing it you bastard, or I'll blow your fucking brains out here and now."

This said the gun's barrel suddenly drooped low. Danno was finding it hard to breathe. David moved forwards seizing his chance.

"Back," Danno called out, his voice betraying the agony in his chest. "Get back, and throw that fucking handle over there," he said, nodding his ravaged head towards the far corner of the dim room.

Danno flicked the gun up to aim at his eyes by way of an insistence and David did as he was told. The handle was hurled and clanged down onto the bare floorboards.

"Good," said Danno, his voice calmed for a moment. "Now I can finish you off. That'll be both of you gone then and I can rest in piece."

Danno could see the questioning expression coming from beyond the fear in David's face.

"Oh yes, I sorted her out years ago," he said, answering the look, "and I'd have got you too, if only you and that girl Ellie hadn't pissed off to God knows where."

As these words hit him David must have stood there open-mouthed. The words sorted her out years ago messed up his mother's history. There was no sense to it.

"Ah! You think she committed suicide, don't you. Good, good. I did a fine job on her singer man. Not even a struggle, so frightened she was, so petrified. I had that noose around her scraggy neck as slick as you please. Dangling from the banister she was, twitching as she turned blue."

David's eyes were brimming with silent horror. Danno could see them, mixed up with his welling tears.

"There was a suicide note," he fought to say.

"There was. In her handwriting too," he said. "Just part of the plan that only half worked, that note," he carried on. "Amazing what you can get someone to do with a knife at their throat. Dictated it to her I did. Made it look like suicide, perfect. I'd have hoped it would flush you out too, or that sprog of mine, so I could, well, I'm sure you get the picture. Everything comes to him that waits don't it? And here you are, as large as life!" he laughed at the last word, laughed through the pains crushing his chest.

Now David's hate for the man was at new depths, vile, bubbling, hatred, fresh and fermenting, amplified by the flashes of lightning outside and the deep angry booms of thunder that followed them. Now, more than ever, he wanted to kill him, kill him with his bare hands. Danno was ranting on about his wedding photo and the difficulties he had in using it to track his mother down, when the most severe pain shot through him like a sabre. Danno had no choice but to crouch down in a foetal position, still upright on the bare floor. With eyes scrunched up in wild pain he beheld David taking his chance, hands out ready to throttle him. Danno raised his gun, crying with the torture of his heart attack. The gun came right up to David's face, stopping him dead.

"Now, fuck off," Danno managed to groan, losing his fight for life.

David heard the little click of the trigger snap. Saw, for one brief microsecond, a bright yellow flash explode straight into his eyes.

Chapter fifteen: The Cyclist

The next flash was big and white, a brilliant white illumination that lasted for less than a second. The sound that accompanied it was not thunder but the less noble rumbling of falling masonry and wood. All I could feel was a sense of falling backwards through the darkness, hitting sludge on a hard floor that somehow broke my fall before what seemed like tons of debris crashed down on me. There was rain falling on my face, upturned as it was.

I lay on my back trying to make out what had happened. A spike had impaled me though the side of my waist. I could hear thunder rumbling in the distance. I was severely hurt all over my body, my ribs, but mostly my jaw. It seemed to be dislocated. More bricks and stone thudded down onto the solid floor trapping me under what I took to be an oak beam. Beyond these simple facts I was in confusion. How could the gun have missed me? The thought ran on a loop inside my head.

The escape from death had left me in a numbed state of shock. It was a feeling like no other. There was euphoria and the stark terror of it mixed up in equal proportions, a concoction that made orderly thinking unworkable. I looked around in the dark wetness to see where I had fallen. Had the rotten floorboards given way? Was I in the cellar beneath the front room? Is that how I had escaped the gunshot? Had the Lord delivered me just in the nick of time?

I heard a groan coming from the right that distracted my puzzled thoughts. It was a man's groan in short difficult breaths. I tried to lift my head to see into the darkness but I was pinned down by heavy, jagged bits of wreckage. All except for my head and right arm I was unable to move. I would rather have died there and then, than to suffer another minute of the biting pain that crushed me. Instinctively, I tried to push at the heap of rubble to ease myself out. It was impossible. A great metal object had pierced me close to where my kidneys were. I could feel it stiff and unyielding. I had no strength to do anything about the weight of stone and bricks bearing down on the beam that straddled my body. Numbing, it was drowning me in a pool of agony. I tried to cry out for help but could not lift my lungs enough for the air. I could not believe my plan had failed so badly. Where was the Lord God? Where was The Almighty when I most needed him? I knew I was going to die. My reprieve had indeed been short-lived.

The groan moaned out a second time awoken by another flash of lightening. Tilting my eyes sideways I could see a head about two feet away, facing down towards the filthy floor. A head was all I could make out. For the brief moment the lightning had flashed its light upon it. I could only see the head emerging from the same line of rubble that was covering me. I laid my head back down on the ground. The floor was covered in sludge of some sort. My head sank down into it and I felt it touch the edges of my ears. Its rancid smell seemed familiar. I had no choice but to lie in the stuff. Exhaustion beckoned me towards sleep. I knew I was dying. So, with no choice left to me, I gave in to its overpowering seduction. All my muscles relaxed. My time had come.

As I began to drift away the groan formed into words. I listened to the voice ask what the hell had happened? I knew the speaker. It was Daniel Harper. He must have been hurled into the cellar with me, I thought. He had obviously fallen on his face. The floor of the front room and the ceiling of the cellar had crashed down on his back. I wondered how long I would have to wait until somebody arrived to help us. I knew it would be too long. It was no use. I was a goner. I was coughing up blood. Danno heard me.

"Christ, can't you die quietly, singer man?" he said.

"You first," I managed to whisper.

"Huh," he snorted. "I should have seen to you long before now."

I was too tired to answer but Danno continued talking.

"And don't bother calling for help. I'll tell them to bugger off, let you die here. No one will lend a hand to you Caruso. They all know which side their bread's buttered on."

"I've told people at the pub that I'm here," I said slowly through a mouth that was broken. "There's a man there, says you owe him ten grand. He'll come looking."

"Ten what?"

"Ten thousand pounds," I struggled to say, "for work on the farm."

"I reckon you're slipping away," he said. "Who told you that?"

"I can't remember his name," I said, closing my eyes.

"I'll ask Harry," he snarled to himself, "he'll know."

I was not listening. All I wanted to do was slip away from the pains. As I drifted towards my oblivion, I heard a sound in the distance. It was a church bell chiming eleven. It was a pathetic ring, more like a set of clanks really. I remember thinking it must have been the sound of Great Rembleton's old church clock carried on the wind. It sounded closer. I thought nothing of it. I knew even as the eleventh clank rang out, that I had never heard midnight's chime.

More time passed. I heard Danno try to extricate himself but he was stuck as fast as I was. He was cursing the building in which we were trapped, saying it was about time the whole place was demolished, that it was an eyesore.

"I'd have got you to fix this place up after the windmill if you'd played your cards right," he said. "Spoils the whole damned village green. It wants pulling down and starting again. We could even have designed a village hall on the site," he said.

I ran his words a couple of times over. What was he on about? The farm was nowhere near the green. We were three miles or so from Great Rembleton. It was not until a flurry of lightening flickers brightened the room enough for me to see the rim of a bicycle wheel poking out from a pile of bricks that I had the first notion of where I was and when. At this, my mind lost its grip. The sight of the wheel rim made me feel almost anaesthetised. The bicycle wheel, maybe I was mistaken though. Maybe it had nothing to do with what I thought it might? It could have come from any bicycle, surely, could it? Who was to say it had ever belonged to me at all? I was hurt and exhausted. Everything was too much. I calmed myself and tried to rein in my tearaway conclusions but they were stubborn, these thoughts. They pestered even as I begged for the pains to leave me be.

I endured five more minutes of agonies. It was an endless term, made worse by the figure an arm's length away. Danno's legs were trapped, he complained over and over. His back hurt him. There was no self-pity, just anger boiling within him at being in such a predicament. I wished he would be quiet. He was not impaled on something as I was. I knew that once the rubble was pulled away he would walk out of this mess scot-free. Out of the side of my body I could touch the metal spike that had run itself through me. I guessed it was a pipe, a remnant from what may have once been the mains water supply to the cellar. My ribs were in severe pain. I doubt that torture could have been worse. All the time Danno's constant swearing became another torment. I turned my head sideways left to face away from his persistent moaning.

I must have lain there for a minute or two when there was an incandescent flash of light and, out of what remained of the building's window, I saw a sight that set the unthinkable into the concrete of reality. Rising high above the house just a few yards away was a tree, exposed in the black night by the flash of the storm. It was the great chestnut tree on the green at Empton. There was no mistake. I knew the tree, knew it as good as if I had drawn it over and over. I could not understand what was going on anymore.

If I was really where my eyes were telling me, then what the hell had the life I had just lived been all about? In the past hour I had come to Bofindle to put an end to an old, frail Daniel Harper, but now that was wrong. I was in the old, derelict house. If it was really true Danno had been kicking me to death only minutes ago. The moment was drenched in nonsense. How was I to believe that in just a few moments, in a state of blackout, I had lived an entire life, full of colour and detail? I could not even believe my own reasoning but what other explanation was there?

Nearly fifty years had passed by in minutes. How could they have run their course in so brief a time? I was David Harper, forty-eight years old. My mind knew who I was, but my brain was telling me that I was still Miller - Miller who had just been beaten up by the man who lay just a couple of feet away, complaining. Gradually, as one thought led to another, I began to grasp the consequences of what my eyes and ears were telling me. If I was in the derelict house and, if I had fallen through the first floor into what had once been the house's kitchen, it could only mean one thing.

If, as I began to accept, I was once more the man the villagers called Miller and the past had been some kind of sickening, long drawn out premonition, then the real David Harper was resting in the womb of the woman I loved, right now. If I was right then, even as I lay here in this rubble, trapped, she was leaving with Ellie, eventually to arrive months from now in the Midlands, thus making the premonition come true. Everything would come true. A life I would not wish on anyone would play itself out just as I remembered it.

Perhaps I was losing my fight for life. My thinking was strange. I could just picture Lotty and little Ellie packing their bags and heading off northward where little Davy boy would live out his miserable life. As one thought made way for another, who could argue that at some point, he would find himself at the old farmhouse where the begetter of all his misfortune lived, intent on smashing his brains out with a jack handle. The whole thing was a long and winding circle. It seemed clear as I lay there in the carpet of bird shit, that, if I died, the circle would just go round again. Perhaps it would only take my death for the cycle to repeat itself over and over, even forever.

I do not know where I got the strength, as I heard the incessant filth pouring out of the mouth of Danno Harper, I was overcome with a blinding rage. It blinded me to my pain. It stiffened my sinews. It was a hot-headed kind of madness. I grabbed hold of his hair at the back of his head, great clumps of it in my hand. He began to scream abuse at me. I was not aware of the words that came out it was all corruption. I remember he said that no one would save me if he told people to keep away - but I was beyond his power. If I was about to die, then this would be the last thing I ever did. At least, baby David would never be able to trace an aged Danno Harper and meet his end from the barrel of a shotgun. The cycle would end.

So I gripped his hair even tighter and angled his head, that was already facing downwards, into the slurry of bird mess and there I pushed, my right arm forcing his mouth deep in, submerging his nostril into the stink. He tried to fight it, but his body was stuck tight and his neck was no match, even for my weak limb. No matter how he tried to move his head to escape me, I held him vice like. I think he tried to hold his breath, because, after a minute or so of struggle, he could hold it in no longer. There was an explosion of air. It sent bird shit splattering into the side of my face. Several seconds passed. I knew he was holding out, trying to fight me, fighting the urge to breathe in. From the pit of his throat there came a desperate grunt but I would not let go. I held him down. It was a grim gurgle when it came, a choking fit of short agonising breaths. I knew the bird mess was being sucked into him, but I held him face down into it all the more. Under the rubble, his body was in convulsions. His breaths were now violent, fearful, ghastly, but no air was getting into him. I was drowning him in the stuff. It must have been a couple of minutes, pushing him down like this then suddenly his head relaxed. I had not appreciated just how tense his neck and scalp had been. Now all that was gone and he was still.

All that remained were the sounds of my exhaustion. I was out of breath, like an athlete, with his race won. I had killed a man. It is quite something to know a fact like that. To know I had extinguished a life infused me with a sickness that I was unprepared for. It did not matter that I believed he deserved it. I was overcome with shame. There was no victory in what I had done, even though the dead body lying next to me belonged to the originator of a host of evils. The fact remained that with my bare hand I had become a killer, a murderer. I wondered how a soldier must feel when he achieved his first kill. Does he feel good that he killed the enemy like I had? Or does he feel for one brief moment, in the heat of battle, an ache of remorse?

It was all pointless thinking really. I was worn out. Impaled on the pipe, racked with pain, my energy depleted, I could do nothing else but give in. It was time to die. My thoughts turned to Lotty. I knew she was leaving but at least there would be no stalker in the years ahead, intent on tracking her down and lashing her neck to a banister. So I let myself drift away. The sounds around me grew quiet. All was still save for the dim voices that seemed to float in the dark, wet night.

"He's here," the voices repeated, over and over then fading away.

Through my closing eyes I beheld a light. It was an erratic point of yellow that grew in luminescence as the voices approached. It was all

I could do to turn my head towards it. Its brightness penetrated the dead, old house, swaying to the sound of boots trampling over the bricks and stone. Someone swore as the light stopped right above me. Its beam was then turned towards the lifeless body next to me and another oath, gleeful this time, rang out in the stench. It was Harry's voice.

I tried to speak but my mouth flopped about trying to work. I heard the voice of the doctor. I think Jack Manders was there too. Harry put the lamp down on the bricks that covered my chest and saw the pipe poking out of my clothes. He said something about blood to the doctor. I was drifting between this world and the next. I had never been so tired.

"Don't say anything old chap," said Harry, almost lovingly, but I had to tell him.

So I tried to talk again. Harry knelt down in the sludge and moved his ear to my face. I could tell he was in awful pain too from the crack in his voice. He asked me what I wanted, repeating that I should take it easy.

"Lotty, Ellie. Don't let them go."

The words were badly formed. I wondered if he understood.

"The farm, they're at the farm."

I knew it sounded gibberish, so I took a breath and in the clearest tones I could muster I managed to say.

"Get Lotty, the farm, quick."

What relief to hear Harry's command barked at the vicar, telling him to fetch Mrs Harper. I heard the clatter of shoes and later the sound of a car starting up. I had done it. If the vicar arrived on time, I would have done it. I could die now. My life's work was over. With big gentle hands, Harry put something soft under my head, as I succumbed to the hurt and said goodbye to the little point of light.

It was the best thing I could have done. I fell into a smooth nothingness. It is hard to describe because there is nothing to describe, nothing except the memory of its smoothness. When I emerged from it I recall it was not the sense of pain that hit me first, it was the warm, tender feeling wrapped around my right hand. Like windows seldom used, my eyelids opened and there she was, smiling, smiling a love that would not die. She was wearing a thin dress that

616

showed her femininity. There was even a hint of perfume mingled in with the smell of the hospital ward. I cried, cried like a child. I could not hold it in. Her tears jerked out of her just as freely, and there we were, crying with joy that we were with one another. Whatever the future might hold, we knew that we would face it together, together with the unborn little David growing within her, who knew nothing of the worlds around him.

The End

About The Author

R. E. Witham's love of writing was kindled when he was just eleven years old. The books of Jules Verne and H.G. Wells inspired him to scribble the adventures of a colossal steam-powered flying machine into four school exercise books. Flight again allowed his sixteen-year-old imagination to write the story of *Imtol*, creator of a winged barrel built to cross a mountain range in search of a missing flock of magical birds. The urge for story telling brought forth a raft of short stories, magazine articles and poems, eventually culminating in his first attempt at a viable book *Albert Dudley Makes His Mark* in 1999.

His work as a graphic designer over a twenty-five year span earned him first place in a National Award competition in 1997 and, following a forty-year career as an illustrator he was granted Approved Status from the National Trust in 2016 for his work on a number of their children's books.

Creativity and imagination have been central to his working life. The generation of copy for commercial clientele through brochures, websites and other promotional literature provided the necessary elbow grease to polish up a self-taught skill. It was this aspect the author's written work that honed his spare time output resulting in the dark and disturbing story of *The Curse Of Beckett's Wood*, written whilst the author held down a full-time job. The mental pressure of that time seems to have infused the book with a brutal honesty that nevertheless charges the reader's mind with the impulse to read on and to delve further into those shadowy places into which it sinks.

Encouraging reviews followed the self-publication of early ring-bound copies but they were accompanied by a universal constructive criticism of its working title. A rethink brought to the fore the intimidating wood as a ground zero from which the eventual curse creeps forth. *The Curse Of Beckett's Wood* therefore seemed to possess just the right tone to evoke a perfect sense of sinister curiosity.

Other works in the pipeline are *The Deadlines of Archibald Crimm* and *The Girl At The Window*.

The author and his wife live in Grantham in Lincolnshire. They have three grown up children and six grandchildren.

Lightning Source UK Ltd.
Milton Keynes UK
UKHW011925100321
380129UK00001B/60